For "Uncle Steve" Griswold, USMC, the "barbarian" who taught me that people are always responsible for their own actions, but that sometimes good people have to take the responsibility for fixing other people's mistakes. You did . . . for thirty-one years. God Bless.

Dedicated to Charles Gonzalez: The sort of person who would discuss quantum mechanics, dialects of Amazonian tribes and garroting German sentries with an impressionable twelve-year-old.

MARDUK

PORT

MARSHALL

TITAN

LANDING

QNKOK

N

CHAPTER ONE

Sergeant Adib Julian, Third Platoon, Bravo Company of The Empress' Own, opened his eyes, looked around the inside of his cramped, one-man bivy tent, and frowned sleepily. Something was different, but he couldn't tell what. Whatever it was, it hadn't twanged his finely honed survival instincts, which at least suggested that no thundering hordes of Mardukan barbarians were likely to come charging through the sealed flaps at him, but that sense of change lingered. It poked at him, prodding him up out of the depths of slumber, and he checked his toot. The implanted computer told him that it wasn't quite dawn, and he yawned. There was still time to sleep, so he rolled over, pushing aside a pebble in the dirt, and shivered in the cold . . .

His eyes snapped wide, and he unsealed the tent opening and popped out into the predawn light like a Terran prairie dog.

"It's cold!" he shouted in glee.

Bravo Company had been marching uphill for the last several days. They had long since passed out of the

1

valleys around the Hadur River, and the city-state of Marshad lay far behind them. In fact, they were beyond any of the surrounding cities that had the dubious pleasure of lying on the borders of the late, unlamented King Radj Hoomas' territory.

They'd made better time than they'd anticipated, yet despite the rigorous pace and steadily increasing upward slopes they faced, they had enjoyed a period of remarkable respite. Between the sale of the captured weapons gathered in Voitan, the remnant funds from Q'Nkok, and the lavish gifts T'Leen Sul and the new Council of Marshad had bestowed upon them, they had been able to purchase all their needs along the way.

In many cases, that had been unnecessary. Several towns had hosted them like visiting dignitaries . . . for more than one reason. The towns had been fearful of Radj Hoomas' ambition and avarice, and were delighted to do anything they could for the aliens who had put an end to them. They'd also been fascinated by the off-world visitors . . . and, in many cases, they'd wanted to get them out of town as quickly as possible.

The trader network in the Hadur had spread accounts of the destruction of the entire dreaded Kranolta barbarian federation at Voitan, the battle at Pasule, and the Marshad coup far and wide, and the message encapsulated in all the stories was clear. The humans were not to be molested. The few times they'd run into resistance—once from a group of particularly stupid bandits—they had successfully demonstrated the effectiveness of classical Roman short-sword-and-shield combat techniques against charging Mardukans without ever being forced to resort to bead rifles or plasma cannon. But thanks to the stories which had run before them, any potentially ill-intentioned locals had known that those terrifying off-world weapons lurked in reserve . . . and had no desire at all to see them any more closely than that.

The Bronze Barbarians of The Empress' Own, veterans all, were well aware of the advantages inherent in a fearsome reputation. This one had come with a higher price tag than they had ever wanted to pay, but it also meant that they'd been able to travel for several weeks with virtually no incidents. That happy state of affairs had given them time to lick their wounds and get ready for the next hurdle: the mountains.

Julian had been off guard duty the night before, but Nimashet Despreaux had had the last shift. Now, as he stood grinning hugely into the semi-dark, she smiled at him while groans sounded across the camp. The female sergeant bent over the fire, picked something up, and walked over to where he was dancing in delight.

"Hot coffee?" she offered, extending the cup with a grin. The company had practically given up the beverage; it was just too hot on Marduk in the morning.

"Oh, thank you, thank you, thank you," the NCO chortled. He took the cup and sipped the brew. "God, that tastes awful. I love it."

"It's bloody freezing," Corporal Kane grumped.

"How cold *is* it?" Julian asked, diving back into his bivy tent for his helmet.

"Twenty-three degrees," Despreaux told him with a fresh smile.

"Twenty-three?" Gronningen asked, furrowing his brow as he sniffed the cool air. "What's that in Fahrenheit?"

"Twenty-three!" Julian laughed. "Shit! I'd set my *air-conditioning* to twenty-three!"

"Something like seventy-three or seventy-four Fahrenheit," Despreaux said with a laugh of her own.

"This feels much colder," the big Asgardian said stoically. If he was cold, it wasn't showing. "Not *cold*, but a bit chilly."

"We've been out in over a forty-degree heat for the last two months," the squad leader pointed out. "That tends to adjust your perspective."

"Uh-oh," Julian said, looking around. "I wonder how the scummies are handling this?

"What's wrong with him, Doc?" Prince Roger had awoken, shivering, to find Cord seated cross-legged in the tent, still and motionless. Repeated attempts to get the six-limbed, grizzly bear-sized Mardukan shaman to wake up had resulted only in slow groans.

"He's cold, Sir." The medic shook his head. "Really cold." Warrant Dobrescu pulled the monitor back from the Mardukan and shook his head again, his expression worried. "I need to go check the mahouts. If Cord is in this bad a shape, they're going to be worse. Their cover isn't as good."

"Is he going to be okay?" the anxious prince asked.

"I don't know. I suspect that he's probably sort of hibernating, but it's possible that if they get too cold something will shut down and kill them." Dobrescu took another breath and shook his head. "I've been meaning to do a really thorough study of Mardukan body chemistry and physiology. It looks like I waited a bit too long."

"Well, we need—" the prince began, only to break off at the sound of shouting from outside the tent. "Now what the hell is that?"

"Modderpockers, let me go!" Poertena shouted. He snarled at the laughing Marines who were crawling out of their one-person tents to sniff at the morning air. "Gimme a pocking hand, damn it!"

"Okay, everybody," St. John (J.) said, slowly clapping. "Let's give him a hand."

"Now that," Roger said, "is a truly disgusting *menage a . . . uh . . .*"

"*Menage a cinq* is the term you're looking for," Doc Dobrescu said, laughing as he walked over to the pinned armorer and the four comatose Mardukans wrapped tightly about his diminutive form.

Roger shook his head and chuckled, but he also waved to the Marines.

"Some of you guys, help the Doc."

St. John (J.) grabbed one of Denat's inert arms and started trying to disengage it from the armorer.

"This really is gross, Poertena," the Marine said as he tried to pull one of the slime-covered arms off the armorer.

"You pocking telling *me?* I wake up, and it not'ing but arms and *slime!*"

Roger began to haul on Tratan as the Mardukan groaned and resisted the pulling Marines.

"They seem to like you, Poertena."

"Well," the armorer's response sounded mildly strangled, "they tryin' to kill me now! Leggo!"

"They like his heat," the warrant officer grunted as he helped Roger heave, then said something unprintable under his breath and gave up. The united efforts of three Marines had so far been unable to get Denat to release his grip, and the bear hug actually did threaten to kill the armorer. "Somebody build a fire. Maybe if we warm them up, they'll let go."

"And somebody help me get Cord," Roger said, then thought about the weight of the Mardukan. "Several somebodies." He looked over to the picket lines where the mahouts made their camp. "Did anybody notice that the packbeasts are missing?" he asked, bemusedly.

❖   ❖   ❖

"We passed through a cold front," the medic said, shaking his head. "Or what passes for one on this screwy planet."

Captain Pahner had called a council of war to consider the night's events. The group sat near the edge of the camp, looking down on the forest of clouds that stretched into the distance from their foothills perch. Above them, the true mountains loomed trackless.

"What cold front?" Julian asked. "I didn't see any cold front."

"You remember that rain we had yesterday afternoon?" Dobrescu asked.

"Sure, but it rains all the time here," the NCO replied skeptically.

"But that one went on for a long time," Roger noted. "Usually, they just sort of hit in short spurts. That one rained, and rained, and rained."

"Right." The medic nodded. "And today, the air pressure is a few points higher than yesterday. Not much—this planet doesn't have much in the way of a weather system—but enough. Anyway, the cloud layer got suppressed," he gestured to the clouds, "the humidity fell, and the temperature . . ."

"Dropped like a rock," Pahner said. "We got that part. Can the locals handle it?"

The medic sighed and shrugged.

"That I don't know. Most terrestrial isothermic and posithermic creatures can survive to just above freezing temperatures as long as they don't stay that way too long. However, that's terrestrial." He shrugged again. "With Mardukans, Captain, your guess is probably as good as mine. I'm a doc, not an exobiologist."

He looked around at the camp, and especially at the *flar-ta*.

"The packbeasts, now, they seem to be better adapted. They burrowed underground last night on first watch and stayed there till things warmed back up. And their skin is different from the Mardukans', scaled and dry where the Mardukans' is smooth and mucous-coated. So I think the *packbeasts* can make it, if we stay below the freezing line. But I don't know about the locals," he finished unhappily, gesturing at Cord and the lead mahout.

They had been speaking in the dialect of Q'Nkok so that the two Mardukan representatives could follow the conversation. Now Cord clapped his hands and leaned forward.

"I can withstand the conditions of last night with *dinshon* exercises. However," he waved a true-hand at D'Len Pah, "the mahouts are not trained in them. Nor are any of my nephews, except Denat, and he poorly. Also," he pointed to patches on his skin, "it is terribly dry up here. And it will only get worse, from what Shaman Dobrescu says."

"So," said Pahner. "We have a problem."

"Yes," D'Len Pah said. The old mahout looked terrible in the light of midmorning. Part of that was the same dry patches that affected Cord, but the greater part was bitter shame. "We cannot do this much longer, Lord Pahner, Prince Roger. This is a terrible, terrible place. There is no air to breathe. The wind is as dry as sand. The cold is fierce and terrible." He looked up from the scratches he'd been making on the ground with his mahout stick. "We . . . cannot go any farther."

Pahner looked over at Roger and cleared his throat.

"D'Len Pah, we must cross these mountains. We must reach the far coast, or we will surely die. And we cannot leave our gear." He looked up at the towering peaks. "Nor can we carry it over the mountains without the *flar-ta*. It's not like we can call Harendra Mukerji for a resupply."

The lead mahout looked around nervously. "Lord Pahner . . ."

"Calmly, D'Len," Roger said. "Calmly. We won't take them from you. We aren't brigands."

"I know that, Prince Roger." The mahout clapped his hands in agreement. "But . . . it is a fearsome thing."

"We could . . ." Despreaux started to say, then stopped. With the loss of most of the senior NCOs, she was being groomed for the Third Platoon platoon sergeant's position. This was the first time she'd been included in one of the staff meetings, so she was nervous about making her suggestion.

"Go ahead," Eleanora O'Casey said with a nod, and the sergeant gave the prince's chief of staff a brief glance of thanks.

"Well . . . we could . . ." She stopped again and turned to D'Len Pah. "Could we *buy* the packbeasts from you?" She looked at Captain Pahner, whose face had tightened at the suggestion and shrugged. "I'm not saying that we will, I'm asking if we *could*."

Roger looked at Pahner. "If we *can*, we *will*," he said, and the Marine looked back at him with a careful lack of expression.

His Royal Highness, Prince Roger Ramius Sergei Alexander Chiang MacClintock, Heir Tertiary to the Throne of Man, had changed immeasurably from the arrogant, conceited, self-centered, *whiny* spoiled brat he'd been before a barely bungled assassination by sabotage had shipwrecked him and his Marine bodyguards on the hellhole called Marduk. For the most part, Pahner was prepared to admit that those changes had been very good things, because Bronze Battalion of The Empress' Own had been less than fond of the aristocratic pain in the ass it had been charged with protecting, and with excellent reason.

Pahner supposed that discovering that a dangerously

competent (and unknown) someone wanted you dead, and then coping with the need to march clear around an alien planet full of bloodthirsty barbarians in hopes of somehow taking that planet's sole space facility away from the traditional enemies of the Empire of Man who almost certainly controlled it, would have been enough to refocus anyone's thoughts. Given the unpromising nature of the preassassination-attempt Roger, that wasn't something Pahner would have cared to bet any money on, of course. And he more than suspected that he and the rest of Bravo Company owed a sizable debt of gratitude to D'Nal Cord. Roger's Mardukan *asi*—technically a slave, although anyone who made the mistake of confusing Cord with a menial probably wouldn't live long enough to realize he'd stopped breathing for some odd reason—was a deadly warrior who had become the prince's mentor, and not just where weapons were concerned. The native shaman was almost certainly the first individual ever to take Roger seriously as both prince and protégé, and the imprint of his personality was clear to see in the new Roger.

All of that was good. But it never would have occurred to the old, whiny Roger even to consider that such a thing as a debt of honor might exist between him and a troop of barbarian beast drovers on a backwoods planet of mud, swamp, and rain. Which, much as Pahner hated to admit it, would have been a far more convenient attitude on his part at this particular moment.

"Sir," he said tightly, "those funds will be needed for our expenses on the other side of the mountains. When we get out of here, we'll need to immediately resupply. That is *if* we don't run out on the way. Or have to turn back."

"Captain," Roger said steadily, sounding uncannily

like his mother in deadly reasonable mode, "we have to have the *flar-ta*, and we will *not* take them from mahouts who have stood by us through thick and thin. You yourself said that we're not brigands, and shouldn't act like them. So, what's the answer?"

"We *can* improve things for them," Gunny Jin said. "Wrap them in cloths so that they don't lose so much moisture. Put them in a tent with a warming stove at night. That sort of thing."

D'Len clapped his hands in regret. "I do not think I can convince my people to continue on. It is too terrible up here."

"If you think we can continue," Cord said, "my nephews will do so. I, of course, am *asi*. I shall follow Roger wherever it leads."

"Let's put it to a vote," Roger said to Pahner. "I won't say that we'll go with it either way, but I'd like to see what everyone thinks."

"All right," the captain agreed reluctantly. "I think, though, that we're going to need all of our funds on the far side of the mountain. Desperately. Still," he added with a shrug. "Despreaux?"

The junior NCO cleared her throat. "It was my idea."

"So noted," Pahner said with a smile. "I won't hold it against you. I take it that was a 'buy the beasts' vote?"

"Yes, Sir, but D'Len Pah hasn't said he'll sell."

"Good point," Roger said. "D'Len? Can we buy them from you?"

The old Mardukan hesitated, drawing his circles on the stony ground.

"We must have at least one to make it back to the forests," he temporized.

"Granted," Roger said promptly.

"And . . . they aren't cheap," the mahout added.

"Would you rather bargain with Captain Pahner or Poertena?" the prince asked.

"*Poertena?*" The mahout looked around wildly. "Not Poertena!"

"We'll strike a fair bargain," Pahner said severely. "If we decide to buy them." He thought about it for a moment. "Oh, hell. When. There isn't a choice, is there?"

"Not really, Captain," Roger said. "Not if we're going to make it over the mountains."

"So," the commander said to the mahout. "Are you willing to bargain for them? In gems, gold, and *dianda?*"

The mahout clapped his lower hands in resignation.

"Yes. Yes, we will. The *flar-ta* are like children to us. But you have been good masters; you will treat our children well. We will bargain for their worth." He lowered his head and continued, firmly. "But not with Poertena."

"Good t'ing they didn't know I was coaching you over tee poc—tee radio, Sir," Poertena said as they waved to the mahouts, slowly making their way back downslope.

"Yep," Roger agreed. "How'd I do?"

"We got pock— We got screwed."

"Hey," Roger said defensively. "Those things are priceless up here!"

"Yeah," Poertena agreed. "But t'ey takin' tee money down t'ere. We prob'ly pay twice what they *flar-ta* is worth. T'at more money than t'ey ever see in t'eir po . . . in their lives."

"True," Roger said. "I'm glad that Cranla went with them. Maybe he can keep people from taking it before they buy their new mounts."

"Sure," the armorer complained. "But now I out a fourth for spades. What I gonna do 'bout t'at?"

"Spades?" Roger asked. "What's spades?"

⋄   ⋄   ⋄

"I can' believe I get taken by my own pocking prince," Poertena grumped much later as he and Denat watched Roger walk away, whistling cheerfully while he counted his winnings.

"Well," Cord's nephew told him with a remarkable lack of sympathy, "you keep telling us there's a new sucker born every minute. You just didn't get around to mentioning that you were one of them!"

Cord raised the flap of the cover as the *flar-ta* came to a halt. The three remaining Mardukans had ridden the big packbeasts for the last several days while the humans had searched for a path through the mountains. To avoid the cold and desiccating dryness, the three had huddled under one of the hide tents. There, in a nest of wet rags, they had spent the day, warmed by the sun on the dark tents.

But as the packbeasts continued to stand motionless, Cord decided to brave the outside conditions. Pushing aside one of the moistened clumps of *dianda*, the shaman slipped out from under the tent and began to walk towards the front of the column, and Roger looked up and smiled as he approached.

"We might have hit a bit of luck," the prince said, gesturing at a pile of rocks. The cairn was clearly artificial, a fairly large pile of stones at the mouth of one of three valleys diverging from the river they'd been following.

The humans had been hunting back and forth in the mountains for a week and a half, looking for a relatively low way across. Several promising valleys had so far yielded only impossibly steep ascents. This valley would not have been considered promising, since it narrowed abruptly up ahead and bent sharply to the south out of sight. However, the existence of the cairn was indisputable.

"Could be some traveler's idea of a practical joke," Kosutic said dubiously. The sergeant major shook her head, looking up the narrow track. "And it'll be a bitch getting the beasts through there."

"But it's the first indication we've had that there's ever been anybody up here," Roger said stubbornly. "Why would anyone lie about the path?"

Pahner looked up at the path the valley might take.

"Looks like there's a glacier up there," he said. He nodded to the stream roaring out of the valley. "See how white the water is, Your Highness?"

"Yes," Roger said. "Oh. Yeah. I've seen that before."

"Snowmelt?" Kosutic asked.

"Glacial runoff," Pahner corrected. "Dust particles from the glacier grinding the mountains. At least part of this stream has its origin in a glacier." He looked at Cord and then back at the *flar-ta*. "I don't see them being able to make it in glacial conditions."

"There is that," Roger admitted, looking up at the snowy caps. "But we still need to check it out."

"Not *we*," Pahner said. "Sergeant Major?"

"Gronningen," she said instantly. "He's from Asgard, so he could care less about cold." She paused and thought. "Dokkum is from New Tibet. He should know something about mountains. And I'll take Damdin, too."

"Do it," Pahner said. "We'll make a solid camp here in the meantime." He looked around at the coniferlike trees. "At least there's plenty of wood."

Kosutic looked around the narrow defile with critical eyes. In the week since they'd started up the valley, they had yet to find a spot the packbeasts couldn't negotiate, but this was pushing it.

"You think they can get through?" Dokkum asked. The little Nepalese was taking the slow, steady steps he'd taught the others when they tried to take off like jackrabbits. The simple method of one step per breath was the only way to move in serious mountains. Anything else would wear humans to the bone between the thin air and steep slopes.

Kosutic measured the defile with the range finder in her helmet and looked at the ground. "So far. Much worse and the answer would be no."

"Heya!" Gronningen shouted. "Heya! By Jesus-Thor!" The big Asgardian was perched at the top of the slope, shaking his rifle overhead in both hands.

"Well, I think we found our pass," Kosutic said with a breathy chuckle.

"Damn," Roger said, looking at the view spread out below the company.

The last of the *flar-ta* were scrambling up the defile as he stepped aside to get a better look. The broad, U-shaped valley at their feet was clearly glacial shaped, and in the center of the deep bowl directly below them was an immense tarn, an upper mountain lake.

The water of the lake, still several thousand meters below their current altitude, was a deep, intense blue, like liquid oxygen. And it looked just about as cold. Given their surroundings, that was hardly surprising. What was a surprise, was the city on its shore.

The town was large, nearly as large as Voitan once had been, and did not fit the usual huddled-on-a-hilltop pattern of every other Mardukan city the humans had yet seen. This town frankly sprawled around the shores of the lake and well up the valley slopes above it.

"It looks like Como," Roger said.

"Or Shrinagar," O'Casey added quietly.

"Whichever it is," Pahner said, stepping out of the way of the beasts as well, "we need to get down to it. We've got less than a hundred kilos of barleyrice left, and our diet supplementals get a little lower every day."

"You're always such an optimist, Captain," Roger observed.

"No, I'm a pessimist. That's what your mother pays me to be," the Marine added with a smile. The smile quickly turned to a frown, however. "We have a smidgen of gold and a few gems left after we paid the mahouts. Oh, and some *dianda*. We need barleyrice, some wine, fruits, vegetables—everything. And salt. We're almost out of salt."

"We'll figure it out, Captain," the prince said. "You always do."

"Thanks—I think," the commander said sourly. "I guess we'll have to." He patted a pocket, but his store of gum was long gone. "Maybe they chew tobacco down there."

"Is that why you chew gum?" Roger asked in surprise.

"Sort of. I used to smoke pseudonic a *long* time ago. It's surprising how hard it is to kick that habit." The last of the *flar-ta* was trotting by, and the captain looked at the line passing down the defile. "I think we'd better hurry to get in front of the band."

"Yep," Roger agreed, looking at the distant city. "I'm really looking forward to getting to civilization."

"Let's not go too fast," Pahner cautioned as he started forward. "This is liable to be a new experience. Different hazards, different customs. These mountains are a fairly effective barrier, especially for a bunch of cold-blooded Mardukans, so these folks may not take all that kindly to strangers. We need to take it slow and careful."

"Slow down," Kosutic called. "The city isn't going anywhere."

The company had been moving through the twisting mountain valleys towards the distant city for the last two days. It turned out that the pass they'd exited from was on a different watershed, which had required some backtracking. The delay meant that they'd run out of fodder for the packbeasts, who were becoming increasingly surly about life in general.

Fortunately, they'd recently entered a flatter terrain of moraines and alluvial wash. It was well forested, and by slowing down they'd been able to let the *flar-ta* forage. But that only worked if the point kept the pace down.

"Gotcha, Sergeant Major," Liszez replied over his helmet com, and slowed down, pausing for a moment to look around.

The path they were following was wide for a game trail, and well beaten. The vegetation was open on either side, and the lower limbs of the coniferlike evergreens had been stripped off by some forager, which permitted good sight distance . . . unlike the damn jungle.

He'd stopped at the edge of an open area. It looked like whatever had been eating on the trees had used the clearing for rooting, because the ground was torn up and turned over in every direction. It was also fairly smooth, however, and the path continued on the other side.

The morning was clear and cool, with the dew just coming off the bushes. This area was a blessed relief for the company, but they still wanted to keep moving. Not only did they look forward to a respite in the city, but the faster they went, the sooner they would reach the coast.

The coast was, of course, only an intermediate stop, but it had begun to loom large in the minds of the company. The coast was an end in itself now, and on maps it looked like they were nearly there. They weren't. At best, it was weeks away through the jungles on *this* side of the mountains, but at least it was getting closer and closer. And that was a damned good thing, Liszez told himself, because good as their nanites were at extracting usable nutrition from the most unlikely sources, there were limits in all things. The severe losses the company had taken at Voitan and Marshad "helped" a good bit, in a gruesomely ironic sort of way, because each dead Marine had been one less charge on the priceless cache of vitamin and protein supplements packed on the animals and on their own backs. Fewer mouths meant they could stretch their stores further, but once the stores were gone, they were gone . . . and the shipwrecked humans were dead. So the sooner they could get their butts aboard a ship and set sail, the better.

Liszez looked over his shoulder and decided the column had closed up enough. He reminded himself to keep the pace down, checked his surroundings for threats, and moved out. On his third step, the ground erupted.

Roger looked at the trees. The stripped bark reminded him of something, and he glanced at his *asi*.

"Cord, these trees . . ."

"Yes. *Flar-ke*. We need to be careful," the shaman said.

Pahner had finally convinced the prince that the lead packbeast was not a place for the commander to be, but Roger still insisted on driving Patty and covering the column with his big eleven-millimeter magnum hunting rifle. So far in the mountains the only hazards had been inanimate, but Marduk had taught them not to let their guards down, and the prince keyed his radio on the reserve command frequency.

"Captain, Cord says that this area is *flar-ke* territory. Like where we first met him."

Pahner didn't reply for a moment, and Roger

remembered the Marine's incandescent rage on that long ago day. The prince never had explained to the captain that the company's free-flow com net had been so unfamiliar—and confusing—to him at the time that he genuinely hadn't heard the Marine's order not to fire at the *flar-ke* which had been pursuing Cord. It had been Roger's very first personal experience with a full-fledged tongue lashing, and Pahner's fury had been so intense that the prince had decided that anything which sounded like an excuse would have been considerably worse than useless.

At the same time, even if he *had* heard the order, he would have taken the shot anyway. He knew that. And he hadn't taken it to save Cord, either—no one had even known the shaman was there to be saved. No. He'd fired because he'd hunted more types of dangerous wild game than most people in the galaxy even realized existed, and he'd recognized the territorial strop markings on the trees in the area. Markings very like those which surrounded them now . . .

"I see," the captain said finally, and Roger knew the same memories had been passing through the older man's mind. They'd never discussed the episode again, and Roger sometimes wondered how much that owed to the fact that the *flar-ke* so closely resembled—physically at least—the *flar-ta* packbeasts with which the company had become intimately familiar. *Flar-ta* could be extremely dangerous in threat situations, but the huge herbivores were scarcely aggressive by nature, and a part of the captain had to have noted the relative passivity of the *flar-ta* and transposed it to the *flar-ke*, at least subconsciously, as proof that he'd been right to order his troops not to fire. The old Roger probably wouldn't even have considered that point, but the new one recognized that Pahner had no more taste for admitting he might have been wrong than anyone else. That was a very natural trait, but one which was an uncomfortable fit in a man like the captain, who had an acutely developed—one might almost say *overdeveloped*—sense of responsibility. Which was one reason Roger had never brought the matter up again. He'd learned not only to respect but to admire the Marine, and he was determined to let sleeping dogs lie rather than sound as if he were defending past actions . . . or trying to rub Pahner's nose in a possible error.

"He's really worried," Roger said diffidently into the fresh silence.

"I know he is," Pahner replied. "He's said often enough that however much they may look like *flar-ta*, they're completely different. I just wish I knew exactly how that worked."

"The closest parallel I can think of is probably the Cape buffalo back on Earth, Captain," Roger offered. "To someone who's not familiar with them, Cape buffaloes look an awful lot like regular water buffaloes. But water buffaloes aren't aggressive; Cape buffaloes *are*. In fact, kilo for kilo, they're probably the most aggressive and dangerous beasts on Terra. I kid you not—there are dozens of documented cases of Cape buffaloes actually turning the tables and hunting down the game hunters."

"Got it," Pahner said in a completely different tone, and switched to the company frequency. "Company, listen up—" he began, just in time for the first screams to interrupt him.

Kosutic never knew how she survived the first few seconds. The beast that erupted out of the ground caught Liszez with a tuskhorn and threw the grenadier through the air to land in a sodden, bone-shattered lump. The Marine didn't even bounce, and the animal couldn't have cared less. It was too busy charging straight at the sergeant major.

Somehow, she found herself propelled to one side of the beast by a muscle-tearing turn and dive that landed her on one shoulder, and she'd flipped the selector of the bead rifle to armor piercing even before she hit the ground.

The tungsten-cored beads penetrated the heavily armored scaled hide which the standard beads would only have cratered, and the creature screamed in rage. It pivoted on its axis, but the NCO had other problems to deal with—an entire herd of the giant beasts had burst out of the ground and was stampeding towards the company.

They were very similar in appearance to the packbeasts, but with months of Mardukan experience behind her, the differences were now obvious to the sergeant major. The *flar-ta* looked somewhat like a cross between a triceratops and a horned toad, but the armor on their forequarters was actually fairly light, their horned head shield did not extend much beyond the neck, and their fore and rear quarters were more or less balanced. These creatures were larger by at least a thousand kilos each, and their side armor was thicker than the cross section of a human forearm where it covered the shoulders and heart region. The head shield extended far enough up and back that a mahout would never have been able to see over the top, and their forequarters were immensely strong.

The sergeant major avoided a stamp from one of those sequoia-thick legs and spun again to dodge the flail of a tuskhorn. She straightened and put three more rounds into the head shield, and watched in disbelief as at least two of them bounced off the unbelievably refractory bone armor.

The corner of her eye caught a flicker that sent her flipping backwards in a maneuver she never could have made practicing, and the space she'd just been in was overrun by another of the giant horned toads. She dodged and rolled twice more as the herd thundered past, then flipped the bead rifle to burst and began hammering the one she'd been battling.

The beast charged at her, and she dodged again. But it had learned the first time and turned with her. The sergeant major knew she was dead and tried desperately to twist aside but she couldn't quite evade the tuskhorn that . . .

. . . suddenly rolled sideways as Patty plowed into the larger beast at full speed.

Roger pumped three fatal rounds into the exposed underbelly of the wounded beast, then leaned over to offer the sergeant major a hand.

"Come *on!*" he shouted, and jabbed the packbeast in the neck the instant the NCO's hand locked onto his wrist. "*Hiya!* Come on, you stupid bitch! Let's get out of here!"

The beast spun on its axis with a bellowing hiss and charged back towards the embattled company. Patty appeared to have forgotten that she was a *flar-ta*. She was on the warpath, and the mountains had better beware.

Pahner swore vilely as Roger's packbeast accelerated straight towards the stampeding giants.

"Action front!" he called over the company frequency. He saw a couple of javelins skitter off the armored front of the charging beasts and shook his head. Most of the company had one magazine of ammunition left. If they used that up, there was no way they could take the spaceport. But if they all died here, it wouldn't matter.

"Weapons free! Armor piercing—do it!" He dodged a milling packbeast as he pulled his own rifle off his shoulder. "Move the packbeasts forward! Use them as a wall!"

He had a brief flash of Roger hitting the avalanche of *flar-ke*. By some miracle, the boy was able to convince his mount to go through the charge rather than ramming one of them head-on. As they passed the head of the column there was a glimpse of the prince pumping fire into the stampede; then he disappeared into the dust.

The experienced CO knew a moment of despair. The charge had hit them from the front and come on, headfirst, down the long axis of the column. That meant the Marines could target only the head shields, which were the most heavily armored part of the attacking beasts, and the fire that was starting to pour into the charge was having negligible effect. He saw a single beast go down, but in another moment the company would be engulfed in a charge of elephants, because nothing was going to stop them.

The first grenades started to fall into the mass, but not even that was enough to turn them. And the only way to kill them was to hit them from the side. It took just a moment for a thought to percolate through his shock, and his sense of guilt for the lives that momentary delay cost would live with him the rest of his life.

"*On the packbeasts!*" he yelled, grabbing for a dangling strap on the *flar-ta* he'd been dodging and swinging himself frantically aboard. "*Everybody on the packbeasts!*"

The stampede hit like a meat and bone avalanche. From his precarious perch, Pahner saw dozens of the Marines go down under the feet and tusks of the giant lizards. But many—most—of the others were scrambling onto the company's mounts.

Even that wasn't the most secure situation, but at

least it gave them a fighting chance as the enraged *flar-ke* charged clear through the company, then turned to charge right back. The good news was that they didn't seem to realize which was the greater danger and directed their fury at the packbeasts rather than the insignificant humans who were actually hurting them, and they slammed into the *flar-ta* like lethal, ancient locomotives. The thudding of massive impacts and screams and shrieks of animal rage and pain filled the universe, but the company's bead rifles were finally able to come into play in the melee. As one of the giant herbivores charged, massed fire from the Marines perched on its flank would smash into it from the side. They were using ammunition like water, but it was that or die.

The situation was a complete madhouse. The Marines, some surviving afoot, some perched on packbeasts, some even having attained the safety of the treetops, poured fire into the rampaging herd. At the same time, the *flar-ke* were charging and slashing at the company's packbeasts and the Marines who'd been dismounted.

Pahner spun from side to side, snapping orders for concentrations of fire where he could, then looked up just in time to see Roger come charging into the melee. Where and how the prince had learned to use a *flar-ta* as a war steed was a complete mystery, but he was the only member of the company who seemed at home in the maelstrom.

He'd apparently picked his target from outside the mass, and he and his mount charged in at full speed. The impact when the galloping Patty hit the larger beast was a carnal earthquake.

The target squealed in agony as the *flar-ta's* tuskhorns penetrated its side armor and slammed it down to its knees. As the sergeant major poured fire into the *flar-ke* to either side of them, Roger pumped rounds into the exposed underbelly of Patty's target. Then, using nothing more than words and thumping heels, he backed the packbeast off its victim and charged back out of the mass to wind up for another run.

Pahner slapped Aburia, who was driving his own beast, on the back of her head.

"Get us out of here! Try to line us up for a charge!"

"Yes, Sir!"

The corporal goaded the beast into a lumbering run, and dismounted Marines dashed in from either side as they cantered through the melee. Pahner snatched them up as they came alongside, snapping orders and passing over his own ammunition.

As he cleared the last embattled pair of behemoths he heard another thunder of flesh headed into the battle. Roger was back.

"I wish the mahouts were here," Berntsen said as he hacked at a ligament.

"Why?" Cathcart asked. The corporal wiped at his face with the shoulder of his uniform. Everything else was coated in blood.

"They used to do this."

The company had halted in the open area created by the burrowing beasts and set up defenses. With this much meat around, scavengers were bound to come swarming in, but the unit could go no further. The casualties had been brutal . . . again.

The friendly Nepalese, Dokkum, who'd taught them all about mountains, would never see New Tibet again. Ima Hooker would never make another joke about her name. Kameswaran and Cramer, Liszez and Eijken, the list went on and on.

"Tell you one thing," Cathcart said. "Rogo was right the first time. These motherfuckers are bad news."

"Yeah," the private admitted, pulling on the heavy skin of the dead beast. "He was right all along."

"You were right back on the plateau, Roger," Pahner said, shaking his head over the casualties laid out inside the perimeter. "These are not packbeasts."

"Like the difference between buffaloes," Roger repeated wearily.

He'd just finished sewing up Patty's wounds, using the kit the mahouts had left and a general antibiotic provided by Doc Dobrescu. He'd been forced to do the work himself, because no one else could get near the grumpy beast.

"Cape and water, you mean?" Dobrescu asked, walking up and sitting down on a splintered tree trunk.

"You were saying something about them just before it all fell into the crapper," Pahner said. "I'd never heard of them before."

"You're not from Earth," Roger pointed out. "Of course, most people on Earth never heard of them, either."

"They have in Africa," Dobrescu said with a bitterly ironic chuckle.

"So what are they?" Pahner asked, sitting down himself.

"They're a ton of mean is what they are," Roger said. "You go out after buffalo, and you take your life in your hand. If they scent you, they'll swing around behind and sneak up on you. Before you know it, you're dead."

"I thought buffaloes ate grass."

"That doesn't mean they're friendly," Roger told the captain tiredly. " 'Herbivore' doesn't automatically equate to 'cowardly.' " He gestured at the mounded bodies of the *flar-ke*. "Capetoads," he snorted.

"What?" Pahner asked. There were a million things

to do, but at the moment they were getting done. He was, for once, going to just let the camp run.

"They look like horned toads, but they're nasty as Cape buffalo." Roger shrugged. "Capetoads."

"Works for me," Pahner agreed. He sniffed at the smells coming from the cooking area. "And it appears that we're about to find out what they taste like."

"One guess," Dobrescu said, with a grunt of effort as he shoved himself to his feet.

As it turned out, they tasted very much like chicken.

CHAPTER TWO

"Now that's something you don't see every day," Julian said tiredly.

"I guess you do around here," Despreaux replied.

The beast looked like nothing so much as a bipedal dinosaur. A *large* bipedal dinosaur, with short forelimbs and extremely atrophied mid limbs . . . and a rider.

"Cool," Kyrou said. "Horse-ostriches."

The rider reined in in front of the company, said something in a loud voice, and raised a hand for them to stop. The reins, which led to a bridle arrangement much like that for a horse, were held with the falsehands, leaving the upper hands available for things like imperious gestures . . . or weapons, and Kosutic walked forward, holding up her own open hands.

"Ms. O'Casey to the front, please," she called over the company frequency. "I can't get a bit of what this guy is saying."

"On my way," the academic's voice replied, and Kosutic returned her attention to the mounted

27

Mardukan. He was clearly a guardsman of some sort, for he was heavily armed and armored. Not that the arms and armor bore any resemblance at all to the equipment in common use on the far side of the mountains. He also looked like a tough customer who wasn't entirely pleased to see them, and the sergeant major clasped her hands before her in the nearest approximation to a Mardukan gesture of polite greeting a human's mere two arms could achieve.

"Our interpreter is on her way," the Marine said pleasantly in the trade tongue commonly used throughout the Hadur. There was no way in the world that the local was going to understand her, of course, but she hoped the tone and body language would get through, at least.

It seemed to work, for the guardsman gave her a Mardukan nod, lowered his raised hand, and settled back to wait. He still didn't seem overjoyed by her company, but his own body language indicated that he was willing to be patient . . . up to a point, at least.

The sergeant major took advantage of the delay to study her surroundings. She rather suspected that the locals had known they were coming at least a little in advance, for the mounted soldier had intercepted them just as they emerged from the dense tree cover higher up the mountain on the edge of their destination's cultivated fields.

The peasants tending those fields had looked up at the commotion, turning from their drudgery for a bit of distraction. They wore dark colored robes that covered them from head to foot. The rough, dark cloth was wet in patches, and as they stopped, several unstopped water bags and wet themselves down. It was obvious how the locals dealt with the, for humans, pleasant dryness of the plateau.

The plants they were tending were thoroughly

unfamiliar, however—some sort of low climbers, staked up on pole-and-string arbors. They were also in flower, and the heavy scent of the millions of flowers drifted across the company like a blanket.

In addition to their odd dress and plants, the locals had the first beasts of burden—other than *flar-ta*—the humans had seen in their entire time on Marduk. The elephant-sized packbeasts were unsuited to any sort of agricultural use, but some of the local peasants were plowing one of the nearby fields, and instead of the teams of natives which would have been pulling the plows on the far side of the mountains, they were using low, six-limbed beasts clearly related—distantly, at least—to the "horse-ostrich" ridden by the guard.

Kosutic looked away from the natives as Eleanora O'Casey walked up beside her and gave the local a closed-mouth smile and a double hand clap of greeting. The march had toughened the prince's chief of staff to a degree the little academic would have thought flatly impossible before she'd hit Marduk, and she'd become thin and wiry as a gnarly root, with knotlike muscles rippling up and down her forearms.

"We are travelers passing through your land," she said, using the same trade tongue Kosutic had used. "We wish to trade for supplies."

She knew the local wouldn't understand a word, but that was fine. The original, extremely limited Mardukan language kernel in the linguistics program she'd loaded into her toot had acquired a far wider database during their travels. It was much more capable than it had been, and if she could only get him to talk to her a bit, it would quickly begin finding points of commonality.

The guardsman gobbled back at her. His tone was stern, almost truculent, but the words still didn't mean a thing, and she concentrated on looking inoffensive as she nodded to encourage him to continue speaking while she studied him. His primary weapon was a long, slim lance, five or six meters long, with a wicked four-bladed head. The lance's point was oddly elongated, and the chief of staff finally decided that was probably to help it pierce the tough armor of the capetoads. It made sense. The giant herbivores were undoubtedly a major pest in the area.

In addition to the lance, the rider had a long, straight-bladed sword sheathed on his saddle. The weapon would have been the equivalent of a medieval two-handed sword, but since Mardukans were nearly twice the height of humans, this weapon was nearly three meters long.

The last two accouterments were the most startling. First, the rider was armored in chain mail with a back and breast cuirass and armored greaves on thighs, shins, and forearms. The overall covering of armor was in stark contrast to the leather and gabardine apron-armor of the Hadur and Hurtan.

Second—and even more interesting—was the large pistol or short carbine stuck in a holster on the saddle. The weapon was of the crudest possible design, but the workmanship was exquisite. It was clearly made from some sort of blued steel, rather than the simpler iron in near universal use on the far side of the mountains, and the brass of the butt was as pale as summer grass. Nor was it the matchlock arquebus she'd expected. Instead of a length of slow match which had to be lit ahead of time and then used to ignite the weapon's priming, this pistol clearly was fitted with the Mardukan equivalent of what had been called a wheel lock on Earth. No doubt that only made sense for a mounted warrior, but coupled with the armor, it clearly indicated a remarkably advanced metal-working industry.

No, they definitely weren't in Kansas anymore.

The soldier reached an apparent stopping point in whatever he was saying, jabbed a hand back the way the company had come, and asked a sharp-toned question.

"Sorry," she told him apologetically. "I'm afraid I still can't quite understand you, but I think we're making some progress."

In fact, the software was signaling a partial match, although it was still well short of true recognition or fluency. The local language appeared to be at least partly derivative of the language used by the natives living around the distant spaceport, but that didn't mean much. The software would have gotten the same similarity between Mandarin and Native American. It just showed that this area was divorced from the region—and language families—across the mountains behind the company. Still, she thought she had enough to make a start, at least.

"We come in peace," she repeated, using as many of the local words as possible and substituting those from the original kernel where local ones were unavailable. "We are simple traders." The last word was part of the language the soldier had been using. "Captain Pahner," she called over her radio, "could you have someone bring up a bolt of *dianda*? I want to show him that we're trading, not raiding. We probably look like an invasion force."

"Got it," Pahner replied, and a moment later Poertena came trotting forward with a bolt of their remaining *dianda*. The beautifully woven silk-flax had turned out to be an excellent trade good throughout the Hadur region, and she hoped it would be as well received here.

Poertena handed one end of the bolt to Kyrou, and the two of them spread it out, being careful to keep the cloth off the ground. The result was all that

O'Casey could have hoped. The guard fell silent, then dropped the reins of his mount to the ground, seated the lance in a holder, and dismounted with the sort of casual grace which always struck a human as profoundly odd in someone the size of a Mardukan.

". . . this . . . cloth . . . where?" he asked.

"From the area we just came from," O'Casey said, gesturing over her shoulder towards the mountains. "We have a large amount of it to trade, along with other goods."

"Bebi," Poertena said, guessing what would interest their greeter, "go get me one of t'ose swords we gots left from Voitan."

The corporal nodded and disappeared, returning a moment later with the weapon rolled in a chameleon cloth cover. Poertena unrolled it, and the ripple pattern of Damascene steel was clearly recognized by the Mardukan cavalryman, who exclaimed at the beauty of the blade. He glanced at O'Casey for permission, then picked up the weapon at her handclap of agreement. It had a broad, curved blade, somewhere between a saber and a scimitar, and he waved it back and forth, then grunted a word in laughter.

"What'd he say?" Poertena asked. "I t'ink it important."

"I don't know," O'Casey said.

The Mardukan saw their evident confusion and repeated the word, gesturing at the sky and the fields around them, at the mountains, and then at the sword in his true-hand.

"Well," O'Casey said, "two things. We now have the local word for 'beauty' and agree on definitions. I'm pretty sure he just said that it's as beautiful as the sky, as beautiful as the flowers of spring and the soaring mountains."

"Oh." Poertena chuckled. "I t'ink we gonna do okay tradin' here."

"Come meet our leader," Eleanora invited, gesturing for the rider to accompany her, and the guard gave the blade back to Bebi reluctantly as he turned to follow the chief of staff.

"I am Eleanora O'Casey," she said. "I did not catch your name."

"Sen KaKai," the Mardukan said. "A rider of Ran Tai. You apparently understand our language now?"

"We have a remarkable facility for learning other languages after listening for a bit," the chief of staff replied, putting enough of a grunt into her laugh to make it clear she was chuckling.

"So I see, indeed." The guard chuckled in response, but his eyes were busy as he examined the small force of humans. "You are . . . oddly armed," he commented, waving at their hybrid Roman-Mardukan weaponry.

"Conditions are very different on the far side of the mountains," O'Casey told him. "But that region isn't our original land, either. We come from very far away, and we were forced to adapt local equipment to our needs. None of these swords and spears are our customary weapons."

"Those would be the guns on your soldiers' backs," the guard guessed.

"Yes," the chief of staff replied briefly. She looked across at the heavily armored cavalryman. "Your armor is closer to what we're familiar with," she said, and he nodded.

"Your equipment is quite unusual," was his only comment, then his gaze sharpened as he saw the bulging skins lashed atop the packbeasts. "Are those *sin-ta* skins?" he asked in obvious surprise.

"Uh, yes. Or, at least, I imagine they are, although we call the beasts *flar-ke*, not *sin-ta*. We were attacked by a herd of them just up the valley." O'Casey paused. "I hope they weren't a . . . uh, protected herd."

"Hardly," Sen Kakai said, his eyes round as he noted the size and numbers of tuskhorns beside the skins. "That herd had just moved into the area. It was one of the reasons I was patrolling up here. I'm sorry about your greeting, by the way. We've been having some problems lately."

"Problems?" the chief of staff asked as they approached the command group. "What sorts?"

"It's been hard, lately," the guardsman replied. "Very hard times."

Eleanora thought about that as the introductions were made all around. She also thought about an ancient Chinese curse which she was beginning to think had been specifically created for Bravo Company. Even if it hadn't been, it was certainly an excellent fit, and speaking simply for herself, she was thoroughly tired of living "in interesting times."

The caravansary was set on the edge of the main market. The cries of the vendors carried over the walls of the large hotel and stable and all the way to the third-story room the command group occupied.

The open window looked out over the flat roofs of the city and the lake beyond. A constant wind blew from the lake and across the city, following the river that flowed down the slope to the distant jungles and carrying the scent of the spices for which the region was famous to the window.

The reason for Ran Tai's existence had become clear on the walk to the town—as clear as the broad, carefully cultivated fields of nearpeppers that spread in every direction. It turned out that the spice, an important component of many of the dishes that Matsugae fixed, could be raised only in high, dry environments. That made it extremely expensive on a planet whose sentient species required high humidity and temperatures, and its cultivation and preparation, along with a few other spices, was the basis of half of the region's income.

The other basis was mining. The mountains were a major source of gold, silver, and iron. There were also small concentrations of gems scattered through the hills around the city, most in alluvial deposits. The combination made Ran Tai a rich, if harsh, town.

But it was a town with a problem.

"Maybe there's been a change in the weather patterns," O'Casey said, shaking her head. "That's one of the few things I could think of that would explain invasions on the scale these people seem to be talking about."

"We don't want to have another set-to with the Kranolta," Roger said definitely.

"Oh, Satan, no," Kosutic agreed, rubbing the still-fresh scars on her arm. "I'd rather go toe-to-toe with a Saint strike force than face up to those Kranolta bastards again. The damned Saints at least know when they're beat."

"Well, these aren't like Kranolta, exactly," O'Casey told her. "Or not like *our* Kranolta, anyway. The Kranolta were a fading force by the time we met them. From the description, these seem to be more like the Kranolta when they first swarmed over Voitan."

"Oh, great!" Julian gave a slightly hysterical chuckle. "New, fresh Kranolta instead of tired, worn-out Kranolta!"

"This group," O'Casey went on, "is apparently coming from the same hill country up on the edge of the northern plains that the Kranolta spread from, but the Kranolta found a gap in the mountain barrier over here, where it flattens out to the east." She gestured at the low detail map, pointing at the far northern region of the huge continent they had been crossing and tracing the dividing mountain range Sen Kakai had called the Tarstens with a fingertip.

"These Boman are pretty much more of the same, but they seem to be distinct from them in several ways. The most obvious one, of course, is that they *haven't* found a way around the Tarstens—they seem to have hit the range and slid along it to the west, instead. They also seem to have started their migration somewhat later than the Kranolta, and their weaponry is significantly different. The Kranolta didn't have gunpowder, but at least some of these Boman use arquebuses, although I suppose they might have gotten them from trading with this area.

"Actually, the Boman—like the Kranolta—seem more like a loose confederation of tribes than anything we might call a unified force, and there appear to be varying levels of technology among different tribes. For example, the tribesmen who apparently act as the leading edge of their movement are considerably more primitively armed than what we might call the 'core' tribes who give their invasion its real weight, with traditional muscle-powered projectile weapons instead of firearms. You might think of them as, um . . . skirmishers, I suppose. Lightly armed and expendable, filtering forward like tentacles to feel out the local opposition and opportunities."

"Great," Pahner said with a dry chuckle. "More Fuzzy-Wuzzies and their shovel-headed spears. So what's driving them? Why have they begun their invasion now? When we're passing through?"

"I can't tell you that," the historian admitted, shaking her head. "Certainly not with any degree of confidence. The motivations of barbarian expansions aren't always clear, but I wasn't joking when I said that there may have been a change of weather. On the other hand, it could be simply a matter of a particularly effective tribal leader looking to carve himself the local equivalent of a Mongol empire. Or it could be that a climate shift has permitted them a higher than normal reproductive rate, providing an expansion in military age manpower. Or it could be the converse—a weather shift which is putting a squeeze on their ability to feed their people where they are and fueling a survival-oriented migration." She shrugged. "Whatever's causing it, they're sweeping down through this region, crushing everything in their path and pushing other tribes ahead of them."

"Which is why the guard was so nervous," Roger said, taking a bite out of something the natives called a *targhas* and which seemed to fill the same niche the ubiquitous kate fruit had filled on the southern side of the Tarsten Mountains. The company had become very fond of the kate fruits, but the kiwi-dates seemed unknown in this region, as did *dianda*. Barleyrice, luckily, was common to both sides of the mountain range, but Roger already missed the kates. The *targhas* had a completely different taste and texture—more like a persimmon crossed with a hairy-skinned crab apple—and he wondered what the troops would dub this one. Persapples? Crabsimmons? Apsimons?

"They've probably got raiders coming up from the jungle as these new barbarians push in," he continued, "and eventually, the Boman themselves are liable to get down here, as well."

"We need to resupply." Pahner looked over at Poertena. "Is that going to be a problem?"

"I been checkin' prices in tee market." The armorer shook his head. "We can get good prices for tee *dianda*. Goood prices. But tee barleyrice is all brought up from tee jungle." He shook his head again. "Food 'round here is expensive."

"So we buy what we need to get to the jungles, then

buy the rest down on the plains," Pahner said, then paused as the armorer shook his head. "No?"

"They harvests is po—messed up." The Pinopan shrugged. "Barleyrice is hard to find, even down on tee plain. We walkin' into another war, Cap'n. Food, it's gonna be hard to find."

"Wonderful." The captain sighed and looked at the ceiling. "Just once, could something go right?" he asked God.

"If it did, you'd figure there was a catch," Roger told him. "Okay, so the bottom line is that we need more cash?"

"We could use it, yes, Sir," the Pinopan said. "Tee barleyrice is gonna be expensive, and t'at don't count tee fruit or spices."

"I would like to get quite a bit of those," Matsugae said. Roger's valet usually attended these meetings, partly to make sure that everyone had refreshments, but also as the expedition's head cook and true logistics manager. "The nearpeppers in the markets around here are absolutely fabulous. Also, there are some other spices that I'd like to get a few dozen kilos of. I've already spotted some very good dishes that I want to try. And we should also think about hiring some camp help, even if they're not mahouts."

"That takes cash, Matsugae," Pahner said pessimistically. "If we hadn't had to buy the *flar-ta*, it would be one thing. But the treasury's pretty bare. We have enough for now, but there's no apparent source in the future."

"So we raise some cash." Roger shrugged. "We've been doing that all along."

"I hope we're not going to have to take any more towns," Gunnery Sergeant Lai said. "The last one was bad enough for me."

"No towns," Roger agreed. "But," he continued,

sitting up, "we need money, and we're a top-notch combat unit. There's a massive migratory movement going on, and lots of fighting because of it. There should be a high-paying mission around here that we can do with minimal casualties."

"You're talking about becoming mercenaries," Pahner said incredulously.

"Captain, what else were we in Marshad? Or, for that matter, Q'Nkok?" the prince asked with a shrug.

"We were Bravo Company of the Bronze Battalion," the captain replied with a tight smile, "forced by circumstances to fight. Then taking payment for services rendered because it made sense to. We were not common goddamned mercenaries!"

"Well, Captain," Roger said quietly, "do *you* have a better alternative?"

The Marine started to open his mouth, then closed it with a snap. After a moment, he shook his head.

"No. But I don't think we've sunk low enough to be mercenaries."

"Poertena," Roger said. "Do we have the funds to buy enough barleyrice to make it to the coast?"

The armorer looked from the prince to his company commander wildly. "Hey, You' Highness, don' get me in t'is!"

"Yes, Roger," Pahner said tightly. "We do. But eventually we'll run out of cash. Of course, we can forage once we hit the jungles. That will eke out supplies a little longer."

"Which will double our travel time," Roger pointed out mildly, one eyebrow raised. "And wear down the *flar-ta*. And use up our dietary supplements. Not to mention that we'll undoubtedly be out of funds when we reach the coast . . . and need to charter or buy ships for the next stage."

"Captain," Kosutic said, and paused. "We . . . might

have to think about this. There's more than just the barleyrice to consider. The troops need a break, and I don't mean sitting in the jungle. They could use some downtime in the city, drink a little wine, do a little shouting. And not having to forage would really speed up the march. It . . . might make sense to look around for a . . . job. But it would have to pay enough to matter."

Roger looked at Pahner and could see that he was thoroughly pissed by the situation. He smiled gently at the commander of his bodyguards and shook his head again.

"What was it you told me? 'Sometimes we have to do things we don't like.' I think this might be one of those times. And I also think that whatever we do to get me home is within the mission parameters. We need cash to do that, so this is within the parameters. And as a last point," he added with a broader smile, "if we don't get Kostas his nearpeppers and spices, he might go all sulky." He winked at his valet, who returned the look blandly.

Pahner regarded the tertiary heir to the throne of the Empire of Man darkly. It had been a vast relief when Roger finally accepted that there truly was nothing—literally nothing at all—more vital than returning him safely to the imperial court on Terra. The captain knew that it had been hard for the prince to come to grips with the notion that his life was that important, given the estrangement which had existed between himself and his mother, the empress, for as long as he could remember. The simple fact was that Roger had believed no one in the entire universe, with the sole exception of Kostas Matsugae, had given much of a good goddamn for him. Which, Pahner had to admit, had been true in many ways. Even, he had come to realize, in Roger's own case, for the prince hadn't much cared for the spoiled, petulant brat he'd seen in his own mirror each day. If anyone had ever sat down and explained to him the reason his father had been banished from court things might have been different, but it had become painfully clear that no one ever had. Personally, Pahner suspected that Eleanora O'Casey was right—everyone had simply assumed that someone *else* had explained his father's inept conspiracies against the throne to him.

No one had, however, and the fact that Roger was the very mirror image of his incredibly handsome, incredibly spoiled playboy father had made things immeasurably worse. Since everyone "knew" Roger was aware of the reasons for his father's disgrace, they'd assumed that the fact that he seemed bent on turning himself into a physical duplicate of that father represented some sort of declaration of defiance . . . or worse. Nobody except Matsugae had ever guessed how much of Roger's "spoiled brat" exterior had been the almost inevitable response of a little boy who had never understood why no one seemed to trust—or love—him to the pain of his loneliness. Certainly no one in Bravo Company had ever guessed just how much more there might be inside him before events in Voitan and Marshad.

But like the other changes in his personality, Roger's new awareness of the realities of the political instability which plagued the Empire of Man, and of the fact that the MacClintock Dynasty truly was the only glue holding that empire together, had proved to have a nasty double edge from the perspective of the commander of his personal security detachment. It meant that the prince had finally learned to accept that there truly was a reason he had to allow his bodyguards to die if that was what it took to keep *him* alive, and also that nothing could be allowed to stand in the way of his return home. But it had also brought the famous

MacClintock ruthless practicality to the surface. If nothing could be allowed to stand in the way, then by the same token, there was nothing he was not prepared to do . . . including turning Pahner's beloved Bravo Company into raggedy-assed mercenaries on a planet full of barbarians.

The captain knew that, and the prince's reasonable and all too logical arguments didn't make him feel one bit better about it. He glowered at Roger for a moment longer, then turned to the two gunnery sergeants.

"What do you think?"

"I don't want to take any more casualties if we don't absolutely have to," Lai said immediately. "We've got quite a way to go and a battle at the end. We need to keep that in mind." But after a moment she shrugged. "Having said that, I have to side with His Highness. We do need the cash. And the downtime."

The captain nodded, then turned to the other gunny. "Jin?"

"Yeah," the Korean said. "I gotta go with the merc idea. But it's gotta pay." He looked up at his CO. "Sorry, Cap'n."

"Well," Pahner said, patting his breast pocket. "It looks like I'm outvoted."

"This isn't a democracy, as I believe you've pointed out once or twice," Roger said mildly, propping himself sideways. "If you say 'no,' the answer is no."

The Marine sighed. "I can't say 'no.' You're right. That doesn't mean I have to like it, though."

"Tell you what," the prince offered, sitting up straight. "We'll handle it. You just sit back and make sure we don't screw up. That way you can imagine it wasn't really Bravo Company that did it." He smiled to take away any sting in the words.

"We can do it 'incognito,'" he continued. "I won't be 'Prince Roger.' I shall be . . . 'Captain Sergei!' And it will be 'Sergei's Raiders' who perform the mission, not Bravo Company of Bronze Battalion." He chuckled at his own suggestion, but O'Casey raised an eyebrow.

"So you'll be incognito, Your Highness?" she said, smiling slightly. "With your *incognito* band of bodyguards?"

"Uh, yeah," he said suspiciously. "Why?"

"No reason," the historian told him. "No reason at all."

"Oh, whatever," Pahner sighed. "Okay, Roger, you take it. Find the mission, plan the mission, command the mission. Just make sure that it's as low risk and high pay as possible."

"Those are usually contradictions in terms," Jin said darkly.

"Maybe we'll come up lucky," Roger told him confidently.

CHAPTER THREE

"Well, I think we came up lucky for the downtime," Kosutic said, floating faceup in the lake. She sat up in her jury-rigged float chair and took a sip of wine. "And with the apsimons. Real lucky."

From the humans' perspective, Ran Tai was a pleasant change from the previous towns they'd visited . . . which meant it was Hell itself for the Mardukans who lived there. Not that they hadn't done their best to make their Hell as civilized and bearable as possible.

The town was wrapped around the stream which led from the lake, and every street had wide gutters that were washed from the same source. These gutters, or *chubes* in the language of the area, were used by street cleaners to keep the well-paved streets clear of manure from their bipedal mounts and packbeasts. In addition, the city had an aqueduct system to provide water that was used for drinking and also pumped throughout the city through clay pipes, and there were fountains and spigots everywhere, drained by the *chubes*. Ran Tai's

infrequent—by Mardukan standards—rains made it the
first city the humans had encountered where the need
to provide water was even a consideration, but the
aqueduct and lake between them made it widely available, despite the climate. That permitted the homes
and taverns to spray the water across mats of grass
specially grown for the purpose, which, in turn,
increased the indoor humidity of the buildings to the
point that it wasn't—quite—a trauma for the mucous-
covered Mardukans.

But the very things which made the city's climate
so unpleasant for its normal inhabitants were what
made it a virtual paradise for the humans. The valley
was above the lower cloud layer, so the sun was frequently visible. In fact, at the moment, it was near
zenith and bathing them in pleasantly damaging UV.
Not only that, the upper layer of clouds rarely produced
rain, which was why the valley wasn't continuously
pounded with monsoonlike downpours. The daytime
temperature rarely got above thirty-two degrees Cel-
sius, and the nighttime temperatures frequently fell into
the twenties.

The waters of the lake were near perfection, as well.
Since the lake was clear, cool, and untroubled by the
large predators which seemed to infest every body of
water in the planet's jungles, the humans had been able
to go swimming on a daily basis—something that had
been impossible on the march. In addition to swimming in it, they bathed in it, an almost forgotten luxury.
The standard issue waterless cleaning cloths provided
by the Imperial Marine Corps had continued to hold
out to an extent, permitting the Marines to avoid the
worst of hygiene problems, but the smooth waters of
the lake and the improvised soaps that Matsugae had
been able to create made the baths heavenly in comparison. Thus, most afternoons found the troops

recovering from their morning sword drill by swimming and floating in the lake.

They'd been surprised to find Mardukans swimming alongside them, but only until they realized how much the locals preferred to be submerged in water rather than exposed to the dry air. The locals had problems with the cool lake temperatures; they had to get out from time to time and warm up. But practically the entire population of the city came down in the afternoons to take a swim.

There'd been a lot of curiosity about the humans at first. It was clear that they were different, but, as in other areas through which the company had traveled, the locals weren't as bothered by their lack of limbs as humans would have been if the situation had been reversed. After the first few days, many of the locals had become well-known to the company, and the humans were accepted as just another visiting caravan.

The Marines also followed the local custom of the afternoon siesta. Pahner, with a few exceptions, had put the company on half-days. Mornings were spent in sword drill, maintaining their advanced weapons, and a thousand and one other minor items that had been neglected out of necessity on the march. The afternoons and evenings, though, were for the troops, and they'd been spending them, to a great extent, napping and soaking up the local culture. Which included its excellent wines.

The upland region supported large groves of apsimon trees from which the natives created a variety of preserves, candies, and wines. The troops had unanimously adopted Roger's suggested name for them, although several of them were of the opinion that the name was entirely too melodious for something so tart and astringent tasting. The natives, including Cord, loved their taste, but as far as Kosutic could determine,

no one in the entire company actually liked the damned
things. Which didn't keep the humans from gobbling
them down by the kilo anyway, for the apsimon had
one huge advantage over the much tastier kate fruit.
It contained a vitamin analogue close enough to Vitamin
C for the Marines'—and Roger's—nanites to actually
make the conversion . . . which meant that the unpleasant tasting apsimon might literally be the difference
between life and death for the company. Vitamin C
wasn't the only dietary supplement humans required
on this misbegotten planet, but it was probably the one
whose absence would have the quickest consequences.
Scurvy wasn't something the IMC normally had to
worry about, but it was just as lethal as it had ever been
for humans deprived of antiscorbutics.

Of course, O'Casey, Matsugae, and the Navy pilot
officers the Marines were lugging around with Roger,
didn't have the same sorts of nanite support. They
couldn't process the Vitamin C out of the apsimons,
but the Marines, who could, no longer required that
particular supplement, which meant that *all* of their
Vitamin C could be rationed out amongst the folks
who still needed it. Better yet, Doc Dobrescu's discovery of the apsimon's unsuspected virtues had given
them all a ray of hope. Their original sketchy data on
the planet hadn't mentioned anything about
apsimons—which was hardly surprising; they had only
fragments of the original planetary survey data, and
any planet was a *big* place, with lots of secrets tucked
away—which suggested that there might be other
things they didn't know about . . . including other native
food stuffs which truly could eke out the off-world
nutritional items they required.

And which might even taste good enough that
humans would enjoy eating them.

In addition to apsimon fruit, however, the area

around Ran Tai also supported another tree whose fruit
was remarkably similar to large grapes. Unlike the
apsimon, the fruit of these greatgrapes, as the Marines
had dubbed them, offered nothing in the way of desperately needed trace vitamins or proteins. On the
other hand, the best wines of the region were prepared
from their musky fruit, and the Marines had become
quite addicted to the light but fruity vintages.

Kosutic sat up again and took a look around at the
frolicking Marines. Gronningen was swimming endless
laps. St. John (M.) had bet the Asgardian that he couldn't
swim two laps across the five-kilometer lake and back.
Which was a sucker bet: Gronningen was a machine at
any physical activity. Another half hour, and St. John (M.)
would be out a quarter-kilo of silver. Aburia looked
miffed, though. The ebony corporal and the Asgardian
had become an "item" in the last month, and she
appeared rather pissed at her oversized boy-toy for
spending so much time on something other than herself.

But however upset Aburia might be, things seemed
to be going just fine for other members of the company. Stickles was making a hard, and so far successful, run at Briana Kane. The brunette plasma gunner
was laughing at whatever the PFC had just said to her
and didn't appear to need any rescuing. Gelert and
Macek also appeared to have come to a mutual understanding and were leaving hand-in-hand. That was
probably going to be tough luck on Gunny Jin, but
she'd held his hand through other heartbreaks.

"You look like you could use a refill," Julian said.

The intel NCO had swum up behind her in total
silence, but she suppressed her automatic start and
nodded at the bottle he held out over her cup.

"Thanks."

"I managed to rig a chiller," he said, rolling onto his
back and propping the bottle on his stomach. The

image he presented, apparently unconsciously, was extremely phallic, she noted as she took a sip of the chilled wine and smiled. The vintage from a minor local winery was flavored with a hint of cinnamonlike spice. It also had a slightly higher than normal alcohol content, as well, and she savored it.

"And where did you scavenge a chiller from?" she asked.

"Russell's armor, of course," Julian replied. He rolled up to stand in the chest-deep water and took a much longer and deeper pull from the bottle.

There didn't seem to be much to say to that. There were a lot of conversations that stopped that way—a quick reference to one of the dead, and a change of topic.

"Any leads on a job?" the sergeant major asked. Because he was the company's intelligence specialist, Julian had been spending his mornings snooping for clues to a job. Along with Poertena, he'd been combing the city, visiting merchants and hanging out in taverns.

"No, and don't think I haven't heard the jokes about it," the NCO said sourly. " 'When are Julian and Poertena going to find a job? When they're done tasting all the wines in the region.' "

"Are you sure?" Kosutic asked with a smile. "There's still all the beer to go."

"Oh, gee, thanks, Sergeant Major!" The squad leader grimaced and took another pull at the wine. "I have to admit that it's a good thing the locals don't distill."

"It's okay," the sergeant major said with a throaty chuckle. "When we get back, you can have your liver replaced."

"*If* we get back," Julian replied gloomily.

"Now, what kind of an attitude is that?" Kosutic rolled over to look at the squad leader, who paused for just a moment.

Since the Marines were drawn from a variety of planets with varying levels of body modesty, it was general practice to reach a minimum societal comfort level. Thus, the females in a unit, except under the exigencies of field conditions, tended to avoid open nudity in front of the males, and vice versa. That meant that the female Bronze Barbarians wore the skin-tight, nearly indestructible undershirts and shorts that went with the chameleon suits while swimming, while the male Marines wore just the shorts. The clothing would have been a capital offense on Ramala, Damdin's home world, and utterly unacceptable on Asgard or Sossann. On the other hand, it would have been considered painfully overdressed for swimming on Earth or Vishnu.

All of which fascinating bits of cultural baggage were no doubt very interesting, but also beside the point. The sergeant major was as hard and flat as a battle tank. Constant exercise and the nanites that all Marines bore had reduced her body fat to the level of an Olympic athlete's. But her basic physiology leaned towards soft curves and relatively large breasts—which became obvious as her left breast slid ever so slightly downward under the V-neck, skin-tight T-shirt and formed the tiniest hint of cleavage.

And totally arrested whatever Julian had been about to say.

Kosutic looked at the squad leader and suppressed a laugh. He looked as if someone had just struck him between the eyes with a hammer, but that was certainly a better direction for his thoughts than where he had been going.

"Centicred for your thoughts?" she said, and Julian almost visibly shook himself. Then he smiled and poured a bit more of the wine into her cup.

"You don't have a centicred. And I don't have a death wish."

"Well, we could think about a trade in kind," the senior NCO told him with a smile. "And I know you don't have a death wish."

The prince was getting used to the local mounts. The *civan* "horse-ostriches" were omnivorous and occasionally vicious, but they were also a quicker way to get out to the mining site than walking, and he reined the beast in and slid off the high-backed saddle. The saddle was stirrupless but had a sort of cup for the thigh that helped a rider balance himself. Of course, it was scaled for a Mardukan and far too wide for a human, but there was nothing to do about that until the new saddles he and Poertena had designed and ordered became available.

He hit the ground with flexed knees, then looked over to watch Cord dismount. The old Mardukan was slower than the prince, and unlike Roger, he'd had absolutely no prior experience with any riding beast other than the *flar-ta*. A lifetime of physical exertion and discipline stood him in good stead, however, and he climbed down carefully until he finally stood on level ground. Once there, he gave his own *civan* a look which clearly indicated that he would have preferred it for supper rather more than he did as a mount.

Roger tied both beasts to the hitching post set outside the low stone building. There were two other *civan* already tied to the same pillar, and the resident beasts snapped at the prince's mount.

When asked what sort of mount he preferred, Roger had sent Poertena to see the guard from their first encounter, and, after questioning the prince at length and trying him out on several potential beasts, Sen Kakai had settled on a proper war mount for him. The beast in question was slightly larger than the norm, and trained for combat duty. It was also extremely aggressive, and it hissed in response to the others' challenges and snapped a foot out. The wickedly clawed hind talons barely missed the closer beast, and were followed by a resounding, guillotinelike snap of impressive teeth. Both of the other *civan* recoiled ever so slightly, and Roger's mount snorted in satisfaction.

Protocol satisfied and hierarchy established, the three beasts settled down to a chorus of back and forth hissing while Cord's milder beast looked around for something to eat.

Roger waited until he was sure the precedence was settled, then glanced up at the two Marines who were still mounted. However much freedom Pahner was prepared to allow his charge in securing employment for "Sergei's Raiders," he wasn't about to relax his insistence that the prince be accompanied by suitable bodyguards at all times. Personally, Roger felt quite confident in his own ability to look after himself, especially with Cord at his side, but he also knew better than to argue. Not only would it have been fruitless, but harsh experience had taught him to understand exactly why no one in his right mind screwed around with the chain of command and authority in what was for all intents and purposes a single gigantic, planet-wide combat zone.

Which didn't mean that he wasn't prepared to *bend* that chain ever so slightly when it suited his purposes.

"You two mosey on over to the barracks, Moseyev," he told the senior Marine in Standard English. "Spread a little silver around in the bar, if they have one, and keep your ears open. I'd like to hear what the grunts have to say about this."

The corporal seemed inclined to argue for just a moment, but the moment passed. Moseyev had no doubt at all that Captain Pahner would remove wide, painful strips from his hide if the captain ever discovered that he'd allowed the prince to send him off on an errand. At the same time, like every other member of Bravo Company, he'd realized in Marshad that the strict letter of the regulations which had made Prince Roger the official colonel in chief of Bronze Battalion was no longer a legal fiction.

He glowered at Roger for a few seconds, wondering just how blithely Colonel MacClintock would have ignored Captain Pahner had the latter been physically present, but then he glanced at the small building awaiting Roger and shrugged. Orders were orders. Besides, every Bronze Barbarian knew that the prince was sudden death on two feet with the bead pistol holstered at his side, not to mention the sword across his back. And that didn't even consider Cord's well-proven lethality. There was no way in the world a building the size of their destination could hold enough scummies to pose a threat to *those* two.

"Right, Your Highness," the corporal said. "Of course, I hope you'll remember not to mention this in front of the wrong ears."

"Mention what?" Roger asked innocently, and Moseyev chuckled and sent his *civan* trotting off towards the barracks.

"That was undoubtedly foolish," Cord observed thoughtfully as he watched the Marines ride away. "In anyone other than yourself, I would probably say that it was *remarkably* foolish, in fact. In your own case, however, familiarity prevents me from feeling the least surprise."

"Yeah, sure." Roger grinned. "You don't like being shadowed everywhere you go any more than I do, you old reprobate!"

"I am not yet so feeble as to require a keeper," the shaman replied with awesome dignity, hefting the long, wickedly bladed spear he continued to carry everywhere. "I, on the other hand, am not the heir of a mighty ruler, either."

"Neither is 'Captain Sergei,'" Roger chuckled, and Cord snorted in resignation as the prince stepped up to the building and clapped his hands for permission to enter it.

The structure sat at the foot of a steep slope that led upward to the opening to a narrow gorge or valley. A series of walls had been thrown up across the opening, and a small army was entrenched before them. It was clear that they'd been there for a while, and were prepared for an extended stay.

"Come in," a voice called from the interior in reply to Roger's clap, and Roger slipped the door catch and stepped into the hutlike building's single room. It was occupied by a trio of guards and two unarmed Mardukans who'd clearly been in conversation when he arrived, and the larger of the civilians grunted in derisive laughter when Roger entered.

"I see the *basik* have heard of our plight," he half-sneered, but the other civilian sliced a true-hand across his chest in a gesture of negation.

"We're in no position to laugh," he said sternly. "You, especially, are not," he added in a pointed tone, and the larger Mardukan hissed sourly, although he made no other response. The smaller native turned to Roger. "I am Deb Tar. And you are?"

"Captain Sergei," Roger said with a slight bow. "At your service."

"And at yours," Deb Tar replied. "What can we do for you?"

"It's more what we can do for you," Roger told him with a smile. "I understand you have a problem."

"That we do," Deb Tar agreed with a handclap of emphasis. "But I doubt you'll be able to do anything about it."

"I don't know about that," Roger said. "We might surprise you."

"Some other time, *basik*," the other Mardukan grunted. "We're about to get the problem solved for us."

"Oh." Roger raised an eyebrow. "I take it there are competitors?"

"For a month's production from my mine?" Deb Tar's snort was perilously near to a snarl. "Of course there are—including my former mine manager," he continued with a distasteful gesture of a false-hand at the other civilian. "Nor Tob seems to feel that it should be easy to take the valley back. Since, after all, it was so easy to take away from him in the first place."

"It was not my fault," the former manager ground out. "Was *I* the guard commander?"

"No, you weren't," the owner agreed. "Otherwise your horns would be over my fireplace. There's still an empty space I could fit them into, though. I would have saved half the cost if you hadn't persuaded me to relocate the refinery there, as well!"

"You made money hand over hand from that!" the former manager shot back, then turned to Roger and Cord. "Come on, *basik*," he snarled. "Let us show you how *real* Mardukans deal with scum like this!"

"Oh, by all means, lead on," Roger invited, waving towards the door. "This I've got to see."

CHAPTER FOUR

"The valley's a fortress," Roger said, and took a sip of wine.

"So, what happened?" Julian asked.

"I've got the whole thing on helmet recording, but the short answer is that it was a farce."

"How?" Kosutic asked. She looked at the schematic of the valley entrance and shook her head. "I don't see anything particularly humorous about the situation. You could take that with a wave of Kranolta, but that's the only way to go over the wall that comes to mind."

"Yep," Roger agreed. "And that was more or less what our friend Nor Tob tried. He gathered up a few hundred out-of-work miners and half-assed mercenaries with a promise to divide the loot when they took the place and threw them straight at it."

He laughed and shook his head.

"They came at the wall with ladders, but it's so damned high that half the ladders broke under the weight of the climbers. Those that didn't got pushed down easily. Basically, they didn't get within five meters of the top."

"How many casualties?" Gunny Lai asked. The gunnery sergeant stood beside Kosutic, looking down at the map and rubbing the side of her nose.

"None," Roger said with another laugh. "Oh, there were a few broken arms and more bruised egos, but no military casualties. The barb mercenaries never even shot back. They just pushed the ladders down and threw stuff. Mostly smelly stuff, like their slop buckets."

"Contemptuous, were they?" the sergeant major asked as she panned the map out to get a look at the entire valley.

"Very," Roger told her. "These guys—they call themselves the Vasin—are apparently a tribe that got displaced by this Boman invasion. Either they were already mercenaries, or else they took up the trade after they got shoved off their homeland originally. Nobody's too sure about that, but whichever it was, it sounds to me like they were looking for work when they hit Ran Tai and they'd gone to the mine as a good place to trade some of their hides for raw gold and silver at refinery prices. As nearly as I can tell, they didn't have any intention of taking it before they got there and realized how wide open it was. No one seems to know exactly what started the ruckus, but they ended up in possession of the place, and according to the owner, Deb Tar, he had over two months of refined output bagged and crated for shipment when they moved in on him. He really, really wants that loot back, but they're not especially eager to hand it over, and since they grabbed it so easily, they're pretty contemptuous of all the locals. Even if they weren't, the city authorities aren't about to take the losses involved in throwing them out—especially when Deb Tar deliberately located his refining facilities right there at the minehead to avoid paying city taxes on them. The way the Council sees it, it's out of their jurisdiction, so good luck to him. And from some of the conversations we overheard, the Vasin have offered Deb Tar a price to get his property back . . . an even *three* months' production."

"Ouch!" Kosutic grimaced. "Still, I'd think giving up an extra month of output wouldn't sound all that unreasonable if it got the mines back for him. He can always dig more, after all."

"But they are bargaining?" Sergeant Jin asked. "That wasn't what we were told."

"Oh, yeah, they're ready enough to deal." Roger smiled broadly. "Deb Tar is just holding out for a better price, which is why he's looking so hard for someone who can kick them out without meeting their demands. Nor Tob was the first to actually try to take him up on it, but when he saw that his own valiant effort was going to be a bust, he decided to haul ass and headed out as soon as it was clear the assault was a failure."

"No wonder," Kosutic laughed. "I bet those miners were some pissed individuals. Anybody know where he went?"

"Nope," Julian said. "It looks like he's gone to ground somewhere. He hasn't left the area, but he hasn't been seen in his usual haunts, either."

"I been lookin' around," Poertena interjected. "T'is Deb Tar, he offering a full month's output to whoever get them out. T'at be something like thirty sedant in gold an' another ten in silver, an' a sedant's nearly half a kilo. Even with tee prices up here, we can load up ever't'ing we need for less t'an twenty sedant of gold." He shrugged. "Tee other gold an' silver be profit."

"So it's a worthwhile operation," Roger said. "If anyone can figure out a method to get in, at least."

"Oh, that's easy enough," Kosutic told him, looking up from the map display.

"Yeah. Getting in isn't a problem," Jin agreed. "The question is how we go about taking on a hundred scummy mercenaries after we do."

"Oh?" Roger looked over the sergeant major's shoulder at the map. "What are you planning?"

"Welll . . ." Kosutic drawled, and pointed at the map. "Your helmet imagery shows that there's a straight cliff at the entrance, right?"

"It widens out further in," Roger said. "But, yes, the entrance is a narrow gorge, nearly fifty meters high. There's a stream that comes out through a metal grate at the base of the wall. It's probably what cut the gorge in the first place."

"Yes, Sir," Gunny Lai said. "But if you get up on top of that plateau at the entrance, you can come around behind the wall and rappel right down on their heads."

"Oh." The prince tugged at a flyaway strand of hair and frowned. "What about getting up the face in the first place?"

"That we can do, Sir," Kosutic said. "But I want to know more about the scummies on the inside. What their pattern is, what sorts of guard posts they set—that sort of thing."

"All right," Roger said. "But we've got some competitors in this. Let's not let them have an edge or tip our own hand. Send a team up to the plateau to check out the route, but tell them to stay low and keep their heads down."

"Kosutic and her great ideas," Julian said sourly.

The windswept plateau was actively cold in the night wind, and the distant lights of the town didn't make him feel any better. If he and Poertena hadn't happened to hear about this job and pass the word to Roger, he could have been down there now, drinking on the prince's decicred.

"Hey, *I* think we lucked out again, Sergeant," Gronningen said quietly.

The big Asgardian was very good in the mountains. He moved like a mountain goat, just as surely and almost as silently. That was why Julian had included him on this little jaunt, and the NCO nodded in agreement with his observation as he took another look at the objective. The mercenaries weren't stupid, and they had guards on the wall against the possibility of a night attack. But they were very complacent, for there were no sentries actually patrolling the camp they'd established in the valley. Or maybe complacent wasn't exactly the right word for it, he conceded after a moment. No Mardukan raiding force could possibly have come after them through these temperature conditions, after all, even if it could have made the climb up the cliffs in the first place, which was questionable.

"This is going to be a cakewalk," he whispered.

"Something's bound to go wrong," the plasma gunner disagreed, getting up carefully to avoid sending a rock bouncing into the valley to give away their position.

The two Marines moved back to the bivouac the team had established. It was an overcast, moonless night, and without the vision systems of their helmets, they would have been stumbling along blind. As it was, the faint reflection of the fires of Ran Tai was enough to give them near daylight vision.

They rounded the small projection of stone that shielded their camp from view from the valley and squatted down by Macek. The private was heating a cup of soup with a resistance heater. Technically, that was a violation of doctrine, since they were supposed to be making a cold camp, but the resistance heater only radiated in infrared, and it wasn't like they had to worry about scummy scan teams picking it up.

"That looks good," Julian observed as he flopped down on his open bivy tent.

"Fix your own, then," the private suggested, and Gronningen chuckled and pulled out a piece of jerked capetoad. The meat from the animals had yielded several hundred kilos of jerky that some of the company relished.

Julian generally found it awful, but he was hungry enough to pull out a piece of his own and start gnawing on it.

"I can't believe that after all I've done for you, you begrudge me a little soup," he said in a whiny tone.

"Yeah? Like dragging me up a mountain to alternately freeze and bake?" the private asked, then chuckled. "Hell, I was making it for all of us," he admitted. "It's not much, just a little jerky and a few leftover pieces of tater."

"Sounds good," Gronningen said. "I'm ready to get off this hill, too," he admitted reluctantly. The Asgardian religion had some extremely stoic overtones.

"Me, too," Julian assured him. "I'm ready for some of Matsugae's cooking." He sighed. "Or even some of the stuff in the town. It's not too bad, you know."

"I want a bitok," Macek said. "That doesn't seem too much to ask."

"Oh, man," Julian said, smacking his lips. "You would have to say that. I want one, too. About an eighth of a kilo. With cheese and onions."

"Yah," Gronningen said, leaning back in his own bivy and masticating the shoe-leather jerky. "A bitok sounds good. Or my mutra's lutefisk." He sighed. "It's been a long time since I had my mutra's lutefisk."

"What's lutefisk?" Julian asked as he took the cup out of Macek's hand and sipped.

"Lutefisk?" The Asgardian frowned. "That is . . . hard to explain. It is a fish."

"Yeah?" Macek took a chew of his own jerky. "What's so special about a fish?"

The Asgardian thought for a moment about trying to explain the attraction of cod soaked in lye, then decided to give up.

"It is a family thing, I think," he said, and retreated into his normal reticent shell after that while Julian and Macek wrangled quietly over the quality of different bitok joints in Imperial City. Eventually, they both agreed that the only thing to do was get back to Earth and go on a bar-crawl to compare them properly.

They finished the soup, then divided up the watches and settled down for the night. One more day of alternately baking and frying on the plateau, and the company should be on its way.

Roger pulled himself over the lip of the plateau and stepped forward to let the next Marine up. The windy tabletop was beginning to fill up with the company, but the Marines stayed well away from the northern wall. One noisy, rolling rock could ruin the entire operation.

Roger nodded to Kosutic as she walked up. The flattened view in the night vision systems worked hand in hand with the helmet's face shields to make everyone anonymous, but the helmet systems threw up little tags as people came into view. The tags were effectively invisible, once you got used to them, unless you consciously concentrated on seeing them, but they provided a way for the user to distinguish who was who.

"How we doing, Sergeant Major?" the prince asked. He looked around as the last Marine hauled herself onto the plateau and checked his toot for the time. "I think we're a little ahead of schedule."

"That we are, Sir," the sergeant major replied. She glanced around and saw that the team leaders were getting their people into position. Everything was working out smoothly, exactly as planned.

Which made her very, very nervous.

CHAPTER FIVE

"Ah, finally something that's working out," Julian said quietly.

The two oversized squads which were all that remained of Bravo Company were lined up along the middle section of the gorge. The gorge snaked back from the entrance for nearly three hundred meters before opening into the mining area, where the majority of the barbarians were bivouacked, but the only guards were on the gates themselves. By landing between the barbarians' camp and the guards, the company could take the mercenaries by the throat . . . assuming everything worked as planned.

"Remember," Roger said over the company frequency, "minimum violence. I want them taken down, and taken down hard, but no killing if possible."

"But don't take unnecessary chances," Kosutic added.

"Right," the prince agreed. "Okay, you all have your targets," he said, clipping his drop line into place. "Let's do it."

The platoon dropped down into the darkness like

the shadows of so many chameleon cloth-covered spiders. The drop clips automatically slowed them as they approached the nearly invisible bottom, then detached as their feet hit the ground. Then the shadows split up, one squad heading valley-ward while the other headed for the gates.

Roger moved through the sleeping encampment and wanted to laugh. The barbarians were pretty clearly a nomadic cavalry outfit, since the recon teams had confirmed that they had their women and children with them, but their picket lines were well up the valley. The *civan* that would have warned them of the humans' approach were well out of sight from the tactical squad.

Julian and his team had determined which hut belonged to the leaders of the barbarians, and the prince had chosen it as his personal target. He hoped that if he took the leader, he could convince him to surrender. He'd been able to negotiate an agreement with Deb Tar and the city authorities of Ran Tai to let the barbarians go free if they surrendered, so he had that to bargain with. If the barbs wanted to fight, though, things could get messy. Whatever else these scummies might be, and however overconfident they might seem, they were also professional warriors, and unlike the Kranolta, they had firearms. As cavalry, they carried the big wheel lock pistol/carbines, not the heavier-caliber infantry arquebuses with their resin-coated slow matches. Developing reliable gunpowder and ignition systems for firearms on a planet with Marduk's predominately humid, one might almost say "saturated," climate must have been a nightmare. It had certainly required more ingenuity than had been the case back on Terra, and from what the humans had been able to discover so far, the several-times-a-day rains which were so much a part of the normal

Mardukan weather experience were a major tactical factor in their use. Armies without arquebuses, or with fewer of them than their opponents, strove mightily to avoid battles under anything except rainy conditions, and no scummy in his right mind would have dreamed of building an army without plenty of old-fashioned, muscle-powered weaponry in reserve.

For himself, Roger suspected that he would never have bothered to try to overcome the all but insuperable difficulties involved with the use of loose-powder, muzzle-loading weapons on a planet like Marduk. But the locals had managed it, and he had no desire at all to see what a two-centimeter pistol ball would do to one of his people, so if it did come to a fight, he was determined that the company would have the upper hand from the start. That was why Aburia's team was busy planting explosives throughout the camp; if the barbarians didn't surrender, the plan was to back off and blow them in place.

Roger and his team froze as a figure stepped out of one of the huts. The small buildings of the mining facility were made of rock rubble from the mine shafts, but their doors were nothing more than hide flaps, and the Mardukan's exit had been silent. One moment, the street was empty—the next the scummy was in clear view. Despite the darkness, they would be spotted in an instant if he looked around, and the entire plan would be blown.

The barbarian scratched at a dried patch on his arm and snarled. Then he relieved himself on the side of the hut, and went back in.

Roger breathed a silent sigh of relief and continued onward. He detoured slightly to get away from the restless barbarian's hut and cut between two of the rough buildings.

His team ended up behind the hut of the mercenary

leader and crept around to its front. Roger consulted his helmet systems and looked around. Aburia's team was nearly done placing their explosives, but not quite, so he held in place to give them a bit more time. The squad headed for the gates was already in position and hadn't been spotted as they set up for an ambush. Their only job was to make sure that the Mardukans at the gates didn't come to the aid of their compatriots when Roger's squad hit the main encampment. If the plan went off without a hitch, their presence would never even be noticed.

Roger consulted the demo schematic and his toot clock again. The charges were emplaced, and Aburia had pulled her team back to provide cover if the entry team needed it. And if that wasn't enough, Roger had a hole card.

He'd lost out on the argument over who went through the door first. Actually, it would have been fairer to say that there'd never been anything which might properly have been called an "argument" in the first place. Pahner might have delegated field command to "Captain Sergei," but there were definite limits to the freedom Roger was permitted in the risk-taking department, and so he waved Julian forward, instead.

The squad leader smiled and waved in turn to Gronningen, who stepped forward quietly and pushed the flap aside. Julian followed him through, and Roger entered behind the NCO. The hut was larger than most, and had a few appointments, including a writing desk, but it was still basically a hovel. Roger shook his head and stepped over to the still-sleeping scummy leader as the team fanned out to cover the other scummies in the room. Two of them were women, but the humans were taking no chances and made certain that *all* of the Mardukans were covered.

Once they were, Roger bent until his helmet was

pointed at the barbarian's face, and triggered the helmet light.

Rastar Komas Ta'Norton of the Vasin, Prince of Therdan, stared up into the light, and all four hands filled with the knives that were his trademark. But he'd hardly moved when he encountered the hard shape of what could only be a gun barrel pressing into his chest. He wasn't sure, because the light in his eyes was the brightest he'd ever seen in his life, but it was unlikely to be anything else.

"Do you want to live?" a disembodied and very peculiar-sounding voice asked from beyond the light. "Or do you want to die, and have your entire tribe die with you?"

"What's the difference?" Rastar snarled. "You'll kill us all anyway. Or make us slaves. Kill us now. At least that's freedom, of a sort."

"Death is lighter than a feather, duty heavier than mountains," the voice, which sounded like no Mardukan Rastar had ever heard, said. "Yet we take up the burden of duty, do we not? I have been given permission to spare you and your tribe if you surrender and leave. You may even retain your weapons. You simply have to pack up and go, taking with you nothing but what you arrived with. If you are in the Vale of Ran Tai at sunset of this day, your lives are forfeit. Your call."

Rastar considered the knives. He was certain he could kill this one, but there were other lights, other guns, and he couldn't kill his women, his tribe. It was the last duty he had, and he could not drop it, even when death beckoned so seductively.

"We keep our weapons?" he asked suspiciously.

"Yes," said the voice. "However, if you try to double-cross us, we'll be forced to kill you all."

"No." The chieftain sighed and put his knives on the

floor. "No, we won't double-cross you. Have this foul valley, and more power to you."

Things were still going too smoothly.

Roger watched the Vasin filing out of their huts and gathering in the central square. He had his own squad moving about in an intricate, flowing pattern that gave the impression he had forces everywhere, when the barbarians actually outnumbered him by three to one, in hopes of keeping things smooth. In fact, the mercenaries outnumbered the force that he had in the camp itself by nearly *ten* to one, and he congratulated himself, in a modest sort of way, on how well the op had gone down.

Of course, he admitted, it had nearly gone the other way. Roger had been terrified by the speed with which the Mardukan had reacted—those knives had seemed to teleport into the chieftain's hands, and he'd had them out and ready before Roger could even blink. If the Mardukan had decided to start the ball, the Empire would have been short one fortunately disposable prince. It had been a sobering experience.

The Vasin's equipment was much better made and finished than Roger had expected, but their nomad background was obvious, for they were packed before Roger had imagined they could even get started. Their *civan* were lined up to leave in less than ten minutes, and Roger approached the chief, Rastar, and nodded.

"It's better this way," he said.

"I hope you won't mind, but if we actually get out of this valley alive, we're planning on being out of the Vale before dawn," the Mardukan told him with a grunt of laughter.

"Not at all," Roger said. "You're not terribly popular. Just one question," he added. The Marines had watched the packing with an eagle eye, and he knew the Mardukans hadn't packed any large amounts of gold and silver. "Where's the shipment?"

"Your guess is as good as mine, *basik*," the chieftain told him. "They keep talking about their 'shipment,' but we've never understood why. There's no large store of metals here." The chief gestured to a heavily built stone shack near a worked-out, abandoned mine shaft. "That's the storehouse. It was empty when we arrived."

"*What?*"

"Hah!" the chieftain grunted. "Let me guess—that was your pay."

"Yes!" the prince snarled. "What happened to it?"

"As I said," the barbarian said in a voice which held a sudden hint of dangerous ice, "it was gone when we arrived here. We don't know what happened to it."

"Sir," Sergeant Major Kosutic put in, "they didn't load it, and there's no way out of the valley, so they didn't carry it out after they got here. Either it left before they arrived, or else it's still here somewhere."

"Shit," Roger said. "Okay, Rastar, you can leave. Pick up your guards on the way out. If you try to come back, I might just get pissed."

"Not as pissed as I am, Lord Sergei," the Mardukan told him. "But for whatever comfort it's worth, I've always heard that the life of a mercenary generally consists of getting stuck with the sword of the paymaster far more often than with the swords of the enemy. From my own limited experience, that's putting it mildly."

He tossed his head in a Mardukan nod, walked over to his *civan*, and climbed into the saddle. In moments, the Vasin column was gone.

"All right, Sergeant Major," Roger sighed wearily. "Let's tear this place apart. Find our gold."

"Yes, Sir," the sergeant major said. But she already had a sinking feeling.

⬧　　⬧　　⬧

"No gold?" Armand Pahner's voice was admirably composed, but he kept his head turned slightly away to hide his incipient grin.

"Nope." Roger kicked one of the low tables. "None. We found a few kilos of silver—hardly enough to outfit us, but maybe if we scrimp . . ." He shook his head angrily. "We searched every mine, as far as we could with the way the groundwater's risen since Deb Tar's people's pumps shut down. Not a bit of gold anywhere."

"Oh, great," O'Casey said. "Stop kicking the table, Roger. We can't afford to break any furniture."

"The worst part is that I'm a laughingstock," Roger said bitterly. "Of course Deb Tar wasn't willing to pay us a red centicred, and the local courts won't touch it. Especially not after the way he kept accusing us of hiding the gold ourselves, as if that made any sense."

"Oh, it's not that bad," Kosutic said. "It was a good op. It went down exactly as planned, and nobody got hurt. Hell, it was basically a training exercise, and a good one. And nobody faults you, Sir. Everybody thought the gold was there, and Deb Tar is furious."

"But where did it go?" O'Casey asked.

"That's the million-credit question," the sergeant major replied, "and His Evilness only knows the answer. It was definitely in the storehouse when the Vasin slipped through the gates, and it's definitely not there now. And the Vasin did *not* carry it out. Unfortunately, none of that tells us what *did* happen to it, and where it went is a mystery. The storehouse was empty, and even the carts they kept the stuff in are gone."

"Carts?" the chief of staff repeated.

"Yeah. They load the stuff into carts to carry it to the storehouse from the refinery, and they just shove the carts into the storehouse to save themselves the trouble of unloading it just so they can load it again when the time comes to haul it down to the city. But the carts weren't there—and they weren't in the refinery or anywhere else, either. We looked just to see if they'd been hidden in the smelters or something."

"There's no way they could've gotten it out of the valley without taking it through the gate," Roger said despairingly. "Mardukans just can't climb that well."

"Well, Your Highness," Captain Pahner said with a smile, "I'm sure we'll think of something. But maybe you want to get some sleep, or even go hit the taverns. Go blow off some steam."

"With what? We're tapped!"

"We're not that tapped," the CO said. "Take the . . . platoon out and have a trooper blast. We can afford it, barely, and it's the best thing to do after a busted op."

"Okay." Roger shrugged. "If you say so."

"Go have some fun, Captain Sergei," the captain told him with a smile.

"That particular ancestor wasn't very lucky," Roger said, summoning a slight grin of his own in return. "I think I'll pick a different moniker."

Pahner chuckled in sympathy, and the prince turned and headed for the door. Behind him, Kosutic looked at the captain and lifted an eyebrow. He was planning something.

Roger was drunk. So was Nimashet Despreaux. And just at the moment, the prince was stone-cold positive that that was a Bad Thing.

The two of them had somehow ended up in a pool of silence in the middle of the roaringly successful party. The inn's owner had been only too happy to have the custom, but most of the Mardukan patrons had gone home early. The off-worlders were too drunk, too aggressive, and, by all means, too loud. A group of Marines in one corner was roaring out one of the dirtiest ditties Roger had ever heard in his life—something about "Three-Ball Pete"—and in another corner, in competition with their theoretically musical efforts, was an arm-wrestling match, complete with chanting cheerleaders. Neither group could have carried a tune if you'd given them a hundred buckets, but everyone was far too plastered to care.

So the little pool of privacy that had formed around him and the sergeant had a queasy setup feel to the high-flying prince's somewhat befuddled instincts. He could feel the little prods from the group even through his wine-induced haze, and, in a way, it was gratifying. Despreaux was by no means ugly, after all. And if the company had decided it was a good thing for them to "get together," it meant a form of acceptance. On the other hand . . .

Roger cleared his throat as Despreaux, apparently oblivious to the little nods, winks, and maneuvers around them, poured him some more wine.

"Nima-sh-sh-shet?" he asked.

"Hmmm?" Her smile was warm, and his resistance wavered for a moment. She was, in fact, quite beautiful. And he'd had that thought any number of times before, he reminded himself, so it wasn't the several bottles of wine he'd consumed at this point.

"I . . . don' ge' involved wi' . . . uh . . ."

What he wanted to say was that he didn't get sexually involved at all. The consequences and ramifications for someone in his position were simply too great, and the two times he'd made the mistake of forgetting that, the public discussion of his sex life had hammered the point mercilessly home. No one outside the Imperial Family could possibly conceive of the intensity with which a public microscope examined the behavior of all MacClintocks, and anyone who thought Roger or his siblings could conduct even the most discreet love affair without the newsies finding out had to be a drug addict. The last thing the dynasty's "bad boy" had needed was to hand the scandal faxes *that* kind of story!

That would have been more than sufficient reason for discretion on Roger's part, but he was honest enough—with himself, at least—to admit that there was another and much more personal reason. His mother had never married his father, and until Eleanora O'Casey had explained the actual train of events to him in Marshad, Roger had always believed deep in his heart that *he* must have been what had driven them apart and led to his father's banishment from court. Looked at logically, the notion that he could be to blame was ridiculous, but the wounded, lonely child to whom it had first occurred had scarcely been in a position to consider it rationally.

And one thing he was totally and bitterly certain of was that he would never put another child into the position of thinking the same thoughts and enduring the same pain. Oh, he knew perfectly well that the drugs and nanites that eliminated the monthly curse for the female Marines also eliminated any possibility of pregnancy, but engaging in a casual affair, especially under these conditions, was as impossible for the prince as it might have been for other scions of the "nobility" to resist banging the servants. And even if it hadn't been, there was no way that he would damage the unit's cohesion that way—no way that he was going to damage his companion-at-arms relationship with the sergeant, one he'd literally shed blood to create, for an evening's romp in the sack.

No matter how badly his inebriated body yearned to throw itself onto the highly trained Marine, rip her uniform off, and bury his face in her high, firm breasts.

But he'd never been able to explain any of his tangled feelings and rational analyses to anyone in his life. Not even to Matsugae, who was, in many ways, the closest thing Roger had ever known to a genuine "father." His personal . . . quirks had led to problems ever since upper school, and he'd still never been able to articulate them. Not even when the commander of his mother's bodyguard had been standing in his bedroom, trying to understand why the stark-naked and raving daughter of a grand duke was calling him a eunuch.

He couldn't think of the way to do it now, either, however hard he tried. And he *did* try. His fuddled brain searched for something—anything—to say to take the sting out of his rejection, but what dropped from his lips was " . . . associateatsh."

Nimashet Despreaux blinked twice and tried to focus on the prince, but all she could see was the target zone just above his Adam's apple.

"Di' you jus' say what I thin' you said?" she enunciated carefully.

"Look, call me weird," Roger said, gesturing with his cup. "But I don' fool around with . . . assoc . . . ass . . . aizoaceae . . . . Look, not tha' it wouldn' be fun. You' gorgeous. Bu' I won'."

"Wha' you mean is you don' fool 'round wi' the help. Tha's wha' you were gonna say, right?" the NCO demanded. "I s'pose a sergeant from a ass en' o' nowhere planet isn' good enough for you!"

"No, is no' *like* that!" the prince protested vehemently, leaning forward to give her a hug. "I like you, an' you're beau'ful, but it wouldn' be right!"

"Kee' you hands off me, you aris-aris . . . aristocratic *worm!*"

"Whaddid I say?" Roger asked in perplexity. "I guess maybe some'ay, but no' tonigh'."

"You're damn' right we won't," the sergeant hissed

as she drew back to strike. "Thas' not somethin' you're ever, *ever* gonna worry abou' again."

"Oh, shit."

For no reason he could think of, Julian had decided to forego the party. Technically, he was off-duty and could've gotten as drunk as a skunk if he wanted to. Unlike Gronningen and Georgiadas, who were supposed to be covering Roger. But they, bless their stupid little hearts, had stepped far enough away to give Roger and his girlfriend some space, some privacy, just like everybody else who'd watched the two of them dance closer and closer all evening. The company was not a unit of voyeurs, but the pool had gone bust twice on when those two were finally going to do the beast with two backs, and if they didn't get it out of their systems soon, somebody was going to squeal to the Skipper.

At the moment, however, Julian was ready to call the pool off. Just as soon as he saved Roger's life—the ungrateful bastard . . .

The hard-driven slap slammed painfully into Julian's forearm as he blocked it.

"Despreaux!"

"Get out of my way, Julian!" the enraged bodyguard screamed. "I won't kill 'im! I'm just going to rip his balls off!"

"That *would* kill him, Nimashet," Julian protested as he blocked another swing. Fortunately, the inebriated Marine was still trying to hit the rapidly retreating Roger rather than deliberately aiming for her fellow noncom.

"No, it wouldn't." Warrant Officer Dobrescu sounded remarkably—and falsely—sober for a man stretched out under a nearby table, bottle in one hand and little black bag in the other. "I'd stop the bleeding. They'd even regrow with enough regen and enough time. I saw it once in a guy that had a bad accident on Shiva."

"See!" Despreaux yelled, trying to force her way past. Roger had retreated into the group of singers in the corner, but the tall, long-haired figure was still easily discernible. "It wouldn't kill him—just hurt. A lot! And it's not like *he'd* miss them!"

She tried for one more moment to shove past Julian, but then, suddenly, all the fury seemed to drain out of her. Her strength went with it, and she dropped back onto a bench and put her face in her hands.

"Oh, Julian, what the hell am I gonna *do?*"

"There, there," he said, patting her awkwardly on the back. The thought crossed his mind—briefly—that this was probably the best time ever to make his own play. But even *he* wasn't that evil a bastard. Probably. He'd have to think about it. He'd done things nearly as low to get laid. But not quite that low. Well, some that were. And, admittedly, some that were even lower. But not to a friend. Had he? "There, there."

"Oooooh." Despreaux groaned and took a long pull out of a bottle. "What the hell am I gonna do? I was willing to be the laughingstock of the company, but this is worse! I'm in love with a man who's unable to screw!"

"He isn't functionally incapable," Dobrescu said carefully. He sat up and slammed his forehead on the underside of his table. "Ouch. Damned low ceilings in this joint. As I was saying. He's functional as a male."

"Oooooh," Despreaux moaned again. "I just wanna crawl under a rock and *die!*"

"Don't tell me this is the first time you've ever been turned down," Julian joked. "You'll get over it. Everybody does."

"It's the first time I've ever *asked*, you idiot! I never

had to before! And I didn't even get to ask—he just
assumed I was going to suggest it! *Assumed!*"

"Were you?" Dobrescu asked, sticking his head out
from between the table and the bench. "Damned odd
architecture in this joint."

"Well, yes," Despreaux admitted. "But that's not the
point! Did you hear what he said to me?"

"Yes," Julian said. "That was when I got the tran-
quilizer gun ready."

"Can you believe the *nerve!*" she spat so furiously
that wine flew out in a spray over the other NCO.

"Yes," Dobrescu said. "I can. And since he turned
you down, I don't suppose you could do with some
comforting from a warrant officer? If, of course, you're
thin enough to fit through the entrance to this cozy
little room I seem to have lucked upon."

Gronningen, fortunately, was large enough to pull
her off the warrant officer. Who complained, vociferously, that since he was the only medic in the company, there was no one else who could work on his
wrenched back and bleeding nose.

The owner, the new manager, and the survey parties had left the valley. The long process of pumping
out the mines and putting them back into production
would start the following day, but for tonight the valley was deserted. Not even the guards had been
replaced.

Which made the fact that three of the windmill-
powered pumps were running all out at the moment
more than a tiny bit peculiar. Their hoses snaked into
the mouth of an abandoned mine shaft, and Armand
Pahner parked himself just outside its entrance and
clicked on his helmet light as a Mardukan emerged
from the opening.

"Why, hello, Nor Tob."

The Mardukan froze in the opening, pinned by the brilliant glare of light. He clutched a chest between his false-hands, while one true-hand carried an uncocked cavalry pistol.

"It was the carts that got me thinking," the Marine continued cheerfully. "If somebody thought really fast and worked quickly, he could wheel quite a bit of this stuff away in just a few minutes. But he couldn't get far with it."

"So he asked me what was right near the storehouse," the sergeant major said from her perch above the entrance behind the Mardukan. "Ah, ah, let's keep those true-hands away from the pistol flint, shall we?" She chuckled. "I nearly kicked myself. Tell me something, did you have them dig this shaft just for this reason?"

"I've slaved in this mine for *years!*" the former manager said. "It was my *right!*"

"And when the Vasin came through the gates, you saw a chance to take your 'right' in the confusion," Pahner observed. "Or did you arrange that, too?"

"No, that was mere chance," the Mardukan said. "But I took that chance when I saw it! Look, I can . . . share this with you. Nobody ever needs to know. You two can have half of it. Hell, forget that foolish child—there are cities on the plains where this much gold will allow you to live like a king for the rest of your life!"

"I don't think so," Pahner said quietly. "I don't like thieves, Nor Tob, and I don't like traitors even more. I think you ought to just go." The captain judged the weight of the chest the former manager was carrying. "You can take that with you, and nobody has to know any different, as you said. But that's it. Time to get on your *civan* and leave."

"This is my *right*," the former mine manager snarled. "It's *mine!*"

"Look," Pahner said reasonably, "you can leave vertical, or horizontal. It really doesn't matter to me. But you're not leaving with more than what you're carrying right now."

"That's what you think!" the Mardukan shouted, and grabbed the cocking arm of his pistol.

"I'm feeling kind of ambiguous about this," Pahner said as the shaft started to fill again.

"Don't," Kosutic said. "His Evilness knows he's no loss."

"Oh, no," the CO said, walking back up the shaft with her. "Not that. It's Roger. How are we going to tell him?"

"I'd suggest that we just pretend there's a magic bag somewhere with more money," Kosutic said. "I mean, he never has to know, right?"

"But what about Poertena?" Pahner asked as he threw one of the cases onto a *turom*. The local draft animals were, indeed, some sort of distant cousin of the *civan*, but they had far more placid dispositions, and this one only whuffled with mournful resignation under the weight.

"What about him?" The sergeant major lashed a bag to a second *turom*. "We tell *him* there's no cash at all; it just brings out his creative side."

"We don't want him getting too creative," the captain pointed out. He paused, trying to judge whether or not the *turom* was overloaded on one side.

"That's always been your problem, Armand," the NCO told him as she picked up another of the heavy cases and loaded it onto her beast. "You're too kind-hearted."

"True, true." Pahner gathered up the reins of his *civan*, swung into the saddle (now equipped with human-style stirrups), and made sure he had a firm grip on his *turom*'s lead. "I need to get over that, I suppose."

"It'll get you killed some day, I swear," the sergeant major said as she mounted in turn. "Take it from me," she added as they headed down the track to town.

Behind them, the water rose over the last of the rock pile at the bottom of the shaft.

CHAPTER SIX

"You know, I really didn't miss this," Roger said as he slid down off of Patty.

"To be terribly honest, Your Highness," Pahner replied, wiping the sweat off his brow, "neither did I."

The first day of travel had been uneventful as the company followed one of the regular caravan trails down out of the mountains. Within a few hours of leaving Ran Tai, however, they'd hit the enveloping, sweltering clouds of the jungle-covered lowlands and passed once more from the region of relative cool back into Marduk's standard steambath.

Cord and the other Mardukans had, of course, been delighted.

There were quite a few of those "other Mardukans," now, including the recently hired mahout who climbed up on Patty and guided her to the picket lines. The mahout and his fellows were only a few of the "camp followers" the company had attached, however. Their stated destination, Diaspra, had been avoided by caravans for the last several months as the advance of the

Boman barbarians made travel out of Ran Tai's high valley increasingly problematical. The riverport city lay on the Chasten River where it broke over the edge of the Diaspran Plateau, and the Chasten drained directly into the vast gulf or inland sea they'd identified from their rough, deplorably undetailed maps as their next objective. The locals called it the K'Vaernian Sea; the humans called it the shortest path to the open ocean which lay between them and their ultimate goal. That made Diaspra their only logical intermediate objective, and their departure had been delayed repeatedly as caravan masters solicited their services for protection on the trip.

All of which explained why the Marines and their beasts were accompanied by two caravans of *flar-ta* and *turom*, along with another two dozen *civan*-riding guardsmen. Between the Marines' heavy weapons and unusual tactics and the additional guards, they might be able to beat off a few attacks.

Roger looked around as the rest of the caravan came to an untidy stop and the Mardukan guards straggled out to assist the Marines. One of Pahner's requirements had been that the guards be willing to follow his orders, even the strange ones, and now the Mardukans began digging foxholes while the Marines laid out mono-wire and directional mines. As always, however, the majority of both groups were on guard, and the work parties hadn't hesitated to conscript liberally from the chaotic mob which wasn't attached to any particular caravan but had simply followed the departing party.

"I don't know about this," the prince said, shaking his head. "There are too many for us to cover, and not enough to really help."

"It'll be all right," Pahner said. "There's a reason the Marines stay around you. They're obviously the best armed and most dangerous of the bunch, so any attacker in his right mind is going to hit the rest of the caravan first."

Pahner patted his breast pocket absently for a moment, then extracted a piece of *bisti* root, sliced off a thin strip, and popped it into his mouth. He replaced the rest in his pocket, and his eyes considered the river that the caravan route followed while he chewed.

"The Boman are also still reported to be on the north side of the Chasten, not our side. But you're right—we still need more guards. I wish we'd been able to hire that group of mercenaries you tangled with. They might have been a tad incompetent, but we could have fixed that quickly enough."

"Well," Roger said with a chuckle, "I understand they had to get out of town pretty quick." He shook his head again at the thought, then frowned. "And I don't know how we could afford a company of mercs, anyway. We're tapped. Remember, Captain?"

"Oh, I don't know," Pahner said with a faint smile as he masticated the mildly stimulating sweet root. "I'm sure something could have been worked out."

"Don't worry, Rastar," Honal said. "We can work something out."

The Vasin prince looked at the strip of overcooked *atul* meat, then out at the encampment. Many of the women had only a scrap of root or bark in their hands, but they were tearing at that avidly, and there was a faint underlying whimper from the young who had already finished their scraps.

"We're just about at our end, Honal," he said quietly, and gestured at the encampment. "We have three times as many women as men, and many of the men aren't warrior bred." He clapped his false-hands in despair. "We might have made it on our trade in Ran Tai. Now . . . I don't know. If we can make it to Diaspra we might be okay. But we couldn't make it the last time."

"I'm sorry about Ran Tai," Honal said. The younger Mardukan looked as if he would like to die. "It was just . . . Those guards were so stupid. And if the gold had been there like everyone said—"

"What?" his cousin asked. "We would have taken it? Are we Boman? Are we bandits, cousin? Or are we Vasin, the last of the war bands of Therdan and Sheffan? The Warriors of the North? The Free Lords? Which, cousin? Warriors or bandits?"

The younger Mardukan didn't answer. He only retreated into his own misery, and Rastar took a nibble of the leathery meat, then stood and walked into the camp. He squatted down in the midst of the nearest group of females, pulled out of one of his knives, and began cutting the strip into very small pieces.

The women remained sitting, looking in shame at their hands as the last Prince of the North shared his meal with the starving younglings.

"That was wonderful, Kostas," Roger said, and took another bite of the succulent drumstick. "What was it?"

"Ah, that was wine-basted *basik*, Your Highness," the valet-cum-chef replied, and Roger looked at him sharply. The only times the prince had heard the term before had been in reference to humans . . . and it hadn't been very complimentary.

"Huh?" he remarked suspiciously and glanced around at the other members of the dinner party.

Cord was doing his best to look inscrutable, but the company had been around Mardukans long enough to recognize suppressed mirth. O'Casey had set down her morsel uneaten as she raised an eyebrow at the cook, but Kosutic—after a look around—ostentatiously popped her next bite into her mouth and chewed with obvious relish.

"What did you say it was?" the sergeant major asked innocently.

"I finally found out what '*basik*' meant when I was shopping in the market," the valet told her with a puckish grin. "It's the Mardukan version of a rabbit. It's apparently shy and somewhat stupid, and it's generally herded into a circle and killed with clubs."

"Hah!" Roger laughed. He raised his glass of the local sweet wine and took a drink. "To the *basik!*"

"Hear, hear," Kosutic agreed, clearing her own full mouth. "And to more *basik*, too!" she added, looking poignantly at the empty serving platter.

"Oh, I imagine something can be done about that," Matsugae told her with a smile, and bowed himself out of the tent to a spatter of applause.

"While we're waiting for the Sergeant Major's *basik*," Pahner said, "I think we need to discuss tomorrow's march."

"You think we'll get hit, Sir?" Gunny Jin asked. The NCO popped a roll of sweetened barleyrice into his mouth and shrugged. "If it happens, what else is there to do? We rally around the prince and form a square."

"Maybe, and maybe not," Pahner said. "We're about out of ammunition for the light weapons, but we have the full loadout, almost, for the heavy weapons. I've been thinking that there should be a way to get them into action quickly."

"Not one that I see immediately, Captain," Gunny Lai said. She leaned back and looked at the ceiling of the tent. "We can't keep the armor going without wearing out the power packs; the little skimp of energy we've been collecting with the solar sheets isn't enough to recharge with. And without the armor, the heavies are pretty impossible to use in a close-contact fight."

"I was wondering," Roger said diffidently. "Do you think that there's a way to mount one on a *flar-ta*? Not a plasma cannon, obviously, but maybe one of the stutter cannons?"

"Uh." Gunny Jin frowned, considering with obvious care. "One of those things has a hell of a recoil, even with the buffers. How are we going to secure it?"

"I don't know," Pahner said. "But that's the sort of thing I was thinking of, and we certainly need to find a way to use the firepower we have left. I'm not sure we'll make it to the coast if we don't."

"We could try it with Patty," Roger said with growing enthusiasm. "Mount it behind the mahout's spot. The driver will just have to keep his head down. I've fired just about everything else off her back by now; firing a cannon shouldn't be all that much worse."

"I don't know about that," Kosutic said with a shake of her head. "There's a whole order of difference between firing a grenade launcher or that old smoke pole of yours and firing a stutter gun offhand."

"You thinking of Old Man Kenny?" Jin asked her with a chuckle.

"Yeah," Kosutic said with a laugh of her own. "That was more or less what I was thinking about."

"Old Man Kenny?" Roger asked. He picked up a sliver of candied apsimon (which didn't taste a lot better to human tastebuds than *un*candied apsimon) and raised an eyebrow. "Care to enlighten us poor mortals?"

"No big story, Your Highness," Pahner told him. "Retired Sergeant Major Kenny is an instructor in the Heavy Weapons advanced course at Camp DeSarge. There've always been war stories about people firing plasma cannons and bead cannons 'offhand' or without them being properly mounted, so he decided to try it and see if there was really anything to them. He's a big guy," the CO added parenthetically.

"Did it work?"

"Well, sort of," Kosutic said.

"He hit the target, Your Highness," Pahner said with a slight smile and another sip of wine. "But he ended up about ten meters from where he started with a couple of cracked ribs and a dislocated shoulder. He wouldn't have been able to hit the next one."

"Hmmm." Roger took a sip of his own wine. "So the straps had better be strong and tight."

"At the least," Pahner agreed. "The gun is going to convey a kick like a *civan* to the packbeast. I don't know what the damned thing is going to do then."

"Damnthings live on a different planet, Captain Pahner," Roger said with a grin. "I know; I've hunted them."

"Nonetheless, Your Highness," the Marine told him, "when we try it out it won't be with Patty and with you as the mahout. We'll have one of the professionals handle Betty, who's a bit more . . . biddable than Patty. And you won't be at the controls of the cannon, either. That's a job for a private."

"Oh, all right," Roger agreed with a small chuckle. "You undoubtedly know best."

"Uh-huh," Kosutic said as one of the mahouts followed Matsugae back into the tent with a huge platter of *basik* legs. "He does. He really does."

"I hope you know what you're about, cousin." Honal looked towards the sound of distant booms and the occasional bugle of a *pagee* in distress. "It doesn't sound good over there."

"These 'humans' should have nothing against us," Rastar said as he mounted his own *civan*. The beasts showed the effects of deprivation almost as badly as their riders did; the pride of his father's stables had become as gaunt as a cheap hack. "And they can undoubtedly do with some additional guards . . . particularly judging from *that*." He drew the first of his pistols and inserted the winding key to test the tension on the wheel lock drive spring. It was ready, and he grunted in satisfaction, opened the sealed pan, positioned the flint striker against the serrated wheel, and then jerked his head in the direction of the sounds of combat while he reached for a second weapon. "If we bargain well, they may not even realize that they can get us for the cost of a barrel of *fredar!*"

Honal slapped the sides of his head in agitation, then sighed.

"All right! Lead on. And this time, I'll make sure not to try to take them over!"

CHAPTER SEVEN

Roger's head jerked up as the first line of scummies burst from the undergrowth. The tribesmen had been hidden in the jungle to one side of the beaten-down path between the two city-states, and their charge had caught the caravan by surprise, perfectly positioned in a narrow channel between the jungle and the Chasten River, with no room to evade them.

The prince checked his immediate impulse to order the mahout to countercharge with the aggressive *flar-ta* and threw his rifle to his shoulder instead. He caught one of the better dressed scummy barbarians in his sights and squeezed just as the ragged line came to a momentary halt and hurled its throwing axes.

It was the first time the company had dealt with that particular threat, but they were ready for it. The Marines on the ground lifted their Roman-style shields (design courtesy of one Roger MacClintock), and the rain of small axes scattered off of them like hail. It was sharp hail, however, as a yelp of pain from one of the riflemen proved. The wounded private hobbled backwards, his calf a bloody mess, and his place was taken by one of the second rank.

The humans were badly outnumbered, and the scummies hit them at the run, but the shield wall stopped them cold. The barbarians had never encountered the technique, and the bristle of spears from the rear rank, coupled with the stabbing short swords of the front rank, baffled them.

They paused, uncertain how to respond, and that momentary check was their doom. The stalled line of tribesmen was perfect meat for a tactic so antiquated to the humans that it was practically prehistoric. The sergeant major barked a command, and the Marines showed that perfect drill for which they were justly famous, jabbing their swords forward in unison and stepping forward to drive the tribesmen back from the vulnerable mounts.

The disciplined dike of shields and swords had also bought time for the single *flar-ta*-mounted bead cannon to be brought into action. Betty had finally been convinced that the noisy thing wasn't going to hurt her, barring some painful strap bruises, and she stood still as a statue while Berntsen and Stickles serviced the cannon. They walked the huge beads across the stalled crowd, killing half a dozen scummies with each shot, and the undisciplined tribesmen, totally unprepared for slaughter on such a scale, could stand the fire for only a few rounds. The rear ranks started to peel away and run back to the jungle almost instantly, quickly followed by the rest, and the less fleet footed of them fell under a brutal avalanche of javelins ordered by the irate sergeant major.

As Captain Pahner had anticipated, however, the majority of the attack had been directed at the remainder of the convoy, not Bravo Company, and things had gone far less well there. The noncombatants had fled to the river, some of them even diving in to escape the attacking tribesmen, while the majority of the guards, fighting as individuals against knots of tribesmen, had been quickly overrun and dragged from their mounts to be butchered despite their armor.

"Julian!" Pahner snapped. "Armor up your team. Bravo Company, prepare to wheel!"

Cord and two of the members of Julian's squad whose powered armor was off-line scrambled up on Patty as Roger rolled her into position behind the thin line of humans. The Mardukan settled into place behind Roger and prepared to wield his long spear while the Marines lifted their shields to cover the prince. Bodyguards or not, they had clearly accepted that his participation was a given.

There was still some fighting going on in the caravan, where armed drovers struggled desperately to hold onto their lives and their livelihoods, but many of the barbarians had already fallen to looting as the short platoon which was all that remained of Bravo Company of the Empress' Own countermarched to the rear.

Roger directed Patty's mahout to a position on the Marines' jungle flank as the cannon-armed packbeast fell in behind the tiny force. The Marines paused again, pulling fresh javelins from the quivers over their left shoulders. Then the sergeant major snapped a command, and they hurled the weapons at the rampaging tribesmen and charged forward with the deep, guttural yell which had been part of the Marine tradition for well over fifteen hundred years.

The tribesmen suddenly found themselves under attack from the flank. The flight of javelins was bad enough, but the bead cannon punching lines of death through their ranks was terrible. They tried to rally to face the charging attackers, but the humans were totally unlike the other caravan guards. Those guards, however courageous or skilled with their personal weapons they might have been, had fought as individual warriors, but the Marines weren't "warriors" in the Homeric tradition. They were *soldiers* who fought not as individuals, but as a deadly, trained and disciplined team, and they'd maintained their interval and dress despite their charge.

They slammed into the scummy force like a hammer hitting glass.

Dozens of the much larger tribesmen were simply bowled over and slaughtered by the charge, falling under the Marines' boots to be finished off by a slash or stab. The few who managed to survive the humans' passage and started to regain their feet were coldly dispatched by the line of mahouts, following the Marines for a chance to loot the dead.

The remainder of the barbarians were pushed to the sides, some of them spilling towards the milling *flar-ta* of the caravan and the Chasten, and others to the jungle side. The flankers on the river side had to contend with now thoroughly confused and angry packbeasts, who trampled several of them underfoot, but the ones on the jungle side were in even worse straits.

Roger and Patty had become a well-oiled machine, expert at the business of slaughter. There were a few ways to attack a *flar-ta* from the front, but most of them required the attacker to stand still to accurately throw a weapon at the beast's eyes or to brace a long spear, and those knots of stillness attracted Roger's attention. When he saw a tribesman ready himself to attack, the prince took him out with a single well-aimed round, but aside from that and an occasional shot at a notably better armed or dressed scummy, he let Patty carry the battle.

The *flar-ta* obviously had a thick strain of capetoad genes. She was not only aggressive, she was *nasty*. She spent no time lingering over kills—she simply spitted and gored enemies on the run, then charged on to the next group. She seemed to live for battle, and it was a terrifying thing to watch . . . so terrible that as she cleared the line of embattled Marines and emerged on its flank, most of the remaining scummies broke off their attack on the company and concentrated on the rampaging *flar-ta* out of simple self-preservation.

It started with a gathering hail of throwing axes. Most of them were poorly hurled, but the constant increase in the sheer volume of projectiles forced the two shield-bearing Marines to intercept them instead of attacking themselves. Next, the barbarians tried to circle the beast, dashing this way and that to get past its deadly horns. The Boman's main close-combat weapon was a long battle ax, and those tribesman who managed to get in close wielded their broad-bladed axes to good effect, inflicting terrible wounds upon the prince's mount.

Roger slid his rifle into its scabbard and drew his pistol, picking off the tribesmen as they rushed in to attack Patty. But there were simply too many of them for one pistol to stop, even in the hand of someone with his skill and enhancements. Patty bellowed in enraged pain as the first axes bit into her thick hide, but retreat was not an option. They were effectively holding the flank of the entire company, and if they fell back, the scummies would pour past them and take the line of Marines in the rear.

The battle hung indecisively in that bloody stalemate which characterizes most hard-fought actions. There was no longer room for maneuver, or tactics; it was stand or die, until one side or the other finally broke and ran.

"Howahah, cousin!" Honal shouted as he threaded his *civan* through the trees. "Maybe this wasn't such a bad idea after all!"

"We'll see," Rastar snorted, dropping his reins and controlling the *civan* with legs alone as he drew four of his dozen pistols. "If we survive."

Honal looked around at the cavalry troop. Most of its men were from his household, since virtually all of Rastar's troop had been killed in the escape from Therdan, and he gestured to either side.

"Deploy when we clear the damned trees!" he shouted. "One volley, then in with sword and lance!"

The heavily armored troopers' answering shout was hungry and edged with hot anticipation. They'd crossed sword and ax with the Boman many times before, and the technique was simple: blast them with one shot from each of your pistols, then charge in knee to knee. Sometimes, they broke and ran. Sometimes, they stood and dragged your comrades off their mounts. But whichever it was, it was always going to be someone *else* dying.

There were nearly a hundred and fifty in the company, including the few survivors of Rastar's guard, and as they came into the open area along the Chasten their column spread expertly to either side and their worn steeds rose to the challenge of battle as usual. The omnivorous *civan* knew a good battle always meant a good feed afterwards, and these *civan* were getting hungry enough to eat their own riders, much less fallen enemies.

Rastar looked to either side as the company took its dress.

"Are you ready, cousin?" Honal asked, true-hands taking up his lance while he held his reins in his lower false-hands.

"As always," the prince replied, and let his eyes

sweep the mounted line. "Let's stick it to these barbarian bastards!" he shouted, and an angry snarl answered him. The few Boman killed today would never repay the loss of Therdan and the League of the North. But it would be a start.

"Volley!"

Roger whipped his leg out of the way as the battle ax sank into Patty's shoulder right where his ankle had been. He finally got the recalcitrant magazine to seat, and shot the scummy in his screaming face as he tried to work the broad ax back out of the wound. The range was close enough for the ritual scars on the scummy's forehead to be clearly visible, and the blood splashing back from the bead impact coated Roger's forearm.

Patty streamed blood from dozens of wounds. Individually, none were immediately dangerous to something her size, but all were deep and painful, and she was becoming increasingly frantic in her attacks, occasionally spinning in place to bring her tail into play. But the Boman had become more expert at avoiding her, or perhaps only those who'd already been experts survived on the blood-soaked ground around her. Whatever the explanation, the mass swarming in on her was mostly dodging her lunges and spins, charging in whenever she paused and dealing steadily mounting damage to her unprotected flanks.

Roger, Cord, and the two Marines had managed to limit even those attacks, but it was becoming increasingly difficult, and more and more of the scummies made it through on every rush. As the intensity of their private battle mounted, the *flar-ta*, her riders, and the scummies attacking her had become so totally focused on the area around her that none of them even saw the deploying cavalry until the first volley hammered into the Boman in front of the Marines. The heavy pistol balls smashed through the packed mass of raiders, driving in against the hard-pressed shield wall, and the tribesmen found themselves once again faced by a flank attack—this one coming straight into their backs from their main direction of retreat.

The bead cannon was still plowing its dreadful holes through their ranks, the rampaging beast on their left flank had laid low dozens of their finest warriors, and the cheating bastards to their front refused to come out from behind their cowardly shields. It was just too much, and the tribesmen turned away from the Marine line and ran up the trail to escape the cavalry charge.

But that wasn't going to happen. The Northern riders slammed into them like an avalanche, firing pistols and spitting them on lances.

Rastar's charge carried his troopers through the caravan, where their ranks were broken by the still-milling packbeasts. Then they turned around and charged back into the fray, dropping their lances and drawing their swords for the best part of any cavalry skirmish. Nor had the Marines been sitting on their hands. As soon as the tribesmen broke, the company began to move forward, cutting down any resistance. The remaining clots of tribesmen in front of them were easily dealt with, and the Marines charged over their bodies to hit the Boman around the engaged cavalry force.

That cavalry was now bogged down, but it didn't seem to care. The mounted Mardukans were hacking at their enemies, seemingly intent on nothing other than killing them. Even as the tribesmen pulled members of the troop off their mounts, the leaders refused to retreat. They'd come to kill Boman, and they went about the business with grim ferocity.

Patty's assigned mahout had survived the first part of the battle by the skin of his horns, and he knew it.

So when Roger ordered him to charge to the aid of the embattled cavalry, the Mardukan decided that nothing was worth heading back into *that*, and slid silently off the packbeast.

Roger snarled in exasperation and climbed into his old, accustomed place and patted the beast on the soft spot under its armored shield.

"Come on, Patty!" he yelled. "Time to get some of our own back!"

The tired but willing *flar-ta* snorted at the familiar touch, and rumbled into a blood-streaming trot. Six tons of mad were about to hit the engaged tribesmen and let the chips fall where they might.

Rastar kneed his *civan*, and the beast did a hopping kick that killed the Boman trying to hamstring it.

The prince, however, was having less luck. The charge had broken through the damned Boman, but it hadn't managed to shatter them cleanly, and barbarians seemed to be everywhere. Worse, they were still fighting hard, despite having been caught between two sets of enemies. Oh, many of them had fled, but others—lured by the obvious wealth of the caravan—had stayed, and the holdouts were intent on killing his men.

Like any cavalrymen, Rastar and his troopers knew that their greatest assets were shock and mobility. Standing cavalry sacrificed almost all of its advantages over infantry, but Honal's force was too bogged down to retreat. Unable to break free and reorganize for a fresh charge, they could only stand and fight, trying to cover their occasional unseated brothers and hoping against hope that the stupid barbarians would realize they were *beaten*.

The prince spun his *civan* in place again, taking the face off of one of the barbarians trying to pull him off from the side. There were two others on the far side, but he was one of those incredibly rare and gifted Mardukans who were quad-dexterous, and that had stood him in good stead in many engagements like this one, where the ability to cover his *civan* was paramount. He whipped all four sabers around himself in a complex and lethal pattern . . . then looked up in half-stunned amazement as a *pagee* thundered through the middle of the battle, bugling like a *pagathar*.

Three humans and a tribesman of some sort were on its back, but they were letting the *pagee* do most of the fighting, and Rastar could see why. The beast tore into the Boman like the poor at a holiday feast, attacking with all the ferocity of a *pagathar* as it gored and trampled its way through the barbarians.

It seemed to be able to distinguish friend from foe as it stepped delicately across a fallen Northerner, somehow managing to avoid crushing him in the press. Or perhaps it was the driver. He seemed to be controlling the beast with knees and voice alone, shouting commands in some sort of gibberish and laying down a heavy fire from a pistol which widened the prince's eyes even in the midst of battle. Rastar loved pistols, especially since he could fire virtually simultaneously with all four hands. But the problem with them was that they had only one shot per barrel. He had twelve double-barreled pistols scattered about his harness and gear, and, at the moment, every one of them had been discharged.

This pistol, however, was spitting shot after shot. Its ammunition seemed limitless, but then he saw the rider pause momentarily, replace a container in the grip, and then start firing again. So easily! In an instant, the weapon was reloaded. With a pistol like that, he could plow through the Boman like a scythe through barleyrice!

He killed another of the barbarians almost absent-mindedly, leaning to the side to scissor the bastard's neck with the two razor-sharp sabers in his false-hands. He might as well not even have bothered; the Boman were running.

He waved to Honal, who lifted a bloody saber in response and ordered his company into pursuit. The *civan*-mounted force would harry the enemy into the ground; if a hand of the Boman remained alive by dark, it would be a surprise.

Now to go bargain with these "humans." Despite his confident words to Honal, Rastar was far from certain that a bargain really could be struck, but at least now he could haggle with references in hand instead of a begging bowl.

Armand Pahner gave the Mardukan cavalryman a closed-mouth smile.

"We appreciate the help," he said as the big scummy swung down from his bipedal mount. "Especially since I think you're the folks we chased out of Ran Tai."

"I would like to say that we came to aid you because we're honorable warriors and couldn't just watch the barbarians destroy your caravan." Rastar removed his helmet and rubbed his horns. "Unfortunately, the fact is that we need a job. We'd like to hire on as caravan guards, and you—" he gestured at the carnage about them and the handful of survivors from the original force of caravan guardsmen "—clearly need more of them."

"Ah." Pahner cocked his head and contemplated the Mardukan for a moment and felt temptation stir. These people were the first Mardukan troops he'd yet seen who'd actually fought as a cohesive, organized force rather than a collection of individualists. They obviously had rough edges, by human standards, but they were head and shoulders above their nearest native competition.

"You're right," he said after a moment, "but there was no gold in the mine. We're as low on cash as you must be."

"We're not expensive," the prince said with a rueful grunt. "And there will be great profit to this caravan when it reaches Diaspra. *If* it reaches Diaspra. We can be paid then."

"How much?" Pahner asked. "When we reach Diaspra?"

"For the rest of the trip?" The prince rubbed the crest of his helmet with one finger. "Board and tack during the trip. Two gold K'Vaernian astar per trooper at completion. Three for each one lost. Five for the commander, and ten for myself." He looked at the pistol at the human's belt. "Although I would personally consider trading quite a bit of that for one of those pistols," he added with a grunt of laughter.

Pahner pulled out his *bisti* root and shaved off a sliver. He offered the leader a slice, but it was refused, so he put the remaining root away while he contemplated the offer. The K'Vaernian coin was about thirty grams in weight. They had more than enough hidden in the packs to meet the Mardukan's price, but he hadn't been born yesterday. Nobody ever went for the first offer.

"One gold astar each, two for the fallen, three for the commander, five for you, and you handle the board," he retorted.

The Mardukan drew himself up and appeared ready to snarl some curse, but paused. It seemed to Pahner that he wasn't used to haggling, which didn't make much sense for a mercenary, but finally he made a hand gesture of negation.

"I agree to the coin, but you must handle board. One

sedant of grain per day per trooper. Five sedant per
civan. An additional ten for our followers, and five for
the commander and ten for myself. And it is not nego-
tiable; we'll have to find another employer if we can't
have the board."

Now it was Pahner's turn to be taken back. He
wasn't sure they had enough barleyrice to support that
all the way to Diaspra, and he chewed his *bisti* for a
few moments, then shrugged.

"We didn't bring that much chow. And I don't know
a way around that. If the damned Boman are on this
side of the Chasten now, we can't afford to go back
to Ran Tai."

"You might have to," the cavalryman told him
soberly. "These are only the outriders, not the main
horde, but they swarm like maggots as they advance.
The way might be impassable."

"If I have to, I'll unload the armor," the captain said
with a feral grin. "I've got enough power and spares
for two uses of it. This might be one of them . . . and
if I unass our powered armor, don't tell me about
'impassable'!"

The Mardukan regarded him levelly, then clapped
hands in resignation.

"I have never heard of 'powered' armor, but you
humans have many things we've never heard of, so perhaps you *can* fight your way through. Yet from what
I've seen of the rest of your weapons, it still seems clear
to me that you will require the aid of a force of guards
who fight with discipline and order, and that is what
we of the Vasin are. So, what can you afford for board?
We wish to go to Diaspra also, mainly because we know
they'll be hiring. But . . . we're out of food. Completely.
We have nothing to bring to the table."

Pahner held the native's eyes, chewing steadily on
his *bisti* root, then nodded finally.

"Okay, we can work with that. We'll share as available, and strip the caravan if we have to. Keeping the fighters in shape is the priority, but nobody starves. How's that?"

The Mardukan commander clapped hands in agreement and held one out, palm outward.

"Agreed. Everyone to share; no one to starve."

"To a long and fruitful alliance, then," Pahner said with a smile, matching the gesture of agreement. Then he chuckled grimly. "Now comes the fun part."

CHAPTER EIGHT

Roger slid off of Patty's back and caught one end of the plasma cannon as it dropped, then handed it off to Gronningen as the plasma gunner jumped to the ground and the mahout moved the packbeast back. The *flar-ta* still hadn't recovered fully from her wounds, and more had been added in the last three weeks, so the prince was keeping her back from this little skirmish.

He waved to the mahouts as the rest of the convoy pounded past towards one of the ubiquitous cities of the lowlands in the near distance. This one sat on a high promontory by the river where the now broad and powerful Chasten descended a series of cascades before reaching the coastal plains, and unless he was sorely mistaken, it must be Diaspra itself. The city was enormous in comparison to the towns of the Hurtan and Hadur regions and sprawled off the promontory and down onto the plains, with its outer portions protected from floods by its massive walls, flood control canals, and sturdy dikes.

It obviously looked good to the packbeast drovers.

They were goading their mounts into a clumsy canter, and the Mardukan children packed on the backs of the beasts looked at Roger oddly as he waved. A few waved back, but with an almost puzzled air, for it was not a Mardukan custom.

The Marines had peeled off from the caravan as well, and now they aligned themselves on the road with a handful of their own, steadier *flar-ta* at their backs. Their chosen location was a narrow way between two thick groves of trees about a thousand meters from the wall, presumably left to provide firewood when the other approaches to the city were brushed back. The pursuing barbarians would be forced to face the Marine line or try flanking it through the heavy wood. No doubt the flank would eventually be turned, but by then the noncombatants would be through the gates of the city and the Marines would be able to *really* maneuver. With the aid of their *flar-ta*, the human force would be able to play hard to get all the way to the walls.

Pahner paced slowly up and down behind his line, gently masticating his *bisti* root, and nodded to Roger. He'd wanted the prince to accompany the noncombatants into the city, but he hadn't bothered to say so. Whether he liked it or not, he'd finally resigned himself to the fact that if there was a fight, Roger would be in the thick of it. As a matter of fact, he *didn't* like it one bit, but that was the bodyguard in him. The Marine in him had to admit (very privately, where Roger would never hear it) that it was far more satisfying to guard someone who refused to hide behind the bodies and lives of other people . . . however difficult that made it to protect the insufferable, headstrong, and often *irritating* someone in question.

Roger himself trotted forward to the line with Cord and Denat in hot pursuit. The two Mardukans had spent the last three weeks learning how to use the large shields the humans had introduced, and the reason was apparent as a storm of throwing axes descended on the human line. The two four-armed Mardukans threw up a double set of shields: one for themselves, and the other for the heedless prince who was carefully judging the approach of the barbarian forces. Roger nodded his thanks to Cord, and looked over at the sergeant major.

"About two hundred or so, don't you think, Sergeant Major?"

"About that, Sir," the NCO replied. "I'm still trying to divide my arm count by four."

Roger smiled and dialed up the magnification of his helmet display, then called up his combat program and put a crosshair on the head of the apparent leader.

"Your call, Smaj."

"Bravo Company will hurl javelins!" the sergeant major announced in a voice which would have carried through the teeth of a hurricane. "*Draw!* Take aim! *Throw!* Out swords!"

The hail of throwing spears didn't stop the barbarians, but it did break up their ranks, and Roger accompanied the javelin volley with three shots from his bead pistol. Like all the rest of the ammunition, pistol ammo was in too short a supply to waste, but Roger very seldom "wasted" ammunition, and his three carefully placed rounds dropped the barbarians' leaders in their tracks. Whether that was good or bad remained to be seen, of course. The company had already discovered that Boman warriors were altogether too prone to a sort of berserk fighting madness once combat began, and sometimes it was only the leaders who would—or could—call for a retreat.

This scummy force had a few arquebuses, and since it wasn't raining (at the moment), the gunners came to the fore as the force approached the humans. There were only six of them, but the rest of the band halted as they laboriously adjusted their waxy, smoking matches and aimed in the general direction of the human company. Three of the firearms, obviously captured from more civilized original owners, were beautifully made, with fancy brass inlay work which had seen better days, but all of them looked incredibly clumsy to a modern Marine. Which didn't necessarily mean they were ineffective . . . assuming that they actually hit something.

The gunners blew on the ends of their matches until the glowing embers satisfied them, then popped open the hermetically sealed priming pans which Marduk's humid climate made essential. They glanced at the priming powder, then grasped the leverlike triggers which would pivot the serpentine metal arms which held the slow matches and dip their glowing ends into the powder.

The weapons were scarcely accurate at anything beyond point-blank range. Of course, this *was* point-blank range, but the Marines were utterly contemptuous of the threat. Cord and Denat ducked behind the humans' line, but the Marines shouted insults at the Boman and actually pulled their shields out of line to expose their bodies to fire.

The reason for their contempt became apparent after the volley. The blast from the relatively few weapons filled the space between the Mardukan and human lines with thick smoke, but it was clear that only a single Marine had been hit. One fatality out of six wasn't a bad average for a Mardukan arquebus volley, so the gunners' fellows shouted approvingly and sprang into a charge. But they checked when the single trooper who'd gone down heaved herself to her feet, swearing, and readied her shield once more.

"Now, now, Briana," Roger admonished Corporal

Kane. "I'm sure that their mothers at least *knew* their fathers."

"Yes, Sir," the corporal said, bringing her shield back around to the front. "If you say so. But I still say I'm gonna gut that stupid bastard. Those damned bullets *smart*."

Roger had to agree. Mardukan arquebuses were wildly outsized compared to any human-scaled weapon, man-packed cannon that fired quarter-kilo balls. The projectiles' velocity was high at short range (which was to say, at any range at which a hit could realistically be anticipated), as well, which imparted a tremendous kick when one hit the kinetic reactive armor of the chameleon suits. But that velocity was what made the chameleon suits effective against them, for the Marines' uniforms were designed for protection against modern, high-speed projectiles. They were relatively ineffective against *low*-speed weapons, like spears, swords, or throwing axes, but arquebus balls were something else. The suits not only "hardened" when struck by the rounds, but distributed the kinetic energy across their entire surface and even around the back. Despite her understandable outrage, the impact was spread widely enough that the most the corporal would suffer was a few bruises.

The Mardukans checked for a moment at the sight of the unexpected resurrection, then charged forward anyway, screaming their battle cries and swinging their battle axes. Many of the barbarians used two axes at a time, and they came windmilling into the human line like four-armed juggernauts.

The Marines were ready for them. Over the last few weeks, they'd fought off repeated small attacks by the roaming tribes who formed the vanguard of the Boman. This was the largest one yet, but it would prove no more of a challenge than the others.

The plasma cannon rolled forward a few steps, placing its barrel just beyond the Marine line as the troopers to either side moved back to give it room, and fired point blank. The belch of ions scorched the fronts of the Marines' wood and iron shields, but otherwise left them unaffected. The same could not be said for the Mardukans.

The plasma cannon had been set at relatively low power, both to conserve energy in its power pack and also because its targets were too frail to require anything more energetic. It was still powerful enough to knock out a modern tank, however, and it tore through the mass of tribesmen like a fusion-powered brimstone battering ram. A ten-meter-wide gap appeared as if by magic straight through the center of their formation. There weren't even any bodies—only a smoking hellhole bordered by blackened, half-consumed skeletons and screaming barbarians, writhing and twisting insanely with the agony of the flash burns seared across their bodies.

There was no time for a second shot . . . or for the howling tribesmen to break off their attack. They were moving too quickly, and the range was too short, for them to change their minds. They had no choice but to carry through with their charge, which actually was the best thing they could have done. At least it got them in close enough to prevent the hell weapon from effortlessly incinerating all of them!

Unfortunately, the fact that closing with their enemies was their "best" option didn't necessarily make it a *good* one.

The plasma cannon pulled back and its flankers closed ranks once more with perfect timing just as the remnants of the shattered formation hit the human shield wall and the Boman learned another lesson: a disciplined wall of shields shrugs off windmilling axes like rain.

Bravo Company was the product of an extremely advanced, high-tech society, but the Marines had been taught in a brutal school since their arrival on Marduk. Only a few of them had really been anything close to what a Mardukan might consider proficient with edged steel upon their arrival here, but those few had passed on all the tricks they knew. Other techniques had been learned the hard way, and Armand Pahner and Eva Kosutic had planned their tactics and training with the fundamentals firmly in mind: keep the shield up, and stab low.

Even as the thundering axes struck downward onto their hard-held shields, the Marines stabbed forward through the narrow gaps between them, aiming for the bellies and gonads of their enemies. The Mardukans had a tremendous reach advantage over the humans, but they were forced to step in close to hack down at the Marines' defensive barrier, and when they did, they also stepped directly into the sweep of the humans' weapons.

The result was a slaughter. The Mardukans, faced by a radically new approach to fighting and unable to find a way through the shield wall, found themselves slipping in the spilled intestines of their own front line instead. Kosutic watched the entire battle dispassionately. She'd become expert at gauging Mardukan morale over the last few weeks, and she saw the point of balance when the barbarians began to waver.

She glanced at Captain Pahner, who nodded. Time to finish this.

"*Bravo Company will advance!*" she called. She looked to the woods to her right, where there was a flash of metal. "Prepare to advance on cadence. *In step! HUT!*"

The company moved forward, calling the time, short swords and spears stabbing with every step, and the Mardukan tribesmen found themselves driven back.

The alternative to retreat was to spit themselves on those dreadful knives the humans wielded.

The plasma cannon had killed perhaps twenty percent of the total Boman force, but the remaining barbarians still outnumbered the Marines by three-to-one, and despite the efficiency of the humans' combat technique, they hadn't really taken many casualties yet in hand-to-hand. They'd still suffered more than the Marines, who'd taken *no* casualties, but the battle was effectively a stalemate, with the edge in quality on Bravo Company's side, and quantity overwhelmingly on the Boman's side.

It came down to attrition and morale . . . but that was easy enough to change. Kosutic looked over at the captain once more, and Pahner nodded in response and keyed his radio.

"Now would be good, Rastar," the communicator clipped to the Mardukan's harness said, and the Therdan prince carefully depressed the talking switch.

"Right-oh," he responded in Standard English. Roger had started using the expression around him a good bit, and Rastar knew it was some sort of joke, but he liked it anyway. He looked over at Honal and wrinkled the skin over one eye in another human expression. "Shall we, cousin?"

The guard commander grunted in laughter and gave a tooth-showing human-style grin.

"Yes, cousin. Let's." He looked at his force and drew his saber. "*Sheffan!*" he cried, slapping the flank of his *civan* with the flat of his blade. Time to show these barbarian bastards what it meant to get in the way of the riders of the North.

The one worry the travelers had had, that the city might not open its gates to them, turned out to be moot. The square beyond those gates was lined with cheering townsfolk, and the guardsmen manning them waved the Marines and their Mardukan allies enthusiastically through.

In fact, the humans found themselves forced to form a perimeter around their packbeasts to hold back the cheering crowds. After a few moments' struggle, the Northern cavalry pushed through to join them, using their occasionally snapping *civan* to open up a space around the human contingent and their animals. It was as well that they had, for the shouts and high-pitched whistles of the ecstatic Mardukans bounced back and forth between the stone curtain wall and the city's structures. The enclosure trapped the bedlam, turning it into a hot, close maelstrom in which all sanity seemed to have been lost as the city guards slammed the gates behind the new arrivals.

The boom of the closing gates could barely be heard over the thunder of the locals, but it still startled Patty, and the overwrought *flar-ta* let out a low rumble and slapped her feet up and down on the cobbles, waving her horns back and forth at the pressing crowd.

"Ho, girl!" Roger yelled over the frenzied uproar, scratching her under her armored shield and patting her on the shoulder. "Steady!"

The huge beast uttered a half-furious, half-querulous bugle, but it was obvious that she hovered on the brink of a berserk response. In another moment she would charge the crowd like a six-ton bull in a china shop, and Pahner shook his head and keyed his helmet.

"Roger, try to keep her under control!" he said quickly, and patted his pockets until he came up with a flash grenade, set the timer for a three-second delay, and threw it straight up in the air.

The tremendous flash and crack of the human weapon had become normal to the packbeasts, who paid no attention to it. But the intense report, magnified by the echoing walls, shocked the crowd into momentary silence broken only by the low rumble of Patty's prebattle fury.

In the hush that followed, a group of guards clad in chain mail and plate pushed their way through the crowd, escorting a pair of elderly Mardukans. At their appearance, the crowd began to fall reluctantly back from the caravan. A few still cheered, but were quickly hushed into silence by their fellows.

Roger waited for several moments, until he was confident that Patty had calmed down at least some, then waved for the head mahout to relieve him on her back and slid to the ground. He walked across to where Pahner stood awaiting the delegation and smiled at the Marine.

"I think they're happy to see us."

"Too happy," the captain replied sourly. "Nobody is that pleased to see the Corps unless their ass is caught in a crack."

"Which means ours is, as well," Roger said. "Right?"

"What else is pocking new?" Poertena muttered, then looked up at his glowering CO and swallowed hastily. "Sir?"

The captain glowered at the armorer for another long moment, but finally relented.

"Nothing, Poertena," he said, shaking his head. "Nothing new in that at all. In fact . . ."

". . . it's getting really old," Roger finished.

"Yep," the company commander said as the delegation finally made it through the cordon of shield-wielding Marines. "Real old," he added, holding out his hand palm up in Mardukan greeting.

The delegation looked terribly pleased to see them. Terribly.

CHAPTER NINE

Gratar, the priest-king of Diaspra, rolled up the document in front of him and crumpled it in his true-hands as he looked at the human visitors. They did not seem happy at the news he'd just imparted.

"So there's no way to the sea?" Roger asked, just to be sure that the information wasn't getting garbled.

"None that is clear." The answer came from the local guard commander, Bogess. The old Mardukan was technically one of the two water priests who held seats on the city council (the other council members were all merchants), but he wore chain mail and the back and breast from the heavy plate armor that was his normal gear. "The Boman swept down within the last ten-day and have encircled the city. Even before then, we had word that the city of Bastar, the port at the mouth of the Chasten, had fallen. Even if you could win down the river, there would be nothing there for you."

Pahner grunted.

"I don't care what city we get to, but we have to

114

cross the ocean. Our destination is on the far side, and the K'Vaernian Sea is our shortest way to the ocean."

The locals at the table traded looks.

"There is nothing on the other side of the water," King Gratar said carefully. "The ocean is an eternal expanse of demon-filled water, placed there by the God to guard the shores of the World Island."

The priest-king's concern for their safety—or perhaps it was for their sanity—was obvious. The local prelate seemed determined to be friendly, despite their heretical notions about just what an ocean was, and the company's appearance immediately after the city's aqueduct had been cut had already been hailed as a sign from their god.

Pahner opened his mouth to reply, but O'Casey laid a warning hand on his arm.

"Perhaps we'll deal with that problem when we reach the sea," she said calmly. "Are there *any* cities on the sea that have held out against the Boman?"

"K'Vaern's Cove," Rastar said instantly. "It could hold out for the rest of eternity."

"You only hope that," Bogess said. "Surely K'Vaern's Cove fell with the rest of the Northern states?"

"It hadn't when we headed this way," the leader of the Northern mercenaries replied.

He'd been looking better since arriving in the city. Once the humans had gotten to know him and his troopers, they'd figured out fairly quickly that the Vasin certainly weren't barbarians, whatever the denizens of Ran Tai might have thought. And once they'd reached Diaspra, they'd found out just how true that was, for it turned out that several thousand troopers from Therdan, Sheffan, and the other city-states of the League of the North had straggled into Diaspra, where they'd reinforced the local forces. Those troopers had been almost pitifully glad to see Rastar alive, and even more so to see how many women and children he and Honal's guardsmen had gotten out. As soon as they'd learned the Prince of Therdan was in the city, the survivors had transferred their allegiance, giving him a quite respectable force and his seat at the table.

"Furthermore," Rastar went on now, "many of the troopers from the League cities have told me that K'Vaern's Cove holds out still. It has enormous granaries—big enough, it's said, to withstand siege for three or even four years if it must—and if that's not enough, it can hold out indefinitely by importing food by sea. More, the peninsula is protected as much by the sea about it as by its walls, and the Boman aren't going to be able to defeat the K'Vaernian Navy. No, K'Vaern's Cove is still there," he finished.

"Well, our granaries are *not* full," the priest-king said, crumpling the damning report once more. "We were unable to get in the harvest before the Boman struck, nor are we a well-prepared border city whose store-rooms are kept filled in anticipation of war. Our fighters, especially with the help of the Northern forces, have held out so far, but we have only a few months' food, and the Boman squat on our fields. If we cannot harvest, we will starve, and they know it."

"They're awaiting the Hompag Rains," Bogess said gloomily. "They should start any day now. Once the rains abate and the land dries, they'll return. And that will be the end of Diaspra."

"Okay, okay," Pahner said, shaking his head. He wasn't sure what the Hompag Rains were, but first things first. "Let's not get negative. First of all, I don't know how familiar you are with sieges. Have you taken control of the granaries?" he asked the guard commander.

"No," Bogess said sourly. "The granaries are privately owned. We can't control them, and the price of barleyrice has already gotten out of hand."

Pahner shook his head again. "Okay, we need to talk about that." He looked around at the small counsel. "Are any of you familiar with sieges?"

"Not really," Grath Chain replied. He was one of the junior council members, one of its many merchants, and his expression was sour as he made a sign of negation. "We've usually managed to avoid wars."

"Usually by swindling the other side," Honal said in a stage whisper.

"It wasn't we who swindled the Boman and started this whole mess!" Bogess snapped. The old warrior's face twitched like a rat in a fury. "It was not *we* who brought this pestilence down upon us!"

"No, it was another scum-sucking Southerner!" the Northern cavalry commander shot back hotly. "Or have you forgotten Sindi?"

"Wait!" Pahner barked as the entire council chamber began to erupt in argument. "We only need to decide one thing at this council: do we want to survive, or do we want to die?"

He glared around the room, and most of the Mardukans turned aside from the heat of his fury.

"That's the only thing we need to know," he went on in a grating voice. "If we want to live, we're going to put aside these arguments and forget the niceties of normal business and do the things we need to do to survive." He turned to the king. "Now, Your Excellency, do you want to live?"

"Of course I do," the priest-king replied. "What's your point?"

"My point is that what I'm hearing is 'I can't,' 'we can't,' and 'it's not my fault,'" the Marine captain told him. "What we need to *start* hearing is 'we can' and 'can do.' Attitude is nearly half the battle in a situation like this."

"What do you mean by 'the niceties of normal business'?" Grath Chain asked suspiciously. "Would one of those things be seizing the privately owned grain?"

"Not at all. But we are going to have to make plenty of decisions that aren't going to be liked, and we can't hold a meeting for every decision and come to a group consensus. You have a problem here, and we have it also. There's no way out of the city, and you don't have enough food for an extended siege. That means we're going to have to bring the barbarians to a decisive battle."

"They won't attack the city," Bogess said wearily. "We've tried and tried to get them to do so. No chance."

"Then we'll have to leave the city with a large enough force to bring them to battle and pin them down," the Marine said. "If we take out a large force, will they attack it?"

"Yes," the king said. "But they'll also destroy it. We've lost half our army trying to fight them for the fields. They'll attack mercilessly as soon as they can concentrate on you outside the walls."

"So we won't have to chase them down?" Kosutic asked in surprise. "I thought we'd have to chase them all over Hell and gone to pin them down."

"Not this group," Rastar said with a grimace. "The Southerners call them all Boman, but this is really the Wespar tribe. You can tell by the tribal markings. The Wespar are uncivilized, even in comparison to the other Boman, and their tribal leader is Speer Mon, a pure idiot even by the standards of *his* tribe. All you'd have to do is say 'meet me here,' and he would."

"Well, they've been smart enough to avoid the walls of the city," Bogess said defensively.

"That's because we bled them white in the north," Rastar said with a grimace. "They learned to feint and hold the fields against us by bitter experience. If we'd had our full grain rations, we'd be holding out still."

"And what happened there, O Prince of the North?" Grath Chain sneered. "What happened to your vaunted stores? The stores that your precious League used as an excuse for its extortionate tolls?"

Rastar was quiet for a long moment. The moment was long enough for the Council to become uncomfortable, and some of them shifted on the cushions scattered around the low table. Finally, the Mardukan prince looked up from his hands at the councilor.

"If you wish to live out the day," he said very calmly, "keep a civil tongue."

"That's no answer, and I'll have you know that no northern barbar—" the councilor started, then froze as he realized he was looking down the barrels of five pistols.

"Put it down, Roger," Rastar said with a harsh chuckle, then stabbed Grath Chain with an eye as cold as the muzzles of his own pistols. "Here is the answer, *feck*-beast. The stores were poisoned. Probably by agents from Sindi; we too had 'offended' that thrice-accursed prince.

"But," he added with a human tooth-showing grin as he put his pistols away, "someone brought that agent to our city. It wasn't a trader from Sindi, for they'd been banned from all the cities of the Northern League." He grinned again at the councilor. "When I find out who it was that brought that agent to my city, I will kill that person. I will do it without asking any permission, or giving any warning. I will do it on the slightest thread of evidence. So I would suggest that you make sure your accounts are in order, *feck*-beast."

The shaken councilor looked to the king.

"I shouldn't have to put up with this from northern barbarians!"

"Your Excellency," Roger said, standing up, "we need to come to an understanding."

The king hesitated, but nodded for him to continue.

"We're in a 'war to the knife,'" the prince said. "What does that mean?" He gestured at Rastar. "Your Northern comrades have told you already. The Boman are here to stay. They'll continue to bleed you until you fall like a hamstrung *pagee*, and then they'll swarm over you like *atul*."

He looked around the council, daring one of them to meet his eye.

"Now, we can win against them. My people have been in wars like this many, many times, and we have a great deal of expertise to offer you. But it has to be a partnership. We'll tell you what we think you need to do. If you do it, we, all of us, might survive. If you don't, we, all of us, will die. And your women and children as well." He looked over at Rastar. "Correct?"

"Oh, yes," the Northerner said bleakly. "The Wespar have no use for 'shit-sitters.'" He looked over at Cord, sitting silently behind the prince, and the tribesman returned the look blandly.

Grath Chain began to sputter something, but the priest-king gestured the angry councilor to silence.

"What do you suggest?" he asked.

"Captain?" Roger invited, resuming his seat.

"Put guards on all the granaries," Pahner said crisply. "Dole out bulk foodstuffs in prescribed portions at fixed prices. This will not only prevent price gouging but prevent hoarding and stretch the available supply. Begin training not only the regular forces but all able-bodied males in new fighting techniques to be used against the tribesmen. Force an engagement at a time and place of our choosing, and destroy the bulk of the barbarian force."

"Where do we get the soldiers?" Bogess asked. "It takes years of training with the sword to make a warrior, and even then better than half are lost in the first battle, if it's a fierce one," he said grimly, and Pahner shrugged.

"I won't say that our methods can make warriors out of them, but we can make soldiers in a few months. It's mostly a matter of training them to obey orders unquestioningly and to stand. If they do those two things, the way we fight can be taught in less than a month."

"Impossible," Grath Chain scoffed. "No one can train a warrior in a month!"

"I didn't say anything about warriors," Pahner told the merchant coldly. "We'll be training *soldiers*, and that's a hell of a lot more dangerous than warriors are. The only thing we need is able bodies." He turned to Bogess. "Can you find several thousand able-bodied men? Ones that can walk two hours with a heavy weight? Other than that, six limbs and a quarter brain is all we need."

Bogess grunted in laughter.

"That we can find, I believe." He turned to the priest-king. "Your Excellency? May we have the Laborers of God?"

Gratar looked pensive.

"The Hompag Rains come soon, and the damage is already extensive. Who will repair the dikes and canals? Who will clean the face of the God?"

Bogess turned to the humans, who were clearly confused.

"The Laborers of God are simple men, common folk. They labor on the Works of God, the canals, dikes, and temples of our city. There are many of them—they far outnumber the small Guard of God—and they're strong-backed laborers. Would they do?"

"Perfectly," Pahner said with a note of enthusiasm. "I assume they already have some sort of structure? That they're broken down into different divisions or companies or something?"

"Yes, they're separated by districts and responsibility," the cleric seated beside Gratar said. The heavyset Mardukan had remained silent throughout the entire discussion so far, but now he leaned forward to meet Pahner's gaze. "I am Rus From, the Bishop of Artificers. The groups are irregular in size, depending on what their responsibilities are."

"And what of those responsibilities?" Grath Chain snapped. "Who will repair the dikes and canals? Who will insure that the face of the God is clean?"

"Your Excellency," Roger responded quietly, "who will do those things if the Boman lay you waste? This is an evil time for your city, one in which you must choose between lesser and greater evils if you are to survive. Yes, repairing and maintaining your city and its temples is important, but you built those artifacts once. You can build them once again . . . if you—and your city—live."

"I suppose," the priest-king mused, then drew a deep breath. "Once again, your truths win through, Prince Roger. Very well. General Bogess, you are authorized to take command of the Laborers of God and turn them into Warriors of God. I suggest that you put the leadership of the Laborers under Sol Ta for this. Chan Roy will understand. Chan is getting old, and Sol Ta has much fire. And may the Lord of Water be with us."

"Thank you, Your Excellency," Captain Pahner said quietly. "We'll do our best to save your beautiful city."

"Hmmm," an older councilor said, rubbing his horns. "I was about to suggest that you'd contradicted yourself on the seizure of grain, Captain. But you didn't. You danced a fine line instead, didn't you? You said you wouldn't seize the granaries, but you didn't say anything about putting guards on them."

"The merchants will still make a profit, just not as large a profit as they thought they were going to. However, it will stretch out the resources and allow us time to train up a force."

"Two months," the old councilor said after a moment. "That's how long until the peasants must begin bringing in the harvest. If we wait longer than that, we might as well all cut our own throats."

"Two months should be more than enough time," Pahner said.

"Good." The councilor nodded at the human, then touched his own chest. "Gessram Kar. I'm one of those shifty merchants you're about to fleece. One of the largest ones, I might add."

"Glad to hear it," Pahner said with a broad smile. "If you don't object, no one else should."

"Perhaps," the merchant grunted. "But I wonder who you'll find to enforce this edict, hmmm?"

"T'ey pocking t'ieves, Sir," Poertena said looking at his pad. "Look, up in Ran Tai, where t'ey can' even *grow* barleyrice, it go for two K'Vaernian copper a kusul."

"At least now we know where all this reference to K'Vaern comes from," Roger observed, then grimaced. "Sorry, Poertena. You were saying?"

"T'ey pocking t'ieves is what I sayin', Sir," the Pinopan repeated. "I find t'ree prices on barleyrice. T'ey between fifteen copper and two *silver!*"

"That would be twenty-to-one on the high end, right?" Pahner asked.

"Yes, Sir. I t'ink t'ey should be around tee same cost as at Ran Tai. Reason is, Ran Tai already got a shortage, so inflation index be about right."

"Inflation index?" Roger repeated with a chuckle.

"Yes, Sir. It tee adjusted cost o' materials in a situation o' limited supply." Poertena glanced at the so far silent chief of staff who gave him a quick and unnoticed wink.

"I know what it is," Roger said. "It's just . . . uh . . ."

"What?" the Pinopan asked.

"Never mind. So, the price should be fixed at about two coppers a kusul? What about other foodstuffs?"

"I got some numbers from Ran Tai, Sir," Poertena said, gesturing at his pad. "Most of t'em're already inflationary, except tee spice. An' most of tee bulk supply for t'at in tee city is on our caravan. I figure out somet'ing for t'at."

"I picked up some information on that from our fellow travelers in the caravan," O'Casey offered. The now whipcord thin chief of staff glanced at her notes. "I think you can use it with the kusul of barleyrice as a base."

"Well, groups of guards have moved to secure all the bulk vendors' supplies," Pahner said. "We'll need to take an inventory and set up a rationing scheme. And I'll also want you to take charge of arming the militia we'll be raising, Poertena."

"Yes, Sir," the armorer replied, his face getting longer and longer.

"Sorry, Poertena," Roger told him with a grin. "We'll have to cut back on the poker games."

"Yes, Sir," the Pinopan said yet again. "But we gonna have problems wit' tee weapons. T'is ain't really a production center. It's a transshipmen' point. Tee caravans come here and load t'eir supplies on barges to send t'em downriver."

It took Pahner a moment to translate that. Then he frowned.

"So if it's not in a warehouse, we probably can't get it?"

"Pretty much, Sir," the armorer said, shaking his head. "We can' no' get steel armor made. T'ere ain't a armory in tee whole town."

"Then we'll have to make do with the shields, assegais, and pikes for the time being," the captain said. "We can have those made up quickly enough to do some good, unlike firearms. And even if we could get them made in time, I'm not about to rely on something as temperamental as a muzzle-loading matchlock in this kind of climate!"

The last sentence woke nods all around. Diaspra's Guard of God had several companies of arquebusiers, but they were essentially a defensive force. Like the huge, multiton hooped bombards made from welded iron bars which dotted the city's walls, their massed fire could be devastating from prepared positions (with overhead cover against the elements) along the city's fortified approaches, but a field battle under typical Mardukan conditions would be something else again. As a matter of fact, Pahner was already eying those arquebusiers as a potential source for the shield-and-assegai-armed companies of flankers his new army was going to require.

"As soon as we get somewhere that has a decent industry, though," the captain went on after a moment, "we're damned well going to see about having some breech-loading percussion rifles made."

"Is that going to be possible?" Roger asked. "I mean, there are a lot of steps between a matchlock arquebus and a breechloader. Spring steel comes to mind."

"Like the spring steel in Rastar's wheel locks?" Pahner asked, smiling faintly. "And have you looked at their pumps?" the Marine went on as the prince's expression turned suddenly thoughtful.

"Not in any depth," Roger admitted. "They have quite a few of them, and they seem pretty damned efficient. I noticed that much."

"Well, I *have* been noticing them, Your Highness— particularly since Eleanora commented on them back at Voitan. I even took one apart when you were running around in Ran Tai. These people have impeller pumps, and the ones in Deb Tar's mines were pneumatically driven."

"You mentioned that before," Roger agreed. "But what does it mean?"

"An impeller pump requires tight tolerances, Your Highness," O'Casey replied before Pahner could. "You have to be able to lathe, which they do with foot-pedal lathes. It also requires spring material—spring steel in most cases, here on Marduk, although that corrodes faster than the alloys we would use in the Empire. However, every basic technology you need for advanced black powder weapons is found in their pump industry. For that matter, as the captain just suggested, anyone who can build wheel locks can build more advanced lock mechanisms. What we call a 'flintlock' is actually a much less complicated device than a wheel lock. In fact, its advantage, and the thing that made it so important when it was introduced on Earth, was that its simplicity made it cheap enough that armies could afford to convert their infantry to it from the even simpler matchlock. Before that, only cavalry units carried wheel locks for exactly the same reason that Rastar and his troopers do—a matchlock is impractical for a mounted man to manage, and cavalry was considered important and prestigious enough to justify the purchase of specialized and expensive weapons for it."

"So we need to go where t'ey make tee pumps, Sir?" Poertena asked.

"That or one of the armories where the gunsmiths make wheel locks," Pahner agreed, then grinned and nodded at O'Casey. "On the other hand, the gunsmiths seem to guard their 'secrets' pretty zealously . . . and they make the pumps everywhere. They have to, with their climate. And I'd rather go somewhere where they have some genuine large-scale manufacturing industry. From what Rastar says, the local gunsmiths are both extremely expensive and pretty damned slow. The ones who make wheel locks spend a lot of time and effort on things like inlay work and decoration—just take a look at Rastar's toys! What we need is someone used to the practical requirements of mass production, or as close to it as anyone on this planet is going to come. When we find him, we'll give him a design for a rifle for the troops and have it produced in quantity. For Rastar's people, too."

"And let me guess," Roger said with a grimace. "That someone wouldn't happen to live in this K'Vaern's Cove, would he?"

"From what I've heard, he probably does, Your Highness," O'Casey said. "Diaspra is a theocracy, and for all that it's also a trading city, it seems fairly typical of the 'mañana attitude' we've seen everywhere else but New Voitan. That's why the Diasprans aren't going to be able to supply us with what we need. But to hear them tell it, this K'Vaern's Cove is the secular center of their known universe. I seem to be picking up a lot of respect for the K'Vaernians, even from the large number of people—mostly clerics—who obviously don't like them. But the Diasprans clearly regard them as not simply heathens, but very peculiar heathens, with all sorts of outrageous notions, including some sort of obsession with more efficient ways to do things which is absolute anathema to something as inherently conservative as a theocratic priest-king's government. So, yes, the logical place to look for the sort of person the captain wants would have to be K'Vaern's Cove."

"Which means he's also right in the middle of this invasion," Roger pointed out. "How are we going to get there to talk to him?"

"Well, first we build us a little army here, then we head upcountry again," Pahner said. "Quickly." He grunted a laugh.

"You got anyt'ing more for me, Sir?" Poertena asked.

"No, Sarge. Thanks for your time," the prince said.

"It's corporal, Your Highness," the Pinopan reminded him. "But t'anks."

"Not any more," Roger said. "I think between the Captain and me, we probably have the juice to get a promotion approved."

"T'ank you, Sir," the armorer said, getting to his feet. "T'anks. I'm gonna turn in."

"Take off, Poertena," Pahner replied.

"Good night, Sirs," the little sergeant said, and headed out the door.

"That was well done, Roger," the Marine CO said when the door had closed.

"He's done a good job," the prince pointed out. "He's been working every night on getting our gear back in shape, and he and Kostas between them have been keeping track of all our supplies, as well. And now this job, without complaint. Well," he corrected himself with a smile, "not any *serious* complaints."

"Agreed," the captain said, then leaned back and scratched the tip of his nose thoughtfully.

"Getting back to the subject at hand," he went on after a moment, "this is a rich city, despite all of the Council's moaning, and this Laborers of God labor force looks top-notch so far. There's over four thousand of them, too." He shook his head. "I don't understand how any city can just set aside twenty percent of its productive male population as a labor force like this, either. Usually, societies like this use farmers in their off time for any required community labor."

"Eleanora?" Roger asked. "Got any suggestions?"

"It's the barleyrice production, of course," the chief of staff said. "Always look to basic production in societies like this, Roger."

"But there wasn't this labor surplus on the far side of the mountains," the prince replied. "Marshad had a fairly normal ratio, and so did Q'Nkok. And Ran Tai, for that matter."

"Ah, but Marshad and Q'Nkok didn't have draft animals like the *turom*. Aside from caravan use, the *flar-ta* might as well not exist as beasts of burden, but that's all they have on the far side of the Tarstens. And Ran Tai—as Poertena pointed out to us at the time—effectively imports all of its barleyrice," O'Casey reminded him with a smile. "I'd say that this place would probably be the center of a Mardukan Renaissance if it weren't locked up tight by the local theocracy."

She glanced at her notes and shook her head.

"The agriculture in this area is phenomenal. The *turom* gives them a remarkable advantage over Q'Nkok and Marshad, and what with the continuously mild weather, an efficient distribution system for nitrates, and excellent crop rotation, they have *five crops* of barleyrice every year. Five. And nearly as many crops of nearchicks and taters, not to mention three of apsimons. Each individual farmer is tremendously productive, which is why all those extra laborers are employed by the temple—they'd be out of work otherwise."

"But that condition has to have existed for some

time," Roger said, shaking his head. "Shouldn't they have been pulled into other production areas by now? That's the normal reaction to technological improvement; one group is left performing the original function more efficiently, and within a generation the rest of the labor force is switched to other markets, usually new ones that become possible because of the freed labor."

"True." Eleanora smiled. "In fact, I'm delighted to see that you remember my lectures so well. In Diaspra's case, however, the society clearly reacted by taxing the farmers still on the land to establish a . . . well, call it a welfare system, and putting the out-of-work ones to work on temple projects. I suspect that if we had a time machine, we'd find that that reaction marked the beginning of the growth of the temple's secular power. And it was probably considered a 'temporary measure,' too."

"Aaargh," Roger groaned. "The only thing more permanent than a 'temporary measure' is 'stopgap spending.' But surely even here they must eventually have the labor shift to new technologies?"

"Not necessarily." The chief of staff waved her hands in a gesture that included the entire planet. "Marduk is a remarkably stable world. There's very little reason for technological improvement. Frankly, I'm surprised that they ever domesticated animals in the first place."

"There's a real lack of wheels," Pahner said in agreement. "There are wheeled carts near the cities, but that's about it. They have the concept—there are all sorts of wheels used in their pumping technology—but they don't use it for transport."

"It's all of a piece," O'Casey said with a quirky smile. "There's very little to drive improvements in this society, and the late Raj Hoomas notwithstanding, most of the city-states—the inland ones, at least—very rarely have major territorial competitions. Wars, yes—lots of those—but by human standards, those wars are pretty small potatoes. And they're not really what we'd call wars of conquest, either. Most of the city-states maintain professional armies to handle the fighting—and do the dying—which tends to insulate the general population from the consequences of combat. And the squabbles between cities are usually over caravan routes, mining sites, and that sort of thing, not over what you might call true life-or-death issues or because some local potentate suddenly got bitten by the notion of building himself some sort of empire. Their climate is fairly constant, too, so they don't have many times when large-scale weather patterns cause big migrations or force technological change. It's a very static society, so any major change probably gets swallowed up by the stasis. Which is probably a large part of the explanation for how devastating a large migration—like the Kranolta or the Boman—is when it finally comes along."

"What about the other cities in this area?" Roger asked.

"We'll have to see," O'Casey replied. "My guess from inference is that the states of Rastar's 'League of the North' were more or less parasitic defensive states. They protected the southern cities from the Boman and their fellow barbarians, and in return, they drew off the excess production from the city-states behind their shield. The next tier of states to the north, like this Sindi place, appear to have been secular despotisms, where the excess labor was involved in glorification of the leadership. I suppose that sort of mind-set might help fuel a potential Caesar or Alexander's ambitions, but so far I just don't know enough to hazard a guess as to whether or not it has, although some of the things Rastar's said about Sindi itself sound fairly ominous.

And I don't know a thing about the societal types to the south of Diaspra."

"And K'Vaern's Cove?" Pahner asked. "That's the one I'm interested in."

"Me, too," the chief of staff admitted. "The more I hear about it, the more fascinated I get. If we think of the K'Vaernian Sea as analogous to Earth's Mediterranean, then the K'Vaernians themselves appear to be the local Carthaginians, or possibly Venetians. Their city is not only *the* major seapower in the K'Vaernian, but it's also the only one which appears to have reacted classically to technological innovation, although even it doesn't seem to have advanced very far by our standards. But I think we can change that. In fact, I wish we were building this army there."

"So do I," Pahner said, chewing his *bisti* root in deep thought. "As it is, winning this war—putting this force together, for that matter—is going to require everyone in the Company to pitch in. And the additional delay makes me really glad we happened across the apsimon. Anything new from Dobrescu on other substitutes?"

"Not yet," Kosutic told him, and the captain grunted. The fortuitous discovery of the apsimon had caused Pahner to reconsider their earlier acceptance of the survey report's insistence that nothing in the local ecosystem could supply their trace nutritional needs. He was still mentally kicking himself for having overlooked the possibility that such a cursory survey, of which they had only fragments, could have been inconclusive, and Warrant Officer Dobrescu had found himself with a new, extra assignment: running every new potential food source through his analyzers with fanatic attention to detail.

"Tell him to keep on it," the Marine CO said now. "He will, of course, but we're going to be too busy training Diasprans to look over his shoulder while he does it."

"And I think I'll just leave that training in your capable hands," Roger told him with a smile. "It's a job for an experienced captain, not a novice colonel."

"More like a job for Sergeant Whatsisname," the Marine responded with a laugh, and Roger smiled with sudden, wicked amusement. As far as the prince could tell, he'd managed to keep his mentor from figuring out that he'd been looking up some of the ancient poetry Pahner so commonly quoted.

"Indeed, 'not a prince, nor an earl nor yet a viscount,' " he said with a butter-won't-melt-in-my-mouth expression, and Pahner looked at the prince sideways and cocked his head.

"'Just a man in khaki kit . . .'" the captain said, ending on a slightly questioning note.

"'Who could handle men a bit,'" Roger responded with a chuckle. "'With his kit bag labelled "Sergeant Whatsisname."'" His smile grew still broader, then faded a little around the edges. "It doesn't seem to change much, does it, Captain?" he said quietly.

"No, it doesn't, Sir," the Marine agreed, with a faint smile of his own. "It never does seem to change. And whether you intend to sit it out or not, I think we'll all have to become Sergeant Whatsisname."

CHAPTER TEN

Krindi Fain wasn't certain exactly why he was standing at the front of a milling group of Diasprans in the dawn rain while three of the odd-looking humans discussed something at the far edge of the courtyard. He was sure that it had something to do with that nice human in the tavern, and he could vaguely remember shouting about teaching the Boman to respect Diasprans and the God. Or something like that. There'd been a lot of shouting. And a *lot* of beer.

But now, just thinking about the shouting hurt his head. He felt as if someone had wrapped thorns around his horn sockets, and from the yelling in the distance, he was afraid there was more coming his way.

There hadn't been any shouting when they were first dragged out into the large square by the chuckling temple guardsmen. They'd been counted off into groups and then given a speech by one of the high priests. The priest had explained that they'd all volunteered for the new forces that were going to be fighting the Boman. That they were the bedrock of the army of the God, and that they would wash over the Boman like a wave. That the barbarians would be as sand before the dreadful tide of their righteous wrath.

Then he'd rattled off the rules under which they would now live. Fortunately for all of the new recruits, keeping track of the punishment for any given offense would be child's play itself . . . since *all* of the rules ended in "guilty party shall be put to death."

The three humans finished their conference, and turned his way. Suddenly, they didn't look nearly as friendly as they had the night before.

"God save me for a drunkard and a fool," Julian said, looking at the crowd of Mardukans.

"You qualify on both counts, Adib." Roger clapped him on the shoulder. "You'll be fine. You've got your notes?"

"Macek does," the squad leader said. "I'm going to give them a few choice words, then turn them over to Gronningen and Mutabi to wear them out."

"That'll work," the prince said, and turned to the crowd of young Mardukans. "Listen up! You men—and I use that term lightly—don't know why you're here or what's coming. Some of you think you do, but you're wrong. If you listen to Sergeant Julian here, and the veterans with him, you might just survive the battle with the Boman! If you don't, I guarantee that you'll end up in an unmarked grave, unpitied victims of a contemptible struggle! So pay attention! Follow orders! And may the God defend the right!"

He glowered at them for a moment longer, then clapped Julian on the shoulder, nodded briskly in the general direction of the thoroughly wretched and confused recruits, and strode off.

❖   ❖   ❖

Julian considered the group like a farmer picking out just the right chicken for supper. Then he pointed to four of the largest or, in one case, most intelligent looking, of them.

"You, you, you, and you." He pointed to marks on the square's cobblestones. Next to each mark was a thirty-meter line. "Here, here, here, and here," he said, and propped his hands on his hips, tapping his toe impatiently until he had the four bewildered nascent squad leaders in place. Then he turned to the rest.

"What the hell are you _waiting_ for? _Breakfast?!_ On the lines, now, _now, NOW!_"

Between them, he and Moseyev's Alpha Team got the milling crowd lined up. It happened neither easily, quickly, nor neatly, and Julian favored the more or less formation with a ferocious glare.

"When I say, 'Fall In,' you will fall in, just like this, on the line, with these four on the marks!" He strode up to the first squad leader and looked him up and down. "_Is that any sort of position of attention?!_" he screamed.

"I, uh . . ." Krindi Fain said.

"When you answer a question, there are _three_ possible answers! They are: 'Yes, Sir!' 'No, Sir!' and 'Clear, Sir!' _Is that clear?_"

"Uh, yes," the miserable and hungover Diaspran said. If this little _basik_ didn't quit shouting at him, he was definitely going to have to do something about it. What, he wasn't sure, since one of those rules had covered the penalties for hitting their superiors. He didn't really feel inferior to this _basik_, but, on the other hand, he didn't want to feel the God's embrace _that_ much.

"Yes, WHAT?" the human screamed at him.

"Sir," Gronningen mouthed silently behind Julian's back.

"_Yes, SIR!_" Fain shouted as loudly as physically

possible, and the Marine noncom glared at him for a moment, then spun in place.

"Gronningen! Ten *Hut!*"

The plasma gunner snapped to attention, and Julian stalked over to him, then turned to face his new recruits again.

"This is the position of attention. Chest out! Stomach in! Heels together! Hands half-cupped and thumbs along . . ."

His mouth clicked shut, and he glared at the Mardukans for a moment in despair as his familiar, well-practiced lecture hit a pothole. Normally, it would have been "thumbs along the seam of the trousers." But that assumed that the sentient in question had only two arms, both of which reached to his thighs . . . and that the aforesaid sentient wore trousers.

"*Macek?!*"

" . . . thumbs of the false-hands aligned with the middle of the outer thigh and true-hands aligned above false-hands," Macek supplied instantly, and Julian grunted in approval and strode back over to the poor squad leader-to-be.

"Got that, four-arms?" He poked the Mardukan in the stomach with his sheathed short sword. The Mardukans had a solar plexus much similar to that of a human, although larger and, if anything, more vulnerable, and the Diaspran partially doubled over, so Julian tapped him on the chin with the hilt of the sword. "Stomach in! Chin back! Chest out! False-hands half-cupped! Thumbs aligned along the thigh! *Do it!*"

So Fain did it. And then, without any ceremony or warning, he threw up all over the little *basik*. He really, really hoped that didn't count as hitting.

Poertena was trying to watch twelve pairs of hands at once, and it just wasn't working.

The group was too large to play spades, so they'd settled on poker. After some initial wrangling about what kind, they'd further decided on dealer's choice, although the initial decision by Chal Thai to start with five-card stud had been greeted with universal suspicion. The local Mardukan factor, who'd become their most prominent supplier of finished pike and spearheads was infamous for bottom-dealing, palming, and that notorious, Mardukan-only technique, "sticking."

It didn't seem to affect the quality of the materials he supplied. The perennially friendly merchant had been on time with every shipment, which had been hard in a city as busy as Diaspra.

The city had been in a night and day fever for the last two weeks. After some token resistance from the senior merchant families, the bulk of the populace, the guilds, and the church had thrown themselves wholeheartedly into the preparations. There was no time to build the kind of armaments the humans would have preferred for the struggle: mobile cannon and flintlocks, as a start. So Pahner, after a series of roundtable discussions, had settled on a modification of their own "Roman" approach.

Since the Boman—and especially their outriders, like the Wespar tribe—had relatively few arquebuses, designing a force to fight arquebuses would hardly have made sense, anyway. Instead, the army the captain envisioned would be designed to handle the threats it did face: the hail of throwing axes which continued to provide the bulk of the Boman missile assault, and their foot charge.

The first tier of what O'Casey had dubbed the "New Model Army of Diaspra" would consist of shieldmen armed with assegais, most of whom would come out of the regulars from the surviving Guard of God (and, oh, but the reassigned arquebusiers had been *livid* about that one!). The second tier would be the pikemen Julian and his henchmen were busy creating out of the recruits from the Laborers of God. Pikes required at least as much discipline but less individual training than assegais would, and just as no one on this planet had ever heard of Roman tactics, none had ever heard of hoplites or classic pike phalanxes. And the third tier would be the *civan*-mounted cavalry Rastar and Honal were teaching a whole new concept of "combined arms" operations.

The short assegais required less metalworking than short swords for much the same utility, plus they could be thrown, in a real emergency, and their broad heads had been readily supplied by the smiling merchant who usually had at least four aces stuck somewhere on his body's mucous covering. Chal Thai was also the main supplier for the needle-sharp awl pikeheads, and he was managing—barely—to keep deliveries ahead of the pike shafts being turned out by dozens of small shops throughout the city. Javelins were another matter. There weren't going to be nearly as many of them as Pahner could have wished, but the hand-to-hand weapons were even more important, so he was concentrating on them and the shields to protect the troops using them.

Those shields were being supplied by the other civilian Mardukan at the table. Med Non had been a minor supplier of custom woodworking and laminated tables until it became apparent that he was the only woodworker in the city with a firm grasp of how to increase production rapidly. Thereafter, he'd become the central manager of the suddenly roaring shield industry in Diaspra. His abrupt elevation and prominence had caused a brief mutiny on the part of one of the larger merchant houses, but Med Non had quashed that quickly by pointing out that none of the changes were going to affect the wealthier merchant's core business, and that his drive to rationalize and speed production gave the other's house many of his own "business secrets," instead. When asked about losing his own business after the emergency was over, he just laughed.

Poertena could understand why; the relatively small Mardukan ran rings around his more established competitors. Accustomed as he was to rapid turnaround of orders—something almost unthinkable to the hide-bound leaders of the larger houses—there was no chance that he would lose any business to those larger houses. Indeed, it would be the larger houses who would have to keep an eye on their rearview cameras.

He also appeared—bizarrely, for a Mardukan—to have no interest in cheating at cards. He'd been raised and trained in a business which required him to calculate lengths and volumes in his head, and he played a conservative game that stuck strictly to the averages. While, of course, watching his opponents' hands.

He was currently peering at the Mardukan in half-armor across from him. Sol Ta, the commander of one of the newly raised assegai regiments, had just laid down a handful of jacks and started to scoop in the pot.

"Card check," Non said, throwing down his cards face up and raising all four hands above his head.

The purely Mardukan variant of poker, which would have made the professionals of New Vegas choke if they ever saw it, said that any player could call a check of all the cards once per game. The rule also required that all the Mardukans at the table throw all of their cards *on* the table and raise their hands above their heads.

"What?" Sol Ta said, then looked at the single jack sitting faceup in the other Mardukan's hand. "Oh." The guardsman raised his hands with the rest as Poertena got up and started checking.

The Pinopan had found that the locals had become downright fiendish about where they hid their cards. One of these days, he half expected to find one with a hollowed out horn, and he looked at Honal, the fourth Mardukan at the table, and raised an eyebrow.

"You wanna 'fess up now?"

The young cavalry commander was notorious, even by Mardukan standards, but he only wrinkled his brow and grinned in the human style.

"I have nothing to hide," he stated, wiggling all eighteen fingers.

Poertena sighed and started with the backs of his hands, then worked his way down. In fact, he was pretty sure the cavalryman wasn't holding—this time—but poker rules were poker rules.

Roger kicked back and laughed silently while he watched. The locals had the oddest approach to cheating he'd ever heard of. If you weren't cheating, they considered you stupid. But if you got caught, they considered you a gross incompetent. As soon as they'd started figuring out the ways they could cheat at cards, they'd leapt in with abandon. Spades and the other whist derivative games were the only ones where they couldn't hide cards, but even then they bottom-dealt, cross-dealt, and stacked decks so cold they froze. And yet they still played for money.

Poertena stood back and shook his head. The cavalryman's harness and tabard were clean. Nothing in his holsters, nothing in his scabbards. The Pinopan knew from experience that it was entirely possible that he'd missed a card somewhere, but he let the Mardukan lower his hands anyway.

Next, he started on Sol Ta. The Diaspra infantry commander wasn't as heavily armed as Rastar's cousin. He had a broad spatha kicked out under the table, and his harness sported only a single wheel lock pistol, but lack of hiding places didn't prevent him from regularly managing to fool them anyway. After a close search, the human stepped back and shook his head, then turned to Chal Thai. The other merchant sat patiently, with an air of benign amusement, while Poertena searched him minutely . . . and without success.

"I gots not'ing," he told Med Non with a shrug, and the merchant looked over at the last Mardukan present as Matsugae quietly entered with fresh drinks. The room was buried deep in the local palace-cum-temple, and had actually been provided by the last player.

Rus From waved the water-colored scarf that was his badge of office.

"What? Surely you don't believe that a humble cleric would introduce a jack into the deck? What possible reason could I have?"

Roger smiled again as he took a glass of cool wine off the tray. He winked at Matsugae, who rolled his eyes in return. The Mardukans seemed to spend better than half their time arguing about who was the more clever at cheating. And the other half denying—purely for the record, of course—that they themselves would ever even *consider* something that dishonest.

"Oh, I don't doubt for a moment that you'd do so," Ta said suspiciously. "I just wonder what involved plot it's a part of."

"I?" the cleric asked, spreading his hands in front of him. "I am but a simple cleric," he added ingenuously. "What would I know of involved plots?"

All five of the others laughed as Poertena carefully counted the cards. The complex hydraulic engineering that was the hallmark of the Diaspra priesthood was managed, almost wholly, by this "simple cleric." There were higher posts to be found in the local theocracy, but "Bishop of Artificers" was arguably the most powerful. And the most technical. This "simple cleric" had the local equivalent of a couple of doctorates in hydraulic engineering.

"Besides," he added, as Poertena silently held up the spare jack from the pile, "I don't understand this human fascination with simple adjustments. Isn't it your own Sergeant Major who says 'If you aren't cheating, you aren't trying'?"

"You cheat you own side, you gonna screw you'self," Poertena said, discarding the jack, sitting back down, and shuffling. As he dealt, he had to stop periodically to unstick cards.

"But we're not exactly cheating, are we?" Sol Ta replied, looking at his hole card. "We're just . . . trying for an advantage."

"Whatever." Poertena shrugged.

"No, seriously," From said. "I'm wondering where you got this odd attachment to 'fairness.' It has very little purpose, and is so very easily used against you. It seems to be a weakness."

"Maybe so," Poertena said with another shrug. He finished dealing and tossed a silver piece on the pile. After a moment, he looked around and realized that they weren't going to let him get away without answering.

He thought about it for a minute. He knew the answer, but he'd never had to explain it to anyone, and he was far from certain how to do so. From his point of view, you either understood it, or you didn't, but he decided to give it a try.

"Okay. Chal, you 'member the firs' time you come and offered you price for spears?"

"Sure," the Mardukan said, tossing a small raise onto the pot.

"You remember what I give back?" the Pinopan asked.

"Sure." The merchant grunted in laughter. "My sales gift."

"Right," Poertena said, and looked at the others. "He hand me a bag of silver an' a nice little statue. An' what I say?"

"'No thank you, and I won't say it twice.' I thought you were hinting that I should offer something a bit larger, but then I realized what you really meant," the merchant said, setting down his cards and picking up the cup of wine Matsugae had left. "So I took the cost off the bid I gave you."

"I had Fri Tar give me a gif' prob'ly ten time as nice as you," the Pinopan told him. "If I made tee call on tee basis of tee gifts, we'd be tryin' to get our gear outta pocking Fri Tar."

"Good luck," Sol Ta snorted. "I've been trying to get him to complete a set of swords for the past six months."

"Right." Poertena picked his cards back up. "That's you answer."

"But how did you decide on Chal, then?" Roger asked, taking a hand in the discussion as he saw the natives' continued puzzlement. "If not by the size of his gift, I mean?"

"He was tee only one take tee cost of tee gif' back out of tee bid, You Highness," the Pinopan said, and Roger nodded and smiled, then looked at the other players.

"I know you Mardukans think this is a quaint custom," he said, "but it's the only way to really build a society."

"We got 'sale gift' some places, too," Poertena said. "It call 'baksheesh.' But if tee size of tee baksheesh is mos' of a salary, people stop workin' for t'eir pay and start workin' for baksheesh."

"And then you have the goddamn plasma rifles,"

Roger growled. "An excellent example of why you *don't* want your procurement people taking little gifts."

"What's that?" Rus From asked, looking at the up cards, then grimaced. "Fold."

"We discovered that we . . . had a problem with one of our main weapons," Roger said, tossing in his own cards. "It would have helped us out several times. In fact, we'd probably have twice the people we do now—if we'd only been able to use it reliably."

"But t'ey blow tee pock up," Poertena said bitterly. "Sorry, You Highness."

"Not at all, Poertena," Roger told him, and looked at the Mardukans. "As he said, they blow the pock up when we try to use them."

"Well," Ta said with a wave of one true-hand, "guns always tend to blow up. But . . . most people survive." He waved his hand again in the local equivalent of polite amusement. Arquebuses were notorious for blowing up, as were the local pistols.

"If one of these were to blow up, it would take out this wing of the palace," Roger said, taking a bite out of an apsimon fruit.

"Oh." The guardsman looked suddenly thoughtful and took another sip of his wine before he tossed in a silver piece to stay in the game.

"Now a situation like that occurs for one of two reasons," Roger went on, leaning back and looking at the ceiling. "Either somebody's been incompetent, or, more commonly, somebody is cutting corners. Usually, cutting corners happens because somebody got greedy. And it usually means that at least one person has had his palm greased."

"'Palm greased'?" Honal asked, raising the stake by a couple of silvers, and Poertena pointed at the pot with his chin and rubbed his fingers together.

"Money," he said bluntly. "Somebody got paid off."

"Ah." Thai gazed at the young cavalryman speculatively, then folded and turned his attention fully to Roger. "That's why you explained in our first game that the next time you caught me cheating in your favor, you could no longer play."

"Right," the prince said. "It's a really strange concept, but it's all about playing fair with your own side. If you don't, since we're all interconnected, you inevitably pock yourself."

"But what about what Sergeant Major Kosutic says?" Honal asked, scooping in the pot without ever showing his hole cards, since everyone had folded rather than stay in the game.

"Ah," Roger said, pulling out a strip of *bisti*. "That's a bit different, you see. The Boman aren't our side. And in that case, 'if you ain't cheating, you ain't trying.'"

Despreaux slid into the spider hole and nodded to Kileti.

"Tell them we've found their main base," she whispered.

The small hole was on a slight elevation, twenty-five kilometers northeast of Diaspra. It was crowded and close with four Marines and the gear for two more. The team from First Squad was one of three sent out to find the main enemy concentration, and Despreaux was pretty sure she knew why she was here. Since her pissing match with Roger back in Ran Tai, Kosutic and Pahner had been going out of their ways to keep her separated from the prince. Since she was a squad leader, that meant keeping her squad separated from the prince. And in this case, it meant putting them out on the sharp end . . . all because His Highness was a stuck up, aristocratic prick.

She pulled out a leather pouch and dumped out the bleeding head of a killerpillar.

"It nearly got me," she said while her quick fingers extracted the valuable poison glands and dropped them into a plastic bottle. Both the neurotoxin and the flesh-dissolver were much sought after by the local apothecaries. Harvesting the bounty of the forests was one of the ways the individual troopers made their drinking money, so patrols had become a privilege rather than a task.

PFC Sealdin picked up his own translucent bottle and shook it.

"One of the mamas came by a few hours ago," he told her cheerfully. The vampire moths had stopped being a danger as soon as the Marines learned to sleep in their sealed personal shelters, but with the invention of a sticky trap, they'd become another source of funds. The anesthetic they produced was one of the most effective available for the Mardukans.

PFC Kileti picked up a plug and jacked it into his helmet com. The microscopic wire attached to the plug ran out of the chameleon cover over their hole and up a nearby tree, from the top of which a small transmitter sent short, directional burst transmissions and bounced them off of the micro meteors that skipped into the atmosphere on a regular basis.

Report complete, the PFC sent a command to his toot, and nodded at the team leader.

"On the way," he said, and the leader, St. John (J.), nodded.

"Okay, Macek and Bebi are going to keep an eye on them for now. We'll switch out tomorrow. In the meantime," he continued, digging into his rucksack and pulling out a strip of jerky, "we wait."

CHAPTER ELEVEN

"You know," Roger said as he hurried from one meeting to another, "they say that the waiting is the hardest part. Does 'waiting' include the preparation, too?"

"Yes, it does, Your Highness," Pahner replied, matching his rapid stride. "You'd do better to quit playing cards all night."

They were passing through one of the outer sections of the vast palace/temple complex, down a cobbled walkway the size of a small street but unoccupied except for themselves. The low wall to their right looked out over one of the city's innumerable canals, and beyond that to the eastern fields. This section used a pumped-out dry canal as a flood preventative, instead of the more normal dikes or walls, and there was a clear view of the vista of fields and trees leading to the purple mountains in the distance. A few farmers could be seen moving in the closer fields with a protective escort of Northerner cavalry.

"Ah, it's not slowing me down," Roger said. "I don't sleep much. It used to drive the teachers at boarding school nuts. I'd be up in the middle of the night, trying to get other kids to play with me."

"You spent a fair amount of time in your cabin aboard the *DeGlopper*," Pahner noted dryly.

"Yeah, well," Roger said with a grin, "I was sulking, not sleeping. Big difference."

They reached the end of the path and started to ascend a series of steps that stretched up and to the left around the central hill. Although the steps were quite shallow for the locals, they were anything but for the far shorter humans, but by now Roger and Pahner had grown accustomed to that, and the prince admired the palace architecture yet again while they climbed. Like most Mardukan structures, the city had started out atop a hill, but over time it had sprawled down to the flatlands, and the Diasprans, as water worshipers, had taken a different approach to the regular flooding to which all of Marduk was prone. Their technique was to work with the water, accepting and controlling it with strategically placed channels, holding pools, and canals rather than fighting it with unbroken lines of dikes. Oh, there *were* dikes—some of them more massive than any others the humans had yet seen—but they were placed more to divert water into other channels than to stand like a fortress in its path. Only the truly critical areas of the city and the areas most vulnerable to flooding had the sort of impervious barriers other cities routinely erected, although Diaspra's were constructed on a far vaster scale where they existed at all.

That relative sparseness of the dikes and coffer dams which served other Mardukan city-states as a sort of additional set of fortified outworks had almost been the Diasprans' downfall when the Boman assault arrived. Fortunately, they'd been able to slow the initial rush of the barbarians by selectively flooding their fields and occasionally artificially inducing flash floods to catch groups of raiders.

In the meantime, the priesthood, accustomed as it was to large-scale public works, had organized vast labor gangs to link the dikes and canals which already existed into one continuous defensive circuit. It wasn't perfect, but the walls, dikes, and canals had combined to stop the barbarians' second, more concerted rush.

It was in the interval after that second assault, when the Wespar had withdrawn to lick their wounds and prepare for a third attempt, that the humans had arrived. And that was also when the barbarians had cut the most prominent and religiously important public work of the entire city-state: the Diaspra Aqueduct.

Roger and Pahner passed under one of the flying buttresses of the massive aqueduct as they continued up the hill, and the prince looked up at it and shook his head in something very like awe, for the aqueduct was a structure fit to make any Roman proud. Normally, it carried water from a reservoir at the foot of the mountains to another reservoir within the city itself, from which it was pumped still further up the hill. At the very summit of the small mountain upon which Diaspra sat was the final reservoir of the city, the source of all its water for use and worship.

The reservoir had originally been a small cluster of very high output volcanic springs which fed a bowl-like lake whose temperature was high even for Marduk. The most ancient part of the city clustered around the lake, and its venerable structures—the oldest the humans had yet seen anywhere—had been carefully preserved. The ancient springs were the focus from which the locals had spread their worship of water, whether it came from the ground, or the rivers, or the sky. They had studied its movement and nature, trying to glean an understanding of their changeable god, and in the process, their understanding of hydraulics had become astounding.

The larger, cooler reservoir below the original lake was tapped for many different purposes. There were public drinking fountains throughout the city, where people came to draw fresh, clean water and make offerings to their god. In addition, there were thousands of decorative fountains, ranging from tiny carvings of Mardukan piscines that spat water a meter or two to a couple of giant structures that fired compressed water jets tens of meters into the sky. There were misting fountains, and playing fountains, and fountains that danced. There were wading pools, and swimming pools, and hundreds of canals.

Or there had been, for all the fountains were dry, now. The Boman had cut the aqueduct at its source, and for the first time in local history, water had to be drawn from the many canals. There was no chance of any Mardukan city running out of water—not with the daily cascades of rain—but for a people who worshiped water, the loss had been devastating.

"I wish there were a way to use water as a weapon," Roger said with a sigh, running his hand over a small fountain carved like a *civan*. "The way these people work with it, the Wespar would be screwed if we could come up with a way to use it."

"I'd considered it," Pahner said, stepping forward to open one of the heavy doors into the temple proper. The temple was a graceful structure over all, comprised of arches, curving lines, and narrow domes like the miters of bishops, but its doors were just as heavy—and Mardukan-sized—as any others. "But aside from the use of strategically placed inundations, which the locals already understand perfectly well, nothing really suggested itself to me."

"So we're still going to have to fight this out with

weapons from the Dark Ages," Roger said, entering the dim corridor beyond the door. The passage was lit at intervals by light wells on the outer side, and although the wells were sloped to prevent water from coming in, it was obvious that another heavy rain had started.

"Well," Pahner told him with a dry chuckle, "it would seem to me that fighting a Mardukan with water would be like fighting a Marine by shooting beer at him."

"Today," Julian told the assembled platoon of Mardukans, "you graduate from your first phase of basic training! And everyone gets a beer."

The recruits had shaped up to a remarkable degree. Despite a disastrous start, Krindi Fain had even turned out to have a head on his shoulders. All four shoulders. The squad leader was, whether he knew it or not, in line for the platoon sergeant position, and his promotion would arrive sooner than he could possibly have expected, for there was a severe shortage of NCOs.

The recruits had learned to make their own tents and even gotten to sleep in them for a day or two. They'd been issued boiled leather and had cut and sewn their own armor. Then they'd marched in it.

All of them—even Erkum Pol, who appeared to have had a lobotomy as a child—had mastered the arts of standing at the various positions, marching in straight lines, and simple column movements. But that had been without weapons in their hands.

Now it was "calculus" time, and from the expressions on their faces (and even more so on their instructors' faces) it was obvious that despite all they had learned so far, the recruits once again had not a single clue. Each of the students held a four-meter wooden shaft in his upper two hands, and a three-meter-square plywood shield in the lower two. And it was abundantly clear that they didn't know what the *hell* to do with either one. Much less both of them.

"But that's for this evening!" Julian continued. "Today, we will begin your real training. Today, you'll be issued your pikes. And the pike simulators you have in your hands. Because if you think we're going to trust you four-armed monstrosities with *real* pikes, you've got another think coming. Until you learn what it means to be a *soldier*, you can just look at them and long for the day you get to hold them! In the meantime, we will begin study of the manual of arms!"

Gronningen stepped forward and began to demonstrate the first movement of the manual of arms, as rewritten for four-armed Mardukans and pikes and demonstrated by two-armed humans. The recruits watched with both intensity and anxiety, and as they did, the blunted pike shaft slipped out of Erkum Pol's nervously sliming hands and hit a second squad team leader on the head. The team leader responded by turning in place and laying out the slightly "slow" recruit with his own four-meter shaft of hardwood. At that point, things . . . devolved.

Somewhere, in the distance, there was the melodious chanting of priests going about their daily rounds. From the city stables came the lowing of *civan* and *turom*, and from the work gangs still laboring on city projects came the sound of deep-voiced work chanties. But the only sounds from the training square were those of wooden pike shafts hitting wooden shields and the coarse bellowing of foul-mouthed Marines.

The line of supplicants approached one by one, each kneeling in turn before the high priest to receive the blessing of their god. Gratar stood before an altar which consisted of a square marble base with a hollow, liquid-filled top. Crystal-clear water flowed up from below through the base, spilling over the edges of the top in a perpetually renewed, glass-smooth cascade that rippled like a living creature as it slid endlessly into the gold and gem-ornamented catcher basin at the altar's foot. Four additional fountains flanked the priest, pouring water into basins of polished lapis, where it was sucked away to join the rest of the underground flows. Spreading his arms to either side, the priest-king chanted as he scooped water from the fountains in a complex ritual and cast the handfuls over the worshiper kneeling at his feet.

The benediction over, the supplicant walked out through a fine shower, signifying that he had been purified, and the next worshiper came forward.

"We should have taken our time," Roger whispered.

"They say the waiting is the hardest part, Your Highness," Pahner joked.

The captain looked across the room and out to the northwest. The audience chamber was at the summit of the hill, a broad theater surrounded by columns and covered only above the stage where the priest-king performed his ritual. Behind him was that holiest of holies, the springs from whose bosom the entire religion had issued. The water from the springs filled the ancient lake and then flowed across natural rock to spill down into the reservoir and away to the north along its endless path to the Chasten River.

The large open area in front of the stage was filled with worshipers and other supplicants, including a delegation of merchants there to protest the rationing plan the temple had imposed. Dozens of the locals stood in the pouring rain, another sign of blessing from their god, patiently awaiting their turn for a moment with the priest-king. The narrow roofs of the surrounding pillars channeled the water into innumerable sprays which interacted with the pounding rainfall to wash down over the worshipers in abundant cascades of shimmering silver.

Roger and Pahner, on the other hand, stood in pride of place under the limited cover at the end of the stage behind the priest-king. Roger noticed that the Marine was distracted, and turned his head to look in the same direction. The rain, like every Mardukan rain, was heavy, but even through the downpour it was possible to see the swollen, dark charcoal clouds blotting the skies to the northwest. Despite their drenching power, it appeared that the current heavy showers were no more than a dress rehearsal for the true deluge to come.

"Usually this would be lightening up by now," Pahner said, "but it looks like we're in for a long one."

The last of the worshipers passed through the spraying water, and Gratar stepped away from the liquid altar.

"Hear now, hear now!" the master of ceremonies bellowed. "His Most Holy Excellency Gratar, High Priest of the Waters, Lord of Diaspra, Chosen of the God, will now hear petitions and grievances."

The stentorian bellow had to compete with the hammering rain and the rumble of overhead thunder. It won the contest, but it was a near thing.

"This reminds me of a Slaker concert," Roger said with a chuckle. He didn't bother to lower his voice, since nothing but a bellow could possibly have been heard more than a meter away over the sound of the storm.

"One of the ones where they use a weather generator to make a hurricane?" Pahner asked. "Ever been to one?"

"Just once," the prince said. "Once was enough. Their groupies all look like drowned sailors."

The two humans stood as patiently as they could. Both of them had better things to do, but they had no real choice but to wait for the petitioners for relief from the rationing. Technically, Poertena could and should have answered any questions which the complainants might pose. Eventually, however, it would inevitably have reached their level anyway, so it made more sense to just get it over with now.

"I wish we could have bugged all the merchant houses," Pahner said. "I feel like we're flailing around without any intel at all."

Roger frowned. While he shared the captain's frustration at the holes in what they knew, he had begun to question the wisdom of depending on eavesdropping for all their decision-making.

"We might as well start getting used to not having that intel," he replied after a moment. "It's not like we could get away with planting bugs everywhere on Earth. For that matter, I'm not even sure it was legal in Q'Nkok and Marshad. This is a Trust World of the Empire, after all."

"True, Your Highness." Pahner smiled faintly. "Believe it or not, I considered that when we first hit Q'Nkok. But the planet is also currently controlled—as much as anyone really 'controls' it—by the Saints, which means that we're in a *de facto* state of war."

"Oh." Roger furrowed his brow, trying to dredge up long-forgotten legal clauses O'Casey and his other teachers had tried to drum into him while he'd paid as little attention as possible. "So we're operating in a wartime condition in a combat zone?"

"Yes, Your Highness." The Marine's grin widened slightly. "So your mother shouldn't have a problem with it," he said, and Roger grinned back.

"Actually, I wasn't thinking about Mother. I was thinking that when we get back, I'm bound to end up somewhere in government. I might as well start learning not to cut corners now."

"I sort of agree, Your Highness. But let's get you off the planet alive before we get *too* ethical, okay?"

"Okay by me," Roger agreed, but then his grin faded. Gratar had dealt rapidly with the first two petitioners—some arguments about dike and canal maintenance. Now it was time for the main event.

The merchants' spokesman was Grath Chain, naturally. He'd remained a thorn in the side of the defense preparations throughout, and his constant carping and complaining were getting worse, not better. It seemed likely that the relatively low-ranked councilman was being used as a tool by the more senior merchant houses—certainly something gave him the confidence to oppose his ruler's decisions, and the only two possibilities which suggested themselves to Roger were truly invincible stupidity or the knowledge that he possessed powerful backers of his own.

Which made him all the more dangerous.

"Your Excellency," the councilor said when Gratar gave him permission to state his grievance, "I come before you as a humble petitioner. I hope that you will deign to listen to my just grievance—a grievance which you alone are able to remedy.

"A month ago, these foreign mercenaries came to our city. They antagonized the Boman beyond the walls and provoked a fresh attack upon the city. They physically threatened me before the entire Council. They have forced upon us the most grievous of measures, whereby the poor starve and the wealthy are impoverished. They have taken the men from the just Works of the God and instructed them in foreign and unfamiliar ways of fighting.

"All of this they do in the name of defending our city against the Boman. But need we make these hasty preparations? The great Works of the God, His dikes and canals, falter beneath the rains, and soon the

Hompag Rains will come. Perhaps they are already upon us." He gestured at the sky, where the downpour continued unabated. "With the men 'training' and the women preparing the barbaric materials of war, who then shall repair the ravages of the God?

"And is this even truly necessary? Have we explored alternatives? Surely, if permitting unnecessary ravages to the Works of the God was an act of apostasy in previous Rains, it must also be apostasy now. And surely this is a time to *avoid* apostasy, not to embrace it! Yet have we explored all other possibilities to avoid angering and outraging the God? No, we have not."

He paused for effect and gestured around at the temple.

"We are a great and rich city, but our strength has never rested in weapons or warlike preparations. Our strength has always been in our riches, and the love of our God, the one running from the other. Our treasury overflows with gold and silver. Certainly, this was offered to the God, but the God calls for sacrifices to serve His greater purposes, and now His temple's walls fall while its treasury is fat. Surely, if a small portion of that treasury were offered to the Boman, they would leave us to plunder other cities. Then the Laborers of God could return to their accustomed duties, preventing the fall of the Works of God."

"Oh, shit," Roger said quietly.

"Yeah," Pahner responded. "Actually, I'm surprised nobody suggested it before. Real surprised."

"Why now?" the prince asked, thinking furiously.

"Probably somebody had a rush of inspiration. Maybe they've even made contact with the barbs already. Who knows?"

Gratar regarded the councilman with obvious disgust but signed official acceptance of his petition.

"Your statement is understandable and has merit,"

he said, not sounding particularly as if he believed his own words. "However, what you suggest is too important to be decided in haste. It shall be considered by the full Council of the city and the temple."

"Your Excellency," the councilor interrupted in a terrible breach of protocol, "there's scarcely time to consider. Surely we must quickly contact the barbarian host, lest they come upon us by surprise and the opportunity be lost."

"You should learn your place, Grath Chain," the priest-king retorted sharply. "Your place is to bring forward petitions and argue their merits. *Mine* is to choose the time and place for them to be debated. Do I make myself clear?"

"You do, Your Excellency," the councilman agreed quickly, lowering his eyes and head in chagrin.

"The Hompag Rains are upon us," Gratar continued, gesturing at the skies. "There is no way for the Boman host to move in the floods of the Hompag, and so we have until the rains pass and the ways dry to make our decision. We shall deal with this petition expeditiously, but without unseemly haste. Yet before that, I wonder if our visitors have anything to say upon this matter?"

The local ruler gestured at the humans standing under the sheltering portico, and the two Terrans barely managed to conceal their surprise. Gratar had obviously had at least some prior information about the petition and its content when he'd asked them to attend the ceremony, but he hadn't shared that information with them. Or not fully, at any rate. His message had made it clear that he would want to hear their responses to any specific complaints the grain merchants raised, but it had never suggested that they might be required to respond to a formal petition to completely abandon military preparations! Certainly no one had suggested they would have to do so in an open forum before Gratar himself reached a decision, and so neither was prepared to make any public statement about it. It was a decidedly awkward situation, which the king seemed to have arranged specifically for their public humiliation.

Roger cleared his throat and stepped forward into the rain. The slight dais at the end of the temple made a satisfactory stage, and he'd been trained since birth in public speaking, but he usually had a script to work from and time to prepare his delivery. This time, he had neither, and he thought furiously for a moment about the proposal and its implications while he gave mental thanks to Eleanora O'Casey for drumming at least some history into his head. Then he looked at Chain and his supporters and smiled. Broadly.

"We have a saying in my country, Your Excellency. 'Once you pay the Danegeld, you will never be rid of the Dane.'

"What does that mean? Like the history of your own home, beautiful, water-washed Diaspra, our history goes back for thousands of years. But unlike the peaceful history of your city, ours is a history drenched in blood. This invasion which is so unusual for you, which makes your skin dry in fear, would be no more than a single bad day in the distant history of my country. Many, many times we have had to face the depredations and devastation of barbarian invasions—so often that our priests once created special prayers for deliverance from specific barbarian tribes. Like the Danes.

"The Danes, like the Boman, were raiders from the North. But they came in lightning-fast boats along the seashore, not by land, and they swooped down upon the coastal villages, killing and enslaving the locals and despoiling their temples. They had particularly gruesome ways of butchering the priests, and mocked them as they died, for they had called upon their god and been greeted only with silence.

"So, in desperation, one of the lands they raided offered up its gold and silver objects, even the reliquaries which had been created to show its people's love for their god, as Danegeld. As a bribe to the Danes, a desperate effort to buy immunity for their own land and people. Lords from all across their land contributed to the goods offered to the Danes in hopes that they might stay far from their shores.

"But their hopes failed. Instead, the Danes, finding that they were offered such tempting wealth without even a fight, moved in. They took lands about the area and became the permanent overlords and imposed *their* gods and *their* laws upon the people they'd conquered. All that society, that beautiful shining land of abbeys and monasteries, of towns and cities, fell into darkness and is forgotten. Of all their great works and art and beauty, only a few scattered remnants have come down to us over the years, preserved from the Danes. Preserved not by the Danegeld, but by the few lords who stood up to the Danes and defended their lands with the cold, keen steel of their swords rather than soft gold and silver and so preserved their people, their gods, and their relics.

"So if you wish to gather your own Danegeld, gather it well. But don't expect to be rid of the Dane."

Gratar considered the prince levelly for a moment, then turned back to the petitioners.

"This measure will be considered by the full Council in ten days. And this audience is now closed."

With that, he turned away from the petitioners and the humans alike, and left the temple by a side entrance, followed by his guards.

"Captain," Roger said as they watched the petitioners

begin to file out of the temple, "you remember what I just said about intelligence and eavesdropping?"

"Julian's pretty busy drilling the troops," the captain replied thoughtfully as he pulled out a slice of *bisti* root.

"He couldn't get in to see the councilmen, anyway," Roger said. "But I know who can."

CHAPTER TWELVE

"Seriously, You Councilship," Poertena said, leaning forward to point out the details of the design, "you can get a much better return from you ores. An' it would be easy to do with you technology. I surprised you don't do it already."

The molecular circuitry fleabug slid down the armorer's finger and across the desk to nestle into a crevice in the wood. It could hear every sound in the room, but detecting it would have required top-of-the-line modern sweeper technology. *Only four more to do*, Poertena thought.

"What's in it for you?" the council member asked suspiciously.

"Well, we not goin' to be back t'rough here. I'd t'ought about some cash up front."

"I thought you couldn't be bought," the Mardukan grunted, leaning back and looking at the water-driven trip hammers in the drawing.

"Well, t'is isn't a material's contract," the armorer told him with a grin. "It off tee books."

Of course, that wasn't, unfortunately, the truth, but the thought of helping to subsidize the company's coffers with bribes from the scummies he was bugging tickled the Pinopan's sense of humor immensely.

"How'd you get Grath Chain bugged?" Roger asked as he watched Julian flipping through conversations. The intelligence AI searched for indexed terms, but sometimes a human could still pull a nugget it had missed out of the sand.

"It wasn't easy, Your Highness." The intel NCO rubbed a blackened eye and winced. "He's refusing to have anything to do with anyone associated with 'the abominations.' He's not even letting most of the water priests in, but Denat finally suggested something that worked."

"What?" Pahner asked. So far they hadn't found anyone pulling Chain's strings, but the puppet master was out there somewhere, and the captain wanted to find him. Badly.

"We used a woman, Sir. Or a brooder-male—whatever. One of the mahouts' women."

"Well, it must've worked," Roger said, pointing at the conversation texts displayed on Julian's pad. Chain was definitely discussing his antipathy for the humans. In fact, he'd discussed it in private with just about every member of the Council. But so far they'd found no meetings in which he was taking orders. Nor, for that matter, was his suggestion of bribing the Boman being well received. He was pitching it as an arrangement in which the church would pay the tribute, but all of his fellow merchants knew where the money would actually come from in the end.

"Huh," Julian said, looking at the index list. "He's been to solicit everyone on the Council except the priests and Gessram Kar."

"Why not Kar?" O'Casey asked. Since the problem they faced was almost purely political, Pahner and Roger were leaning on her to untie whatever knot was threatening to strangle them. "He's in our corner, but so is Welan Gor, and Chain visited him."

"I've been thinking about that, Ma'am," Julian said. "The only explanation I can come up with is that the communication must already have been made before our bugs came online. Either Chain got a firm no, or . . . not."

"You mean that Kar could be conspiring against the throne?" Pahner asked.

"I submit that it's a possibility we can't afford to overlook, Sir," the intel NCO replied.

"We actually seem to have two different things going on here," the sergeant continued, pointing to the transcripts. "We have a debate taking place behind closed doors about the most effective method to deal with the Boman. Don't get these locals wrong; they all seem to think that they're doing the right thing. There are so many good intentions around here that you could mark a superskyway to Hell with them. Even Grath Chain is well intentioned, in his own—you should pardon the expression—scummy, self-centered, underhanded, devious, and treacherous sort of way. Oh, he's also upset about some economic losses and his loss of privilege, but mostly he just wants things to be back to normal. That means putting him back into the catbird seat, of course, but it also means a return to a situation in which the Boman aren't a threat to Diaspra, which isn't exactly a 'bad' thing."

"I'm perfectly willing to accept that all the parties involved have the best possible motives for everything they're doing," Roger told him. "Given the mess we're in, though, what does that have to do with anything?"

"Maybe not a lot, Your Highness, but then there's this other conversation going on in the shadows."

"What other conversation?" O'Casey asked.

"Here's an example. Welan Gor to Fan Pola. 'I think Grath's plan is an interference. We should use the humans for the Great Plan.' The caps are mine to reflect the emphasis all of them seem to be placing on it," Julian said.

"What's the 'Great Plan'?" Roger asked.

"That's a very good question, Your Highness. There's not much confusion about what it means among the five or six, Gessram Kar included, who apparently know about it. But if they ever get together to discuss the details of whatever it is, they haven't done it anywhere that we have monitored." Julian looked around the ring of puzzled and slightly worried faces. "Any ideas?"

"Have our bugs just missed it because of bad luck in their placement, or does there seem to be a particularly high level of security consciousness where this 'Great Plan' is involved?" O'Casey asked.

"Security consciousness is *definitely* high on this one," the sergeant said promptly. "At one point, a council member wanted to discuss something peripheral to it with Gessram Kar, and Kar got very upset. He said that not only was the conversation finished, but that such discussions could only take place 'at the times and places so designated.' Security's very tight on whatever it is. About the only thing I can tell you for sure is that whoever is orchestrating the 'Great Plan' is always called the 'Creator'."

"'Creator'?" Roger repeated, then chuckled sourly. "Well, that certainly has a fine godlike ring to it, doesn't it?"

"Yes, it does, and that means it's probably something targeted at the hierarchy," O'Casey said with a nod.

"I'll need to look at all the relevant conversations. Maybe I can pick something out."

"What do we do about Chain?" Roger asked. "That was the original point of this meeting, if I remember correctly."

"So far, he doesn't appear to be a viable threat, Your Highness," Pahner said. "Until he reaches the level of a viable threat, let's not do anything which would foreclose any of our options."

"Agreed," Roger said. "I think we ought to talk to Gratar again, though. Get a feel for what he thinks."

"About Grath Chain, or about the 'Great Plan'?" O'Casey wondered.

"About Chain . . . and whether or not he realizes there's anything else going on," Pahner replied grimly.

Honal waved his hand, and the hornsman trumpeted the call which brought the unit of *civan* to a stop.

"Damn it, Sol Ta! You were supposed to open out!"

"We're trying!" the infantry commander shouted back. "It's not as easy as it looks!"

"Yeah? Well, you ought to try pulling a thousand *civan* to an unexpected stop before they stomp all over your infantry allies!"

"Enough!" Bogess shook his head as he trotted his own *civan* over to where the two leaders were arguing. "Enough," he repeated more calmly. "It's the timing, Honal. And training. That's why we're out here, in case you didn't notice."

"Oh, I've noticed, all right," Honal said sharply, then drew a deep breath and waved over his shoulder at his troopers. "But my cavalry doesn't need training in basic movement orders. So we're going to cut back to just the minimum—myself and a company of about a hundred. Something that can stop unexpectedly if it has to without turning into this sort of confused mess . . . or walking on our allies."

"Fine." Bogess gave a handclap of agreement. "But this is important. I can see the humans' point about a charge at the end, rather than the beginning, but can you keep your cavalry under control? Wait for the order?"

"Easily," Honal grunted. "The ones who weren't with us on the trek down from the mountains might have been a problem before we got hold of them, but not now. Those humans know what they're talking about, and their tactics have never failed. As long as we can hold up our end, everything will be fine."

"Good," Sol Ta said. "But for that to happen, we have to get this maneuver right. And that means—"

"Back to training," Bogess finished for him. "In the meantime, I'm going to see how it's going with the recruit forces. If we're having this much fun, you can just imagine what training them must be like!"

"On the square!"

Krindi Fain groaned and stumbled wearily to his feet. For three endless weeks from hell, they had assembled on this accursed square at the edge of the city and practiced the simple drills of how to stand and march as squads and platoons. Then they'd been issued their sticks in lieu of pikes and taught to march and stand with their sticks and shields. And then they'd learned more complex countermarches, company and battalion formations, and how to form and break. How to move at a trot with pike and shield in hand. How to do the approved Mardukan pikeman squats. How to live, eat, sleep, and defecate while carrying a pike and shield.

For every endless hour of each long Mardukan day, they'd trained for fifty minutes with a single ten-minute break. Then, at night, they'd been mercilessly hounded by the human demons into cleaning their encampment and gear. Finally, in the middle of the night, they'd been permitted to get some rest . . . only to be awakened before dawn and chivvied back onto the square.

He gave Bail Crom a hand to his feet.

"Don't worry, Bail," the squad leader said with mock cheerfulness. "Just think—a couple more weeks of live pike training, and then, when it's all over, we get to fight the Boman."

"Good," the former tinker grumped. "At least I'll get to kill something."

"We're going to kill something anyway," Erkum Pol said nervously.

"What do you mean?" Fain asked as he led them to their places. If you didn't make it to your mark before the humans, there was punishment drill: trotting around the square with lead weights on your pike and shield while chanting "I am a slow-ass! I want to kill my buddies!"

"Somebody told me we gotta kill something to graduate," Pol said sadly.

"What?" Bail Crom asked. "A *civan*? A *turom*?"

"No," the simpleminded private said with an expression of great woe. "We have to kill a member of our family."

"What?" Fain stared at him. "Who told you that?"

"Somebody," the private said. "One of the other squad leaders."

"From our platoon? Who?"

"No," Pol said. "Just . . . somebody."

The squad leader looked around the mass of troops on the square and shook his head in a gesture he'd picked up from their human instructors.

"Well, I don't care if it was another squad leader, or Sergeant Julian, or Colonel MacClintock himself. We are *not* going to have to kill a member of our own family."

He reached his position just as Corporal Beckley came up to take over the formation.

"Are you sure?" the private asked, his confused face still a mask of woe.

"Positive," the squad leader hissed out of the corner of his mouth. "We'll talk about it later."

Frankly, he sort of wished the job of squad leader was someone else's. This leadership stuff was for the *atul*.

Roger stepped through the door at a gesture from the guard, then stopped in surprise. He knew that this wasn't a throne room, but he was shocked by the informality of the setting. The priest-king of Diaspra was invariably surrounded by dozens of attendants and lesser priests, but this room, although large, was virtually empty. There were five guards along the inner wall, but Gratar stood alone by a northeastern window, looking out at the rain.

The room echoed to the rumble of thunder. The Hompag Rains had come, and the city had been buried under the deluge for two days. The rain gurgled in the gutters, chuckled in the *chubes*, and filled the flood canals. Sheets of water wrestled with the dikes and threatened to overwhelm the defenses of the fields at every turn. The Chasten, once a clear blue-green from its mountain origin, now ran swollen and brown with the silt of the forests and plains, and everywhere the rains poured down and down and down.

After a glance at the guards, Roger walked to the window and stared out at the downpour beside the priest-king. The room was on the highest level of the citadel, and on a good day, the mountains were clearly visible from its heights. Now, the view was cloaked with rain.

The gray torrent gave patchy views of the fields to the east and of the dikes which protected them. That area was the drier upland of Diaspra's territory and should have been more or less immune to flooding, but beyond the dikes a sheet of water at least a meter deep—two meters, in places—washed across the landscape, hurrying to plunge over the cliffs and into the rivers and thence to the distant sea. That swirling sheet seemed not so much to spread from the river as to *be* a river a hundred kilometers wide; the actual Chasten was just an incidentally deeper channel of it.

The bluff line that created the normal Falls of Diaspra was now a hundred-kilometer-wide Niagara, clearly visible to the north. The mist from that incredible cascade should have filled the skies, but it was beaten down by the rain, and that same curtain muted the rumble of the plunging tons of water. The sight was both impressive and terrifying, and the prince suspected that that was the reason for having the audience here.

After a moment, the king gestured out the window without looking at the prince.

"This is the True God. This is the God all Diasprans fear—the God of the Torrent. We worship the placid God of the Spring, and the loving God of the gentle Rains, but it is the God of the Torrent we fear. This is the God we strive to placate with our dikes and canals, and so far, that has always worked, but only with unceasing toil.

"Your preparations for war take our workers from that toil. Already, the walls of the canals crumble, and the weirs are not turned in their proper times. Already, the slopes of the dikes erode, and the pumps fail for lack of maintenance.

"This, then, is our God, and our worship is a battle against Him." The king turned at last to look at the prince. "So, which enemy do we face? The Boman, who can be bought off with a few coins and pretties? Or our God, who can only be fought through toil and preparation?"

Roger stared out at the brown flood and the yellow lacework of its foam and understood the trouble in the priest's heart. It was only too easy to imagine how quickly the first Mardukan to look out at that sight must have gotten religion. Even as he watched, in the distance one of the massive forest giants slowly toppled and was swept over the cliffs. It looked like a toothpick in the distance, and was pounded into fragments that size in moments.

It was impressive and terrifying, yes. But a look to the east told a different story. The inhabitants of Diaspra had spent generations expanding their fields and making preparations for the annual rains, and it showed. There were dozens of flood canals between the city and the edge of the fields, with dikes interspersed between them. The primary purpose of the dikes was to break the force of the flooding water so that the weakened waters could be gathered by the canals and drained to the north and south. To the south, they drained into the swollen Chasten; to the north, they drained into an even more impressive native-made river, which, in turn, drained over the bluffs and into the lowlands.

A concentric set of three dikes protected the fields themselves. All of them led back to the city upland, and between each was a flood canal that led to an enormous storage basin which was kept pumped dry during the "dry" season, when it only rained four or five hours a day, not thirty-six. During the Hompag, however, the inflow outpaced the pumps, although not by much. The level of the reservoirs rose by only a handful of centimeters per day, and there was little likelihood that they were going to be overwhelmed before the end of rains.

Given that everyone had been commenting on how intense this season's Hompag Rains were, it looked to Roger as if the city could have made do quite handily with about half the defenses against flooding that it actually had. But trying to tell Gratar that was probably futile, so . . .

"There are several aspects to consider, Your Excellency," he said delicately, after a moment. "I've already referred to one: once you pay the Danegeld, you're never rid of the Dane. The Boman will take your treasure until you can't pay anymore, then they'll wipe you out anyway and plunder what they can from your ruins. And that treasure is what pays for all of this." The prince gestured sweepingly at the flood defenses. "If you're forced to give it to the Boman, there will be no funds to maintain all of this, anyway.

"But there's another issue which must be faced, Your Excellency. A delicate one which I've been reluctant, as a foreigner, to address." The prince continued to gaze out over the foam-streaked brown and amber torrents, but he no longer truly saw them. "Perhaps, though, it's time that I speak of it and tell you the story of Angkor Wat."

"Angkor Wat?" the priest-king repeated. "Who is he?"

"What, not who, Your Excellency," Roger said with a sad smile. "Angkor Wat was a city long, long ago on my . . . in my land. It was, and is, one of the most beautiful cities ever to exist—a paradise of gorgeous, ornate temples and lovely public buildings.

"It, too, was ruled by a priest class which worshiped water, and it was filled with magnificent canals and bridges. As you know, no doubt better than anyone else, such things take manpower to maintain, and in addition, the temples needed to be kept clean and the public buildings needed to be kept clear of greenery, as well. But the priests accepted that, and they dedicated themselves and their treasury—and their people—to the tasks of building and maintaining their magnificent city, and thus they lived for many, many years.

"They were a shining gem among lesser cultures, a splendid and beautiful vision, but there came a day when one of their neighboring rulers joined a group of fractious tribes. That neighbor saw the richness of Angkor Wat and was jealous. He had no fear of the wrath of their god, for he had his own gods, nor did he fear the people of Angkor Wat, for they were priests and temple workers, and Angkor Wat had few warriors.

"And so that shining gem fell before those barbarian invaders and its treacherous neighbor and was lost in the depths of time. So complete was its fall that its barbarian conquerors even forgot where it was. For thousands of years, it was no more than a rumor—a city of fables, not reality—until, finally, it was found again at last, and our searchers for antiquities cleaned the ruins. The labor required was immense, but they did the work gladly, out of the sheer joy of uncovering and restoring the beauty and magnificence which once had been and then had been destroyed.

"In the end, they made the entire city into a museum, a showcase of splendid temples and public buildings, and I went there, once. I was forced to go by a tutor to see the architecture. But I didn't come away with a love of the beauty of the buildings . . . I came away with a bitter contempt for the leaders of that people."

Roger turned and faced the priest-king squarely.

"Those leaders weren't just priests of a god. They were also the leaders of their people—a people who were slaughtered and enslaved by barbarians, despite the tribute that they paid and the battles they fought to build and preserve their city. They were butchered because their leaders, the leaders charged with keeping them safe, refused to face reality, for the reality was that their world had changed . . . and that they were unwilling to change with it."

The prince turned back to the window and the flood beyond.

"You can prepare for the water if you wish, Your Excellency. But if that's the enemy you choose to face, the Boman will kill you—and all of your people—before the next Hompag Rains come. The choice is yours."

The priest-king clapped his hands in agreement. "It is indeed *my* choice."

"The Council doesn't have a say?" Roger asked. O'Casey had been of two minds about that, and it wasn't as if there were a written constitution she could refer to for guidance. Not in a society which was based entirely upon tradition and laws of the God, which mostly bore on small group interaction and maintaining the dikes.

"Not really. They may advise, and if I discount their advice too many times and my decisions are shown to have been in error, I could be removed. It has happened, although rarely. But, ultimately, it is my choice."

The king rubbed his hands in distress, which was something to see in a four-armed Mardukan.

"There is a festival at the end of the rains," he said finally. "A celebration of rejoicing that the God has chosen to allow us to break ground again. I will make my announcement at that time, either to fight the Boman or to pay them tribute."

The monarch regarded the prince levelly.

"I have valued your advice, Prince Roger, and that of your adviser, the invaluable O'Casey. Yet I also understand your bias. You still must travel to the sea, and if we do not fight the Boman for you, that trek will be impossible. The Boman will never let you pass after your actions against them."

Roger's eyes rested once again upon the distant, thundering cascade. He said nothing for several moments, then he shrugged.

"Perhaps it *will* be impossible, but if you think the tales from the north are terrible, you never want to see the Empress' Own in true fury." He turned his head and smiled at the monarch. "You really, really don't, Your Excellency . . . and neither do the Boman. Better to face the wrath of your God of the Torrent armed only with belief, because when He's done, those of you who survive will still have silt in which to plant. When the Empress' Own are done, there will be no one to care."

CHAPTER THIRTEEN

"Today is your first taste of war."

Julian pointed to the four-armed dummies set up on the frames. They were the simplest possible effigies of a Mardukan: a head, two horns, four arms, and two legs, all connected by a long, dangling tube. Ropes ran to the tops and bottoms of the frames so that they would stay in place, and two more ropes ran to either side. The sergeant watched the recruits regard the dummies with perplexed and very cautious eyes and grinned ferociously.

"Now we get to have the fun of good training!" he told them loudly. "Fain! Front and center."

The Mardukan squad leader marched up to the human and came to a position of order arms with his pike. It was the real thing now, wicked meter-long steel head and all.

"You've been instructed in the use of the pike, correct Squad Leader?" Julian asked as St. John (M.) and Kane gripped the ropes attached to either side of the center dummy.

177

"*Yes, Sir, Sergeant Julian!*"

"You are now going to demonstrate your proficiency. On command, your job is to advance at a steady pace and drive your pike through the dummy, just as you will in combat against the Boman enemy. Can you do that?"

Fain didn't even look.

"*Yes, Sir, Sergeant Julian!*"

"Very good. Now, I will be behind the dummy. If it makes it easier for you to stick it all the way through by thinking that you might get me, too, you can feel free to envision that. Clear?"

"*Clear, Sir!*"

Julian stepped around behind the dummy and waved to Corporal Beckley.

"Take it," he said.

"Private Fain! Order arms! Private Fain, advance arms."

The Mardukan automatically dropped the butt of the weapon to the ground at the first command, then pointed the weapon at the target on the second.

"Private Fain will advance with determination at my command. Advance by half-step! Two, three, hut, hut, hut . . ."

The private stepped forward at the slow, balanced advance of the pike regiment until the pike was in contact with the dummy. Despite the simplicity of its construction, it was difficult to drive the weapon into it, and realistic enough to make him feel as if he were committing murder, but he put his weight behind the slow-moving weapon and tried to press it into the thick leather of the dummy's "body."

At the first hard thrust of the pike, the two Marines began to yank on the ropes while Julian, out of sight behind the dummy, set up a horrible, heart-wrenching wail as if from a soul in Hell.

The Mardukan private, horrified by the dummy's "reaction," flinched backward. And—inevitably—the instant he did, he found the diminutive Corporal Beckley at his side, screaming as loudly as Julian.

"What the fuck do you think you're doing, you four-armed *freak?!*" she shouted. "We told you to *kill* that bastard! You *will* advance with determination! *Advance*, two, three . . . !"

The shaken Mardukan grasped the pike firmly in two sliming true-hands and raised his shield as he advanced. This time, he expected the reaction of the team behind the dummy and drove forward despite it as the dummy apparently died in shrieking agony. For his pains, as the pike penetrated, a concealed sack of blood burst and went spurting out on the ground.

That red flood was enough to send him stepping back again, only to be verbally assaulted from behind. He drove forward once more, and this time, with a final, desperate thrust he stabbed the razor-sharp pike all the way through the target.

Julian's screaming ended . . . so abruptly that Fain was afraid he'd actually skewered the squad leader. His momentary fear, followed by elation that he might truly have killed the sadistic little two-armed shrimp, was short-lived as the sergeant came around the blood-drenched dummy.

"Listen up!" the Marine barked. "What we've just demonstrated here is the training technique you will all use. Two of you will pull on the ropes while a third stands behind—well behind—and simulates the sounds of a person dying. This will prepare you, as well as we can, for actually doing it. We will be participating in other training to prepare you, as well.

"This may seem hard, but hard training saves lives—*your* lives. And if you think that this is hard, wait until you actually face someone with a weapon in his hands, trying as hard as he can to stick it into you before you stick yours into *him*.

"You won't like it, because killing a person with steel, up close and personal . . . well, that really sucks."

"Their drill sucks," Honal groused as he waved for his company to wheel to the left and take the opposition cavalry in the flank.

The other contingent, also from the Northern League but from Shrimtan in the far east of the Ranar Mountains, tried to react to the flanking maneuver, but the ill-led mass of *civan* became tangled in its own feet and reins. The leader of the troop, who'd been a very junior officer when he led his own band of refugees south looking for any shelter from the Boman storm, waved his battle flag to call for a halt.

"True," Rastar said. "But we'll change that, won't we?"

"We'd better," the Therdan cavalry leader grunted. "From what I've been hearing in the city, it might be just us and the humans in the end."

"May the gods forfend," Rastar said with a grimace. "We've taken their gold and their food, and I would be bound to our agreements. But I truly wouldn't care to try for K'Vaern's Cove with the Wespar between us and the hills."

"Aye," Honal said as he spurred forward to "explain" to the other Northern lordling that "drill" meant doing things in a certain way, at a certain time, the same way, every time. And beyond the hills? The rest of the fucking barbs—including the true Boman.

CHAPTER FOURTEEN

"What are you guys so enthused about?" Roger asked.

There'd been little change in the week since his inconclusive meeting with Gratar. Training went on, and the inexperienced workmen were slowly turning into drilled units under the tutelage of the Northerners and the Marines, but other than that, things seemed to be coming slowly but inexorably apart.

More and more of the Council had begun siding with Grath as the floodwaters rose and dikes washed away without workmen to maintain them. From all reports, these were normal events precipitated by heavier rains than usual, yet each fresh inroad was another nail in the coffin of the policy of using the laborers as a military force. The calls to have them out in the rain working on the failing flood controls had already become clamorous, and every sign said that it was only going to become still worse.

At no point were the city, its inhabitants, or even the fields seriously threatened by the water, but that didn't seem to matter. The combination of the endless, enervating rains and a constant drumbeat of pressure from the cabal of carefully orchestrated tribute proponents eroded the confidence of the Council further with every failing dike, however inconsequential.

At the same time, the company's bugs provided constant tidbits of information about the second cabal working on its unknown "Great Plan." Whatever that plan was, it was large, for Julian had already identified no less than ten Council members, including several on the tribute side, among the conspirators. Whoever the Creator was, he'd amassed a sizable following and had excellent operational security, and so far no one who might have been in the know had used his actual name where the bugs might have overheard it. One of the reasons for that, apparently, was a suspicion that the humans might have listening devices like those they were, in fact, actually employing. All of which made the pleased expressions on everyone's faces seem particularly out of place to the gloomy prince.

"We think we intercepted a message to the Creator," Julian said, tapping at his pad. The handheld device was attached to the top of the all-purpose tactical intel computer the NCO had packed along, a helmet-sized, half-kilo device which contained fifteen terabytes of multiuse memory and a host of Military Intelligence software.

"What? It had an address on it?"

"No, Sir," Kosutic said. The sergeant major and Poertena were watching the intel NCO as if he were a woman giving birth to their first child. "We had an intercept that said a message was going to be passed, and we decided to have Denat stake out the pass in hopes of seeing who got it. But they used a dead drop, so Denat went ahead and picked it up."

"Won't that tip them off?"

"Dead drops go missing," Pahner said with a shrug, chewing calmly on a *bisti* root slice and pointedly ignoring the intel NCO. "Often. But one of the Council members who's involved in the Great Plan called this 'a very important message,' which seems to be a code phrase for messages directly to and from the leader. So Denat followed the messenger until the guy dropped the tube with the message in it into a *chube*. When I realized it could be going anywhere, I told Denat to pick it up. I doubt that we could have rolled up the whole line to the Creator no matter what happened; as crafty as this guy has been, there were probably a half dozen links in the chain. Not to mention that it would have been obvious that we were onto them with Denat trying to trot after it watching it float along."

"What's running?" Roger asked, watching the cavorting critters on the tiny screen of Julian's handheld. The device was running a query program, and the NCO had replaced the ubiquitous purple sundial of most programs with the graphics from a popular game program. The spinning and dancing hedgehogs formed into lines, and once all of them were in place, they blew up. There looked to be only about five or six explosions to go, which suggested the program was nearing the end of its run.

"Pocker was in code," Poertena said.

"I had to load the local written language before we could do anything else," Julian added. "We'd never gotten around to doing that. Then I scanned in the message, and now we see if it decodes it." The intel NCO beamed. "And it seems that it does," he added as the hedgehogs performed a final unnatural act and then exploded. "God, I love that game."

"B-T-H was a favorite of mine when I was a kid, too," Kosutic agreed. "Which I suppose says something about my childhood. So, what does it say?"

"Hmmm," Julian murmured. "Flowery for a secret message. 'Estimable Leader. Attempts to suborn human Marines have thus far failed. It is recommended that

direct contact with their senior officers be made at the
soonest possible moment. Aid in the Plan from the
humans would be useful. Their resistance to the Plan
might be disastrous.'"

"Well," Pahner said, climbing to his feet and beginning to pace in the small room, "that was refreshingly
cryptic. What attempts to suborn our Marines? Sergeant Major?"

"Nothing reported to me," Kosutic said, pursing her
lips.

"Maybe tee people tryin' to pay me off?" Poertena
asked.

"Maybe," Julian said. "Anybody in particular come
to mind?"

"Nah," the armorer replied with a shrug. "T'ey all
try to give me gif's. I said 'no.'"

"Maybe he should have said 'yes,'" Roger suggested.

"For that to work, he would have had to do it from
the beginning," Pahner disagreed with a frown, "and
we didn't know we were going to have these problems
when we started here. Twenty-twenty hindsight."

"Something we need to think about as an operating procedure for the future, though," Roger said.
"Maybe the order should be 'Take the bribe and report
it so we can find out where the string leads.'"

"The standing orders of the Empress' Own already
call for anyone who's 'tapped' for an intel request to
report it," Pahner told him, still frowning. "But the
Sergeant Major says no such reports were made. Right?"

"Right," Kosutic confirmed. "I'll ask around and make
sure." She got to her feet. "Keep me updated, Julian."

"Bet on it, Smaj," the NCO said. "I want to know
what they mean by 'direct contact.'"

Roger stood by his window, watching the pike units
forming up and drilling, and frowned. The morning of

Drying had dawned unusually hot and steamy, but the newly minted soldiers appeared unaffected by the heat or humidity.

The units were colorful. They'd scared up enough leather to make a short leather cuirass of sorts for each soldier, and the Leathermakers' Guild had dyed them in the colors of the different companies. The company shields matched, turning the gathering forces into a panoply of colors as the companies wheeled and formed like a huge kaleidoscope. The casual observer might have concluded that all that martial color was simply to make a splendid show, but Roger had enjoyed more personal experience than he'd ever wanted of just how difficult it was to keep track of who was who in the howling bedlam of combat. Identification of who was a friendly and who a hostile was always difficult from inside the furball, even for the humans with their sophisticated helmet sensor systems. For Mardukans fighting other Mardukans and equipped only with Mark One Eyeball scanners, it would be even worse, but the strong visual cues of the company colors ought to help greatly. Or that was the idea, at any rate.

The new troops' drill was excellent, he reflected. The days of pounding rain had rung to the sound of marching formations as the Marines first drilled the original cadre and then acted as advisors as the cadre trained the next layer of units. Roger had participated in that as well, while trying to run down support and supplies and figure out what cabals they faced. All in all, it had been a good time, despite the unrelenting workload and the sense that, apsimons or no, their supply of diet supplements was steadily dwindling, but now it was time to find out if the new companies and regiments would be used as planned, or if it had all been for naught.

For that matter, there still had been no contact from the cabal of the Creator, and the prince wondered if he would ever know whether that was because their interception had prevented the critical message which might have initiated that contact from reaching the Creator, or because follow-up messages suggesting the same thing had gotten through only to be ignored.

He turned from the window and started preparing for the ceremony. There would be a parade to start, then an invocation of the God of Water by the high priest, followed by any number of other ceremonies. The festivities were to continue through the night, and he'd been invited to over sixty separate parties. He would be attending about five; the rest had been farmed out to O'Casey and various Marines.

He buckled on his pistol belt and had just checked the chamber when there was a knock on the door.

"Enter," he called, holstering the pistol.

PFC Willis stuck her head in the door.

"Sir, Bishop From is out here. He requests a moment of your time."

Roger frowned and tugged at the front of his tunic. It was one of the *dianda* outfits Matsugae had had made for him in Marshad, and its light, lustrous saffron complemented his golden hair and the intense tan he'd developed.

"Show him in," he said, and turned as the artisan-priest entered and looked around the small and spartan room.

"Pardon my intrusion, Your Highness," Rus said, smiling and gesturing in self-deprecation. "It was but a small matter. I believe that you wish to have conversation with the Creator?"

Roger froze in shock. Of all the people who might have contacted him from the cabal of the "Great Plan," the second or third highest ranking priest in the temple was not who he would have picked as most likely.

"We wish to speak to you, and there is not very

much time at all," the cleric continued. "You may bring two guards. Or you can continue in blissful ignorance. 'Your choice,' as you would say."

Roger thought very hard for a moment, then nodded.

"We'll go. Let me get the guards and brief them."

He stepped out into the hall, and the two Marines guarding his door looked at him in surprise as he pulled his bead pistol back out to check the charge. Roger wasn't sure if the meaning of his action was plain to Rus From, but he knew it would communicate his own seriousness to the Marines. He looked at the power indicator, then nodded, holstered the weapon once more, and looked at the troopers.

"We're going to a surprise meeting. Just me, you two, and the priest. And we're leaving now."

"Sir," Georgiadas said, "shouldn't we inform Captain Pahner?"

"I don't have time to call him, Spyros," Roger said, with a very slight emphasis on the first-person pronoun. "We have to go now."

"Yes, Sir," the grenadier replied. "Let's do it, then."

"After you, Bishop From," the prince invited, gesturing down the corridor.

"This should be interesting," Willis muttered as they left their post and accompanied the prince on his latest harebrained excursion.

"Yeah," Georgiadas whispered back as he used his toot to key his communicator for a subvocal message. "Like the Chinese curse."

"Roger just left for an unspecified location with Rus From!" Pahner snapped, as he slammed open the sergeant major's door.

"Shit," Kosutic responded, throwing on her tunic. Unlike the prince, the rest of them had to wear their battle-worn chameleon suits, but they'd finally had the time to really attack the stains and tears. There were also spares available from the wounded and the dead, and they'd been put to good use. The final patchwork suits had clearly seen hard usage, but they were no longer the stained rags they had been.

"Not good, Sir," Julian added from the other side of the camp bed. The intel NCO pulled on his boots and sealed them to his uniform, then picked up his bead rifle and checked the chamber. "Do we go after him?"

"And does he have any guards at all?" Kosutic demanded harshly.

Pahner looked from one to the other and not quite visibly shook himself. It wasn't that seeing two Marines together was unusual, but the Regs were very specific about relationships between two people in the same direct chain of command. There were, in Pahner's opinion, very good reasons for that regulation, given that Marines were still people and that favoritism—or the need to keep one's loved ones out of harm's way—remained an ineradicable part of the human condition. And whether the captain agreed with them or not, the Regs made any such relationship a "crash and burn" offense. If two people in the same chain of command wanted to marry or become lovers, that was just fine with The Book . . . as long as one of them transferred out of that chain of command.

But there was nowhere on Marduk for anyone to transfer *to*, and Pahner felt a moment of absolute fury at Kosutic for allowing such a thing to happen. The sergeant major was his right hand. It was part of her job to make sure that *other* people weren't in violation of military law, not to go around violating it herself! Besides, she was forty years older than Julian—not, Pahner had to admit, that she looked it.

And Julian . . . Julian was an experienced troop who'd

been around the block a few dozen times. He damned well knew as well as Kosutic did just how far out of line they were and what a dilemma their actions were going to create for one Armand Pahner!

But even as those thoughts flashed through his mind, the captain knew it wasn't that simple or cut and dried. What were people supposed to do with themselves, with their emotions and their sex drives? Turn them off? Pretend they didn't exist? The Regs had never envisioned a situation in which a unit this small would be this isolated for so long, and what were two people to do when there was no place either of them could transfer to? And even if that hadn't been so, what was he supposed to do in this specific case? Oh, sure, Kosutic and Julian were both supposed to be setting examples to their subordinates, which meant holding their conduct to a higher standard, but how could he justify lowering the boom on them when he knew that *they* knew that he knew there were plenty of other similar relationships cooking away out there. Christ, there was even Despreaux and the prince to think about! God only knew where *that* mess was headed, and what was Pahner supposed to do if the two of them decided that the solution was to give in and do what they both so obviously *wanted* to do? Order them to behave—like that would do any good at all? Charge a member of the Imperial Family with violation of the Regs? Court-martial just Despreaux?

Besides, he thought as his initial, shock-born fury faded just a bit, he couldn't think of a single person less likely than Kosutic to let anything that was happening in her bed affect her decisions and actions in the field. Or, for that matter, less likely than Julian, despite the intel NCO's well-earned reputation for bending the rules. So if it wasn't going to have any negative side effects on the way they did their jobs, and if making a point out of jumping all over them was only going to unsettle his command structure and force him to take note of other, potentially even stickier relationships, then shouldn't he just keep his mouth shut and pretend he hadn't seen a thing?

"Derail your train of thought there, Armand?" the sergeant major chuckled.

"He has two guards," Pahner replied somewhat coldly. It was the first time Kosutic had ever addressed him by his given name in front of another member of the company, but the comment had been as effective a way to restart his mental processes as a slap to the face. Which was what the NCO had intended, he was sure. This whole situation was just going to have to wait, he decided firmly. Like maybe for the next ten standard years or so.

"Willis and Georgiadas, Sir?" Julian asked, apparently (and falsely, Pahner felt certain) unaware that there was any particular reason he ought to be sweating bullets. Or maybe he just had his mind totally focused on the job in hand. He was buckled up and ready to go, waiting only to be told where, so maybe that was all he was thinking about.

Yeah. *Sure* it was.

"Right. Georgiadas called it in," the captain said after only the briefest of cold-eyed pauses. "Rus From was the contact from the cabal," he added.

"Oh, my." Kosutic sat back down on the camp bed with a thump.

"So, no, we're not going in guns blazing," the captain continued. "We need to know what's going on before we make any decisions."

"We need to get Eleanora," the sergeant major said. "This is her area of expertise. And we'll need to crossfeed from Spyros to Roger."

"Julian," the NCO said.

"I'm on it, Sir," the intel sergeant replied, keying

his helmet communicator. "I'll get her headed for the command post."

"Let's get to it, people," Pahner said, and stepped back out the door. Once it was safely closed against observation, he stopped and shook his head. Julian and Kosutic. He snorted. God. Like he had time to think about that right now.

CHAPTER FIFTEEN

Rus From led the prince and his bodyguards to a back corridor of the temple/palace and an inconspicuous door that revealed a long spiral staircase which appeared to have been hammered from the bare rock of the Diaspra outcrop. The dank, Mardukan-sized stone steps were both steep and slippery with condensation, and as the party descended, the temperature dropped precipitously.

The stairs seemed to spiral downward forever, but they finally reached bottom at last and emerged into a dark, soot-streaked room illuminated only by a few sputtering torches. The cleric led them from there down a curving hallway/tunnel that was at least partially natural. There were chisel marks in places, but most of the walls seemed to be natural, water-worn limestone.

Then they turned a curve, and the priest paused as the passageway disappeared ahead of them into a curtain of plunging water.

"I must ask your warriors to leave their helmets at this point," he said.

"May I ask why?" Roger asked, eying the curtain of water dubiously. "And am I to take it that we have to pass through that waterfall?"

"Yes, we do," From said. "There are two reasons to do so. We are about to enter one of the most holy of the Secrets of the God. Beyond that Curtain of the God is His other self: the Dark Mirror of the springs above.

"We chose to use this place as a meeting ground for that reason, but also for the same reason you must first remove your helmets then pass through the curtain. It is believed that this will disable your 'transmission devices.' They are, I believe, susceptible to damage from water, yes?"

"Yes," Roger said with a sinking feeling in the pit of his stomach.

"Georgiadas!" Pahner snapped. "Tell the Prince to agree. Then set your helmet on retrans and we'll monitor the feed from your toots."

"Sir," Georgiadas said with a swallow, "it would probably be best to go with the priest's suggestion. That's what my . . . intuition says, anyway."

Roger looked at the lance corporal, then at his helmet.

"Right. Georgiadas, Willis, off helmets." He looked down at his practically new suit and winced. "Kostas is going to kill me."

"We can monitor, Sir," Julian said as he manually adjusted the gain on the video, "but we can't send them audio."

Pahner nodded in understanding. The toots pulled video and audio off of the appropriate nerves and rebroadcast them, but while the broadcast could be picked up and boosted by the helmet systems, the

Marines' toots were not designed to *receive* audio and video. Marines were fighters, not intelligence agents. As such, they were supposed to have their helmets on whenever it might be necessary for them to receive anything like that. Roger's toot could both send and receive audio and video, but he couldn't retransmit through the Marine helmets, largely as a consequence of the enormously redundant security features built into the implant hardware of any member of the Imperial Family.

"We can send them text if we need to," the captain told the sergeant. "Bounce it through the helmets, then to the guards' toots, then to Roger. Input isn't that big a deal; I think Roger's going to be walking out of that meeting unmolested, and I've got the rest of your squad armoring up in case he doesn't."

"I hope it doesn't come to that," O'Casey said pensively. "If Rus From is being used as a messenger, we can assume that the group behind this plot is even larger and more powerful than we'd thought. If we have to use force, it will gut Diaspra at exactly the moment it most needs solidarity."

"If we know that, then *they* know that," the NCO said stolidly. "They have to, and they won't do anything to jeopardize the preparations."

"Let's hope so," Kosutic said, then smiled. "But, take it from me—His Evilness knows partisans aren't always reasonable."

"Well, that was refreshing."

Roger shook the droplets from his fingers and wrung out his hair, then looked around the torch lit room at the circle of hooded, lantern-carrying figures and fought down a smile.

The room was part-cavern and part-construct. The back wall had been mined out to enlarge a natural grotto, but the far wall was mostly natural, and a small spring welled up at the base of a wall of sculpted limestone. It was surrounded by stalagmites and stalactites, and the light of the lanterns shone through the stone and water with a hollow translucence. Behind the spring was a small, natural ledge, the edge of a dry waterfall. It had been scrubbed immaculately clean, but fine discolorations indicated that something other than water flowed over it from time to time.

The site was probably as secret as they came. And it was still lousy tradecraft.

"This is the Dark Mirror," Rus From said, stepping up to the spring. "It is the brother of the God of the Sky." He nodded at the gathered figures and waved his lower hands in a gesture of deprecating humor. "And this is the dark mirror of the Council."

"Unless I'm much mistaken," Roger said dryly, glancing around the gathered figures in turn, "it *is* most of the Council."

"Whether it is or not, is beside the question," one of the robes replied.

"Chal Thai," Julian said. The voice print recognition was almost instantaneous. "Shit."

"We represent the dark mirror of the surface," the robed figure continued. "On the surface all is agreement, but in the shadows there are questions."

"We seek to change the society of our city," From clarified. "To break it of its dependence on the temple."

Roger blinked.

"But . . . you're a *priest*," he blurted.

"Yes," the cleric replied with a gesture of resignation. "So I am. But what I am more than anything else is an artisan. An . . . artist. I create things with my hands, things that move and work, and that is my true calling. But to do that?" He made the gesture of resignation again, this time with a negative emphasis. "To be a creator of things in Diaspra, I must be a priest."

"The Creator," Julian said.

"*Nicht scheisse*," Pahner responded. "Send a message to Roger. Do not agree to anything, but don't turn them down flat, either."

"Yes, Sir."

"So why am I here?" Roger asked.

"We feel there is a need for change," another figure said. "The power of the temple has grown too great. It is . . . choking us. We could be a great city, a city as powerful and well-regarded as K'Vaern's Cove, but we have this great choking beast of the temple on our backs."

"We don't hate the God," another voice chimed in. "But we feel that it's time and past time for the power of the temple to be reduced."

"Gessram Kar and Velaum Gar," Julian read the voice print identifications aloud as he hit the "send" button.

"Hail, hail, the gang's all here," Kosutic whispered.

"Yes," Eleanora said with a note of desperation. "It's a 'quorum of the Senate of Rome.' "

"What?" Pahner asked.

"One of the arguments for Caesar's assassination having been legal was that the conspirators who effectively signed his death warrant constituted 'a quorum of the Senate,' " the history professor said.

"Oh," Pahner said. Then, "*Oh.*"

Roger read the text message received by his toot and tried, again, not to smile. They must be having gibbering fits at the command post.

"To an extent, I agree," Roger said carefully. "And I'm sure—" actually, he was positive "—that my advisor on such things, Ms. O'Casey, also agrees."

"She does," From said. "Eleanora and I have had long discussions about the local political situation and your human political history. Our conversations and the points she raised were what convinced us to arrange this meeting. They gave us hope that you would . . . assist us in this endeavor."

Pahner's head turned like a tracking tank turret. His eyes nailed the chief of staff, who shrugged and held her hands out, palms up.

"How was I to know?" she asked.

"You didn't happen to give them a copy of Machiavelli or Permuster while you were about it, did you?" the Marine growled.

"The . . . precautions that we took on the way in were, of course, to defeat your 'electronic' transmitters," the priest/technician continued. "Conversations with your Marines indicated that they were susceptible to water damage. I presumed that your helmets were sealed, however, which meant they would have been unaffected by the Curtain."

By now, Roger was familiar enough with Mardukan expressions and body language to easily recognize smugness when he saw it. The question was whether he ought to pop the bubble or permit blissful ignorance, and he decided to go with ignorance for the time being.

"This is all very interesting," he said, "but you still haven't indicated what you want us to do."

"Isn't it obvious?" another voice practically hissed from the shadows. "This 'New Model Army' looks up to you. The people see you as saviors sent from the

God. If you were to overthrow the temple, it would
be over without the slightest bloodshed. Over in an
instant."

"Grath Chain," Julian said in a surprise.

"No way!" Kosutic said, then glanced over his shoulder at the voice print labels and shook her head.
"But . . . he couldn't have been in on the plot from the
beginning, could he?"

"A recent and ill regarded addition, unless I miss
my guess," Eleanora told her. "Note the distance
between him and the others, his position in the group,
and Rus' body posture. Not well regarded at all, at all."

"It's a bit more complicated than that," From said
with a quelling glance at his fellow conspirator.
"Gratar is a revered figure, what your chief of staff
would call a 'saint,' although we have no such des-
ignation. Overthrowing him will be *hard*, but because
he's so well-regarded and because he's so deeply and
genuinely devoted to the God, he's doing more
damage than any ten previous prelates."

"The taxes required to create and maintain the
public works of this madman are choking us," the figure
identified as Gessram Kar said.

"And whatever the taxes," From put in, "the lack
of innovation is stifling us. The temple has always
been conservative, which is death on the habits of
thought which produce innovation. That's bad
enough, but its narrow focus on the Works of God
reduces ambition, as well. It's almost impossible to
get capable young people to take up the crafts
these days. Why should they, when they know
they're going to do nothing but spend their days
building and repairing pumps . . . and that many of
those pumps are no more than backups to the

backups to the backups? Pumps which will never be used?"

The cleric gestured at Roger and his two silent body-guards angrily.

"And all of this when it is so clear that there's so much more to learn and to do and build! Those tiny, tiny transmitting devices we found in Gessram's office. The weapons you bear. The 'simple' devices that your Captain Pahner has described to me. There's an entire world of inventions there to be made; a world of learning to be drunk from! And what do we do? *Pumps!*"

"Oooo, that's got to be frustrating," Kosutic said.

"Obviously," Pahner said, with a shake his head.

"No," she said. "I don't think you've quite got it yet, Sir. I've got the feeling that this guy is like a Taketi or a da Vinci . . . stuck fixing pumps."

"Oh." Pahner rubbed his chin, then nodded. "Oh, yeah."

"And let's not forget the security aspects," another figure said. "Had you not arrived, there's no way we could have gotten the Laborers of God released to bolster the Guard of God, yet with the Northern states overrun, we can expect other waves of barbarians to follow this one like plagues. Without you, we would already have lost to the Wespar; unless we change the direction of the city, we *will* lose to the next wave."

"You don't have to tell me," Pahner said sadly. "Bogess. I recognized his voice."

"That tears it," O'Casey said. "The only major figure not there is Sol Ta."

"Who could just be one of the quiet ones, or not in the conspiracy because of his relatively low rank before we arrived," Pahner responded. "It really doesn't matter.

If it weren't for the position Gratar holds in the eyes
of the populace, they would've already moved. Damn."

"And they want us to counterbalance his prestige,"
O'Casey agreed. "What do we do?"

"Normally, I'd say 'tell them to at least wait until we
leave,'" the Marine said, rubbing his chin once more.

"But Gratar is on the fence about fighting the
Boman," Kosutic said with a raised eyebrow.

"If they kick off a civil war now," Julian put in, "we
have serious problems. We'll be forced to choose sides."

"Teach your grandmother to suck eggs, Julian!"
Kosutic snapped, then inhaled sharply. "Sorry, Sergeant," she said contritely.

"Not a problem, Sergeant Major, but it's so much
more complex than that."

"Yep," Pahner agreed. "We'd be absolutely against
it under almost any other circumstances, but . . ."

"Yes, 'but,'" O'Casey said. "But we don't know if
Gratar's going to support fighting the Boman."

"We don't know, for sure, that this cabal is going
to support fighting them, either," Kosutic pointed out.
"Not if it includes Chain."

"We need clarification," Pahner said, but Roger had
given up waiting for a message.

"Rus From, the rest of you," the prince said, smooth-
ing back his hair, "you're under a few false impressions.

"We're not here to cure all of this world's ills. We
weren't here to fight the Kranolta. We didn't come here
to put down a coup in Q'Nkok, nor to install a rational regime in Marshad. We especially aren't here to
interfere in internal Diaspran politics.

"We're wrecked here, and just trying to get home.
And, frankly, kicking off a coup just before a major
battle against an external enemy is *not* an action that
favors that."

"Gratar doesn't favor fighting the Boman," the figure the computer—and Pahner—had identified as Bogess said.

"Neither does Grath over there!" Roger snapped. "What? You thought I wouldn't recognize his voice, Bogess?"

There was a moment of silence, and then Bogess threw back his hood and made a gesture of resignation.

"You humans all sound alike to us. We assumed you wouldn't be able to distinguish *our* voices."

"He cannot be allowed to talk!" Chain squeaked furiously. "We've come too far; we're too exposed."

"And what would you have us do, merchant?" the war leader asked with a grunting laugh. "Kill him? Have you seen those weapons of theirs in action?"

"I wouldn't suggest trying it," Willis said, unprompted. "I really, really would not."

"Yes," From agreed. "We are exposed. And that's the point. We've advanced our timetable on the basis of our hope that you would intervene."

"Well that was certainly silly," Roger said. "Until the battle's over, we're not about to interfere."

"But *we* must," Bogess told him. "Other cities had begun eyeing us with greed even before the Boman advanced upon us. With the damage we're certain to take from the Boman, they'll surely take advantage of us."

"Yeah," Roger said. "But not until after the battle. And they might not even then. If we beat the Boman soundly—which is possible, if we're not fighting a damned civil war at the same time—it will give them pause."

"And continue to leave businesses stagnant, if there's no change within the city," Gessram Kar said, still without lowering his hood.

"And our technology," From agreed. "Not to mention

the fact that we who have sought to change things will undoubtedly be sent to visit the God."

"Guys, I don't know the answer to that," Roger said. "All I can say is, let's get the battle done. Then we can try to work something out. But until we get rid of the Boman threat, a civil war is out of the question."

"What if Gratar says we won't fight the Boman?" Bogess asked. "What then? As you've pointed out, we will have them as an *astain* on our necks for the rest of eternity."

"Oh, not that long," Roger said with a chuckle. "Just until they drain you dry and decide to finish overrunning you."

"But if Gratar decides to appease the Boman?" Kar asked.

"Then . . . we'll see," Roger said. "There are some ways we might be able to make a fast strike through to K'Vaern's Cove. We might not have to fight the Boman at all. And we'll know Gratar's decision soon enough," he added, directing a thought at his toot. "In fact, if we don't hurry, we'll all be conspicuously missing from his speech."

"If he says 'no,'" Chain hissed, "you'd better hope the Boman give you time to escape!"

"Captain Pahner, Sir," Private Kraft said from the door of the intel room. "Sir, St. John (J.)'s team has been trying to get hold of you, Sir. It looks like the Boman are moving."

CHAPTER SIXTEEN

"What've you got, Despreaux?"

The Drying Ceremony was about to start, and virtually everyone who was anyone wasn't going to be there on time. Pahner shook his head at the black humor of the situation, wondering what, if anything, Gratar was going to think when half his Council and all of his alien advisers arrived late from every direction, out of breath, and clearly disturbed. The fact that the long-awaited Boman offensive could actually be used to cover domestic shenanigans which should never see the light of day appealed to the captain's sense of irony.

Which, unfortunately, didn't necessarily make that offensive good news.

"Captain, we've got loads of trouble," the sergeant responded over her com. "I sent Bebi and Kileti out to eyeball the encampment just as soon as it started to dry out at all. They'd just gotten into position—they hadn't even had time to start a proper hide—when the Boman started pouring out of their camps on the hills."

"Tell them to pull back," Pahner snapped as the head-quarters group turned the last corner to the court where the audience was to take place. The solid wall of Mardukans in front of them forced them to pause briefly, and he could hear the intonations of the opening ceremony on the other side. Things weren't quite out of hand yet. If Gratar decided against engaging the Boman, though, it would be a near run thing.

"I did, but they're stuck. They were setting up on a little ridge leading to that group of hills the Boman are on. Now the barbs are using the ridge to stay out of the muck down in the lows. They're headed right for Bebi and Kileti, and they both say if they move it would give them away. They're stuck, Sir."

"Right." The captain had been in enough screwed-up situations to know exactly what his Marines were thinking, and he agreed. If they were even slightly hidden, it would be better for them to stay still than to try to move. "What about you?"

"We're not on their direct line to Diaspra, Sir," the sergeant replied. "Right now it looks like they're going to bypass us. If they don't, well, we'll see what happens."

"Okay," Pahner said as the Marines began to push their way through the throng of scummies. "Get a movement estimate and count, then report back. Patch it to the Sergeant Major, though. I'm going to be kinda busy."

"Aye, Sir," the patrol leader said. "But I can already tell you, the count is 'a shitload.' "

"There's a shitload of 'em," PFC Kileti whispered.

"I know, Chio," Bebi whispered back. "Now shut up."

The team had just reached the observation point when they spotted the oncoming Boman horde. The barbarians flowed without any semblance of order, a vast mass of walking Mardukans that seemed to move in extended family groups. A senior male or two and several younger males would be accompanied by nearly as many females and a gaggle of young from "snot-sucker" infants up to preadolescents. There were some purely male groupings, and a few of unescorted younger females, but, by and large, the horde was centered around the familial groups.

They appeared to be carrying all of their worldly possessions on their backs. The males all supported large bundles—personal goods and loot from earlier conquests—while the females carried children and smaller bundles. There didn't seem to be any groups of "slaves," nor did they use many beasts of burden. There were pack *civan* scattered through the group, and *turom*, but they were few and far between.

The reconnaissance team wore not only their hard-used chameleon suits, but also an ancient invention called a gill suit. The genesis of the gill suit was lost in the mists of time, but in its simplest form—which these were—it was a net tied through with strips of cloth. The local cloth used for sacks had turned out to have all the properties the humans were looking for; the strips broke up the human outline, making it almost invisible in any sort of cover. The projectors of the combat armor did the same thing, but the recon team didn't *have* armor . . . and gill suits didn't require batteries.

Captain Pahner nodded to Roger as the prince slid into position beside him. Roger had taken time to slip back to his room and change clothes, replacing his ruined saffron outfit with a black one, and Pahner hoped the color wasn't an omen.

"We have another problem," the CO whispered.

"Julian told me," Roger replied, his nostrils flaring

wide and white. "What the hell are we going to do, Armand? We can't fight the Boman by ourselves."

"We'll do whatever we have to, Your Highness," the Marine commander told him flatly. "If we have to fight the Boman with just ourselves and Rastar's troops, we will. And we'll win."

"How?" Roger asked hopelessly.

"'Our strength is as the strength of ten,' Your Highness," the captain said with a slight, sad smile. "We'll win because if we don't, we'll never know it. That world won't exist for us, and that's a form of winning, if you look at it from just the right angle."

"Go out in a blaze of glory?" the prince asked. "'Death is lighter than a feather'? That's not your style, Captain."

"And the alternative is?" The Marine grunted. "Your Highness, we *will* get you home . . . or die trying. Because whether it's death from lack of supplements because we didn't get home in time, or death from an alien spear on some battlefield, our swords will still lie in the heather. There's no other possible outcome if Gratar chooses not to fight."

"We can work the conspiracy angle," Roger said.

"Eleanora and I discussed that," Pahner replied. "But if the conspirators start their coup just after Gratar calls for an offering of tribute, it will appear as if the whole purpose of the rebellion is simply to avoid the cost that will fall on the merchant class."

"Ouch. I hadn't considered that."

"Nor had I, until Eleanora pointed it out," the CO said with a smile. "And as she also pointed out, that would make it seem as if all the rebels are really after is simply to shift the monetary loss from the rich merchants to a far higher cost from the poor soldiers. If Gratar doesn't come up with that line of reasoning, I'm sure someone—Chain perhaps—will adduce it."

"And that would really kill the coup," Roger grunted. "The largest single military force would be on Gratar's side, and so would moral supremacy."

" 'God favors the side with the most cannon,' " Pahner agreed. "But, of course, in this case, just who has the most 'cannon' might be a debatable matter. I've got the platoon standing by. Julian and everybody else in his squad is in armor; the replacement circuits are ready to put in place as soon as I pass the word."

"You're going to back them?" Roger asked, eyeing him askance.

"If it's that or face the Boman in our skivvies, hell yes!" the Marine said, turning to look at the prince. "You think I'm crazy? If Gratar says no, it's our only shot . . . even if it won't work."

"Well, I guess it's blaze of glory time, then," Roger said with a wince. His own death he could face calmly, but the continued loss of Marines was something else, and he found himself wondering if getting as close to them as he had was for the best after all. When they'd started this long journey, they'd been mere faceless automatons; now each and every member of the dwindled company was a face and a soul, and the loss of each of them was a wrenching pain. Even as he and Pahner discussed the loss of the rest of the company, he was fretting for the two Marines in the reconnaissance patrol, pinned down by the passing Boman. And he continued to fret as the annual and extremely long Drying Ceremony, with its distribution of grain and blessings upon the fields, continued through the endless Mardukan day.

Between the out-of-the-way position of their hide and their gill suits, the two cowering Marines had managed to remain unseen as the tide of barbarians passed them. And it was a tide, indeed—a flow that continued through the morning and long into the afternoon. There were a couple of times, as groups used the lee in which the humans sheltered for a pause, when it seemed that they must be detected. One time, a warrior walked up to the bush they lay under and peed on the side of its trunk. The urine splashed off of the root and onto Bebi, but still they managed to avoid detection.

Their helmets automatically processed targets seen and heard, using that for max/min estimates of hostiles. The processors had some problems separating the noncombatant females from the male combatants, but even the most conservative estimate was overwhelming.

"Over twelve thousand warriors," the team leader subvocalized with a slight shake of his head. The comment was picked up by his throat mike and transmitted to his companion.

The flood was beginning to trickle off as stragglers wrestled with the churned path the army had created. Those stragglers were mostly individuals: older females, and wounded who'd been cast out as unfit. There were some younger Mardukans, as well—orphans who hadn't been absorbed by other families and weren't old enough to fight for space in one of the bachelor groups. Yet, varied as they were, all of these scavenging stragglers had one thing in common; they survived solely on the leavings of the family groups . . . and no one else in the tribe gave a single, solitary damn what happened to them.

"What a fucked-up society," Bebi whispered. "Look at those poor people."

"Not so unusual," St. John (J.) radioed back from the base camp. "Until it was brought into the Empire, Yattaha practiced the tradition of casting out the old just as their ancestors did. Once he was no longer useful to the community, it was customary for an old person to voluntarily take himself away somewhere and starve himself to death.

That was the tradition, anyway. What actually happened was that they got tossed out of the house and wandered around the camp until the winter killed them."

"That's barbaric," the Mausean protested.

"That's why they call 'em 'barbs,' Bebi," St. John (J.) retorted. "People like the Saints make like barbarism and tribes and living hand-to-mouth is so great. Until they look at what that actually means, anyway. Then half the time they don't pay attention to what they're seeing, 'cause if they *did* pay attention, it'd knock all their pretty dreams right on the head. Living like this is just living in Hell for everybody in the society every single day, whether they know it's Hell or not."

There was silence over the communications link, and then St. John (J.) inhaled deeply.

"Time to call it in. Looks like upwards of twelve, fifteen thousand hostiles. Sounds like Voitan all over again."

"And this time with a shitload of poor, noncombatant sad sacks added," the PFC said, shaking his head again as an emaciated Mardukan with only one arm sat wearily down in view and rolled over on his side. The pink scars on the new-made corpse clearly indicated that he'd been a warrior until recently.

"They're all sad sacks, Bebi," the team leader said. "Just some worse off than others."

Gratar completed the last ritual blessing of the barleyrice and ascended the dais through the crowd of lesser priests to stand by the liquid altar and dancing fountains. He remained there, silent, head bowed, as the crowd patiently awaited his pronouncement. Despite the tension in the air, the vast square was silent but for the hushed susurrus of thousands of lungs breathing the humid atmosphere and the occasional shuffle of feet.

For Roger, it was a moment of odd transcendence.

It was as if he were perched on a precipice, without any control over his immediate future. He felt as if he were leaning into a strong wind, storming up the cliff into his face to support him. It was a mighty wind . . . but at some point, it would fail, and he would fall. That was inevitable, beyond his control, and whether he fell to death or to victory would depend on the words about to be said by someone else.

Finally, the prelate turned from his devotions and looked out over the crowd. He raised his arms as if to call for even deeper silence, and when he spoke, the exquisite acoustics of the temple square carried his voice clearly to the farthest ear.

"We are the People of the Water. The People of the Water are ancient beyond memory. When the first prospectors came to the Nashtor Hills, the People of the Water were here. We remember."

"We remember," the gathered priests chorused.

"We remember the Autean Empire. We remember when the Auteans, consumed by the pride of their own power, threw off the strictures of the God and spread their crops to the farthest distance, the better to extend their might. We remember how they built their roads and leveled mountains. How they dammed and bridged the rivers.

"We remember how the long, dry times that allowed them to flourish ended in eternal rains, and how the Auteans fell before the Wrath of the God. How their cities and crops flooded, their roads washed away, their fortresses sank into the mire. In time, northern barbarians drifted down upon them, driven by hunger. They found the ruins of the Auteans, conquered their scattered survivors, and founded their own cities where once the proud Auteans ruled.

"Thus was born the Northern League . . . and we remember."

"We remember," the crowd responded somberly.

"We remember when K'Vaern's Cove was nothing more than a barren place of temporary respite for fishermen from distant ports. No more than a rocky, unusable place where fishermen would gather to ride out the storms . . . until a clumsy fisherman named K'Vaern wrecked his boat on the rocks and, being bereft of support, charged fees from other boats who wanted to tie up to his wreck that their crews might come ashore and stretch their legs. And in time, on the ruins of that wreck, he built a dock, and a shelter from the storms. Then an inn. Then a city. We remember."

"We remember."

"Through it all, the People of the Water remember. We remember when Sindi was founded, and when the Auteans themselves came from the north. The founding of Ran Tai, and the wars of the south. Through it all, the People of the Water have watched, and remembered, and been true to themselves. We worship our God, and teach the ways of worship to all and sundry, and that has been enough.

"Now come the Boman, the latest in the unending river of time, and we are threatened by them, as has happened before in our long history. First, by the early Auteans. Then by the Sartan, dread riders of the *civan* they brought with them, who, in time, became the Vasin of the League of the North. And now, by the Boman.

"The Auteans never pressed upon us. They found civilization, something they had never seen, and in time they founded their own cities and became contemptuous of us. But we survived when they perished by staying true to the worship of our God.

"The Sartan came down from the north in their shrieking thousands, wielding long spears and mounted upon their fierce *civan*. The Sartan we fought, and kept from our lands until they finally returned to the north to found their own cities. And, in time, they, too, became contemptuous and forgot the God, to their shame."

"To their shame," rumbled back from the crowd.

"Now come the Boman. Many say that we should take the Laborers of God, now recreated into the Warriors of God, and face the Boman in battle. That we should throw them back to the northern wastes through our power and knowledge and faith in the God.

"Others say that we should set our Laborers of God to the tasks of the God, rebuilding our Works of God, that our God may not turn His face from us, or, worse, come upon us with the Eternal Wrath that destroyed Autea. That we should pay the Boman from the monies that are set aside for the temple and from additional taxes upon our merchants. That the Boman will turn aside if we give them gold without battle."

"This, then, is the dilemma. Shall we be a nation of Warriors of God, who go forth and crush the enemy while the Works of God waste away? Or a nation of Laborers of God, making and maintaining the Works of God, while an enemy threatens us with destruction of all the God holds sacred?

"Whatever my decision, there will be misery. If I decide for tribute, the monies taken from the merchants will mean mouths that go unfed and crops that are never planted. Money is the lifeblood of a city, and giving it to the Boman in an amount that will appease them will cripple us as a people. And however much we give, still it may not prevent the destruction of all we hold dear.

"Yet fighting the Boman will not be bloodless. We will certainly lose sons to the fury of battle, with all the misery and grief that will bring upon us. We will lose sons who have grown up in our midst, and will be sorely missed. And if we fight, we might yet lose, and then all would be lost to no avail."

"If he doesn't make up his mind, we're kicking off anyway," Julian said, rattling his armored fingers on the helmet on his knees.

"You're a fine one to bitch," Cathcart said. "You got any fucking idea how hot this shit is when it's shut down?" The plasma gunner looked like a gray statue with a sweating, animated head. His plasma cannon was pointed up over his back, as if threatening the ceiling with terminal prejudice unless it surrendered.

"And you know the fucking plumbing doesn't work, right?" Pentzikis snapped. "I've gotta pee like a *flar-ta!*"

"You shoulda gone before you suited up," Poertena said. He fingered the baggies of capacitors nervously, waiting for Pahner's orders to open the bags which were the components' only protection from the destructive humidity and molds of Marduk. Without them, only the four suits of armor with the old-style capacitors—the ones fortunate enough to have escaped the last "upgrade" cycle—were operable. But if the little armorer was forced to install them, their serviceable lifetime could be counted in days, or weeks at most. Certainly, they would never last long enough to retake the planetary spaceport from the SaintSymps who controlled it.

"If we gotta use tee armor, it'll be peein' time for sure, anyway," he added grimly.

"I'm still gonna kill the old fart if he doesn't get this over with," Julian snarled.

"There is a third way," Gratar intoned. "We could send emissaries to the Boman with gifts. Lesser gifts than the Boman might like, but followed by the

Warriors of God. We could try to buy peace with them at a lesser price even while we dissuade them from war with the might of our army and the power of our God.

"Yet this would leave the Boman, and ourselves, unsure. Incomplete. Waiting to discover what ultimate resolution awaits us both if the tribute should be demanded a second time. Or a third. In the long run, it would be no more than the first choice—to maintain the Laborers and hope for peace rather than to accept the burden of war.

"The God tells us many things about the world. He tells us that there are ways of greater and lesser resistance. That all is change, even if it appears eternally the same on the surface. That rocks come and rocks go, but eddies are eternal.

"And above all else, our God tells us that when we are faced with a challenge, we must understand it and confront it squarely, then do whatever is necessary to meet the challenge, no matter the cost.

"When a flood comes, one does not ask for it to go away. One might pray to the God for it to be lessened, but even that is usually in vain. The God calls for us, as a people, to build the Works that are necessary to meet his Wrath, and thus we have always done.

"And today, we have built a new Work of God, one called the Army of God. . . ."

CHAPTER SEVENTEEN

Roger pulled Patty to a stop and nodded to Captain Pahner and General Bogess.

The two commanders stood on a tall mound at the center of a solid redoubt. One nice thing about using the Laborers of God for their core force was that the Mardukans had, by and large, been digging ditches and building levees one shovelful at a time for their entire working lives. Constructing a fortification was simply a matter of laying it out and letting them get to work; a Warrior of God was never happier than when he had a shovel in his four hands.

The commanders had put that willingness to good use. Once the battleground—a shallow valley at the edge of the sprawling fields of Diaspra—had been determined, construction had begun. The New Model Army had built a central bastion to hold the Marine reaction force and some of the *civan* cavalry, and then the Warriors had gotten to work on their own lines.

A hedge of stakes, pointed forward, had been set up in front of the pike regiments. The sharpened stakes ranged from one to two meters in length, and created a prickly forest in front of the Diaspran regiments.

There were regular breaks in the hedge. Blocks of Northern cavalry waited at their ease behind the pike regiments, resting their *civan* yet ready to sally through the lines. The stakes were spaced widely enough for the *civan* to squeeze through them going out at almost any point, but the openings in the hedge were the only gaps through which the cavalry might come back. Which was why the steadiest of the pike companies, flanked by the shield and assegai-armed regulars from the pre-Marine Guard of God, had been stationed to cover those openings.

One end of the battle line was anchored on a canal, while the other abutted the forest. Although the Boman could conceivably flank them from that direction, it was unlikely. The ground was rough, the forest was thick, and the Wespar were not well known for fancy battle-field maneuvers. They were lucky if they could all arrive at the same battle on the same day, and even in a worst-case scenario, any movement to flank the Diaspran line should be obvious, and the Marines or Northerners could beat it off.

"It looks good," Roger said as Dogzard slid down off the flank of the packbeast. Although he'd made great strides in mastering the art of *civan*-riding, Roger had also firmly grasped that pearl of veteran wisdom: stick with what you *know* works in combat. He and the *flar-ta* had worked out the rules for a lethal partnership he had no intention of breaking up. Besides, the dog-lizard could ride behind the *flar-ta*'s saddle, a practice which no *civan* would tolerate, and the prince's pet—now a veritable giant for her species—refused to be separated from him. Not that her devotion or increased size had made her any less importunate, and Roger watched her sidle up to Bogess and accept a treat from him as her due.

"It could be better," Pahner replied. "I'd prefer more ranged weapons, but even if we had more arquebuses . . ." He waved a choppy gesture at the drizzling rain. The Hompag had passed, but "dry season" was a purely relative term on sunny Marduk, and at the moment, the relationship was distant, indeed. "If the Boman are smart," the Marine went on, "they'll stand off and pound us with those damned hatchets."

"We've got the javelins," Roger pointed out, frowning at Dogzard. She finished off Bogess' treat, licked her chops, and jumped back onto the *flar-ta*, which snorted its own disgust.

"Yes," Bogess said, absently wiping his fingers on his armor. "But only one or two per soldier. The Boman carry several axes each."

"It's not that big a deal," the prince insisted. "The pikes have their shields, and if they really do stand off like that, we can hammer them with plasma fire."

"Some of the companies could be steadier," Pahner commented pessimistically.

"Jesus, Armand," Roger laughed. "You'd bitch if they hanged you with a golden rope!"

"Only if it were tied wrong," the captain told him with a slight smile. "Seriously, Roger. We're outnumbered three-to-one, and don't think the Diasprans don't know that. It will affect them, and the Boman are bogey men to them. They're all . . . six meters tall. I was going to say three meters, except that that's about the height of a normal Mardukan. But that ingrained fear is something we have to be prepared for."

"Well," Roger said, waving as he prepared to ride down the line, "that, as you've told me, is what leadership is for."

"When they going to come, Corp?" Bail Crom asked. Krindi Fain tried to keep his expression calm as he surreptitiously wiped one hand on his cuirass. It wouldn't do for the troops to see that his palms were sliming.

The pikes stood at rest on the battle line, awaiting the arrival of the Boman. They'd been there since just after dawn. They'd prepared the defenses well into the night and then gotten back up after only a brief rest for a sketchy breakfast. Now, between the up and down stresses and the physical labor of marching to the battle site and digging in, the entire New Model Army was adrift in a hazy, semi-hallucinatory condition, the mixture of physical fatigue and sleep deprivation that was the normal state of infantry.

"If I knew that, I'd be up in the castle, wouldn't I?" he snapped.

The drums from the Boman encampment just over the ridge had been beating since dawn. Now it was moving into late morning, and their enemies' refusal to appear was making the Diaspran noncom far more anxious than he cared to appear.

"I was just wondering," Crom said almost humbly. The normally confident private was a sorry sight to see in the morning light.

"Don't worry about it, Bail," Fain said more calmly. "They'll come when they come. And we'll be fine."

"There's supposed to be fifty thousand of them," Pol said. "And they're all five hastongs tall."

"That's just the usual bullshit, Erkum," Fain said firmly. "You can't listen to rumors; they're always wrong."

"How many *are* there?" Crom asked.

"Bail, you keep asking me these questions," Fain said with a grunt of laughter. "How in the Dry Hells am I supposed to know?"

"Well, I was just wondering," the private repeated . . . just as a burst of intense drumming echoed from the opposite ridge line.

"And I think you're about to find out," Fain told him.

"Quite an interesting formation," Pahner remarked as he dialed up the magnification on his visor.

The Boman force was at least fifteen thousand strong, yet it didn't stretch as wide as the smaller Diaspran army. Its narrowness would have invited a devastating flanking movement if he'd had the forces for it, but he didn't, and if it wasn't as wide as the Diaspran battle line, it was *far* deeper. It flowed and flowed across the ridge, a seemingly unending glacier of barbarians, and it was obvious that the New Model Army was badly outnumbered. The captain watched them come for several more moments, then keyed his communicator.

"Okay, Marines. Here's where we earn our pay. These scummies have to stand."

"There's a million of 'em!" Pol wailed, and started to back up.

"*Pol!*" the squad leader barked. "Attention!"

The days and weeks of merciless training took hold, and the private froze momentarily—just long enough for the squad leader to get control.

"There are *not* a million of them! And even if there were, it wouldn't matter. They all have to come past your pike, and my pike, and Bail's! Stand and prepare to receive! Stand your ground!"

The private in front of Bail Crom started to turn around—then froze as a chilly voice behind them echoed through the thunder of the drums.

"Sheel Tar, I will shoot you dead if you don't turn back around," Lance Corporal Briana Kane said with a deadly calm far more terrifying than any enraged shout. The private hesitated, and despite the drums and the approaching shouts of the Boman, despite the odd, visceral sound of thousands of feet pounding down a far slope, the sound of the Marine's bead rifle cycling was clear.

Sheel Tar turned back toward the onrushing enemy, but Fain could see him shuddering in fear. The mass of enemies advancing towards them was horrifying. It seemed impossible that anything could stop that living tide of steel and fury.

Pahner saw the occasional flicker of a face turned towards the bastion. It was a nervous reaction he was used to, yet this time was different. He was a Marine, accustomed to the lethal, high-tech combat of the Empire of Man and its enemies. Prior to his arrival on Marduk, he had *not* been accustomed to the ultimate in low-tech combat—the combat of edged steel, pikes, and brute muscle power. Yet for all of that, he knew precisely what he had to do now. An ancient general had once said that the only thing a general in a battle needed to do was to remain still and steady as stone. Another adage, less elegant, perhaps, but no less accurate, summed it up another way: "Never let them see you sweat." It all came down to the same thing; if he gave a single whiff of nervousness, it would be communicated to the regiments in an instant . . . and the Diaspran line would dissolve.

So he would show no anxiety, despite the Boman's unpleasant numerical superiority. Even with the arguably superior technique of the phalanx and shield wall, and the advantage of the stake hedge, the battle would be a close run thing indeed.

And like so many close run battles, in the end, it would come down to a single, all-important quality: nerve.

❖   ❖   ❖

Roger sat on Patty, eleven-millimeter propped upright on one knee, his hand resting on the armored shield of the *flar-ta*, and watched the oncoming barbarians. He knew as well as the captain that he should be presenting a calm front for the soldiers of the regiment he was parked behind, but for the life of him, he couldn't. He was just too angry.

He was tired of this endless battle. He was tired of the stress and the horror. He was tired of facing one warrior band after another, each intent on preventing him from getting home. And more than anything else in the universe, he was tired of watching Marines who had become *people* to him die, one by one, even as he learned how very precious each of them was to him.

He wished he could pull the Boman aside and say, "Look, all we want to do is get back to Earth, so if you'll leave us the hell alone, we'll leave *you* alone!"

But he couldn't. All he and the Marines could do was kill them, and it was at times like this that the rage started to consume him. It had started at the first battle on the far side of this Hell-begotten planet, and just seemed to build and build. At the moment, it was a fury so great, so bottomless, that it seemed it must consume the world in fire.

And he was especially angry that Despreaux was out there somewhere. Most of the Marines were as safe as they could be in a battle on this misbegotten world. They were standing at the back of the formations, providing "leadership," and if the enemy broke through the lines, they had a better than even chance of escape. Losing the battle might well mean starvation would kill them all slowly in the end, but not today.

But Nimashet was out there, somewhere, with her team. Cut off, with nowhere to run. All she could do was hide and wait for her orders, and Roger knew what those were going to be and wished—wished as if his soul were flying out of his body—that their positions could be reversed. Despite what had happened in Ran Tai, he'd realized that he had to face the fact that he was madly smitten with one of his bodyguards. He had no idea whether that was only because he'd been beside her in good times and bad for the last few awful months or whether it was something that would inevitably have happened under any conditions, nor did it matter. Right now, all that mattered was that he wanted to kill every stinking Boman bastard before they could put a slimy hand upon his love.

Frightened Mardukan pikemen who knew human expressions, looking over their shoulders for reassurance from their leaders, took one look at Prince Roger Ramius Sergei Alexander Chiang MacClintock and turned instantly back to face their foes, for even the Boman in their fury were less frightening than the face of their human commander.

"Don't mind us!" Honal called out to the nervous Diasprans as their hands shifted on their pikes and their anxious faces turned to the rear. "We're just here as observers, after all! Still, we're glad you're here, too . . . and we definitely prefer for you to stay right where you are."

The muttered, grunting laughter of a hundred heavily armed cavalry rose hungrily behind him, and the wavering faces turned back to the storm.

Bogess watched the surges of uncertainty ripple through the pike regiments. He was totally confident in the steadiness of his assegai-armed regulars. Despite their earlier losses to the Boman, they had demonstrated their determination often enough even before the humans had taught them their new tactics and discipline. Now they truly believed what the human

Pahner had been telling them for weeks—that no organized force of *soldiers* was ever truly outnumbered by any horde of barbarians.

Nor did the Diaspran general harbor any fears about Rastar and his cavalry. No one had ever called a Northern cavalryman a coward more than once, and these Northerners had a score to settle with the Boman. Like his own men, they were supremely confident in their own leaders and the humans' tactics, but even if they hadn't been, the only way the Boman would have taken this field from them would be to kill them all.

But the new regiments . . . They were the complete unknown at the very heart of the "New Model Army." The human Marines had accomplished a miracle Bogess hadn't truly believed was possible just by bringing the ex-Laborers of God this far, but there was only one true test for how any army would stand the stress of battle, and that test was about to be applied.

Assuming that his regulars, Rastar's cavalry, and the Marines could make the regiments stand in place long enough.

He looked over at Pahner, who nodded.

"I'd say it's time, General," the human said, and Bogess gestured to the drummer by his side and looked back out over the field.

The drum command sent an electric shock through the standing ranks of the pike force. The first thunderous rumble brought them to attention, and the second fierce tattoo lowered their forest of pikes into fighting position.

Suddenly, the charging Boman were faced with a wall of steel and shields, and that thundering charge ground unevenly to a stop just out of throwing ax range. A few individuals came forward and tossed the odd ax at the wall of shields, but the light hatchets rattled off uselessly, demonstrating the efficiency of the simple, ancient design. Insults followed the throwing axes, but the regiments stood in disciplined silence, and the Boman seemed confused by the lack of response. Then one of them, a chieftain of note, to judge by his ritual scars and necklace of horns, came out of the mass and shouted his own incomprehensible diatribe at the motionless wall of pikes.

Roger had had all he could take. He slid the eleven-millimeter into its scabbard, pulled out a whistle, and kneed Patty into a trot.

"Roger!" Cord called from where he stood at the *flar-ta's* side, startled out of his calm assessment of the incipient battle. "Roger, where are you going?"

"Stay here, *asi.*" For the first time since he'd saved Cord's life, it wasn't a request. It was an order, and he also snapped his fingers abruptly for Dogzard to unload. "I'm going to go teach these barbs a lesson in manners."

"Oh, shit!" Julian said. "Captain!"

"Roger," Captain Pahner called calmly, calmly. "Where do you think you're going?"

Even as he spoke, he saw the prince remove his radio-equipped helmet and sling it from the *flar-ta's* harness.

"I'm going to kill him," Pahner whispered, maintaining a calm, calm, outward demeanor. "See if I don't."

The ranks in front of the packbeast parted at the shrill whistle to let the behemoth through, and Roger trotted towards the still-shouting chieftain, slowly raising the gait to a canter as the ancient Voitan steel blade whispered from its sheath. His rage against the obstacles of the long journey had gone icy cold. All the world had narrowed to the blade, the *flar-ta*, and the target.

As Patty neared the Boman lines, he kneed for her to turn, and rolled off her back. Hitting the ground at that speed was risky, but he was far too focused to worry about something as minor as a broken ankle, and it brought him to his target in a full charge.

The three-meter native was armed with a broad iron battle-ax which had seen long and hard service. The scars on the barbarian's body and the condition of his ax told his story as well as any chanted saga might have. This was a chieftain who'd conquered half a world and smashed the finest fighters in the Western Realms to dust.

And Prince Roger MacClintock could have cared less.

The Mardukan was fast. The first, furious slash of the prince's katanalike blade was parried by the heavy iron ax. The razor-sharp steel sword sliced a handspan-thick chunk out of its relatively soft iron, but the blow was blocked.

The second, backhand blow, was not.

The Mardukan was as good as dead, with a cut half-way through his torso, but that wasn't enough for the prince. As the body crumpled, slowly, oh so slowly to its knees, the sword whistled back up and around in a perfectly timed slash, driven by all the power of his shoulders and back, that intersected the native's tree trunk-thick neck with the sound of a woodsman's ax in oak. That single, meaty impact was clearly, dreadfully, audible in the sudden hush which had enveloped the entire battlefield. And then the Boman chieftain's head leapt from his shoulders in a geyser of blood and thudded to the ground.

Roger recovered to a guard position, then looked at the thousands of barbarian warriors standing motionless in the drizzle a mere stone's throw away, and spat. He gave a single flick of his blade, spattering the blood of their late chieftain halfway to their lines, then turned his back on them contemptuously and started back to his own lines in near utter silence . . . which erupted in a sudden, thunderous cheer.

"I'm *still* gonna kill him," Pahner muttered through his own forced smile. "Or make him write out 'Arithmetic on the Frontier' until his fingers bleed."

Beside him, Bogess grunted in laughter.

It took another fifteen minutes for the Boman to work themselves back into a frenzy once more. Other chieftains stepped to the fore and harangued the stolid Diaspran lines. Many of them waved the bloody souvenirs of past conquests at the pikemen, while others spat or urinated in their direction. But the ones who cast nervous glances at Roger, once more sitting atop Patty and glowering at the barbarian swarm, weren't much help to their cause.

Eventually, the barbarians began to move forward once more, in a creeping, Brownian fashion. A few axes arced out and thudded down, a few warriors charged forward and menaced the pikes, and then, finally, when some magic proximity had been reached, the entire mob flashed over into a howling fury and charged forward, shrieking defiance and hurling axes.

A storm front of javelins answered them. The New Model Army's javelin supply was severely limited, because there simply hadn't been time—or resources—to manufacture them in anything like the numbers Pahner could have wished for. Not if the artisans of Diaspra were going to provide the pikes and assegai he needed even more desperately, at any rate. There was only a single javelin for each pikeman, and three for each assegai-armed regular, but they did their job. The avalanche of weapons, hurled in a single, massed launch at the shrieking mob, ripped the charge into broken blocks. Given the numerical disparity between the two sides, the effect was actually more psychological than anything else. In absolute terms, the Boman's numbers were more than sufficient to soak up the javelins and close, but the holes torn in the front of the charge proved to the pikemen that they *could* kill the barbarians, and the object lesson worked. The pikes held their ground as the enemy charged forward . . . and was stopped again.

It was deadly simple: there was no way for the Boman to make their way through the thicket of pikes. The weapons were layers deep, jutting through every interstice. Stakes could be pulled up or knocked down, even if that meant stopping long enough for the shit-sitters to try to kill one, but those pikeheads were another thing entirely. Pushing one of *them* aside was no more than a temporary solution . . . and only left another to drive into an attacker's vitals, anyway. That became horribly obvious very quickly, yet some of the barbarian horde tried anyway. Some even succeeded . . . for a time.

Fain wasn't sure who'd started the chant. It wasn't he, but it was a good chant, as such things went, and it was simple—which was even better. "Ro-*Ger!*" with a poke of the spear on the "Ger!"

"Ro-*Ger!* Ro-*Ger!*"

The whole force, or at least the regiment he was a tiny part of, was chanting the prince's name. And it seemed to be working. The ferocious Boman, who'd been a source of such terror before the battle, weren't so terrible, after all. What *was* terrible was killing them.

Fain's regiment was one of the ones guarding the openings deliberately left in the hedge of stakes. Had he considered it, he might have realized that their position was a form of backhanded compliment, a decision based on the fact that their commanders considered his regiment steady enough to be entrusted with responsibility for holding such an exposed and critical position. At the moment, however, the squad leader wasn't thinking about compliments; he was thinking about how the absence of any stakes in front of them seemed to have drawn the attention of every demon-cursed Boman in creation . . . all of whom were running straight at *him*.

Which meant that the only way for him to live was for *them* to die.

When the barbarians had first charged forward, that hadn't been a problem. Given his place in the front ranks of his pike company, Fain had been too busy getting his own pike into fighting position and keeping an eye on the rest of his squad to worry about throwing any javelins. That had been the job of the ranks behind them, and of General Bogess' regulars. Despite his own hatred for and fear of the Boman, it had been ghastly to watch the savage storm of javelins rip into them, but at least *he* hadn't had to throw one. And those of the barbarians who'd survived and kept coming had balked when they first confronted the leveled wall of pikeheads. Clearly, they hadn't had the least notion of how to proceed, but the pressure from behind them had been too great for them to stop and figure out what to do next. That pressure had driven them forward . . . and Fain had been forced to kill them.

The experience had been far worse than the simulation. The first Boman who'd been spitted on his pike had been young, barely old enough to sire sons. He'd clearly been trying to claw his way to the rear, anything to avoid the wall of pikes. But the young barbarian had lacked the strength to force his way through the seething mass behind him, and that mass had driven him remorselessly onto Fain's spear.

The Mardukan noncom's true-hands had tightened on his pike shaft like talons, yet they'd seemed weak, so weak, as if the frantic contortions of the shrieking Boman transfixed on the wicked head of his pike must wrench the quivering shaft from them. In that unique, private instant of hell, Krindi Fain was all alone with the young warrior, who dropped his weapons and seized the steel-headed wooden shaft driving into his guts with all four hands and tried desperately to wrench himself off of its agonizing sharpness.

But then the training came to the fore. Fain put a wall of disbelief up around his senses. The shrieking on the other end of his pike became a teammate, playacting in the background. The frantic shudders transmitted up the spear were just two of his friends, pulling on the ropes that suspended the training dummy. With the spear well and truly stuck in, the squad leader could turn aside and not see the bulging eyes or the lolling tongue as the barely scarred young barbarian gasped out his life on the end of the wickedly sharp spear.

Then, for the first time in his life, he blessed Julian and all the other Marine bastards who'd trained him. And as he looked around at the other members of his squad, he knew that they all had to do the same, or his own killing would be for nothing.

"Stick it in!" he shouted. "You just have to *get it stuck in!*"

Pahner flipped up his visor and nodded.

"Pikes are like bayonets. They're terror weapons. The Boman can't force themselves onto the pikes to drive forward far enough to reach the pike*men*. We're not really killing that many of them, but we have them well and truly stopped."

"But we *will* kill many of them if the ones behind keep pushing the ones in front forward," Bogess demurred. "They don't have anywhere else to go, and in time, they'll push the spears down by the sheer weight of dead bodies. And when that happens, they'll walk over the corpses and kill us all."

"And not everyone can stand it from *our* side, either," Pahner agreed harshly.

"No!" a private in the front rank cried. "No, *no!*"

The Diaspran was shuddering as he dropped his pike and turned to the rear. The dropped weapon, coupled with the way his flight knocked the men to either side of him out of their own positions, opened a momentary gap into which a Boman inserted himself. The warrior was well-nigh crazed with fear, surrounded by a wall of sharp steel and the smell of death, but the only escape from his own terror seemed to be up the suddenly opened path before him.

The path that led straight to Bail Crom.

The private blocked the first hack of the Boman's ax with his shield, but the second frantic slash licked over the shield's upper edge. It bit into his lower shoulder, severing the muscles that lifted the lifesaving piece of plywood, and after that, it was all over. Half a dozen pikes stabbed forward to fill the gap, thrusting at the crazed Boman, impaling him even as he hacked and hacked at the body of the private, but the fact that the barbarian joined him in death was lost on the happy-go-lucky Crom.

"Bail?" Pol called hesitantly. The simpleminded private tried to look around the intervening squad members. "Bail?"

"Stand your ground, Erkum!" Fain shouted. The humans had a mechanism for sadness and grief. They "cried." The liquid of the God Himself flowed from their eyes in moments like this. Strange that people who did not worship the God should be given such a gift.

"Stand your ground and get it stuck in, Erkum Pol!"

But not everyone was a Krindi Fain, and not everyone could stand.

"Captain, we've got ourselves a situation here!" Kosutic called.

Pahner spotted the sergeant major's icon on his HUD and looked off to the left. Some of the brighter Boman had realized that their best chance was to go around the hedge of pikes, since they couldn't get *through* it. Most of their flanking efforts had been defeated by Bogess' regulars, wielding their assegais with deadly effect. Whether Crassus or Shaka would have approved more strongly of them was difficult to say, but any barbarian who had expected it to be "easy" to get past their shorter weapons quickly discovered that he'd been dead wrong.

Yet for all their skill, the regulars lacked the standoff reach of the conscripted pikemen. The Boman were paying at three or four to one for each spearman they managed to hack down, but here and there they managed to batter their way through, however extortionate the cost. An isolated squad of regulars suddenly found itself under overwhelming assault and went down under a blizzard of throwing axes and the thundering blows of battle-axes. Its fall opened a brief but deadly hole in the line, and dozens of howling barbarians lunged through it and flung themselves onto the flank of a pike regiment.

The pikemen, already dazed and bewildered, despite their training, by the howling holocaust of battle, were taken at a deadly disadvantage. It was impossible for them to swing their long, heavy weapons around to confront their attackers in time, and the sudden onslaught was too much for them.

They broke.

The sergeant major's radioed warning turned Pahner's attention to the regiment just as it shattered like crystal under a hammer. The ground was suddenly scattered with the pikemen's shields and weapons. And bodies. As was always the case before the advent of artillery, the majority of casualties were inflicted when one side finally turned its back and tried to run.

Bogess followed the direction of Pahner's gaze, and then looked at the captain.

"Cavalry?"

"Not yet." The laconic Marine shook his head. "Let the armor handle it." He keyed his communicator. "Sergeant Julian, left wing, please."

The four fully functional suits of armor were already moving when the command came in. As they swung past the bastion, it was clear that the Boman were well and truly into the rear areas, and Julian couldn't understand why Pahner was so calm about it.

The Marines to either side of the breach were down, although it looked like they were only wounded, not dead, and the pike regiments to either side of the breakthrough, stiffened by a reserve of Bogess' regulars, had re-formed to protect their own flanks. But all they could do was hold their ground and cling to their own positions, and the flood of barbarians pouring through the seventy-meter-wide hole swept past the formed units and threatened to fan out and take still other regiments from the rear. And if that happened . . .

Clearly, it was time to show the locals what "peace through superior firepower" meant.

The four armored Marines spaced themselves across

the salient with the two plasma cannon in the center, since they had the worst secondary effects, and opened fire.

The ten-millimeter bead cannon were loaded with flechette rounds. Each shot pumped out a half dozen narrow darts with moly-blade edges instead of a single normal bead, and the darts cut through the packed barbarians facing the four armored suits like horizontal buzz saws. Their molecule-wide edges would have cut through chain mail and steel plate, and they shredded the totally unarmored natives effortlessly into so much constituent offal . . . which the plasma cannon flash fried.

The fire wasn't widespread enough to stop all of the barbarians, but it ripped straight down the center of the breakthrough, and the hammer of it was a shock that sent the majority of those to either side—those who survived—into screaming, terrified flight. They turned and clawed and fought, not to advance, but to run from the Hell-spawned demons who had appeared in their very midst. The few warriors who'd been forward of the main damage, and out of the zone of effect of the plasma rounds, continued their charge, because there was nothing else they *could* do, only to find that iron was no match at all for ChromSten.

Julian casually backhanded a barbarian half again his own height who was obscuring his vision, crushing the unfortunate native's skull like an eggshell, and shifted the team's fire.

"Captain, we have the hole closed again, but we can't really keep it plugged. Can we get some cavalry over here to handle the leakers?"

"Will do," Pahner responded as he prepared to call Rastar on another channel. "Good job, Julian."

"Just another glorious day in the Corps," the squad

leader replied stonily, tracking his flechettes back across the shrieking barbarians. "Every day's a holiday."

"Yes," said the captain sadly. "Welcome to the Widow's Party."

"Still a stalemate," Bogess said. "We hold, and they do not quit. We could be here day after day."

"Oh, I think not," Pahner said dryly. "Roger obviously doesn't have the patience today for us to squat here in a game of chicken." He glanced at his pad, nodded, and keyed his communicator once again.

"Okay, Despreaux. It's about time."

The team had crept past the lightly defended encampment and down the reverse slope of the ridge. If anyone had looked hard for them, they would have been obvious, but none of the Boman were watching their own rear. Why should they? All of their enemies were in front of them, and so the Marines were overlooked, just a few more odd bits of flotsam left by the passing horde.

Until, that was, they calmly stood up at Pahner's command, took off their camouflage, and opened fire into the backs of the entire Boman force.

At first, their efforts were almost unnoticed. But then, as more and more of the barbarians pushing towards the front fell under their fire, some of the Mardukans looked over their shoulders . . . especially when the grenades began to land.

"*Yes*," Pahner whispered as the rear of the enemy formation started to peel away.

"They're running?" Bogess asked. "Why?"

"They aren't running from their perspective," Pahner replied. "Not that of their rear ranks, at any rate. They're chasing the Marines behind them. But from the point of view of the ones in the front rank, they *are* running, and we're not going to disabuse them of that notion." He turned to the drummer. "Order a general advance of pike units. First, we drive them out of position, then we harry them into the ground.

"But they haven't broken," Bogess protested.

"No? Just watch them," Pahner said. " 'And then along comes the Regiment, and shoves the heathen out.' "

Fain heard the drum command with disbelief, but he passed it on verbally, as he had been trained to do, to ensure that the punch-drunk soldiers had the orders.

"Prepare to advance!" he bawled wearily.

His arms felt like stones from holding the pike for what seemed like all day, poking it into the screaming, twitching dummies—or so his mind told him. And now the command to advance. Madness. The enemy was as thick as a wall; there was nowhere to advance *to*.

The New Model Army's losses had been incredibly light. The front rank of his company had only lost a handful, the next rank less. Of his own squad, only Bail Crom had fallen, but to advance on the enemy, who'd stood their ground the entire day, was impossible.

He knew that, and nonetheless he took his pike firmly in hand and prepared to step forward to the beat. It was all that was left in his world—the Pavlovian training the human sadists had put them all through.

"You know, Boss," Kileti gasped, slithering down the slope toward the distant canal, "I used to wonder why we were always running in training."

"Yeah? Well, as long as we don't twist an ankle in our court shoes," Despreaux managed to chuckle grimly.

It seemed that all the hounds of Hell were on their trail as they approached the canal. But the rope bridge—the blessed, blessed rope bridge—was in place as promised, with a grinning Poertena already starting across to the other side. Denat was there, too, and saluted Marine-style as they approached.

"Permission to get the hell out of here, Sir?" the Mardukan called as the Marines thundered towards him.

"Just don't get in my fucking way," St. John (J.) yelled, leaping for the ropes as the rest of the team clambered on behind him.

"Not a problem," Denat said, inserting himself into the midst of the team. The team had split into two groups and taken opposite sides of the two-rope bridge, each group leaning out to balance the other side. The much more massive Mardukan was a bit of a hassle, but not too terribly so.

"What's to keep them from crossing the canal?" Kileti asked. "I mean, we cut the rope once we're on the other side, sure. But, hell, it's not that wide. You can swim the damn thing."

"Well, Yutang and his little plasma cannon, for one thing," Denat said with a grunt. "Heavy bastard, too. But he promised me I could try to fire it 'off-hand' if I agreed to carry it for him. And, of course, Tratan brought Berntsen's bead cannon."

"You're kidding," Despreaux said. "Right?"

"About Tratan carrying the bead cannon? Why should I kid? He's not all that weak," the Mardukan said with another grunt of laughter. "Seriously, I've wanted to try it for some time. And what time could be better?"

"This is gonna be fun," Macek said.

"Are we having fun yet?" Julian asked. The rear of the Boman force might have run off in pursuit of the recon team, but a solid core of the front ranks had stood against the advance of the pikes so far. He was fairly sure what Pahner would use to break the stalemate.

"Julian," his communicator crackled. "Get in there and convince them that they don't want to stand there."

The four armored figures advanced through the open salient toward the Boman force to their front. That area already had a slice cut out of it, a line written in blood on the ground, beyond which only the most stupid and aggressive barbarian passed. Briefly.

Now the Marines opened that hole wider, firing their weapons in careful, ammunition-conserving bursts. The dreadful fusillade cleared a zone deep enough for them to actually pass the front of their own forces and step onto ground held by the Boman.

The friable soil was greasy with body fluids blasted from the Marines' previous targets, and their path was choked with the results. But the powered armor made little of such minor nuisances, crunching through the hideous carnage until the four turned the corner and pivoted to face the flank of the Boman still massed before the Diaspran pikes.

Once again, the armor burped plasma and darts, soaking the ground in blood and turning the churned field of the watershed into an abattoir.

"You know," Pahner mused as the cavalry sallied out in pursuit of the Boman force, "if that pike regiment hadn't broken, it would've been a lot harder to get the armor into the middle of the Boman. That's a case of the fog of war working *for* you."

"So now what?" Bogess asked.

"The force that took off after the recon team will be pinned against the canal. Detail about half the pikes to keep them pinned in place, and we'll pound them with plasma from the far side of the canal until they surrender. As for the rest—"

He gestured in the direction of the pursuing cavalry.

"We'll put in a pursuit. They'll break up in the face of the *civan* forces; they don't have polearms of their own, so they'll have to. We'll follow up with the rest of the pikes, and any groups the cavalry can't hammer into *feck*-shit, we'll hit with the pikes and armor. Next week, the Wespar Boman will be a memory."

Bogess looked out over the field strewn with corpses. There was an obscenely straight line of them where the two forces had grappled throughout the long day. They were piled in blood-oozing windrows, yet there weren't really that many bodies for a fight which had lasted so many hours. But the field *beyond* that line more than compensated. The ground there was littered with them where the Northern cavalry had ruthlessly cut down the fleeing barbarians.

"Why don't I feel happy about that?" he asked.

"Because you're still human," Pahner replied, and the native general turned to him with a quizzical expression.

"You mean Mardukan, don't you?"

"Yeah," Pahner said, watching the prince's *flar-ta* disappear over the crest of the far ridge with the Northerners. "Whatever."

CHAPTER EIGHTEEN

"You asked to see me, Your Excellency?" Captain Pahner asked.

From Roger's description, the room was the same one in which he'd met with Gratar during the Hompag. The previous meeting, however, hadn't included Grath Chain, who stood by the far wall. Mardukans didn't go in much for facial expressions, but the councilor looked like a three-meter cat who'd just swallowed a two-meter canary . . . or *basik*.

"Yes, Captain," the priest-king said, stepping away from the window and walking to the small throne on the far side of the room. His guards eyed Pahner nervously; obviously, something was up.

Gratar sat on the throne and rubbed one gem-encrusted horn thoughtfully as he looked at the floor. Then he raised his eyes to the human and clasped his hands before him.

"I have been given unpleasant news by Grath Chain," he said.

"I could play dumb," the Marine responded, "but there wouldn't be much point."

"Then you admit that you were—are—aware that there is a plot to overthrow the Throne of God?" the king asked very quietly.

"We were, and are. And if you hadn't decided to fight the Boman, we would have supported it," the captain told him. "My armored platoon was prepared to assault the Drying Ceremony, with orders to seize you and terminate Sol Ta and Grath Chain with prejudice."

The king clasped his hands again and lowered his head in regret.

"I have come to know and trust you, Captain, and as for the traitors of whose actions Grath has informed me . . . Many of them are men I know and trust and, yes, love as brothers." The king raised his head and looked at the human with sorrow, reproach . . . and building anger. "How could you be so disloyal?"

"I'm not disloyal, Your Excellency," Pahner told him levelly. "Nor, however, am I a Diaspran. My loyalty is to my mission, and my mission, as we explained to you on our arrival, and to the conspirators when they finally approached us, is to deliver Roger, alive and sane, to his mother. Any action we have to take to secure that reunion is an act of loyalty on our part. *Any* action, Your Excellency, no matter how personally repugnant it may be."

"So you would have overthrown the Throne of God?" the king snapped. "I should have your head for this! And I *will* have the heads of every member of this cabal!"

"The head of your recently victorious war leader?" Pahner asked with a raised eyebrow. "And of your second in command, the architect of so many of your favorite Works? The heads of the leaders of the

Warriors of God? The head of your own guard force? Most of the members of your Council, all of whom manage businesses or farms that are the lifeblood of this city?"

"I—" Gratar paused. "Tell me the rot isn't so deep," he said despairingly.

"What rot, Your Excellency?" Pahner asked.

"The hatred of the Throne of God!" the priest snapped. "And through that, the hatred of the God, Himself!"

"Who said they hated the Throne of God?" the Marine inquired with a slight smile, pulling out a length of *bisti* root. "And who said that they hate the one who sits on the Throne of God? Do they chafe at the restrictions imposed by your defenses against the Wrath? Yes. Do they think those defenses are far more extensive and costly, in both time and effort, than they need to be? Yes. But they all swore to the depth of their admiration for you, personally, and not one of them has mentioned hatred of the God."

"Then why do they seek to overthrow me?" Gratar asked in confusion.

"I suppose I have to ask another question to answer that," Pahner said, popping a slice of the *bisti* root into his mouth. "How many canals and dikes does the God want?"

"Listen to him not, Your Excellency!" Chain exclaimed. "He but seeks to blind you with the false words of his people!"

"Shut up, Grath. Or I'll feed you your left horn through your butt-hole," Pahner said mildly. "You've obviously had your say. Now it's time for somebody else to talk."

Gratar seemed to pay the interplay little attention. He only waved vaguely at Chain, and his eyes were fixed on the human.

"How many dikes?" he asked. "As many as necessary to secure the city against the Wrath. We were lucky in the Hompag and lost only the outermost defenses, despite our inattention. But we must not depend upon 'luck' or forget the lesson of the Auteans."

"Lucky?" Pahner shook his head. "Your Excellency, I was under the impression that these rains were particularly fierce. That it had been twenty rains since last they were this heavy, and that only two rains in all of your recorded history have exceeded their intensity."

"Yes, but we were given a reprieve by the God," the priest returned. "We fought the Boman in His name, and so he forgave us for our inattention and chose not to overwhelm us as He could have. He might not always be so forgiving."

"Or, possibly," Pahner said carefully, "the outer defenses were sufficient against the threat. Isn't it possible that the God was satisfied with just them?"

The priest-king leaned back and clasped all four hands once more.

"Is this the crux of their argument? That there are too many Works to the Glory of the God? That we should follow the path of Aut and spread ourselves to the winds?"

Pahner looked that one over carefully before he replied.

"I'd say that that *is* the crux of the argument, more or less, of those who are honest in what they say," he admitted after a moment. "There are some," he gestured with his chin at Chain, "who were in it only for power or profit, no question; there are those among the conspirators that are the Sons of Mary to be sure. But even some or all of those believed that Diaspra would be a greater city if there were fewer Laborers of God and more . . . 'Laborers of Diaspra,' I guess you could put it. Laborers free to find their own work. Artisans free to work on something besides 'pumps, pumps, pumps that are never used.'"

"Rus From," Gratar sighed. "My oldest and, I thought, best friend. I'd heard his complaints before, but I thought them nothing more than . . . mild blasphemies."

"Rus *is* your friend, Your Excellency," Pahner said seriously, "and he certainly worships the God. True, he worships the art of technology, as well, but there's no real need for the one to exclude the other. It's just that he needs a greater challenge than, well, 'pumps, pumps, pumps.'"

"What shall I do?" the priest-king asked in a near wail. "My Council is against me, most of my soldiers are against me, the merchants are against me. . . . My back is to the wall, Captain Pahner!"

"Not quite," the Marine said. "Sol Ta supports you."

"Grath tells me otherwise," Gratar said, looking at the Council member.

"The human lies," Chain said. "Sol Ta has professed his hatred for you. He seeks your overthrow, that he might keep command of this accursed 'New Model Army,' and Bogess has promised it to him for his support."

Pahner gazed at him speculatively for a few seconds, then shrugged.

"That's the first I've heard of this, Your Excellency, and once we figured out what was going on we used some of our devices to infiltrate the cabal pretty thoroughly. We knew almost everything that was happening, I think, and all we've heard says that Sol wasn't even approached because he thinks darkness comes and goes at your command. Which was why, despite the feelings of the conspirators, he had to go to the wall right away. I can't, of course, explain why the testimony of such a selfless and trustworthy soul as Grath Chain might contradict that of every single other person involved, but perhaps some explanation for that might occur to *you*."

He and Gratar gazed into one another's eyes, and the beleaguered priest-king actually grunted a ghost of a laugh, but then the human continued.

"If you want a serious suggestion about what you should do, though, I have one. Several actually."

"I'll listen," Gratar said. "I've always found your advice to be, I believed, honest and well thought out."

"That's my job," Pahner told him, and clasped his hands behind him.

"Whatever happens, things are going to change," he began. "You took four thousand menial workers and turned them into pretty fair soldiers, and when the wounded heal, there will still be well over three thousand of them left. Some are going to be willing, even eager, to go back to their old jobs, but many others will be discontented. They'll feel that since they and their mates saved the city, the city owes them a living from here on."

"That isn't a logical conclusion," Gratar interrupted. "They saved the city because otherwise they themselves would have been killed when the city fell."

"But it's a conclusion they'll reach," Pahner said flatly. "In fact, some will already have reached it. It's common, almost inevitable, among veterans, and however illogical, it's still something you'll have to deal with. They've . . . changed. They've seen the high and the wide, and they can't go back to just rolling the lawn for the abbott."

"This is a nightmare," Gratar muttered, shaking his head.

"Don't think of it that way, Your Excellency," the Marine advised. "Instead, regard it as a test—one like the Wrath. You must put dikes where they're needed to stem the flow of change, and canals where *they're* needed to divert it into other channels. And, of course, you must learn to embrace change even as you embrace Water, recognizing both its light side and its dark."

The priest-king gazed at him, his body language arrested, and Pahner smiled.

"The other issue, of course, is the cabal and their feelings about the Works of God. Now, there's a saying in my land, that 'when you have one problem, you have a problem; but when you have a bunch of problems, sometimes they solve each other.' You're going to have to do *something* with your veterans. Many societies, placed in a similar pressure cooker, end up with an army they have to use, and so they proceed to go out and conquer everything in sight until stopped. For example, you realize that you could take over Chasten's Mouth and most of the other broken city-states rather easily?"

"We could," Gratar agreed with distaste, "but we wouldn't. The God is not a god of battle."

"From what I've seen and learned of your people, that would be my observation, as well, Your Excellency," Pahner said, then shrugged. "But if some other, less honest priest deposed you, he might not be so honorable, and a dishonorable priest can achieve terrible things by manipulating a people through cynical misuse of their faith. 'The God demands worshipers. These heathen cities have suffered at the hands of the Boman as His punishment for their worship of false gods. It's our duty to bring them to an understanding of the true God, if only to save them from His further just and terrible Wrath. And if they refuse to embrace the true God, then it's our duty to send them to their false gods!' "

"Is that a quote?" Gratar asked.

"More like a mosaic of quotes," Pahner admitted. "We humans have a . . . more varied palette to draw upon then you do."

"I couldn't see Rus doing that," Gratar objected. "He's no more a believer in conversion by the sword than I am."

"Oh, I agree, Your Excellency. But it's rare for the original revolutionaries to get to enjoy their revolution. Often they're too focused on fixing the things they see as 'wrong' to manage and maintain the structure and organization their societies require, and everything collapses into chaos for a period. In other cases, the idealism which got them to act in the first place makes them vulnerable to betrayal in turn. In either case, the *feck*-beasts any society contains generally pull them down and install one of their own."

The human very pointedly did not look at Chain.

"So are you saying we should go forth and conquer to keep our army out of mischief at home?" Gratar asked curiously.

"No. I said it's sometimes done. Raiden-Winterhowe in my own . . . land is an excellent example. They were a peaceful people until they were invaded by barbarians, much as you were by the Boman. And, like you, they had to learn war, fast. In fact, they were much more damaged by their attackers before they learned their lessons than you've been, but they learned them well in the end. In fact, they got much better at it than their enemies, and they won. Now they're aggressively expansionist . . . and a real pain in the ass to their neighbors. They know it, too, but they've established a tradition of expansion, and they can't stop. To them, the only question is how much air they can blow into their divers' air bladders."

"One could make an argument there," Gratar said

slowly, rubbing a horn in thought. "We could blow up quite a large bladder at the moment, and without requiring our new subjects to embrace the God. I would never force them to convert to a faith they don't truly hold, but the payment of some tithes, now . . ."

"The problem," Pahner said with a grim smile, "is that you have no administrative structure for it. Question: Who administers the cities you conquer? Local officials, or a governor appointed from here? And how do you choose the governors? Is Grath here one? And what about military forces? Some of the locals, the ones with a degree of power, especially, are going to object to your control. Do you raise forces there to keep their opposition suppressed? Or do you raise forces here, or from your other conquests, and send them to keep the peace? And if you raise forces there, and keep them there, and the governor is from there, how do you convince them to send you tithes?"

"Ah . . . These are . . . interesting points."

"Interesting or not, the logic of empire would require you to answer them, Your Excellency," the Marine said. "And don't even get me started on roads. One of the reasons you guys don't have empires is because you can't move your forces over large distances or support them logistically on field operations, and you won't be able to without decent roads."

"There are many problems with roads," Gratar said. "As I suggested in my sermon, the God does not, apparently, favor them."

"Given your climate, Your Excellency, I'd have to call that a fairly drastic understatement." The human shook his head. "But without roads, forget empire. I doubt you could make it work. Hell, I don't think *I* could make it work on Marduk, and even if someone *could* hammer an empire together, it wouldn't last more than a generation. Transportation is simply too tough. No, you need another way."

"And you have a suggestion?" the priest-king asked. "Or are you just going to ask impossible questions?"

"Yes, I have a suggestion," Pahner told him. "But I wanted you to have a feel for your constraints before I put it to you.

"Some of your veterans are going to want to go back to their old jobs. Take them back. Repair the dikes and canals. Drain the overflow lakes. Fix the washouts on the roads.

"But some of them *won't* want their old jobs. They'll want to continue their new career. Some of them will have developed a taste for it. Soldiering isn't a career for the weak of heart, but some have a mentality—which isn't, mind you, a bad thing for society as a whole—that finds soldiering better than digging ditches. We Marines are going from here to K'Vaern's Cove, and there are Boman yet to be engaged on the far side of the Nashtor Hills. Send the veterans who don't want to leave the army with us as an 'Expeditionary Force' to help us relieve K'Vaern's Cove. That gets them out of the city while you work on some of the other problems, and it also raises your profile with your neighbors as an ally, instead of a threat. Or a potential victim. There will be other city-states who use the Boman and their defeat as an opportunity for expansion, and convincing them not to expand in your direction ought to be high on your list of priorities.

"Now, rather than sending Sol Ta with these forces, send Bogess. That gets the most sticky military threat off the board without kicking off a revolution by killing him. And send Rus From, as well. We're planning on giving the people of K'Vaern's Cove the designs for a variety of weapons. We would prefer to avoid engaging the Boman ourselves, if we can help it, but the secrets of those weapons should be worth the price of the trip across the ocean to the people who have no choice but to fight the barbarians. However, creating those weapons, especially in quantity, will be difficult, and tinkering with those problems will give Rus a chance for something other than 'pumps, pumps, pumps.'"

"You would have me *reward* them for their treachery?" Gratar demanded angrily.

"What reward? Do you think they love this city any less than you do? What I'm proposing is, effectively, exile from their home—the home in whose interests, as they saw them, at least, they were willing to risk traitors' deaths. Or would you rather try to fight them in a civil war? Bogess is no slouch as a military commander, and in a war in the city, I could see Rus From being remarkably dangerous. Whatever happened, it would be bloody and nasty, not to mention expensive. And without Bogess or Rus on your side, you'd probably lose."

"But without the Laborers of God . . ."

"And that's my final point, Your Excellency," Pahner said quietly. "You *have* to pull back on the Works of God. They were beautiful symbols during the time of stasis you've just been through, but this invasion is going to shake things up, and you're going to need those workers in other areas. You'll need them as soldiers, and as artisans working on things you don't even know yet that you have to produce. Even with your climate, we should have been able to fight this war with muskets or rifles, not pikes!

"You know now, if you think of what the God has told you, the extent of the Wrath of the God. Consult your temple's records, Your Excellency. Compare the worst ravages of the Wrath to the Hompag Rains which have just passed and judge what is the very worst flooding your God will send upon you, then design your dikes and canals to resist that degree of Wrath. That's what your God is asking for, no less and, probably, no more. But surely He doesn't expect you simply to go on building redundant dikes, digging redundant canals, and manufacturing redundant pumps forever when there are so many other things that His people also require."

"Now he presumes to speak for the God!" Chain snapped. "Haven't you heard enough treason and blasphemy yet, Your Excellency?"

"Grath," Gratar said mildly, "if you say one more word without my asking, I will have a guard . . . what was it? Ah, yes—'feed you your left horn through your butthole.'" He gazed at the council member coldly for several seconds, and Grath Chain seemed to shrink in upon himself. Then the priest-king turned back to Pahner.

"And what of the Council?" he asked.

"The Council is a snake pit," Pahner admitted. "But without Bogess and Rus From to give them legitimacy, they're a snake pit which will fang itself to death. Dump the problem of the displaced Laborers of God on them and watch them scramble for cover."

"Make the Council's members responsible, individually, for their maintenance?" Gratar mused. "How very . . . elegant."

"So long as you insure that it doesn't become a form of slavery," the Marine cautioned. "But, yes, that should work. This sort of thing is more O'Casey's area of expertise than mine, and I would certainly advise you to discuss the details with her, but I believe that the points I've laid out will defuse almost all the major problems. It won't be an easy time with all the region recovering from the Boman, whatever you do. But if you treat the changes as a challenge to be worked with, it should also be a profitable time. For the city and for the God."

"And Grath?" Gratar asked, looking once more at the conspirator standing by the wall.

"Do what you will," Pahner replied. "If it were up to me, I'd say give him a thankless job and all the worst people to do it with, and impose severe penalties for failure. But he's really a treasure if you use him properly. For example, you'll probably be threatened by another city-state soon, whatever you do. If that happens, send him there with some funds to destabilize it. If he succeeds, reward him. If he's found out, disown him and swear that whatever he did, it was never by your orders."

"But he has done me a service in warning of the coup," Gratar said. "Surely I owe him something for that."

"Okay," Pahner agreed. "Give him thirty pieces of silver."

"This way is probably for the best," Bogess said, gazing out over the canals and dikes in the first, faint light of dawn. "However early it is."

"Well, we need to be to the Nashtor Hills by nightfall," Rastar pointed out with a shrug. "Better to be hit there by the scattered tribes rather than caught out in the open."

"And how much of this precipitous departure is to prevent the people from seeing half their army and two of their leaders hustled off into the wilderness?" Rus From demanded with a growl.

The cleric shifted the unfamiliar weight of the sword baldric on his shoulder as he stood between the general and the Northerner prince and looked upon the flood-control works. He wondered if he would ever again see the Bastar Canal. It was the first project he'd worked upon as a young engineer under that old task-master, Bes Clan.

"The Boman are no threat to Diaspra; we made sure of that," Rastar replied, and it was true. The Northern cavalry, with the pillage and destruction of their own cities fresh in their collective memory, had been merciless to the retreating foe. If a thousand Wespar ever made it to their distant cousins, it would be astonishing.

"I had plans," From half-snarled.

"And now you'll have new ones!" the Therdan prince snapped. "You're the one complaining about nothing new. Haven't you heard the plans of the humans? Rapidly firing guns? Giant ships? Light, wheeled cannon? A 'combined arms force'? What do you have to complain about?"

The artisan turned slowly to look at the prince.

"What would you give to see Therdan or Sheffan once more? See them shining in the morning light as the *tankett* calls? See their people going about their business in peace and plenty through your actions?"

Rastar turned away from the cleric's hot gaze and looked out into the growing light.

"I see it every night in my dreams, priest. But I cannot return to my home; it's no longer there." He shrugged, the gesture picked up from the humans, and fingered the communicator on his harness. "Perhaps, in time, things will change and for some there will be a homecoming."

"Centicred for your thoughts?" Kosutic's voice was quiet, for Roger was definitely looking grim.

The prince leaned into the armored head of the *flar-ta* as his memory replayed again and again the sights and sounds and smells of the pursuit. It had been necessary. He knew that. But it had also been hideous . . . and the pleasure he'd taken in it as he poured out his anger and fear and frustration upon an enemy who'd really had nothing to do with creating his predicament in the first place had been still worse. There were dark places in his own soul which he'd never before realized were there, and he didn't like the look at them he'd just been given.

There was no one else in hearing distance. The Marines and Mardukans were engaged in final preparations for the fast march to the Nashtor Hills, and he turned his head to meet the sergeant major's eyes.

"I wanna go home, Top," he whispered. "I just want to go home."

"Yeah," the sergeant major sighed. "Me, too, Boss. Me, too." She gave Pahner a thumbs-up as the captain looked down the long line of march. All the mahouts and cavalry leaders gave the same signal, and she inhaled deeply. It was time to move out.

"The only way to get there is to put one foot in front of the other," she said, "and I guess it's that time." She looked up at the somber prince with a shrug and a crooked smile.

"Time and high time to be trekkin' again, eh?" the prince said. "Well, here's to the last march. To the sea."

CHAPTER NINETEEN

Dergal Starg waved at the bartender.

"Give me another, Tarl. Nothing better to do."

It was the fifth time he'd said that, and Tarl was probably getting tired of hearing it. Not that the bartender was going to say anything.

Ownership of the Nashtor mines had been disputed between three different city-states right up until they and the armies they'd kept glowering at one another might actually have been some use. Right up until the Boman had smashed two of the city-states into rubble and cut the mines off from K'Vaern's Cove, the only one of the three which had ever been worth a solitary damn. But none of those cities had ever believed they could *control* Nashtor, whoever might officially claim ownership. Those mines were the province of one Dergal Starg. Merchants could merch, warriors could war. But it took a by-the-gods miner to mine, and in all the lands of the Chasten and Tam, in all the Nashtor Hills, there was no miner to match Dergal Starg.

Which was what made the present situation so bitterly ironic, of course. Because what was needed right now was one of those iron-head Northern war princes. Or a K'Vaernian guardsman. Or even an idiotic war priest from Diaspra. Because no matter how good a miner you were, a mine without markets was just a hole in the ground that you poured money into.

Sure, a few hundred miners and a group of engineers had been able to create defenses the Boman avoided. Sure, they were able to keep mining, even with the occasional probing foray by the barbarians. But even though the sounds of the surrounding mines and smelters continued to echo through the tavern, they weren't quite right. At any other time, he would have been down Shaft Five in a heartbeat, for example. He could tell the lazy bastards were lying down on the job down there, but what was the point of working yourself to death, of building inventories, when there were no buyers?

There was none, of course, but Dergal Starg still ran the mines and smelters. And the miners were, by the gods, going to keep on mining right until the mines ran out of food, new picks, and the thousand and one other things they got from the stupid, cheating merchants.

And the bartenders were, by the gods, going to tend, which was why he glared at Tarl when his mug of wine wasn't immediately refilled. But then he noticed that the bartender was staring over his shoulder with wide eyes and all four hands thrown outward in a gesture of surprise.

Starg turned around to see what the nincompoop was staring at, and froze. The crew which had just walked under the roof of the wall-less structure was a flatly amazing sight, and not just because the mines were sealed off from everyone else in the entire world by the Boman, yet he'd never laid eyes on a single one of them before.

Four of them were obviously Northerner iron heads, two of them wearing some of the nicest ironwork it had ever been his pleasure to admire. The fluting on one of the cuirasses followed the new trend coming out of K'Vaern, picked up apparently from some outlandish place which had never heard of steel on steel. No doubt it reduced the weight of the armor by a good bit, but traditionalists—and Starg, by the gods, put himself in that category—thought it was likely to backfire. The damned stuff was bound to catch the point of a weapon or crack under any heavy pounding, although he had to admit that this armor was as hacked about as any he'd ever seen, and it seemed to have stood the test well. From the look of the wearer, it would probably be a better idea not to make any sarcastic remarks about it, either.

But the ironmongery, however impressive, wasn't the most interesting thing about the group. One of the iron heads' companions was a lightly armed, gods-be-damned *priest*. One of the damned water boys, no less, unless he was mistaken, and a senior one by his gear. Starg had seen a couple of water boy missionaries in his time, but most of them had been youngsters. This fellow was anything but, and the wrench he wore on the golden chain about his neck made him an *artisan* priest. Artisan priests were like *legends*; you never saw one outside Diaspra. But that still wasn't the most interesting thing about the group—that had to be the *basik* in the middle.

It couldn't be an actual *basik*. For one thing, it was too gods-be-damned big, but it sure as the gods *looked* like a *basik*. No horns, no claws, no armor—just soft and pink all over. Well, it was wearing some sort of covering, and its skin had an ugly dry look, like a *feck*-beast's. But other than that . . . and the helmet . . . it certainly looked like a *basik*.

The iron head in the fluted cuirass held out one hand, palm up to indicate friendship.

"You are Dergal Starg?" he asked.

"Yeah," the miner snarled. "Who by the gods wants to know?"

"Ah," the Northerner said with a weird facial grimace that exposed his teeth. "The famous Starg personality. Let me introduce myself. I'm Rastar Komas Ta'Norton, Prince of Therdan. King, I suppose now. I believe you once met my uncle under better circumstances."

Starg slumped suddenly, even his belligerence temporarily muted. Kantar T'Norl had been one of the only damned outsiders who hadn't been totally, by the gods, idiotic. Unlike all too many others, Kantar had always been a voice of reason in the region.

"I'm sorry, Rastar Komas Ta'Norton. I shouldn't have been so abrupt. The loss of your uncle was a terrible blow to the Valley of the Tam."

"He died as well as could be permitted," the Northern prince said, "leading a charge to cover our retreat. We were able to get many of the women and children out of Therdan and Sheffan because of his sacrifice and the willing sacrifice of his house warriors."

"It's still a great loss," the miner growled, taking a sip from his now refilled mug.

"Yes, and hardly the way he would have preferred to leave us," the prince agreed with another of those odd grimaces. "I suspect that he would have preferred drowning in a wine vat," he said, and Starg grunted in laughter for the first time.

"Yes, he was a bit of a drinker. It's a recent vice on my own part, of course."

"Not according to my uncle," Rastar disagreed. "He said you could drink a *pagee* under the table."

"High praise, indeed," Starg said. "And now that we've covered the pleasantries, where did you come from? The trails are swarming with Boman."

"The ones to the north may be," the thing that looked like a *basik* said, "but the ones to the south are . . . clearer."

"Who's the *basik*?" Starg asked, gesturing at the odd creature.

"This is Captain Armand Pahner of the Empress' Own," Rastar said with yet another of those odd grimaces. "And calling him a *basik* to his face could be a mistake of cosmic proportions. A *brief* mistake."

"Captain Pahner and his 'Imperial Marines' are the reason that there no longer *are* any Boman to the south," the cleric put in, and extended one palm-up true-hand of his own in greeting. "Rus From, at your service," he said, administering the mining engineer's second intense shock of the day.

"*The* Rus From? The Rus From who created the two-cycle pump system? The secondary aortal injector? The Rus From who designed the God's Lake runoff entrapment system? That was a thing of beauty! I used a modification of it in our Number Nine shaft trap."

"Um," the momentarily nonplused cleric said. Then, "Yes, I suppose that was I."

"So you came up from the south?" Starg asked. "What happened to the Boman?"

"Wespar, actually," Rastar said, and clapped hands in a shrug. "We killed them."

"That's a somewhat simplistic explanation," From noted reprovingly.

"Accurate, nonetheless," Rastar argued. "They don't have enough left to burn their dead."

"They don't burn them, anyway," Starg said distastefully. "They *bury* them."

"True," From said. "A terrible use of land. Can you

imagine what would happen if *everyone* buried their dead? Before long, all the dry land would be overrun with dead bodies!"

"Could we debate social customs at some other time?" the maybe-not-*basik* asked with a grimace which, allowing for the differences in shape and form, was remarkably like the one Rastar had been making, and Starg finally remembered where he'd seen it before. It was the exact expression a *basik* made when you had it cornered and were just about to club it. Like it was trying to talk you out of it or something.

"Indeed," Rus From said. "We brought a caravan through with us. It includes some of the items you ordered from the merchants of Diaspra before the Boman closed the roads."

"We appreciated that last shipment of pig iron, by the way," the maybe-not-*basik* said. "It would have been tough to do everything we had to without it."

"Yeah, well, normally we do most of our trading with K'Vaern's Cove," Starg said. "But they were cut off by then. We just had to hope a caravan would make it back from Diaspra, instead."

"And indeed it did," From said. "I'm afraid that few of the mining implements you ordered are included, however. Most of the ones that were complete were converted into weapons. We do have a goodly load of food and wines, spices, and so forth, though."

"That's all well and good," Starg protested. "But we're going to need those tools soon."

"And they'll be completed in time," From said dryly. "With all the weapons we recovered from the Wespar, there's much more than sufficient iron to replace the material we commandeered."

"And with any luck, we'll be able to get the Boman's attention so centered on us that they won't be a problem between here and K'Vaern's Cove much longer, either," Rastar added. "There were none on the south side of the hills. Where are they?"

"Mostly still gorging on the corpse of Sindi," Starg said. "But there are many bands just wandering around, some of them quite large. You'll find it difficult to pass through to the Cove, if that's your target."

"Oh, I don't know about that," said the maybe-not-*basik*. "I think we might just give them pause."

"You see," Rastar said, "we're not *exactly* a caravan."

The forces from Diaspra sprawled everywhere around the mines. Most of them were inside the hasty walls the miners had thrown up against the Boman under Starg's direction. Those of them who were not, lightly armored figures carrying incredibly long spears or lances, were busy erecting another camp adjacent to the mining area. They dug with incredible energy and precision, as if they'd been doing it their entire lives.

"What, by all the gods, is this?" Starg asked, rubbing a horn furiously.

"Well," the maybe-not-*basik*, Pahner, said, "I'm afraid we weren't quite sure who held the mines, so we took the liberty of securing your guards until we were sure. They're unharmed," the not-*basik* added hastily.

"So you just snuck in and took over?" the mine manager demanded, wondering whether he was angrier at the newcomers or at the guards who were supposed to have prevented such things from happening.

"It's . . . something of a specialty of ours," the not-*basik* said with another of those strange grimaces.

"They did it to us once," Rastar confirmed with a weird move of both shoulder sets.

"So now what?" Starg asked. "You can't do any good here; the Boman just avoid us."

"We may leave a few groups of our soldiers with

you," Rus From replied. "Some of our Diasprans haven't taken as well to conditions on the march as they thought they might. That doesn't make them poor soldiers, though, and they can be helpful training and supporting your miners. The rest of us are going to K'Vaern's Cove."

"You'll never make it," the mine manager warned. "You might have made it on a straight shot from the south, but it's different between here and the Cove."

"Yes, it is," the not-*basik* agreed with one of those weird grimaces. Suddenly, he looked much less like a *basik* than an *atul*. A hungry *atul*. "There's a road."

"We'll be moving very fast," Rastar added. "You might have noticed that we have a large number of *turom* and *civan* along with the *pagee*. The humans have shown us that an infantry force can move much faster than we ever believed possible if the spear-carriers take occasional rests by holding onto the packs of the *turom* and *civan*. Also, many of them, and all our wounded, ride on the *pagee*. I wouldn't have believed it before they proved it, but we can travel nearly as fast as *civan* cavalry."

"We should get through without problems as long as we can avoid their main force," the "human" noted. "You said that they're in and around Sindi. I've seen that on a map, and it's well out of the way of the direct route to K'Vaern's Cove. How sure are you of their location, and where do you get your information?"

"Some woodsmen still move among the Boman," Starg replied. "Charcoal burners and the like who simply give them whatever they want and survive as best they can. We help them out with whatever we can spare, and in return they keep us fairly well informed on where the barbs are and what they're up to. Also, Sindi is the largest and richest city they've conquered. They aren't done looting it even yet."

The humans shared a look with the Northern prince, but Rastar seemed to agree.

"They would know, Armand," the Northerner said. "The woods are filled with half-wild workers, and I doubt that they'd care much for the Boman. Their lives are never easy, but they must be truly impossible in the midst of this invasion."

"Then we need to factor them into our next move," said the not-*basik*, Pahner. "Intelligence cuts two ways."

"What?" Starg asked. "They're not particularly smart—"

"He means that they could talk to the Boman as well as to you," Rastar translated. "It's a human term meaning all that you know about your enemy."

"We don't want our axis of advance communicated to the Boman," Pahner added.

"I doubt that they'll be talking to the Boman," Rastar demurred. "They're insular even under normal conditions, and I'm sure they're staying as far away from the invaders as they can."

"That's truth," Starg said. "We've traded tools and weapons to them for food and other supplies. Otherwise, they'd have nothing to do with us, either."

"Tools," Pahner said. "That we're not in need of. But how much refined iron do you have on-site?"

"Why?" Starg asked suspiciously.

"Because we're taking it all with us to K'Vaern," Pahner said, looking out over the building Diaspran camp. "K'Vaern's Cove will need it if they're going to survive, and we need them happy with us. It's why we came this way, really."

"Oh, you are, are you?" Starg said angrily. "Just how are you going to pay for it? It's not like you even brought all that was already owed!"

The not-*basik*'s head turned towards Starg like a machine. The human was scarcely half the miner's size, and Starg had been in more fights as a youngster than his old bones cared to remember. But at that moment, he was as sure as the gods had made him that he did not want to test the human commander.

"Worry not," Rus From said calmly. "I'll guarantee payment for the material from the temple."

"Oh," Starg said, his hostility disappearing abruptly. "In that case, I suppose it will be all right. And in answer to your question, there are several tons waiting to go. We've been smelting most of the time."

"Pig iron, or wrought?" Rastar asked.

"Pig," the miner said with a shrug. "I've got a puddling forge, but I don't have the charcoal to make it worthwhile to run it."

"We can make steel from this?" Pahner asked. "That's important."

"You can," Starg said shortly. "At least they can in K'Vaern's Cove . . . if you get it there."

"Great," Pahner said, nodding as he slipped a slice of *bisti* root into his mouth. "Give him a chit or whatever, Rus, and let's get loading. I want to be able to pull right out in the morning."

Dergal Starg stood watching the receding column in the morning light. The humans and half the *civan* cavalry had left earlier to sweep the path of the caravan, and about a third of the "pikemen" were holding onto straps dangling from the pack *turom* and *civan*. The rest were spread out to either side and in front, screening the caravan as it headed for the broad, stone road to K'Vaern's Cove.

The head of the miner guard force walked up to Starg as he stood by the rough rock wall guarding the entrance to the mine.

"I'm sorry about yesterday, Dergal. We just weren't vigilant enough. It won't happen again."

"Hmmm?" the manager said, then shook himself. "Oh, don't worry about that, T'an—it's the least of our worries. I just got scammed by a human who spent half his time talking about pits, or pocks, or something. He also taught me an interesting game of chance, and I now owe him about four days' output. In addition to that, we've just sent all the metal we've processed since the invasion into the very midst of the Boman solely on a promise of payment from a priest who, I have since discovered, left home under . . . less than auspicious circumstances. And we can only collect it if we manage to get word back to Diaspra that they owe it to us. And if a caravan makes it back through to us, of course."

"Oh," said T'an. Then, "This isn't good, is it?"

"By the gods, I don't know," Starg said, with a grunt of humor. "But I *think* it's grand."

"Is Gratar going to pay?" Pahner asked. "We would've gone ahead and loaded the iron whether he would or not, but will he?"

"Yes," From said. "He will, and he'll know that I knew that he would. I regard it as it is— What's that phrase you humans use? 'A parting shot'?"

"And a nice one, despite Poertena's best efforts," the Marine agreed.

"Yes, it is," the priest said with a note of obvious satisfaction as he visualized the priest-king's reaction to the bill Dergal Starg was about to present to him. "But what matters is that we have the iron, which should be well-received in K'Vaern's Cove. Now all we have to do is get through with it."

"Oh, we'll get through," Pahner said. "Even if I've got to break out the armor, we'll get through. It's after we get through that it gets interesting."

CHAPTER TWENTY

"Where's the city?" the sergeant major asked. All she could see from the top of the *flar-ta* was walls and hills.

"Beyond the hills," Rastar said. "This is just the outer wall."

The city was on a peninsula between the ocean and a broad bay, and the peninsula narrowed to a low, very narrow neck where the wall closed it off before spreading out once more beyond it. If it hadn't been for a breakwater and some low dunes, the half-hearted waves on their left would have been washing over the road.

A fresh, onshore wind blew in from the sea, carrying away the scent of rot from the bay to their right. The shoreline on that side edged almost imperceptibly into a salt marsh, over which four-winged avians croaked and hissed. The salt marsh blended in turn into a small delta from the Selke River—more of a creek, really—which the road had paralleled all the way from the Nashtor Hills.

The wall itself was immense, the largest Kosutic had seen since Voitan. It stood at least ten meters tall and was nearly that broad. The gateway was a massive, double-turreted affair, with a dogleg and clearly evident murder holes, and massive bombards loomed from the walls at regular intervals. Either K'Vaern's Cove had common everyday enemies in plenty, or else it had entirely too much money and had needed something expensive to use it up on.

The ends of the wall were anchored by bastions, studded with more bombards, where it met the sea and the marsh, respectively. The seaward bastions apparently served double duty as lighthouses, and the wall continued back along both coasts until the land rose and became rocky enough to make a landing difficult or impossible.

"Bloody serious defenses," Kosutic muttered.

"K'Vaern's Cove has participated in numerous wars in the region, at one time or another," the Northerner prince told her. "Sometimes in alliance with the League, at other times in opposition. It's never been interested in conquest, though. Most of its wars have had to do with maintaining freedom of trade . . . or pressing for it."

"Was Sindi one of the ones it fought?" the sergeant major asked. "And what is the story there? You keep referring to it, but you've never explained."

"I assume that your Ms. O'Casey is familiar with the story by now, but, in short, Tor Cant, the Despot of Sindi, was a bloated *feck*-beast. He was also a fool whose desires far outweighed his vision or ability, and the foremost of those desires was to be the ruler of all the land around the Tam and Chasten.

"He began his efforts by moving against the League of the North. Since we were the greatest military threat to his plans, he attempted to cause trouble between our cities in the hope that we would turn on one another and destroy ourselves for him. Then, when that plot was revealed and even he realized it was a complete failure, he sent embassies to the Boman. After much placation, some of their senior chiefs agreed to come meet with him, and he also gathered representatives from many of the Southern states who chafed at our trade taxes. The official reason for the meeting was to negotiate a treaty with the Boman, because if the Boman were no longer a threat, then the League would no longer be required. And if that happened, he reasoned, all the lands of the South would unite to rise up against our taxes.

"It became clear, however, that he had no intention of negotiating in good faith with the Boman. I said that his desires outweighed his vision, and that was probably overgenerous of me. The Boman are barbarians, but Tor Cant *treated* them like barbarians . . . and not very important ones, either. Instead of offering concessions, he put forward demands which anyone, not just the Boman, would have considered insulting. And when the Boman chiefs rejected them, he completed his idiocy by throwing a fit and ordering them killed in his very throne room, in front of the Southern ambassadors.

"It was, I've heard, quite a scene. His guards were Southern weaklings, so the Boman chiefs and their guards nearly cut their way to the throne, despite having been taken completely by surprise. Unfortunately, they didn't quite reach it, and when word of what had happened reached the northern clans, they swore blood feud against all the 'shit-sitters' in the cities.

"They came upon the League first, and all of us had been sabotaged, one way or another, undoubtedly by agents of Sindi. In Therdan it was poison in the grain stores. Sheffan had its water supply fouled. Others had mysterious fires in their granaries, or found the fodder for their *civan* poisoned.

"The intent, probably, was for the League and the Boman to destroy each other. Then Sindi would move against both, coming as a savior to what remained of the League and destroying the Boman. Then the League would have been absorbed, and the warriors who were left would have been used against the other cities."

"But that's not what happened," Kosutic said.

"No," the native prince responded very quietly, gazing at the approaching walls. "Tor Cant was a fool, and he underestimated the Boman. He obviously expected them to attack us as they always had before, clan by clan and tribe by tribe, and he reasoned that, even crippled by his treachery, our cities would be able to hold long enough to bleed the barbarians and weaken them fatally before they could move further south. But the Boman were united, and their strategy was far better than it had ever been before. They came upon Therdan in a wave, for we were the chief city of the North, and their new leaders realized that if we fell, it would not only open the way south but dishearten the rest of the League, as well. They besieged us for barely a month and a half, and we took good measure of them. So long as we were able to man our defenses, we killed many of them for every warrior we lost. But in the end, we were starving, and before we lost the flower of our *civan*, my father had me fight my way out, with as many of the women and children as we felt we could take.

"My uncle, whom Dergal Starg spoke of . . . He and his household opened the way, and we went forth over the carpet of their bodies. The youngest of the cavalry, on the best *civan*, with the women and children clinging to us as we ran."

"We didn't bother going to Sindi; it would have been pointless. Instead, we struck for Bastar, thinking that we might find aid there. But the Boman were before us, and behind us. We could only flee before them.

"And so, in the end, you found us. A starving band of ragged fugitives, washed up as flotsam in the mountains."

"And Therdan?" the sergeant major asked softly.

"It fell shortly afterward. And Sheffan, and Tarhal, and Crin. And D'Sley and Torth. And Sindi."

"But not, apparently, K'Vaern's Cove."

"No," the Mardukan agreed. "The Cove is impregnable."

Bistem Kar peered through the telescope at the approaching column. There had been more than sufficient time to make his way from the Citadel to the wall, for the column had been sighted before First Bell by the sentinels, but he still didn't have a clue as to who this was. It clearly wasn't the Boman horde, as he'd first assumed. In fact, the lead units appeared to be Northern League cavalry, but just what the rest of the ragtag and bobtail might be was another question. And the matter of what its purpose here might be was yet another. Assuming that those glittering points were on the ends of extremely long spears, this force was far too large and well armed to be a mere supply caravan, and, by the same token, probably wasn't another column of refugees.

He slid the device shut and made a gesture of frustration.

"It makes no sense."

"More refugees?" Tor Flain asked. The second in command of the K'Vaern Company of the Guard glanced sidelong at his commander. Kar was called "The Kren," not just for his immense size, but for his speed and cunning, as well. The *kren* was a water beast, but the commander had proved that its tactics worked just as well on land.

Kar had turned out in his habitual wear—the armored jerkin and harness of a Guardsman private, without the glittering emblems of rank to which he was entitled. It was a uniform he'd worn for many seasons, and one he was comfortable in. He would wear it to all but the most formal meetings, and in all but the most pitched battles, for it was a badge to him, and one that the Guard appreciated. Many was the time that he'd proved himself a guardsman to the very heart, fighting for the resources to keep the Company in top form, whatever it took. And everyone knew that it was only his regular, unceasing battles for a decent budget which had permitted the Guard to repulse the first assault of the Boman.

But the Boman had sworn that no city of the south would remain standing after that stupid bastard in Sindi's actions, and the fact that none of the other cities had had anything to do with Tor Cant's massacre didn't seem to matter. So now it was up to the Guard, and the rest of the capable citizenry, to make that barbarian oath fail, and the odds against that were heavy.

Kar opened the telescope back up and looked through it once more, and Tor Flain took a moment to admire the device. Dell Mir was a wizard with contraptions, but the war against the Boman had seemed to bring out the genius in him. From the device that squirted burning coal oil to changes in the smelters that had steel coming out of their ears (when they could lay their hands on raw materials, at least), the quirky inventor had proved a priceless resource to the defenses. Another example of the sort of genius the Cove seemed to produce almost spontaneously.

Tor Flain loved his city, although he, like many others, had not been born here. His parents had moved from D'Sley when he was young and started a small fish-processing business. He'd grown up with the K'Vaernian bells in his ears and worked long hours as a child and teen, gutting the daily catches and running the results from Great House to Great House. His father was a good salesman, but it was his mother who'd really run things. She'd had an eye for the best fish, and the best way to do things—what some were now calling "efficiency"—and it was the efficiency of the House of Flain which had permitted them to rise from a tiny processor, one among hundreds, to a noted provider of luxury goods. They weren't a major house, by any means, but they were no longer living in a shack on the docks, either.

And as a result of that, their daughters had married well and their sons had spread into many major positions throughout the city and its varied businesses. Positions such as that of second in command of the Company. That hadn't seemed such a good move once; now, Tor Flain's position was arguably among the ten most important ones in the entire city. And while he wasn't about to use his influence to give business to the family, it wasn't really necessary for him to. Anyone who wanted to deal with the Guard assumed that while dealing with the House of Flain wasn't a requirement, it couldn't hurt, either.

Genius inventor from apprentice smith, commander of the Guard from simple guardsman, second in command from a family of fish-gutters. That was K'Vaern's Cove . . . and it was why he would willingly lay down his life for it.

Kar slid the telescope closed again and tapped it on one true-hand, his lower arms crossed in thought.

"It's a relief column," he said.

"Damned small one, then," Flain responded. "Barely three thousand."

"But what three thousand?" Kar mused. "The Northerners' lead banner is that of Therdan."

"Impossible," Flain scoffed. "It was overrun in the first wave!"

"True. But there were rumors that some of them had escaped. And the banner next to it is Sheffan's. They're all supposed to be dead, too, you know. But the really interesting thing is the banner at the head of those spearmen." Tor looked a question at him, and Kar grunted a chuckle. "It's the River."

"Diaspra?" Flain said in astonishment. "But . . . they would *never*. They don't involve themselves in wars at all."

"This war is different," Kar pointed out. "But what I don't understand are all the *turom* and *pagee*. There seem to be an awful lot of them for a relief column that size. It's almost more like a giant caravan, and there are some figures out there—strange ones that look a bit like women but are obviously something else. Many of them are on the *pagee*, too."

He opened the telescope yet again, peered through it for long, thoughtful minutes. Then, suddenly, he gave a whoop of delight.

"*That's* what they're packing!"

"What?" Flain asked.

"Iron, by Krin! Those beasts are loaded with iron bars!"

"They must've come by way of Nashtor," the second in command mused. "Somebody was using his head for something besides holding up his horns."

"Send out a rider," Kar said. "Let's find out what we have here. I think we're going to like it."

The Mardukan who greeted them was the biggest damned scummy—with the possible exception of Erkum Pol—Roger had ever seen. Which, given the size of normal Mardukan males, was saying something. Not only was this one damned near four meters tall, he was disproportionately broad even for that towering height and looked as if he could bench press a *flar-ta*.

"Bistem Kar," Rastar said with obvious relief. "You live."

"Yes, Prince Rastar," the monster responded in a deep, rumbling grunt of laughter. "And as amazed as you are to see me, I'm ten times as amazed to see the heir of Therdan at the door."

"We tried to win through to you when first we fled, but there were too many Boman," Rastar admitted. "And, as the gods would have it, perhaps that was for the best." He turned from the K'Vaernian commander and gestured to Roger. "Bistem Kar, Captain of K'Vaern's Cove, may I introduce His Royal Highness, Prince Roger MacClintock of the Terran Empire."

"I greet you, Prince MacClintock, in the name of the Council of K'Vaern's Cove," the Mardukan responded, admirably restraining his obvious curiosity about just what in hell a "Terran Empire" might be. "And I greet your loads with even greater happiness," he added.

"That's why we stopped by Nashtor," Roger said. "And may I introduce my senior commander, Captain Armand Pahner, who was the one who insisted on retrieving the metal."

"I greet you as well, Captain Pahner," the Guard commander said, casting a close eye over the human. He looked from the chameleon-clad CO to the similarly clad Marines spreading out to either side of the caravan and suppressed an audible grunt of pleased laughter. "Welcome to K'Vaern's Cove."

"K'Vaern's Cove," Rus From said with more enthusiasm than he'd shown since leaving Diaspra. "We're here."

"Wonderful," Bogess responded in a much grumpier tone. "Another city, another battle. Just wonderful."

The area between the inner and outer defenses was given over to agriculture. There were crops of barleyrice and apsimon fruit, mostly clustered on the bay side of the narrow neck of land. On the seaward side there were fruit vines, the famous sea-plums of the coastal region that produced sea-plum wine.

"But this is *K'Vaern's Cove!*" the priest said. "K'Vaern of the Bells! All the world meets in K'Vaern's Cove! This is where over half the devices in the entire Chasten Valley come from. This is where the impeller pump system was *invented*. There's no other city like it!"

"Uh-huh," the general scoffed. "And all the streets are paved with gold. It's still just another city and just another battle."

"Well, we'll see," the cleric replied, refusing to be suppressed by the pessimistic soldier.

"And another new way of doing battle," Bogess continued. "It's not as if we can just teach them pikes and be done with it. No, we have to create these 'muskets' and 'mobile cannon.' Then we have to learn how to use them ourselves."

"Not quite," From corrected as the two representatives from Diaspra were called forward. "In fact, you'll have to, somehow, learn how to use them while they're still being created. And without the help of the humans."

"Podder mocker," Poertena muttered as the column rounded the first hill.

The basis of the city's name was immediately clear. Far below them lay a perfect natural harbor—a cove cut off from the worst effects of weather by hills on either side. All of the hills were extremely steep, with sheer-sided inlets or fjords between several of them, and the bay and the inlets had been linked to create a sheltered, multipart port. Clearly, some of the smaller side harbors could support only small craft, but there were hundreds of those circulating around the city.

The deep-water portions of the port were packed with ships. The most common was a single-masted, square-rigged, round-hulled design very similar in most respects to a medieval Terran cog. There were differences—the beam to length ratio was a bit better—but generally, the resemblance was remarkable. Most of them were about twenty meters from stem to stern, but a few larger ones ran to a bit over thirty, and one of the larger ones was being towed out by a galley, assisted by the slight puffs of the land wind coming over the hills.

One of the side-harbors seemed to be given over to military vessels, of which there appeared to be two basic types. At least two-thirds of them were sleek, low, needle-slim galleys armed with rams, but with no apparent sign of seagoing artillery. The remaining warships were larger, heavier, and clumsier looking. Like the galleys (and unlike most of the merchantmen in the harbor), they carried both oars and masts, but their main armament was obviously the batteries of heavy guns bristling from their heavily built forecastles above their long-beaked rams. Their banks of oars precluded any sort of broadside-mounted artillery, but they were clearly designed to lay down a heavy forward fire as they closed in on their enemies, and there was something very peculiar about those guns. Poertena dialed up the magnification on his helmet and grunted in sudden understanding and surprise, for the guns he could see weren't the built-up, welded-together bombards they'd seen on Diaspra's walls. These guns were *cast*, by God!

The four major hills around the port were part of a series of hills that ran for kilometers to the north, and all of them were covered by interlocked buildings. Houses were built on warehouses were built on shops, until virtually all the open spaces were filled with places of work or living, and often both simultaneously in the same structure.

And everywhere the eye looked, there were bell towers.

Sergeant Julian stood beside the little Pinopan and shook his head in bemusement. It surprised him a bit to realize that nowhere else in all their weary trek had he seen a single Mardukan bell. Not one. But now there were dozens—scores—of bell towers in sight from his single vantage point. God only knew how many there were in the city as a whole . . . or what it must sound like if they all tolled at once. He could see little bells, like carillons, in some of the towers, but there were also medium bells, big bells, and one great big giant bell which must have weighed as much as eight or nine tons in a massive tower near the center of the city, and he wondered why there were so many of them.

Roads twisted through the architectural crazy-quilt, packed with Mardukans. Everywhere Julian and Poertena looked in the city, there were Mardukans selling and buying and going about their business. From the edge of the sheltering hills, the city looked like a kicked anthill.

But anyone who actually wanted to kick this anthill had his work cut out for him. The city was encircled by another immense wall, much larger and stronger than the outer defense work and crowned with artillery which probably threw nine- to twelve-kilo roundshot, with bastions every sixty meters or so. The harbor mouth itself was protected by immense citadels, each liberally supplied with its own cannon, and those guns were massive. In fact, they looked big enough to throw seventy-five- to eighty-kilo shot, although Julian hated to think about the appetite for gunpowder those monsters must have. The only open space in the entire city was a large formation area on the inner side of the wall, which extended the full length of the fortifications' circuit. The area outside the wall had also been cleared, although there were some temporary buildings in that space now, especially near the water and around the main gate, where a virtual shanty town had sprung up.

The wall extended upward on the highest hill, bisecting the city, and connected to another massive citadel, a many-tiered fortress, obviously carved out of the mountain it sat upon. The stones of its exterior portions blended into the background rock so cleverly that it was difficult to tell where the fortress started and the mountain ended, and it, too, boasted a soaring bell tower, this one crowned with an elaborate gilded weathervane in the shape of a ship with all sail set.

"I can see why everybody thinks this place is impossible to take," Julian said.

"Yeah," Poertena said, then thought about it. "But, you know, you gotta wonder. Where's tee supplies?"

"Huh?" Gronningen asked. The stolid Asgardian seemed unaffected by the immensity of the city.

"Well, as long as you can be supplied by sea . . ." the intel NCO said.

"Sure, but where tee supplies gonna come from?" the Pinopan asked. "T'ere's no place to grow food for all t'ese people on t'is peninsula, even wit' all the fish they prob'ly catch. My guess is t'ey used to get most of t'eir food from t'is Sindi place or some such. Where's it comin' from now?"

"Ah," Julian said. "I see your point. And it's not

coming from the next city downriver from Sindi, because that one's been overrun, too."

"So t'ey shipping t'eir supplies from where? A hundred kilometers? Two hundred? A t'ousand?"

"Yeah."

"Instead of just barging it downriver an' across tee bay. And t'at goes for all tee other stuff t'at isn't luxury stuff, stuff you usually get from nearby. Wood, leather, metal, stuff like t'at. And what you gonna bet most of t'eir trade used to be with t'ose cities tee Boman took?"

"But you can depend on distant supply sources and get away with it," Julian argued. "San Francisco did back in the old, old, old days on Earth. And everything it needed mostly came in on ships, not overland."

"Sure," the Pinopan agreed. "New Manila's not'ing but a seaport and a starport, an' it's as big as it gets on Pinopa. T'ey gets ever't'ing but fish from tee ass-end of nowhere. But two t'ings. You see t'ose ships?" He pointed at the oversized cog making its cumbersome way out of port.

"Yes," Julian said. "So?"

"T'at's tee worst pocking ship I ever see. Any kinda deep-water blow, an' it's gonna roll right over an' sink like a flooded rock. An' it's gonna be slow as shit, an' if it slow, it cost more money to run, an' t'at means tee grain gonna be expensive. And t'at means in tee end t'ey starve unless t'ey gots some big source o' pocking income. Which is what leads to tee other t'ing, which is t'ey not'ing but a market. Sure, t'ey might make some stuff here. T'ey might be a reg'lar New Dresden, but it's gonna be not'ing compared to tee stuff t'at's just waiting to ship to somwheres else. An' if not'ing coming down tee Chasten *or* tee Tam, t'en t'ey gots not'ing to sell. An' if t'ey gots not'ing to sell, t'en t'ey gonna starve."

❖   ❖   ❖

"How are you supplied?" Pahner asked. "If you don't mind my asking."

The relief column had attracted remarkably little attention as it passed through the large shanty town around the gate and the outer wall. If a war threatening their very survival was going on, the people of K'Vaern's Cove seemed not to have noticed.

The main thoroughfare on which they were traveling was packed. Only the force of guardsmen calling for way and physically pushing blockages aside permitted the caravan to keep moving, and the side streets were just as crowded, with carts or kiosks set up every few meters selling a mixture of products from food to weapons.

The city was packed onto the slopes surrounding the cove, and the surrounding hills virtually stopped the sea winds, which turned the city into a sweltering, breathless sauna even hotter than the Mardukan norm. The still air also trapped the scent of the streets, and it closed in on the column as it passed through the gate. The effluvia was a combination of the cooking and spices of the side streets and the normal dung smell of all Mardukan cities, subtly flavored with a hint of clear salt air and the rot smell which was common to every harbor in the known universe.

Most of the buildings, aside from the soaring bell towers, were low and made from stone or packed mud, with plaster walls which ranged from blinding white to a glaring clash of painted colors. It was the first place the humans had seen where extensive use had been made of pastels, and the combination of riotous colors, furnace heat, and heady smells dazed some of the Marines.

Single doorways fronted directly onto the street, and children darted out into traffic without heed. One particularly reckless youngster was almost turned into paste by Patty, but the *flar-ta* made a weird five-legged hop and somehow avoided treading on the scrambling waif.

The corners of the buildings all sported elaborate downspouts that led to large rainwater containers. Some of those had markings on them, and Pahner watched as a person dipped from one of them and dropped a metal coin into it. Clearly, someone had just made a sale, and he wondered for a moment why, of all the cities they'd visited, only K'Vaern's Cove seemed to have some sort of water rationing.

The same emphasis on providing water was apparent in the occasional larger pools they passed. The pools, slightly raised above the level of the street and about two meters across and a meter deep, ranged from five to ten meters in length and collected water from the larger buildings' downspouts. They were covered with half-lids and clearly were kept scrupulously clean, for the water in them was as clear as any spring, and they, too, had copper and silver coins on their bottoms.

"Supplied?" Kar turned to look at the human, then gave the handclap of a Mardukan shrug. "Poorly, in all fairness. And, no, I don't mind your asking. Gods know we've crossed swords with the League before, but I don't think they're less than allies now."

"Indeed," Rastar said. The Northern cavalryman grunted in harsh laughter. "Many's the war which we waged against the Cove, or the Cove against us, over its control of the Tam Mouth, or our control of the Northern trade. But that's all past, now. The League is no more, nor will it arise once again in any strength in our lifetime. We're all in this together.

"But tell me," he continued, "why are you short? Don't you have nearly unlimited storage under the Citadel?"

"Yes," the K'Vaernian general agreed. "But we

don't keep the granaries filled to capacity in peacetime, because stock—"

A sudden, deep, rumbling sound, like the tolling of bronze-throated thunder, interrupted the Guard commander. All of the bells, in all of the towers, sang simultaneously, in an overwhelming outpouring of deep, pounding sound that swept over the city—and the astounded column—like an earthquake of music. But it was no wild, exuberant cacophony, for the bells rang with a measured, rolling grandeur, every one of them giving voice in the same instant. Four times they tolled, and then, as suddenly as they had begun to speak, they were silent.

The humans looked at one another, stunned as much by the abrupt cessation as by the sheer volume of the sound, and their companions from Diaspra seemed only a little less affected. Rastar and his Northern fellows had taken it in stride, however, and the native K'Vaernians seemed scarcely even to have noticed, but then Bistem Kar grunted a chuckling laugh.

"Forgive me, Prince Roger, Captain Pahner. It didn't occur to me to warn you."

"What *was* that?" Roger asked, digging an index finger into his right ear, where the echo of the bells seemed to linger.

"It's Fourth Bell, Your Highness," Kar told him.

"Fourth Bell?" Roger repeated.

"Yes. Our day is divided into thirty bells, or segments of time, and Fourth Bell has just passed."

"You mean you get *that*—" Roger waved a hand at the bell towers "—thirty times a day?!"

"No," Kar said in a tone the humans had learned by now to recognize as tongue-in-cheek, "only eighteen times. The bells don't chime at night. Why?"

Roger stared at him, and it was Rastar's turn to laugh.

"Bistem Kar is— What is that phrase of yours? Ah, yes! He's 'pulling your leg,' Roger. Yes, the bells sound to mark each day segment, but usually only the ones in the buildings actually owned by the city, not all of them!"

"True," Kar admitted, with the handclap which served Mardukans for an amused shrug, but then the titanic guardsman sobered. "We are at war, Prince Roger, and until that war is over, all of Krin's Bells will sound in His name over His city at the passing of each bell."

Roger and Pahner looked at one another expressionlessly, and Kar chuckled once more.

"Don't worry, my friends. You may not believe it, but you'll become accustomed more quickly than you can imagine. And at least—" he gave Rus From a sly look "—we won't be constantly pouring water over you!"

The cleric-artificer chuckled along with the others, and Kar returned his attention to the humans.

"But before the bells interrupted us, I believe, I was about to explain to you that we don't keep the granaries fully filled during peacetime because stockpiling like that hurts the grain trade, and we normally have sufficient warning of a war to purchase ample supplies in time. But this time the Boman came too quickly, and we were having the same problems with Sindi everyone else was. That bastard Tor Cant actually started stockpiling last season, which makes me wonder if his murder of the Boman chiefs was really as spontaneous as he wanted us to think. But he wasn't interested in sharing any of his surpluses, and he went as far as putting a hold on all grain shipments out of Sindi 'for the duration of the emergency.' We got in some additional stores from other sources before Chasten's Mouth was overrun, but not much. There's no real shortage, yet, but it will come.

Many of the merchants are rubbing their hands in anticipation."

"What of Bastar?" Rastar asked, gesturing to the north. "I've heard nothing of their people."

"Almost all of them escaped to us when it was clear they couldn't hold against the Boman." Bistem Kar made a gesture of resignation and frustration. "Another drain on our supplies, both of grain and of water, but not one that we could in good conscience reject. And we'd had our problems with D'Sley, as well as all the other cities, but again . . ."

"One for all, and all for one," Pahner said.

"Indeed," the general agreed, and turned his attention back to the human. "But what is your place in all of this? I'm told that these long spears are your innovation, and the large shields. I can see their usefulness against the Boman axes. But why are you here? And involving yourselves in our plight?"

"It's not out of the goodness of our hearts," Roger said. "The full story is long and complicated, but the short answer is that we have to cross that—" he pointed to the sea beyond the harbor "—to reach the ocean, and then cross *that* to get back to our home."

"That's a problem," Kar said forebodingly. "Oh, you can get passage from here to the Straits of Tharazh if you must. It will be expensive, but it can be arranged. But no one will take you beyond the Straits to cross the Western Ocean. The winds would be against you, and no one who's ever tried to cross the ocean has returned. Some people—" the K'Vaernian glanced sideways at Rus From "—believe that the demons which fill the ocean to guard the shores of the world island are to blame, but whatever the cause, no ship has ever succeeded in crossing it and returning to us. There's an ancient tale of one ship having arrived from the *other* side—a wreck, rather, for it had been torn to pieces by something. According to the tale, there was a lone, crazed survivor who babbled in an unknown tongue, but he didn't live long, and no one was ever able to determine what had destroyed the ship."

"Storm?" Pahner asked.

"No, not according to the tale," the general said. "Of course, it might be a fable, but there's an ancient log in one of the museums here. It's in a tongue no one I know of can read, but it's accompanied by what purports to be a partial translation—almost as old as the log itself—and you might find it interesting. The translation seems to describe monsters of some sort, and the tales of the ship's arrival here are very specific in saying that it had been bitten and torn by something."

"Goodness," From murmured provocatively. "You don't suppose it might have been one of those mythological demons, do you?"

"I don't know what it might have been," Kar admitted cheerfully. "Except that whatever it was, it must have been large. And unfriendly. Either of which would be enough to convince *me* to stay well clear of it, by Krin!"

"You know that there's something on the other side, though?" Roger asked.

"Oh, yes," the K'Vaernian replied. "Of course. The world is round, after all; the mathematicians have demonstrated that clearly enough, though not without argument from some of our, ah, more conservative religions. That means that eventually you must come back here, but the distance is immense. And in all honesty, there's never been much incentive for anyone to go mucking about in the open ocean. Quite aside from wind, wave, and possible sea monsters," he grinned at From, who chuckled back at him, "there's the problem of navigation. How does a seaman know where he is unless he can close the shore every so often and compare local landmarks to his charts? And what merchant would go voyaging beyond Tharazh? We know of no cities or peoples to trade with there, and we have—had, at least—all the trade we can service right here in the K'Vaernian Sea. As to what's happened to the one or two lunatics who *have* tried to cross it, no one truly knows, so it's a fertile subject for, um . . . imaginative speculation."

"Well, we'd heard that you're unable to sail across it," Pahner said, "but we've done quite a few things on this world that no one has ever done before."

"They crossed the Tarsten Mountains," Rastar interjected.

"No! Really?" Kar laughed. "And is the land beyond really filled with giant cannibals?"

"I think not," Cord said. The old shaman had a strong gift for languages, but without a toot of his own, he lacked the translator support the humans enjoyed, and the K'Vaernian general looked at him sharply at the sound of his pronounced and highly unusual accent.

"D'nal Cord is my *asi*," Roger said, "my, um, sworn companion and shield mate. He's from the People, who live in the Hurtan Valley. It's not only beyond the Tarsten Mountains, it's actually farther from the Tarstens than they are from here."

"Pretty close to a fourth of the way around the world from the Tarstens," Pahner agreed. "And the people on the far side of the Tarstens didn't look much different from you. No *civan* or *turom*, though."

"Truly, we live in a time of wonders," Kar said. "And I meant no offense to your people, D'nal Cord."

"And I took none," the *asi* said haltingly. "Far we have come, and much have I seen. Much is the same from one side to the other." He glanced around for a moment. "Although this is by far the largest city I've

ever seen. Voitan was just as . . . alive before its fall,
but it wasn't *this* large."

"Voitan?" Kar asked.

"A long tale," Roger said. "And a cautionary one."

"Aye," Cord agreed with a handclap of emphasis, and
looked at the K'Vaernian levelly. "Voitan, as everyone
knew, was invincible. Until the Kranolta."

CHAPTER TWENTY-ONE

Roger looked around the room and nodded in satisfaction. The space was relatively small but comfortable, placed on the seaward side of the citadel and looking out over the blue K'Vaernian Sea, and the sea breeze that blew in from the windows on that side blew back out through inner windows which overlooked a courtyard on the other side. The citadel's bell tower was less than fifty meters from those windows, and the prince winced inwardly at the thought of what it would be like whenever the K'Vaernians' "clocks" went off, but he was willing to accept that as the price of the windows. There wasn't anyplace in the entire city where he could realistically have hoped to escape the bells, anyway, and the breeze wafting through the room felt almost unbelievably good after the sweltering steambath of the city streets.

The chamber contained the ubiquitous low cushions and tables, but Matsugae had already set up his camp bed and acquired a taller table from somewhere. Together with his folding chair, it made for a comfortable place from which to contemplate their next steps.

The plan was simple. They would show the K'Vaern's Cove people some of the military technologies from humanity's bloody past which would be within reach of their current capabilities in return for a trip across the ocean. It had sounded reasonable when they worked it all out before leaving Diaspra, but Poertena had already given his opinion of the seaworthiness of the local boats, and it wasn't good. Roger's head was ringing with such phrases as "deck stiffness," "freeboard," and "jib sails," most of which he already knew from his own yachting days. Poertena, however, seemed to be a veritable mine of information on practical, sail-powered work boats, and that mine was saying "No Way."

So it looked like simply putting a better sail plan on one of the local boats might be out, which would mean months of time spent building new boats. Or at least refitting one of the local boats from the keel up.

The rest of the plan was beginning to look iffy, as well. They hadn't yet met with the local council, but Bistem Kar clearly felt that K'Vaern's Cove wasn't as unconquerable as Rastar and Honal had believed. If his attitude was shared by the Council in general, simply saying "Hey, here's a few tricks. Have fun, and we're out of here," might not work.

All of which sounded as if it might mean yet another battle, and Roger wasn't sure he was ready for that.

He gazed out over the sea and sighed. He'd spent most of his seventeenth summer blue-water sailing off of Bermuda, where, unlike Pinopa, sailing was the recreational province of the rich rather than a matter of economic survival. The blue-water races in the Atlantic were comradely competitions between members of the monetary elite and their handpicked crews, and the yachts used bore as little resemblance to what was needed here as a race-flyer bore to a hover-truck, but given the choice between sailing a cargo sloop through a Mid-Atlantic gale and battling the Boman, Roger was sure what his answer would be. Even with the possibility of sea monsters thrown in for good measure.

Someone knocked on the door, and he turned towards it. The guard outside was Despreaux, and she refused to meet his eye when she opened the door to let Matsugae enter. The incident in Ran Tai still lay between them like a minefield, and he had to get past it. Ran Tai had proven that it wasn't smart to get *too* close to the troops, but it was even less smart to have a bodyguard who was poisonously angry with you. And it wasn't as if Despreaux could ask for a transfer, so, sooner or later, he had to talk to her about it and try to smooth the waters.

Besides which, he was still deeply confused about his feelings for her.

He sighed at the thought, then smiled again as he heard Matsugae puttering around behind him. The little clucks as the valet straightened the eternal mess were soothing.

"Are you glad to be out of the kitchens, Kostas?"

"It was a very interesting experience, Your Highness," the valet replied, "but, all things considered, yes, I'm quite glad. I can always go back and putter there if the mood takes me, and it's not as if I'm really still needed at this point." With over five thousand total persons, human and Mardukan, with the column, cooks were easy enough to find.

"But we'll all miss your *atul* stew," Roger joked.

"I'm afraid you'll just have to suffer, Your Highness," Matsugae responded. "It's funny, really. I gave that recipe to one of the Diasprans, and he just stared at me in shock. I suppose it's the equivalent of Bengal tiger stew to humans. Not what they'd consider normal fare."

"'Skin one Bengal tiger . . .'" Roger murmured with a chuckle.

"Exactly, Your Highness. Or perhaps, 'First, fillet the Tyrannosaurus.'"

"I can just imagine Julian's stories about this little jaunt once we get home," the prince said.

"Perhaps, but the jaunt isn't over yet," the servant retorted. "And on that subject, you have the meeting this afternoon with the K'Vaernian Council. I obtained some cloth in Diaspra. It's not as fine as *dianda*—the threads are somewhat coarser, and the weave isn't as tight. However, it made an admirable suit, and I found enough *dianda* to line it and provide two or three *dianda* shirts to go with it."

Roger glanced at the proffered garments and nodded, but he also cocked one eyebrow quizzically.

"Black? I thought you always said black was only for weddings and funerals."

"So I did, but it was the best dye Diaspra had available." The valet looked uncomfortable for a moment, then shrugged. "It's what they make their better priestly vestments from."

"Works for me," Roger responded with a smile. "You know, you really have been a tremendous boon throughout this entire hike, Kostas. I don't know what we would've done without you."

"Oh, you would've made do," the valet said uncomfortably.

"No doubt we would have, but that doesn't mean we would have made do as well as we have."

"I suppose it *is* fortunate that I learned a little something from all of the safaris on which I've accompanied you," Matsugae conceded.

"A vast understatement, Kosie," the prince said fondly, and the valet smiled.

"I'll go make sure the arrangements for this afternoon are in place," he said.

"Very good," Roger said, turning back to the window and allowing Matsugae his space. "And pass the word for Cord, Eleanora, and Captain Pahner, if you would. We need to have our positions clear before the meeting."

"Yes, Your Highness," the valet replied with a small smile. The Roger who'd taken off from Earth would never have given that order with such certainty, assuming that the need to worry about preplanning would have occurred to him at all. Which it wouldn't have. At least this "little jaunt" had been good for something.

The council chamber was rather smaller than Roger had expected. The long room at the foot of the city's central and tallest bell tower was low-ceilinged (for Mardukans) and filled to capacity by a cross-section of the city. The actual Council—fifteen representatives of various groups within the city—sat at one end, but the other end was a public gallery, open to any voting citizen of K'Vaern's Cove, and there wasn't enough room to sneeze at that end.

The city-state was a limited republic, with the franchise restricted to those who paid a vote tax, which amounted to ten percent of a person's yearly income. It was the only direct tax levied upon the citizenry, but there were no exceptions from it and no exemptions for the poor. If you wanted to vote, you had to pay the tax, but even the poorest of the poor could come up with that much if they were frugal. It was obvious to Roger that although the vote tax provided a goodly chunk of income for the city, it was really intended primarily to limit the vote to those willing to make a

genuine sacrifice to exercise their franchise. Other taxes
and duties levied on warehouses, imports, and port
usage by ships not registered to a K'Vaernian citizen
provided the majority of the city's operating capital.
Which, of course, raised interesting questions about
future budgets now that the Boman had managed to
eliminate at least two-thirds of the Cove's usual trading partners.

The Council was elected "at large," with the whole
body of citizenry voting for all council members. In
effect, however, each represented the particular social
group from which he came. Some were guild representatives, while others represented the entrepreneur
class that was the economic lifeblood of the city. Still
others represented the class of hereditary wealth, and
a few were even representatives of the poorest of the
city's multitudes.

All of which meant that the Council was a diverse
and—to Roger's eye—fairly hostile bunch as it greeted
the human and Diaspran representatives.

The spectators behind the visitors were an even
more diverse lot . . . and considerably more lively. The
public gallery was open to all voters on a first-come,
first-served basis, and while there were tricks the rich
could use to pack the chamber if they really wanted
to, the current audience seemed to be a pretty good
cross-section of the city. And a raucous lot they'd been
as the Diasprans began their presentation.

Bogess had started with a precise report on the
Battle of Diaspra, complete with a long discussion of
the preparations, including some of the more contro-
versial training methods introduced by the humans.
Those preparations had occasioned some loud and
derisive commentary from the crowd of onlookers, but
it was his description of the battle which had drawn
the most responses. As seemed to be the case for the

entire planet, the K'Vaernians had never heard of the concept of combined arms or, with the sole exception of the League cavalry, disciplined mass formations. Bogess' description of the effectiveness of the shield wall had been scoffed at so loudly by the raucous crowd that the chairman of the Council had been forced to call for order. His description of the effect of the Marines' powered armor, however, had drawn the loudest response. At first, his account had been greeted with stunned silence, but that had quickly given way to loud derision and the mockery of disbelief.

"They are very noisy," Cord commented to Roger.

"Democracy is like that, Cord," the prince responded. "Every yammerhead who thinks he has two brain cells to rub together gets his say." As he spoke, he noted that there were many Mardukan women in the group. They were just as vociferously involved in the debate as any of their male counterparts, and he decided that that was probably a good sign. It was certainly unlike anything they'd seen elsewhere on Marduk, with the sole exception of the reconstituted government of Marshad.

"I must say," the old shaman grumped, "that I would prefer some less noisy method of doing business."

"So would I," Roger agreed, "and the Empire is a bit less wide open and raucous than these people are. We're a constitutional monarchy with a hereditary aristocracy, not a direct democracy, so I guess you could say we're more representative than democratic. Then again, direct democracy wouldn't work very well for something the size of the Empire of Man, and all of Mother's subjects get to vote for their local representatives in the Commons. Every citizen is absolutely guaranteed the rights of freedom of speech, public assembly, and the vote, too, which means sometimes we get just as loud and noisy as these folks are . . . or even worse."

"Then you should make changes. Much *quieter* changes," Cord sniffed.

"Funny, a lot of people keep saying that . . . whatever form of government they have. The only problem is, if you tell the yammerheads to shut their gobs, you don't have real representation anymore. If everyone isn't free to speak his mind, then, ultimately, *no one* is, and in the end, that will come home and bite everyone involved on the ass. Noise and disagreement are part of the price you pay for freedom."

"The People are free," Cord said. "And they aren't noisy."

"Cord, I hate to break this to you, but the People *aren't* free," Roger disagreed. "The People are locked into a system in which there are two choices: be a hunter, or be a shaman. Well, three, since you can choose to be neither and starve to death, instead. Freedom entails the making of choices, and if you only have two choices, you aren't free. For that matter, the People's lives are no picnic. Doc Dobrescu's determined that the tribal clans have an average life span two-thirds as long as the townsmen. They also have twice the death rate among their young. That isn't freedom Cord. Or, to the extent that it is, it's the freedom of misery."

"We're not miserable," the shaman argued. "Quite the opposite."

"Yes, but that's because you don't know, as a group, any other way to live. And, let's face it, the People are very tradition-bound. All cultures at that tech level have a tendency to be that way, and traditions and customs help restrict your choices and inhibit change. Look at your own case. You studied in Voitan before the Kranolta wiped out the original city, and you came home a scholar and a sage, but you also came home still a shaman of the People. I don't doubt for a minute that you loved your life and your tribe, however many worthwhile things you may have found during your stay in Voitan. And I certainly agree that the 'shit-sitters' in the People's neck of the woods weren't exactly shining beacons of the very best that civilization—and democracy—can offer. But the traditions which brought you home again may also have blinded you to the fact that the People as a whole simply have no concept of how much better their lives—or their children's lives—could be."

Roger shrugged.

"There are some humans—like the Saints—who think it's always best to let native peoples continue in their native conditions without 'corrupting' them by suggesting any sort of alternative. Despite the death rates, despite the pain and suffering they experience in day-to-day life, it's better to let them 'seek their own paths' and 'retain their cultural integrity.' Well, the Empire disagrees. And so do I. We don't want to come in and force any culture to embrace social forms which are anathema to its values or to impose some 'one size fits all' cultural template by force, but we have a moral responsibility to at least make them aware of the alternatives. There are many problems with our modern human society, but dying of malnutrition or an impacted tooth isn't one of them, and no other sentient should have to die of them, either."

"So it's better to have this?" the shaman asked, gesturing to the screaming matches at the back of the room. Bailiffs had been busy while Roger spoke, breaking up the handful of fistfights which had broken out. Now they were in the process of throwing out the terminally vociferous and combative, but it was still a noisy lot.

"Yes, Cord, this is better than life in the tribes," Roger said. "Most of the people in this room saw all of their littermates survive. Most of them are going to live twenty to thirty years beyond your own relatively long life span. Very few of them go to bed hungry at night because the hunters failed to find game, and very few of them have suffered from scurvy, or rickets, or lost teeth, or been reduced in stature because they were hungry all the time as children. Yes, Cord. This is a better life than the tribe's."

"I don't think so," Cord said with a gesture of disagreement.

"Well, see?" Roger grinned. "We've got a disagreement. Welcome to democracy."

"If this 'democracy' is so splendid," the shaman said, "why is it that Captain Pahner does whatever *he* feels is right without constantly calling for discussion and votes?"

"Ah. That's a bit different," Roger said with a shrug. "Democracies need militaries to protect them, but no effective military is a democracy."

"Oh, I see. It is yet another internal human contradiction," Cord remarked with a certain undeniable edge of satisfaction. "Why didn't you simply say so at the beginning?"

"Order! We're going to have order here!" Turl Kam banged his heavy staff of office on the floor. The burly ex-fisherman had been a minor boat owner until a clumsily run line had removed his lower leg. He might have been able to continue with the peg which had replaced it, but he'd opted to sell the boat and go into politics, instead. After years of wheeling and dealing, he had attained the pinnacle of power as head of the Council, only to have the Boman invade on his watch. It was very frustrating. His constituency was the local fishermen and short-haul cargo sailors, and there was little or no good to be extracted from the situation for them. There was, however, a great deal of ill to be expected from it, which was why they were so restive at the moment, but that was no reason for them to take it out on him.

"There's been a bunch of stuff said by the folks from Diaspra that's hard to believe," he agreed, "but—" One of his own constituents jumped to his feet and started yelling, but the chairman stared him down. "The next one of you lengths of fish-bait spouts off, I'm gonna eject you. And the guard's gonna dip you in the bay for good measure! Now, I got the floor, so everybody just shut the hell up and stop interrupting the speakers! We're gonna give our visitors their say, by Krin!"

Someone else began a shouted objection—which ended abruptly as Turl Kam nodded and two of the bailiffs booted the loudmouth out of the chamber. One or two others looked as if they were contemplating saying something, but mouths closed all around at the chairman's glare, and he snorted in satisfaction.

"As I was saying, what they're saying is hard to believe. But it's also gonna be easy to prove or disprove, and when the time comes, we'll get some proofs. But now isn't the time or place.

"And, furthermore, there ain't no reason for them to be lying. They got nothing to gain by coming here—K'Vaern's Cove is less important than spit to Diaspra, so you just keep that in mind when they speak.

"Now it's the turn of the Cleric-Artisan Rus From. Rus From, if you would give us your words?"

From stepped forward and bowed to the Council, but instead of speaking to them, as Bogess had, he turned to the common citizens packing the chamber. "You wonder at the statements General Bogess has made, and that's hardly surprising. We speak of miraculous-sounding events—of walking walls of spears and shields that broke the Boman like a twig. We speak of the very lightnings of heaven striking the enemy from the weapons of our human companions, and you wonder and doubt.

"Some of you know my name, and if you've heard aught of my own small achievements as an artisan, I ask you to remember that when I speak to you now of wonders beyond wonders. These visitors, these 'humans,' bring marvel after marvel. Their own devices and weapons are as miracles to us, yet in many ways, what they can tell us about our own crafts and technologies is even more miraculous. We cannot duplicate their lightning weapons, or the devices which allow them to speak and act as one over vast distances, but they've brought us new methods of doing, new methods of thinking, and new methods of making other things which we *can* duplicate and use. And by showing us the thinking behind those other things, they have opened up, for me, at least, a vast panorama of new ideas and new inventions. Ideas and inventions that will change our way of life forever.

"Many of these ideas and inventions would not have been well regarded in my own land. The Boman invasion has shaken up my city, but you know it well. It's a city of priests, where the responsibility of new thought is rigorously maintained. One is absolutely required to have a new thought once in one's life. No more, and no less."

He waited for the audience's grunting laughter to die, then continued.

"So when I was told 'Go to K'Vaern's Cove,' I was awash with excitement, for of all the cities between the mountains and the sea, surely K'Vaern's Cove would be the one where the reality of these new ideas and new devices could reach its fullest flower. Surely, in K'Vaern's Cove the people of Krin of the Bells would greet new ways of sailing and learning and manufacturing with the same enthusiasm I did! Surely, in K'Vaern's Cove, if anywhere, I could find thinkers and doers to rival my own thinking and doing! Surely, in K'Vaern's Cove, if anywhere, I could find people ready and eager to accept the challenge put before them! For the people of K'Vaern's Cove have never quailed before any challenge, and surely they would not quail before this one."

He paused and looked around at the assembled group.

"And now I am in K'Vaern's Cove, and what do I find? I find disbelief," he gestured at one of the more vocal locals, "derision," he gestured at another, "and mockery." He gestured at a third, and clapped hands in a gesture of grief and surprise.

"Was I, a foreigner, wrong in my opinion of your city? Is it in fact the case that K'Vaern's Cove, as noted for its acceptance and open-mindedness as for the majesty of its bells, is unwilling or unable to accept new ideas? New ways? Is K'Vaern's Cove unwilling to face new challenges? Has it fallen into the slothful trap of the lesser cities—the traps of fear, insularity, and complacency? Or is K'Vaern's Cove still the shining beacon that it seemed to be from distant Diaspra?

"The answer is up to you," he said, pointing at individuals in the audience. "It's up to you, and you, and you. For K'Vaern's Cove is not ruled by an oligarchy, as Bastar. It isn't ruled by a priest, as Diaspra, or by a despot, as Sindi. It is ruled by the people, and the question is, what are the people of K'Vaern's Cove? Fearful *basik*? Or courageous *atul-grak*?

"The answer is up to you."

He folded all four arms and gazed levelly at the suddenly much more thoughtful audience for several long moments, then turned to the Council and gave a very human shrug.

"For my own presentation, I have only this to add. The humans have given me designs for weapons which can fire bullets farther and straighter than you can imagine. They can also be reloaded far more quickly than any arquebus or wheel lock, and, perhaps even more importantly, they can be fired even in a rain to rival the Hompag and strike targets accurately from as much as an *ulong* away. They've showed me how to reduce the size of our bombards to such an extent that they can be pulled by *civan* or *turom* and be used against the Boman at short range in the open field of battle. I don't say that producing these weapons will be easy or fast, for we lack the skills and the techniques which the humans would employ in their own homeland, but I do say that they can be produced using our own artisans and our own resources. Given all of that and the support of the people of this glorious city, we can *destroy* the Boman, not simply defeat them. Or you can huddle here like *basik* until your grain runs out and the Boman come and take your horns.

"It is up to you."

"And what does Diaspra gain from this war against these invaders?" one of the Council members asked skeptically.

"Not much," Rus From admitted. "Everyone is fairly certain that the Boman are uninterested in the lands south of the Nashtor Hills. Once they've reduced K'Vaern's Cove, most of them will return to the North. Others will settle in these lands. Eventually, we might have to settle the Nashtor Hills with fortified cities against them, as the Northern League once protected the cities north of the hills, but that would be a far day in the future. Soon enough, we would be able to negotiate the reopening of Chasten Mouth, which would give us our sea trade back. Actually, without the competition of K'Vaern's Cove, we'd be the center for trade from the Tarsten Mountains and the Nashtor Hills. Financially, we would be well set.

"On the other hand, without your landward trade, there's little use for K'Vaern's Cove. In time, the trading ships will stop coming, and you will dwindle. Even if you reach an accommodation with the Boman and survive, you are bereft without the downriver trade of the Tam through D'Sley. In time, you will be nothing but a ruin and memory."

"Well, that's all the reasons you *shouldn't* be here," Turl Kam ground out between clenched teeth. For all of the K'Vaernians' legendary volubility, no one, not even Bistem Kar, had been so brutally honest about their predicament. "So why *are* you here?"

"I'm here because my master sent me," From replied. "I was happy to come in many ways, but I must admit that I also had projects and plans which would have kept me fully occupied in Diaspra." He chose—tactfully, Roger thought—not to go into exactly what all those projects and plans had been. "But Gratar had other ideas, and I'm here at his orders," the cleric finished.

"And what was his purpose?" the Council member who'd spoken earlier asked, and From remembered his name. He was Wes Til, a representative of some of the richer merchant houses. *Anything to get me out of town*, the priest almost replied, then thought better of excessive candor.

"I think that the words the humans gave me fit best," he said instead. " 'In the face of evil, good persons must band together lest they fall one by one, unpitied sacrifices of a contemptible struggle.' Certainly, we could make an accommodation with the Boman. But that doesn't mean such an accommodation would be just, or right, in the long run or the short. And even leaving the question of justice aside, that accommodation might or might not hold. If it doesn't, and we've allowed those we should have aided—and who might have aided us in our need—to fall through our inaction, then whatever disaster comes upon us will be no more than we deserve.

"And so we bring iron, purchased from Nashtor by the guarantee of Diaspra's temple, and we ask only that its purchase be repaid after the war. However, I also come with two thousand infantry which must be kept and maintained, and we brought no great sums of treasure beside the iron. If, after the war is over, you have supported our 'Expeditionary Force' with food and goods sufficient to pay for the iron, then the account will be considered balanced by Diaspra.

"Thus we bring you your much-needed iron and a force to aid you, and effectively ask only for maintenance.

"Personally, I think Gratar is insane to be so generous in such a time of peril for us all. But then, I'm not as nice as he is."

"You sure are blunt, Rus From," Turl Kam said, rubbing his hands in worry.

"I'm a priest, not a politician," the cleric responded. "Worse, I'm an artisan, and you know what they're like."

"Indeed," Wes Til grunted in a laugh shared by the citizens behind the priest. "But where are these wonder weapons of the 'humans'? And what of the humans themselves? They have yet to speak."

"Yes," Kam agreed. "Who's gonna speak for the humans?"

Roger recognized his cue and stepped forward with a gracious nod to From as the priest relinquished the floor to him.

"Members of the Council," the prince said, half-bowing to that group, "and citizens of K'Vaern's Cove," he added, turning to give the crowd of spectators the same bow, "I speak for the humans."

"Why are you humans here?" Kam asked bluntly. The Council had already been informed of the humans' plans, in general terms, at least, but only informally.

"We aren't from around here, and we want to go home," Roger said. "That may sound fatuous, but it's important to understanding our needs and objectives. In order for us to return home, it's necessary for us to reach a city in a land which lies beyond the Western Ocean, and our time, frankly, is running out. Because of that, it's our intention to purchase passage—or ships, if necessary—and depart for that distant land as soon as possible. Our ship expert is of two minds about how best to proceed. He's of the opinion that the local ships aren't well designed for blue-water sailing, despite their excellent construction, and he's uncertain whether or not we could convert them to our needs. If he decides that we can't, and I believe he's inclining in that direction, then it will be necessary for us to build ships from the keel up."

"That will take time," Til said. "Time you said you don't have. And the cost will be substantial, especially in time of war."

"We have funds," Roger said, and managed—with difficulty—not to glare at Armand Pahner, who'd finally gotten around that very morning to revealing the true fruits of Ran Tai to him. "I'm sure," the prince went on, "that we can afford the construction or modification."

"Maybe you can, and maybe you can't," Kam said. "There's a shortage of building materials, and our navy had a short and nasty fight with the Boman out on the Bay after D'Sley fell. The stupid bastards seemed to think they could get through from D'Sley using rafts and canoes. We taught 'em better, but however dumb they may be once you get them on the water, they don't have a lot of give up in their nature. We took some pretty heavy damage of our own, and most all our timber, especially for masts, comes down the Tam. There aren't masts to be had for love or money, and there won't be none until we retake the lands where the cutting is done."

"We'll manage," Roger said with determined confidence despite a severe sinking sensation. "We've crossed half this world. We've fought our way across rivers in the face of an army of *atul-grak*. We've destroyed tribes almost as numerous as the Boman without support. We've crossed unscalable mountains. We've driven paths through the burning deserts. One stinking little ocean isn't going to stop us."

"The sea's a lady, but that lady's a bitch," Kam told him reflectively. "I turned my back on that bitch just once and lost a leg to her."

"You turned your back more than once, you old drunk!" one of the crowd shouted.

"I ought to have you ejected for that, Pa Kathor," Kam said with a grunt of laughter. "But it's almost true. I wasn't drunk—I was hung over. But the point is that the sea *is* a bitch, and a mean one when the mood strikes her, and the ocean's worse. Lots worse. You might want to bear that in mind, Prince Roger."

"We're aware of the difficulties and dangers, Turl Kam," Roger replied. "And we don't underestimate her. But whatever her mood, we must cross her, and we have many things going for us. For one thing, we have a technology, a simple rigging innovation, which permits us to sail far closer to the wind than your own ships can."

"What?" Wes Til asked in the suddenly silent room. "How?"

"It isn't difficult," Roger told him, "although it would be easier to demonstrate than to explain. But it permits a ship to sail within thirty or forty degrees into the wind."

"How?" Turl Kam took up Til's question. "That's impossible. No one can sail closer than fifty degrees to the wind!"

"No, it isn't, but as I say, it's something better demonstrated than explained, and we will demonstrate it. We'll teach your sailors and your shipwrights how it's done while we prepare for our own voyage, but that's only one of our advantages. Another is that we have much better navigational arts than you, and we know where we're going. We know approximately where we are on a map, we know where our destination lies, and we know how to keep track of our position while we sail towards it, so when we set out, we'll be heading for a specific destination on a course we can plot reliably, rather than making a blind voyage of discovery."

"And this destination lies across the ocean, does it?" Til mused aloud.

"Yes. It's a large island or small continent, a piece of land the size of the lands between the mountains and the sea."

"So you'll be building a ship . . . ?"

"Or ships," Roger corrected. "Precisely how many will depend on their sizes and the quantity of supplies or pack animals we must take with us."

"Or ships," the Council member accepted the correction. "But you're going to build them, then sail across the ocean to this other continent. And once you get there, you'll find a port waiting for you. And then what?"

"We'll probably sell the ships. Our eventual tar— destination is in the interior."

"Ah," Til said. "So you won't need the ships on the far side. So if someone were to participate in building the ships, perhaps pay for it entirely, and then give you passage for a nominal fee . . . ?"

"Someone wouldn't be thinking about getting a lock on a new market, would someone?" Kam asked through the scattered laughter.

"I'm sure that something could be worked out with someone," Roger said with a closed-lipped, Mardukan smile. "Which is an example of what I meant by not letting things get in our way. We have much to offer, but we also have priorities which, however much we might like to vary our plans, call for us to proceed on our way without delays."

"But you could stay and fight?" Til persisted.

"If we did, it would change several equations," Roger replied cautiously. "A delay to fight here would mean we would have to make a faster passage, which would require different ships. And we wouldn't be fighting directly, because there are too few of us to matter against a foe as numerous and geographically dispersed as the Boman. What we could do would be to act as trainers and leaders for your own forces, as we did in Diaspra. And although we're too few in numbers ourselves to fight the war *for* you, perhaps we could act as shock troops in one or two critical battles, again, as we did in Diaspra.

"But that isn't our intention. If K'Vaern's Cove throws its weight into the battle against the Boman, you should win, even in an open field battle, without us. And if you *don't* throw your full weight into the fight, it would hardly be in our interest to support a half-hearted war."

"But with your aid, would our casualties be lighter?" Til pressed.

Roger opened his mouth to reply, and stopped. He thought for a moment and almost turned to look at Pahner for an answer, but he already knew what the answer was.

"If we threw our full effort into it, your casualties

would be lighter. We've described the new weapons to Rus From, but their construction is complicated, and we weren't able to tell him exactly how to solve all of the problems he would face in building them. Not because we deliberately chose to conceal or withhold information, but because we're simply not fully familiar with your manufacturing capabilities. Our own land has many technologies and machines which yours doesn't, and we don't know the best and most efficient way to adapt your own capabilities to solving the problems.

"To be honest, we didn't worry about that aspect. Rus From's reputation is well known, even here in K'Vaern's Cove, and from our own observation in Diaspra, that reputation is well-deserved. We were confident that he would be able to overcome any difficulties in time, and, unlike us, time is something which he—and you—possess. Not as much as we thought before we learned the true state of your supplies, perhaps, but still longer than *we* have if we're to reach our destination alive. Even without us, Rus From—and your own artisans, of course—would almost certainly be able to produce sufficient of the new weapons to defeat the Boman before lack of supplies defeats *you*.

"If, on the other hand, we remained in K'Vaern's Cove, our own artisans would be available to help with that production. We'd be able to learn what we don't currently know about your capabilities, and with that knowledge we could probably save a great deal of time in putting those weapons into your warriors' true-hands. Also, at the risk of sounding conceited, our Marines would be far better trainers than the Diasprans. We have an institutional memory to draw on, and a degree of personal experience which they lack. As an analogy, the Diasprans would be apprentices teaching unskilled people to be apprentices,

while our Marines would be master craftsmen teaching others to be journeymen."

"How would you go about the actual fighting?" Til
asked. "Would you go to some point and dare the Boman
to attack you? Or would you try to draw them forward
against our own defenses? Would you attack Sindi?"

"I can't answer those questions," Roger said,
"because we haven't discussed the matter among ourselves. As I've repeatedly stressed, we aren't here to
fight the Boman. We need to cross the ocean. Having said that, if we did take the field against them, we
would probably begin by recapturing D'Sley to use as
a base of supply. Trying to supply around the Bay would
open you up to interdiction."

"Uh," Turl Kam said. "What was that last word?"

"Sorry." Roger realized he'd used the Standard
English word and pulled up the translation software
on his toot, then grimaced when he discovered that
there *was* no translation. "You don't seem to have a
word for it, so I was forced to use our own. Let's just
say that packing stuff all the way around the Bay opens
you up to having your supply line cut. Interior lines
of supply are always better."

"So you'd want to retake D'Sley as a start," Til said,
rubbing his horns. "What then?"

"Any moves after that would depend on what intelligence we'd gathered."

"What . . . thinking you'd brought together?" Kam
said carefully. "Are you saying it would depend on what
you decided as a group?"

"No," the prince said. "Look, this is getting complicated. What I meant was that when we knew where the
Boman were and how they were moving, or *if* they were
moving, then we could think about what strategy to use.
But we're not going to be doing any of those things
because—"

"Because you have to cross the ocean," Kam said. "Right. We got that. So what we've got is some soldiers of dubious worth and some half smelted iron from Diaspra. We're supposedly going to get some new toys—but not the *best* toys—from you humans by way of the Diasprans. And with these gifts, we're supposed to go out and beat up on the Boman. Because if we don't, Rus From tells us, the Cove is going to die on the vine."

"Don't know when I've ever heard it put more clearly," Wes Til said. "Krin knows, we've clearly died on the vine in every other war we've been involved in! So I guess that just about sums it up."

"Yes, it does," Roger said, grinning widely and this time letting a mouthful of pearly teeth show. "Now, as I was saying. Since from what you just said you guys are clearly having *no* problems with the Boman, perhaps you can tell me where I could buy a dozen masts?"

CHAPTER TWENTY-TWO

"Okay, Poertena, what've you got?" Roger asked.

The council meeting had adjourned without reaching any decisions, so the humans were continuing with their plan to modify or build a ship and the Diasprans were in limbo. If the K'Vaernians decided that fighting the Boman wasn't worth what it would cost, the Diasprans' trip would have been in vain, but Roger had a gut feeling that that wasn't what would happen.

"I went down tee harbor wit' Tratan, Sir. Just nosin' aroun'," the Pinopan said, and pulled out his pad. "We gots problems."

"There's a materials shortage," Pahner said. "We got that much at the council meeting. How bad is it?"

"Say t'at t'ere ain't no materials, an' you closer, Cap'n," the sergeant replied. "'Specially masts and spars. I see t'ree, four shipyards—t'ey shut down: no wood. Tee two I see working, t'ey workin' slow, just killin' time."

"Worse than I thought," O'Casey muttered. "The city didn't look all that depressed on the way in."

"Oh, tee parts we come t'rough, t'ey busy. It's tee docks t'at's idle. You go down tee docks, you gots lots o' people jus' hangin' around. Lots of tee porters, normally unload tee ships, t'ey just hangin' around. Lots of tee guys work in tee warehouses. And tee sailors. Hell, even tee taverns is shut down—no business."

"And the docks have got to be the linchpin of this economy," O'Casey said. "It's not like they produce much."

"I don't know about that," Julian said. "I was nosing around, too, and there's a large industrial sector beyond the first set of hills. The entire peninsula is short on ground water—that's why they've got all those catcher cisterns—but they've got some pretty good powered equipment running over there. A lot of it's wind-powered, but they use some water-driven machinery that draws on really big cisterns. Hell, I even saw one shop that uses tidal catcher basins to drive wheels with the outflow—they've got two moons, and that makes for some hellacious tides even on an inland sea like the K'Vaernian. But for all the equipment they've got, things seemed slow," he admitted. "Lots of people around, and all the foundries were active, but . . . slow. I think the city's probably a 'value added' economy. They get raw materials, work them into goods, and sell the goods. But there aren't any materials to rework right now, and more than half their markets are gone."

"Can we buy a ship and cross the ocean?" Pahner asked.

"No, Sir," the Pinopan answered promptly. "We can buy a ship, no problem. But we no can cross tee ocean in one of t'ese tubs. We might make it, an' we might not. You wanna take a maybe-maybe not chance with tee Prince?"

"No," Pahner said with a grimace. "So what's the alternative?"

"We can buy a ship, strip it to tee keel, an' use tee timbers to build a new one," the Pinopan told him. "T'at sound like a good idea, but it make it nearly twice as long to build t'an if we starts fresh, an' we ain't got an infinite supply of supplements."

"Is it just the masts that are in short supply?" Julian asked.

"No. Oh, tee masts're tee worst part, but ever't'ing's short. You build ships out o' wood, you needs seasoned timber. You can use green, but t'ey ain't gonna last very long. T'at's maybe not a problem for us, but t'ere ain't *no* timber in tee city—not where anyone gonna sell it to us, anyways."

"And there won't be any from their internal resources, either," O'Casey said grimly. "It's a classic problem for any seapower based on wooden hulls. Once you cut down all of the usable timber in your immediate vicinity, you become dependent on an overseas supply for your shipyards. And the overseas suppliers K'Vaern's Cove has depended on just got hammered under by the Boman."

"T'at's right," Poertena agreed. "Oh, I t'ink we can maybe pry loose 'nough timber for one ship, but no more."

"Well, can't the platoon fit on just one?" Julian asked, wincing as he used the term for the surviving Marines. Mostly because "platoon" was exactly what Bravo Company had become.

"Yeah," the Pinopan answered with a sideways glance at the captain. "But is t'at all we taking?"

"Captain Pahner?" Roger glanced at the CO. "Is there something I should know?"

"I've been talking with Rastar," Pahner said quietly. "The Boman didn't just sack Therdan and Sheffan—they razed them to the ground, and the surviving League forces are generally uninterested in returning to rebuild. There's nothing there *to* rebuild, and I think there's also an aspect of not wanting to see their dead in it. If they don't see them, don't see the ruins with their own eyes, they can remain in denial deep down inside. And the *civan* unit has also bonded well to us and, to an extent, to your person as a leadership figure. In addition, Bogess has mentioned that some of his forces aren't interested in returning to Diaspra. Again, for some of them it's that they've developed an interest in learning and seeing new things, and for others it's a basic change of allegiance."

"You're thinking of taking some of the Northern and Diaspran forces with us?" The prince chuckled. "Her Majesty's Own Mardukan Sepoys?"

"I cannot secure your person with thirty-six Marines, Your Highness," the captain said in a much more formal tone than usual, meeting the prince's gaze levelly. "Certainly not in this environment. I could barely manage with a full company . . . and I don't have a company anymore. As Sergeant Julian just said, I have a platoon. That simply isn't enough, and that means I have to do it through some other means."

Roger's chuckle died, and he nodded soberly.

"I hadn't intended to make light of your predicament, Sir. Or your losses. I was simply anticipating Mother's reaction."

"Indeed," Pahner said, and shook his head with a sudden grunting Mardukan-style chuckle of his own. "I can see our return now. Her Majesty will be most . . . amused."

"Her Majesty," O'Casey said, "after she reads the reports, will be most . . . amazed. There's never been a saga to equal this one, Captain. At the least, you've placed your name in the military history books."

"Only if I get him back to Her Majesty," Pahner pointed out. "Which requires crossing the ocean, making our way through whatever political zone we hit on the far side, and recapturing the spaceport with only thirty-six Marines and a half dozen suits of problematical powered armor. And that's why I would like to take a unit of *civan* cavalry and another of Diaspran pikemen, or riflemen or musketeers, whichever it turns out, with us."

"Which means how many ships?" Roger asked.

"Six," the Pinopan answered. "Six thirty, thirty-five-meter schooners. Lots of sail area, pretty good cargo volume, good sea legs, an' weatherly. Maybe topsail schooners. Square sails on tee main an' fore won' help much on tee trip over, but t'ey be good for tee trip back wit' tee prevailing winds behind you."

"You can build one of t'ose—those?" Pahner asked.

"Wit' a little help. T'ey gots most of tee techniques we need, they jus' use 'em all wrong. T'ese ships t'ey make are tubs—not all t'at bad for what t'ey does, but t'ey don' do much. Never sail out o' sight o' land, run for shore whenever a storm blow up, t'ings like t'at. T'at's why I don't t'ink nobody's gonna make it 'cross tee ocean in one o' t'ese toy boats. But smooth out tee lines, give some deadrise an' some more dept' of hull, lower tee freeboard fore an' aft an' bring it up some in between, an' you gots you'self a real tiddly ship. On'y real problem is, t'ey don' use buildin' drafts—t'ey designs by eye an' uses half-models to fair tee lines."

"Do you have any idea at all what he's talking about?" Roger asked O'Casey plaintively, and the chief of staff laughed.

"No, but it certainly sounds like *he* does," she said.

"It not so dif'rent from some o' tee little yards back home," the Pinopan said, "on'y we use 'puter wire drawings, instead. You build you'self a model—tee scummies, t'ey do it out o' wood, 'cause t'ey gots no computers—an' t'en you takes tee lines direct from tee model to tee finished ship wit'out detailed plans. 'Course, tee scummies, t'ey don' know nothin' 'bout displacement an' stability calc'lations, an' t'eir mouldin' lofts suck, but I can handle t'at no sweat."

"All of which means?" Pahner pressed.

"I wanna make a half-scale model to test my numbers," Poertena told him. "T'at take about a month. T'en, if it good an ever't'ing go smooth, t'ree months for tee rest."

"*Four* months?" Roger demanded, aghast.

"Can't do it no faster, Sir," the sergeant said apologetically. "T'at's as fast as we can go, an' t'at's after we gets tee materials. I can start on tee model as soon as I gets some funds. Talked to a pretty good shipbuilder today, an' I t'ink we can work wit' him. But we gotta get timbers, an' more important, we gotta get a dozen or so masts—an' spare masts an' spars, too, an' sails, now I t'ink about it—from somewheres."

"You were prophetic, Your Highness," Pahner said sourly. "This shipbuilder, Poertena—he didn't happen to have anything to do with a fellow named Wes Til, did he?"

"Don' know, Sir. Is t'at important?"

"Maybe, but not for the model, I think. Okay, you're authorized to draw funds as necessary. If it isn't terribly expensive, buy a small craft to unstep the mast for the model. And get that shipyard to work. I want the model completed in three weeks."

"I try, Sir," the Pinopan said mournfully, "but I don' t'ink it gonna happen in t'ree weeks. I only say a mont' 'cause I know you not gonna let me have two. But I try."

A quiet knock at the door interrupted the discussion, and PFC Kyrou poked his head into the room.

"Captain Pahner, Sir, we have two Mardukan gentlemen out here with what I think are dinner invitations."

Pahner raised one eyebrow and made a pointing gesture with the index finger and cocked thumb of his gun hand. The private shook his head in reply, indicating that neither seemed to be armed, and the captain nodded to let them in.

Both of the Mardukans wore enough jewelry to open a shop, but to Pahner's admittedly inexpert eye, it didn't appear to be of very high quality.

"I'm Captain Pahner. And you are?"

"I am Des Dar," the first said, bowing slightly in the local fashion with clenched fists brought into shoulders. "I bring Prince Roger an invitation to a personal dinner with my employer, Wes Til." The messenger proffered a tied and sealed scroll. "The location and time are within. May I tell my employer that you accept?"

"*My* name is Tal Fer," the second Mardukan interrupted quickly, proffering an equally ornate scroll, "and I am sent from Turl Kam with an invitation to Prince Roger to join *him* for dinner. May I tell him you accept?"

Kyrou saw three more functionaries, scrolls in hand, approaching the prince's room and judiciously turned off his toot's translator function. Then he leaned back in through the door and caught Captain Pahner's eye.

"Three more scummy flunkies inbound, Sir."

Cord, who'd learned enough English to recognize the untranslated human term for the locals, turned a grunt of laughter into a cough.

"Sorry," he said when Des Dar and Tal Fer looked at him. "Age is catching up with these old lungs."

Pahner frowned at the private and gave the old shaman a very speaking glance, then turned back to the first two messengers.

"Sirs, please convey to your employers our delight at their invitations and—"

He stopped, out of both polite phrases and his depth, and looked appealingly at Roger's chief of staff. O'Casey's eyes creased in a smile as she looked back at him, but she took over smoothly.

"However, we are unable to respond immediately," she told the messengers. "Please convey that to your employers, along with the fact that we will reply to them as soon as possible."

The messengers jockeyed for position as they handed their scrolls to the chief of staff. She took them smoothly, with a courteous refusal to give either precedence, then gave the same message to the trio Kyrou had spotted when they arrived. Two more turned up after those, and at that point Pahner ordered Kyrou to repeat the mantra for O'Casey and closed the door. Firmly.

"We need some local input on these," O'Casey said, as she perused the documents. The text was readable, thanks to her toot, and the invitations were not only from Council members, but also from major merchants. She suspected that some of those might be more important in the long run than the Council members themselves.

"Cord, could you pass the word for Rastar, please?" Roger said. "We're going to need to get his input on these invitations and some sort of stronger feel for whether or not his forces really intend to accompany us overseas."

"Yes, My Lord," the shaman said obsequiously, and climbed to his feet. "Your *asi* lives only to obey, no matter what the dangers he must face. I will brave the hordes of messengers for you, although my heart quails within me at the very thought."

"It *is* your duty, now that I think about it," Roger said with a grin, then touched the Mardukan on a lower shoulder. "Seriously, I'm not sure I dare go out there at the moment."

"Not a problem," the *asi* said. "After all, I'm not the one they long to entice into their power."

" 'Yea, though I walk through the valley of the shadow of death, I will fear no evil,' " Roger quoted with another grin. "I'll meet you at the room after this madhouse subsides."

"I'll see you then," Cord agreed, and opened the door and forced his way into the crowd of shouting messengers.

"And tell Kosutic to send some spare guards down!" Pahner yelled to Kyrou as the door closed, then looked at Roger with a crooked smile. "Ah, the joys of civilization."

CHAPTER TWENTY-THREE

Rastar shook his head over the invitations laid out on the floor.

"Some of these I can only guess at, but you're right. Whether or not we get any support is going to depend more on these invitations than any Council meeting."

"Am I reading these right?" Roger asked. "Do they really say something like 'and bring a date'?"

"Yes." Rastar chuckled. "The local custom, decadent in the eyes of my people, is to have men and women at the same dinner. The women are supposedly there to lend an air of grace to the proceedings. I think the idea is for them to keep us from spitting on the floor."

"Bloody hell," Roger said. "Do they realize that one of my main advisers is a woman? And one of my senior officers, as well, for that matter?"

"I'm not sure," Rastar said. "But it's going to be very important for you to attend at least three of these if you hope to achieve anything here in the city. How you divide them up is going to be . . . interesting."

"Eleanora . . . ?" the prince said plaintively.

"I'll do my best," the chief of staff sighed. "I wish I understood the position of women in this society better, though. I'm getting this queasy feeling that we've arrived in the middle of the suffrage movement, which means that any time a female opens her mouth in a definitive manner, as I tend to, it's going to be taken as a political statement."

"Well, let's go on as we intend to end," Roger told her. "We're a mixed unit from a mixed society, and I don't intend to convey anything else, whatever the societal norms. Also, there's this story of a woman who organized the evacuation of D'Sley."

"There are three invitations from D'Sley nobles," Rastar noted. "But none from a woman."

"Julian," Pahner said. "Track down that story and get us some clear intel on it."

"You think it's important?" Roger asked.

"If we have to stay and fight, it will be," the captain said. "If she can organize a sealift one way, she can organize one the other way."

"Ah." The prince smiled. "Rastar, I get the feeling that D'Sley wasn't a democracy?"

"No," the Northerner said. "It was controlled by a council of nobles and a weak king. From what I've heard, the king is dead, and many of the nobles as well, but many of the commoners escaped, especially the women."

"And they're clogging the city," Julian added. "That's one of the sore points at the moment—all the D'Sley refugees."

"Just once," Roger said, shaking his head. "Just damned once, I would like *something* to go smoothly *somewhere* on this planet."

"There is a sense of *déjà vu* here, isn't there?" O'Casey laughed. "I'll set about divvying up these invitations with Rastar. You go discuss clothes with

Matsugae. I'm going to need a clean and presentable dress or suit, as are several of the Marines. We can . . . elevate their social importance for the evening."

"Oh, Lord," Roger said, grabbing his head. "Just once. Please God, just *once*." He shuddered. "Poertena. At a formal dinner? The mind boggles."

Kostas Matsugae shook his head and grimaced.

"You really don't appreciate me enough," he said.

"Probably not," Roger agreed wryly. "But we need dresses or suits for myself, Pahner, O'Casey, Kosutic, and some of the other Marines."

"Why here? They seemed to do just fine with chameleon suits everywhere else."

"The locals are a bit more sophisticated in K'Vaern's Cove," Roger said. "They deal with so many different cultures that they're more likely to notice the . . . poor condition of the uniforms, even if they don't wear clothes themselves. Unfortunately, we can't afford to create anything but the very best impression, because we need something from these guys, like a fleet of ships, so Armand wants you to coordinate with Eleanora to see to it that any appearance we present is a good one."

"Oh, very well," the valet said with a sudden twinkle. "I'll think of something. There are a couple of bolts of *dianda* left, and I'm sure the locals have some of that serge-like material I found at Diaspra, if nothing else. And I've already seen some very nice wall hangings and tapestries here, so if I look really hard . . ."

His voice trailed off thoughtfully, and Roger stood.

"Right, well, I'll leave you to it," he said.

"Hmmm," Matsugae said with an absentminded nod, but then his eyes sharpened. "Do we know who's going to be attending these events? And when are they?"

"Uh, no," Roger said as casually as possible. "We're not quite certain yet who's on the guest list from our side. But the dinners are mostly tomorrow evening," he finished brightly.

"Tomorrow!"

"I guess I'd better get going now," Roger said, beating a hasty retreat.

"*Tomorrow?!*"

"Have a good time, Kostas. Use whatever funds you need," the prince said, and disappeared out the door like smoke.

The valet stood staring at the closed door, jaw still half-dropped, for several fulminating seconds, but then he began to smile.

"Whatever funds I need, hmmm?" he murmured. "And coordinate with Eleanora, is it?" He chuckled evilly. "*This* one you're going to pay for, Roger," he promised the absent prince. "In fact, I think it's two-birds-with-one-stone-time, young man!"

Eleanora O'Casey glanced up as Matsugae walked into her office, took one look at his expression, and chortled. Then she gestured at the scrolls scattered over the floor around her.

"Look at this before you complain to me about *your* problems," she warned him.

"Oh, I wasn't going to complain," he said with a decidedly wicked grin. "I was only wondering if you'd decided on who was escorting whom?"

"Well, we've got a minimum of two separate categories of meetings going on, and probably at least three. The first category consists of the ones which are going to be crucial to getting overall political support, so those are the most critical and I'm assigning senior officers and in some cases some of our more . . . polished NCOs to them."

"All right. And the others?"

"The second category are the dinners where I can reasonably expect the majority of the conversation to revolve around military-technical issues. Bistem Kar is hosting one of those, for example. For those, I feel comfortable sending experienced but slightly less polished NCOs. Then there's a dinner invitation from a shipyard associated with Councilor Wes Til. In fact, Til is hosting the banquet."

"So he'll be there in person?"

"Yes, and I'm not entirely certain whether that one ought to be considered overall political or military-technical . . . or possibly in a third category all its own. Call it, um, logistical. Or maybe financial. Whatever, I'm assigning it the same priority as category one. Particularly since Tor Flain, the local Guard's second in command, is also going to be present."

"So who's going to that one?"

"Oh, Roger. Technically, the Council chairman is higher in rank than Til, but given the fact that we're going to have to build our own ships, the combination of economic and military aspects make this the more important meeting, I think. And if military questions arise, I'm sure Roger can field them."

"And who's he going to be escorting?"

"I haven't decided yet. Given its importance, I suppose I should go with him, but there's another that fascinates me more. One of the other Council members, who's nearly as wealthy as Til, has arranged for a dinner to which a D'Sley nobleman will be bringing the female who arranged the D'Sley sealift."

"That does sound fascinating," the valet said. "Have you decided who'll be escorting you to it?"

"No, I hadn't," she said, then looked up and raised an eyebrow at his expression. "Really?"

"I would truly like to meet the . . . formidable lady

who organized that evacuation," Matsugae said honestly. "And I believe my calendar is open."

"Okay," she agreed, pulling out an invitation scroll and making a note on it. "That's that one filled."

"Excellent. And, if I may, I believe I might have an appropriate suggestion for Roger's companion, as well."

"Christ on a crutch," Roger grumbled as he tossed his helmet on the bed the following afternoon. "I just came back from the harbor, and I see what Poertena means about tubs—those things must roll in a bathtub!"

"Well, some of us weren't able to go gallivanting about the city," Matsugae sniffed, and Roger smiled as he took in the valet's appearance. Matsugae wore a suit of dark blue velvet that was both extremely handsome and much too heavy for the local weather, and the glittering MacClintock crest of a palace servitor in personal service to the Imperial Family sparkled brightly on his breast for the first time since they'd arrived on Marduk. Its brilliance would have been sadly out of place on a chameleon suit, but it was also a proud award very few could claim, and the valet brushed it absently with his fingers as he returned the prince's regard.

"Nice outfit, Kosie! I take it Eleanora shanghaied you for the guest list, too?"

"I would scarcely choose the term 'shanghaied,'" Matsugae said primly, "but, yes, I will be attending one of the dinners tonight. In fact, Eleanora and I will be going together, thank you."

Roger's smile turned into a grin, and Matsugae sniffed again.

"It's certainly an evening out which I've earned," he said, pointedly. "While you were out playing in the harbor, I've had half the platoon cycling through my own private tailor's shop." Roger's eyebrows rose in surprise, and Matsugae gave him a triumphant smile.

"I am—justifiably, I feel—quite proud of it, since I created it in a single day. And it's undoubtedly the largest tailor's shop I've ever seen, since I had to buy an entire idled sailmaker's loft to put it in!"

"Good work, Kostas! I knew we could count on you. Now all we have to do is replicate your outfit a few dozen times over, and we'll be able to attend all the boring dinners we have to to save our own buns and K'Vaern's Cove both! When am I scheduled for a fitting?"

"You will no doubt be happy to know that you won't require a fitting, despite the fact that you chose to spend the entire day playing hooky down at the harbor instead of assisting with the preparations. As it turns out, the St. John twins are both very nearly your size and build, so I was able to use one of them as a breathing manikin. You now have a new suit. Congratulations."

"Man, you were really upset at getting this dumped on you, weren't you?"

"Not as much as it might seem. You are, I believe, attending the small dinner party with Wes Til?"

"And Tor Flain," Roger agreed, unbraiding his hair and stripping off his chameleon suit. "I don't suppose there's time for a bath?"

"One has been drawn, Your Highness," Matsugae assured him. "And who are you taking to the party?"

"Eleanora, I'd presume," Roger said with a suddenly wary expression, one foot still in his trousers as something about the valet's tone sounded warning signals. "But you said you were going with her, didn't you?" he asked suspiciously.

"Actually, I did. The two of us are going to meet with Sam Tre and Fullea Li'it, the lady who arranged the D'Sley sealift."

"Oh." Roger finished stepping out of the uniform. "Kosutic, then?"

"Being accompanied by Sergeant Julian to a meeting with Bistem Kar, I believe."

"That should be interesting," Roger observed. "Too bad I didn't draw that one. So if not Kosutic, who? Gunny Lai?"

"Accompanying Captain Pahner to his dinner with Turl Kam."

"Okay," Roger said, turning to face him and planting his hands on his hips. "Spit it out, Kosie. Who?"

"Actually, I believe Sergeant Despreaux is the next most senior female Marine," the valet said with a bland expression.

"*Oh*," Roger oofed, his expression remarkably like that of a poleaxed steer. Then he shook himself. "Oh, Kostas Matsugae, I had no concept of the depths of wickedness lurking in your soul. You are an evil, evil person!"

"*Moi?* Well, perhaps. I can state without fear of contradiction, however, that she cleans up pretty. For one of the 'help.'"

"Such an evil person," Roger whispered to himself as Despreaux came through the door.

The sergeant's blouse was a lovely shade of off-white. The sleeveless and collarless garment was made of an opaque, white linenlike material that was almost paper thin but had an odd translucence, like mother-of-pearl. The base fiber was something called *halkha*, and it came from the pods of a hemplike plant unknown on the east side of the Tarsten range. The locals used it very much as Terrans had used cotton in the days when there were no synthetic fibers, for everything from wall hangings, to sacks and coarse-woven bags used to hold tubers and grains, to sailcloth. There was, however, an enormous difference between those rough, sturdy utilitarian fabrics and the fine threads and tight weaves required to make such lovely cloth, and Roger wondered where Matsugae had found enough, on no notice, to create several outfits.

Rather than buttoning up the front, the blouse was sealed with soft, beautifully tanned leather ties up the sides and at the shoulders. Roger supposed that was because it had been impossible even for Matsugae to introduce buttons and buttonholes to the generally unclothed Mardukans in the time available to him, but the ties lent the outfit an air of barbarism that was somehow in keeping with the whole crazy affair.

The simple peasant skirt that accompanied the blouse was also white, although a shade darker than the blouse. Its pleats swirled around her long legs, and Roger winced as he looked at her footwear.

"Court shoes? Where in the hell did he find court shoes?"

"Is that all you have to say, Your Highness?" the sergeant snapped, fiddling with the unfamiliar weight of the skirt. It was the first time in months that she'd worn anything but her uniform and skivvies.

"Uh," Roger replied, suddenly tongue-tied.

"I hope your 'associate' meets with your approval," Despreaux said in tones of deadly sweetness, and Roger grimaced.

"Look, I wasn't at my very best that evening, and that wasn't the word I really wanted. But neither was 'servant,' 'help,' or 'slave.' Sometime, maybe, I can explain what I did mean to say, and why. But right now, we have a mission. If it helps, I didn't ask for this, either."

Despreaux's eyes flashed, and she threw her hands up in the air.

"Oh, sure, that makes me *really* happy, 'Milord'! Now I'm not just stuck with *you* all night, I'm stuck with somebody who doesn't want his 'associate' to sully the evening!"

Roger grabbed his hair and started to pull it, then drew a deep breath and shoved the disarranged strands back into place.

"Sergeant Despreaux. Truce, okay? I'm sorry. Does that help? I'm sorry for offending you. I'm even sorry for not taking you up on your implication, or at least seeing if what I *thought* was an implication was, in fact, an implication at all. I am very attracted to you. Was, am, and will be. I was that night. I am tonight. I will be at some future date when perhaps we can sit down and discuss the . . . problems of one Roger MacClintock and why they cause him to keep making an ass out of himself in front of beautiful women."

He drew another breath and held a hand up before Despreaux could get a word in edgewise.

"But tonight, we have a mission to complete. A very important one. And that requires that we not be clearly at odds for the entire evening. Now, can we manage to *act* like we like each other? A little? For a few hours?"

Despreaux closed her mouth and let out her gathered breath through flaring nostrils, then nodded.

"Yes, Sir. We can."

"Very well. In that case, I think it's time." Roger started towards the door, only to be blocked by the sergeant's automatic reflex action—the Empress' Own *always* went through a door before its principal.

The prince looked at her and smiled. He also noticed that the court shoes, whose high heels had come into fashion once again, made her nearly as tall as he was. He still didn't have a clue how Matsugae had managed to find shoes, but he discovered that it was distinctly pleasant to have Nimashet Despreaux's eyes on a level with his own.

"Sergeant," he said, "tonight you aren't a bodyguard. Tonight, I'm your escort to dinner, and, as such, it's my job to open the door for *you*."

Despreaux smiled back and let him open it. Then she went through first, automatically scanning from side to side.

That's what you think, she thought. *And where did the Sergeant Major get that holster? Try to get between these thighs tonight, Your Highness, and you've got a hell of a surprise coming!*

It took her a moment to realize that she assumed both that he would try . . . and that she would let him succeed.

Oh, Nimashet, you've got it bad.

CHAPTER TWENTY-FOUR

The restaurant at which Roger and his "date" arrived after a long journey from the Citadel appeared to be little more than a shack right on the edge of the water on the seaward side of the city's peninsula. North of the main portion of the city, the location was a perfect half-moon bay, partially sheltered from storms by a reef of rock clearly demarcated by the swirl of luminescence where marine organisms glowed in the gentle swell washing over it. The bay, with its strip of rock and sand beach at the foot of the high limestone cliffs soaring up to the city wall, was quite pretty, if a trifle exposed. The haphazardly built structure of gray, weathered wood perched out over the water on piles driven into the rocky shore, open on the bay side and with two small fishing boats tied up in the shelving water beside it.

Roger slid down from their *howt'e* and turned to give Despreaux a hand down. The Triceratops-like beast was a smaller version of the *flar-ta* that stood "only" two meters at the shoulder, which was still amply large to make it just a *tad* ostentatious as a mode of transport through the streets of K'Vaern's Cove. Fortunately, like most *flar-ta*, *howt'e* were remarkably placid. But they were also expensive, and the fact that Wes Til had sent one to collect his human guests was both a statement of his wealth and—Roger hoped—a deliberate gesture of respect.

Despreaux would normally have handled unloading from the beast with athletic grace, but the fifty-millimeter heels the valet had somehow cobbled together got in the way of easy dismounts from Triceratops look-alikes.

Roger smiled at the thought, then smiled again as his squad of guards spread out around him and a team went in ahead to sweep the restaurant. He found the dichotomy odd. In battle, and even on the march, Pahner and the rest of the Marines had become accustomed to letting him risk his life alongside the lowliest private. They might not like it, but they'd finally accepted that it was going to happen. Get him into a "normal" situation, though, and their reflex protectiveness clamped down like armor.

The point team returned and nodded approval, and the remainder of his guards deigned to allow him and Despreaux to enter the restaurant themselves.

The interior of the shack was far superior to its inauspicious exterior. The building was broken into several smaller rooms, separated by simple woven walls that permitted the fresh sea breeze free run of the building. There were at least two dozen Mardukans in the first section, gathered around long, low tables, picking at trays of food and sipping from bulbous containers.

Roger's nose was assaulted by the scent of cooking as he entered, and he knew immediately that whatever else happened that evening, he was about to have a superior gustatory experience.

"Smells good," the sergeant whispered.

"Now I wish we'd brought Kostas," Roger said, as a jewel-bedecked Mardukan female approached.

"He's eating with Eleanora, remember?"

"That's what I meant."

"Welcome, gentle sir and madam, to Bullur's." The speaker seemed young to Roger, possibly the equivalent of a Terran teenager. "Did you make a reservation?"

"We're here with the Wes Til party," Roger said, handing over his invitation. He was moderately surprised by the fact that their greeter was female. It was the first time since Marshad that he'd spoken to a Mardukan woman, aside from exchanging a few words from time to time with one of the mahouts' women, although his observations in the markets and at the Council meeting had already confirmed that O'Casey was right in at least one respect. Here in K'Vaern's Cove, women clearly enjoyed at least some status.

"Very good, sir," the young lady said after a glance at the scroll. Her examination of it had been long enough, and purposeful enough, to indicate that she could read the angular script. "If you'll follow me?"

"Where are we going?" Despreaux asked, planting a restraining hand on Roger's forearm before he could move.

"Through here," the hostess replied in a slightly questioning tone.

"St. John," the sergeant said, and pointed with her chin.

"On it, Nimashet," the big Marine said, following the hostess with a grin. "Why don't you just let your hair down for the evening?"

"I don't think so," the NCO said primly as she and

Roger followed St. John (J.) across the restaurant at a more leisurely pace, giving him time to check out the other room without being any more obvious about it than they had to.

"I think that would be an excellent idea," Beckley put in from behind the prince. "Letting your hair down, that is. Although, come to think of it, letting down *his* hair might be even more fun."

Roger drew a deep breath and bit his tongue rather firmly, but Despreaux's head whipped around and she gave the corporal a look like a solar prominence.

"I don't recall asking for your opinion, Reneb," she said in a dangerous tone, and the corporal chuckled.

"Nope, but them as needs help are usually the last to realize it. Just think of it as a friend trying to help you out."

"Reneb!" Despreaux began in a voice of mingled wrath and amusement, but she clamped her jaw when Roger put a hand on her forearm.

"It's not like she's the only one who thinks we're both being idiots, Nimashet." He sighed. "And the hell of it is, they're probably right! But," a wicked gleam entered his eyes, "if you won't tell them the deep dark secret of what passed between us in Q'Nkok, *I* won't!"

They reached the door opening into the last section of the building as he spoke, and St. John reappeared to nod that the room was clear just in time to see Sergeant Despreaux turn an interesting shade of crimson.

"My, my, my!" Beckley said in interested tones. "Whatever *did* happen in Q'Nkok, Nimashet?"

"Never you mind!" Despreaux snapped. "I mean, nothing happened in Q'Nkok! I—"

"*Nimashet!*" Roger's tone was one of shocked reproach. "How could you possibly have forgotten that wonderful morning?"

"There *wasn't* any wonderful morning!" Despreaux snarled, and then, as Beckley burst out laughing, the sergeant closed her eyes, drew a deep breath, and smiled in spite of herself. "Damn you, Roger," she half-chuckled. "I was willing to let you live for Ran Tai, but for that . . . ?"

She looked around the private room, the bodyguard reflex making personally certain that the room was indeed cleared, then relaxed ever so slightly. The area took up about a quarter of the interior of the restaurant, and it was occupied solely by the Councilman, his invited guests, and a few flunkies.

"Hey, you gotta catch me first," Roger told her with a wink as the Councilman and the K'Vaernian Guard's second in command came to their feet. "And kicking off those heels will give me at least a second's head start."

"Prince Roger Ramius Sergei Alexander Chiang MacClintock," Wes Til said, giving a shallow bow, "I believe that you've already met Tor Flain. May I introduce my life-mate, Teel Sla'at?" The woman beside him bowed at the waist and gave a gesture of greeting. She wore something Roger had never seen before, a magnificently worked harness of gold and lapis lazuli, and he returned her bow gracefully.

"Teel Sla'at, I greet you. And you as well, Wes Til. Well met."

"And may I introduce *my* life-mate, See Tra'an?" Tor Flain added. The guardsman had doffed his armor and instead was heavily bejeweled, with at least five necklaces, and bracelets on all four arms. His lady was even more heavily jeweled, with enough assorted metals and gems to be considered half armored. About half the total outfit consisted of a single sort of pearly gemstones, most of them greenish in cast and skillfully set in a pattern which emphasized the subtle gradations in their coloration. It made her look like some sort of Mardukan mermaid, and Roger wondered if the locals had that myth.

"I greet you, See Tra'an, Tor Flain," he said. The humans hadn't worked out the protocol for introductions at these dinners, although Eleanora had been sweating blood trying to figure it out. The biggest question was whether or not the women, who in virtually every other Mardukan society they'd encountered had been voiceless pseudo-slaves, should be greeted or even acknowledged. So far, none of the K'Vaernians had reacted with shock or outrage, and the female greeter and the conversations in the rest of the restaurant, which had involved mixed genders, also suggested that he'd hit just about the right note.

"And may I introduce Sergeant Nimashet Despreaux," he went on, gesturing to the sergeant . . . who, to his amazement, dropped a very creditable curtsy.

There was a momentary awkward pause, and then Teel Sla'at made a hand gesture of humor.

"Could you, perhaps, enlighten us as to your relationship to the 'sergeant'?" she asked politely.

Roger's eyebrows rose in a combination of surprise and dismay. Surprise because, despite the conversations that had gone on in the other rooms, he'd somehow assumed that the women would be along as a sort of window dressing. Dismay because he now had to explain his relationship to Despreaux, and even he wasn't sure what it was.

"Prince Roger and I are trying to determine if we're compatible to mate," Despreaux answered while he was still grappling with the question.

"And you have a choice?" Til asked. His tone indicated interest rather than distaste or shock, and Despreaux smiled as Roger chuckled ruefully.

"Oh, yeah, we sure do," the prince answered.

"Please, be seated," Til invited.

" 'Compatible to mate,' " See Tra'an repeated. "I understand that you humans are capable of mating at any time. Is that true?"

"Yes," Roger said uncomfortably, as he and Despreaux stretched out on the pillows scattered around the low tables. The escorting Marines took positions around the room, and Cord dropped into a lotus position behind Roger. "We can."

"Pseudo-mating is a form of social interaction and even recreation among us," Despreaux added. "On the other hand, it's a taboo subject in several of our subcultures."

"Is that a hint to drop the subject?" Teel Sla'at asked. The Councilor's mate slid a platter of thin, cooked slices of something in front of Despreaux and followed the motion by popping a slice from a similar platter into Wes Til's mouth.

The sergeant looked at the platter in front of her, then picked up one of the slices and ostentatiously ate it herself.

"Not at all. Neither Roger nor I are from one of those subcultures." She paused and picked up another slice. "This is good."

"Calan," Tor Flain said. "A shell-covered species that lives on the rocks. Preparation is laborious, but the result is excellent. How does one tell the difference between human males and females? You and R—the Prince are almost the same size."

Roger smiled as Despreaux fell momentarily silent. He picked up one of the slices and offered to feed it to her, and his smile became a grin despite himself as she glared silently at him.

"The easiest way to tell is to look for protuberances on the chest," he told the K'Vaernian guardsman. "There are other clues, but they're difficult to explain."

"Protuberances?" Flain repeated. "What are they? Or is that a taboo subject, as well?"

It was Despreaux's turn to laugh at the prince as his face flushed, and she kept her mouth shut, waiting to see how he would answer.

"It's a taboo to some people, but not to me," the prince said determinedly. "They are . . . similar in purpose to the heavier secretions on the backs of your females. They secrete a thin substance that's consumed for sustenance by human young."

"May we see them?" See Tra'an asked.

Roger rolled his eyes, and Despreaux smiled sweetly at him.

"Certainly," she said, and undid the ties at her shoulders.

"Hmmm." Til leaned forward and prodded the exposed breasts gently with his finger. "And you say these are used to produce food for your young? Is that their only purpose?"

"That and turning men into babies," Despreaux said with a silvery laugh as she did the ties back up, and Tor Flain looked at the prince.

"Your face has changed colors. Does that mean you and Sergeant Despreaux are going to mate?"

"*No!*" Roger said as Despreaux started laughing uncontrollably. "Oh, shut up, Nimashet."

"Is that a command, Your Highness?" the sergeant asked with a throaty chuckle.

"No, just a desperate attempt to steer the conversation onto less sensitive ground, I suspect," the councilor observed. "Unless I miss my guess, it seems that we've offended our guests."

"Only the more important one," Flain said. "Quick work. This is why I think inviting women to sensitive negotiations is insanity."

"Ah, my fine D'Sley import!" his mate said with a grunt of laughter. "You are so up-to-date."

"Well, it's true. You women are just too flighty."

"I wouldn't advise telling that to Eleanora," Roger said, taking another bite of the calan.

"She's your, what is the term, 'chief of staff'?" Til asked.

"Yes. She's my senior political adviser, as opposed to Captain Pahner, who's my senior military adviser."

"And a woman?" Flain asked.

"A woman," Roger agreed. "She's meeting with Lord Sam Tre and Madame Fullea Li'it this evening. And the person who's 'escorting' her isn't a senior adviser."

"So she'll be the one carrying the weight of the discussion?" Til asked.

"And any actual negotiations, political or financial, that might come up," Roger agreed, and didn't notice the looks that passed between the K'Vaernians at the word "negotiations" as he offered another bite to Despreaux. She accepted unthinkingly, and then they both froze as she nipped the slice off just short of his fingers.

"Ah, look," Tor Flain said. "He's turning red again. I say they're going to mate."

"I hope they can wait until after dinner," See Tra'an added. "I've heard wonderful things about the grilled *coll.*"

Roger cleared his throat.

"We are *not* going to mate."

"Certainly not here, that is," Despreaux corrected.

"This is an interesting restaurant," Roger said, managing not to sound—quite—desperate as he changed subjects.

"One of my family's," Flain said, accepting the change. "Most of the employees are cousins."

"It's not much to look at on the outside," Despreaux said. "I take it that was deliberate?"

"Part of its charm," Teel Sla'at agreed. "If you don't know about it, you don't come here."

"It has excellent food, though," Til added. "Tor Flain's family is well known for their fish."

"It's what we do," the soldier said with a gesture of agreement. "Father started off small, concentrating on quality. He was sure there was a market for much more expensive and higher quality products than are usually available, and there was."

"And you, Wes Til? What's your background?" Roger asked.

"The Til are one of the oldest families in the city," the councilman's mate answered.

"We bought K'Vaern's dock from him the second time he went bust," the councilor said with a grunt of laughter. "And we've managed to keep a grip on our properties. Unlike most families."

"And didn't fade away," Roger said with a nod. "That's unusual over more than three or four generations. On the other hand, we're having a hard time getting much of the feel for time with you guys."

"And you, Prince Roger?" See Tra'an asked. "You're part of a politically powerful family? How long has it been in power?"

"The MacClintocks have been the Imperial Family for nearly a thousand years now," Despreaux answered for him. "However, we're long-lived, so that's only—" She paused.

"Twelve generations," Roger concluded. "Our family can be traced back for many more generations before that, with various members holding positions of power, but there was no Empire, which meant no emperors."

"So you grew up with the exercise of power," Til said. "Interesting."

"Yes and no," Roger replied as a group of servants entered bearing steaming platters. The centerpiece was a large fish with a broad, flattened head resembling a stonefish. The head was intact, but the body had been gutted and skinned and the entire fish had been grilled with some sort of glazing.

"I'm the youngest child," Roger continued as the platters were scattered around the low tables. "I have two very competent older siblings to manage the family affairs."

"Ah," Flain said, carving a section off of the fish as the servants moved around placing small bowls of side dishes by each diner. "So you became a military commander? That's what happened to me. There was nowhere in the family that fitted my interests, so I joined the Guard."

"Not really," Roger said. "The Marines are my bodyguards. I'm their ceremonial commander, but Pahner is the actual military professional."

"You've improved," Despreaux said, taking a bite of a sliced orange root. "Yow! That's hot."

"Thanks, but I'm still not a real commander," Roger pointed out. "Just because the Marines will obey me doesn't mean I'm a Marine."

"They no longer obey you for reasons of coercion," Cord said. "You are a commander in fact, whether the law supports you or not."

"Whatever," Roger said uncomfortably. "But my 'career' isn't yet set."

"You're a sailor, as well?" Til asked.

"Only a dabbler," the prince responded, taking a slice of orange root of his own. "Wow! That *is* hot. But sweet, too." He took a sip of wine to reduce the burn, and shrugged. "I've sailed with people for whom it's a hobby, but one of our junior personnel who's meeting with your shipyard manager and the owner of the boatyard that's producing our model comes from a land of professional seamen. He's our real expert, and he worked for some years in a shipyard in his land while he was attending school, but I can talk about seafaring generalities, which is one of the reasons I'm meeting with you."

"It's a tradition among our people to assure that if any decisions are to be made at a meeting, no one there knows what they're talking about," Despreaux said. "Do your people have the same tradition?"

Roger choked on his wine, and Til grunted.

"I take it that that's a joke," the laughing councilman said.

"Unfortunately, it has a measure of truth to it," Flain said. "An inefficiency that my father expertly exploited."

"We will be making no decisions tonight," Roger said after swallowing more wine to clear his throat. "We might discuss some of the things that need to be worked out, but no decisions are going to be made."

"It isn't our tradition to make decisions over food," Teel Sla'at pointed out.

"But you do discuss things of importance?" Despreaux asked. She took a bite of the flaky fish and raised her eyebrows. "That's excellent. What's that glaze?"

"It's made from the same orange root," Flain said. "Ground very fine and mixed with wine, sea-plum juice, and some other spices which are a family secret."

"If you really want the recipe, I can get it," See Tra'an offered. "All it takes is scratching at the special place at the base of his horns."

"Is the fish a bottom feeder?" Roger asked, glancing at the centerpiece. He knew a good time to help someone by drawing fire when he heard one.

"Somewhat," Flain said quickly. "They lie on or near the bottom in large schools and rise to herd bait fish and clicker schools. They're generally caught on lines, although they can sometimes be netted with drift nets, and care is required in their preparation. They have a gland which must be removed before cooking, since it produces an oil which is quite poisonous."

Despreaux looked up quickly at that, and Roger chuckled at her expression.

"We have a similar fish in our own land," he assured the guardsman. "Some of our people actually prefer to sample small doses of the toxin it produces, though, and I gather from your tone that that's not the case here?"

"Hardly," Tor said with a grim chuckle. " 'Quite poisonous' is a slight understatement, I'm afraid. 'Instantly fatal' would probably be better."

"I see." Despreaux swallowed a mouthful, her expression uneasy, and Roger took pity on her.

"Remember Marshad and Radj Hoomis' cooking, Nimashet," he told her, and she glanced at him, then visibly relaxed at the reminder of the inept Marshadan monarch's attempt to poison his "guests" . . . without any notion of how alien their physiology truly was.

"Please, feel no concern," Flain said earnestly. "I assure you, our people—and especially my own family—have been preparing coll for many, many years. Care is required, but the preparation process is relatively straightforward, and no one has actually been poisoned in as long as I can recall."

"I'm sure we'll be fine, Tor," Roger said, and smiled encouragingly at Despreaux as the sergeant gamely helped herself to another generous bite of the fish.

"Yes. In the meantime," the guardsman went on with the air of someone once again seeking a deliberate subject change, "I'm fascinated by these ships you envision. Triangular sails?"

"We'll have a model built fairly quickly," Roger told

him. "We could do one on a smaller scale as a demonstrator, I suppose. I was down at the harbor earlier, watching some of your shipping, and I saw that you already know how to beat to windward."

"'Beat to windward'?" Til repeated.

"Sorry. A human term for tacking back and forth across the wind."

"Ah. Yes, we know how to tack, but it's a laborious process, and in light winds, especially, our ships often get caught in irons."

"'In irons'?" It was Despreaux's turn to repeat a phrase, and Roger nodded.

"He means their ships lose way before they can carry across the eye of the wind onto the opposite tack. Actually, I was a bit surprised that they tack instead of wearing ship." The sergeant rolled her eyes, and he grinned. "More sailorese, Nimashet. It means turning away from the wind in a near circle instead of turning *across* it when you change tack."

"And why should that be a surprise?"

"Because they use square headsails instead of the fore-and-aft jibs we use, and those are a pain to manage," Roger told her.

"Indeed they can be," Til agreed. "And you're quite right. At least half the time, our captains do prefer to wear rather than tacking. It takes more time, but especially in light breezes, it's often the only way to be sure you get clear around. But you have a new sail plan to allow us to avoid such difficulties?"

"I wouldn't go quite that far," the prince said, "but it should certainly make tacking a lot easier. You'll be able to sail much closer to the wind, too, so you won't have to tack as often, either. It'll still be easier to sail *with* the wind, but this ought to simplify things for you. A lot."

"So you can sail across the sea," Flain said.

"If there are any materials to build your ships," Til added.

Roger took another bite of *coll*. "Poertena believes we can purchase and cannibalize some of the local ships for parts."

"Still, that seems unnecessarily complex," Flain said, swallowing a bite of barleyrice. "It also will take some time."

"True," Roger agreed. "But there doesn't seem to be an alternative."

"Well, if the Boman weren't squatting on the forests, you could get all the masts and lumber you wanted," Wes Til pointed out. "For that matter, there's a huge stockpile in D'Sley. We've sent small raids over to recover raw materials, but the Boman are onto us now. They don't want to destroy the naval supplies, either—they may be barbarians, but they understand the decadent concept of money, and they intend to sell them at some point, no doubt. But taking any more would require an army."

"Hmmm," Roger said. "We weren't aware of that. It must be making the discussion with Eleanora interesting."

"Indeed," Flain agreed. "What are they discussing, do you know?"

"Eleanora wanted to meet the person who organized the D'Sley sealift."

"Ayeiii!" Til said. "When you mentioned that they were meeting with Fullea Li'it I hoped you were jesting."

"Why?" Despreaux asked. "Is there something wrong with her?"

"She's just—" The councilor paused, searching for a word.

"She is very direct," Teel Sla'at said with a laugh. "She speaks her mind. And D'Sley wasn't nearly so open with their women as we are, so a D'Sley woman speaking her mind is . . . unusual."

"She's also stubborn as a *turom*," Til put in.

"Then that ought to be an interesting meeting," Roger said with a smile.

"Fullea will press for your support in retaking D'Sley," Til said.

"There's no need for us to participate in that," Despreaux said. "We've done our fighting already."

"You have Bogess and Rus From to lead you," Roger pointed out, picking up another slice of orange root. "How does this do if you sauté it?"

"Quite well, actually," Flain answered. "But it's more piquant with the *coll* fish if it's raw. The problem is that no one trusts Bogess' understanding of the weapons or the tactics. Not like they trust you and Captain Pahner."

"Ha!" Roger laughed. "You'd trust unknown aliens over a known general?"

"We would when that's the reaction of the general's own army," Til said quietly. "And the reaction of the general himself. I doubt that the Council is going to be willing to leave the safety of the walls without the support of you Marines, your commander, and your 'powered armor.' "

"Bloody hell." Roger shook his head. "We're not here to fight your wars for you."

"Oh, I think we could fight our own wars, thank you," Flain said just a bit tartly, but then he paused and gave the Mardukan equivalent of a sigh. "Or we could, if we could build the support for it," he admitted unhappily, "and it will require some impetus to convince the populace that leaving the safety of the walls is the best plan. Which it is, since hiding behind the walls is a death sentence for the city, whether it comes by starvation or assault."

"Hmmm," Roger said, finishing off his fish. "Convincing populaces is one of Eleanora's specialties."

"That it is," Despreaux said. "I think that the meeting with the D'Sley contingent is going to be interesting."

CHAPTER TWENTY-FIVE

"So you are a female." Sam Tre's tone made the statement a question, and a fairly tentative one, at that. Despite his role as escort to the redoubtable Fullea Li'it, the D'Sley nobleman seemed confused at finding himself carrying on a serious conversation with a human woman, especially one who'd been represented as one of Prince Roger's senior officers.

"Yes," O'Casey said sweetly. "I am."

"And the 'Chief of Staff,'" the D'Sley female reclining on both left elbows across the low table said. "Fascinating."

"And your companion? Kostas, you are a senior officer also?" Tre asked.

"I don't think so," the valet replied with a smile.

"He's one of our logistics and supply experts," O'Casey said tactfully.

"That's one way of putting it," Matsugae said, picking at his rubbery *basik*. "Tastes like chicken and twice as many ways to prepare it," he muttered, then looked back up at his host with a slightly apologetic smile.

"Excuse me. I can't help noticing the food, which is fair enough I suppose. For want of a better explanation, I'm the cook for this expedition."

"He's in charge of support for the Marines," O'Casey corrected. "He was Roger's body servant, and was pressed into service for his present job. Which, I might add, he's performed admirably."

"Ah," Fullea said. "So we have a D'Sley nobleman, a female chief of staff, a D'Sley fisherman's widow, and a human cook." She grunted in laughter until Eleanora was afraid she would choke. "This is quite a party."

"I wish you had cooked, Kostas Matsugae," Tre said. "You're correct—there are many good ways to do *basik*, and this isn't one of them."

"I fear I made a poor choice of restaurants," Fullea admitted ruefully. "I'm learning as fast as I can, but hosting important dinners in foreign cities wasn't part of the station to which I was born."

"You're a fisherman's wife?" O'Casey asked.

"I was," the D'Sley woman replied. "Not a poor fisherman; he owned his own boat and shares in his brother's cargo barge. But not . . . rich. Not a noble by any stretch, nor a man of means."

"And he was killed by the Boman?" Matsugae asked.

"Earlier, actually," the widow said. She made a gesture of resignation. "Swept off the deck by a line. Never found the body."

"' . . . The men who go down to the sea in ships,'" O'Casey quoted softly. "I'm sorry."

"The sea gives and takes away," Fullea said. "But the problem was his brother. Tareim felt he should take over the business. I was, after all, just a woman, even if I had been advising my husband for years. In fact, he'd far surpassed Tareim in gain, and it wasn't because my husband was an astute businessman. But Tareim didn't want to hear that. He didn't want to hear anything which might have made him 'subservient' to a mere woman, and the law favored him. There was little I could do, when he took over, except watch everything start coming apart, and things kept right on going from bad to worse until I . . . persuaded him to let me advise him. After which the business recovered."

"Our device translated that as 'persuaded,'" the chief of staff observed, toying with her wineglass. She supposed, given the restaurant's obviously costly fixtures and the jewelry of the other patrons, that the wine must be an expensive vintage, but it was also thin and tasteless as vinegar. "Would that be an accurate translation?"

"The term she actually used has overtones of gentle persuasion," Tre agreed. "However, in the context, it can be assumed that the reverse was true."

"I had two thugs accost him and threaten to break both his false-arms if he didn't put me back in control." The widow made a dismissive gesture. "Of course, they never said they were working for me. In fact, they didn't know they were. I'd hired them through a friend of my husband's, and they believed they were from a moneyman Tareim owed money to. Since part of the arrangement that put me back in charge also put me in direct contact with the moneyman and left me controlling all of Tareim's payments to him, no one was ever the wiser."

She chuckled softly, and the humans joined her.

"A neat solution to the problem," O'Casey said. "But what did this have to do with the sealift?"

"I'd built up a small fleet of ships by the time the Boman swept down from the north. When Therdan was surrounded and I realized the barbarians had no intention of stopping with the cities of the League, I decided that it would be good to move my base of operations,

so I'd already arranged to shift everything to the Cove."
Fullea picked at her dinner for a moment. "At first,
when the Boman surrounded D'Sley in turn, there was
a great deal of money to be made from ferrying rich
nobles to the Cove. But then all of those who could
pay to go were gone, and there were still all those
people left."

She made another gesture of resignation.

"She organized the fishermen," Tre took up the story.
"And the cargo barges. Begged, bullied—whatever it
took—and started moving anyone who turned up at the
docks across to K'Vaern's Cove."

"Not able-bodied men," the widow countered. "Not
until the Seven tried to leave, anyway."

"Yes," the nobleman agreed with a grimace of distaste. "The Council tried to flee in the middle of
Fullea's evacuation—on private boats, and without
telling the military commanders, most of whom were
mercenaries, anyway."

"That's when it all came apart," Fullea sighed. "We
still refused to take soldiers if there were women and
children, but more and more of the soldiers turned up.
Then they started seizing the boats and not coming
back. Finally, we called it off."

"You could see where the Boman were by the burning houses," the nobleman said quietly. "It was raining, hard, so the flames didn't spread from house to
house—not on their own . . . but you could see the fires
marking their line of advance."

"You were there," Kostas said.

"Sam held the rearguard for quite a time," Fullea
responded. "But then he was wounded, and some of
his men brought him down to the docks and loaded
him on one of the ships. It was almost the last one
out."

The nobleman clapped his hands in a Mardukan

shrug. "After that, it got very bad. The final ships out . . . what they saw wasn't good."

"Sacks of heavily defended cities are like that," O'Casey said. "Fortunately, we humans, as a society, are pretty much past that. We had a bad period about a thousand years ago—the Dagger Years that caused the formation of the Empire. But since then, we haven't experienced organized pillaging. Not of major cities, at any rate."

The chief of staff toyed with the limp vegetables of a side dish.

"Are you going to go back?" she asked. "When the Boman settle down or move back north?"

The nobleman made a gesture of uncertainty.

"The Boman have vowed to remain on the southern lands until all of the cities of the south are destroyed, including K'Vaern's Cove," he said. "So we can only return if the Cove survives, and even if the Boman don't overwhelm the city walls, the Cove is weakening day by day while they squat on the timber and ore and fields. When the Boman leave, there may not be any reason to return."

"For me, I don't know," Fullea said. "I lost everything in the ferry efforts and the Battle of the Bay." She pointed at the two small necklaces she wore. "Would I wear a pair of simple *coll* pearl necklaces if I had more left? No bracelets, no rings. No ships, no funds. For me, it's all to do over." She made another gesture of regret. "I'm old. I'm not sure it's in me to start over again."

"There's also a labor problem," Tre pointed out. "We lost much of our population fighting the Boman. At least, much of our labor force. All we have left are . . ."

"Women and children," O'Casey said with a glance at Matsugae.

"Yes," the nobleman confirmed.

"And then there's the whole sticky political question," the widow added with a grunt of laughter, and the nobleman sighed.

"Too true. The Council lost all its political capital when its members tried to flee, and all the noble houses are now stained with the same reputation."

"But the nobles had portable funds," Fullea pointed out, "so they're the only ones with the money to rebuild the city."

"And no one trusts them to rebuild it and stay the course?" the valet murmured. "I can think of half a dozen ways to fix that."

"So can I," O'Casey said. "More, of course, but I think your half dozen are probably the same as the ones on my shortlist. Just one would be to offer shares in ownership to K'Vaernian interests. That's your funding problem solved right there. Offer lesser shares and a small stipend to volunteers from K'Vaern's Cove interested in rebuilding the city. Things like that. You'd end up with a limited corporation managing the city. However, it would be an economic vassal of K'Vaern's Cove."

"That's the weirdest thing I've ever heard of," Tre said. "Who's in charge?"

"The chief executive, strictly limited by a binding charter," Matsugae said, and glanced at O'Casey. "Therean Five?"

"Something along those lines, anyway," the chief of staff replied, taking an absentminded bite of limp vegetables. "But, in general, societies like that are lousy in wartime. Therean Five was a special case of a homogenous militaristic agrarian society." She paused and chuckled. "With a really funny charter, if you're a history buff."

"'And this time, we really, really mean it,'" Matsugae

quoted. "And the majority and minority opinions of the framers are required for every amendment."

"Right," O'Casey agreed, then turned back to Fullea and Tre. "But if that wouldn't work here, you could try a limited monarchy, like the Empire. The nobles get an upper house with specific powers, the commoners get a lower house with specific powers, and there's a hereditary executive that must be approved by both houses. Various other restrictions and controls have to be cranked in as well, of course. The judicial branch, for example. And it's very important for long-term success to provide for ongoing periodic replenishment of the upper house. Like I said, lots of details, but that's the broad outline."

"Do you *know* all the details?" Fullea asked after a moment's pause.

"You could say I have a firm academic grasp of them," O'Casey replied with a smile. "One point about it—whatever system you use, you really need to have either unlimited suffrage or citizenship through service. Muzzling half your population won't work as technology advances."

"You're speaking of giving women political power," Tre said.

"Yep."

The nobleman glanced over at his dinner partner, his body language clearly troubled.

"While there are certainly *individuals* . . ."

"Oh, shut up, Sam," the widow said tartly. "There was no reason—outside of some truly stupid laws written by *men*—why Tareim should have inherited, and he squandered it all until I forced him to give it back. And there are other women who could do just as well as I did—possibly better."

"But few are prepared for it, or able for that matter," the nobleman argued.

"How do you know until you try?" O'Casey asked. "I've heard this argument throughout this entire journey, but look at K'Vaern's Cove."

"Well, the Cove isn't necessarily what we'd want to become," Fullea said. "But it *is* a good argument and case in point."

"You're going to need them as a work force," Matsugae told the nobleman. "And I think they'd probably surprise you. I've worked with women from many of your people's societies on this trek, and almost all of them were more than their men were willing to admit. Even the 'open-minded' ones," he added.

"Ayiee. I get your point." Tre picked up one of the overcooked tubers. "But I'm definitely choosing the restaurant next time."

"All of this is extremely interesting, and probably valuable, but doing anything about it depends on retaking D'Sley," Fullea pointed out.

"What we don't have is the funds to hire enough mercenaries to do that," Tre said with a sigh. "Even if there were enough mercenaries in the entire world."

"So you have to convince K'Vaern's Cove that it's vital to them," O'Casey countered. "Everyone seems to agree that if the Boman squat on the resources, K'Vaern's Cove is going to wither away. So why aren't they taking the fight to the Boman?"

"Because the Boman have smashed every army that's dared to face them." Tre made a gesture of resignation. "They far outnumber the K'Vaernian Guard, and this branch, at least, is ably led. Leaving the walls would be suicide."

"And you don't have the traditions, techniques, or tactics for conscript armies, so there's no structure to allow for rapidly increasing the size of the Guard," O'Casey said, nodding in understanding.

"But all of those are easy enough to get," Matsugae put in. "Right?"

"If you're willing to pay the political cost," the historian agreed. "But for that to happen, someone with a significant political base has to see the light."

"I think that you'll find it difficult to have ships commissioned under the current conditions," Fullea said. "And *you* have some political capital."

"No," O'Casey corrected gently. "Rus From and Bogess have some political capital, and we've given them sufficient information to be able to take the fight to the Boman. Perhaps the wrong people are having this dinner?"

"No," Fullea retorted flatly. "Neither Bogess nor Rus From show a clear understanding of the techniques and technologies you've given them. It's unfortunately clear that they're still feeling their own way into adapting to these new ways of war, and because it is, the K'Vaernians are understandably reluctant to depend on them. They won't follow the direction of Bogess in the field the way that they would your Captain Pahner, who Bogess has told them is a military genius."

"Captain Pahner is very good," O'Casey said with a smile, "but not a genius. He does have that ability to stay calm in a crisis which is critical in a military commander, but generally he draws on historical background to fight his battles. 'Genius' implies innovation."

"But Bogess doesn't know the same history," Tre observed shrewdly. "Does he?"

"No."

"There you go."

"Fullea, Sam Tre," O'Casey said, "I understand your desire, but we have a schedule to keep. We *must* keep that schedule, and we're already far behind where we need to be. We can't dally in K'Vaern's Cove to help you fight your battles, and we most especially are not going to fight the Boman for you. We're not mercenaries."

"What would it take to convince you to help?" Fullea asked. "Besides a decent dinner, of course."

Eleanora smiled faintly. "I'm not the person who makes those decisions, and if I told you anything it would be the minimum requirements for us to *consider* assisting."

"Understood," Tre told her. "And those minimum requirements are?"

"We'd require more information about the Boman, their location, and numbers. We'd require a real plan, and the wholehearted support of K'Vaern's Cove, and that would have to include full support for the building of our ships and the outfitting of the army. We'd need to ride roughshod over some of the largest businesses in the city, and they'd have to take it and smile."

Tre winced and sat back, but Fullea remained leaning forward, all four hands clasped, as still and calm as a Vedic statue.

"And if all those requirements were met?"

"Impossible!" Tre exclaimed. "The K'Vaernians just aren't like that!"

"And if all those requirements were met?" the widow repeated.

"If all of them were met, Pahner would consider it," Matsugae said. "Especially if the campaign took no longer than building the ships did."

"There's no way to guarantee that," Tre said firmly.

"No, but by the time the ships were finished he'd have been able to train someone else and help them develop the experience and knowledge to take over," O'Casey pointed out. "And by then either the Boman would've been pretty well shattered or else they'd be at the walls."

"So we have to get the whole Council behind it?" the widow asked. "I can see getting *most* of them . . ."

"Even more important, you have to get the whole body of the citizenry behind it," O'Casey clarified. "Not because they control the Council, but because they'd have to work willingly for the cause."

"Do you have any ideas about that?" Fullea asked, taking a sip of wine.

It's not going to be a short dinner, is it? O'Casey thought.

CHAPTER TWENTY-SIX

Roger slumped onto the pillow and nodded to Despreaux. The sergeant had arrived early, and she looked up from her own pillow to nod back. At least her stiff acknowledgment was no longer actively hostile, but it wasn't exactly brimming over with joyous welcome, either, he reflected. Sooner or later, they were going to have to sit down and iron out their problems . . . assuming they ever managed to find the time to.

His *asi* settled quietly behind him as Julian and Tratan entered. They were followed by the rest of the staff and senior commanders, until the spacious room was rather full. Fortunately, it had large windows open on two sides to the sea breezes, so it wasn't stuffy even with the gathered staff.

Pahner arrived last, accompanied by Rastar and Rus From, who quickly took their seats.

"All right, we have to make some decisions," the Marine CO said. "Or, rather, *I* have to make some decisions. But we all need to know the parameters, so

I want everyone to present what they've learned as succinctly as possible. Then we'll decide what we're going to do.

"Poertena, you start."

"*Si*, Cap'n." The Pinopan checked his pad. "I'm gonna say t'is one more time: we don' wanna cross no blue water in t'ose tubs. We could convert one o' t'em to a schooner sail plan in about a mont', but it'd turn turtle in tee first good wind, no matter what we do."

"Can you explain that for us nonsailors?" Julian asked. "They sail them just fine now, right?"

"Sure, but t'ey only sail in t'is little millpond," Poertena replied, gesturing out the window at the K'Vaernian Sea, "an' t'ey don' get out o' sight o' land, either. T'ey can't, even if t'ey wanted to, 'cause t'ey gots no way to navigate. What t'ey gonna use for noon sights on t'is planet?" This time his gesture took in the solid gray overcast. "So t'eir ships're buil' for shoal water an' what t'ey calls 'Mediterranean conditions' back on Terra."

"Mediterranean?" Kosutic repeated, and the Pinopan shrugged.

"You see any surf on t'ose rocks?" he asked, pointing to the rocky coastline far below the citadel. "No? T'at's cause t'is little puddle of a K'Vaernian Sea ain't big enough for real swells to build—not wide enough for tee wind to build a good, heavy sea. Oh, shallow water like t'is, it can blow up nasty quick when a heavy wind does come 'long, but t'at's not what tee normal conditions are, an' if t'ey sees a blow comin' up, t'ey heads for shore or drops anchor an' lies to to ride it out. 'Cording to all t'eir hist'ries, t'at's how come K'Vaern's Cove ever got settled in tee first place, an' I believe it. But you ain't gonna be able to do t'at out on no ocean, Smaj."

"Um." The sergeant major nodded slowly, and Poertena shrugged again.

"T'ese ships is shoal built," he went on. "T'ey gots no depth of keel an' t'ey flat-floored as hell—t'at's partly so's t'ey can beach t'em jus' 'bout anywheres t'ey wants to—an' t'ey still figurin' out how sail plans work. Frankly, I surprised t'ey uses square sails an' not a lateen rig, and t'at's part o' tee problem."

"'Lateen'?" Julian repeated plaintively, and O'Casey chuckled.

"Sailor technospeak is much older than your kind of jargon, Sergeant," she said, not unkindly but with a wicked glint in her eye. "Sailors have had thousands of years to develop it, so you're just going to have to ride it out."

"But what does it *mean?*" the intel NCO pressed, and the chief of staff glanced at Poertena.

"I don't know the nuts and bolts as well as you do, Poertena, but perhaps I can help establish a context for what you're telling us?" The Pinopan nodded for her to continue, and she turned her attention back to Julian.

"Back on Earth, two different types of ship designs evolved before the emergence of steam power and propellers. Think of them as the 'Mediterranean type' and the 'Atlantic type.' The Mediterranean is very much like the K'Vaernian: essentially landlocked, shallow, and with very moderate normal wind and wave conditions. The Atlantic is a much rougher body of water, and typical mid-Atlantic conditions would be extremely dangerous for a ship designed to survive only in Mediterranean conditions.

"So the Mediterranean powers developed galleys and, later, galleases—light, shoal-draft, low-freeboard vessels, very like the K'Vaernians'—and with sail plans which utilized what was called a lateen rig, a single, loose-footed sail on a yard set across the mast at a fairly sharp angle.

"The Atlantic type evolved as a much deeper-hulled ship, to provide the sort of stability a vessel would require under typical conditions there, with more freeboard to move the deck higher to keep it clear of normal wave conditions. And unlike the Mediterranean sail plans, the Atlantic type gradually evolved a multimasted rig with two or three square sails on each mast and triangular fore-and-aft headsails—the 'jibs' Poertena and Roger keep talking about. It was a much more powerful arrangement, allowing the Atlantic type to depend primarily upon wind power rather than muscle power delivered by way of the oars, which also meant that they could be built bigger, heavier, and sturdier. Not to mention freeing up the sides of the ships to mount heavy batteries of cannon once the oar banks were out of the way."

She considered what she'd just said for a moment, then shrugged.

"It's not really my area of expertise, so I'm sure I didn't get it all right, and I've probably left out a good bit, but that may give you some idea of the kind of design incompatibilities Poertena has to overcome."

"Yep," the diminutive armorer agreed. "Even t'eir merchies, t'ey too shallow draf' for blue-water conditions, an' as for t'eir warships—!" He rolled his eyes. "Forget it. You gets a good blow, an' t'ey goin' over, no matter what you do. An' t'ey ain't never heard o' jibs or foresails—all t'ey gots is t'ose big pock—I mean, all t'ey gots is t'ose square spritsails t'ey sets under tee bowsprit. T'ose help some beatin' to windward, but not a lot. An' t'ey gots no drivers—no fore-and-aft sails on tee stern to help t'ere, neither. Nope, t'eir sail plans, t'ey suck for blue-water. T'at's why t'is design go 'way on Eart' after t'ey learn tee jib sail."

"So we teach them." Julian shrugged.

"Mebbe," Poertena conceded. "But we gots to do

it pretty quick if we gonna get t'ese ships built. An' even if we do, I been down to tee local museum and took a look at tee log from t'at one ship t'ey say crossed tee ocean from tee ot'er side. We not only gots to worry 'bout building somet'ing can handle blue-water, we gots to build somet'ing can stand up to whatever ripped up t'at ship, too."

"Ripped it up with what?" Roger asked. "Tentacles? Claws?"

"Seem like a big fish, You' Highness," Poertena said. "You gotta remember, I didn' read it direct, only tee partial translation tee locals worked out, an' tee guy writin' tee log was half outta his mind even t'en."

"Great," Julian said. "So even if we make the ships in time, we have to fight sea monsters?"

"More arguments for a fast ship," Roger said with a crooked smile. "But was this sailor sure it wasn't a submerged reef, Poertena? You can get those in what looks like open water."

"I know, You' Highness, but it real specific. 'As a grea' jaw, tearin' tee craft asunder, a demon o' tee dept's,' an' like t'at."

"Bloody hell," Kosutic said mildly. "And I thought *atul-grak* were interesting."

"So we'll have to build," Pahner said, pulling the conversation firmly back into focus. "And that's going to take at least three months. Where does that put us in terms of rations and supplements?"

"It puts us in trouble, Captain," Matsugae replied quietly, and all eyes turned to the valet. "The apsimons are helping a lot, but we're still running shorter and shorter. Warrant Officer Dobrescu is checking everything we come across in hopes of finding additional substitutes, but if he can't, we've got about four months, four and a half at the most, before we begin facing very serious dietary deficiencies."

"Time to cross the ocean once we get the ships built?" Pahner asked, turning back to Poertena.

"Hard to say for sure," the Pinopan replied. "I t'ink we prob'ly lookin' at at least a mont', t'ough, Sir."

There was complete silence as everyone in the room digested those figures. Assuming that Poertena's estimates were as accurate as everyone there knew they were, then even if everything went perfectly, with no delays at all, their supplies would run out the moment they reached their final objective. And the one thing they'd all learned here on Marduk was that things were not going to go perfectly.

"Okay," Pahner said after a moment, "we have a look at our transportation and supplements constraints. I think the term to use is 'narrow.' Rus, how do the K'Vaernians look from the point of view of large-scale weapons production?"

"There's good news and bad," the Diaspran bishop told the humans. "The good news is that the K'Vaernians are much more capable metalworkers than we of Diaspra. Much of that may be due to their worship of Krin, for just as we've learned to work with the God's water, they've learned to cast the bells which give Krin his voice. Also, their reliance upon seapower has inclined them in different directions. We of Diaspra use bombards and arquebuses mainly as defensive weapons from our fortifications, but their heavier warships rely upon artillery, and even their light galleys carry many arquebusiers and light, swivel-mounted bombards along their rails, because they use the fire from those weapons to decimate enemy crews before they board. Thus, even though the K'Vaernian Guard isn't huge, the city has great store of arquebuses aboard its ships, and great experience in the casting of naval artillery.

"Their navy depends upon privately owned merchant ships to serve as auxiliaries and to support their regular warships in battle, and so many of those merchant vessels also carry artillery and arquebuses. The bombards and arquebuses of their warships, however, are all provided by the city government, and all are built to common calibers, which isn't true of the privately purchased small arms aboard the merchantmen.

"According to the figures Bistem Kar has been able to provide to us, there are some eleven thousand arquebuses between the Navy and the Guard. All of these are of the same caliber, and 'rifling' them as you've shown us wouldn't be difficult. There are more than sufficient skilled craftsmen in the city to deal with that part of the problem. There's a large stock of wrought iron and steel on hand, as well, and although much of it has already been made into weapons and armor, it could be handily converted by the city's foundries.

"Spring steel for the mechanisms will be somewhat more difficult to produce, but not impossibly so. The breech mechanisms which you've described to us will present much graver difficulties, however. Producing them in quantity shouldn't be overly complicated, but it will take time to develop a design suited to our capabilities, to produce the machine tools required to manufacture them, and to turn them out in large numbers.

"I've discussed the problem with some of the local artisans, and in particular with Dell Mir, however, and I believe an alternative solution can be worked out. Manufacture of 'percussion caps' will actually be much simpler than the production of a suitable breech mechanism. The city's alchemists are quite familiar with quicksilver, which is also used by some of the local physicians, and there's rather more of it in K'Vaern's Cove than I'd feared would be the case. No one here fully understands the production of the 'fulminate of mercury' you've described, but Sergeant Despreaux assures us that she can teach us how to make it, and the local mint will be able to produce the caps in very large numbers, although much care will be required in actually making them.

"Frankly, the greatest problem lies in the provision of rifle ammunition. We must design new bullet dies and get them into production, but that's only a part of the problem. If we're able to put eleven thousand rifles into the true-hands of our soldiers, and if we issue sixty rounds of ammunition to each, that will require us to provide *six hundred and sixty* thousand rounds of ammunition, and I see no way we can produce that many 'cartridges' in the time available to us. I'm considering possible ways around the problem, but so far I've been unable to think of one. Of course, we could always issue muzzle-loading rifles, which would both avoid the problems of machining breech mechanisms and alleviate much of the pressure in the area of cartridge production, but it would also cost us much of the advantage in rate of fire which we'll require to face the Boman's numbers in the field.

"There's also the question of gunpowder supplies. Because the K'Vaernian Navy uses bombards and arquebuses in such quantity, and because the shore batteries use such heavy bombards, there are much greater stores of powder in K'Vaern's Cove than there were in Diaspra. Unfortunately, no one in the known world has ever contemplated the expenditures of ammunition which would be required by an army like the one we propose to build. Bistem Kar is still inventorying the contents of the city's magazines, but it seems likely that we'll be unable to meet all of our needs out of current supplies. The powder mills stand ready, and, in fact, continue to produce small additional quantities of powder even as we speak, but the raw materials—in particular the sulfur—are all imported, and the Boman have already overrun the customary sources of supply. Alternative sources exist, but it will take time to develop them and transport the needed resources to the city.

"The best news may well be that because their metalsmiths already understand the casting of bombards—and bells—they will be able to produce your new 'horse artillery' much more rapidly than I'd believed would be possible. Their gun foundries already understand the mysteries of sandcasting and other techniques you described to me, and they have much more capacity than I'd dreamed, primarily because the Cove has long since become the major supplier of artillery to all of the navies of the K'Vaernian. None of them have ever considered the innovations you've suggested, however, and their master gunsmith had something very like a religious experience when my sketches demonstrated the idea of trunnions to him. That innovation by itself would have completely transformed the use of bombards, but the addition of percussion locks for the guns and the idea of mobile land artillery has thrown the entire gun casting industry of K'Vaern's Cove into a furor. My best estimate is that there is sufficient metal already here in the city to produce two hundred bronze and iron pieces to throw six to twelve-*sedant* shot—say three to six of your 'kilos'—although doing so will require the navy to sacrifice many of its existing larger bombards to provide the required metal.

"Once again, however, the problem is time. Not so much for the Cove, as for your own timetable. The actual casting of the pieces could be accomplished within one and a half or two of your months, but boring and reaming them will take considerably longer. They have the technology, but they don't normally produce weapons in the caliber ranges we need, nor do they normally have to work under such tight time constraints, and boring a gun is a long, painstaking process."

"We can help there," Julian grunted. The Diaspran looked at him and wrinkled the skin above one eye, and the intel sergeant chuckled. "All we need is to set up a 'Field Expedient Post Hole Cutter,' " he said, and Kosutic and Pahner startled everyone else present by bursting into laughter.

"Satan, yes!" the sergeant major chortled, and laughed even harder when Roger and O'Casey stared at her in obvious perplexity. She managed to get herself under control relatively quickly, however, and shook her head as she wiped her eyes.

"Sorry, Your Highness. It's just that Julian's absolutely right. All we need is our bayonets, and we've got plenty of those."

"Bayonets?" Roger blinked, and Kosutic nodded.

"Sure, Sir. They issue us with those nice memory plastic bayonets . . . you know, the ones with the same molecular edge they put on the boma knives."

"Oh." Roger sat back on his cushion, his eyes suddenly thoughtful, and Kosutic nodded again, harder.

"Absolutely, Sir. Those things'll cut *anything*, which is damned handy, since we use them a lot more for tools around camp than we do for sticking people close up and personal. But the point Julian's making is that the field manuals tell us exactly how to build 'post hole cutters' that'll cut nice, perfectly circular post holes in anything from clay and dirt to polished obsidian. We can sure as Satan set them up to bore and cut anything the locals can cast, and they'll do the job in hours, not days or weeks."

"Smaj's right, Sir," Julian said. "Give us a couple of days to get set up, and we can bore out the barrels one hell of a lot faster than the foundries can cast them!"

"That would be wonderful news," From said enthusiastically. "It would allow us to build up a much heavier artillery train than I'd believed possible, and that should help enormously. But even if that's possible, we still aren't going to be able to field the sort of rifles-only army you want, Captain Pahner. Not in the time available. Because we can't supply the quantities of ammunition required in the time available, Bogess and I have discussed with Bistem Kar the necessity of raising additional pike regiments to make up the required fighting force. There are more than sufficient metalworkers here in the city to manufacture pikeheads and javelins in very large numbers. Indeed, from what Bistem Kar has told us, it seems very likely that we'll run out of able-bodied soldiers well before we run out of the ability to equip them with pikes, assegais, javelins, and the new shields.

"Taking everything together, then, I believe that given two months with which to work—and the sergeant's 'post hole cutter'—the foundries and artisans of K'Vaern's Cove could equip a field army with some four to five thousand breech-loading rifles, assuming that we use Dell Mir's suggested design alternative, with sufficient ammunition, supported by two hundred pieces of artillery and ten to fifteen thousand pikemen and spearmen. Allowing for gunners, engineers, and other support troops, that would come to something on the order of thirty-six thousand troops. K'Vaern's Cove is a large and populous city, but that number probably represents the maximum force which the city can muster, even assuming that the entire manpower of the Navy is brought ashore and pressed into service with the Guard and that all of the refugees here in the city capable of military service are also placed under arms. There might be a few more able-bodied men available, but larger numbers cannot realistically be removed from the city labor force without cata-strophic dislocation."

"Good God," Roger said, turning to Pahner. "Did you come up with all of that?"

"Yes," the Marine said. "If we have to stay and fight, I want to do it with the best possible equipment and the best possible field force. I'd hoped that we could put more riflemen and fewer pikemen into the field, but it sounds to me as if Rus, Bogess, and Bistem Kar have probably come up with the best practical mix of weapons and manpower numbers."

"How do you intend to train anyone on all those new weapons when none of them even exist yet?" O'Casey asked.

"I still don't *intend* to train them," Pahner said. "But the way it would be done if we ended up with no choice but to do it would be with simple wooden mock-ups until the real thing became available. Again, from the grunt's eye view, it would be primarily a matter of instill-ing the discipline the troops need and giving them confidence in their new equipment. For the officers, it would be a matter of a lot of sand table exercises to make them familiar with the capabilities—and weaknesses—of their new army. The real problem is that this would be a much larger battle to administer than Diaspra was, which means we'd be spread accord-ingly thinner and that a more comprehensive organi-zational infrastructure would be required."

"I'm very impressed with Kar," Rastar said. "And with Bogess, of course. But I'm not sure that they can both develop an understanding of the tactics and simul-taneously manage the training, particularly in the time available. For that matter, this whole concept of a 'staff' is very odd."

"All right," the captain said. "There's sufficient pro-duction to create the weaponry to equip a small field

army. We don't have a fixed number on the enemy at
this time. The time required to create the weapons
would be approximately the same as the time to train
the individuals in their use, but doing either or both
of those things would narrow our window to reach the
spaceport before the supplements run out. Sergeant
Julian, could you give us your report on the political
situation in K'Vaern's Cove?"

Julian pulled out his own pad, keyed it alive, and
scratched his chin.

"It's a pretty open democracy, so the political situation is complex, Sir. There are about fourteen major
positions on the matrix, and most have a party of adher-
ents prepared to support them at the expense of their
competitors. However, the majority parties are pretty
well represented by Wes Til and Turl Kam. Til represents old money, shipyards, and land-based mercantile
interests in general, while Kam represents the labor
groups and the actual sailing community.

"Tratan," the intel NCO continued, nodding at the
Mardukan, "has spent some time on the streets, feeling out the attitudes and opinions here in the city. I'll
let him talk about it."

"It's amazing what people talk about around a dumb
barb," Cord's nephew said. "My only problem has been
keeping up with the local dialects. You humans aren't
able to really hear it because of however those 'toots'
of yours do the translating, or so I understand from
Julian, but the locals speak a very fast pidgin of several of the coastal languages. I didn't know any of them
before we arrived in Diaspra, and I only speak one of
them with any real fluency, even now, so talking to
these people has been . . . interesting.

"In the long run, though, I think that the fact that
I don't speak the local language very well probably
helped, because it contributed to the 'dumb barb'

image and let me eavesdrop on a lot of conversations without anyone really thinking about the fact that I was there.

"What I can tell you is that the city is *very* worried. In the abstract, everyone is hostile towards the notion of taking in all the refugees from the mainland, too. The reason I say in the abstract, is that most of the refugees are staying with distant relatives, acquaintances, or what have you, and everyone thinks that *their* refugees are just fine. It's all the *other* refugees they want to run out of town."

"It's a branch of Turl Kam's party that's agitating against the refugees," Julian said. "A splinter party, really; I haven't seen any sign that he personally supports the agitation."

"True, but everyone is also extremely worried about the Boman," Tratan continued. "Because of the stories from all the refugees, they have a clear picture of what having the Boman come over the wall will mean, and no one wants to see that here in K'Vaern's Cove. Most people aren't willing to admit that they don't really buy into the idea that the Cove isn't an impregnable fortress, but the nervousness is growing, and when the food begins to run out, I think it's likely to turn into panic. At the same time, though, there's a significant voice—a very quiet one, but persistent and very widespread—that wants full-scale war against the Boman as the best way to keep them away from the city walls in the first place."

"Does it have any spokespeople?" Kosutic asked intently.

"No," Julian and Tratan replied simultaneously, and the Mardukan shrugged and gestured for Julian to continue.

"None of the arguments in favor of all-out war have a spokesperson because the idea itself seems to cross party lines," the sergeant said. "It's like an undercurrent, a strong one, that keeps turning up in all discussions of the Boman crisis. 'If only someone would face them . . . We can face them . . . We could use our might to destroy them, but . . .' That sort of thing. *Anytime* you discuss the Boman, it comes up, and the few who I've talked to who were against taking the offense were pretty defensive about their opposition."

"Same here," Tratan agreed. "This land blockade is strangling the city, and everyone knows it. They're blaming the refugees for their problems, but they really know it's the Boman."

"Also, D'Sley might or might not have the resources we need to build the ships," Julian noted. "There were significant stockpiles of raw materials there that hadn't been shipped at the beginning of the war, including seasoned wood and masts. No one's positive that the Boman haven't destroyed them since, but the consensus seems to be that they haven't because they recognize the value the stockpiles represent."

"We got that, too," Roger said.

"Tor Flain and Wes Til were very careful to point it out," Despreaux added.

"Yes," O'Casey said. "Our couple were careful to make the point, too. But they were also careful to point out that getting access to those supplies would require more than a raid."

"That depends on your definition of 'raid,'" Pahner said, "but I agree in general."

"And if there aren't sufficient materials here in K'Vaern's Cove," Roger added, "cutting the needed timber upriver from the city would require a military covering force to keep the Boman off the woodcutters, and managing that would be almost as difficult as taking and holding D'Sley in the first place."

"Let me make one thing clear," Pahner said. "In my

opinion, there's no way to face the Boman with Marines and Northern cavalry alone. Any kind of confrontation in the field would require the backing, at the absolute minimum, of the K'Vaern's Cove Guard and everyone we could pry loose from their Navy, and that would be a dangerously slim field army, with virtually no margin for any sort of losses. It would take a fully mobilized citizenry to field the much larger army Rus is talking about building, and, frankly, even that would be none too heavy a force to go up against someone as tough as the main Boman horde sounds to be."

"We actually put it that way in our conversation with Sam Tre and Fullea Li'it," O'Casey said. "No support without a fully mobilized citizenry."

"You think we could take them . . . if we had to, that is?" Roger asked.

"With artillery and breech-loading percussion cap rifles added to the pike and assegai regiments?" Pahner nodded. "Yes."

"Excuse me, Sir," Kosutic said, "but are you suggesting that we stay and fight?"

"I'm suggesting that we consider it," the CO said. "Tratan, what do you think?"

"Fight." The Mardukan shrugged. "You need the willing support of the K'Vaernians to build your ships, and their construction requires materials that are on the other side of the Bay, underneath the Boman. Also, I think kicking their barb asses would be a good idea on general principles."

"Poertena?"

"Fight, Sir," the Pinopan said. "We need tee pocking timber."

"Sergeant Despreaux?"

"Fight, Sir," the NCO responded. "We're going to be here, either way you look at it, when the Cove goes head-to-head with them. However it looks *now*, I don't think we'd get away with sailing off into the sunset *then*."

"Julian?"

"Fight, Sir. All the other reasons, and I've developed a real case of the ass about barbs, Sir."

"Let's cut this short. Anyone against?"

"Not against, really," Kosutic said, "but the troops are getting worn close to the ragged, Captain. Nothing against the boys and girls, but we saw a lot of over-reaction in Diaspra. It's something to keep an eye on."

"Noted," the CO said. "But that's not an objection?"

"No, Sir," the sergeant major said, and the captain leaned back on his pillows and looked around.

"All right. If the Council can build a consensus for all-out war against the Boman, elements of the Empress' Own will participate as cadre trainers and advisers in return for full-scale support in building a fleet of fast, blue-water ships. Preproduction of the ships should begin at the earliest possible moment."

"We need intel," Roger said. "We don't really know what the barbs' main force is doing. We think it's sitting in Sindi, but we don't really know that for sure."

"Absolutely," Pahner agreed. "And when we know where it is, we'll start to plan. Right now, however, the basic plan is to start from D'Sley. Retaking that will be the first step however the intel stacks up; after that we can work the rest out."

"Recon teams?" the sergeant major asked.

"Yes. Use Second Squad and send Gunny Jin out to coordinate it. Keep Despreaux here, though; we need her to work with the alchemists." Pahner leaned back and his eyes went unfocused. "And add shovels to that list of vital materials."

"And maps," Roger said. "And axes. And we probably need to get Poertena or Julian involved with Rus and Bistem Kar to be sure their projected numbers for raw materials are accurate. No offense, Rus, but we're talking about a production scale like nothing that's ever been done around here before."

"No offense taken, Your Highness," the Diaspran assured him. "Having someone double-check our estimates would make both of us feel much better, actually."

"A thousand and one questions, people," Pahner said, picking up his pad. "Including how to get the K'Vaernian in the street solidly behind the war. We need them all answered. Sergeant Major, get the reconnaissance out. Don't just use the squad. There's too much area to cover, so use local woodsmen and some of Rastar's cavalry, too, and pass out all the communicators you can scrounge. Eleanora, get to work on a propaganda program to get these K'Vaern's Cove people fighting mad. Poertena, we need you on the ships, so that leaves you, Julian, as our premier armorer."

"Joy," the NCO said with a grin.

"That's 'Joy, Sir,'" the captain told him, eyes on his pad as he entered notes. "Look over the materials numbers and production estimates with Rus, then work with Rus and this Dell Mir on designs. I suggest that you get His Highness involved in that, as well, and I'll be looking over both of your shoulders."

He made another entry on his pad, then looked up and raised an eyebrow.

"Why are you all still sitting here?" he asked mildly, and various people found themselves pushing to their feet almost before they realized they were moving. The Marine smiled wryly as they began filing out, but then he raised one hand.

"Stay a moment, Roger," he said.

"Have you been naughty again?" Julian whispered as he passed the prince on his way to the door. Roger only smiled and shook his head, then walked back to the company commander.

"Yes, Captain?"

"Sit down," Pahner said, pouring a cup of wine. "I want to discuss a couple of things with you."

Roger accepted the wine warily.

"I made up with Despreaux . . . sort of," he said. "Or, I think I have, at least. In a way. Kind of."

"That's not the point of this discussion," Pahner told him with a frown, "although we do need to discuss that sometime, too. But this is a 'professional development' counseling session."

"Professional development as a prince?" Roger asked with a grin. "Or as a Marine."

"Both," the captain said, and Roger's grin faded as the Marine's somber expression registered. "I want to talk you about your actions since . . . Marshad, basically."

"I've been holding up my end," Roger said in a quieter voice. "I . . . think I've even gotten most of the troops to like me."

"Oh, you've done that, all right," Pahner said. "In fact, you're a fine leader, from an officer point of view. You don't undercut your NCOs, you lead from the front, all that stuff. But one of those good qualities is also a hell of a problem."

"Would that be leading from the front?" Roger asked.

"In a way." Pahner took a sip of his wine. "Let me tell you a little story. Call it 'This Is No Shit,' since it's a space story. Once upon a time, there was a Marine sergeant. He'd seen a few engagements, but one day he did a drop on a planet after a pirate raid had been through."

The captain took another, much deeper sip of wine, and Roger suddenly realized he'd never seen the Marine really drink. Until today.

"It wasn't pleasant. I think Despreaux talked to you once about coming in behind pirates. We seem to do it too often, and you only have to do it once to get real excited about pirate hunting.

"So, after that, the sergeant in our little story did just that—he got *real* excited about pirate hunting. In fact, the sergeant got so excited that one time he took a bunch of buddies and raided a ship that they just *knew* was a pirate at a neutral station.

"And it was one—a pirate, that is. But so, it turned out, were about half the spacestation's permanent personnel, and the cruiser the sergeant and his buddies were assigned to ended up having to fight its way off the station and nearly took a shitload of casualties. All because a sergeant couldn't figure out when it was appropriate to go hunting pirates, and when it wasn't."

Roger watched the captain take yet another drink of wine.

"What happened to the sergeant?"

"Well, all sorts of things went wrong at that spacestation. Among other things, the commander of the cruiser hadn't really been supposed to dock there in the first place. So nothing, officially, happened to the sergeant. But it took him a while to make gunny. Quite a while. And even longer to make captain."

"So I should quit chasing barbs," Roger said flatly.

"Yep," the captain said. "There's too many of them for the few you kill to matter a hill of beans. And when you're killing barbs, Cord and the platoon are trying to keep you alive . . . and having a damned hard time of it.

"But that's not all I'm getting at, either. Another reason that sergeant went on a private expedition was that he'd been on combat ops too long. After a point, you start trying too hard, not caring about what happens, whether you live or die. I think most of the platoon is there right now, Roger. That's what the Smaj was getting at a few minutes ago. But, frankly, son, you're showing the worst signs of all."

"And I'm the worst one to be showing them," Roger said very quietly.

"Yep," the Marine said again. "Want to talk about it?"

"Not if I can avoid it." Roger sipped his own wine and was silent for several seconds. Then he shrugged minutely. "Let's just say that I feel somewhat responsible for the entire situation."

"Let's just say that you feel *very* responsible for the situation," the captain told him. "Which is bullshit, but telling you that doesn't help, does it? And now you see the Marines as people—*your* people—and even the new, native troops to an extent, and every one of them you lose is like a piece of skin ripped off your body."

"Yeah," Roger half-whispered, peering down into his wine.

"Didn't they have a class about that—several, actually—at the Academy?"

"Yes, Captain, they did. But I'm afraid I didn't pay as much attention as I should have," the prince answered, "and I'm having a difficult time applying the lessons."

"I'm not surprised," the Marine told him almost gently, and Roger looked up quickly. Pahner smiled at him. "Roger, don't take this wrong, but part of the problem is that at heart, you're a barbarian yourself."

"I'm what?" Roger blinked in surprise.

"A barbarian," Pahner told him. "Mind you, being a barbarian isn't always such a terrible thing. There are barbarians . . . and barbarians, you know, and you don't have to be a butchering maniac like the Kranolta or the Boman to have what the Empire thinks of as 'barbarian' qualities. Just like some of the most 'civilized' people you're ever going to meet would cut your throat for a decicred if they thought they could get away with it. The thing is, the Empire has gone all civilized these days, and the qualities of a barbarian warrior aren't exactly the ones your lady mother's better classes of subjects want to see when they invite someone over for a high tea. But the qualities the people at those teas denigrate as barbaric are the ones the soldiers who keep them safe have to have. Courage, determination, discipline, loyalty, passion for your beliefs, and the willingness to lay it all on the line—and lose it, if you have to—out of a concept of honor and responsibility, rather than looking for compromise and consensus because 'violence never settled anything.' The military has always been out of step with the mainstream culture in most wealthy societies which enshrine individual liberty and freedom, Roger. It has to be, because those sorts of societies don't have the natural 'antibodies' against foreign and domestic enemies that more militaristic ones do. By and large, I think that's a very good thing, even if I do sometimes wind up thinking that most civilians are over-protected, under-educated drones. But the reason I think of them that way is that *I'm* a barbarian by their standards, and they keep me around because they need someone with barbaric qualities to keep them safe in their beds at night. I don't imagine you ever really realized that you had those qualities, too, before we hit Marduk, and I hope you won't be offended if I say that no one else realized that either. Except for Cord, maybe."

The captain sipped from his cup once again, his expression thoughtful.

"I hadn't really thought about it before, but you and he are almost mirror images, in a way. You come from the most protected place in the most powerful and civilized empire in the known galaxy, and at the moment you find yourself on a barbarian planet at the ass end of nowhere, and in some ways it's like you were born to be here. Cord comes from a bunch of ragged ass barbarians in the middle of a godforsaken jungle full of *flar-ke, atul-grak,* and killerpillars, but he was educated at Voitan, and there's a sage and a philosopher down inside him, as well. There's some sort of weird resonance there, one I don't imagine anyone outside the two of you really understands, but it's certainly real. Maybe that resonance is why he slipped so easily into the mentor role for you. Or maybe it was just that, unlike any of the rest of us, he had no preconceptions where you were concerned, which let him see you more clearly than the rest of us did.

"But whatever it is, Roger, you need to be aware of what you really are. You can't afford not to be, because of *who* you are. I'm not just talking about the situation we're in here on Marduk and your place in the chain of command, either. You're the Heir Tertiary to the Throne, and somehow I don't think you're just going to fade into the woodwork again when we get you home. But you're going to be up against some operators who are used to manipulating people with a lot more life experience than you have, and if they have a better read than you do on who you are and how you think, you're screwed."

"I don't guess I ever thought that far ahead," Roger said slowly.

"I'd be surprised if you had. However you got here, you're in the position that every junior officer worth a flying fuck finds himself in sooner or later, Roger. To work with your troops, you almost have to love them. If you don't give a damn about them, that comes across, and not caring is like an acid that corrodes whatever you have inside that's worth keeping. But you also have to be willing to let them go. People die, son.

Especially Marines, because we're the ones who volunteer to be at the sharp end of the stick. That's what we do, and sometimes we crap out, and sometimes the mission means that we have to die or, worse, we have to let our *people* die . . . or choose which of them are going someplace we know some of them won't be coming back from and which of them aren't buying a ticket this time. Either way, Roger, when it's time, it's time."

Roger crossed his arms and looked away, his mouth a stubborn line, and despite his own sincerity the captain almost laughed at how hard the onetime royal brat was fighting against accepting what he knew was true. There was nothing at all humorous about it of course, and Roger would never have forgiven him for even the driest chuckle, yet the irony was almost overwhelming as the captain reflected on how the mighty had fallen . . . and how much Roger had discovered that losing *his* people hurt.

"Roger, here's the bottom line. If you stick yourself out on a limb, everybody else climbs out there with you, and now it's less because they have to than because they *want* to follow you into whatever desperate situation you've managed to find. There are times when that's good, but only when things are *already* desperate. So quit climbing out on the limb, okay? It might make you feel a little better, because you're sharing the danger, but it just gets more troops killed in the end."

"Okay."

"For what it's worth, you seem to be a natural born leader, and it's not just your hair. The Marines are bad enough, but the Diasprans seem to think you shit gold. It's an unusual commander who can cross species like that. I can't. They respect my judgment, but they don't think I walk on water."

Roger inhaled deeply, then nodded.

"So what you're saying is that if I go out and do something stupid, it's not just the Marines I'll imperil."

"No, it isn't," the captain agreed. "So start letting other people take point, all right? We all know you care, so put down the rifle."

"Okay," the prince said again, then met the Marine's eye. "How does this affect my command?"

"Like I said before, it's going to be a reserve. If I need you, I'll use you, and you'll go out with the scouts if everything works out right. But *behind* the scouts, right?"

"Right," Roger said. "Behind the scouts."

"Take care, Your Highness," Pahner said, nodding in dismissal, and Roger set aside his wine and rose.

"Good night, Captain."

CHAPTER TWENTY-SEVEN

"It worked," Wes Til said as he swept into the room, and Turl Kam looked up from the letter he was drafting.

"They agreed?"

"They're willing to agree, with some tremendous qualifiers—the most serious of which is that we have to demonstrate our willingness to fight a 'war to the knife,' as Prince Roger puts it. He seems awfully fond of that phrase . . . I wonder if it could be the motto of his House?" The councilor thought for a moment, then made a throwing-away gesture. "At any rate, that's what they demand—that we throw the entire power of the city into the war. No faction fighting, no politicization of the commands, and no graft."

"That won't be simple," Kam said, sitting back. "To get agreements, we're going to have to make promises, give favorable contracts, that sort of thing."

"As long as it doesn't have any negative effects, I think anything goes." Til sat on a cushion. "They also require us to throw our support behind building these ships of theirs. They want them completed while the campaign is actually underway."

"Where do they expect us to get the materials?" the Council chairman demanded in exasperation.

"Well, they've already said that the first stage has to be the retaking of D'Sley to use as a base, so the materials will be available. And let's be honest, Turl. Sure, materials are tight here in the Cove, but they're not as tight as we've been telling them. The Navy is still sitting on its minimum stockpiles, and if the Council officially agrees to help build their ships, you and I can pry at least the keels and ribs out of old Admiral Gusahm if we have to."

Kam grabbed his horns and pulled at them.

"Krin! I *hate* trying to get things out of Gusahm. He seems to think he invented the entire concept of navies and that everything that floats is his own private property!"

The chairman stared into space, trying to suppress a shudder as he pictured the looming confrontation with Gusahm, yet he knew Til was right. Eventually, Gusahm would yield, however gracelessly, to the direct orders of his civilian superiors. The real problem was going to be lining up the political support to meet the *rest* of the humans' demands.

"Can you swing your faction? I *think* I can convince the fishing contingent, and the trade faction is already screaming for me to do something."

"We need to do more than convince them," Til said. "We need to get them enthusiastic. To raise an army the size of the one the humans insist is necessary, we're going to need every able-bodied sailor from the Navy, and we're going to have to triple the Guard, as well, and that will require volunteers."

"Our citizens are very civic minded, but I'm not sure we can get all the volunteers we need with a straight appeal to civic duty. You have any suggestions?" the former fisherman asked. "Because I'm not sure those kinds of numbers are possible."

"Yes, I do have a suggestion. Or rather, O'Casey had some," the merchant said. "Very good ones, at that. That human is tricky."

"Suggestions such as what?" the chairman asked skeptically.

"You know," the councilor said pensively, "the Cove has a reputation for pinching coins till they squeal. I'm certain a lot of that reputation comes from jealousy among other cities that can't seem to pinch quite as tightly as we do, but there may be a little truth to it. So what we have to ask ourselves is what one factor could convince our mercenary countrymen that taking on the Boman would be a good thing?"

"So are we going to fight, or not?" Chem Prit asked as the squad of New Model pikemen navigated the streets of the city.

"I don't know, Chem," Krindi Fain said. This was the first evening their company had had off, and he didn't really care one way or the other about what the high command was thinking. He and Erkum Pol had a pouch of silver each, and he was far more interested in the fact that somewhere up the street was a tavern that served soldiers. "When Bogess tells us to fight, we fight. Until then, we wait."

"I hate waiting," Prit complained.

The private was a replacement, and not much of one, for Bail Crom. He'd been at the Battle of Diaspra, but not with Fain's squad, and he wasn't fitting in well.

"You hate everything," Fain responded. His tone was absent, for he'd spotted the tavern he'd been told about. Most of the drinking places in the town had prominent signs denying entry to thieves, itinerant singers, and soldiers. Unless they wanted to go all the way down to the docks, this was one of the few taverns available.

"Keep your hand on your cash," the corporal said as they approached the open door. "I hear a singer."

The dirt-floored room was long and low. Something about the setup made Fain sure it had been a stable at one time, but if there was any remnant of the stable smell it was overwhelmed by the stench of urine and rotting beer. Drinkers lounged on piles of barleyrice straw, their drinks and food propped on low tables that were no more than heavy planks set on split logs, and listened to the crack-throated singer in the middle of the room.

The bar, such as it was, was at the far end—a broad plank laid on a set of upended kegs. The corporal led the half-dozen pikemen through the gloom, stepping over and around vomit and less identifiable substances, until they reached their objective.

"What've you got?" Fain asked the barkeep, turning sideways to the bar to keep an eye on the scene behind him. With itinerant singers around, there were bound to be thieves, as well.

"Beer or channy leaf," the bartender replied. "There's a mite of plum wine, but I doubt you've the pocket for it."

"How much is the beer?" Prit asked.

"Three silver a mug."

"*Three silver?* That's outrageous!" the replacement snapped. "By the God, I never should've left Diaspra! These damned K'Vaernians are all thieves!"

"Shut up, Chem." The corporal backhanded the loudmouth on the ear. "Pay no attention to the idiot," he told the barkeep. "He hasn't got the wet out from behind his horns."

"You need to keep him muzzled, then," the bartender

said, setting down something heavy and pulling his false-hand out from under the plank. "In case you Diaspra fuckheads hadn't heard, we've been cut off from most of our supply for fucking months. He'd better be glad there's beer to be had at all. And another shitass remark like that, and I'll have you out the door."

Prit started to open his mouth, and Fain backhanded the private again before the retort got out.

"We only have bar silver," he told the bartender.

"I've the weights," the barman said, opening a lockbox.

"You don't mind if I take your measure, do you?" the corporal asked. "Not that anything would be off, of course."

"Not if yours are right, there wouldn't be," the bartender replied with a grunt of laughter.

Fain pulled a sculpture of finely carved sandstone out of his pouch and compared it to the silver-piece weight on the K'Vaernian's scales. The two pans balanced almost perfectly, and the corporal grunted in satisfaction at the proof that the bartender was fairly honest in his scale and base measure.

"There's a law against illegal measures in the city," the barkeep said as he measured out the silver in the corporal's pouch. "I'll give you a hair over standard measure on the silver if you want to change it all for coin," he added.

"Why? Because you love our faces?" Prit asked.

"By Krin, you really are a walking invitation to have your face smashed, aren't you?"

"All the same, he's got a point," the corporal said. "Why give us better than standard measure?"

"My littermate's a silversmith. A bit over standard is still better than he has to pay for bar silver."

"Done," the corporal said. "I'd rather have it in coin, anyway."

"Where'd you come up with all this?" the barkeep asked, serving out mugs as he weighed and changed the contents of their pouches. The bulk silver was in irregularly shaped thumb-sized nuggets that looked like shiny knucklebones.

"Them Boman was rolling in it," Prit said. "We just got our pay from that last fight."

"Thought so," the barkeep said. "You Diaspra guys are the only silver we've seen in a while. Surprised to see infantry with cash, is all."

"It's why I came in with these twerps," the private told him. "I'm for some more loot, loot, loot! These Boman took Sindi, they're going to be shitting gold."

"You'll be shitting yourself when you finally see them, you gutless infantry bastard," a Northern cavalry-man said, looming out of the darkness. "Give me some more channy leaf, you K'Vaernian thief."

"You'll be keeping a civil tongue in your head, or you'll be chewing with one side," the bartender snapped. "Five silver."

"It was two before," the cavalryman snarled.

"The price goes up with the aggravation," was the reply. "Make that seven."

"Why you pissant thief!" The cavalryman's hand dropped to his sword.

"Let's not get carried away here," Fain said, look-ing to see if there were any cavalry NCOs in the joint.

"Fuck off, you infantry maggot," the cavalryman slurred, spinning on the slightly smaller junior NCO. "It wasn't for you fucking Southerners, we wouldn't be in this mess."

"Hey, forker, we're all soldiers together," the cor-poral said with a grunt of laughter. "Let me stake you to a round of beer."

"I don't need any of your damned silver, either!" The Northerner slapped the corporal's hand and sent the

freshly counted coins, more than an infantryman's pay
for a month, spinning into the gloom. "Short leg bastards. Do nothing but slow us up."

"Corp," Pol said slowly. "He knocked . . ."

"I know, Erkum," the corporal said calmly. "Look, fellow, that was uncalled for. Now, I know you've got
problems—"

"*I* don't have any problems," the cavalryman growled,
picking the junior noncom up by his harness. "You do!"

The corporal hit the low table sideways, spilling beer
and less mentionable products of the local economy
across the revelers. He rolled away from the group as
it surged to its feet and tried to come back upright
himself, only to run into another set of backs instead.

"*DIASPRA!*" Prit yelled, and plowed into the cavalryman, all four arms windmilling.

Fain took a kick to the ribs and flipped the kicker
onto his back, then came vertical with a twist and a
heave, but by the time he regained his feet, the bar
had turned into a giant free-for-all. A club hit him in
the side of the face, and he felt a hand pulling at his
pouch.

"God bedamned minstrels!" he snarled, and grabbed
the itinerant singer by the horns and spun the thiev-
ing bastard off into the melee. He ducked another
swinging club, catching it on his own horns, and kicked
the club swinger in the balls. His assailant went
down . . . and he suddenly found himself faced by the
Northerner and three of his larger friends.

"It's time to clean up this bar," the original trouble-
maker snarled.

"Let's be sensible about this, folks," the infantry corporal said, although sense seemed to be in short supply.
"Nobody wants to get hurt."

"And nobody's gonna get hurt," another of the
cavalrymen said. "Except you."

"Leave my friend alone." Erkum Pol's voice was so quiet it was almost inaudible through the tavern's bedlam, but the order was accompanied by a whistling sound.

"Why?" the original cavalryman scoffed, never looking away from Fain while he raised a large chunk of wood purposefully overhead.

If there was a verbal answer from the simpleminded soldier, it wasn't audible over the sodden thump and the crunch of bones as the hard-driven plank crashed into the foursome.

Fain stepped back as the cavalrymen hit the ground, then grabbed the tabletop before the improvised battering ram could be drawn back for another swing.

"Good job, Erkum. Now, eet's time to pocking leaf."

"But I never got a beer," the private complained.

"Take one," the proprietor said from behind his pile of kegs. "Take a keg. Just get out of here before the Guard arrives."

"They destroy our taverns and inns, carousing day and night," Dersal Quan complained. The Council member twisted his rings in frustrated exasperation. "And the stench!"

"Yes, and that's another thing. What with the shortages and all, we don't need all these soldiers waving their money around. It's just driving up prices and leaving the penniless . . ."

Sual Dal, the representative for the cloth merchant's guild, paused, trying to find the word he wanted.

"Pennilesser?" Wes Til suggested. "Yes, yes. It's a terrible thing. People having money to spend is quite awful. Fortunately, that's not much of a problem in a city like K'Vaern's Cove just now."

"Don't take this so damned lightly, Til!" the

guildsman snapped. "I don't see any of these folks buying sails or any of their silver lining the pockets of my guild. It's all going for beer and channy leaf."

"And fish," Til countered. "And whatever other consumables can be found in the city. For that matter, there was a large purchase of fine woven materials lately, wasn't there?"

"It was all material bound for Sindi," the guildsman said with a gesture of resignation. "We practically took a loss."

"Practically and actually are two different things," Til replied. "The problem isn't the soldiers from Diaspra. Nor is it the Northerners. Or even the refugees. The problem is the Boman, and until we get rid of them, we're all going to be taking a loss."

"That's all well and good to say, Til, but it's not so easy to do," Quan said, twisting his rings again.

"No," Til agreed. "It won't be easy, and it won't be cheap, but until it's done, we're all going to do nothing but lose money. Sooner or later, it's going to catch up with us. I'm set pretty well, but I understand that you, Quan, had already paid for a large shipment of copper ore coming out of Sindi. Yes?"

"Yes," the businessman growled.

"And are you ever going to get that shipment?"

"No."

"And how are the rest of your investments doing? Well?" He paused, but there was no answer. "Thought not. As for sails, I don't see *any* ships being built, do you, Sual?"

"No," the guildmaster admitted.

"On the other hand, the humans are planning at least six very large ships with a *brand-new design of sail*. A very special kind of sail whose new shape and size will, I'm sure, require only the best of weavers and sailmakers."

"Ah?" the guildmaster grunted. "Really? That's . . . interesting news."

"But to build those ships, they need materials—*lots* of materials. They were going to just buy some of the ships that had been laid up and take them apart, but if we could retake D'Sley and get the materials from there, it would be much better for them. And, of course, that would mean that they wouldn't be cutting up the already available sails from the ships they'd purchase to make their new, special sails."

"Ah."

"And as for you, Quan, they're discussing a radical new version of arquebus and a new-style bombard. All of them will have to be made somewhere, and if I recall correctly, your foundries aren't doing a lot of business just this minute, are they?"

"Ah." The industrialist thought about that for a moment. "Where's the money for all of this going to come from?"

"Where did the money all these soldiers have been throwing around come from?"

Wes Til leaned back and watched as the concept settled into their minds. Oh, yes, that Eleanora O'Casey was a sly one. Better to do anything to get her on her way before she decided to just go ahead and take over K'Vaern's Cove lock, stock, and barrel! But for now, at least, they were all headed the same way, and O'Casey's shrewd contributions were pushing the ship along nicely.

CHAPTER TWENTY-EIGHT

Krindi Fain stood braced outside the company commander's office and willed his heart to stop. It had been three days since the fight in the bar, but he was certain the Guard had finally tracked them down. He'd heard through the grapevine that the cavalry shits were still in the hospital—one of them had been touch and go, according to the scuttlebutt—and two guardsmen had been in with the CO since early morning. That could only mean one thing, and when the summons had come, he'd nearly run for it. K'Vaern's Cove was an easy city to get lost in, after all, but he'd finally decided it was better to face his punishment.

"Fain. Come!" the CO called.

The commander was a regular, a young officer who'd been a sergeant in the Guard of God before the humans turned up. He'd initially resented being placed with the pikes, until it became clear that the New Model Army was where everything was happening. He had, however, already had quite a career before his posting to the regiment, including a brawl in the distant past with some Northerner cavalry that had left him with only one horn and blind in one eye. Maybe that would mitigate the punishment.

"This who you're looking for?" the commander asked one of the guardsmen with a head jerk in Fain's direction.

"You Krindi Fain?" the guardsman asked.

The corporal knew he was in trouble now. It wasn't just a couple of guardsmen, but one of the Guard's underofficers.

"Yes, I am," he answered. Best to keep it simple. The more you said, the more likely you were to make a mistake.

"Good," the underofficer said. "Little thing, aren't you? Sergeant Julian made it sound like you were five hurtongs high and breathed fire."

"I don't know how I'm possibly going to run a company if my best people keep getting pulled out from under me," the CO groused.

"So this isn't—" Fain stopped and backed up before an over-active mouth could get him in the trouble he might just have skated out of after all. "What is this about? Captain?"

"We're going to change weapons again—you knew that, right?" the company commander asked.

"Yes, Captain. Muskets, or some word like that."

"Well, that's been changed again," the Guard underofficer said. "The weapon's still being designed, but it's going to be something else—something called a 'rifle.'" He snorted. "Arquebuses may be all very well for those pussies in the Navy, but they've never worked half the time in the field, so I don't see these 'rifles' working any better. But you're one of the ones pointed out by the humans as a good person to participate in what they call 'weapons development.'"

"Oh," Fain said faintly.

"You're to take one other member of your squad, as well," the CO informed him. "Who?"

The young NCO hesitated for only a moment.

"Erkum," he said.

"Are you sure?" the CO asked with a laugh.

"Yes, Captain," Fain replied. "I know it sounds funny. But I also know I'll take care of him, and I don't know that about my replacement."

"Good enough." The officer stood up behind his low desk and offered his true-hand, human fashion. "Good luck, and do the Regiment proud."

"I will, Captain." The NCO turned to the guardsmen and made a gesture of question. "What now?"

"Get your gear loaded up," the underofficer said, and jerked a true-hand's thumb at his fellow guardsman. "Tarson here will escort you to your new quarters." The officer grunted a laugh. "Congratulations, you're moving down in the world."

The workshop was deep beneath the Citadel, a natural cavern filled with the whisper of winds flowing through ancient limestone passages. Besides a long, deep light well, at least partially manmade, the room was also lit by torches, candles, and lanterns until it was nearly as bright as day. All, apparently, to support the eyes of one Mardukan.

That person was standing in front of a large wall of limestone which had been smoothed to the consistency of glass. The white wall was heavily overlaid with black charcoal scribbles, and those scribbles were getting thicker as the ancient Mardukan covered the wall in meandering doodles like a cave painter of old.

Most of the scribbler's constant mutter was directed at Rus From, who was following him around with a bemused expression. Other than that, Fain recognized a couple of other members of the pike regiment. And, especially, a couple of the humans.

Pol followed him like a shadow as he walked up behind sergeant Julian.

"Pardon me, Sergeant," he whispered. "Do you perhaps remember me?"

Julian turned and gave him one of those strange human tooth-baring smiles.

"Fain, glad you could come," the human whispered back. "Hell, yes, I remember you. I was the one who suggested you for this."

The sergeant turned back to the show and waved at the gathering around the white wall.

"Look at that guy, will you? Amazing."

"Who is it?" the corporal asked. He knew better than to ask why he was here; the humans would tell him that when they were ready.

"Dell Mir. The local equivalent of Rus From, except that that's like comparing a hand grenade and an antimatter missile." The Marine shook his head again. "Rus From had barely started showing him a couple of outlines of what we were talking about, and he just took off, dropping ideas like rain."

"So is he going to make all the stuff they're talking about?"

"Nah. See the people following him around?" The sergeant pointed to a group of Mardukans with scrolls and tablets trailing along behind the two mechanical geniuses.

"Priests?"

"Nah. More like technicians, or maybe mechanical engineers. This guy, Wes Til, apparently set this up. Dell Mir spouts ideas all day long, and those guys write them all down and then go see how well they really work."

"Cool," Fain said. It was a human expression that

meant "interesting" and "unusual" and several other things. Like "okay" it was such a good expression that it had been adopted by the entire New Model Army, and Julian gave a grunt of laughter when he heard it.

"We're going to be on the trigger team. Once the design is finalized, we'll be working with the job shops that are going to make the trigger mechanisms."

"I don't know anything about triggers or mechanisms at all," the Diaspran confessed. "Just because I'm from Diaspra doesn't mean *I'm* some sort of mechanical genius."

"Don't worry," Julian replied. "I'll handle all that. You're going to be a gofer."

"Gopher?" the Mardukan asked in some confusion. The human translating device sometimes used words that were just as alien as the humans themselves, but it was odd the way that even the strangest word seemed to carry hints of other meanings. "Some sort of *basik?*"

"No, a 'go-fer,'" Julian corrected. "'Krindi, go-fer coffee. Krindi, go-fer lunch.'"

"Oh," the corporal said with a laugh. "Okay."

"Don't worry, it'll be more than that. In fact, we'll probably be bumping you up to sergeant to give you a bit more weight dealing with the locals. We'll be making sure the shops are supplying quality parts and that assembly shops are using only the specified materials. Everything's going to be standardized with interchangeable parts, so we can produce it in quantity."

"Big . . . ummm," the Diaspran struggled for a word.

"'Project' would be the human term. Like building a dam or a major dike. Yeah, it is, and a rush one, too. We're about out of time."

The Marine broke off as Captain Pahner stepped to the front. The Marine CO looked at the sketches on the wall and shook his head.

"Simpler, Rus, Dell. Simpler. This thing has too many parts. Every one of them will tend to break in the field, and every one has to be made, adding to cost and time. So look at something like this and say to yourself 'How can I get rid of parts?'"

The slight K'Vaernian with the piece of charcoal in his true-hand turned and looked at the Marine with his head cocked to one side.

"But your techniques of industry and mass production will cut the production time, surely?"

"True," Pahner said, "but they're not magic, and there's something called lead time to allow for. The more time we spend here, working out potential bugs in the designs, the less time we spend working them out in the foundries, and the fewer we get into the field. Don't forget, 'mass production' requires us to design and set up the production lines before we get to the 'mass' part of the equation, and the more parts we have to make, the more setup time we'll need. So cut down on the complexity and find some way to get rid of parts. You did a good job of that with the new breech design, so I know you can do it here, too. Let me show you what I'm thinking about."

The captain stepped forward, took the charcoal from the Mardukan's unresisting hand, and began marking on the wall.

"See this? You've got a double set of springs *here*. But if you move the lever to *here*, you can eliminate one spring entirely."

"Yes!" the K'Vaernian said, taking the charcoal back. "And eliminate this—what did you call it? Sear? Take this one out, and extend *this* lever . . ."

"As you can see," Julian whispered again, "we have our work cut out for us."

"Sergeant, how are we going to train on these if they're not even produced yet? And how long are we going to have? I mean, the Boman could move out at any time."

"That's somebody else's problem," the Marine said with an evil grin. "You concentrate on ours."

The long, low boat grounded on the mud of the riverbank, and D'Estrees slipped over the side and into the underbrush.

Gunnery Sergeant Lamasara Jin consulted his pad as he checked position before he inserted the last team. There were five more two-person teams scattered along the line of advance from D'Sley to Sindi, where the Boman main host supposedly was. This team was the furthest forward, and along with some local woodsmen, would probe still further forward until they reached Sindi or made contact with the Boman force.

Personally, the gunny really doubted that *all* of the Boman could be at Sindi, whatever the locals thought. The best premassacre population estimate Julian and O'Casey had been able to put together for Sindi gave the city a total population of only around seventy thousand. Which, Jin was willing to admit, was a really huge number, even allowing for the efficiency of Mardukan farmers, for a society which made virtually zero use of the wheel. It might not seem like much for the Empire, where that entire population could have been put into a single pair of residential towers in downtown Imperial City, but for a barb planet like Marduk, it was huge.

And it was also no more than a third of the total numbers people kept throwing around for the Boman.

Jin hoped like hell that the enemy force estimates were excessive, but he didn't really think they could be off by too much. Like all the Marines, he'd developed a pronounced respect for Rastar and Honal, neither of whom seemed at all inclined to inflate enemy numbers to excuse their own defeats, and they both insisted that the combined clans of the Boman could put at least a hundred thousand *warriors* into the field . . . which suggested a total population, including women and children, of at least half a million. And given that, like the Wespar, all of the Boman clans brought their women and children along rather than leaving them at home and undefended while the men were away, that meant one hell of a lot of scummies had descended on what used to be the League of the North and the other cities on the northern shore of the K'Vaernian Sea.

According to all reports, those scummies had been sitting more or less motionless for at least three or four months since taking Sindi, and that many mouths would have eaten the countryside around a city Sindi's size clean in far less time than that. Not to mention the fact that a city of seventy thousand could never provide even minimal housing for six or seven times that many invaders.

All of which suggested to the veteran noncom that—as always seemed to be the case—he and the rest of the company were about to find out that the backroom intelligence pukes had screwed up again. Fortunately, the captain had been a Marine long enough to be very cautious about how much trust he put in intelligence his own people hadn't confirmed. *Un*fortunately, there was only one way to confirm this intelligence.

Jin tapped the pad off and stepped ashore as D'Estrees reappeared and gave a thumbs-up. Normally, as Bravo Team leader, D'Estrees would have been teamed with Dalton, the team's plasma gunner. The only problem with that was that Dalton was now . . . dating Geno. If Jin put the gunner out on the point of the spear, everybody was going to think he was trying to kill his rival for Geno's affections. So instead, the plasma gunner was nice and safe and in the center of the deployment of the recon teams . . . and the overall commander of the insertion was taking point. Which, when Captain Pahner found out, would bring up words like stupid and suicidal. Instead of favoritism.

Damned if you do, and damned if you don't. But nobody was going to accuse Mamma Jin's boy of favoritism. Stupidity, though, okay, maybe.

But somewhere out there was the target, and right now he didn't care if that target was Saints or pirates or Boman. Because sooner or later, he was going to get a chance to kill something, and the closer he was to the action, the more likely that was to happen. And if he didn't kill something else soon, he just might start on one too-good-looking plasma gunner.

Two klicks to the track that ran from D'Sley to Sindi. It paralleled the river, so it never saw much traffic, since barges made so much more sense than land transport. But it was there, and if the Boman came to play, it would be along that track.

And if they didn't come out to play on their own, then they were just going to have to be called.

"I don't care if you do think it's a waste of time," Bistem Kar told the skeptical underofficer in a deceptively calm tone. General Bogess stood beside the K'Vaernian CO, but the Diaspran was being very careful not to involve himself in the conversation. "I don't even care if your *men* think it's a waste of time. *I* don't think it is, and this—" he tapped the ruby-set hilt of the sword at his side, the one only the commanding officer of the Guard Company was permitted to wear "—means that what I think is all that matters, now doesn't it?"

The underofficer closed his mouth and straightened both sets of shoulders. The thought of being ordered

around by Diaspran "soldiers" so new they still had
canal mud on their feet was enough to infuriate anyone, and he sympathized perfectly with his men. And
even if the idea of being instructed by jumped-up
common laborers hadn't been hard to swallow, the
sheer stupidity of what they were supposed to be
learning was almost intolerable. Damn it, they *knew*
how to do their jobs, and they'd done them well
enough for decades to make K'Vaern's Cove the most
powerful city-state on the entire K'Vaernian Sea! And
they hadn't done it by hiding behind any silly shields
and refusing to come out and fight like men!

Even granting the incontestable truth of all of that,
however, Kar's tone of voice had just forcibly reminded
him that there were other considerations, as well. "The
Kren" was a guardsman's guardsman, always willing to
listen—to a point at least—to the opinions and con-
cerns of his men, but anyone who'd ever been stupid
enough to think that that mild tone was an invitation
to further discussion never made the same mistake
twice.

Kar gazed at him for a moment, clearly waiting to
see if he'd finally found someone stupid enough to keep
pushing. He hadn't, and after waiting a bit longer to
be sure the point had been adequately made, he
allowed his own manner to ease.

"I admit it seems a bit . . . bizarre," he conceded
then, "but I've watched the Diasprans drilling. I've
never seen anything like it, either—not for infantry. But
much as I hate to admit it, now that I've seen the
humans' notions of how infantry should drill and
maneuver, I can't understand why the same ideas never
occurred to us."

"Sir, it just seems . . . wrong," the underofficer said
in a carefully dispassionate tone, and Kar grunted a
chuckle.

"It isn't the way our sires did it, or our grandsires, or *their* sires," the Guard commander agreed, "and I suppose it's inevitable for us to feel some sort of, um, emotional attachment for the way things have always been. But it's worth thinking about that the League, which spent the most time fighting the Boman instead of other civilized sorts of armies, already used tactics a lot closer to these new ones of the humans than ours. Now that *we're* the ones up against the barbs, maybe it's time we considered the fact that we can't take them on one by one. Even if they were willing to play by the old rules, there are so many of the bastards that we'd run out of bodies before they did, no matter how good we are. But these new tactics—all this teamwork with these 'rifles' and 'pikes' and 'assegais,' and those big shields the humans have invented—are going to change all that *if* we can figure out what in Krin's name we're doing with them. The problem is, we don't have a whole lot of time, and we're going to have to *un*learn almost as much as we have to learn.

"So I don't have a lot of time to spend arguing with my underofficers," Kar went on in a slightly harder tone. "We're all going to be much too busy listening to General Bogess here. And we're also going to be busy making sure that our noncoms understand that they're going to be listening to the Diaspran training cadre. I don't care if most of the Diasprans *were* dam builders and canal diggers four months ago. What they are *now* are soldiers. More than that, they're combat veterans who've done something none of us ever have: met the Boman bastards in the field and kicked their miserable asses all the way into whatever Krin-forsaken afterlife they believe in.

"So you *will* go back to your unit, and you *will* tell them that they really, really don't want me to come explain all of this to them in person. Is that clear?"

"Yes, Sir!" the underofficer said quickly. "Perfectly clear, Sir!"

"Good." The Guard commander gazed at him once more, then nodded dismissal. "I'm glad we had time for this little conversation," he told the underofficer. "Now go back and get that mess straightened out."

"Yes, Sir! At once, Sir!"

"We're going to train them *how*?"

St. John (J.) would much rather have been out in the field probing for the Boman camps. Anything but trying to explain the captain's brainstorm to this evil-looking scummy.

"The weapons are going to be something like an arquebus, Sir," the Marine answered. "But they're going to need to be aimed, not just volley-fired in the target's general direction, and Marines know all about teaching aiming. The most important part is breath and trigger control."

He picked up the contraption which had been leaning against the wall, brought it to his shoulder, and pointed it.

"We teach them about sight picture, then we put a K'Vaernian copper piece on this carved sight mockup and have them practice squeezing the trigger. When they can do it time after time without the copper falling off, they'll be halfway there."

The company commander picked up the wooden carving of the rifle and tried to point it while balancing the copper piece on the narrow width of the sight. The coin chimed musically as it promptly hit the stone floor, and the Mardukan snarled in frustration.

"This is madness. Is this supposed to be war?"

"Oh, yeah," the Marine breathed. "You have no idea. Just wait until you see the cannon."

❖   ❖   ❖

"You want them to what?"

"Your company is going to be cadre for the artillery corps, Sir," Kosutic told the Mardukan who stood looking at her incredulously with all four arms crossed. Until that very morning, the scummy had been the executive officer of the *Sword of Krin*, the galleass flagship of the K'Vaernian Navy, and he didn't seem particularly delighted by his new assignment.

"This is ridiculous," the naval officer grunted. "Bombards are shipboard weapons—they're too heavy, too slow, and eat too damned much powder and shot to be practical for any damned mudpounder to use!"

"Sir, I understand why you feel that way, but I assure you that these 'bombards' aren't anything like the ones you're familiar with."

The Mardukan made a skeptical sound, and Kosutic drew a deep breath. She was the only member of the company besides Captain Pahner himself who had been through crew-served heavy weapons training. In Pahner's eyes, that made her the logical senior trainer for the envisioned artillery. The fact that, unlike this dubious scummy, she'd never fired a muzzle-loading, black powder artillery piece in her life was apparently beside the point. And, in a way, it was, because no one on this miserable mudball of a planet—including the four-armed pain in the ass glowering at her—had ever heard of the concept of field artillery.

"Sir," she went on after a moment, "the main reason you were assigned to this duty is that unlike the Guard officers, you do have experience with artillery. But you have to realize that the bombards you're used to aboard your ships are very different from the field guns we're going to be producing."

"Bombards are bombards," the Mardukan said flatly, and Kosutic bit her tongue firmly.

Part of the problem, she knew, was that K'Vaern's Cove was accustomed to being the supplier of the finest artillery around, and the K'Vaernian Navy was even more accustomed to considering its gunners to be the best in the world. Which meant that none of them were very happy to be told that the smart-ass humans were going to show them how artillery *ought* to be made and used.

That reaction was inevitable, at least initially, and not simply among scummies. Human military types through the ages had reacted negatively to suggestions that what they knew had worked in the past might not still be the best technique or weapons available in the present. The big problem here was that they simply didn't have time to bring people around gradually, which meant that Turl Kam and Bistem Kar had been fairly direct and brutal in laying down the law to their more doubtful subordinates. And that meant that a certain degree of tact was absolutely required.

"Sir," she began diplomatically, "I wouldn't know where to begin to tell you how to go about fighting a naval battle. Frankly, I don't know shit about that particular subject, but I understand that your standard tactics for heavy bombards are to row directly at your target and to fire a single, close-range salvo from all of your guns just before you ram and board them. Is that about correct?"

"In general terms, yes," the Mardukan said grudgingly.

"And why is it that you don't fire more than one shot per gun, Sir?"

"Because it takes seven chimes to reload them," the naval officer told her with exaggerated patience. A chime, Kosutic knew, was a K'Vaernian time measurement equal to about forty-five seconds, so the scummy was talking about a five-minute reload time. "And," the officer went on, "because relaying the guns for a second shot would take even longer."

"Yes, Sir, it would," the sergeant major agreed. "But the guns that we're going to be using can be reloaded much more quickly than that. In fact, using bagged charges and fixed antipersonnel you'll be able to fire them once per chime—maybe even a little more rapidly—under maximum rate conditions at short range."

The Mardukan stared at her incredulously, and she showed her teeth in a thin smile and continued.

"In addition, the new carriages we're going to be building, coupled with how much lighter the cannon themselves are going to be, will make them a lot more mobile than any bombard you've ever seen. We figure a single pair of *turom* should be able to haul even the bigger ones around without much trouble. And this new feature here—" she tapped the trunnions of the wooden mock-up someone from ancient Earth might have recognized as remarkably similar to something which had once been called a "twelve-pounder Napoleon" "—will actually let you make changes in elevation between shots."

The Mardukan uncrossed his lower arms and leaned closer. It was apparent that he was truly looking at the new weapon for the first time, and Kosutic hid a smile as some of his truculent skepticism seemed to fade. If they could just get the scummies to really *see* the advantages, three quarters of the job would be done.

The K'Vaernian Navy's bombards were very well made from the standpoint of their metallurgy and casting techniques, but as practical artillery pieces they left a lot to be desired. In fact, they were simply huge bronze or iron tubes which were strapped to heavy wooden timbers and then chained or roped to the deck of a ship. They looked more like big, clumsy rifles than they did anything a human would have called an artillery piece, and it was impossible to adjust their elevation in any way. As for recoil, the K'Vaernian gunners simply stood as far to one side as they could and touched off the priming. The heavy hawsers which fastened the bombards to the deck and bulwarks kept the gun from jumping clear overboard, and the friction between the wheelless "carriage" and deck acted as an extremely crude recoil damper. Hauling the guns back into position for the next shot without any sort of wheels under them was a backbreaking process, of course, but they accepted that as the price of doing business because that was the way it had always been done before.

The new guns, on the other hand, were a very different proposition. Their carriages, with large spoked wheels with extra-wide rims, and lighter weight, would give them a degree of mobility no Mardukan had ever dreamed was possible, and the introduction of trunnions and elevating screws would completely change their tactical flexibility, both afloat and ashore. With the addition of premeasured, bagged charges and fixed rounds of grapeshot and canister, their rate of fire would also be enormously increased. If the team working on ammunition actually managed to get the bugs out of a decent shrapnel round in the time available, the guns would be even more effective, but the sergeant major had no intention of holding her breath while she waited. In fact, she had a pretty shrewd notion that the more optimistic visions of explosive filler for cast-iron shells were doomed to disappointment. The rocket batteries were a different matter entirely, of course, but no one really knew how well that project was going to work out either. And in the meantime . . .

"Sir, as you know much better than any of the Guard officers, the important thing with crew-served weapons like this is for everyone to perform their jobs precisely according to a standard drill. What we're going to add to what you already know is speed, because it will be possible to load and fire the new guns much more quickly . . . if the crews are properly trained.

"You know what your bombards do to the hulls of enemy ships. Try to picture what a weapon like this will do to a mob of Boman. Each shot will punch right through them and kill anyone who gets in its way, and when dozens of these guns are massed, there's nothing like them. In our society, artillery was called 'The King of Battle,' but for the guns to be effective, their crews must be drilled to exhaustion. They have to be able to clear, load, and fire the weapon under the most extreme circumstances, then limber up, move on, and do it again. So you learn the steps, then you practice them again and again.

"That means that there's no need, initially, for the cannon themselves. A training mock-up, or even a few marks on the ground to show its outline, will do in a pinch, because it's how you move around the gun that really matters. The trick is to teach the gunners how to do it right before they ever *see* a real cannon—teach them never to stand behind it once it's loaded, to do their jobs in a certain sequence, and to do them *fast*.

"So we're going to show you how. You and your people were chosen because you're already familiar with artillery. Whether you realize it or not, you already have most of the basic knowledge you need, and all we have to do is to teach you to see that knowledge a little differently and adjust to a whole new tempo. So once we've shown you that, your people will show others, and those people will show still others, and so on. And when we're finished, we'll have ourselves a tiddly little artillery corps that will pile up Boman like barleyrice."

The skeptical naval officer was listening much more closely now, and she hid another smile as she turned to the six Marines standing around the carved wooden model. The end of the barrel was slightly scorched, because it had just finished double duty as a model for the mold and been left a bit too close to a furnace afterward.

"These fine young Marines, who just spent the last few hours learning what to do, are going to demonstrate," she continued. "What they can't demonstrate is that there are some things you Mardukans can do, with four arms, that they can't do with just two. We'll have to work that out, with your assistance, as we go along."

She drew a deep breath, and nodded to the senior Marine.

"Squad!" she barked. "Prepare to place the gun into action! Gun in action . . . Move!"

And the six Terran Empire Marines, born on planets circling five different stars, began the ritual of service to the artillery—a ritual which had been old before the first rockets lifted beyond the atmosphere of Terra and looked to be going on when the last star cooled.

Some things just never seemed to change.

CHAPTER TWENTY-NINE

Something hard and circular socketed instantly into Fain's temple as he trotted through the doorway, with Erkum hard on his heels, and ran straight into the human prince.

The newly promoted sergeant heard a deep rumble of displeasure behind him and reached back to very carefully put a restraining hand against Pol's chest until Roger could reach out and push the bead rifle muzzle aside.

"It's all right, Geno. He's one of ours," the prince said, then tapped the sergeant on his mid-shoulder. "Krindi Fain, isn't it? You did well at the Battle. Held your squad together admirably."

"Thank you, Your Highness," Fain said, braced to attention and trying not to show his relief *too* plainly.

"Not so formal, Sergeant—we're all old soldiers here. Sergeant Julian making sure you're getting fed right? I can't promise sleep; none of us are getting much of that."

"Yes, Your Highness."

"Good. Remember to take care of your troops, and they'll take care of you." The human turned to the sergeant's shadow and craned his neck to peer up at the towering giant. "And the inimitable Erkum Pol, I see. How are you, Erkum?"

"Yes, Your Highness," the private said.

"I'll take that as 'doing well,'" Roger said with a smile. Apparently he knew about the soldier's simplemindedness. "And, Erkum, next time use a smaller plank, right? I need all the cavalry I can get."

"Yes, Your Highness," Fain heard himself say.

"Carry on," the prince said, striding off with a wave, followed by his bodyguards, and the Diasprans braced back to attention.

"Lots smaller plank," the last Marine guard whispered with a human-style wink as he passed Fain. "Fuckers are *still* in the hospital."

Roger shook his head as he turned the corner to the training ground. That lad Krindi was going to go far . . . assuming he could keep Pol from killing someone at an inopportune moment.

He chuckled, then turned his attention to the company of riflemen-to-be. The ranks were lined up in an open formation, with each soldier holding a wooden mock-up of the final rifle design. As the prince entered the area, the cadence of fire was being called.

"Open. Load. Close. Cock. Cap. Aim. Fire."

The bull-throated Mardukan giving the orders saluted as Roger went past. Another veteran of the New Model pike regiments, the Diaspran, like most of that force, had been broken off for cadre for the new units.

The numbers for those new units were looking much better than Roger had feared they might, if not quite as good as he could have wished in an ideal world. The

core of the new and improved K'Vaernian army would
be the veterans of the Guard, their less than enthusiastic fellow citizens temporarily reassigned from the
Navy, Rastar's Northern cavalrymen, and the Diaspran
pikemen. But that would account for little more than
a third of the total numbers they needed, and volunteer levels had been gratifyingly high. Some of the local
volunteers were in it only for the expected loot, which,
however mercenary, was certainly understandable. The
Boman on this side of the Nashtor Hills had conquered
the northern cities and Sindi, all of which had been
wealthy and powerful states, so it was only to be
expected that they would be swimming in treasure as
a result of their victories. Other volunteers had come
forward because they perceived the Boman as a threat
to their own city, and some had volunteered because
they were refugees from other cities who wanted some
of their own back.

Whatever their reasons for joining, the troops were
being formed into a tidy little army. Now if they could
only get some weapons for it.

And maybe they were doing something about that,
he thought, looking up to see Rastar grinning as he
waved something and trotted towards him from the
other side of the square.

"First production unit out of the Tendel foundry,"
the Northerner said as he reached the prince, and
handed him a massive rifle.

The weapon was gigantic and starkly utilitarian. The
twenty-five-millimeter bore made his own eleven-
millimeter look like a toy, and the breech was the size
of a plasma cannon firing chamber.

The final design was very different from the one the
Marines and Rus From had sketched out before leaving
Diaspra, and almost equally different from the new,
improved cartridge version Pahner had wanted to

produce once they actually got to K'Vaern's Cove. The original design had been very similar to the old Sharps breechloader from the ancient American Civil War, with a moving breech block that clipped the end off of a linen cartridge when the breech was closed to expose the powder charge to flash from a priming cap. Although gas leakage would probably have been a problem, just as it had been with the original, From and Pahner had rather doubted that it would seriously inconvenience anyone already accustomed to the godawful priming flash of a Mardukan arquebus.

The much more advanced design Pahner had wanted once he decided to stay and fight, on the other hand, would have used either a brass cartridge case or a composite brass and paper case, either of which would have been a centerfire percussion design with a metallic base to provide an excellent, flash-proof seal at the breech. One look at the manufacturing complexity and lead time required to produce that ammunition in quantity had knocked that idea on the head, however, and everyone had gone looking for some workable compromise solution. One had been found—and finally put into production—in a design which had been suggested by Dell Mir and owed more to local expertise with pumps than even Pahner had believed might be the case.

The prince gripped the protruding bolt handle, which looked very similar to that of his own hunting rifle when it wasn't configured for semi-auto fire, and raised it, turning the bolt through a half rotation. K'Vaern's Cove's pump makers had developed a standard fixture for use as an inspection/cleaning port for their pumps, which was closed by what was in effect a big, coarse-threaded bolt with a washer at one end. Mardukans spent a lot of time doing maintenance on their flood control pumps, even in a place like K'Vaern's Cove, where the steepness of the slopes (which promoted very rapid runoff) and the absence of a readily tapped aquifer made potable water scarce, and the inspection port had been designed for ease and speed of access. It was fitted with a crank-style handle on one end, and moved in a cam-mounted sleeve, so that when the bolt was run out of the threads, the entire plug pivoted downwards and hung from the underside of the pipe it normally closed.

Mir, with an eye to practical adaptation which explained much of his reputation for genius, had seen no reason not to use a perfectly sound existing design rather than get bogged down in esoteric new concepts. Of course, there had been some changes. The two biggest ones had been to convert the fittings from bronze to steel and his decision to cut away the threads on two sides of the threaded bolt plug and to interrupt the threads that the plug seated into so that only a half turn was required to engage and disengage the threads. He'd also made some other minor changes, including moving the bolt handle to the side (an idea he'd borrowed from Roger's eleven-millimeter) and machining a guide onto the rifle bolt to ensure that it followed the proper mechanical path, but the overall effect had been to take a simple plumbing fixture and use it to manufacture the most deadly weapon K'Vaern's Cove had ever seen.

The cartridge design had also been simplified. There wasn't much question that the K'Vaernians would have been able to produce Pahner's brass cartridges . . . eventually. Certainly, their tech base and metallurgy were capable of making the jump to manufacture the captain's design, but setting up to produce it and experimenting to come up with exactly the right alloy for the cases would have taken considerably longer than K'Vaern's Cove—or its human visitors, at least—had. So instead, Dell Mir had turned to a local plant.

The Mardukans called it *shonash*, but after one demonstration of its properties, the Marines had instantly christened it the flashplant, because on any planet without Marduk's daily rains, it would have been a deadly fire hazard. The K'Vaernians crushed its stems to extract a fine, clear, hot-burning oil, which they used in industry and as lamp fuel, and the large, flat leaves were sometimes used to wrap packages where wetness was an even greater than usual danger. They were so heavily impregnated with volatile oils that they remained tough and flexible even after they'd been "dried" and were almost totally impervious to water. That was good, but, unfortunately, they were also extremely combustible, which made it somewhat dangerous to use them for packaging in conditions which wouldn't keep them fairly wet.

Dell Mir had recognized instantly that those very qualities made flashplant leaves almost ideal as a cartridge paper substitute. A little experimentation had quickly demonstrated that the flash from one of Despreaux's early percussion caps would burn straight through a double layer of leaf almost instantaneously. So the K'Vaernian inventor had produced a design in which one of the new hollow-based bullets and its propellant were wrapped together in a flashplant leaf cartridge. The base of the cartridge was a thick, disklike, heavily greased felt patch, and when the rifle bolt was driven forward and engaged in its threads, the explosion of the cartridge drove the felt back against the face of the bolt to complete the seal and prevent any gas leakage. The next round loaded pushed the remnant of the previous round's patch forward and out of the way, and the rifle was ready to fire again. The final product of his efforts adhered very closely to Pahner's drive to reduce the number of parts, yet worked with a robust simplicity Roger had to admire.

There was still plenty of room for improvement, but this design had the three most important virtues of all: it worked, it would be hard for even a soldier to break, and it could be produced quickly.

The workshops of K'Vaern's Cove had sprouted rifling benches like toadstools, and the Guard and Navy's arquebuses had been hauled in and handed over to the machinists for modification. The rear ends of their barrels had been sliced off, they'd been rifled, the exterior of the back end of the barrels had been run through thread-cutting dies, the modified pump inspection ports had been screwed on, and a redesigned trigger mechanism taken from the existing wheel lock pistols had been modified to control a side-mounted hammer for a percussion lock. And that had been that. Well, aside from the provision of bayonet lugs on the ends of the barrels.

Now the prince finished opening the breech and flipped the rifle up to his shoulder to take a good look at the breech mechanism and the barrel. Although there were a few burrs on the exterior from the hurried work of the shops, the interior was beautifully machined and the bolt's threads engaged and disengaged with smooth precision.

"Very nice," he said. "The only thing that would make it better would be proper metallic cartridge cases, but this will more than do the job."

Despite what Rus From had told them, the volume of production that was in the pipeline still amazed Roger. The effective blockade of the city from the land side had idled hundreds of small foundries and shops throughout the peninsula on which K'Vaern's Cove sat. All of them, it seemed, wanted in on the new government contracts, which had given the designers some leeway to stray from the "simpler, simpler, simpler" mantra. They hadn't wandered far, but the provision of a proper bayonet had been one of the "frills" Pahner had been prepared to forego. The K'Vaernians, on the other hand, found the notion of parking a sixty-centimeter blade on the end of their new rifles *very* attractive. One of the great disadvantages of the arquebus had always been that it was essentially little more than a clumsily shaped club if the arquebusier found himself forced into a melee. Now each of the new riflemen would be able to look after himself in the furball if he had to, which had proven extremely reassuring to soldiers who were still none too sure about the effectiveness of all these newfangled ideas. Roger was a strong supporter of the bayonet, but he personally found the ladder sight even more useful, and the butt-mounted cleaning kit was nothing to sneer at, either.

The logistics bottleneck, as From had predicted, lay far less in the rifles than in the manufacture of their ammunition. There was plenty of lead for bullets, and the new bullet dies hadn't been a problem, but actually putting the cartridges together—even using Dell Mir's flashplant design—was a delicate, time-consuming, hand labor task, and not one that could be trusted to off-the-street casual labor. Even if simple assembly hadn't been a problem, no one in K'Vaern's Cove had ever imagined the rate of ammunition expenditure Pahner was projecting. An arquebusier did well to fire one shot every two minutes, and under normal circumstances probably wouldn't fire more than five to ten rounds in any engagement. Pahner was talking about issuing sixty rounds per day as the new riflemen's standard unit of fire, and he wanted a reserve of no less than four units of fire for the entire army before committing to action, and that didn't even consider the rounds they were simply going to have to expend in training. While each individual cartridge used very little gunpowder, hundreds of thousands of them used tons of the stuff, and given the competing needs of the artillery, the claymores, and the new rocket batteries, there simply wasn't enough powder to provide ammunition for the numbers of rifles which could, in theory, have been produced.

But what they *could* produce, Roger thought with a wicked smile, was going to be more than enough to give the Boman serious problems.

"And look at this," Rastar told him with an even more wicked grin of his own as he brought another weapon around from behind his back . . . then froze when three bead rifles instantly snapped up to cover him.

"Hey, come on!" he said. "It's me, Rastar."

"Yeah," Roger said, taking the pistol from the cavalryman, "but we've had another death threat. And the attempted assassination of Rus From. So they're a little twitchy." He looked the weapon over and smiled. "Again, very nice."

The weapon was a revolver, very similar in appearance to what had once been known as a Colt Dragoon, but much larger and with some significant design peculiarities to fit the Mardukan hand. It was lighter than the rifles—with no more than a mere twenty-millimeter bore—and it was also a seven-shot weapon, not a six-shooter. The rear of the cylinder had nipples for the copper percussion caps the alchemists' guild was producing in quantity under Despreaux's direction, but the biggest differences (besides an odd indent in the grip so that it could be held more easily with a false-hand) were the fact that it was double action, not single, and that it was a swing-out cylinder design. Obviously, the firer was supposed to swing the cylinder out and slide more of Dell Mir's flashplant-bagged cartridges into place from the front, base end first, then cap the chambers, and lock the cylinder back into place, which would make it much quicker to reload than the cap-and-ball revolvers of ancient Earth.

"Really nice," Roger said, handing it back. "Of course, it would break my wrist if I tried to fire it."

"It's not my fault you're a wimp," the Northerner said, taking his prize back.

"Ha! We'll see who's a wimp in a month's time," Roger replied. "How many of these are we producing?"

"As many as possible," Rastar said with a gesture of dismissal. "The machining is more complicated than for the rifles, and we can't just convert existing arquebus barrels, and there are some problems with about a quarter of them—they break for some reason, after a couple of shots. I got the first four."

"Of course," Roger said. Rastar was not only the commander of the Northern cavalry but also far and away the most dangerous pistoleer, himself included, the prince had ever seen. "I suppose we should thank goodness for pumps, pumps, and more pumps. Those industries are certainly coming in handy. Are you scheduled for the exercise this afternoon?"

"Yes," the Northerner replied with a grimace. "Maps, maps, and more maps."

"It's good for the soul," Roger said with a grin.

"So is killing Boman," Rastar said. "Although, at this point, anyone would do."

"I think we're going to have to kill somebody, Sergeant," Fain said.

"Why?" Julian asked, looking up from the meal on the low table. He couldn't wait to get back to someplace that had decent chairs. Hell, he couldn't wait to get back to someplace that had decent food.

"Show him, Erkum," the Diaspran noncom replied.

The huge private held up a spring to show it to the Marine, then started to stretch it. The heavy spring resisted at first, then began stretching outward . . . until it snapped with a brittle sound.

"Skimping on the springs again, huh?" Julian said, dropping his fork and picking up his sword. "You'd think they'd learn."

"Yeah, but this foundry's owned by one of the members of the Council," Fain said. "Which was very carefully pointed out when I saw the shop foreman about this."

"How much did he offer?" the Marine asked, taking out his pad and punching a message into it.

"A kusul of silver," the Diaspran replied with a shrug. "It was insulting."

"Damn straight," Julian laughed. "Maybe up front, or weekly, but a one-time offer after they'd already been caught? Jesus."

"So what are you going to do?"

"I guess we're just going to have to explain to him what the words 'quality process improvement' mean. You, me, Erkum, and a squad from the New Model. Get it set up."

"Who is," Julian ostentatiously consulted the scrap of paper in his hand, "Tistum Path?"

"I am," said a heavyset Mardukan, appearing out of the gloom of the foundry.

The forging room was hot. Unbelievably hot, like a circle of Hell. Julian could have sworn that water left on any surface would start to boil in a second. There were two ceramic furnaces where steel—spring steel, in this case—was being formed over forced-air coke fires, and the fierce flames and bubbling steel contributed to a choking atmosphere that must have been nearly lethal to the Mardukans working in it. Which wasn't going to dissuade Julian one bit from his appointed duty.

"Ah, good. Pleased to meet you," the sergeant said cheerfully, walking up to the foundry manager ... and kicked him in the groin.

The squad of riflemen behind him were all from the New Model Army's Bastar Battalion of pikes. As the workers in the foundry grabbed various implements, the Diasprans' brand-new rifles came up and the percussion hammers clicked ominously as they were cocked and leveled at the workers. There had been enough demonstrations of the weapons by now that the workers froze.

The mastoid analogue behind a Mardukan's ear wasn't quite as susceptible as the same point on a human, but it would do. The hardwood bludgeon bounced off it nicely as the shop manager was driven to his knees.

Julian ran a length of chain around the stunned foreman's ankles and gave a thumbs-up to Fain, who began hauling on the pulley arrangement. The sliding crane was designed for lifting multi-ton crucibles of boiling steel, and it made short work of lifting the three-meter Mardukan into the air. As the manager recovered, Julian threw a rope about his horns and used it to drag him along until he was suspended in the flaring heat over one of the furnaces.

"Here's the deal!" the Marine shouted to the head-down Mardukan. "Springs are very *important* in weapons, and *you*, Tistum Path, are very important in the manufacture of *springs*. This is a *vital* position you hold, and one that I *hope* you are worthy of! Because if you're not—" the human hawked and spat into the furnace, but the glob of mucus exploded before it hit the surface of the bubbling steel "—it would just be a *senseless* waste of Mardukan life."

"You can't do this to me!" the Mardukan screamed, coughing and squirming frantically in the fumes blasting up from the furnace. "Don't you know who *owns* this place?"

"Of course we do, and we're going to be visiting him next. He's going to be *terribly* disappointed to learn that one of his employees misunderstood his orders to produce the best quality material, and damn the cost. Don't you think?"

"That's not what he said!"

"I know *that*." The Marine shook his head. "But there's no way he's going to admit that he told you to cut the cost, no matter what kind of shit you produced. So we're going to explain to him, in a gentle way, that while profits are the lifeblood of any economy, the contract he signed was supposed to include a reasonable profit margin *without* cheating. And we're already paying top dollar, so since we can't figure out which springs are shit and which ones aren't, he's going to be taking them *all* back. And replacing them. With good ones."

"Impossible! Who's going to pay for it?"

"Your boss," the Marine hissed, stepping into the blazing heat from the furnace. The red light of the boiling steel turned his angular face into a painting of Satan gloating over a new-caught sinner. "And the next time I have to come back here, both of you are going to be nothing but trace elements in the steel. *Is that perfectly clear?*"

"These humans are insane!" the councilor complained hotly.

"All the more reason to support getting them on their way," Wes Til replied, rolling a bit of spring in his fingers.

"They threatened me—*me!* They said they'd melt me in my own steel! I want their heads!"

"Hmmm?" Til looked up from the spring. "Wouldn't

have anything to do with cracked revolver frames, broken springs, and exploding barrels, would it?"

"Those aren't my fault," the other Mardukan sniffed. "Just because a few of my workers were cutting corners, probably to line their own pockets—"

"Oh be quiet!" Til snapped. "You signed contracts. From the point of view of the humans, you're responsible, and you know as well as I do that the courts would back them up if there was time for that. But there *isn't* time, and they don't really seem to be very interested in half-measures, now do they? So, under the circumstances, I suggest that you do exactly as they say, unless you want your heir to be the one who does it."

"Is that a threat?"

"No, it's more on the order of a statement. They seem to have the most remarkable intelligence system. For example, they've already tracked down the person who ordered the attack on Rus From. Or so I would guess. You notice that Ges Stin hasn't been gracing us with his presence lately?"

"Yes. You know something?"

"No. However, it's lately become common knowledge that it was Ges Stin who ordered the attack. It's even common knowledge who planned the attack at his orders and actually paid those unfortunate assassins. None of them, however, are anywhere to be found."

"Ges Stin has many shipping interests. He could be in the southern states by now."

"Hmmm. Perhaps."

"What does Turl Kam think of this?"

"He thinks that he's down one competitor for the fisherman's guild vote," the merchant said with a grunt of laughter.

"I will not be intimidated," the other councilor declared defiantly.

"The sliming on your forehead gives you the lie. But you don't need to be," Til replied. "Just make sure your shops produce what they promised. Instead of weak crap." The spring he'd been flexing broke with a pop. "You really don't want a few thousand people with rifles in their true-hands . . . discussing the problem with you. Do you?"

CHAPTER THIRTY

Dersal Quan stood on the foundry floor and watched in disbelief as the human-designed device sliced through his best bronze as if it were *qwanshu* wood. He'd had even more doubts than he'd cared to express to Wes Til when he discovered just how many pieces of artillery the insane humans and their Diaspran henchmen expected to cast in the ridiculously short time limit they'd imposed. Now it looked to him as if they might actually manage to meet their preposterous production schedule.

The Quan foundries had been among the largest and wealthiest in K'Vaern's Cove for generations. They'd provided over half the Navy's total bombards since Quan's father's time, and at least a third of the bells hung in the Cove's towers to the glory of Krin also bore the Quan founder's stamp. Quan had never doubted that his modelers and patternmakers could produce the forms or that his casters could pour the guns, but pouring bronze wasn't like pouring concrete. It had to be done right, and there were no corners that could be cut unless one really liked bombards which were honeycombed with flaws and failed when proofed . . . or blew up in combat, always at the most inopportune time possible. And even after that time requirement had been allowed for, the need to bore out the guns was the single most time-consuming element of the entire process.

The true secret to a bombard of superior accuracy lay in the care taken in the preparation of its bore and the shot it would fire, although it had taken the gunners generations to realize how critical things like windage and uniform bores truly were. In fact, Quan's own father had begun his apprenticeship in the family business manufacturing cannonballs out of *stone*, and the art of cutting and reaming bores properly had been practically invented by one of Quan's uncles. It was a multistage process which required days for each piece, and no one had ever imagined that someone would demand so many guns in so short a time period, which meant that no one had the machinery to bore out more than a half dozen or so guns simultaneously. Not only that, but the crazy humans had insisted on a shot size which no one in K'Vaern's Cove had ever used, which meant that none of the boring equipment which already existed was the right size, and that the foundries also found themselves forced to produce new shot molds even as they cast the gun tubes themselves.

But the humans had insisted that there were ways around the problems, and so Quan had accepted their contracts, trusting Krin to prove the diminutive foreign lunatics knew what they were talking about. And trusting in the Cove's courts to absolve him of legal responsibility for failure when it turned out that they didn't.

As it happened, they *had* known what they were talking about, and now he watched in lingering disbelief as the ebony-skinned human called Aburia switched off her device and pushed the transparent goggles up on her forehead while one of her K'Vaernian assistants spun the handcrank which retracted the boring head from the new piece.

"What did you say this is called?" Quan asked, waving a true-hand at the device.

"I don't know that it really has a name," Aburia told him with one of the "shrugs" humans seemed so fond of. "It's sort of a bastardized field expedient, actually. The cutting head is only three of our bayonet blades, and Julian and Poertena made the shaft by welding a couple of broke-down plasma rifle barrels together and then splicing in a powerplant from Russell's powered armor. Your own people put together the rack-and-pinion system to move it, and your shop foreman and I worked out the clamps and brackets to hold everything still while we drill."

She shrugged again, and Quan clapped hands in a gesture of profound, respect, tinged with surprise.

"I didn't believe you could really do this," he admitted. "Even watching you, I'm not sure I believe it now! Seeing a shaft that thin—" he gestured at the slender rod, no thicker than a human finger, which Julian and Poertena had welded together with something called a laser kit "—take that sort of load without even flexing isn't just impossible, it's preposterous! It ought to be wobbling all over the place, especially since you had to piece it together in the first place out of hollow tubing. There's certainly not any way that it should be allowing you to cut such uniformly true bores! And I've never heard of any knife blade that could pare away bronze like so much soft cheese and never even need sharpening."

"Well, sir," the human said with one of those teeth-showing smiles Quan still found mildly disturbing, "we haven't used bronze for something like this in close to two thousand of our years. We've got a lot better alloys now, and a blade with an edge a single molecule wide will cut just about anything without dulling down so's anyone would notice!"

"So your Julian said," Quan agreed, "although I'm still not very certain just what these 'molecules' you keep talking about might be. Not that I suppose it really matters all that much as long as your wizards' spells keep working as promised."

"The Regiment usually manages to hold up its end, sir," Aburia assured him. "Especially when we've got a member of the Imperial Family with his ass in a crack!"

"How about the rocket batteries?" Pahner asked.

He, Rus From, and Bistem Kar stood on a catwalk watching Dersal Quan talk to Corporal Aburia.

"They are progressing better than I'd anticipated," From told him. "The Cove's pump artificers have set up to machine the 'venturis' in quantity, and the test rockets have performed well. The biggest problem, of course, is that they consume even more gunpowder than the new artillery will."

"Price of doing business if we want a decent bursting charge at the terminal end of the flight," Pahner said with a shrug.

"That's understood," Kar rumbled in his subterranean voice, "and I've been most impressed by the weapons' effectiveness. Yet that doesn't change Rus's point. We have only so much powder, and at the moment we have at least three different things to use every *sedant* of it on. We're doing our best to get production levels back up, but even if we had every powder plant working at full capacity, we would still feel a serious pinch." He shook his head in one of the gestures the K'Vaernians had already picked up from their human visitors. "You humans may be the most deadly fighters anyone has ever seen, but the strains your way of fighting put on the quartermaster are enormous."

"You only think they are," Pahner replied with a chuckle. "Actually, the logistics for an army equipped with such simple weapons as this are child's play compared to the supply problems we normally have to deal with. You folks are the most advanced and innovative society we've come across yet on our journey, but you're only really getting started on what we call the 'Industrial Revolution.' Trust me, by the time you hit your stride, you'll look back on this as a relatively minor effort!"

"Assuming that we survive the Boman, of course," Kar pointed out.

"Oh, I feel confident that you'll survive them," Pahner said. "Whether we succeed in crushing them in a single campaign or not, we're going to do so much damage to them—and you guys are going to learn so much in the process—that their poor barbarian butts are pocked in the long run, whatever happens."

"Perhaps," Kar agreed. "Yet for that to happen, we must do enough damage and give our people enough confidence in the final outcome for them to see the wisdom in sustaining the struggle to that point."

"Which is where we come in," Pahner said with a nod. "Believe me, Bistem, we've figured that out. Don't worry. We'll give you and your people the basic skills and tools you'll need, and we'll play the 'Krin-sent champions' to get your army into the field in the first place. But don't sell yourself or the Guard short. Between you, Bogess, and the Diaspran cadre, you'll be able to hold up your end without us just fine if you have to after we leave."

✧   ✧   ✧

"But what do they *want* all these wagons for?" Thars Kilna demanded in the tone of a person who knew no one could answer his question.

"Do you know, I think they forgot to tell me," Miln Sahna told him sarcastically. "I'm sure it was only an inadvertent oversight though. Here—you put the wheel on this end of the shaft, and I'll run ask Bistem Kar. When he explains it to me, I'll come right back and tell *you*."

"Very funny," Kilna growled. "You keep right on telling yourself you're a wit, Miln—at least you're *half* right. In the meantime, I still want to know why in Krin's name they need so many wagons! It just doesn't make sense."

"Um." Sahna grunted sourly, but he had to admit his fellow apprentice had a point. Not that either of them was complaining, precisely. The cart-makers' guild usually had orders to fill in a place like K'Vaern's Cove, but they were seldom as busy as they would have liked. Carts and wagons were very useful within the confines of a city, but they weren't a lot of use anywhere else, given what weather tended to do to roads on Marduk. Once you got off a paved surface, it made much more sense to rely on pack *turom* or *pagee* than to drag a wheeled vehicle through hub-deep mud. The fact that wheels would let a single beast pull a far heavier load than it could actually carry when paved surfaces were available was beside the point when those surfaces *weren't* available . . . which was virtually all the time.

Of course, the new wheels the humans had designed were different from the heavy, solid ones Kilna and Sahna had been learning to make before their arrival. Like the wheels for the new gun carriages, their spoked design was both stronger and far lighter, and if their steel rims were preposterously expensive, they should also make them last much longer. Not to mention that those rims were almost three times as wide as the rest of the wheel, which offered a huge decrease in ground pressure and should make them at least a little less inclined to sink into soft ground than traditional ones. But still . . .

"I don't know what they want with them," Sahna admitted finally. "All I know is that they told us they were important, they're paying us to make them, and we're learning new techniques no one else ever heard of." He gave the handclap of a Mardukan shrug. "Aside from that, all I can tell you is that they must have a lot of stuff they want to haul somewhere!"

Krindi Fain looked on with interest as Prince Roger examined the rifle. It was a tiny thing, compared to the weapons equipping the new rifle battalions, but the native sergeant had been around humans long enough not to nurture any foolish theories about "small" meaning "not lethal."

"Nice work, Julian," Roger said, trying the balance of the rifle. Unlike the Mardukan-scaled weapons, this one hadn't been made by converting existing arquebus barrels, which meant it represented far more man hours than one of the mass-produced weapons. On the other hand, the rifle shops had produced only forty of them.

The prince shouldered the rifle, checking the weld between cheek and buttstock, and grunted in satisfaction. It wasn't the custom-fitted stock of his hunting rifle, but it was excellent for a one-size-fits-all military weapon, and he lowered it once more to open the bolt.

There were distinct differences between that bolt and those of the Mardukan-scale rifles. In fact, aside from the fact that it was made out of old-fashioned steel and had no provision for conversion to semi-auto mode, it was effectively identical to the bolt of Roger's own rifle, complete to the small electronic contact on the bolt face, and he laughed.

"Remember that little bet beside the river, Adib?" he asked, and Julian chuckled just a bit sourly as he recalled the day he and Roger had perched in adjacent treetops, posted to cover the troops swimming a Mardukan river against the voracious predators who called that river home.

"Yes, Sir, I do," he said. "Cost me quite a few push-ups when I lost, as I recall."

"Yep," the prince said with a grin, closing the bolt and admiring the smoothness of the action. "But what I was thinking about was your suggestion that I should get myself a bead rifle because of its magazine capacity. Seems to me there's just a smidgeon of ironic humor in the situation now."

Julian snorted, but he also had to nod in agreement, and it was hard not to chuckle himself as he remembered all the times Captain Pahner—and Sergeant Adib Julian, for that matter—had groused about the way the prince's old-fashioned, nonstandard "smoke pole" complicated the ammunition supply problem. The fact that the prince would be unable to fire military bead rounds out of it when he ran out of chemical-powered ammo had been a big part of it, but so had the sheer grunt work involved in lugging along the cases of ammunition the prince (still in original, patented, pain-in-the-ass mode) had insisted on bringing down to the planet. It hadn't been all that bad once they got pack animals to take the weight instead of carting it on their own backs, but Roger had brought over nine thousand rounds down with him, which had represented a pretty severe case of overkill . . . at least until the company discovered just how nasty Mardukan jungle fauna truly was.

Most of the Marines had been prepared to forgive

Roger his foibles when it turned out that his big magnum was the most effective antipredator armament they had, particularly in his skilled hands, but there'd still been the odd grumble over his habit of policing up his brass. Modern military weapons left no cartridge cases to worry about, but Roger's personal cannon littered the ground with thumb-thick brass cases every time he used it, and he'd flatly insisted on picking up after himself.

Most of it, Julian was certain, went back to the fact that even the old Roger had always taken his responsibilities seriously when in the field on safari, whether anyone else had realized it or not. But there'd been another reason, although no one had known it, since no one had bothered to ask the prince about his motives.

The Parkins and Spencer was the crown jewel of big game rifles, and Roger's cherished weapon had probably cost more than most luxury aircars. But it was also intended to be taken on safari in places so far out back of beyond that ammunition shops might be few and far between, and because of that, its ammunition had been designed for reuse and ease in reloading. The electronic igniter built into the base of each case was certified for a minimum of one hundred discharges without replacement, and although the cases themselves were still called "brass," they were actually a much more advanced alloy which could be reloaded almost infinitely without deforming, cracking, or splitting.

Which meant, given Roger's mania for cleaning up his shooting stands, that the company still had well over eight thousand perfectly serviceable rounds of ammunition, once they were reloaded with black powder. True, they wouldn't generate the velocity and kinetic energy the same rounds had when filled with the considerably more sophisticated propellant they'd been designed to use, but the cases were strong enough to take maximum capacity loads of black powder, which still produced something no one in his right mind wanted hitting him. And a kick like an irritated *flar-ta* . . . not to mention a smoke cloud from Hell.

Still and all, that ammo's existence had certainly justified manufacturing forty custom rifles to provide each surviving human with one, plus spares. It gave the company around two hundred rounds per rifle, too—more like three hundred and fifty for each of the surviving riflemen. That wasn't a spit in a hurricane compared to the sort of ammunition expenditures bead rifles used up on full auto, or even in three-round burst mode, but it was a hell of a lot for a bolt action rifle. Not to mention the fact that at the moment the company had a total of exactly one hundred and eleven bead rifle rounds.

And Julian knew *exactly* how much it amused the prince to see the entire surviving company carrying around *his* ammo after all the grief the Marines had given him over his choice of weapon.

"I still say it's a pain in the ass," the sergeant said after a moment. "Yeah, yeah—I know all about 'field expedients.' But the projectile drop on these things is a bitch!"

"That's because you Marine pussies are spoiled," Roger told him smugly as he handed the weapon back over. "The muzzle velocities on those bead rifles of yours are so high they've got about the same ballistic profile as a laser over their effective sight range. This kind of weapon takes a *real* marksman!"

"Oh, yeah?" Julian challenged. "In that case, let's see you fire some of these black powder monsters out of something besides that Parkins and Spencer of yours!"

"A petty thought, Sergeant," Roger said loftily. "Very petty."

Both of them grinned at that, because unlike the rifles the K'Vaernians were making up for the humans, Roger's big magnum had a built in system to measure projectile velocities without a chronograph. Better still, it automatically fed the information on the last round fired to the rifle's holographic sight unit, which, in turn, automatically adjusted the sight's point of aim. Just knowing exactly where to aim wasn't enough to make a crack shot out of anyone who hadn't mastered the techniques to make sure the bullet actually went there, but it did help to explain some of Roger's uncanny ability to make the really long-range shots.

"Well, I never thought I'd admit it," Julian said, "but I guess I really am glad you brought that smoke pole along. Mind you, I'd still prefer a bead rifle—or to have the damned plasma rifles on-line!—but if I can't have that, this is a pretty damned good substitute. Thanks, Your Highness."

"Don't mention it, Sarge," Roger said, clapping him on the shoulder. "Remember, it's my imperial ass, too, if we come up short against the Boman."

Julian nodded, and the prince smacked his shoulder again, nodded briskly, and strode off, followed by Cord and his assigned bodyguards.

"Sure it is," the NCO said, so quietly that Fain could barely hear him. "Sure it is . . . and the only thing you're worried about, too, I bet!"

The human laughed, shook his head, and turned back to the native sergeant.

"Now, Krindi, about those bayonets—"

Poertena stood beside the building ways and watched the swarming K'Vaernian shipwrights at their work.

There was no real possibility of completing the vessels the humans would require for their transoceanic voyage out of the resources currently available in K'Vaern's Cove. But there was enough seasoned timber to begin laying down the keels and frames, and the fairing battens were already in place. The light planking ran over the frames Poertena had selected to establish the lines of the hull, and the local shipwrights were busily setting up the intermediate frames within the template so established. All in all, the little Pinopan was more than satisfied with how quickly his teams were working. And they *were* "his" teams.

Once the Council had committed to full-bore support for the shipbuilding project, that carefully hoarded, officially "nonexistent" timber had started falling out of certain artfully concealed stockpiles, and the shipwrights' guild had turned out hundreds of trained shipbuilders. At first, enthusiasm had been limited, despite the Council's insistence and financial support. However, even the grumpiest and most conservative of the workers had been delighted to have work at all, given the current besieged state of the city, and there'd been a certain excitement over building such large ships to such a novel design. And what Poertena had been able to show them about molding lines and lofting hulls properly had been devoured with a burning passion. But for all that, there'd also been a great deal of skepticism, for no one had ever suggested the hull form and, particularly, the rig Poertena had designed.

Most of that skepticism had disappeared once he got his "technology demonstrator" into the water, however. Given the support of the Council, he'd been able to get the ten-meter test vehicle built and launched considerably more quickly than he'd anticipated. In fact, he'd managed it almost as quickly as Captain Pahner had demanded, and he was justifiably pleased with himself for the accomplishment.

He was also deeply satisfied with how well the new craft had performed. Some adjustments had been required, but the basic hull form was a well established and thoroughly proven one, used all over Pinopa and virtually identical to what had once been called a "Baltimore clipper" on Earth. Although Poertena had worked for almost four standard years in his uncle's yard on Pinopa to help defray his college expenses, this was the first time in decades that he'd turned his hand to any sort of design work, and he was actually a bit surprised that he'd gotten it as close to right as he had. He'd been forced to move the mainmast of his twin-masted design about one meter aft, and there was a little more hoist to the big gaff foresail, which was actually the primary sail for this rig, than there really ought to have been, as well. Like most Pinopans, all of whom had a certain mania for fast ships, Poertena had a tendency to over-spar his designs. Unlike some of his fellows, though, he also recognized that he did, and he'd modified his sail plan accordingly.

Despite those minor flaws, however, the demonstrator had been a complete success, particularly when it came to laying the doubts of the local maritime community to rest. The expressions and consternation of the Cove's grizzled captains as they watched the half-sized topsail schooner go bounding across the dark blue of the K'Vaernian Sea, leaving a ruler-straight wake of creamy white as she sailed almost twenty degrees closer to the wind than any other ship in the world could have, had been priceless. And well they should have been. The ability to sail a single compass point—just a hair over eleven degrees—closer to the wind than another ship meant that the more weatherly vessel would be almost four minutes ahead, all other things being equal, after sailing a mere thirty kilometers. Beating dead to windward, a ship which could sail no closer than fifty degrees to the wind (which was better than any of the locally produced designs could manage) would have to travel fifty-two kilometers to make good thirty-two, whereas Poertena's new design would have to travel only forty-two kilometers, or only eighty percent of the same run. That was an advantage, over a voyage of many hundred kilometers, which no merchant skipper could fail to appreciate, and it didn't even consider the fact that being able to sail closer to the wind than a pursuer could would provide an invaluable insurance policy against pirates . . . or that the new rig required a much smaller crew of sail-handlers. Those thoughts had suggested themselves almost instantly to the captains watching Poertena's design go through her paces, and when she spun on her heel, shooting neatly across the wind to settle on the opposite tack and go racing onward at a speed no other ship could have sustained, those same captains had been ready to kill for ships of their own like her.

To the Mardukans, Poertena's little ship was pure magic, and they regarded him with the sort of awe which was the just due of any irascible wizard. There might be questions about the humans' endless store of innovations in some quarters, but aside from two or three dyed-in-the-wool reactionaries, there were no longer any in the shipbuilding community. And while the Cove's seamen still had enormous reservations about the wisdom—or sanity—of any attempt to cross the ocean, they were thoroughly prepared to embrace the new rigging concept and hull form, and Poertena had used their desire to master the new techniques unscrupulously. He was perfectly willing to teach them to anyone . . . as long as his students agreed to sign on for the voyage. More than a few would-be students disappeared into the woodwork when he explained his conditions, but a much larger number agreed. Not without trepidation, and not—he was certain—without comforting themselves in many cases with the belief that the voyage might never happen, but they agreed.

He suspected that Wes Til's strong backing had more than a little to do with that. As Til had half suggested he might at the first Council meeting, the canny merchant had agreed to subsidize the cost of building the new ships in return for Pahner's promise that the ships and crews would be his once the humans were delivered to the far side of the ocean. The fact that the Council had also agreed to pick up a third of the construction cost, and that his shipyards were building them (and thus acquiring an enormous headstart on his competition where the new techniques and technology were concerned *and* recouping a good chunk of his own outlays) had been a factor as well, of course, but Poertena had no problems with that. Even with the Council's contribution to the cost, Til was picking up the tab on an enormously expensive project, and he certainly deserved to show a handsome return on the risk he was running. Besides, his contacts in the seafaring community, especially with Turl Kam's backing, had been essential to recruiting the sailors which the expedition would require.

Now the Pinopan stood in the dockyard, watching the work progress, and hoped that the campaign Captain Pahner and the Mardukan commanders were putting together would come off as planned.

If it didn't, he was going to run out of timber in about another two weeks.

Roger was devoutly thankful for his ear plugs as he walked behind the line of firing Mardukans with Cord.

The concussion from each shot was chest-compressing, which was hardly surprising, since the "rifles" would have been considered light artillery by most humans.

Each firing pit held a firer, a trainee coach, and a human or Diaspran safety coach. The targets were outlines of a Boman warrior, including an outline of an upraised ax. Many of the axes had been blown away by an avalanche of bullets over the last few weeks, but the system still worked. When a recessed metal plate in the primary target zone was struck, the target would fall, then rise back up a moment later. Hits anywhere else, even in the head, wouldn't drop the target.

Roger saw a spark on the head of the target in front of him and lay down on the ground behind the firer. It gave him a better perspective on the shooting while he listened to the safety coach.

"Get your barrel lower." The trainee coach was a Diaspran, a former Laborer of God, to judge from the muscles in his shoulders and back, with a deep, powerful voice which managed to carry through the thunder of rifle fire. "Shoot that barbarian bastard in the gut! It hurts them worse."

"Also," Roger put in from behind the pit, "a bullet shot low will tend to hit *something* even if you miss your target. One that goes flying overhead does nothing but let that barbarian bastard through to kill you. And your buddies."

"Excuse me, Sir!" The Diaspran started to scramble to his feet. "I didn't realize you were back there."

Roger waved all three back down.

"Continue what you're doing. We don't have time for all that saluting and scraping and bowing. We pull out for D'Sley in three days, and every one of us had better be ready." He turned to the K'Vaernian private in the fox hole. "A few days—a week—and you're going to be in one of these facing *real* Boman. Barbarians with axes that have no purpose in life but to kill you. Every single time you squeeze that trigger, I want you to keep that in mind. Got it?"

"Yes, Your Highness," the K'Vaernian said.

From his looks, the rifleman had been a fisherman until a month and a half ago, with nothing to worry about but whether his boat's nets would bring in enough fish to keep the wolf from the door, or whether a sudden storm would send the boat to the bottom, like so many before it. Now he was faced with radically different stresses, like the possibility that someone he'd never met, and had never hurt, would try to kill him, and the question of whether or not he could kill in return. Roger could see the confusion in his face, and produced a smile.

"Just keep your aim low, and follow the orders of your officers, Troop," he said with a chuckle. "And if your officers are dead, and your sergeants look white, remember, it's ruin to run. Just lay down and hold your ground and wait for supports, like a soldier."

"Yes, Sir, Your Highness!"

Roger pushed himself to his feet, nodded to the other two, and continued down the line with his *asi*.

"There was something suspiciously polished about that last statement, 'Your Highness,'" Cord observed, and Roger smiled.

"More of the Captain's Kipling," he said, "I ran across it in a book at the Academy, but I'd almost completely forgotten about it. It's called 'The Half-Made Recruit.' 'Just take open order, lie down and sit tight, and wait for supports like a soldier. Wait, wait, wait like a soldier. Soldier of the Queen.'"

"Ah," the shaman said. "A good sentiment for them, then. And it sounds familiar."

"Really?" the prince looked up at his *asi*, wondering

just how much Kipling Pahner had shared with the old
shaman, but refrained from repeating the last stanza
of the poem:

> When you're wounded and left on Afghanistan's
>   plains,
> And the women come out to cut up what remains,
> Just roll to your rifle and blow out your brains,
> And go to your God like a soldier.
> Go, go, go like a soldier.
> Soldier of the Queen.

Turl Kam copied the posture of the humans around
him, standing with his foot and peg not too far apart
and all four hands clasped behind his back. The blocks
of fresh-minted soldiers striding by were impressive. He
had to admit that, yet he wished that he was as inwardly
confident as his outward appearance proclaimed.

"We've poured out money and political capital like
water," the one-legged ex-fisherman said. "I've bullied
friends, tormented enemies, and lied to everyone but
my wife—and the only reason I didn't lie to *her* was
because she agreed with me and was busy helping me
lie to everyone else. So tell me one more time that
you're going to be able to do something with this army."

Captain Pahner looked at the ranks of four-armed
natives, brand-new harnesses polished, their freshly
made pikes, assegais, or rifles gleaming under the bright
pewter sky.

"There are no guarantees in war, Sir. The troops
have trained hard in the time they've had, we've
picked the best officers we could find, and we've got
pretty damn good initial intelligence on the enemy.
That puts us in the best position we could realistically expect, but all I can absolutely promise is that
we'll try. Hard."

"Your plan is complex," the chairman grumped. "Too complex."

"It is," Pahner agreed. "Especially for a green army. But if we're going to take the field with you, we've got to come up with a way to hit them hard and do it fast, and at least there are three bullets in our gun. Any one of them could—probably would—kill the Boman. Certainly we should eliminate them as a threat for the remainder of this year if even one of them works properly. If all three work, then we should eliminate the Boman threat permanently . . . and reduce our own casualties enormously."

"I suppose that will have to be good enough," the chairman said, sighing.

"I will tell you this," Pahner said, after a moment. "You, and your society, will never be the same again. Once the genie's out of the bottle, you can't put him back."

"Excuse me?" Kam looked at the human in perplexity, and Pahner shrugged.

"Sorry. It's an expression my own people use. What it means is that once a new idea or a new invention is turned loose, it takes on a life of its own, and you can't get rid of it. These weapons won't just go away, and using any new weapon just gets easier and easier . . . especially if they let you kick the shit out of your enemies on the cheap."

"I suppose so," the chairman said. "But perhaps this will be the last war. Surely we'll learn from this, put away these toys, and become a society devoted to peaceful trade."

The Marine looked up at the towering Mardukan, and it was his turn to sigh.

"Let's talk about this after the battle, okay?"

"Bravo Company?" Fain stepped up to the sergeant assembling the riflemen.

"Yes, Sir," the K'Vaernian NCO said, and snapped to attention.

The docks behind the group of K'Vaernian riflemen were a picture of frenzied activity. Hundreds of watercraft, from barges barely fit to navigate across the Bay to grain ships that normally plied their trade along the coast, were lined up, disgorging soldiers and cargo. As Fain watched, a column of pikes formed up and marched inland. Beyond them, one of the new bronze "field pieces" was being swayed out of a grain ship's hold and down to the dock, where its limber and team of draft *turom* were already waiting for it.

D'Sley's whole lifeblood had been trade. Located in the swamps created by the Tam River as it neared the sea, the city had controlled the estuary of that vital waterway. Since the estuary was relatively shallow, most seacraft had unloaded their cargo on these docks and cross loaded it to barges designed for river trade. Most of the latter had been destroyed or stolen by the Boman, but there had been numerous shipyards and stockpiles of building materials scattered around the city, most of which hadn't been lost, stolen, or burned.

"Don't call me 'Sir'!" the Diaspran sergeant snapped. "I work for a living. This is your guide. You know where you're supposed to go?"

"Southwest wall," the K'Vaernian NCO said, and nodded to the D'Sley woman who was to guide them to their positions.

"You don't have a problem with following a woman, do you?" Fain asked. There damn well would have been problems for a Diaspran unit, and he knew it, but these K'Vaernians didn't seem to mind.

"Not at all," the K'Vaernian said.

"Okay, move out when you have eight out of ten of your people. We'll round up the stragglers back here and send them along."

"We're ready to go now, then," the other NCO said. "Except I don't know where our captain is."

"He'll be along. Most of the officers are in officer's call at the moment." Fain handed the other sergeant a hastily prepared map. "Here. There's been some damage to the city. This should help, if you get lost. Move out."

"Yes, Si—Sergeant," the K'Vaernian said as he took the map, then turned to the company of riflemen. "Okay, you maggots! Fall in and get ready to move! Act like you've got a pair!"

"You're ready?" Fain asked the guide, who kept her eyes on the ground but made a gesture of agreement.

"Yes, Lord."

"Don't call me— Oh, never mind. Just don't let anyone bully you, and guide them well, all right?"

"Yes, Lord," the woman said. "I won't fail you."

"Don't fail *yourself*," the Diaspran responded. "Good luck."

The infantry marched off on the guide's heels, merging with the swarm of pikemen and spearmen funneling into the city, and Fain looked over his shoulder as the first troop of cavalry pounded past towards the distant, shattered gate. Someone in the next regiment raised a cheer, and the officer at the head of the cantering troop flourished his sword until they were out of sight in the ruined city.

"And good luck to you, you poor bastards," the sergeant said softly.

Roger looked out at the city through the open flap of the command tent. D'Sley had been much smaller than K'Vaern's Cove, but it had, by all reports, been quite beautiful in its heyday. The construction of the city on a rise in the middle of the tree-filled swamp had run heavily to wood, however, and when the

Boman horde washed over its low walls, not even the Mardukan climate had been able to prevent the fires from getting out of hand.

Some of the piles of corpses near the docks, most of which were, thankfully, done decomposing, showed clear signs of having been heated to the point where bone burned. It must have been a veritable firestorm, so there wasn't much to be found in the way of sights. Just scattered chimneys, blackened stubs of pillars, and the curtain walls. Most of the lumber and shipyards, though, had been *outside* the walls, fortunately.

"It looks like the city was stripped before being burned," Julian was saying. "There are no signs of grain in the ruins of the granaries, and all the worked materials are gone from the ironworks. All the ore that should be there is, though."

"So did they use boats, or carry it out by land?" Pahner asked.

"Land," Rus From said. "The trail to Sindi is badly damaged from heavy traffic, and there are no indications of barge construction. I'd say everything left by land."

"What's available in the shipyards?" the Marine CO asked, swiveling his head to look at Poertena.

"Ever't'ing we need," the Pinopan said with a huge grin. "We can get to work shippin' it back home to tee Cove right away."

"Do it," the captain said, and turned to Fullea Li'it. "How's the transfer going?"

"Well," the widow answered, consulting a scroll of notes. "All of your infantry regiments are across. The cannon and rockets are all unloaded, and most of the provisions are across. We're cross loading to the barges, and that will be completed by tomorrow."

"Tor?"

"We're still pushing the field force through," the

Guard's second in command and designated CO for the D'Sley garrison said. "My people will be coming ashore starting tomorrow. Don't worry, Captain. Whatever happens at Sindi, D'Sley is going to stay firmly in our hands."

"Rastar?"

"We had to take the long road around the end of the Bay," the pistol-covered Northerner said, taking a sip of wine, "but we're all here. We didn't run into anyone on the way, either, and we'll be ready to move out again in the morning."

"Get used to long days in the saddle; there are lots more to come," Pahner told him, and looked back to Julian. "The Boman haven't moved?"

"No, Sir. Not *en masse*. Parties of them have come and gone from the city, some of them quite large, but the main force there is sitting tight, and those nodal forces of theirs are sitting just as tight on what used to be other cities."

"I still don't understand that," Bistem Kar admitted candidly. "It's not like them at all."

"We already knew the bastards had learned not to throw themselves straight at fortified walls at Therdan," Rastar told him with bleak pride. "Obviously, they're sitting in place and waiting for starvation to weaken the Cove before they hit it."

"Oh, that part we understand," Tor Flain assured him. "They've never been smart and patient enough to try it before, but there can't be much doubt that that's exactly what they're doing. But it's the way they're deployed while they wait that bothers me."

"There could be several reasons for it, Tor," Bogess suggested. "For one thing, Julian was right about the additional security it offers their women and children."

Bistem Kar gave a hand-clap of conditional agreement, but he still looked decidedly unhappy, and

Pahner didn't really blame him. The comfortable belief that all of the Boman were clustered in and around Sindi had turned out to be somewhat less than accurate once Gunny Jin and his LURPs got into position. Actually, smaller forces of a "mere" ten to fifteen thousand warriors each had been deployed to the sites of several of the other conquered League and non-League city-states . . . all of them on the far side of Sindi from D'Sley. But so far as Jin and his human and Mardukan scouts had been able to determine, those satellite forces had only a relative handful of women and children as supporting camp followers. At least half of all the Boman dependents were packed into Sindi with "only" thirty or forty thousand warriors to keep them company. What was more, the women and children in the city apparently came from every Boman clan and tribe, not just from those of the warriors deployed there.

"No doubt the sergeant is correct, at least in part," Kar told Bogess after a moment. "Certainly Sindi had the best fortifications of any of the states outside the League, and from all reports, they took the city—and its walls—pretty much intact. So, yes, it probably *is* the best and most easily defended place from which to protect their families. But Boman clans *always* stay together, and they trust no one—not even tribes of the same clan—to protect their women and children." He shook his head in a human-style gesture. "We've seen entirely too many innovations from the Boman to make me happy, and this strikes me as another. I would be much happier if I understood precisely what it's intended to accomplish."

"We're trying to figure that out, Sir," Julian told him, "but we haven't been able to get any of our listening devices actually into the city . . . yet. From what the shotgun mikes have picked up from the troops' bull sessions, though, it's pretty clear that this Kny Camsan has a whole bunch of new ideas, and this seems to be one of them. Lot of the troops aren't too crazy about some of his notions, either, but Camsan's the one who took over after Therdan, and he's kicked so much ass since then that he's almost like God. Or he was right after they took Sindi, anyway. It looks like some of the shine may be starting to wear off from the troops' perspective—kind of a 'but what have you done for us lately' sort of attitude."

The intel NCO gazed down at the map on the table for a few moments, then shrugged.

"Whatever he's up to, at least we know where the bastard is, and the whole Boman position is still pretty much a holding one. Mostly, they seem to be busy foraging around the cities, and I imagine they'll sit right where they are until they finish eating the countryside bare and don't have any choice but to move on out. In the meantime, though, we know where they are and, so far as we can tell, they *don't* know where *we* are.

"The scout teams report that the maps are fairly accurate," he continued. "There've been some changes—like the damage the roads have taken from the Boman's use, like the track from here to Sindi. But in general, the cavalry should be able to trust them."

"Good," Pahner said. "Better than I could've hoped. Rus, is the damage to the track going to slow up your work crews' transit?"

"Not appreciably." The cleric took a bite of apsimon. "They'll be mainly foot traffic, and they can keep to the shoulders if they have to. By the time we're ready for the caravans, we should have all the road repair gangs in place."

"You need to make the timetable," the Marine said warningly. "If you don't, that whole part of the plan is out the window."

The cleric shrugged all four shoulders.

"It's in the hands of the God, quite literally. Heavy storms will prevent us, but other than that, I see no reason to fear. We'll make the schedule, Captain Pahner, unless the God very specifically prevents."

"Fullea?"

"We'll be waiting," the D'Sley matron said. "We're already repairing the dock facilities, and things will go much quicker once we get some decent cranes back in action. We'll make *our* timetable."

"Rastar?"

"Hmmm? Oh, timetable. Not a problem. Just a ride in the country."

"I swear, you're getting as bad as Honal," Roger said with a chuckle.

"Ah, it's these beautiful pistols you gave me!" the Northerner prince enthused. "With such weapons, how can we fail?"

"You're not to become decisively engaged," Pahner warned.

"Not a chance, Captain," the Northerner promised much more seriously. "We've fought this battle before, and we didn't have any friends waiting for us that time. Don't worry; we aren't planning on leaving our horns on their mantels. Besides, I want to see what cannon do to them, and we won't have any of our own along."

"Bistem? Bogess?"

"It will be interesting," the K'Vaernian said. "Very interesting."

"A masterly understatement, but accurate," the Diaspran agreed.

"Interesting is fine, but are you ready?" Roger asked. "Some of the units still seem pretty scrambled."

"They'll be ready by tomorrow morning," Kar assured him, and Tor Flain nodded in agreement.

"All right," Pahner said, looking at the tent roof.

"We'll transfer the bulk of the cavalry tomorrow. Once they're off, we'll embark the infantry. As we're doing all of that, we'll also push out aggressive patrols on this side of the river to screen our advance. Starting tomorrow."

He gazed up at the roof for a few more seconds, obviously running through a mental checklist, then looked at Roger.

"One small change," he said. "Roger, I want you to take over the Carnan Battalion of the New Model. That and one troop of cavalry—Rastar, you choose which."

"Yes, Captain." The Mardukan nodded.

"They're going to be moving with the infantry. Roger will command the combined force as a strategic reserve. Roger, look at putting *turom* under all the infantry."

"If you're thinking of a mobile infantry battalion, *civan* would be better," Roger said. "Also, aren't we going to need the *turom* elsewhere?"

"We'll see. If you can get them on *turom* in the next three days, they'll go upriver behind the cavalry screen. If you can't, they'll go with the infantry."

"Yes, Sir," the prince responded.

"Okay," the captain concluded. "Get as much rest as you can tonight. There won't be much from here on out."

CHAPTER THIRTY-ONE

The gentle current of the river was barely enough to make the barge bob, but the war *civan* was having none of it.

"Get *on* there, you son of a bitch!" Honal snarled, but the *civan* was remarkably impervious to his rider's gentle encouragement. Finally, the cavalry commander gave up. "Get some ropes!"

Enough lines on the horse-ostrich and enough hands on the lines finally managed to drag the recalcitrant beast onto the barge.

"Last one, Rastar!"

"Good, we're already behind schedule," the Northern prince replied, and turned to look over his shoulder as something moved up behind him.

"Good luck, you two," Roger said. The prince was riding his huge war *pagee* again, with that weird creature from the far lands and his war slave up on her back. It was fortunate indeed, Rastar reflected, that the captain's plan didn't require Roger to cross the river. Getting that huge beast on a barge would have been far worse than unpleasant.

The last prince of fallen Therdan looked past the human and his odd companions to the troop of cavalry following along behind the *pagee*. Chim Pri, the troop leader, was a cousin of sorts, a distant one, but he'd shown great promise on the retreat and in Diaspra. He also worshiped the ground Roger strode on, so detailing his troop as bodyguards—whatever the captain might call it—had been an easy decision.

Rastar was hard put not to grunt in laughter at the sight of the brand-new banner snapping in the breeze beside Patty. It had been Honal's idea to have the thing made, but Rastar had gotten behind and pushed once his cousin suggested it. It hadn't been easy to get it made without Roger's discovering that they were up to something, but the expression on the prince's face when it was formally presented had made all of the secrecy and skulking about eminently worthwhile. Rastar hadn't been certain whether Roger wanted to laugh or shoot them on the spot, which was more or less what he'd expected. What he hadn't expected was the fierce pride the prince's new personal cavalry troop took in their banner.

Rastar watched the stiff breeze blow the *dianda* standard straight out to display the *basik* head. Of course, it didn't depict *quite* a standard *basik*. This one lacked the timidly inoffensive and stupid expression of the original, and the mouthful of needle-sharp fangs—clearly exposed in a particularly nasty-looking human-style grin—were hardly part of the issue equipment of the garden-variety *basik*.

On the other hand, they went very well with the incredibly deadly *basik* who commanded the cavalry riding under it.

"Good luck yourself," Rastar told him now. "And try not to get killed. Captain Pahner would do all manner of incredibly painful things to me if you did something that stupid."

"Coward," Roger said, and Rastar shook a playful fist up at him.

"Just make sure you're ready when we come scampering back," Honal put in with a grunt of laughter.

"We will be," Roger said. "I swear it."

Rastar stuck out a true-hand, and Roger leaned down to take it.

"Keep your powder dry," the human said in a voice which was only half-teasing.

"We will." The Northern prince spurred his war *civan*, and the beast easily trotted down the planks onto the barge beside Honal's recalcitrant mount. "See you in Sindi."

"No!" Kny Camsan, paramount war leader of the Boman, slammed a fisted true-hand onto the table hard enough to send half the cups flying into the air and spill wine everywhere. Not that it mattered particularly, for the floor of the former throne room was well over a centimeter deep in food and other debris. The once splendid chamber reeked like a midden, but the barbarians lying on mats of straw atop the mire paid no more attention to the muck than they did to the stench.

"We have those K'Vaernian bastards right where we want them," the war leader continued in grating tones, "and I, for one, have no intention of throwing myself at their walls until they're a hell of a lot weaker than they are right now. I am *not* letting anyone repeat Therdan."

There was a mutter of agreement at that. The war leader who'd decided that Therdan could simply be overrun with enough bodies had died in the second wave, but Boman in fighting frenzy weren't precisely noted for tactical flexibility, and the waves had continued while the tribal leaders argued over who would replace him. And while they argued, nearly a tenth part of the combined clans had died.

"K'Vaern's Cove isn't Therdan," Knitz De'n argued. "And they're just sitting there like *knivet* in a burrow. They obviously aren't going to send forces out, and if they won't come out to fight, we should strike them now. Instead, we sit in our own shit in this foul city when we should be on the trail to war, not hiding behind walls!"

"He has a point," Mnb Trag said mildly. The old chieftain was Camsan's closest adviser, but he was also smart enough to appear receptive to the suggestions and demands of others. It was, as he'd shown Camsan, one of the most effective ways to *defuse* those demands. Unfortunately, it worked better for an adviser or the chieftain of a single clan than it did for a paramount war leader, and Camsan glowered at De'n.

"Let the damned shit-sitters break *their* teeth on walls for a change!" he shot back. "If you want to attack K'Vaern's Cove, go ahead, but I shall remain here until they're on their knees. And when they're weak enough, then we'll destroy *that* city and return to our homes. That's what we swore—that's what *you* swore—to do. To remain as long as it took to destroy the Southerners once and for all."

"And that's what we want to do!" Knitz De'n snapped. "Let the shit-sitters hide inside their walls if they want—*we* are the warriors of the Boman!"

The women came out with new cups of wine and more cooked meat. The herds of *turom* and *pagee* which had supported the city now feasted on its fields, and the Boman feasted on them. When they were gone, the clans would have to move as well, but not yet. And when they did move, Camsan intended to accomplish something no other Boman chieftain had ever accomplished. Which, of course, was the true reason so many of the other clans' women and children were here at Sindi under the "protection" of his own clan and its closest allies.

Not that he was prepared to explain any of that to De'n. The young firebrand was too arrogant and ambitious to be admitted to all of Camsan's plans. Unfortunately, Camsan knew De'n spoke for a growing fraction of even those warriors in Sindi, so he dared not simply ignore him, either.

"Perhaps there's some point to your argument," the war leader told the younger tribesman as one of the women replaced his own wine cup. "I won't rush to attack the walls of K'Vaern's Cove, but we are Boman, and even the sharpest ax grows dull if it's allowed to rust too long upon the wall. I would not have you grow rusty when I'll soon have need of your strong arm, Knitz De'n, and there are reports of League cavalry on the land road from K'Vaern's Cove to D'Sley. Why don't you take your band and go see what's happening? If you find any of those League shit-sitters, kill them for us, and take their goods for your own. Then check D'Sley and make sure the shit-sitters aren't trying to rebuild it or something."

De'n looked at him for a long moment, obviously aware that he was about to be dispatched on a task which was little more than make-work designed to get him out from under Camsan's feet. Yet his own demands for a more active policy left him little choice but to obey, and so he stood and walked out without another word.

Mnb Trag rubbed his horns as he watched him go.

"We do need to do something soon," Trag said much more quietly to Camsan. "He's not the only one complaining."

"I know he's not," Camsan responded, equally quietly. "And I also know that if we sit here long enough, the plague demons will begin to carry off our warriors." The nomadic Boman had developed very little of the resistance to diseases which city dwellers required, particularly on a planet like Marduk, where no one had ever heard of the germ theory of disease or the necessity for public hygiene. "But if our prisoners spoke truthfully, then K'Vaern's Cove isn't nearly so well supplied as we'd feared, now is it? And," the war leader added with an evil chuckle, "I feel confident somehow that they were truthful with us, don't you?"

It was Trag's turn to chuckle. The greatest prize the Boman had taken in their entire campaign had been the capture of Tor Cant, the shit-sitter whose treachery had united the clans—however temporarily—at last. It was hard to believe that even *he* could have been stupid enough to allow himself to be taken alive, but Trag had come to the conclusion that there was nothing Tor Cant hadn't been stupid enough to do. It was a pity, in some ways, because for all of his stupidity the one-time Despot of Sindi had possessed a certain devious cunning. He might have amounted to something if he'd had a single *sekr* of brain or even a trace of backbone to go with that quality.

Fortunately for the Boman, he'd had neither. It had taken him almost six days to die, but he'd told them everything they could ever have wanted to know about his betrayals of his fellow shit-sitters before the first iron had even begun to glow. Most of the "councilors" and advisers they'd captured with him had taken their cue from their despot . . . not that their efforts to buy their lives with their information had worked, of course. But it did mean that Kny Camsan knew all there was to know about both the strengths and weaknesses of his last remaining foes.

"I share your confidence in their . . . honesty," Trag said after a moment, "and the K'Vaernian Guard is far too small to be a threat in the field. All they can do is hold their walls, and they won't be able to do even that once starvation sets in properly. But their accursed navy remains intact. Can we be certain that they'll be unable to fill their granaries?"

"From where?" Camsan chuckled scornfully. "We've destroyed all of the other shit-sitter cities around the sea and throughout the Tam Valley, and the other clans sit on their fields and devour their animals. All they can offer K'Vaern's Cove is more mouths to feed and no food to feed them with." He clapped hands in a gesture of negation. "No, Trag, hunger will begin to bite them long before the demons weaken us. Then they'll come out and fight, or they'll go aboard their stinking boats and flee, and either way, we'll take their city and burn it to the ground."

"And the League cavalry?" Trag asked.

"We'll see," the war leader said, taking a bite of half-raw *civan*. "True, the iron heads had more guts than these worthless Southerners, but there can't be many of them left. I doubt there's anything to the rumors, but we'll see. And if there isn't, we'll send some of the youngsters out to K'Vaern's Cove to see how it's defended. If it looks weak, or if they're beginning to run low on food already, we'll put in an attack to probe their defenses. But I am *not* going to repeat Therdan."

Not, at least, until I've taken K'Vaern's Cove, as well . . . and made my position as paramount war leader something more permanent, he added silently. He didn't say it aloud, although that wasn't because he distrusted Trag. His older ally knew all about his plans, he was sure, despite the fact that they had never openly discussed them, and if Trag had disapproved, one of them would already be dead.

"All right," Trag said after only the briefest moment, "but be warned. Hungry or not, those damned K'Vaernians have always been too tricky to make me happy."

"I can't believe we've gotten this close without these idiots even guessing we're here," Honal said.

After being ferried across the river, the cavalry had taken back trails up to a point just outside Sindi. Thanks to the reports from the Marine long-range reconnaissance patrols, the Northerners had been able to avoid the scattered clusters of Boman on the north side of the river between D'Sley and Sindi. Not that there'd been many of those clusters to avoid.

Sindi, the undisputed queen of the upper Tam, had originally been built on the south side of the river, but it had long since spread to both banks, taking its impressively fortified walls with it. Before the Boman came, it had been surrounded by vast fields of barleyrice, which the constant rains were rapidly destroying, now that no one tended them any longer. But its true wealth had lain in the fact that it had controlled the only bridge across the river for *hurtongs*. The bridge itself was a massive stone construction at the heart of the city, wide enough for four *pagee* or twenty warriors abreast, whose completion, generations before, had really begun the history of Sindi.

Although Sindi had drawn most of its wealth and power from its position on the Tam, the city was actually located at the confluence of three rivers. A smaller stream, the Stell, flowed into the Tam on the western side of the city, where the road to D'Sley crossed it on a narrow stone bridge and then continued on through spreading fields to the distant jungle. The third river, the Thorm, joined the Tam just upstream from the city, flowing down from the northeast and eventually becoming unnavigable not far from one of the Northern League cities.

The cavalry troopers had turned progressively more grim as they drew closer to the destroyed cities which had been their homes, but Rastar wasn't worried. He knew they were fully focused on their target, and he was confident that they understood the mission brief. Which seemed to be working out almost perfectly—so far, at least—he told himself, because Honal was right. The Boman clearly didn't have a clue that they were anywhere near. Before the barbarian invasion, there would have been Sindi cavalry patrols this far out to spot them, or at least workers in the fields, but now there was nothing at all on the north side of the river beyond the city gates themselves. All of the field huts had been burned, and nothing moved here but an occasional *basik*.

So far, so good.

"It's a *hurtong* to the gates," Rastar said. "Clande, your group will stop here and hold. Get the surprise set up along the trail, and don't let anybody we may have missed sneak up behind us, or we're all pocked."

"Yes, Rastar." The young cousin might have argued once that rear area security was hardly the job of a warrior. But the only survivors of the League of the North were those who'd learned the lessons which had made their survival possible, and the hotheaded "warrior" who would once have argued was one with last season's rains.

"The rest of you," Rastar went on, sweeping Honal's subordinate officers with his eyes, "remember why we're here, and don't get too enthusiastic. It's not like there's all that much we can really do if they're hiding inside the city, after all! We'll make a charge at the gate and see if that works. It probably won't, so we'll put some grapnels on the walls. When they start throwing their damned axes, shoot a few of them—but don't, for the gods' sake, let them realize how effective the rifles and revolvers are. When they get their shit together, we back off and taunt."

"We've heard this before, Rastar," Honal said patiently and squinted up into the gathering light as the morning drizzle began. "Let's go."

The last prince of Therdan looked at his cousin and nodded.

"Let's all be charming lures, shall we?"

"Absolutely," Honal said. "Sheffan! Front!"

"Julian," Gunny Jin whispered into his radio, "give me the Old Man."

"Pahner here."

"The cavalry are starting the demonstration, Sir."

"Good. Give me an update if the situation changes."

The massive gates shrugged off the thunderous explosion with scarcely a quiver.

"Oh, very nice," Rastar said. "They should be convinced they're impregnable now."

"Yes," Honal agreed. "And so far, we haven't even lost anyone."

That, Rastar knew, would change as soon as the sun rose above the eternal clouds. Already, the Boman could be seen on top of the high wall, running around without apparent direction. A few groups of cavalry had gotten grapnels up on the battlements and were swarming, slowly and carefully, up the lines. As the two commanders watched, a group of barbarians got one of the heavy hook-and-line arrangements unfastened and hurled it over the side. The grapnel, fortunately, didn't hit anyone, but the shower of throwing axes which followed it emptied a few saddles. Nor had all the Boman activity been as pointless as it had looked, and more than one Northerner flinched as a pair of massive hooped bombards fired from a bastion of the main gate in a huge belch of lurid flame and thick smoke. Fortunately, the Boman gunners had only a vague notion of how artillery was supposed to work, and they hit nothing. The arquebusiers who'd finally begun assembling in their covered positions were another matter, however. They were no more accurate than the bombards, individually, but there were far more of them, and more saddles began to empty, while here and there a *civan* went down bellowing in pain.

"Time to call them back," Rastar ordered.

"Got it."

The high call of the *glitchen* horn rang out through the rain, signaling for the cavalry to pull away from the walls and out of ax range, and Rastar watched with an approving eye as his troopers obeyed.

"Now to do the real work," he said with a grunt of laughter.

"They're taunting us," Mnb Trag said.

"Yes," Camsan agreed. "But *why* are they taunting us?"

The Northerner cavalry had been at it all morning. Their initial attack had been a complete failure—the bags of gunpowder had barely even scratched the gates. But the small band hadn't given up, though precisely what the idiots thought they could accomplish was beyond Camsan. They'd been riding around the walls and hurling taunts at the guards for the last few hours. No scatological or genealogical detail had been left out of the suggestions which could be clearly heard on the walls, and the taunts were working, judging by the furious anger of his warriors.

"They want us to chase them," Camsan said, "so we won't."

He turned to look back over the city with a proprietary eye. Although it had taken some damage in the sack, it was still the crown jewel of the upper Tam, with rank on rank of low stone houses rising up the central hill to the citadel. Whatever else anyone could say, *he* had taken Sindi, and the horns of that hated bastard Cant. Nobody was going to take either of those accomplishments away from him, and he'd already decided that Sindi would make an appropriate capital for the new, powerful empire which would shortly replace the weak and gutless shit-sitters who had dared to challenge the Boman clans.

But his contemplation of the future was interrupted when Trag gave a handclap of negation.

"I don't think you have that choice," the older chieftain told him, and pounded on a merlon of the granite wall with one false-hand. "If you sit here much longer, looking like you're afraid to face a couple of hundred League shits in the open, you might not have a position by tomorrow."

"That bad?" the war leader asked his adviser. Trag grunted, and as Camsan turned to look at the warriors around them, he was forced to admit that his ally might have a point. "All right, take the Tarnt'e and go chase them down. There was never a group of cavalry Boman couldn't run into the ground—not even old, worn out Boman," he added with a grunt of laughter, but Trag didn't join his amusement.

"I don't think that will work either," he said somberly. "If I go out, by the time I get back, you'll have been deposed, and Knitz De'n will have taken your place."

"But if we do what De'n wants and storm K'Vaern's Cove head on, it will be the death of thousands of them," Camsan said. "Do they want that?"

"No," the older chieftain said, "but most of them

figure it'll be someone else who does the dying. Besides, what they really want, most of them, is to return to their villages. But we made this stupid pact to destroy *all* the cities of the south, which means they can't go yet, so they want to destroy K'Vaern's Cove and get it over with. They're frustrated, and that's why they want to gut these iron head pukes."

"Don't they realize that the iron heads wouldn't be riding around out there all by themselves unless they *wanted* us to come out and chase them? There has to be a reason they want to lure us away from the city, Mnb."

"Of course there does, and most of our warriors know it. But if they can't burn K'Vaern's Cove to the ground, then killing these Northerners will have to do. They know perfectly well that the Northerners want them to come out from behind the walls, and they don't care. At least it would be an honorable battle. Besides, there's only three or four hundred of them."

"That's exactly my point," Camsan said. "The Tarnt'e alone would be more than enough to crush them all."

"That's *not* the point," Trag replied patiently. "You have forty thousand warriors in this stinking city, all of whom want to kill something . . . and most of whom are starting to think thoughts you'd prefer they didn't. You think they don't know some of the other clans are beginning to mutter about how many of the women and children are here under our 'protection'?"

Camsan's eyes narrowed, and this time it was Trag who grunted a harsh laugh.

"Of course they do! Fortunately, most of them think you're only trying to keep the other clan leaders in line, and I think most of them actually admire your ruthlessness. It's what we need in a war leader. But our warriors are Boman, too, and their axes have been unbloodied too long. If you don't give them—all of them—a chance to kill something else, then they're going to start thinking very hard about killing *you*. Kny, you're one of the finest war leaders ever to think for the clans, and I believe you truly have the chance to accomplish what you and I both know you desire. But you don't pay enough attention to the way our warriors *feel*, and that's going to get you killed if you keep it up."

Trag didn't add that it would undoubtedly get him killed right alongside Camsan. Both of them knew it was true, but that didn't invalidate anything he'd just said. More than one Boman war leader had been removed by the clans if he seemed too timid, and the retirement of Boman war leaders was an . . . extremely permanent process.

"Oh, very well," Camsan said at last. "It's ridiculous to take so many to defeat so few—how many iron heads do the fools think there are to go around?—but you probably have a point. I'll give them their chance to kill something. But if I go out to play chase-the-*basik* in the woods, can you stay here with your tribe? At least I can trust you not to totally screw up."

"I can hold the city," the older chieftain agreed. "Besides, I have to admit that I'm a bit old for a *civan* chase."

Julian updated the situation map on his pad and transferred it to the captain.

"It's looking pretty good so far, Sir. The main Boman force is headed out the gates now. Only bad news is that we had another batch of barbs head southwest earlier—about two thousand. We don't have any idea where they were going or where they are at the moment."

Pahner tapped his foot on the barge deck and spat his chewed-up *bisti* root over the side.

"Have the cavalry screen echelon to the south. And throw the patrols out a little farther to keep an eye out for the strays. We need to make sure they don't show up at the wrong time."

"Not good," Kar said. "We're on a slim margin. If your 'strays' turn up during the attack, they'll make things difficult."

"Difficult, but not impossible," Pahner said. "Fog of war. You have to figure that something will go wrong even in the best case, and if that's the worst that happens, I'll be delighted. I'm more worried about them hitting us *after* the assault, anyway."

He looked out over the river. It was filled with barges and boats for over a kilometer in every direction as the army of K'Vaern's Cove made its slow way up river.

"If we get compromised from the north bank, we can land on the south side, where we've got the cavalry screen and the Marine LURPs to cover us. The only part I'm really worried about is the possibility of having this Camsan get word to his detachments too quickly and assemble the main host to come back while we're still landing, and even then the cavalry should slow them up long enough for us to finish landing or retreat."

"Or to get hit during the transfer," Bogess said quietly.

"We can break that part of the operation off at almost any time," Pahner replied with a shrug. "As long as Rastar does his job and the screen stays alert, we're golden."

CHAPTER THIRTY-TWO

"There's something very familiar about this," Honal said. "And I'm getting tired of running away from these fellows."

"Shut up and spur!" Rastar laughed. The wood line was rapidly approaching, and he hoped everything was in place. If it wasn't, things were about to get interesting.

Behind them, the Boman host was still pouring out of the city. It was going to take a while to get them all out, even with the three huge gates in Sindi's northern wall, but at least ten or fifteen thousand were already outside the fortifications. Rastar was relieved—and a bit surprised—to see that so many of the bastards were already coming after his troopers. He and Pahner had both expected a relatively small force to be sent out at first, and they'd figured that the rest of the horde would sit still until the original pursuit force suffered a mischief. But the Boman seemed to be in a bit of a hurry, and from the looks of things, at least sixty or seventy percent of all the warriors in Sindi intended to go chasing after a mere three hundred Therdan and Sheffan cavalry. It didn't seem fair.

"Horns!" Rastar called as they approached the edge of the jungle. The road, such as it was, continued on under the dense trees and tangled lianas, a muddy track that had been the main route to their former homes. In better days, it had seen regular caravans carrying the raw products of the Boman, leather and drugs mainly, to the south, and the return flow of manufactured products—jewelry and the very weapons the cavalry now faced.

The cavalry responded instantly to the call of the horns, narrowing into a double line as it approached the wood line.

"I can see the spare mounts," Honal called. "Now to get it stuck in!"

The two leaders broke to either side of the road, and Rastar dismounted from his wearied *civan* as the rest of the troopers of his "bait force" thundered past them with a yell.

"Time to pock them all!" Rastar shouted to them, swinging up into the saddle of a fresh mount.

"Give 'em hell, Sir!" one of the troopers called back, still headed for where their own remounts waited. "We'll be right behind you!"

"Up the banners!" Rastar bellowed in a grunt of laughter. "Let's get it stuck in!"

"Up the banners!" Honal passed on the order in a voice fit to wake a dozen generations of the dead as he bounded up onto a fresh *civan* of his own. He drew the first pair of his revolvers and raised them overhead.

"*SHEFFAN!*" he howled like a hunting *atul-grak*, and the voices of four thousand additional heavy cavalry thundered their own deep warcries as they burst out of the edge of the jungle behind him.

✧   ✧   ✧

"Aha!" Camsan's head came up as the baying voices sliced through the pattering rain and he recognized the standards at the head of the charging force. "*That's* what this is all about."

"It's that stupid, gutless prince who led the escape from Therdan when he ran away," one of his henchmen grunted as he, too, recognized the banners. "Good. It's time to finish that line off once and for all."

The war leader gazed across at the standard of fallen Therdan, coming at him through the rain, and felt considerably less sanguine than the subchief.

"His uncle wasn't so easy to kill . . . or gutless," he pointed out. "Neither was his father, and I think we're about to get mauled. But you're right—we'll hunt them down at our leisure now. There's not much else to do. Besides, if we don't kill them now, they'll just be back next week."

Camsan made no effort to coordinate the actual attack. There would have been no point in trying, since Boman warriors in hot pursuit of a foe did not respond well to direction. The two or three thousand arquebusiers had already fallen begrudgingly back from the front ranks, since the rain made their matchlocks effectively useless, but the rest of the host only quickened its pace.

Camsan was right about what was going to happen to his leading warriors, but not even he realized how bad it was actually going to be. The Boman were old hands at fighting League cavalry, and they should have known better, but they were also individualists who fought as individuals. And, as almost always happened when the enemy ran away from them, they were more concerned with overtaking their fleeing foes before anyone else caught up and stole the honor of the attack from them than they were with maintaining anything remotely like a formation. The first five or six thousand out of the city gates had opened a relatively wide gap between themselves and their fellows as they pounded through the rain after Rastar's troopers, and—as also happened with unhappy frequency—they were about to get reamed when the "fleeing" cavalry turned on them, because none of their fellow clansmen were in range to support them.

It was all rather depressing to Camsan, who'd spent the last half year fighting an uphill battle to teach his tribesmen at least some modicum of caution and discipline, but it was hardly surprising. And to be fair to his warriors, they knew exactly what was going to happen. But they also knew that the rain would take most of the Northerners' wheel locks out of action, and they still boasted half again the cavalry's numbers. They were going to take losses, but they would also *inflict* losses, and they should be able to at least keep the enemy occupied and pinned down until their slower compatriots could catch up. Besides, this would be their first opportunity to kill something in almost five months, and they bellowed in hungry anticipation.

Some of that anticipation turned to surprise moments later, when the charging cavalry opened fire despite the rain. Mounted troops' wheel locks usually worked at least a little better than matchlocks in typical rain conditions, but these cavalry troopers' weapons weren't working "a little" better. They were working a *lot* better, and Camsan grunted a curse as he watched bullets slam through his warriors. The League cavalry's fire was *much* heavier than normal, and despite the bounding gait of the bipedal *civan*, it was also damnably accurate.

"How the hell are they firing those damned things in the rain?" Camsan demanded as he and the rest of the main body ran after the vanguard, and then snarled a fresh curse as Hirin R'Esa, chieftain of the Ualtha and one of the war leader's staunchest supporters, went down with a fist-sized hole in his chest. "However they're doing it, I'm glad they don't have more of them!"

"It won't do them much good now," his henchman replied with a feral grin. "They're down to ax range, now."

"What's that prayer Roger taught you?" Rastar grunted as he holstered his smoking revolvers.

" 'Gods, for what we are about to receive, may we be truly thankful,' " Honal shouted back. He grinned in the human way, bare-toothed in the rain, as the troopers around him laughed.

"Whatever," Rastar muttered as he couched his lance. The rain of axes was tearing holes in his ranks, and he wasn't prepared to take *too* many casualties in what was really nothing but a giant feint.

The cavalry slammed into the first rank of the barbarians and carried them away. The Boman were already shocked and disordered by the massed pistol fire. Rastar's troopers had discharged well over twenty thousand rounds of twenty-millimeter fire into them. Firing from the back of a moving *civan* had never done much for accuracy, but the Boman had been a big target, and the avalanche of pistol bullets had killed almost a third of their front rank outright and wounded even more of them.

The Northerners' long lances easily took out the rest of the first rank. Snarling, war-trained *civan* slashed and tore as they rode over the wounded, snapping off arms and even heads with vicious delight, and the Broman howls of anticipation of a moment before became shrieks of raw agony as the survivors of Therdan and Sheffan wreaked bloody revenge. Almost better, at least half of Rastar's troopers managed to recover their lances as they slammed through the front rank, and they used them to good effect on the next, slaughtering the barbarians in front of them. And then the cavalry broke through into the gap between the Broman main body and what had been the vanguard. Two-thirds or more of that vanguard were now corpses, and aside from a few who'd been taken by battle frenzy, most of the survivors were running as hard as they could.

By Rastar's most conservative estimate, his four thousand men must have killed at least that many barbarians, and the shrieks of rage and hatred from the rest of the Boman host were music to his ears. Clearly, he and his troopers had accomplished their main goal; whatever happened now, the barbarians would never stop chasing them. Typical Boman bloody-mindedness would see to that, but it never hurt to make sure they got the hint, and Clande and the rest of the reserve were waiting to do just that . . . assuming that he and Honal could get their men back on the trail before the next wave of barbarians caught up to them. That next wave was larger—*much* larger—and for all their frenzy, Boman weren't stupid enough to offer him another opportunity like the last one. No, this wave would concentrate mainly on pinning the cavalry while other warriors swept around on their flanks, and that meant it was time to go.

"Back!" he shouted. "Sound the horns! Back to the forest. Time to run for it!"

His troopers had already managed the hardest part of the maneuver; they hadn't allowed themselves to be sucked into chasing down the fleeing survivors of their first clash. Now they responded instantly to the horn calls and wheeled once more to thunder back up the muddy road towards the woods.

"This is where it gets tricky!" Honal shouted beside him.

"Get to the front. Don't let anything slow us down," Rastar ordered, and Honal nodded acknowledgment and slapped his spurs to his *civan*. Rastar watched him go and crossed the fingers of his left true-hand in yet another gesture acquired from the humans. Timing, he thought, was everything.

The cavalry's lead ranks bogged up a bit as they reached the opening in the woods, but they were all veterans who'd been in nearly continuous battle for half a Mardukan year. Their commanders had learned their own trade well and added the benefits of human notions of discipline to their own, and they handled the maneuver with an aplomb that would have been frankly amazing before the long war against the Boman. Troops interleaved with troops, and squadrons formed into columns, until all three thousand-plus surviving riders were pounding at a gallop down the mud-slick track.

They got themselves sorted out not a moment too soon, for the second wave of Boman had kept right on coming, absorbing the fragments of the first wave as it came. The front ranks of at least twelve thousand howling warriors were fewer than fifty meters behind the rearmost trooper, and Rastar—holding his position near the rear of the column—felt a moment of intense anxiety. The barbarians were close enough to keep up a shower of throwing axes, although their accuracy left a great deal to be desired, and the slower pace the *civan* were forced to adopt as they thundered along in close proximity was allowing the Boman warriors to close the remaining range slowly.

"This is where some artillery would have been nice," he muttered to himself. But if he didn't have field guns, then he had the next best thing . . . assuming that it worked.

An ax clanged off of his backplate, and he gave his

mount the spurs, leaning forward in the saddle to urge
the beast onward. Another handful of his men went
down, but only a handful, and the Boman were beginning to slow themselves down in turn as they packed
solid in the relatively narrow slot of the track. Which
was exactly what Rastar wanted and the humans had
planned on.

The explosions, when they came, were like the end
of the world. Rastar had never heard of "directional
mines" or "claymores" before the humans came along,
but he'd seen them tested in K'Vaern's Cove. It was
amazing how murderous such a relatively simple concept could be, but not even the tests he'd observed
had prepared him for the reality of what a few score
old musket balls packed atop a half-*sedant* or so of
gunpowder could do.

Clande and his reserves had been busy while Rastar
and Honal trolled for Boman, and the trail was lined
on either side with the infernal human devices. The
troopers had placed one every two meters, and there
were almost two hundred of them. The Boman were
running three and four abreast as they pursued their
enemies, and over six hundred of them were in the kill
zone when Clande touched off the fuse and the rolling explosions marched down the trail to envelop them.

There were, perhaps, a dozen survivors.

Six hundred, or even six thousand, casualties were
scarcely a fleabite against the total numbers of the barbarian host, but not even the Boman were immune to
the sheer shock and horror of such heavy losses so
instantaneously inflicted. The howling war cries turned
to screams and shrieks, and the headlong pursuit slith-
ered to a broken-backed halt amid the bodies and bits
of bodies, shattered tree trunks and fallen branches, and
the drifting smoke that shrouded the hell-spawned carnage of the ambush.

Rastar reined his *civan* back to a walk, looking over his shoulder at the destruction and agony, and bared his teeth in a hungry, human-style smile. Another small payment on the enormous debt Therdan owed the Boman, he thought viciously, and stood in the human-designed stirrups he and his troopers had adopted.

"Kiss my ass, you Boman pussies!" he shouted, slapping his rear end. "See you in Therdan—and bring your pocking friends!"

"What in the name of all the demons was *that?*" Camsan's henchman demanded as the two Boman stopped in stunned disbelief. The war leader had been no more than forty or fifty meters outside the kill zone, and he shook his head, half-deafened by the unexpected fury of the explosions.

He'd never imagined anything like the torn and mangled pieces of what had been warriors—certainly not that such carnage could be wreaked in an eyeblink! He stared at the wreckage for several moments, then shook himself again as he felt the matching consternation and disbelief of the warriors surrounding him.

He looked around quickly. The morning had not gone well. He and his warriors had killed perhaps two hundred of the shit-sitter cavalry, but their own losses had easily been fifteen or twenty times as great, and the sheer shock of this last hammer blow only made the pain of their casualties bite deeper. The clans had lost far more men in taking any one of the shit-sitter cities he'd conquered, but losses were expected when storming sheer stone walls. This was something else, and he recognized its potentially deadly effect on his warriors' morale.

"It was clever of the iron heads," he grated loudly enough to be clearly heard as he made himself walk forward into the blood and torn flesh. "Clever, but only gunpowder, not magic or demons. This is why they wanted us to follow them."

"Exactly as you *did*," a subchief accused, and Camsan turned slowly to face him. The war leader said nothing, only looked the subchief in the eye, and then Camsan's battle ax, the ceremonial ax of the paramount war leader, flashed up in a lethal arc and the subchief's head thumped heavily into the bloody mud of the track.

The silence which followed its impact was profound, and Camsan turned in place, sweeping every warrior in range with his hard gaze.

"For months you've whined and complained like children deprived of sweets because I would not lead you to battle," he said flatly. "I've warned you again and again that K'Vaern's Cove will be no Sindi—that the Cove's walls are high, and its people cunning. And for warning you, I have been repaid with mutters that I am no fit war leader. *I*, who took Therdan and crushed the League under our feet. I, who took D'Sley and even fabled Sindi! I, who have led you to triumphs our sires, and their sires, and *their* sires before them, never dreamed of!

"And now, when the iron heads rode around the walls shouting insults at you, and you demanded that we go forth and take their horns, you cry like little children because I gave you what you wished. I see that the warriors of the Boman are become *women!*"

He felt their sullen resentment, but none dared to meet his iron gaze, and he spat on the ground.

"There's no magic here, only cunning from our enemies and the foolishness of warriors who can see no response to any challenge but to rush to meet it. Do not blame me for the consequences of your own rashness! And don't think for an instant that any man who questions my decisions and my orders again will not be *atul* meat before nightfall!"

He kicked the dead subchief's head contemptuously off of the trail, and glared at all of them, one warrior staring down the shock and defiance of thirty thousand others, and the fiery elixir of his own power as he crushed any challenge to his authority filled him like fine wine. The silence stretched out, singing with tension, until, finally, he grunted in satisfaction at their submission.

"Now," he went on then, his voice calmer and more businesslike, "it's clear that the iron heads have returned to plague us, and this—" he gestured at the chaos of the ambush site "—proves that the K'Vaernian shit-sitters are supplying them with new weapons. There can be no more than a few thousand iron heads left in all the world after the feasting of our axes in their cities, but it would seem that the K'Vaernians mean to use them to bite at us. No doubt they hope to lure us into traps and ambushes like this one again and again. Perhaps they even believe that they can somehow drive us into leaving the Cove unburned if they strike us often enough.

"But we are the Boman! We are the warriors of the North, the power of the wind itself, and we will hammer our enemies into dust! We won't give these iron heads the time to sting us again and again, won't let them choose the moment at which *they* will attack *us*. Mnb Trag and his clan hold Sindi behind us, and the K'Vaernians will never risk their own precious hides beyond the safety of their walls. Nor could all the iron heads who still live take the walls against Trag and his warriors. Even the full strength of the K'Vaernians would require a siege to break those defenses, and the iron heads will have no chance even to try if we stay close upon their heels. They know that as well as we do, too, and so they will have spare mounts hidden ahead somewhere. They know us of old, even as we know them, and so they know that without such remounts they will never outdistance the Boman in the long run. They think to leave us behind here, at the beginning of the chase, or to exhaust us until we give up, but their hope is in vain, for we will take the time for a true *basik* hunt! You wish blood on your axes? Very well, I'll give it to you!"

He wheeled to the messengers who always attended upon the paramount war leader. Picked runners all, carefully chosen from their own clans and tribes, they waited only for a nod from him to dash off with messages to any of the clan leaders, and he waved them closer.

"These new toys of the iron heads," he said, careful to put only contempt into the word "toys" and to conceal the shock he himself still felt at their effectiveness, "will be far more dangerous if they're able to choose the time and place to use them against us. So you will go to the leaders of your clans, and you will summon them to the field. We will pursue the iron heads wherever they may go, and the other clans will join us, closing in and driving them like *basik* before the beaters. Even if still more of them wait out here somewhere, and even if all of them are gathered together in one place, we'll have the numbers and the strength to sweep them aside as if they were so many grains of sand. Let them flee where they will, even unto the ruins of Therdan and Sheffan themselves! There will be no escape, and we will overwhelm them even if they find some worthless fortification to hold against us!

"Go! Summon the clans, for we have enemies to kill!"

"Christ," Pahner said. "Thirty-two thousand? What did they *leave?*"

"Far less than that," Bogess opined. The Diaspran had become Pahner's chief of staff, for all intents and purposes, as his own forces were integrated firmly into the K'Vaernian force structure, and he frowned thoughtfully as he considered the LURPs' report. "Most of the warriors would have insisted on chasing the Northerners. The Boman and the Vasin are enemies of old, with so many scores to settle that no one on either side could possibly count them all up."

"Jin says there are still some wandering around in the fields," the Marine said, consulting his pad.

"Looting," Bistem Kar said with a wave. "They'll be gone by the time we land. And we'll be landing out of sight of them, anyway."

"Something's going to go wrong," Pahner said.

"Who now is taking council of his fears?" Bogess asked with a grunt of laughter.

"Not taking council, just worrying," Pahner grumped. "And where the hell did Roger get to?"

"Start to forget our real job there, Boss?" Julian asked with a grin, and glanced at the heads-up display on his helmet visor. "Reports have him with the forward cavalry screen on the D'Sley-Sindi road. Track, rather."

"Good," Pahner said. "He's staying back like I told him to." The Marine paused and frowned. "If the report is accurate, anyway."

"Hey, Gunny! How ya doing?" Roger said quietly.

Jin suppressed his start and turned to look at the prince. The dying light of afternoon revealed Roger, lying on his stomach, covered in a gill blanket and with his face coated with camouflage paint while he grinned at the gunny's jump.

"Any news?" he asked.

"Jesus, Sir," D'Estrees said. "You scared the shit out

of me. You ever heard of giving a poor Marine with a loaded rifle a little warning?"

"Gotta keep that old situational awareness, Corporal," the unrepentant prince said. "The night will soon be alive with little creepy-crawlies." He turned back to Jin. "So, what's happening?"

"Rastar says they're well into the chase," Jin replied. "The cavalry's about twelve klicks to the north, with the Boman from Sindi in hot pursuit. And it looks like this Camsan fellow's taken the bait, hook, line, and sinker." The noncom patted the directional shotgun mike on the side of his helmet and grinned. "Gave a hell of a little speech after the claymores turned about two hundred meters worth of scummies into sausage filling, Sir. Sounded to me like he figures he got his dick caught in a drill press and the only way to keep somebody from challenging his position is to go personally nail Rastar's horns up on a wall somewhere."

"So he called in the other clans?"

"That he did, Your Highness, that he did. I just hope Rastar and Honal are half as good as they think they are, 'cause if those bastards ever *do* catch up with them, it's gonna be ugly."

"Don't sweat it, Gunny," Roger advised. "As a matter of fact, Rastar is probably at least two thirds as good as he thinks he is. Besides, we only gave him enough claymores for one good ambush. Didn't want him getting too creative on us, after all! So any other little unpleasantries he wants to send the Boman are going to have to come out of his rifles and revolvers, which ought to encourage him not to let them get *too* close." The prince shook his head. "He'll play tag with them, just like we planned, until we're ready for them to head on home, and it looks like they'll be bringing all their friends with them when they come."

"Hope so," Jin said, and waved in the direction of

Sindi's barely visible walls. "Meanwhile, there's nothing stirring in Sindi Town."

"Are you out here by yourself, Sir?" D'Estrees asked.

"I dropped most of the troops about four kilometers back and came forward with half a troop of cavalry. They're back about a half klick."

"Who's in the group, Sir?" The gunnery sergeant asked. "Just Mardukans?"

"Four hundred cavalry from Chindar, four hundred or so infantry from the pikes, and Beckley's team. Oh, and Cord and Matsugae."

"You brought Kostas?" D'Estrees asked. "Don't go getting our cook killed, Sir!"

"I told him he ought to stay home in the Cove, where it was safe," Roger said with a grin, "but he pointed out that since the army now had real cooks, he could go back to being my valet. 'Just because you're sleeping on the ground doesn't mean we can't keep up appearances.'"

"Ha, that's Kostas!" Jin said. "How long you going to stay, Sir?"

"You mean potentially giving away your hide? Not long—I can take a hint. I'll head back to the troops in a minute. I just wanted to look at the city."

"What're you going to call them?" the corporal asked.

"The Mardukans?" Roger gave a quiet chuckle. "I don't know. Maybe 'Her Majesty's Own Mardukan Guards'? Whatever I call them, I need to be getting back before they come looking for me."

"Take care, Your Highness," Jin said. "And for Vishnu's sake, keep your head down and out of the line of fire."

"Will do, Gunny," the prince said. "See you in Sindi."

CHAPTER THIRTY-THREE

Mnb Trag looked out over the fields in the growing light. Somewhere to the north, he knew, were Camsan and the rest of the clans, perhaps closing in on the presumptuous iron heads even as Trag stood here on the walls of Sindi. It irked him immensely to be left behind, as if he were too old or lazy to go chase cavalry, yet he had to agree with Kny.

It was never wise to do what your enemy wanted you to do. Presumably that iron head cavalry had known the Boman would chase them, and presumably they'd also known that no heavy cavalry could outrun the Boman indefinitely. So there had to be a trap waiting for the host, and Camsan had been right to be wary.

Yet Trag knew that *he* had been correct, too. Trap or no trap, Camsan had no choice but to pursue the Northerners and destroy the challenge to his authority their mere presence represented. And whatever the iron heads had hoped to accomplish, they would fail in the end. No shit-sitter Southern army survived, aside from the relatively tiny force of the K'Vaernian Guard, and the Guard was far too weak to endanger any Boman force in the open field. So, in the end, the trappers must be trapped and destroyed. Judging by the dangerous deviousness of that first ambush, the K'Vaernians had obviously devised new weapons in a desperate attempt to make their League mercenaries more effective, and that undoubtedly meant casualties would be heavier than they ought to have been before the host managed to trap and destroy the iron heads, but their fate was ultimately sealed. And in their destruction, Camsan would add yet another triumph to the matchless string of victories he'd produced for the clans, and so further consolidate his grip upon the power he and Trag both knew lay almost within his grasp. "Barbarian" the shit-sitters called the Boman, and there was truth to the sneer, Trag admitted proudly. But "barbarians" could build empires, too.

Yet for all his satisfaction, something still felt wrong. He couldn't quite lay hold of what it was that concerned him, but it was there.

And then, as the light gathered, it became clear what it was.

A small host emerged from the forest on the D'Sley Road—small, but obviously much larger than any force the shit-sitters should possibly have been able to assemble. Block after block of infantry marched forward, moving in regular lines more precise than even those K'Vaern's Cove Guard bastards. He was too old to see what sort of weapons they carried at this range, but there were at least two shit-sitters for every warrior he still had in Sindi, and he had no doubt that they carried scaling ladders in plenty.

"Where did *they* come from?" one of his warriors gasped.

"K'Vaern's Cove," the chieftain answered. "I guess

they must have put a sword into the hand of every shit-
sitter who could see lightning or hear thunder and just
brought them out." He grunted in laughter at the
thought of the enemy's obligingness at bringing the soft,
gutless—and untrained—city slugs into the sweep of
his own ax. Still, it looked as if there were an awful
lot of them.

"We should be able to pile them on the wall like
bales of barleyrice," he said, "but it will be a fight to
tell the grands about."

More and more of his fellow tribesmen gathered on
the parapet as the regular ranks of shit-sitters
assembled just out of bombard range. The groups
walked in step, their odd march broken only when they
crossed the small bridge over the Stell, and formed in
neat blocks on the city's side of the stream.

"I've never seen spears that long," someone said.
"You don't suppose those gutless Wespar were telling
the truth when they said . . ."

The voice trailed off, and Trag grunted a deeper,
harsher laugh at the edge of nervousness which had
sharpened the remark.

"I've never put much faith in the lies Wespar pussies who got their asses kicked by a bunch of shit-sitters
tell to cover the way they must've fucked up," the
chieftain said. "And even if they were telling the truth,
how would the same spears have gotten clear to
K'Vaern's Cove this quickly?"

"You're probably right," one of his own tribesmen
said, "but those really are awfully long *pagee*-stickers
out there, Mnb."

"Maybe someone from the water boys told them
how to scare the Wespar off," Trag scoffed, "but we
aren't Wespar, are we? We're the Tranol'te! And even
if we were Wespar, do you really think there's any way
they could get something as long as those damned

things up *scaling* ladders?" He laughed more loudly than ever.

"No, I don't," the tribesman said.

"Of course you don't," Trag said, and waved dismissively at the small army which had now taken up position in front of the gates on the northern side of the river, close enough that even Trag could see them clearly. "And I don't see any battering rams over there," he went on, "so there isn't really much they can do to us as long as we're not stupid enough to go out and meet them head-on, now is there?"

"I don't know, Mnb," the tribesman said. "We don't have enough warriors to man the walls. Not the way we ought to, anyway."

"Doesn't matter," Trag said confidently. "*They* don't have enough scaling ladders to swamp us, either. We've got more than enough to hold this part of the walls until the end of the world, and they don't have enough time for anything like a proper siege. Kny Camsan is out there behind them, and it won't take him long to realize why the iron heads wanted to lure us out of the city. When he does, he'll come right over them, and that will be the end of K'Vaern's Cove! All we have to do is keep them right where they are until he gets here. So get your warriors moving—we need them here on the walls!"

Messengers dashed off to summon the warriors of the clan to battle, and Trag leaned on the battlements, watching the shit-sitters. His confidence was genuine, but he was honest enough to admit that he didn't have a clue what the shit-sitters were up to as scores of them began pushing some sort of wagons up behind the blocks of infantry.

No doubt it was some new fancy trick the K'Vaernians had devised, but no trick was going to get them magically through the massive stone walls of Sindi.

❖   ❖   ❖

"Move, move, move!"

Rus From and General Bogess were an eye of calm in a hurricane of effort as the specially trained companies manhandled the wagons into position. Those positions had been very carefully selected and surveyed by the Marine LURPs who'd kept Sindi under constant surveillance while the K'Vaernian army was equipped and trained. As well as both Diasprans had come to know their remarkable human allies, they'd been astonished by the routine, matter-of-fact way in which the Marines had roamed Sindi's environs under cover of night. Everyone knew the Boman barbarians could hear the whine of an insect's wings at seventy paces, yet the humans had penetrated effortlessly to the city's very walls, and their unobtrusively placed stakes had guided each wagon to its preselected position under the Diasprans' watchful eyes.

"Do we really think this is going to work?" Bogess asked the cleric under his breath, and From chuckled.

"Oh, I'm certain it will *work*," he said. "Once, at least, that is, given our gunpowder situation. Whether or not the Boman will cooperate by being where we want them to when it does work isn't my province, however, thank the God!"

"You're always so reassuring," Bogess muttered.

"Of course I am, that's my job!" From said cheerfully, then frowned thoughtfully. "It looks like we're just about ready," he observed. "Time for our last inspection."

"Let's get started then," Bogess replied, and the two of them separated and headed in opposite directions along the arc of wagons arranged before the northern walls of fallen Sindi.

"The bastards are up to something," one of Mnb Trag's subchiefs muttered.

"Of course they are," Trag shot back. "What? You thought they'd marched all this way just to stand there and scratch their asses at us?"

"Of course I didn't," the subchief retorted. "But I don't hear you telling us what it is they *are* up to, either!"

"Because I don't know," Trag conceded. "On the other hand, what does it matter what they're up to as long as they're out there and we're in *here?*"

He stamped a foot on the massive, solid stone of the parapet, and the subchief joined him in grunting laughter.

"The carts are laid in, Armand," Bogess said as he and From trotted up to Pahner and Bistem Kar. "The LURPs' stakes were exactly where they were supposed to be, and we're ready whenever you give the word."

"Good," Pahner replied, but his tone was a bit absent. Kar stood beside him, studying the city's walls through Dell Mir's telescope, but the Marine had the magnification of his helmet visor cranked up to give him a far clearer view than any primitive telescope could hope to match.

"They're a bit more spread out than I could wish," Kar said after a moment.

"Well, we can't expect the other side to do everything we want it to," Pahner pointed out. "And it probably doesn't matter all that much in the long run—these aren't exactly precision weapons, so there's going to be enough spread in the impact zone to cover a good bit of target dispersal. I'm more concerned about how many may still be under hard cover in the bombard and arquebus galleys. We're going to get good coverage, but we don't have anywhere near as much overhead penetration as I wish we did."

"According to Jin's count, there can't be very many

arquebusiers left in the city, Sir," Julian pointed out over his powered armor's radio. "And if they aren't blind, then they must've seen all our nice scaling ladders. Which means they have to have moved just about everybody they've got left up onto the battlements to repel boarders."

"Nice and logical, Sergeant," Pahner agreed with a sour grin. "Unfortunately, logic is still a really good way to be wrong with confidence."

"Yet I think he's right," Kar said, closing his telescope with a click.

"If he isn't, we'll find out soon enough." Pahner sighed, and turned to From. "All right, Rus. They were your babies in production, so I guess it's only fitting to let you be the one to send them on their way. Light 'em up."

"What *are* those stupid shit-sitters up to?" Mnb Trag groused. "I'm not as young as I used to be, damn it, and these old legs are getting tired!"

"Sure they are," the subchief laughed. "You're a Boman, 'old man,' so don't think you can fool *us* into thinking you need a rest! No sitting down until you've killed your quota!"

"If I must, I must," Trag agreed with a theatrical sigh, and tested the edge of his ax with a thumb. "Still, I wish the *basik* would go ahead and poke their heads up here where I can cleave them!"

"Oh, they'll be along, I'm sure," the subchief told him. "Either that, or they'll slink back downriver like the cowards they are."

Trag grunted agreement, but his attention was on those odd wagons the shit-sitters had pushed into position with such care. Now crews were stripping the canvas covers off of them, and the old chieftain rubbed at a horn in puzzlement as the pewter-gray, late-morning light gleamed dully on strange, stubby cylindrical shapes. He couldn't tell what they were made of, but there were scores of them in each wagon, arranged in some sort of wooden frames that held them upright. Each of them was perhaps a handspan in diameter, but at least as long as a warrior's forearm, and the work crews seemed to be fussing over them with a ridiculous attention to detail.

Whatever they were doing, it didn't seem to take them long—this time, at least—and the crews scampered back to their positions. In fact, Trag realized, the wagons were widely separated from the waiting shit-sitter army. The closest of them was at least a hundred paces from the nearest block of infantry, and he suddenly wondered why that was.

Rus From made himself wait until the last wagon crew had completed its work and confirmed that they were safely back behind the danger lines. Then he glanced at Pahner one more time, turned to the K'Vaernian artillerist standing beside him with a lit torch, and nodded.

"Light it," he said flatly, and the K'Vaernian touched his torch to the waiting quick match.

A small, bright, hissing demon flashed along the lengths of fuse, racing across the damp ground in a stink of sulfur, and throughout the ranks of the army, men covered their eyes or ears, depending on their individual inclinations. And then the hissing demon reached the first wagon.

Mardukan societies of all types and stripes boasted enormous and detailed bestiaries of demons and devils—not surprisingly, probably, given the nightmare creatures which truly did walk the planet's jungles. Yet not one of the collections of monsters the humans had yet encountered had included anything remotely like the Terran dragons of myth.

Until today.

The wagons seemed to explode, but that wasn't quite what had happened. Each wagon contained a wooden frame, and nested into each frame were two hundred and forty twenty-centimeter rockets. Two thirds of those rockets were fitted with time-fused fragmentation/ shrapnel warheads—a bursting charge of black powder surrounded by a shaped matrix of musket balls which turned each missile into what was, effectively, a huge, self-propelled shotgun shell. The other third were pure blast weapons, with simple contact fuses designed courtesy of Nimashet Despreaux and warheads charged with two kilos of black powder each.

There were fifty wagons outside Sindi, for a total of twelve *thousand* rockets, and the blast warheads alone carried eight metric tons of gunpowder, exclusive of the propellant charges. The projectiles roared heavenward in an incredible, choking column of brimstone-flavored smoke and flame, then arced over and came screaming down. The fragmentation warheads burst in midair, and although the jury-rigged time fuses were crude, to say the very least, the vast majority functioned approximately as designed. A deluge of almost two million musket balls hammered the battlements and a zone fifty meters deep on either side of the walls, like the flail of some outraged war god that turned every exposed Boman into so much torn and shredded meat. No one on Marduk had ever so much as contemplated such a weapon, and so none of the barbarians had even considered taking cover. Instead, they'd crowded together, almost literally shoulder-to-shoulder, to await the anticipated assault, and they couldn't have offered a better target if they'd tried to. Here and there a small group or an isolated individual happened to have had sufficient overhead protection to avoid annihilation, but they represented only a minute proportion of Mnb Trag's tribe and its allies. When that dreadful broom of fire and fury swept across the walls of Sindi, almost ten thousand Boman warriors perished in a single screaming moment of devastation.

And on the heels of the fragmentation warheads, came the blast weapons. Compared to modern human weapons, the quaint, crude black powder rockets were mere children's toys, but the earth trembled underfoot like a terrified animal as those "toys" came crunching down on the walls and the buildings behind them. A terrifying drumroll of explosions threw fire and smoke, bits and pieces of barbarian warriors, roofing tiles, building stone, and shattered wood higher than the walls themselves, and the soldiers of K'Vaern's Cove looked at one another in shock and awe at the sheer havoc of the humans' weapons.

Mnb Trag never had the opportunity to share their shock and awe. Along with virtually every warrior of his tribe, he was wiped out of existence before he had time to grasp, even dimly, what horror lurked within the despised shit-sitters' wagons.

"Damn," Julian said almost mildly. "Think we used enough dynamite, there, Gronningen?"

"We can hope," the big Asgardian replied stolidly, watching the incredible pall of smoke and dust rising like some loathsome beast above the broken stoneyard which had once been the northernmost portion of the city of Sindi.

"Guess we find out now," Julian said as his HUD flashed. "Time to saddle up, troops."

Mnb Trag was dead, but by some fluke of ballistics and fate, the subchief who'd stood barely ten paces from the old chieftain still breathed. That wouldn't be true very much longer, and the subchief knew it, for he felt his strength fleeing with the blood pulsing from his savagely mangled legs. But the anesthesia of shock kept him from truly feeling the pain, and he pushed himself up onto his elbows with his fading strength and stared about him in total disbelief.

The wall itself still stood, virtually intact and gruesomely decorated with the torn and dismembered bodies of his fellow clansmen, but the neat houses and streets behind the walls had been threshed and shattered under a club of fire. Flames roared from the broken structures, bellowing and capering like demons above a broken wasteland of rubble, and the dying subchief felt an icy stab of terror as he surveyed the wreckage. Not for himself, for a man who knew he was dying had very little else to fear, but for the host following Kny Camsan in his pursuit of the League cavalry. If this dreadful devil weapon could unleash such devastation upon solid stone and masonry, what would happen if it caught the host in the open, completely without protection?

That thought shuddered in the back of his fading brain, and he turned away from the vista of ruin. He found himself facing the massively bastioned main gate of the city, instead . . . just in time to see magic.

Before the Mardukan's dying eyes, four demons appeared out of nowhere in a ripple of distortion, like the wavering of heat above a flame. They were mottled gray and yellow, with only two arms and bulbous heads and bodies, and their skins looked like wood or metal. As the subchief watched in amazement, one of them made a sword appear from nothing and struck it deep into the gate. Into the gap between the leaves of the gate, actually, and metal screamed as the demon sliced downward. Massive locking bars of bronze and iron parted like thread, and then the demon made his sword disappear, reached out to grip one huge bronze-sheathed panel in each hand, and pulled them apart.

The subchief watched in horror as a second supernatural apparition began to assist the first. Those gates were incredibly heavy, and slightly warped from the Boman's own assault on the city and the iron heads' bags of gunpowder. Dozens of stout warriors were required to open or close either one of their panels . . . slowly. But those two powerful demons, all by themselves, were—

And then, he died.

There were still a few Boman survivors, and some of them were actually on their feet as Julian threw the full weight of his armor against the gate and it came fully open. The huge hinges were twisted top and bottom, but the soft iron couldn't resist the powered "muscles" of the suits. Only the fact that, massive as they were, the suits were much lighter than the gate panels had prevented the armored Marines from flinging them open instantly, but instantly wasn't really required.

The first barbarians were already charging forward to regain the gateway, and Julian wondered whether it was courage or stupidity—or if there was a difference between them—that kept the barbarians on their feet. Or perhaps it was only the battle fury for which the Boman were famed. Not that it made any practical difference what kept the survivors coming.

The army behind him was also charging for the gates, and his HUD showed a tide of blue icons racing to support him. But the K'Vaernians had kept well clear of the impact zone, which meant they had considerably farther to go, and it was clear that the surviving barbs were going to get there first.

Not that it was going to do them a bit of good.

Julian didn't even bother to unlimber his bead cannon. He and Moseyev were still busy opening the gates, anyway, but that was all right. The only way the scummies could reach the gate was down the long, narrow gate tunnel, and anything his stutter gun could have added to the carnage of Gronningen's plasma cannon in such confined quarters would have been superfluous.

The phlegmatic Asgardian squeezed off a single shot that filled the tunnel's bore from wall to wall with a sliver of a star's heart. Half the tunnel roof disappeared as the upward angled plasma bolt slammed into it and sliced a huge wedge out of the back face of the city wall. For a few moments, the rest of the tunnel roof looked as if it might hold, but then it, too, collapsed downward, taking half of one of the gate bastions with it. The avalanche of plunging masonry looked as if it might be going to bury the Marines, but it fell clear . . . and Gronningen's *second* shot blew straight down the gaping, roofless cut through the curtain wall which had once been a tunnel.

The bolt of nuclear fire hit the new-made rubble before it even had a chance to settle properly, and the broken walls and falling stones simply lifted back into the air. Some of their mass was converted to slightly cooler plasma, but most of it simply added its weight to the shrapnel flying from the explosion, as if the city itself was rising up against its invaders.

The same actinic fire, mixed with bits of half-molten stone, washed over the surviving Boman . . . who promptly stopped surviving.

"Krin," Bistem Kar half-whispered as the first battalion of K'Vaernian infantry slid to a skidding halt behind the armored figures it had intended to relieve. No unarmored individual was going to be able to survive in the blast-furnace fury of that shattered gate tunnel for some hours to come, and the Cove's senior guardsman shook his head in slow disbelief. The humans had never demonstrated any of their energy weapons for the K'Vaernians, who'd had only the reports from Diaspra to go on, and despite himself, Kar had never really quite believed those reports. Oh, he hadn't doubted them intellectually, but what Bogess and Rus From and other veterans of the New Model Army had described to him had been so far beyond the limits of his experience that he'd simply been unable to grasp the reality.

Now, he'd seen it . . . and he still wasn't certain he believed it. The power of the plasma cannon was even more shocking, in an odd sort of way, because it came on the heels of the rocket bombardment. The dreadful, overwhelming hiss and roar and crackle and thunder of the rockets had been the most cataclysmic thing he'd ever experienced. In the instant that those howling missiles slammed home, he'd felt, however fleetingly, as if the very lightnings of the gods had been placed in his true-hands. Yet that single shot from Gronningen's weapon had sliced effortlessly through the massive stonework even the concussive thunder of the rockets had left virtually untouched, and the tough, confident guardsman felt something tremble inside him as he realized that every single word the Diasprans had told him was true.

He turned to Pahner and shook his head.

"Why don't you use them to clear the whole city?" he asked, jerking his head in the direction of the armored Marines, still standing unconcernedly in the inferno of the gutted gate tunnel. "We're going to take casualties in those warrens, prying the Boman holdouts out one by one."

"Power," Pahner said. "Not enough of it, that is."

"Ah," the K'Vaernian commander said with a gesture of puzzlement. "I'm just a simple old soldier, of course, but—"

"Ha!" the Marine laughed. "Some 'simple old soldier'!"

"I stand by that description," Kar said with a dignity which was only slightly flawed by the twinkle in his eye. "But, simple old soldier or not, *that*—" he waved at the gaping wound which had once been a gate tunnel "—seems ample power to deal with anything these barbarians might bring to bear."

"Not that kind of power," Pahner said. "Or, not directly, that is." The K'Vaernian regarded him with obvious confusion, and the Marine shrugged. "You know how some of the hammer mills in K'Vaern's Cove use wind power, and others use water power from your storage cisterns?"

"Yes," Kar said, his expressions suddenly thoughtful. "Are you saying those things—" he nodded at the quartet of armored Marines once more "—don't have enough rainwater stored in their cisterns?"

"In a way," Pahner agreed, trying to figure out how to explain "potential energy." "The suits run on very powerful energy storage devices. We don't have many of them, and we need those we have for later use. And the weapons themselves only have so many charges, so we can't afford to use them unless we really need them. And we *are* going to need both them and all the power we've got left soon enough; there's a *real* battle waiting for us down the road."

"I can see that you wouldn't consider this a battle," Bogess said, glancing at the carnage of the gate. "But that's because we pulled the main force away from the city, *and* because the Boman were considerate enough to assemble right in the middle of our kill zone, exactly as we'd hoped. Unfortunately, we've used up the rockets now, so we won't be able to blast them this way again. Although," he added thoughtfully, "I still don't know how useful the rocket wagons would be in a real mobile battle. We knew where the city was, so we could plan exact trajectories. And better yet," he chuckled grimly, "Sindi couldn't exactly dodge."

"That's true enough," Kar acknowledged, "and it's also the reason I agreed that we should use them all now—there's not any point in holding back weapons which might not work later if their use now helps to assure a victory we have to have."

"Agreed," Bogess nodded. "But it still looks like there were at least ten thousand warriors still in the city, and that's only a small fraction of what's out tramping around chasing Rastar and Honal. Sooner or later, we're going to have to face up to the rest of the horde, after all, and I suppose that *would* qualify as a battle in almost anyone's eyes."

"I wasn't talking about the rest of the Boman," Pahner said, pulling out a slice of *bisti* root. "We haven't been totally up-front with you guys. Oh, we haven't *lied* to you, or anything like that, but we've . . . neglected to mention a couple of things. Like the fact that the port we keep saying that we have to reach on the other side of the ocean happens to be held by our enemies."

"*Your* enemies?" Bistem Kar said carefully. "With similar weapons, I assume?"

"Yes."

"God of Water preserve us," Bogess said faintly.

"Anyway, there won't be many holdouts to find in there," the Marine observed. "As you said, Bogess, most of them were right where we wanted them, waiting for us on the walls. Most of the ones we missed there got themselves killed in the gate tunnel, and the ones who didn't are probably still running . . . and will be, for a while. So keep the troops in hand and fight them through the city, but you shouldn't have that much trouble punching through. Just remember we have to get in before everybody else refugees out. And while you two get that moving, it's time for Rus to bring up the labor teams so we can get down to the real work."

"Well," Bogess said, "now I understand why you Marines don't look upon a battle with the Boman with dread. This *isn't* much of a battle to you, is it?"

"In a way," Pahner said, "but it's not just a matter of scale, you know. That—" he gestured with his chin at the huge pall of smoke and flame still billowing above the rocket strike "—is just as destructive, in its way, as any plasma cannon. It's not as . . . efficient, I guess, but those poor Boman bastards are just as much dead, mangled meat as if we killed them with bead rifles or smart bombs. Blood is blood, when you come right down to it, and it's not the thought of the battles that lie in our future that makes this any less dreadful. Not really. It's just that once you've walked through Hell a few times, it takes a lot for anything to get past your shell.

"Even something like this."

CHAPTER THIRTY-FOUR

Roger squatted by the side of the trail and tied his hair up in a knot. A *crint* called in the jungle, and he smiled.

"It's good to be back in action," he said.

"Maybe so," Cord replied repressively. "But I wish you would at least stay behind the scouts . . . as Captain Pahner instructed you to."

"I *am* behind the scouts," Roger said with a grin, and pointed to the south. "See? They're right over there."

The thrown-together force whose cavalry component had taken to calling itself—unofficially, at least—"The *Basik's* Own" had pounded up the muddy track from D'Sley as fast as the infantry's *turom* could go while the main army made the same trip by water. Now they were about a half-day short of the city itself, and a thin line of screening cavalry stretched south from them, bending back in an inverted "L" to cover the track from just west of Sindi back to the Bay while the labor gangs who couldn't be crammed into the available water craft completed the march from D'Sley behind it.

Roger had chosen an encampment along a shallow stream that cut the track. The waterway, no more than thigh deep to the *turom*, flowed out of the jungle to join with the Tam River just to the north. It would provide a landmark to place the force around and water for the *civan* and *turom*.

The prince himself had just climbed down from Patty when Turkol Bes, his infantry commander, rode up on his *turom*, dismounted, and clutched the inside of one thigh.

"God of the Water, none of the troops will be able to fight! They'll all be too busy rubbing their groins!" he groaned.

"You'll get used to it," Chim Pri laughed as he slid off his *civan*. "After a week or so, you'll get used to it."

"How are the *turom*?" Roger asked.

"They'll be okay," Bes said. Not long ago, the young battalion commander had been a simple wrangler working on the Carnan Canal in Diaspra, but only until the Carnan Labor Battalion had been drafted for the New Model Army at King Gratar's orders. Of all the workers in the battalion, Turkol Bes had repeatedly shown the greatest ability to think on his feet and make good decisions under pressure, and promotion had been rapid.

"It's not like they're carrying much weight," the former laborer continued. "But they're not used to going so fast."

"Too bad we couldn't put you on *civan*," Chim Pri said with another laugh. "You'd really love that."

"But they needed all the spare *civan* in the Cove for the main cavalry force," Roger pointed out. "Maybe after we get them back we can upgrade."

"Oh, no," Bes said. "I'll sit on a *turom*, if that's the cost for keeping up with the *civan*-boys. But I am *not* going to try to ride one of those vile and ill-tempered beasts."

"You do whatever it takes to complete the mission, Turkol," Roger pointed out. "Speaking of which, right now we don't have one. But we can expect to get used pretty soon, I think. Now that the labor force is in Sindi, the Captain's going to start spreading the cavalry screen back out to cover the troops still working on the road gangs, and he'll need us then. Maybe even sooner. So we need to start thinking about how that might work. This is ground we could be fighting over, so I want everyone to keep a close eye on it."

The two battalion commanders traded looks.

"Do you think we'll actually be used?" Pri asked.

"Yes, I do," the prince said. "You might think you're just an oversized bodyguard, but Pahner is going to use us. Our mobility will be a key factor, if the Boman are hard on someone's heels."

He took a sip out of his camel bag, then pursed his lips and grimaced when it ran dry. It was time for a refill, but he looked at the nameless stream without enthusiasm. It was choked with mud stirred up by the hundreds of *civan* and *turom*, and although the bag's osmotic filter would take out the mud, some of the taste always got through.

"We need to keep an eye out all around," he continued, playing with the nipple of the empty camel bag. "Just because we think we know where the threat is, doesn't mean we're right."

"Let me fill that for you, Roger," Matsugae interrupted, gesturing at the camel bag. "You're just going to distract them playing with it if I don't."

"Thanks," the prince said, pulling the bag out of his day pack and handing it over.

"There *is* a cavalry screen out there," Bes pointed out to the prince, gesturing with his false-hand.

"Yes, there is," Pri said. He handed his own canteen to Matsugae at the valet's gesture. "Thanks, Kostas," he said, and looked back at the infantry commander. "It could probably stand to be pushed further out, though, if we want real security. And even if we do push it out, it could still be wiped out before we got the word . . . if there was a force coming up from the south, at least."

"So keep an eye on the terrain," Roger said, nodding in agreement. "The roads and the streams and where they are, shortcuts, and spots that would slow you down. Or slow the Boman. And most of all, make sure everyone stays on his toes."

Matsugae walked upstream, waving at the occasional soldier he knew. He recognized quite a few of the Diaspran riflemen from work details which had been assigned to the kitchen—a surprising number, really. It just showed that they'd been on this godforsaken planet too long, he thought. But he had to admit, hellhole or not, it made good people. The Mardukans were a fine race, and it would be interesting to see what Roger made of the planet after he got back to Earth.

The valet finally reached the edge of the picket lines and turned to the stream. There was a small team of scouts a bit further upstream, but they weren't fouling the water, and the hovering cavalry screen didn't seem to be doing so either. It was running quite clear, and actually a bit cool, which would help the chiller on Roger's camel bag.

He stepped onto a root and dropped the camel bag into the water. Its active osmotic system could absorb the water directly through its skin, but using the chemical filter took several hours. Fortunately, there was also a simple pump which could fill and filter it rather quickly, but Matsugae suddenly realized that although he *knew* about the pump, he'd never personally used one. He'd seen the Marines use them enough times, but this was actually the first time he'd fetched water on the entire trip; he'd had his own duties, and there'd always been someone else around to do that.

He looked down at the camel bag, fiddling with the pump fitting for a few moments until he finally figured out the release. Then he dropped the snorkel tube into the water and started pumping. To his delight, the bag started to fill instantly, and he grinned. *Got it right in one*, he thought cheerfully, watching the bag swell.

What he forgot to watch was the water.

The fastest reactions in the universe couldn't have gotten Roger across the encampment in time, and the finest neural combat program couldn't have killed the damncroc any deader than the two dozen rounds from the cavalry outpost.

None of which made any difference to Kostas Matsugae.

By the time Roger got there, it was all over but the bleeding. The *atul* had taken the valet in the throat, and even Doc Dobrescu's little black bag couldn't have done anything for the imperial servitor. More was gone than just the throat when one of the cavalrymen rolled the limp body over.

Roger didn't bother checking for life. He'd become only too intimately familiar with death, and no one could live with his head half severed from his body.

"Ah, Jesus, Kostas," St. John (J.) said, coming up behind the prince. "Why the fuck didn't you look? There's always crocs."

"I don't think he'd been outside a secure perimeter before," the prince said quietly. "I didn't think about that. I should have."

"No one can be right all the time," Cord said. He knelt by Matsugae and picked up Roger's camel bag. "Mistakes happen. You have to accept it when they do, but this was not your mistake, Roger. Kostas knew the jungle was dangerous. He should have been more cautious."

"He didn't understand," Roger said. "Not really. We all spent our time wrapping him and Eleanora in foam packaging."

"The foam packaging we should have wrapped *you* up in," Beckley said. The team leader shook her head. "We need to bag him, Your Highness."

"Go ahead," Roger said, then knelt and removed the palace badge from Matsugae's tunic. "I promise you, Kostas. No more mistakes. No more dawdling. No more dandying."

"Maybe dandying," St. John said. "He liked you to wear nice clothes."

"Yes, he did." Roger looked at the much patched chameleon suit the valet was wearing. "St. John, look in his packs. Knowing Kostas, he's got one good outfit packed. Beckley, if he does, dress him in it. Then bag him, and before you tab him, I want to say a few words."

"Yes, Your Highness," the corporal said quietly. "We'll take care of him."

The prince nodded, but before he could reply, his helmet gave the minor ping of an incoming call.

"Roger, it's Pahner. The engineers are getting down to it here in Sindi, but it looks like we're going to need a bigger labor force to pull this off. That means I'm going to have to draft more infantry, which means what cavalry we have is going to have to take on an even bigger share of responsibility for our flanks and the convoys. I'm going to have to bring them close into the road and spread them thinner to cover the extra footage, so I need you to swing further down to the south to anchor the line. I want you at Victor-One-Seven by nightfall."

Roger looked down at the body of his friend and shook his head.

"Could we have a couple of hours, Captain? We have a . . . situation here."

"Are you under attack?" Pahner asked.

"No . . . No we're not, Captain," Roger said.

"Then whatever it is, handle it and get on the road, Your Highness," the Marine said crisply. "You're a mobile unit, and I need you mobile. Now."

"Yes, Sir," Roger said quietly. He keyed off his mike and looked at the corporal. "Can the ceremony, Reneb. I promised no more mistakes and no more dawdling. Bag him and burn him; we're moving out." He switched back to the captain. "We'll be on the trail in ten minutes," he said.

"Good," Pahner said.

Rastar slid off his *civan* and moaned.

"I'd kill to be able to take off this armor," he groaned, and Honal grunted in laughter.

"You Therdan people are too soft. A mere forty *kolong*, and you're complaining!"

"Uh-huh," the prince replied. "Tell me *you're* not in pain."

"Me?" the cavalry commander said. "I think I'm going to die, as a matter of fact. Why?"

Rastar chuckled and rubbed his posterior gingerly while he looked at the stream.

"Thank goodness for accurate maps," he said. "I never appreciated them properly before."

"Yes, knowing where to water and where to hide—as opposed to where to fight—is *very* important," Honal said a bit tartly.

"Don't worry, cousin," Rastar told him. "There'll be

plenty of fighting before this is done. Send back skirmishers with a communicator. Have them find the Boman, but tell them not to get too close. Just give them a few shots to sting them; then pull back. Make sure they have plenty of remounts and know where to go." He pulled out his map and studied its markings. "The turnoff for the first group is just ahead, and I especially want to know if the Boman split up when we do."

"Will do," Honal agreed. "I still say this plan is too complicated, though. Splitting ourselves up is crazy."

"We need to keep the Boman interested until it's time to lead them back home again," Rastar said, not looking up from the map, "and Boman are simple sorts. If we just run in a straight line, they may lose interest and start heading back too soon. That would be bad. But if we run all over the countryside like headless *basik*, their uncomplicated little souls should find the puzzle irresistible and keep them coming right behind us. We hope."

"Can I still not like it?"

"Yes . . . as long as you *do* it. And speaking of doing, it's time to go."

Fresh *civan* had been brought up from their string of spares while the officers talked, and Honal looked up at the towering expanse of his new mount with a sour expression.

"I don't know if I can climb clear up there," he groaned.

"Here, let me give you a boost," Rastar offered. "You Sheffan super-trooper, you."

Camsan cursed.

"*Another* group splitting off!" he complained.

"And in a whole different direction," Dna pointed out. "They must have cut their numbers by half with all this scattering."

"Hard to tell," the war leader said. "They're keeping in line to confuse our trackers about numbers, but I think you're right—there are fewer headed toward Therdan than there were."

The Boman leader rubbed a horn in thought.

"Have all of the messengers reported back yet?" he asked.

"All but the one to Hothna Kasi," Dna replied. "He had the farthest to go, but he should have arrived there by midnight of last night." The other Boman glanced up at the overcast, estimating the time. "By now, all of them should be on the trail."

"Good," Camsan grunted, "because that means all this splitting and scattering isn't going to do them any good in the end. It's just going to break them up into even smaller bits and pieces when our warriors finally start catching up with them. But I think we need to split off some parties of our own to go directly after these groups. I want to know where they're all *really* headed."

"Break up ourselves?" the scout leader asked.

"Yes. This isn't like the iron heads," the war leader said quietly. "They're being more devious than normal, and I smell a trap. Something, somewhere, is going on. Something big."

CHAPTER THIRTY-FIVE

"Damn," Beckley said. "I didn't believe it could be done."

"Neither did I," Chim Pri said.

"You have no faith in the Laborers of God," Turkol Bes told them with quiet pride. "When the God rains destruction, you have to build and repair *fast*. It's what we're best at."

The road from D'Sley to Sindi, which had been reduced to so much soupy mud by Boman foot traffic, had changed. Engineering crews, working to Rus From's careful plans and equipped with giant cross-cut saws, axes, sledgehammers, and splitting wedges, had altered the landscape almost beyond recognition. Massive trees, some of them more than a meter in diameter, had been cut off close to the ground, sawn into lengths, split, and dragged out to the side of the roadbed. Wood wasn't the best material for covering a road, especially on Marduk, because it rotted and broke too quickly. But this road was being designed for one purpose and one purpose only, and it only had to hold up for a few days of heavy use.

Behind the woodcutters and splitters had come other teams of Mardukans, including civilians impressed from D'Sley and K'Vaern's Cove, leveling and grading the beaten track and filling in the deepest bogs with gravel and gabions of bundled barleyrice straw. When they finished, a third group had taken the split logs by the side of the grading and laid them down to form a corduroy road. The entire project had been one continuous motion, and now that it was done, the first wagon loads of supplies and materials liberated from Sindi were creaking along it towards D'Sley.

Ther Ganau, one of Rus From's senior assistant engineers, trotted up on a *civan* and waved two hands.

"Stay out of the right-of-way, if you will. I don't want anything to slow traffic." He gestured at the heavy flow of nose-to-tail wagons. "What do you think?" he asked Roger.

Pri looked over at the silent prince, and sighed. "Brilliant, Ther Ganau. Truly amazing. I've never seen such a sight in all my days."

Roger remained silent, and Cord dug a thumb into his back.

"Say something," the shaman hissed, and Roger looked up at last.

"Very nice, Ther," he said listlessly. "The Captain said he wants us anchoring this end of the line. Where's the best place to dig in?"

The engineer began to reply, then paused for a moment as he noted the roll of material lying on the withers of the prince's *flar-ta*. He recognized one of the humans' devices for cremating their dead, but all the people who would normally have been around Roger in the field were still there, and he brushed the question aside. He could deal with that mystery later.

"Yes, Your Highness. The Captain has called most of our infantry forward from this end of the line, so if I could borrow the Carnan Battalion for close security and push your cavalry a bit further out to the west, I'd be grateful."

"Whatever," Roger said. "Take whatever you want." The prince kneed Patty towards the river and lifted his rifle from the scabbard. Unless the Tam was totally abnormal, there were bound to be damncrocs in it.

"What happened?" Ganau asked quietly, gazing after the *flar-ta*.

"A croc got Kostas," Beckley replied.

"The God take him," the priest-engineer said sincerely. "A terrible loss."

"Especially to the prince," the Marine pointed out. "Kostas was with him for years. And he's blaming himself."

"What should we do?" the engineer asked. "Is there anything?"

"I don't know," Beckley said as a shot rang out from the river bank. "I just don't know."

The incoming call's priority code said it came from the sergeant major, and Pahner told his toot to accept it.

"Pahner."

"We have a situation with His Highness," Kosutic said without preamble. "Beckley just called it in. She says Kostas bought it this morning, and Roger's in a total funk. He's turned over his command to Ther Ganau and isn't answering calls. Reneb says he's sitting down by the Tam shooting crocs and won't talk to anybody."

Pahner carved off a slice of *bisti* root and popped it into his mouth.

"You know," he said after a long moment, "I'm trying and failing to decide which part of that I like the least."

"Me, too. I'm gonna miss Kostas' damnbeast casserole. And I'm not sure I'll be able to eat croc again."

Pahner looked out over the gathering heaps of material outside the gates. The stores of Sindi, which soon would be the stores of D'Sley and K'Vaern's Cove, were unbelievable. Despite the tremendous inroads the Boman had made upon them, the food supplies of the city remained enormous. Sindi had completed its own massive harvest just before the invasion began, and it was also a central gathering point for the products of the entire region. More than that, it seemed obvious that the rumors that Tor Cant had been stockpiling grain for at least two full harvests in anticipation of the present war had been accurate.

The result, when gathered in one place, was a truly awesome mountain of barleyrice, and the Boman had barely begun to devour it. The barbarians had been too busy eating the draft animals of the city and its satellite communities to waste much time with mere grains and vegetables. All of which meant that even with the barges which had moved the infantry upriver, there was no way to recover those supplies before the Boman returned. The barges would have time to make one, possibly two, trips, but if he committed them to that, they would be unavailable in the event that the plan came apart and a precipitous retreat from Sindi became necessary. Which didn't even consider the fact that there had never been enough barges to lift the combat troops *and* Ther Ganau's engineers.

The city's magazines had also contained several dozen tons of gunpowder, but that posed no particular transportation problems, since From and his engineers were busily expending it as they completed the destruction of northern Sindi.

If they were going to get all the other captured supplies out, though—and God knew K'Vaern's Cove could use every scrap of food in Sindi, especially if things worked out to leave a Boman field army still active in the area—then that corduroy road through the swamps *had* to be held. And while this would-be Boman Napoleon, Camsan, seemed to be chasing Rastar and Honal as fanatically as one could wish, there were still other bands of barbarians wandering around out there. If one of them should hit the convoys of wagons and *flar-ta* lumbering back and forth between Sindi and D'Sley, the results could be catastrophic. Which meant he needed Roger functional. Now.

He thought about a solution and grimaced. The obvious one—which wouldn't work—was to call Roger and tell him to get over it. The one which *would* work, unfortunately, wasn't a good answer in the long-term. The consequences could be literally cosmic, but it was the only one that might work in less than the couple of days it would take Roger to get over his funk without it.

"Eva," he said, "I'm gonna have to break every rule in The Book. As a matter of fact, I'm gonna have to throw it away."

"Okay," the sergeant major said. "What are we gonna do?"

"Get me Nimashet."

Nimashet Despreaux paused.

The prince sat on the river bank, rocking back and forth, his rifle across his lap. She knew, intellectually, that there was no way he would use it on her, but she also knew that he wasn't tracking very well at the moment. So she cleared her throat just a bit nervously.

"Your Highness?"

Roger looked out over the rippling water. He was scanning for "v"s in the fading evening light, but even as his eyes watched the stream with the alertness and intensity of the hunter he was, he wasn't really present. His mind, to the extent that he was thinking at all,

was in a brighter past. A past that wasn't filled with
blood and death. A past where his mistakes didn't kill
people, and where all he had to worry about was
getting his mother's attention, if not approval, and not
completely screwing up in the process. Not that he
ever had. God knew he was a screwup. He always had
been. It just did not make any sense to give him the
slightest shred of responsibility. All he ever did was
fuck it up.

He started without turning his head when someone
laid a hand on his shoulder.

"Go away. That's an order. I'm busy."

"Roger. Your Highness. It's time to leave." Despreaux
wondered if she could get the rifle away from him
without inflicting—or suffering—damage, then decided
to shelve that question. Even if she'd been able to get
the rifle, he'd still have his pistol, and facing Roger
with a pistol in his hand was a losing proposition. "We
need to get your cavalry into position," she said.

"Fuck it," the prince said in a flat voice. "Let Ther
tell Chim what to do. And Turkol. I'm done giving
orders, or even making requests. All I ever do is fuck
things up. Even us."

He looked up over his shoulder at last, and the sergeant almost stepped back at his expression.

"Look at us, what there is of 'us.' " He snorted bitterly. "I can't even carry on a fucking conversation with
a woman I love without totally screwing up."

"You didn't screw up, Roger," the sergeant said, sitting down at his side. Her heart had taken a tremendous lurch at the word "love" but she knew he didn't
need her throwing herself at him at the moment. "I
did. I realize that now. In fact, I've realized it all
along—I just didn't want to admit I have, because it
was so much easier to go on being mad at you, instead.
But all you were trying to say was that fraternization

is a bad idea, and you were right. If you don't watch it, it screws up a unit faster than anything else ever could."

"That wasn't what I was trying to say," the prince said. "It *is* a bad idea, but with so much fooling around going on in the Company, what damage could one more affair do?"

"So what did you mean to say?" Despreaux asked warily. "I assume you *weren't* going to refer to the hired help?"

"No." Roger rubbed his face and looked out on the water again. "What I meant to say was: I don't fool around. Put a period on the end of that sentence. I did a couple of times, and they were outright disasters. And I felt like a shit each time. All I could think about was that I didn't want another bastard in the world. I didn't want to betray someone like my father and mother had."

He pulled his helmet off and set it on the ground. The river bank was covered in a low, soft ground cover, somewhat like short clover, under the shade of a massive jungle giant. It was as comfortable a place as any on the planet to deal with bleak despair.

"I didn't know what the relationship was between my mother and the bastard formerly known as 'my father,'" he said. "But I did know that wondering what the relationship was, and blaming myself for whatever it *wasn't*, had to be the worst way for a kid to grow up. And there are places in the Empire where it matters how 'pure' you've been, and I had to think about that, too. Most people think I never gave a good goddamn about my obligations as a prince, but that's not true, either. Of course, it's not surprising they think that way—I managed to screw up those obligations, too, after all. But that didn't mean I didn't care, or that I didn't recognize that the risk was too great for me to justify fooling around."

"At all?" the incredulous sergeant asked. "For how long? And, I mean, uh . . ."

"I lost my virginity when I was fifteen. To a younger daughter of the Duke of New Antioch. A very ambitious daughter."

"I've heard about that one," Despreaux said carefully. The "scene" was a minor legend in the Emperor's Own and the cause of one of the few resignations of a company commander in its history. "And I've heard that nobody had ever seen you 'with' anyone else. But, I mean, what do you—I mean, that's a looong time."

"Yes, it is. Thank you for pointing that out."

"It's not good for you, you know," the Marine said. "It's not healthy. You can develop an enlarged prostate even while you're young. Sure, they can fix it, but prevention is a much, much better alternative."

"Do I really have to discuss the details of my non-sex life with you?" the prince asked. "Especially right now?"

"No, you don't," Despreaux admitted. "But didn't anybody ever talk to you about it? Didn't you have a counselor?"

"Oh, sure. Plenty of them. And they all took the same position: I needed to release my bonds to my father, put my sense of his betrayal of me behind me, and take responsibility for my own life. This is referred to as 'reality therapy' or 'quit being such a fucking whiner.' Which would have worked real well, except that it wasn't my *father* I resented the hell out of."

"Oh." The sergeant tugged at an earlobe. "That has to be weird. Everybody in the Empire regards the Empress like, well, like a goddess, I guess."

"Yep," Roger said bitterly. "Everyone but her son. I never, ever forgave her for the fact that I didn't have a dad. She at least could have remarried or something.

I finally figured out that was one of the reasons I went into sports—look at all those father figures."

"Oh," Despreaux said again, and then, very, very carefully, "And Kostas?"

"Sort of," Roger said with something halfway between a chuckle and a sob, then drew a deep breath. "Kostas was hard to see as the kind of larger-than-life pattern kids want in their fathers, I guess. But in every other way that counted, he was the closest I ever got. Could have gotten, maybe. He was always there when I needed him . . . and I wasn't there when *he* needed *me*. Of course."

Despreaux's arms twitched as she listened to his ragged breathing, but she made herself pause and think very carefully about what she was going to do. The intensity of Roger's emotions, and the jagged edges of his grief and self-hatred hit her like a fist, and she was more than a little frightened by the dark, pain-filled depths which stretched out before her. But fear was only a part of what she felt, and not the greatest part, and so, finally, she gave a slight shrug and gently took the rifle out of his hands and set it on the ground. Wordlessly, she wrapped her arms around him and pulled him down to lie with his head on her lap . . . and ran her fingers through his sweaty hair as he began, very quietly, to cry.

Her own eyes burned, and she wondered how many lonely years it had been since he had ever let anyone see him weep. Her heart ached with the need to reach out to him, but she was a Marine, a warrior. She knew what needed to be said, but not how to say it, and so she crooned wordlessly to him, instead, and somehow, he seemed to understand the words she couldn't find.

"I don't know what to do, Nimashet," he told her. "I . . . I just can't kill anybody else. I've killed so many of you already. I just can't do that anymore."

"You didn't kill anybody, Roger," she said gently, the words coming at last because she needed them so very badly. "We're Marines. We all volunteered for the Corps, and we volunteered again for the Empress' Own. We knew the score when we signed up, and we could've quit at any time."

"You didn't sign up to be marooned on a planet full of four-armed barbarians while trying to protect a dead-beat prince!"

She smiled, and if that smile was a bit misty, that was her own business.

"Not a deadbeat—more like a dead-shot. Your Highness, there are so many ways to die as a Marine that it's not really funny. This is near the top of the list of odd places and ways, but it's not clear at the top."

"Kostas didn't sign up to be a Marine," he said softly. "He didn't sign on to die."

"People die all the time, Roger." The sergeant combed the tangles out of his hair with her fingers. "They die in aircar accidents, and of old age. They die from too much parsan, and from falling in the shower. They die in shipwrecks, and from radiation poisoning, and by drowning. Kostas didn't have a monopoly on dying."

"He had a monopoly on dying from my mistake," Roger said in tones of quiet, utter bitterness. "I made a simple request and didn't think about the consequences. How many times have I done that—and not just to him? How many times on this march have you Marines been put in jeopardy—or killed—because of my stupid actions? My stupid *unthinking* actions?"

"Quite a few," Despreaux said. "But I think you're being a bit unfair to yourself. For one thing, I've talked to Turkol and Chim. You didn't ask Kostas to get you water; he *offered*. I know, I know," she said, laying one hand lightly across his mouth in what wasn't quite a caress. "That doesn't change what he was doing, or the fact that—just like always—he was doing it for *you*. But I think it does matter that it was his choice, not yours. And while we're on the subject of fairness, do you really think Kostas didn't know about the risks? Know the jungle is dangerous? Roger, he was along for every single step of the march. He was the one who oversaw the mahouts butchering the damncrocs when you and Julian had that shoot-off crossing the damned river before Voitan—you think he didn't know they lived in rivers? For God's sake, he's the one who was on safari with you on all those godforsaken planets none of the rest of us ever even heard of!"

"What are you saying? That it was *his* fault?"

"I'm saying it wasn't *anyone's* fault. Not his, not yours. He went to perform a routine task—not just for you, but for Chim Pri—and somehow, for some reason, he was too distracted to pay attention. It happens, Roger. It happens all the time, every day of our lives. It's just that here on Marduk, if your attention wanders at the wrong moment, you end up dead. You didn't kill him, and he didn't kill himself—the fucking planet did."

"And the Marines? What about *them*?" Roger demanded in a harsh, almost spiteful tone.

"Two things," Despreaux told him calmly. "One, every time you've 'put us in jeopardy' it was a relative danger. This planet is no place for a right-thinking Marine who wants to die in bed, preferably while getting a leg-over, but you didn't pick it, and you certainly didn't order us to come here. Second, a lot of those 'stupid unthinking actions' are the reason we love you. Looking at it sensibly, I guess it really isn't very smart of you, but you just throw yourself at the enemy and keep moving forward until you come out on the other side, and in some ways, Marines aren't all that different from Mardukans. We know the object is to kill the other guy and come home afterward, and we don't have any use at all for officers who keep hanging themselves—and us—out just to prove what great big brass ones they have. But for all that, we respond to COs who *lead* us a thousand times better than we do to those who send us out ahead. And whatever other faults you may have, we've discovered on this shit ball of a planet that you're one hell of a leader. You've got a lot to learn, maybe, about thinking your way through problems—I swear, if you ever faced a Rasthaus wartbeast, you'd throw yourself into its mouth and try to tunnel out the other end!—but you wouldn't do the one thing a leader can never do in combat: hesitate."

"Seriously?" Roger rolled over on his back and looked up at her, and she stroked his face and smiled.

"Seriously. The only thing a Marine truly hates is a coward. Hold still." She leaned down and kissed him. It was a hell of a bend, but she was limber, and Roger released her lips reluctantly.

"What are we doing? And how did we get from Kostas to here?"

"What? They didn't cover that in the Academy?" she asked with a soft laugh. "Call it the desire for life renewal in the face of death. A strong desire. The need to hold back the ferryman in the only way we know." She paused and ran a hand down his side. "Ten years, huh?"

Roger sat up and wrapped his arms around her. As he did, he noted that his tactful bodyguards had discreetly withdrawn out of sight of himself and their squad leader. Which made him wonder what would happen if another damncroc, assuming there were any left in the entire river after his extermination efforts, slipped up out of the water while they were engaged.

Which made him wonder where his cavalry detachment had gotten to. He remembered giving the infantry to Ther Ganau, which made him wonder who was covering the supply convoys.

Which made him groan.

"What?" Despreaux asked huskily.

"Oh, God, Nimashet. We just don't have time. Where's my cavalry? How are Rus From's engineers doing at Sindi? What's happening with Rastar? Are the barges all in place, and who in hell is covering Ther's caravans?"

Her eyes flared, and she grabbed him by the front of his chameleon suit.

"Five minutes," she ground out through gritted teeth.

"More like thirty seconds," the prince told her with something almost like a laugh. "If we can get our clothes off in time, that is. But it's thirty seconds we need to *not* take. I've already lost hours with this despair shit, and we don't need to lose any more with the reverse."

She stuck her hip into his and rolled him over onto his back with the grip on his chameleon suit.

"Listen to me, Prince Roger Ramius Sergei Alexander Chiang *MacClintock!*" she hissed. "I want a promise. You can make it on anything you care to name, but you *will* make it! And that promise is that as soon as we get somewhere safe, and all the crises are past, you will take me to bed. And take your time at it. And do it *well*." She picked him up and pounded him lightly on the ground with each phrase. "Do you swear?"

Roger wrapped his legs around her, pulled her down on top of himself, and kissed her.

"When we're back on Earth. When all of this is behind us, when we're back in the Imperial Palace, and we can be sure it's not the situation. When I'm sure that I love Nimashet Despreaux more than life itself, and that it's not unbridled lust from all the pain and death and blood. Then I'll take you—as my wife, if I can get away with it, or as a senior partner, if I can't. And I will love you until the day I die. I swear it on my dead."

She pounded her head into his breastbone.

"All I want to do is to screw you, you idiot! You're supposed to be telling me you'll love me and marry me to get me to bed—not telling me that to get *you* into bed *I* have to marry you. That's *my* line!"

"Do you accept?" Roger asked.

"Of course I do!" she snapped. "I'd have to be an idiot not to. I love you so hard it hurts, and don't think I'll get over that just because we get back to Earth. Hell, I was so far gone I loved you when you were just an overblown, brainless, arrogant prick of a clothes-horse and I damned well should have known better!"

"Speaking of clotheshorses," he said, fingering the placket of her chameleon suit, "these uniforms could use some work. That's the second thing I'm going to do when we get back to Earth." He looked into her eyes. "So we wait?" he asked in a quieter voice. "You're okay with that?"

"I wouldn't use the term 'okay,'" she said. "'Okay' is definitely not the adverb, or whatever. As a matter of fact, if there's a direct opposite of 'okay' for this situation, that's about where I am. I'm not exactly 'bad' with it, I guess, but I'm definitely sort of 'anti-okay.' On the other hand, I'm a big girl. I'll live."

Roger rolled over, then stood, and pulled her to her feet.

"You ready to go?"

"Sure," she answered sharply. "Let's go find something for me to kill before *you* start looking any better."

"Okay," Roger said with a smile. "I want you to

know, I really do want you. But I don't get any easier with time."

"I've noticed," the sergeant muttered darkly. "Stubborn as a Mardukan day is long." She shook her head. "I have *never* had this much trouble getting a man to bed. For that matter, I've never had *any* trouble getting a man to bed. It was always the other way around."

"Frustration is good for the soul," Roger said. "Look at what it's done for me!"

"Yeah," Despreaux said with a sigh. "No wonder you're so dangerous. Ten years?"

CHAPTER THIRTY-SIX

Armand Pahner stood on the walls of Sindi and gazed out over the muddy, trampled fields. Work crews, wagon trains, and infantry pickets marching out to relieve other pickets stretched as far as the eye could see with a helmet visor set to max, but even as he gazed at them, the activities outside the walls weren't what occupied his mind.

He was thinking about women and children.

The Boman host traveled with all the (limited) comforts of home, including its women and young . . . and Kny Camsan's ambitions had concentrated over half the total host's dependents right here in the city. In fact, it was that bit of intelligence, discovered by Gunny Jin's LURPs and confirmed by reports from a handful of the primitive woodsmen who continued to linger in the forests, despite the Boman's presence, which had shaped the captain's entire strategy.

Pahner had given the strictest orders that every one of those dependents was to be taken into custody, and that none of them were to be molested in any way. The biannual "heat" of the Mardukans eliminated, for all practical purposes, the issue of rape from the local art of war, which—given humans' history—he thought was a very good thing. But that didn't necessarily make war nice and sanitary, and the Boman's depredations and the sheer, horrifying scale of the massacres they had perpetrated had left the locals perfectly willing to slaughter their women and children in return and be done with it. K'Vaernians didn't have the expression "nits make lice," but there was general agreement that the only good Boman was a dead Boman, and the age or sex didn't matter.

Those qualities did, however, matter to Pahner. Leaving aside the clear proscription in imperial regulations against atrocities, leaving aside even his own personal repugnance for unnecessary slaughter, he needed those dependents. He needed them alive, and in good condition.

They were bait.

Normally, the Boman didn't besiege a city the same way a "civilized" army might have. If they failed—or chose not to—overrun its walls with their first, concerted rush, they fell back on their own sort of investment. They didn't call up the engineers to dig trench lines, and they made no effort to batter down walls or tunnel under them. Nor did they encamp outside a city's walls to hold it under a close envelopment. Instead, they just . . . existed, like some vast, slowly swarming sea which had inundated all of the lands about their enemies yet offered no fixed camps which might be assaulted to force them into battle. Their presence, and overwhelming numbers, prevented any organized movement on the part of the besieged city. Anyone trying to break out or escape was caught and overrun. Laborers trying to work the fields were massacred, draft animals were slaughtered or run off.

If large forces sortied against them, they avoided their foes until enough barbarians gathered to pull them down and destroy them. If a city was weak enough, they were willing to simply pile up to the wall and assault it, but in general, they took their time and let it fester and rot . . . *then* assaulted it.

Part of the reason for that was logistical. The Boman were herdsmen, of a sort, which helped sustain their population levels, but they also depended on large areas for hunting and gathering, like other Mardukan barbarians. Even without the need for hunting, their flocks of meat animals—the closest to "farming" they came—required vast grazing areas. At home, they moved their flocks constantly, allowing the grazing in any one area to recover between visits, and they were generally forced to do exactly the same thing when they went to war, assuming they intended to actually feed their warriors. There was no way they could organize a supply train, so staying put for any extended period wasn't really practical, except for the times—like Sindi—when they were able to capture supplies someone else had stockpiled.

True, they had chosen to begin this war with a series of frenzied, massive assaults which had suffered huge casualties, but that had been because this time they were working to a comprehensive strategy which had been designed to annihilate *all* of the southern city-states, not simply to take a single town. They had recognized their need to smash the Northern League quickly, before it could recover from Sindi's treachery and its cities could come to one another's aid as they always had in the past.

The sheer surprise of their coordinated tactics had done almost as much to defeat the League as anything agents from Sindi might have accomplished, Pahner suspected, although he had no intention of suggesting anything of the sort to Rastar or their other Northern allies. After generations of fighting Boman in the same old way, no one in the League had anticipated such an overwhelming onslaught . . . and neither had the Southern city-states behind it. The terror effect of the League's sudden collapse, coupled with the sheer size of the Boman host and the fact that most of the Southerners, secure in the League's protection, had settled for modest defensive works of their own, had made it relatively simple to storm each successive city in turn, and Camsan had done just that. Sindi had been a tougher nut, but the war leader had made no real effort to restrain his warriors' enthusiasm in Sindi's case. He couldn't have, given the reason the war had been decreed in the first place, but casualties in the storm of Sindi had actually been worse than they had in the attack on Therdan. The Northerners had been far tougher opponents, but Sindi had been much larger, and its authorities had been given sufficient time to prepare before the hurricane howled down upon it.

But after Sindi, the Boman had reverted to their more normal tactics rather than attempt an extremely unwise storm of K'Vaern's Cove. The only real difference was that their capture of Sindi gave them a powerful, heavily defended forward base, and—coupled with their conquest of the other Southern city-states—enough captured food to stay in place for several months. Eventually, of course, they would eat their captured larders bare and have to begin thinking about more aggressive ways to take the war to the Cove, but until the humans and their Diaspran allies arrived, Camsan's strategy of letting the K'Vaernians rot and deplete their already limited food supplies feeding the floods of refugees had been working quite nicely. It had been almost certain that, assuming he could hold the Boman together as a cohesive force, he could have sat where he was long enough to reduce the Cove to starving near impotence and then poured his warriors over the walls the Guard would be too weakened to defend.

Which was the whole reason Pahner was out here now. Whether or not the Cove would be fatally weakened before starvation forced the Boman to move themselves, *he* couldn't wait to see the outcome. He needed to bring the barbarians to decisive battle now, so that he and his Marines could get the heck out of Dodge before their food supplements ran out, and to do that he needed to do two other things. First, he needed to present them with a threat which appeared less formidable than it actually was, and, second, he needed to give them a reason to attack that threat.

A reason like rescuing all of their women and children.

The captain didn't much like his own strategy, but it was the only one he could think of which had a chance of working within the time constraints he faced. And if there were things about it that he didn't like, *he* wasn't the one who had decided to level every city-state north of the Diaspra Plateau and the Nashtor Hills.

He snorted, once more amused by his own perversity. Here he was, protecting thousands of women and children from massacre at the hands of his own allies, and all he could think about was how despicable of him it was to use them as bait to lure their menfolk into battle. On the other hand, he suspected he was also dwelling upon that thought to avoid considering one that worried him even more, and it was probably time he stopped doing that. He shook his head, then checked the time and decided that he couldn't put it off any longer.

He drew a deep breath, sent a command to his toot to bring up his communicator, and spoke.

"Roger?"

"Here," the response came back, almost instantly, and the Marine felt his shoulders relax ever so slightly.

"You sound better," he said. "Are you?"

"It comes and goes," the prince said over the radio. "I'm tracking again, if that's what you mean. Whose idea was it to send Nimashet?"

"I felt that you were a bit too exposed," the captain said. "So I augmented Corporal Beckley's team with the rest of the squad. They'll stay with you for the remainder of the operation."

"I see." There was silence over the com for several seconds while both of them digested a great many things which hadn't been said and probably never would be. "So, how're we doing?"

"Pretty much on schedule," Pahner replied. "Eva is working with Rus on the preparation of the defenses. That only seemed to make sense, given her involvement with the artillerists. And Bistem and Bogess have their infantry fairly well organized on the approaches to the city, given that we've had to tap each regiment for a labor battalion to help out Rus's engineers."

"And Rastar?" Roger asked.

"So far, so good," Pahner told him. "He's having a bit more trouble than we'd hoped he would opening the distance between himself and their main force, and it's pretty obvious that they're trying to catch him between the pursuit from Sindi and forces from the other occupied city-states. So far, they haven't been able to hit him with anything he couldn't handle, and his ammunition supply seems to be in pretty good shape, but his whole diversion looks like turning into one big running battle."

"Are we going to have to go in after him?"

"I don't know. I hope not, and so far it looks like we can probably avoid it. But I'm keeping an eye on the situation."

"Good. And what do you want us to be doing?"

"Pretty much what you are, Your Highness. From what Beckley and Despreaux told me yesterday evening, you've got your cavalry about where I want it on that southern flank. I'm going to peel the Carnan Battalion back off from Ther's close cover force on the convoys and send it back to you. We'll let the other cavalry cover him; I want those rifles back out there with you."

"Just to keep my precious hide intact?" Roger asked a bit tartly, and Pahner snorted.

"I'm sure that's somewhere in the back of my mind," he said, "but it's not foremost. Mainly, I just want to be sure that the anchor at the far end of my line isn't going to come loose if somebody runs into it."

"I see. Well, in that case, Captain, we're just going to have to see to it that we stay put, aren't we?"

Dna Kol swallowed a bite of parched barleyrice and leaned down to suck water from the stream.

"If we don't find these damned shit-sitters soon, we head back to the city. I'm out of food and patience," he growled.

"What are they doing?" one of the warriors asked. "First they head west, like they're going back to wherever they crossed. Now they head east."

"They're scattering to avoid us," Dna Kol said. "And somewhere, they're gathering again."

"How can they find each other out here in the woods?" the warrior asked. "I don't know where I am. Oh, I could find the city easily enough if I headed in the right direction long enough, but I certainly couldn't tell anyone else how to find *me*. So how do *they* know where they are? Or where to go to find the rest of them?"

"Maps," another of the warriors spat, drawing his

head up out of the stream. "Damned shit-sitter maps. They map everything. They'll know where every stream crossing is before they get to it."

"Which is how they're managing to lead us around by the nose," Kol agreed. "But we'll track them down soon enough . . . and bring the whole host down on them when we do."

"I could do with some new armor," the first warrior said. He pulled a throwing ax from its belt loop and made a chopping motion. "And I know just how to get some."

"Let's move," Kol said. "I can smell them. They're near."

Rastar ran another patch through the barrel of one of his revolvers, examined the weapon carefully, and decided he was satisfied. In some ways, the last prince of Therdan missed Captain Pahner's pistol. It held far more rounds than the seven-shot revolvers, its recoil was less, and it was a *lot* easier to clean. But for all that, he still preferred these new weapons. There was something about the spit of flame and the trailing smoke from gunfire that added a deeper dimension to the battle. And Pahner's pistol had been too much like magic. These pistols were clearly the work of mortal hands, yet they spoke with all the sound and fury of a gunpowder thunderstorm.

"Time to change *civan* again," he announced as Honal rode up to him and reined in.

"I'm not sure I can dismount," his cousin groaned. "I *used* to think I was tough."

"I believe you mentioned that yesterday morning," the Northern leader said. He finished loading cartridges into the cylinder, carefully plugged the mouth of each chamber with the heavily greased felt pad which prevented flash-over from detonating all seven rounds at once, and began fitting the copper caps over the nipples at the rear of the cylinder. "Change your mind?"

"I think I've figured out a translation for that joke that bastard Pahner told us before we set out," Honal said in indirect reply as he slid gracelessly out of the saddle and fell onto his back. The *civan* delicately stepped away as a groom came up to unsaddle it.

"Oh?" The prince finished capping the cylinder and swung it back into place and looked up inquiringly. The humans' toot translations were usually excellent, but they made a hash of jokes . . . which had been obvious in the case of Pahner's statement.

"You just have to make a terrible pun out of it, and it's really quite funny," the Sheffan cavalry commander said, still laid out flat on the ground. "If, of course, you haven't spent three days at a fairly constant trot. Try it this way: 'A Manual for Cavalry Operations, Forty *Kolong* a Day, by Princely Arseburns.' "

"Ah!" The Therdan prince gave a grunting laugh. "Har! That's pretty good, actually. Feel better?"

"No," his cousin said. "I have princely arseburns. I have armor chafe. I have dry-slime. And I think my legs just fell off."

"Nope," Rastar said with another grunt. "They're still there. Hey, think of how the *civan* must feel."

"Pock the *civan*," the cavalry commander said with feeling. "When we get back to K'Vaern's Cove, I swear I'm going infantry. If I never see another *civan* again in my life, it will be too soon. I'm going to personally eat every one of them I've ridden in the last three days. It'll take a couple of seasons, and I think I've already killed two the cooks didn't get gathered up, but I'll get all of the others. I can do it. I have the determination."

"We have lost quite a few," Rastar said softly. "A lot more than I'd like, in fact. But as long as they hold up for the last run, we're golden."

"Not necessarily," Honal said, finally sitting up with another groan. "One of my scouts caught a group on our back trail."

"*Now* you tell me?"

"They're a few hours back," Honal told him unrepentantly. "But we do need to ready a reception."

Dna Kol paused at the edge of the clearing. The spot was a regular stopping place on the Sindi-Sheffan caravan trail, an open area created by a thousand years of caravans' cutting undergrowth for firewood, and a medium-sized, fordable stream ran through it. A heavy rain was falling, reducing visibility, but it was still clear that more iron head cavalry than he ever wanted to see again waited on the far side of the clearing.

"Crap," he snorted. "I think we've been suckered."

"There's more of them moving off to the right," one of his followers said. "Let's hammer this group before the others get into position."

"I think we're the ones who're going to be hammered," the subchief said. "But that does seem to be the only option."

Rastar grinned in the human fashion as the Boman burst from the tree line, screaming their tribal war cry. His only worry had been that they might move back into the trees, taking cover from the cavalry's fire, but perhaps the pounding rain explained why they hadn't. Surely, by now, the Boman must have realized that the League troopers' new firearms were remarkably unaffected by precipitation! Still, he supposed the ingrained habits of decades of experience against matchlocks couldn't be overcome in a mere three days.

"Load up, but hold your fire!" he shouted as he spurred his *civan* into the clearing. "I want to try something."

He drew up, turned his *civan* to present its flank to the barbarian line, and pulled out four of his eight pistols as the Boman charged to get into throwing ax range. His true-hands pointed right and left, to the outside of the charging barbarian line, while the false-hands pointed at its center. He let all four eyes defocus, drew a deep breath, and opened fire.

The astonished barbarians' charge shattered as all four pistols blazed simultaneously and the accurate, massed fire piled up a line of bodies for the following warriors to stumble over.

The prince's grin was a snarl through the thick fog of rain-slashed gunsmoke as he spun his *civan* and galloped back through the positions of his waiting cavalry.

"Okay," he called, smoking pistols held high, "now *you* can try!"

He holstered two weapons and started reloading the other two as the cavalry about him began to fire.

"Wyatt who?" he grunted.

"Are you going to get all the supplies out?" Roger asked over his helmet com.

"I sure hope so," Pahner replied with a snort. "Although, we're retaining a good bit more than I'd originally planned. Got to feed these women and children something."

"I'm surprised the troops are staying in hand so well," Roger said, studying the video feed from the captain's helmet and taking in the orderliness of the city's occupiers.

"Me, too," Pahner admitted. "I'd assumed at least a twenty-five percent loss rate from AWOLs in the city, but we're at nearly one hundred percent present as of the morning report."

"That high?" Roger sounded surprised, and Pahner chuckled.

"Bistem Kar gave them an incentive," the Marine explained. "Before he released the troops to glean, he paraded them in front of the huge piles of stuff from the main storerooms and promised each of them a share on return. Some of them never even left—why go hunting through the city, when you can be handed a bag of gold and silver for staying put?—and the rest came back soon enough."

"That Kar is one smart cookie," Roger observed with a chuckle.

"That he is," the captain agreed. "And there's an important lesson here, Roger. Smart allies are worth their weight in gold."

"So what's the game plan at your end?" the prince asked.

"Rus's people are recovering from their engineering efforts. As soon as they have, I'm sending half of them back to Tor Flain to man the D'Sley defenses for him and help Fullea cross load the Sindi loot from the river barges and caravans to the seagoing vessels for transit to the Cove. The other half will move over and begin helping to load the barges from this end."

"And Bistem and Bogess?"

"I'm putting half of their people on the stores, and the other half on security. We're going to have Boman filtering back from the north soon, and I want a good security screen dug in to deal with them until we're ready."

"And after that, we wait," Roger said.

"And after that, we wait," Pahner confirmed.

Kny Camsan's head went up as he heard the firing to the north.

"Another skirmish, while all the time this group gets smaller and smaller and further and further away," he growled.

"What else can we do?" one of the subchiefs asked. "We have to run them to ground."

"Of course we do," the war leader said, "and we can. I have yet to find a group of *civan* that can outlast the Boman over the long run. But they're scattered all over the landscape, and we've been letting them dictate where we go by chasing directly after them. No more! Tell the warriors to spread out and head back towards the southeast. Instead of chasing them, we'll sweep on a broad front while the other clans join up with us. When our full strength is assembled, we'll be a wall, moving through the jungle, and whenever we encounter one of these accursed groups of theirs, we'll hammer them into the earth!"

"That sounds better than chasing along their back trail day after day," the subchief agreed. "But we're running low on food."

"We are the Boman," Camsan said dismissively. "The host can go for days without, and when we've run them down, we'll fill our bellies on the meat from their *civan* and go back to Sindi in triumph."

"Some of the host have tired of the chase. They're already going back to Sindi."

"Fine by me," Camsan grunted. "I didn't want to chase these shit-sitters in the first place, but be damned if I'll head back now until I have that Therdan pussy's head on a spear!"

CHAPTER THIRTY-SEVEN

"Armand?"

Pahner looked up in surprise as Eva Kosutic stepped into his commandeered office in the Despot's Palace of Sindi. He hadn't actually seen her face-to-face since their arrival here. They'd stayed in touch through their coms, of course, but the sergeant major had been buried in her own portion of the preparations for the "Sindi Surprise Party," as most of the army was calling the battle plan, which had kept her busy with the engineers and the artillery corps. It wasn't her physical presence that surprised the captain, though; it was the tone of her voice and her expression. He hadn't seen a grin that huge since well before Bravo Company ever heard of a planet called Marduk.

"Yes?" he replied, arching his eyebrows, and her grin got even bigger.

"Just got off the radio with Doc Dobrescu," she said, and laughed. She didn't chuckle—she *laughed*, with a bright, almost girlish delight that deepened his surprise even further. "He's got some . . . interesting news," she added.

"Well, would you care to share it with me, or are you just going to stand there with that stupid grin all day?" he asked just a bit tartly, and she laughed again.

"Sorry, Boss. It's just that I've always known His Evilness had a really perverse sense of humor, and now He's gone and proved it!"

"And how, if you ever intend to get around to it, has he done that?"

"You know that little job you gave the Doc? The one that's had him running everything he could get his hands on through the analyzers?"

"Yesss," Pahner said slowly, leaning further back in the camp chair behind his desk.

"Well, he just hit pay dirt," the sergeant major told him. "He's found something the nanites can process into the protein supplements we've got to have."

"He *has?*" Pahner snapped back upright in the chair.

"Yep, and you'll never guess where he found it," Kosutic said with another huge grin. Pahner cocked his head demandingly, and she laughed once more. "You remember that poison gland in the *coll* fish? The one that's absolutely lethal to any Mardukan, no ifs, ands, or buts?" Pahner nodded, and she snorted. "Seems the Doc remembered how Radj Hoomis failed to poison us and said, what the hell, let's check it, too. And when he did—"

She shrugged, and Pahner stared at her.

"Let me get this straight," he said slowly. "This deadly poison no one else on Marduk can eat is like . . . like *cod liver oil* for humans?"

"Not a bad analogy at all," she agreed with a nod. "From what he's saying, it tastes just as bad—or even worse. But all his tests say it's the real stuff. Of course, it won't work for anyone who doesn't have the full nanite loadout, but when you couple it with apsimons, the troops—and Roger—are good to go almost indefinitely. And we've got enough regular supplements to keep everyone who doesn't have the full spectrum nanites going for a good year or more, as well. Which is what I meant about His Evilness and His sense of humor."

"Hmmm?" Pahner was still too busy grappling with how Dobrescu's announcement had changed his constraints to realize what she was saying for several seconds, but then he laughed harshly. "I see what you mean," he said, shaking his head slowly. "We agreed to kick off this entire operation, built the damned army, pissed off every merchant in the Cove, turned K'Vaernian society on its ear, pushed the training, drove everyone into the field, and set up this whole trap just because we were running out of supplements and couldn't afford to wait around. And now we find out we've got all the time in the fucking world!"

"Absolutely," she agreed with a laugh of her own.

The two of them stared at one another for almost a full minute without saying another word, and then Pahner sighed.

"I wish we'd known sooner," he said slowly. "Kostas would be alive right now if we hadn't had to go back into the field, for one thing. But at the same time, maybe it's for the best. If I'd known about this, I would've been a lot more willing to sit things out and look for other options as the safer way to get Roger home, and if I'd done that, there wouldn't have *been* a K'Vaern's Cove in another six months."

"From what we've seen of these Boman bastards since we actually hit the field, I think you're probably right," Kosutic said more somberly, "and I wouldn't like that. I've decided I can really get along with these K'Vaernians, almost as well as with Rastar and his *civan* boys. So I guess I'm glad we didn't leave them in the lurch, too. And speaking of Rastar," she went on, changing the subject, "just how are he and Honal doing?"

"Don't know," Pahner admitted, and checked the time on his toot. "They're about due for another check in, but the last time I talked to them, even Honal was starting to sound a little frayed around the edges."

"Honal? The original Mardukan Hotspur?" Kosutic chuckled. "That'll be the day!"

"It looks like they're spreading out," Honal said. The most recent group of Boman to encounter his troopers were stretched out on the ground, riddled with pistol bullets or spitted on lances and sabers. This time, however, almost a dozen of his own men were down to keep them company on their trip to Hell. "This is the largest bunch we've run into yet."

"And I think they're closing in on us," Rastar agreed unhappily. "They're getting thicker as we head south."

The native prince eased himself in the saddle and looked around. It was raining again, which didn't do much for visibility, but he was reasonably confident of his present location. Thanks to the fact that each group to split off from the main force had included at least one trooper with a human communicator, he also knew roughly where all the rest of his men were. The good news was that his entire force should be reformed within the next several hours. The bad news was that the Boman seemed to have figured out roughly where he was headed for his rendezvous.

"We're not going to be able to make it back to Sindi," Honal said. "Are we?"

Rastar pulled out a map and grimaced accusingly at it, although it really hadn't told him anything he didn't already know.

"I don't know," he sighed. "We're so close I hate to give up. I don't doubt that they'll go ahead and head back for Sindi even without us to chase, but if we have to give up on the city, we'll have to head all the way up to the Sumeel Ford, instead, and that means heading up the Tam to the Chandar Fords. We'd be completely out of it. By the time we could cross the river, we might have to head all the way to Nashtor to avoid the Boman."

"So much for that plan, then," Honal said. "And I don't know that we could make it, anyway. The *civan* are just about worn out."

"I know," the prince said. He grimaced again, and keyed his communicator. "I think we need to tell the captain."

Pahner looked at the map and managed not to swear. It wasn't easy. From the reports, there was no way the cavalry on its own was going to break through the Boman who'd swept around to get between it and Sindi. Only a fraction of the total Boman force had managed to bottle them up, but a fraction was all it took, when they'd been outnumbered the whole time by nearly thirty-to-one.

If he sent them east, on an end run to the fords on the upland plateau, they would be out of play for the entire battle, depriving him of the huge bulk of his cavalry. That probably would have been endurable, given the battle he intended to fight, but it would cost him any real possibility of a pursuit if—when—the Boman broke. Worse, it was almost certain that all or some of the main host would go right on chasing them. Not only would that mean that whatever percentage of the barbarians kept chasing the cavalry would miss the reception he'd so carefully prepared for them here at Sindi, but it was also likely that the Boman would manage to run them down before they could reach safety.

Yet there were reports of Boman everywhere between Rastar's force and Sindi, not just farther out, where the cavalry was in light contact with the barbarians. Some of them were even starting to hit the guards he'd pushed out from the northern gates of the city, and he had damn all information on their numbers. If he sent out a relief force to rescue Rastar, he risked having it defeated in detail by an enemy whose strength he was unable to accurately evaluate.

He gazed at the map for several more silent moments, then straightened and turned to his command group.

"Bistem, you have the most forces present and on security," he said. "Take all the Diaspran forces that aren't broken up as stevedores, add them to First Division, and go relieve the cavalry. Take Julian and his team, as well. We'll worry about power for the armor later."

"Yes, Captain," the K'Vaernian commander said. "We won't fail."

"Make sure you don't," Pahner said, "and don't stint the fire. We've been saving the full power of the rifles for a surprise, and I think it's about time to start showing these bastards how surprising they are."

"Yes, Captain." The K'Vaernian gave a human-style nod, ducked out of the command tent, and started forward, calling for messengers. Pahner watched him go, then keyed his communicator again.

"Rastar, I'm sending out a relief force. The K'Vaernians are going to head for your position. Dismount and fight as infantry and push your way through to link up."

"Yes, Captain," the distant prince said over a background crackle of pistol fire. "The woods are thick enough out here that we've already had to dismount, but we can't keep our flanks secure enough to push forward. I've tried twice, and been badly outflanked each time. If you don't mind, I think I'll wait for the K'Vaernians to draw some of the attention off of us."

"Do as you see fit," the Marine said with a face of stone. Clearly, it was getting tight in the woods. "The relief column is on the way. However, be aware that if more forces press down on you, I might have to tell them to retreat."

"Understood," the embattled prince said. "We'll try to cut down the opposition as much as possible. Rastar, out."

Pahner looked around the fields before the city. The piles of cured leather, sacks of barleyrice, cloth, coal, ores, charcoal, refined metals, and a thousand and one other things vital to K'Vaern's Cove's economy were being slowly reduced by the line of bearers carrying them to the barges, the caravans of packbeasts, and the long line of wagons creaking down the corduroy road. Whatever happened here, the Cove desperately needed those supplies if it was to survive while its trading partners rebuilt themselves from the ruins. Yet every one of the stevedores loading the booty was also a soldier who was as much out of the battle as if he'd been shot through the head.

He could take some of them off of the loading duty, but that would slow down the loading operation. Which would be fine, if his overall plan worked. But as Rastar's predicament pointedly illustrated, plans had a tendency to spring leaks, and if the master plan collapsed, the Cove would need those supplies worse than ever.

Finally, he decided to take the gamble. The majority of the Boman were on the north side of the river, but they clearly were closing in on the cavalry, which had turned out to be too good as bait. There should be enough pickets covering the northern approaches to the city itself, even after Kar's departure, to hold anything else which might come at them from that direction. The caravan route to D'Sley on the south bank couldn't boast anywhere near the same amount of security, but it was covered by its own thin cavalry screen, and it seemed—so far, at least—to be isolated from the main threat area. If there were any formed Boman on the south side of the river, they couldn't possibly be present in numbers as great as those to the north, and the screen would just have to take them on as they came.

"Rus, get in the middle of that," he said, gesturing to the lines of Mardukans loading stores, "and see if you can find some way to speed things up."

"Will do," the engineer said.

"Come on, Rastar," the captain said quietly. "Keep your ass alive until Bistem can drag your butt home."

Honal swung out the cylinder of his revolver and grunted.

"I love these things. Where has Pahner been all my life?"

"Flying between suns, according to the Marines," Rastar said, hammering a stuck bullet out of the barrel of one of his own pistols. The cartridge had succumbed to the eternal humidity, despite its flashplant wrapping, and the damp gunpowder had only sparked enough to drive the slug into the barrel. "I wish he were here at the moment, though. What a screwed-up situation."

More Boman had trickled up behind the cavalry unit, encircling it. Fortunately, most of the force had reformed before the Boman pinned it, which had at least prevented the detachments from being annihilated in detail. The bad news was that it put them all in one place, which meant that better than three thousand riders and nearly eight thousand *civan* were trapped in a single pocket which the barbarians could now close in upon. Most of the true war *civan* were on the perimeter, squatting like ostriches on nests as cover for their riders, and the cavalry had managed to fell trees to simultaneously expand their fire zones and form a crude abattis covering most of their front, but the eddies of barbarians were sweeping inexorably closer.

Honal took another breath and squeezed the trigger.

"Got you, you Boman bastard," he muttered, then chuckled sourly. "You know, much as I love these revolvers, I could wish we had more rifles to go with them!"

"Some people are never satisfied," Rastar grunted. "We've got a helluva lot higher rate of fire than rifles, and with all these pocking trees, it's not like the bastards are out of range when we see them at all!"

He got the barrel cleared and closed the cylinder once more. There'd been times during the pursuit when he would have agreed wholeheartedly with Honal, but there simply weren't enough rifles to go around. Dell Mir's simplified cartridge design had allowed the humans to somewhat better Rus From's original estimates on the numbers of rifles which could be supplied with ammunition. Instead of five or six thousand, K'Vaern's Cove had managed to put eight thousand into the field, but that still fell far short of any number the K'Vaernians and their allies would have liked to see. It also meant that virtually the entire production of rifles had gone into the hands of the infantry units, who—if everything worked out the way it was *supposed* to work—would be doing the majority of the fighting. Rastar's troopers had been issued only four hundred of the new weapons. On the other hand, they'd had six thousand revolvers—virtually the entire production of that weapon.

They'd also gone through well over two thirds of their total ammunition by now, but Rastar decided not to think about that just at the moment.

"Oh, I'd never want to trade my revolvers in," Honal told him, eyes searching for another target. "I was just thinking that if we had more rifles, that would mean we also had more rifle*men* to carry them. Which would be very comforting to me right now."

"To me, too," Rastar admitted. "But I think there's a fair chance that we'll be seeing them sometime soon."

"I hope so," Honal said more somberly. "And I think I'm glad about who the Captain chose to send to relieve us. If *I* had to choose between Bogess, bless his thick head, or Bistem Kar, I'd take Kar any day."

"I have to agree," Rastar grunted, "but I wish he'd hurry up and get here." The Boman were massing for another attack as he finished reloading his pistols. "It's not like we've got an infinite amount of ammunition."

"He'll be here soon," Honal said. "Quit fretting."

Krindi Fain clasped all four hands behind him and stepped in front of Lieutenant Fonal. The adviser sergeant turned his back so that the company of forming infantry couldn't see what he was saying and cleared his throat.

"You need to quit fretting, Lieutenant."

"Is it that obvious?" the officer asked nervously.

"Yes," Fain said. "There are many ways to lead well, and twice as many to lead poorly. Looking nervous and uncertain is in the 'twice as many' category."

"So what do you suggest, Sergeant?"

"Take a breath, look at your map, and don't rub your horns every few seconds. There's a worn patch forming. Laugh. You can talk to the troops, but only about stuff other than whether or not they're ready. Your best bet is to stand there like a rock and just look as certain as the rainfall. If you go talk to Colonel Tram or General Kar for a moment, then come back and look really relaxed, it would help."

"But what about getting the company ready? We've got half a platoon missing!"

"Leave the worrying about that to Sergeant Knever. Either he's the right man for the job, and the company will perform for you when you need it, or you should have replaced him before now. Either way, it's too late to be thinking about changes. And if we have to leave without half a platoon, we leave without them."

Fonal started to rub a horn once more, then checked the movement.

"How can you be so calm, Sergeant? There are a lot of Boman out there, and not many of us." The officer leaned closer. "We're going to get slaughtered, in case you hadn't realized it," he hissed.

The sergeant tilted his head to the side and studied the lieutenant.

"Would you prefer to round up the missing ranks, Lieutenant?" he asked, wondering what the response would be. He wasn't very surprised, unfortunately.

"Frankly," Fonal said, squaring his shoulders, "if *we're* missing half a platoon, I suspect most of the other units in the regiment probably are as well. And it would be a good idea if an officer stayed behind to gather them up and send them forward."

"You have a very good point, Lieutenant," the Diaspran said. "Could you excuse me for a moment?"

Fain gestured at Erkum Pol and walked over to the quartet of armored Marines.

Julian was monitoring the commander's briefing. Kar had been handed a difficult tactical problem and not much time to solve it, but he was going about the preparation as professionally as anyone Julian had ever seen. Some of his regimental and battalion commanders, on the other hand, didn't seem all that happy about the mission, so the NCO wasn't feeling particularly happy in turn when someone rapped on his armor to get his attention.

"Hey, Krindi. How they hanging?"

"One lower than the other, as usual, Sergeant," the Mardukan answered soberly. "We've got ourselves a little situation over in Delta Company. The company commander just told me he thought it would be better if he stayed behind and rounded up stragglers."

"Oh, shit," Julian said. "Anybody hear him?"

"Aside from Erkum and me? I don't think so."

"Good," Julian said. "I won't have to kill him."

The Marine thought about it for a moment. The only person who could relieve the commander—and that commander definitely needed to be relieved—was Bistem Kar, but the K'Vaern's Cove Guard commander was far too busy to bother with a single cracked officer.

"Tell the company commander that, pending confirmation from General Kar, he's temporarily assigned to rear detachment duties. He should report to General Bogess while the rest of the force is in the field."

"Are we going to be able to get away with this?" Fain asked. "I mean, I agree and everything, but can we get away with it?"

"I can," the Marine said. "I'll tell Pahner about it, but that's about all I need to do. You don't send an officer out if he can't keep it together in front of the troops. Maybe you make *him* a troop, but that's for later. And I'll explain it to Kar and the guy's battalion commander when the time comes."

"Last question," Fain said. "Who takes the company? There's no subordinate officers—just a sergeant seconded from the Guard, and he's running around getting everybody in line and making sure they all have ammo."

Julian was just as happy that there was no way to see into his armor as he grimaced. After a moment's additional thought he gave an equally unseen shrug.

"You take it," he said. "Tell the sergeant that you're standing in until a qualified officer can be appointed. I'll get with Kar right after the meeting and tell him what's going on."

"Joy," Fain said sarcastically. "You know, if I'd known this day was going to come, I'd never have taken that pike from you."

"If *I'd* known this day would come, I never would've handed it to you," Julian said with a laugh.

"They're moving out now," Roger said, picking at the food in his bowl. The new cook simply didn't have Matsugae's way with Mardukan chili.

"That's half the force," Despreaux said, doing a quick count with her own helmet systems. "Who the hell is guarding the store?"

"There are still seven regiments in and around Sindi, even if two thirds of their personnel are busy humping crates. South of the city? Us. There are six, maybe eight hundred cavalry in the screen from here to the D'Sley swamps, with a few pickets to the east. If anything ugly comes our way, of course, the troops acting as drovers and mahouts will do their best, but they're going to be pretty scattered out. And then there's the crate-humpers back at Sindi."

"Just getting them into formation would take a couple of hours," Beckley put in. "By the way, I'm glad you two finally kissed and made up."

"Is that what we did?" Roger asked, regarding the corporal with a crooked eyebrow.

"According to the pool it is," Beckley replied with a complacent smile. "Won me almost five thousand credits, when I get home to collect it, too."

"I thought you looked revoltingly cheerful, you greedy bitch," Despreaux said with a grin.

"Me? Greedy?" Beckley shook her head mournfully. "You wrong me. I'm just delighted to see that, once again, the course of true love cannot be denied."

"Let's hope not, at any rate," Roger said, suddenly somber. "It would be nice if *something* about this trip stayed on course."

CHAPTER THIRTY-EIGHT

"Where in the hell did all this shit-sitter cavalry come from?" Sof Knu demanded, glaring at the ten- or fifteen-man cavalry picket from the undergrowth while rain drizzled down from an ebon sky.

"It must have been the 'marsh gas' we were chasing," Knitz De'n replied.

The last five days had been a period of utter frustration. De'n's tribe had arrived on the K'Vaern's Cove road to find absolutely no sign of any iron head cavalry, although there had been some tracks, washing away in the rain. They'd found a few of the damned wood runners and tortured them for information, but most had denied knowing anything, no matter how much they screamed. Finally, one had admitted to seeing some cavalry, but the place he claimed to have seen them was so close to Sindi that De'n had ordered his torturers to give him special attention to punish his lies. But the worthless creature had continued to shriek the same lie over and over again until he died, so the subchief had decided he had no choice but to check it out . . . only to find these damned patrols between him and the city. The only good thing was that the shit-sitters hadn't spotted him in return. Yet.

"We can sweep them aside easily," Knu said. "Just give the word."

"The word is *given*," the subchief growled, pulling out a throwing ax. "As soon as the tribe is assembled, we'll run right over them. And anything else that stands in our way."

"What was that?" Roger looked up from his map and cocked his head.

"What was what?" Despreaux asked. "I can't hear a thing but the rain."

"Shots," the prince replied. "To the southwest." He stood up, trying to triangulate the source by turning his head from side to side, but the brief crackle of gunfire had already died.

"Somebody shooting a damnbeast?" Chim Pri suggested uncertainly.

"Maybe one of the cavalry pickets," Roger said. He looked out at the rain-soaked, night-dark woods and shivered despite the unending Mardukan warmth. "Chim, saddle up. I want you to head southwest and see what you find. Push skirmishers out front, but find the picket that was shooting if you can, and find out what it was shooting at."

"No more shots," Turkol Bes pointed out.

"I know," Roger said wiping the rain out of his face. "And I don't care. I still want to know what they were shooting at."

"I'm going," Pri said, looking into the water-filled, Stygian blackness. "But if it's trouble, you'd better be ready to follow us up sharpish."

"We will," Roger assured him, keying his helmet com. "Sergeant Jin?"

✧　　✧　　✧

"We heard it, too, Sir," the gunnery sergeant said. The majority of the LURP teams had been left out to supplement the cavalry screen. "It was almost due west of us. All we could hear were the shots, but it sounded like one of the screen patrols ran into something heavy."

"*Atul*?" the prince asked, and over the radio, Jin could hear Mardukans bellowing what sounded like orders in the background. Clearly, the prince was on the ball.

"I don't think so, Sir," the NCO said. "I was just about to call it in to Captain Pahner when you called me."

"Right," Roger said, and Jin could almost hear the wheels turning. "I'm pushing my cavalry down there to see what they find. I'll go ahead and orient the Carnan that way, as well. Call the Captain and give him a situation report. MacClintock out."

The NCO smiled in the darkness. Whatever was going on in the deep woods seemed to have galvanized the prince, thank God. He truly sounded like himself for the first time since Matsugae's death . . . and that was the first time the gunnery sergeant had ever heard Roger refer to himself unthinkingly as a MacClintock.

Patty burbled unhappily as the mahouts threw on her harness.

"I know, girl," Roger said, soothingly. He patted her behind her armored ruff. "I know it's dark. Deal with it."

It *was* dark—very dark. The double cloud layer had set in with a vengeance, and the moons weren't even up above it. Once they got away from the fires, most of the force would be nearly blind. The cavalry would be depending on their *civan* to find the way, and many of them would get lost. But the *civan* would eventually find their way back, at least. The same could not be said for the infantry.

He looked up to see Bes coming towards him in a way which demonstrated the point. The infantry leader had been reading a map in the tent, and now, in the shadows of the *turom* assigned to the mobile unit, he was walking with all four arms thrown forward, questing for anything which might loom unseen in his way.

"Over here, Turkol," Roger said. His own helmet systems, of course, made the area almost daylight-bright . . . which gave him an idea.

"God of Water, Your Highness," the infantry commander said. "How are we going to find our way through this?"

"I was just thinking about that," Roger told him. "I think I'll have to break up my Marine squad and let each of them lead a section of the column. We'll move in line until we find out what's happening, and each of the troops will have to hold hands with the men in front of and behind him."

"Okay," Bes agreed, his eyes starting to adjust at least a little. "The good news is that the Boman don't like to move in the dark, either. And they do it slowly. I'll go get the troops lined up."

"And I'll get the Marines," Roger said.

"*No!*" Despreaux snapped. "We're your bodyguard, not seeing-eye Marines!"

"Sergeant Despreaux, that's an order," the prince said coldly, "and if I bring it to Captain Pahner's attention, which I should *not* have to do, he'll back me on it. We may very well have a hostile force of unknown size on our flank, and no forces on this side but *us*. I don't have time to debate with you."

"Who covers your back, *Sir?*" the squad leader demanded.

"Two Marines," Roger answered, "one of whom will *not* be you. And you won't be leading a group, either, nor will I. That leaves eight. Go get them ready, and have them report to Turkol. We need to have left already."

Despreaux threw up her hands.

"All right, all right. I get the picture. Yes, Sir, yes, Sir, three bags full. Just do me one favor, Your Highness."

"What?"

"Don't go riding into the middle of a thousand Boman screaming a war chant, okay?"

Roger snorted. "Okay. And do me one favor back."

"What?"

"Don't get yourself killed. I've got plans for you."

"Okay," the sergeant said. "I'll be going now."

Chim Pri reined in at a small stream and strained to hear. The jungle was always alive with sound, yet this time there was something extra. The rain had stopped, temporarily at least, but a wind was blowing through the treetops. It probably presaged yet another rainstorm, which would be irritating enough, but it was also blowing noisy spatters of water off of leaves and vines. It made hearing difficult, yet there was something else, another rustling half-lost in the background sound, but there.

He turned around and realized he could barely see two mounts behind him.

"First three troopers. Move forward and see what that is. And try not to get yourselves killed."

A trio of *civan* trotted obediently forward, and he heard one of the all-but-invisible troopers grunting in laughter.

"Yes, Sir. We'll try real hard not to get killed."

"You'd better," the cavalry commander said with a

grunt of his own. "Anybody who gets killed tonight is going on report!"

It took only a few moments for the *civan* to thread their way between the trees. But their approach, quiet as it was, was detected, and the night rang with barbarian warcries from hundreds of lungs.

"Gods of Fire and Darkness!" Pri snapped. "What in the three hells did we run *into*?"

One of the troopers he'd sent forward let loose with all seven shots in one of the newly issued revolvers, and the brilliant lightning bolts of the muzzle flashes showed the cavalry commander dozens of barbarians . . . and probably hundreds more behind them.

"Spread out!" he shouted. "I need some sort of accurate count!"

The commander spurred his *civan* to the south, searching for the tail of the barbarian column as the Boman charged straight into the swirling cavalry of the *Basik*'s Own. Finally, as the shots rose to a crescendo, he decided he'd seen enough.

"Sound the recall!" he ordered the hornmen, who'd somehow kept up through the woods. "Sound a general retreat. Hopefully, they'll fall back to the infantry."

He picked the communicator off his breast as he turned to the northeast, wondering how to tell Roger that the entire force was apparently cut off. Behind him, the horns began to sound.

The enemy was upon them.

"Well, gentlemen, this is what happens when you draw to an inside straight," Pahner said.

"It might not be that bad," Bogess said. "If it's a small force, we can beat it off."

"According to Chim Pri, it's at least a thousand or two thousand," the Marine said, "and our last sizable cavalry force—his—is scattered through the woods and all mixed up amongst them. So it's not going to be easy to stop them."

"Should we stop the loading?" Rus From asked.

"Not unless we have to," Pahner said. "Pull one regiment off of loading duties just in case, but basically, it's up to Roger now. If he beats them, we'll continue as we're going. If he's forced out of position or flanked, we'll start pulling troops off of loading to form a front facing towards D'Sley." The Marine paused and shook his head. "Did I just say what I think I said?"

"You said we should pull a battalion off of loading and that it's up to Roger," Bogess said. "Is that what you mean?"

"Yes," the captain said with a grimace. "I'm supposed to be protecting *Roger*, not the other way around. This is *not* going to look good in my report."

"You have to write the report for it to look good or bad," Rus From said with a grunt of laughter. "Let Roger look out for himself."

"Lord, Lord, Lord," the Marine groaned. "His mother's going to kill me."

Roger dropped his pad into its pouch and shook his head. He already knew the terrain, and there was nowhere to anchor his flank. There was a stream not too far behind them, though, that would work to control the line.

"Turkol, we're backing up to the far side of the stream. Put one company in reserve, spread the other three in a line, and start working out a light defense work. Have them dig in good; we're not backing up any further."

"Got it," the infantry battalion commander said. "What about the flanks?"

"If we can get the cavalry back in, we'll have it cover them. Until then, I'll split the Marines and put them in place as security teams." He thought about it for a moment more, but there wasn't much else to do. "Move."

"Roger," Pri said into the communicator, "where the hell are you? And where the hell am I, for that matter?"

"Do you remember crossing a small stream on your way out?" the prince responded, gazing at the icon the location transponder in Pri's communicator had thrown up on the map on his pad.

"Yes, I'm on the same trail we followed on the way out, I think." The cavalry commander looked around. He heard occasional pistol shots behind him, but he had at least half his command regrouped.

"We're setting up on the stream. Are you in contact with the Boman?"

"No," Pri said. "Not as an organized body, at least. Some of my people are still out there, and I can hear them shooting, but it's blacker than the inside of an *atul*'s nest, and I can't see crap. We broke contact as soon as we realized we were outnumbered, though, and I'm pretty sure my stragglers all know which way to head."

"Well, get back down there. Stay together this time, and hit them hard, then fall back in contact. We need them to come to us from the direction of our choice, and the only way to make sure they do is for you to lead them right in. We've got you on our pads and helmet HUDs, and Despreaux or I can guide you, roughly, at least, if you lose orientation on our position."

"Got it," the cavalryman said, glad to have orders, even if they were mildly crazy. "You do realize that there are over two thousand of them, right?"

"Fine," Roger said. "Just get them to the stream, and

Turkol will do the rest. Oh, and when you get close, you'd better start sounding your horns."

Roger strode along the line of digging riflemen and grinned.

"I thought you New Model Army boys could *dig!* What are you, a bunch of women?"

A shovelful of wet dirt, half mud, came flying out of the darkness and hit his chest in answer.

"We're so good we can hit you in the dark, Sir!"

"As long as you can hoist them as well as you throw them," Roger said with a laugh. "We've got about two thousand Boman coming at us, so I think you're going to appreciate a wall in a little bit."

"Don't worry, Your Highness," one of the riflemen said. "We're not afraid to die for the God."

A quote came to mind. Roger couldn't remember who'd said it, but it sounded like Miranda MacClintock.

"You're not supposed to die for your God, soldier. You're here to make sure the other poor sod dies for *his*."

"Nice," Bes said as Roger walked back to the command post. The low wall and fighting trench the soldiers were erecting was backed with a small bastion for the commanders. Considering that they'd only been working on it for half an hour, it was quite an accomplishment.

"It was a quote," the prince admitted. "I swear, every good military line has already been used by somebody." He looked at the developing defenses and shook his head. "Very nice. I suppose if we can't win with this, we don't deserve to. I wonder how it's going north of the river?"

CHAPTER THIRTY-NINE

"Yes, Sir. I understand," the sergeant said.

"If I had a 'qualified officer' to replace you with, I would," the Marton Regiment's adjutant said. "To tell the truth, if I'd had a qualified officer to replace Lieutenant Fonal with, I would have."

"Yes, Sir. I understand."

"You don't sound like it," the battalion commander put in with a serious expression. "You sound petrified."

"I'll handle it, Major Ni," Krindi Fain said. "I'd just expected to be replaced. At most, I'd figured I'd handle the route march. But fighting them? I'm not sure I know how."

"Just do what you're told, soldier," the CO said. "I'm giving you a temporary rank of full lieutenant. You taught most of them the drill, so don't tell me you don't know it yourself. Just do what you know."

"Yes, Sir," the Diaspran began again, then checked himself. "I really do understand. And will comply."

"Okay," Ni said with a gesture of support. "Get to it."

Fain found himself walking back through the

temporarily stopped division, wondering where and how he'd gone wrong.

"What's wrong, Fain? You look like somebody shot your dog."

He looked over at Julian and made a gesture of resigned horror.

"I'm in command of the company."

"Yeah," the Marine said. "I thought that might happen."

"I'm not real sure about this," Fain admitted. "It's a lot of responsibility."

"So was the training you gave them," Julian pointed out. "Same deal. Just get up there, and do what comes natural. Remember every good leader you've ever known and copy them. Slavishly, if you have to. And never let them see you slime." For some reason, the Marine found this last humorous.

"Okay," the Diaspran said.

"Here." The human dug into a pouch and pulled out a twisted piece of metal.

"What's this?" Fain asked, turning it over and over in a true-hand.

"First battle I was ever in," the Marine said, "I caught that piece of shrapnel. I held onto it for good luck. I sort of figured if I had it, I'd never get hit again. Don't know why. But it's always been a lucky piece for me."

"What are you going to do without it?" the Diaspran asked.

"I'm not going to need it for this battle," Julian said, tapping his armor. "The Boman hasn't been born that can crack this stuff. You take it. I'll be okay."

"All right," Fain said. "Thanks. And may the God of Water protect you."

"It's not me you have to worry about," the squad leader said, hefting his stutter gun.

❖   ❖   ❖

Kny Camsan grunted in laughter.

"So that's what those shit-sitters were doing! There's an army back at Sindi, and they were trying to get back to it."

"That's nothing to laugh about," a subchief said sharply. "All our loot is back there, not just the loot from Sindi. And our women."

"Sure," the war leader replied with another grunt. "And so are ten or twelve thousand warriors with Mnb Trag to keep them on their toes. Which means their stupid army is still going to be sitting in front of the walls waiting when we get back. This was just a big spoiler raid. They wanted to suck us away from Sindi so they could get the rest of their army into position."

"Maybe," the subchief said. "If that was the idea, it worked, though."

"Of course it did," Camsan agreed. "And how much good is it going to do them? We've got the entire host almost fully assembled now, and the shit-sitters aren't just outside their walls, they're outside *ours*, with every warrior we have ready to come right up their backsides. They probably figured that they'd get all of our warriors out of Sindi to chase their cavalry, but they didn't, and their smart-ass plan has them stuck out where we can get at them in the open!"

"Maybe," the subchief repeated. "But we're having a hard enough time with these shit-sitter cavalry. Those new weapons of theirs are tough."

"Not tough enough now that we know where they are and what they're trying to do," Camsan shot back. "When we overrun the iron heads, we'll take their new weapons for our own. And then we'll overrun their army at Sindi and take *their* weapons, too. And when we've done that, there will be no army to man the walls of the Cove, and we'll overrun *them*, as well!"

"Let's hope it goes that way," the subchief said gloomily, "but so far, the iron heads have been doing much better out of this than we have."

"Listen up!" Bistem Kar's powerful voice boomed over the gathered infantry division. "So far, this whole war has been going for the Boman, but we're taking it to them now. The only thing that stands between us and victory is that the cavalry is trapped in there."

He gestured over his shoulder to the deep woods.

"We're going to go in there and find them. It won't be hard." There was an uneasy chuckle at that, for the crackle of gunfire was clear in the distance. "Then we're going to open up a hole and let them out. Then we march back to the city.

"I won't kid you; this is going to be a tough fight. But we can do it. All you have to do is aim low and obey your officers. Now, let's go give the Boman a little taste of what war with K'Vaern's Cove means!"

"Lieutenant Fain," the battalion CO said, "we've been tasked with putting out a company of skirmishers. Do you know the difference between skirmishing and regular fighting?"

Light was just beginning to filter through the trees, but there still wasn't enough to see your hand in front of your face, much less distinguish a white thread from a black. The entire march from the city had been made in inky darkness, and only the sheer insanity of it had prevented complete disaster. After all, the Boman had known no one would be crazy enough to try it, so why bother to set up ambushes along the route? Now, with dawn approaching, the infantry was arrayed to pry the cavalry out of its trap. If it could.

"Skirmishing means to spread out and move slow," the Diaspran said in reply to the question. "Move from cover to cover. You're trying to find the enemy force. When you do, you engage them at maximum range from cover. You try to slow them up and figure out how they're deployed, but you can't let yourself get pinned down by them, or they'll kill you."

Major Ni sighed.

"As I suspected, you know far more about it than my other company commanders. Congratulations, you just volunteered."

"Sir, this isn't a skirmisher unit," the Diaspran protested. "You use woodsmen for skirmishers. Or trained forces. It's a job for . . . crack shots and experts!"

"Nonetheless," Ni said with a gesture of command. "Get out in front."

Fain went trudging back to his new company, wondering how to pass on the word.

"Straighten up," Pol said. "Don't let them see you slime."

"Where did you hear that?" Fain asked. It was more words than Pol usually used in a week.

"Sergeant Julian," was the only reply.

Fain started to think about that. How would Julian handle the situation? Well, first of all the sergeant would be hard as nails. No protests would be allowed. Julian would explain what they were going to do in a way that made clear he was a past master of the technique . . . whether he'd ever heard of it before in his life or not.

Fain had trained with the Marton Regiment, so he knew, in general, who were the crack shots. There were quite a few who were good in Delta Company, and that was important with skirmishers.

Before the recently promoted lieutenant knew it, he'd practically walked into his formation.

"All right, you yard birds!" he snapped. "We've been

detailed as skirmishers. And *we're* going to show the rest of these shit-for-brains what that means . . . !"

Roger had just taken a sip of water from his camel bag when the skirmishers pelted back from their sentry posts.

"Here they come!" one of them shouted as he tumbled over the hastily constructed wall.

The former laborers of the New Model Army had worked hard through the night, and the fortifications were as well constructed as anyone could have done in the time available to them. They consisted of a shallow wall and a trench behind the stream, all covered by a thin line of infantry pickets. Most of the cavalry had made it back and was forming up at the rear, and as soon as Pri pronounced them ready, they would head for the flanks to reinforce the Marines.

Cases of spare ammunition and rations from the pack *turom* were spaced along the wall, runners had been assigned, and most of the pack animals—including a recalcitrant Patty—had been sent to the rear, up the road towards Sindi, to clear the fighting position.

All that was left to do was fight.

"Captain Pahner, Roger here," Roger said into his radio, considerably more lightly than he actually felt. "We're about to engage an estimated two to three thousand screaming barbarians. I have, as usual, created numerous bricks without straw. And might I say once more how incredibly much fun this whole Mardukan Tour has been. We really must try it again sometime."

Despite himself, Pahner chuckled, but the chuckle had a grim note.

"Just finish them off and sit tight," he said, "because it doesn't look like I'm going to have anyone to send you for a while. The north bank is heating up."

❖   ❖   ❖

One of the skirmishers paused, raised a hand, and made the sign for lots of good guys. Then he corrected it to bad guys.

Krindi Fain grunted and motioned for the spread-out company to move over to the left. The Marines had a term for the movement he wanted, but at the moment, he couldn't think what it was. The idea, though, was clear. When they opened fire, the Boman would know they were being attacked, and if the skirmishers attacked from right in front of their own main force, the Boman would know where their enemies were and where to counterattack. But if the skirmishers moved over to the side, the Boman might be suckered into attacking in the wrong direction.

In which case, they were *basik* on toast.

Most of the lead scouts, all people who'd at least been in the woods a couple of times, started making signals that they were seeing Boman, and Fain waved the rest of the company to a halt. Clearly the enemy was concentrating on the cavalry, but sooner or later they were bound to notice the force at their back. It was time to get it stuck in, so he grabbed a messenger and scribbled a note.

"Verbal to the Major. Tell him we're engaging . . . enfilading the Boman from the west flank."

"Enfil . . . enfol . . ."

"Never mind. Just tell him we're hitting them from the west. Get going."

The messenger disappeared into the undergrowth, and Fain looked around. He caught the company's sergeant's eye and made a gesture across his throat, followed by a complicated and terribly rude one.

Time to get it stuck in.

Honal looked up at the sudden sound of a light crackle of riflery from the south.

"About time," he grunted.

The Boman had gotten increasingly aggressive even as windrows of their dead built up around the perimeter. The undergrowth beyond the crude abattis was now so shot torn that the jungle forest had been opened up from the ground to about five meters up, and it was all swarming with Boman.

"Just in the nick," Rastar agreed, tightening a bandage around one of Honal's upper arms. "Spread the word to get ready to move out. When we do, I want the sick, the halt, the lame, and the dead on saddles. And we need to be ready to cover the retreat. These bastards are going to be really irritated to see us leaving, and it isn't going to be easy to convince them to say goodbye."

Fain looked to both sides. The Boman in front had gone to ground under the hail of fire from the skirmishers, but more were probing around the flanks.

"Tell First Platoon to fall back and south," he said, and turned to Erkum Pol. "Get the reserve to the south and make sure our way home stays open. Don't let them run, and make sure they shoot low."

"Okay," the private said, and loped off.

"Come on, Major," the newly promoted company commander whispered. "Where's the rest of the pocking army?"

"Colonel," Bistem Kar growled, "what seems to be the problem?"

"I'm ordering my lines, General," the Marton Regiment's commander said. "It will take a bit more time."

The officers of the regiment were in a huddle by the side of the Therdan-Sindi trail, and it was apparent from their expressions that the K'Vaernian commander had appeared in the midst of an argument. A heated one, from the looks of things, and that was never good news in a combat zone.

"Ask me for anything but time," he muttered. Unfortunately, Colonel Rahln, the regimental commander, like too many of Kar's senior officers, was not one of his long-term Guard officers.

The field army had been organized into five divisions, each of three regiments, plus the attached League cavalry. Each regiment consisted of one four-hundred-man rifle battalion, two four-hundred-man pike battalions, and two hundred-man companies of assegai-armed spearmen for flank protection. That meant each regiment represented almost a third of the entire prewar Guard's manpower, and there were fifteen of them in the army. Kar had kept command of the First Division for himself, and he and Pahner had at least managed to ensure that all of the other divisional commanders were Guard regulars. But despite everything they'd been able to do, all too many of the regimental commands had gone to political cronies of influential councilors or merchants, and Sohna Rahln, the Marton Regiment's CO, was one of them. Prior to the war, Rahln had been a merchant involved in several businesses, notably shipyards, but not a sailor . . . and definitely not a soldier. The appointment had been a sop designed to persuade him to support the operation, and now it was endangering it.

"Colonel Rahln, could I speak to you for a moment in private?" the general rumbled.

"I have no secrets from my officers," the former merchant said loftily, and Kar gritted his teeth. One thing he particularly disliked about Rahln was that, like many of the wealthy political appointees scattered through the force, he could never quite seem to forget his prewar contempt for the Guard. After all, if the Guardsmen hadn't been stupid—or lazy—they would have gotten *real* jobs during peacetime, wouldn't they? "You can have your say here."

"All right," Kar said. "If that's the way you want it. We have skirmishers out there, from *your* regiment, who are in contact with the enemy and need your support. We have cavalry trapped out there that needs to be relieved. You have the point regiment, and you are personally responsible for the movement of your units. You will begin the assault in the next ten minutes, or I'll have you shot."

"You can't do that!" Rahln snapped. "I'll have you broken for even suggesting it!"

The K'Vaernian general reached out and lifted the lighter officer into the air by his leather harness. The colonel squawked in shock at the totally unexpected assault, but his shock turned to terror as the Guard officer flipped him over a hip and then slammed him onto the ground on his back so hard that everyone within three meters actually heard the air driven from his lungs.

Kar dropped to one knee and took the colonel by the throat with one false-hand.

"I could squash you like a bug," he hissed, "and nobody would care. Not here. Not in K'Vaern's Cove. Now get a spine, and let your officers—who, unlike you, know what they're doing—get to work!

"Nine minutes," he added, with a shake of the throat.

"Are you sure that was a good idea?" his aide asked as they headed back to the command post.

"The only problem with it was getting that cretin's foul slime on my clean harness," the general snorted. "His battalion commanders are professionals. If he leaves them alone, he'll make the deadline. But cut orders to replace him with Ni if he continues to fuck up. And send a team of Guards . . . with revolvers and a watch."

CHAPTER FORTY

Fain looked around. The remnants of his company were gathered by the side of another of the numerous streams found in the Sindi Valley. They'd managed to pull out of the developing pocket, but they'd left some bodies behind. Pol was here, though, with the reserve which had hammered the Boman trying to flank them from the south. The company had found it necessary to watch its footing on the way out to avoid tripping over the bodies of dead barbarians.

The brass, naturally, had failed to provide a map, so Fain had only the vaguest notion of where they were. He did know, however, that the Boman had pulled back for the moment. They were maintaining their perimeter around the trapped cavalry, and they appeared to think the skirmishers were the only threat. That was nice, since it presumably also meant that the barbs still didn't have a clue where the *real* threat was coming from, which was precisely what Fain had hoped he and his people would accomplish.

The only problem was that they weren't skirmishing anymore. He needed to keep the Boman aware of Delta Company's presence if he wanted to keep them from figuring out where the rest of the relief force was, and he knew it. But he also knew that, ultimately, raiding on the flanks like this didn't do any good, however much it confused the enemy, unless there was an immediate follow on assault, and an assault was exactly what had failed to materialize. It was obvious that if the company went back, the Boman would be on them like *atul* on a stray *turom*, but unless the rest of the regiment got its head out of its ass and actually moved when he headed back in, it would only get his people killed without even doing any good.

It wasn't supposed to work this way. There should have been an assault. The Major had *said* there would be an assault, not just his single company thrown out here in the middle of nowhere without support.

It wasn't supposed to be this way, and he hoped it was going better elsewhere.

"Captain Pahner, Roger here."

The voice sounded in the captain's mastoid implant, and he keyed his helmet.

"Ah, Prince Roger! Still alive, according to the little chip in my brain which I suspect detonates if you die."

"I see everyone is in a good mood," the prince said. In the background, Pahner could hear continuous and heavy rifle fire. "I'd like to revise that previous estimate of mine. Make that three thousand-plus Boman."

"I really love this business," Pahner said conversationally. "I know that no plan survives contact with the enemy, but have any plans ever gone this awry?"

"I'm sure they must have," Roger said in an encouraging sort of way. "Somewhere. But I digress. I don't suppose you have anything resembling a reserve back there?"

"Actually, I did," Pahner said. "I'd detached half the laborers back to combat duties. But I just sent them north of the river to back up Bistem. It would take at least a couple of hours just to get them back to this bank, much less to your position. Why?"

"Just wondering," Roger said, and Pahner heard the distinct sound of a bead pistol firing. "We got a bit flanked here."

"Roger," Pahner said in a very calm voice, "are you surrounded?"

"I prefer to call it a target-rich environment," the prince replied. "But the good news is that they seem bound and determined to wipe us out rather than bypass us and head for the city or the D'Sley road. So we're succeeding in our mission, aren't we?"

"But I'm not," Pahner said calmly, very calmly. "I'm pulling the rest of the infantry off of the stores."

"Yeah, well, don't bother on our account," Roger said. "You couldn't get infantry here for hours, and this is gonna be over, one way or the other, in another thirty minutes."

Roger ducked as Despreaux fired over his head. Particles of black powder stung the back of his neck, the muzzle flash singed his ponytail, and only his helmet kept him from being permanently deafened.

"Careful there, honey!" he said. "I've always wondered what a toot looks like, but I don't want to look at my own."

"Screw you, Your Highness," the sergeant said as a rifle volley hammered the latest charge into offal. "That one was too close."

"Not so bad," Bes said, sticking his head out of the slit trench they'd gouged out of the muddy earth behind their original positions. "Would have been nice if we'd been able to hold the original line, but this one isn't bad, except on the flanks."

"Speaking of which," Despreaux said. "Reneb, check in. Everybody still here?"

"Still here," the team leader confirmed. "No casualties in the team so far, and we're piling them up."

"Same here," Roger said, looking out of the slit trench.

There were only twelve humans in the entire force, but each of them had begun the day with thirty ten-round magazines for their new rifles. They were conserving that ammunition as much as they could, letting the Mardukans' single-shot rifles carry most of the fight at long range. But whenever the barbarians began another charge, the sheer volume of fire from those magazine-fed rifles and the cavalry's revolvers wreaked dreadful carnage.

The ground on both sides of the trench for as far as Roger could see into the jungles was littered with Boman bodies. The barbarians had learned that the only way to get into ax range was to charge forward blindly, seeking to break through the fire zone by sheer weight of numbers. A few times, it had gotten down to hand-to-hand, but even there the Carnan Battalion and the *Basik*'s Own had managed to hold their own, and the assaults had been repulsed.

"Here they come again!" Bes shouted, closing his rifle breech and firing at the first of the charging Boman.

This time the barbarians had managed to coordinate their attacks, which made things tougher. They came from both sides, but not directly at the flanks, which probably would have rolled up Roger's entire embattled position. The prince looked to the nominal "rear" and shook his head as the aiming reticle appeared in his vision. He tossed his magnum to Cord, who'd become quite a respectable rifle shot himself, drew his bead pistol once more, took up a two-handed stance, and began a timed fire sequence. One shot per second cracked out for each of the fourteen seconds it took the Boman line to reach the trench, and each shot took out a barbarian.

The riflemen to either side, Marine and Mardukan alike, had been hammering out fire in both directions. The rifles' black powder filled the little clearing with gray-white smoke and a smell like the breath of Hell itself, and as the Boman jumped into the trenches or struck down with their two-handed battle axes, it seemed as if Lucifer had arrived in person.

The majority of the defenders switched to their long bayonets, and Despreaux blocked the swing of an ax, buttstroked the axeman in the groin, and then ducked as Turkol Bes bayoneted someone over her shoulder. She sprang past him as Cord missed a block and was slammed into the wall of the trench. The bleeding shaman had been the last thing between Roger and an ax-swinging Boman easily as large as Bistem Kar, and the sergeant felt an instant of pure despair as she realized she could never reach him before he reached Roger.

Patty had been sent back with the other pack animals, but Dogzard had evaded all efforts to corral her and send her back, as well. As the barbarian's ax rose for the fatal stroke, ninety kilos of hissing lizard ripped into his leg from the side. The dog-lizard's attack slowed the Boman just enough for Roger to twist sideways and get a shot in. The hypervelocity bead took the axeman almost dead center, but despite the slamming impact, the barbarian still managed one last swipe at Roger. The prince blocked the blow with the sword in his right hand, then stepped out of the way as the giant toppled at his feet.

The axeman had been the last enemy alive in the trench, and Roger stepped back again as a pair of Diaspran infantrymen heaved the body out of the trench and added it to the parapet of corpses.

"God damn these stupid, four-armed bastards," Despreaux cursed wearily, wiping blood out of her eyes. "Don't they know when they're beat?"

"Sure they do," Bes grunted in laughter. "Almost as well as oversized *basik*."

Knitz De'n grabbed both his horns and shook them back and forth in anger. A scout had just brought back word that Sindi had actually fallen—that the city was being looted to the ground and that all of their women and children had fallen into shit-sitter hands—and this tiny group had repulsed *five* charges by the finest ax wielders in the Valley of the Tam. It wasn't possible.

"One more time," the subchief hissed. "One more charge, and we can destroy them all."

"No, we can't," Sof Knu said flatly. "These new arquebuses of theirs are impossible, and they fight like demons. Let us go west; surely some warriors must have escaped the fall of the city. We can find them—join with them, and harass these K'Vaernians. Harass them, and pull them down like *kef* do a *turom*. It's how we always face greater forces."

"No!" Knitz De'n shouted. "We'll kill them here and now! This is our land, taken by our arms, and no one will take it away!"

"Do as you wish," Sof Knu said, "but I'm leaving, and taking my warriors with me. I'm not insane."

The ax entered between Knu's shoulder and neck, almost severing his right true-arm. He fell, and Knitz De'n dragged the ax free with a wrench and waved it in the air.

"Do any others dispute my right of command?" he

snarled, looking around the group of sullen barbarians. "One more charge! Into the face of death I fly! With the heart of an *atul* and the strength of the *pagathar!* *Wesnaaar!*"

"I don't believe it," Despreaux said, and Roger looked up from bandaging Cord.

"This is a joke, right?" he said as he watched four Boman charge out of the brush. The unsupported quartet was about as much threat to the combat veterans dug in to await it as a similar number of children.

"Either berserk, or doing it for honor," Pri said. He gave the barbarians another look and grunted. "Berserk."

"Well? Is anyone going to shoot them, or are we just going to let them kill us all?" Despreaux asked tartly.

Four bead pistol shots cracked out before a single rifle could speak, and the Boman flew backwards in explosions of gore.

"What?" Roger said, holstering the pistol and returning to his *asi's* bandage. "Like that?"

"Yeah," Despreaux said quietly into the sudden silence. "Like that."

"You know," the prince said, never looking up from the bandage, "one of these days, I'm going to be in a fight where I don't kill anything."

"That'll be the day," the sergeant replied sadly.

"You know, this could turn out to be a nice day after all," Krindi Fain said as regular volleys started hammering to the east.

Despite the lack of support, the former sergeant had sent snipers forward to peck at the Boman line. The response had been violent, but uncoordinated, with nearly three hundred Boman chasing the snipers into the woods . . . where the survivors of his hundred-man company had finally ambushed them at the edge of a thicket. The company's fire had piled up most of the barbarians for very little loss, which had been one of the first things to go right all day. But nice as that had been, the sudden, massive firing crashing out to the east now was the most blessed sound he'd ever heard.

"Our job's done," he said. "Let's go find the good guys. And for the God's sake, keep an eye out! The Boman are going to be swarming around the flanks, and we don't want to get shot by our own people, either!"

"Can we loot the ones we killed, Lieutenant?" one of the troopers asked.

"Not until after the battle," he snapped. "Now let's move out while the moving's good."

"But we're gonna retreat," the trooper protested. "We won't be able to get nothin'."

"You're gonna get my foot up your ass if you don't shut up," Erkum Pol said. "You heard the Lieutenant. Move it!"

"Time to leave, people," the company commander said, pointing slightly to the south of the firing. "About there should be good."

"Right there!" Rastar shouted as the *civan* lurched to its feet. He spurred to the west, revolvers streaming smoke and flame. Half a dozen of his troopers rode with him, their massed fire tearing a hole in the Boman line, and then all of them dodged aside as the herd of stampeding *civan* thundered past them.

The loose *civan*, driven by Honal and a dozen more mounted troopers and maddened with fear from the firing and blood smell behind them, smashed into the already breached Boman line, throwing it even further into chaos. The regular volleys from the south, when most of the previous firing—light as it had been—had come from the south*west*, had thrown the enemy totally off balance. Caught between two fires, the barbarians on the south side of the perimeter hadn't known which way to turn.

The barbarians on the other three sides had no such doubts. They charged forward when they saw the cavalry slipping out through the hole in the line, but only to run into regular, slamming volleys of aimed rifle fire. The three thousand cavalry in the pocket had been low on ammunition, and barely a tenth of them had been armed with rifles. The men of the five rifle battalions Bistem Kar had peeled off and assigned to Major Dnar Ni, who had replaced the recently deceased Colonel Rahln as CO of the Marton Regiment, suffered under no such handicap. There were two thousand of them, and they slammed volley after volley into the packed barbarians. The four-armed Mardukans could load, prime, and fire their weapons without even lowering them from the firing position, and their rate of fire was incredible by any human standard. The Boman were crowded so closely together a single bullet could kill or wound as many as three, or even four of them, and each rifleman was sending six aimed rounds per minute straight into them. Not even the famed Boman fighting frenzy could carry them forward into that vortex of destruction, and the warriors in front of the firing line were driven to ground.

The warriors to either side of the relief force riflemen spread wider, seeking to find and envelop their flanks, only to encounter assegai-armed spearmen and recoil afresh.

"Message to Colonel Des," Kar said. "He's to refuse his right flank and withdraw. Same message to Colonel Tarm, but he's to refuse his *left*."

The K'Vaernian general looked up with a nod as Rastar reached his command group and reined in.

"Prince Rastar."

"General Kar," the prince said with a matching nod. "Nice of you to show up."

"Had a few problems with a subcommander," the K'Vaernian admitted. "They're solved. How many are we looking at?"

"Not the entire host, thank the gods." The cavalry officer slid off his *civan*. "I think Camsan figured out where we were headed sooner than we'd planned. Whatever happened, he scattered his own troops and the first ones to reach him through the woods here in an effort to keep us from getting back to Sindi, and that's all we've got to worry about right this minute. The rest are still back there, coming down from the north to join up. Only a few of them actually found us, I think, but that, unfortunately, seems to include Camsan himself, so the coordination's been fair. And all the rest of them are undoubtedly coming on from behind him."

"As long as it's not the full hundred thousand already, we should be fine," Kar said. "We need to retreat smartly, though."

"Oh, yes," Honal agreed fervently, riding into the conference. "I don't want to spend another night like that last one."

CHAPTER FORTY-ONE

"This is actually beginning to look halfway decent," Pahner said.

"I'm glad to hear it," Rus From said. The Diaspran who'd become the chief field engineer of the K'Vaernian army stretched wearily. "We managed to get almost all of the exposed stores aboard the boats and sent them off downriver," he reported. "There's still a lot to go, but it's all on the south side of the river now, behind the surprise."

"Good," Bogess said. "Now if we can just get the army back together here before Camsan turns up—and assuming, of course, that Bistem gets back here intact—things will definitely be looking up. And it looks like Roger has smashed the Boman to the south quite handily."

"Yep," Pahner agreed. "Gotta love competent subordinates. Of course, that begs the question of who's the subordinate in this case. Speaking of which." He keyed his communicator. "Prince Roger, Captain Pahner."

Roger groaned as the attention signal pinged.

"Roger," he said. "Take that however you prefer."

"I hate to break this to you, Your Highness, but I need you to bring your butt back to Sindi. I imagine we'll be entertaining the main host here sometime tomorrow morning, and I'd like you to be present for the party."

"Gotcha, Captain," the prince said with another groan, and surveyed the troopers lying all around the reclaimed original trench line in exhausted heaps. No doubt it was all dreadfully untidy, and not at all the way it was supposed to be according to The Book, but at least all the bodies were out of the trench, and all the wounded had been bandaged.

"We'll head out in a few minutes," Roger went on. "But be aware that we had to send all of our *civan* and *turom* back already, so we're on foot. That's going to slow us down."

"Understood," Pahner said. "I'll send some troops out to meet you with your mounts. Move out, Your Highness."

"Roger, out." The prince smiled as he got to his feet. "Take that however you prefer," he whispered, and then poked the sergeant who'd lain half-asleep beside him with a toe. "Despreaux! What the heck are you doing lying around snoring when your prince is in danger?"

Krindi Fain wasn't lost, he simply didn't know where his battalion—or his regiment—had gotten to. No one else seemed to know either, but, since seeing their company commander stumbling around in the middle of a retreat looking for their parent unit would be a bad thing for morale, he'd parked the company with the supply packbeast guards and gone a-hunting.

He also wasn't asleep, simply sort of numb. Which was how he came to be walking with his eyes sort of closed when he slammed into the obstacle.

"What are you doing here, soldier?" Bistem Kar's aide-de-camp demanded as the acting lieutenant bounced off of him, and Fain's eyes went wide at the sight of all the brass standing about.

"Krindi Fain, acting lieutenant, Delta Company, Rifle Battalion, Marton Regiment!" he said, snapping a salute. "I'm looking for the Battalion, Sir!"

"Fain?" Kar himself rumbled. "Weren't you an instructor sergeant not too long ago?"

"It's a long story, General," the braced acting lieutenant said. "I think I'll let Major Ni and Sergeant Julian explain it, if I may, General!"

"Delta Company?" one of the other officers said. "I thought that was Lieutenant Fonal. I was surprised he got picked to command those skirmishers on the southwest flank, but that was you, wasn't it?"

"Yes, Sir," Fain said. "We're just trying to find our way home now, Sir."

General Kar grunted in laughter.

"That's the best description of this madhouse I've heard yet," he said, and his command staff joined his laughter. Fain was pretty sure that his participation in their humor wouldn't be appreciated, but he was too tired to really care, and he raised all four hands, palms upward in a purely human gesture.

"I'm just trying to find our unit, Sir," he said tiredly. All these clean staff officers, who'd undoubtedly had to suffer through a hot breakfast and forego the pleasure of being covered in smoke stains and blood, were making his head ache.

"Not anymore," Kar said. "Go back, get your people, and bring them up here, instead. I'll be moving around, but I'm sure you can find the headquarters. I'm sorry there's no sleep for any of us, but make sure they get a bite to eat . . . and then replace the command group security company. *Colonel* Ni is just going to have to figure out how to spare you, because I'd rather have combat-proven veterans watching my backside!"

"Thank you, Sir," the former NCO said.

"No," the general said firmly. "Thank *you*. When we hit the Boman, they didn't know which way to turn, and that was due in large part to you. So thank your company for me. When we get back to Sindi, I'll do it personally."

"Yes, Sir," the acting lieutenant said. "I better go get the Company."

It took hours to retreat through the trees. The Boman seemed endless as the long Mardukan day wore on; for every one they killed, two more seemed to spring up out of the earth. The cavalry was essentially useless, since not only were its *civan* all but exhausted, but it lacked the clear space to work up to a charge even if they hadn't been. The few mounted troopers with rifles had been sent to fill gaps in the line, but Rastar and Honal kept one troop in the saddle, ready to plug any sudden holes.

The pikes weren't much more use than cavalry in the close confinement of the jungle, but the assegai-wielding spearmen proved their value again and again during the chaos and confusion of the withdrawal. The Boman probed around the flanks, and even turned them a few times, only to be driven back and pounded into the ground. It seemed, as the choking pall of gun smoke rose like thick fog through the canopy, as if the withdrawal would never end. The nightmare struggle, crash of rifles, scream of bullets, and shriek of the wounded and dying were all part of some eternal, unending purgatory from which there could be no escape, and all anyone knew of it was the tiny part that he himself endured.

But, in the end, the withdrawing regiments finally

reached the edge of the trees, and the whole, dreadful engagement could be seen.

Pahner saw it from the walls of Sindi, and shook his head as the units began to emerge. Bistem Kar had pulled out most of his dead, and all of his wounded, and he'd taken a fraction of the casualties he should have. Of course, he'd had an enormous advantage in terms of his troops' weapons, but Pahner suspected that the K'Vaernian general would have succeeded in a battle against an equally armed force, as well. There was a name that hovered on the edge of his consciousness, something about a wall. That was what Kar reminded him of, a stone wall nothing could break, even as he moved his units like dancers in a thunderous ballet of battle.

The pike battalions came first as the K'Vaernian forces began to clear the edge of the jungle. It was clear to Pahner that Kar had been forced by the combat environment to reorganize his forces on the fly, and the rifles continued to fire further into the jungle as the pike units shook out into line and dressed ranks. From the looks of things, they hadn't been heavily engaged in the previous fighting, and it was likely that the Boman had not yet discovered just how hard a target an unshaken wall of pikes was.

As the pikes settled into place, other units began to emerge from the jungle. Rastar's cavalry came first, much of it dismounted by now. The wounded and the dead came next, covered by walking wounded and spearmen. The riflemen came last of all, falling back with an iron discipline Pahner could feel all the way from the walls. It was a discipline he and his Marines had trained into them, but he knew only too well how that discipline could have vanished if the troops had feared for one moment that their commander was irresolute. Obviously, they had no such fear where Bistem Kar was concerned.

The trickiest moment came when the pike blocks had to open ranks to let the riflemen pass through, but Kar managed the maneuver so adroitly that the Boman never even seemed to recognize the moment of opportunity.

By the time the Boman realized what was happening, the retreating army had reformed itself into a huge, hollow square of pikes. In effect, there were no flanks for the barbarians to attack, any longer, and the entire formation marched slowly but steadily towards the gates of Sindi. Time and again, masses of Boman swept outward, hooking around in an effort to find an open flank to exploit, only to find themselves held well beyond hand-to-hand range by the pikeheads while aimed volleys tore them apart. Once or twice, enough barbarians managed to circle around the pike square to bring it almost to a halt, but each time, Kar concentrated his riflemen to bring a devastating fire to bear and literally blasted a path through them.

In the end, even the Boman were forced to admit that they could not overwhelm their enemies, and the triumphant relief force broke free of the sea of barbarians and began to funnel back through the gates while a steadily contracting shield of pikes, covered by rifles on the ground and on the walls alike, held off the barbarians' last, despairing charges.

Throughout the endless, exhausting day, Krindi Fain had stood at the edge of the command group and watched the general work. Kar had stood still and calm, hands clasped behind his back, and only occasionally snapped out an order. But whenever he did give an order, aides and messengers scurried to obey.

Fain didn't have to worry about that, though. He'd

deployed his company around the general, and that was that. The new company commander realized that his own blundering into the group around the general was at least partially to blame for the change in his command's assignment, since it had pointed out a certain weakness in Kar's security arrangements. There was no way he should have been able to, more or less, sleepwalk past the command group's previous guards, and he was determined that no one else would sleepwalk past *him*. Not that it required a great deal of personal effort from him. Delta Company's skirmishers, their rifles held muzzle-down and to the left, like some of the Marines, glared balefully at anyone who approached the general. Nobody was going to sleepwalk past *these* guards.

That eager alertness had left Fain free to watch the progress of the battle, and he'd recognized that in Bistem Kar he saw someone operating on a level of competence he could recognize and appreciate but never hope to approach himself. Now he watched the Boman attacks trickle off as darkness finally fell and the last of the relief force, including the command group, withdrew behind the walls of Sindi.

Kny Camsan stood in the evening rain and stared in disbelief at the walls of Sindi.

It couldn't be true. It was impossible! Yet the evidence was there before his eyes, impossible to deny.

He had trusted Mnb Trag to hold Sindi in his absence, and he wanted to blame the old chieftain for failing him. But no one could look at those walls and blame Trag. Even all that the shit-sitters had done to the host throughout this long and terrible day paled beside what they'd done to Sindi. Camsan could not imagine what had torn and ripped the massive walls that way, but there were dozens of breaches through them—huge wounds through which the shit-sitters must have stormed to wrest the city from Trag and his warriors.

"What do we do now?" one of the other chieftains demanded harshly.

"We gather our numbers throughout the night," Camsan replied, never taking his eyes from the ravaged walls of the city which was to have been his capital.

"And what then?" the chieftain pressed, and Camsan turned to face him.

Tar Tin was of the Gestai, one of the larger Boman clans, and the Gestai had been among the most restless under Camsan's leadership. Tar Tin himself was a chieftain of the old school, one who believed in the exalted power of the battle frenzy to carry warriors to victory over insurmountable odds, and that made him dangerous. Worse, he'd been one of the stronger supporters of the war leader Camsan had replaced after the debacle at Therdan, and his resentment at being pushed aside by those who'd supported Camsan ran deep.

"And then we pin the shit-sitters and starve them," Camsan said sharply.

"And starve our women and children right along with them?" Tar Tin more than half-sneered. "Truly a plan of rare genius!"

"It's the only way!" Camsan shot back forcefully. "The losses we've taken charging into their guns again and again today are proof of that!"

"I say that it is *not* the only way," Tin spat. "The shit-sitters themselves have broken and torn the walls which might have held us out, and they hold our women and children hostage against us. Do you think that they'll hesitate for a moment to kill those women and children—the women and children you gathered together here that they might be '*safe*'—once they realize they themselves are doomed? We must attack—*now!* We must storm through the gaps they made for us in their own foolishness and overwhelm them before they destroy the entire future of the Boman!"

"That is madness!" Camsan protested. "Didn't you see what their new weapons *did* to us in the forest? Don't you realize that if they can tear such rents in walls of stone and mortar, they can do far worse to our warriors if we allow them to catch us in the open? No, we must find another way!"

"We must *attack!*" Tin snarled, even more loudly. "That's what true Boman do—they charge, and they die. And then other Boman charge over their bodies, and still others, until a charge strikes home and we triumph!"

"We've lost thousands this day!" Camsan snarled back. "And if we assault those walls, today's losses will seem as nothing. It will be Therdan all over again, only many times worse. What good will we do our women and children by charging to their rescue only to be destroyed ourselves? Do you think the shit-sitters will hesitate to kill them once they've destroyed the host, and the threat of our vengeance no longer hangs over them?"

The war leader clapped his hands in a gesture of violent negation.

"To charge a prepared enemy with the weapons these shit-sitters possess would be as stupid as it would be pointless! We must find a better way!"

"It is your 'better ways' and your clever stratagems which have killed more of us than anything else," Tar Tin said in a flat, deadly voice. "I think you have lost the respect of the clans. This disaster is *your* doing, even more than the shit-sitters'."

The Gestai chieftain stepped back and raised his hands.

"Who is the origin of our grief? The walls of the city lie broken and open! Our warriors lie dead on the field for nothing! Whose hesitation and refusal to overwhelm K'Vaern's Cove gave the shit-sitters the time to prepare these 'new weapons,' and who led our warriors out to face them while our women and children were stolen from us?" Tin glared savagely at Camsan, and his voice dropped to deadly softness as he repeated, *"Who is the origin of our grief?"*

The other chieftains gathered around the argument. Most of them were far older than Kny Camsan, and more than a few had resented his relative youthfulness when he was named war leader. They'd supported his ascension after Therdan because the horrible casualties suffered trying to storm that city's walls had been enough to frighten even Boman. But now, with casualties almost as heavily piled on the field and scattered through the jungle, and with the bulk of the clans' women and children in the hands of shit-sitters, they were willing to consider another change.

"What do you think they're doing over there?" Roger asked wearily.

His mobile force had reached Sindi shortly after nightfall. Even many of the infantry had learned how to doze in the saddle now, for utter exhaustion was an excellent teacher, yet Chim Pri and his cavalry had somehow managed to dress ranks and trot jauntily through the southern gates under their snarling *basik* standard. Now the prince stood on the battlements, most of his weight propped on a merlon while he and Pahner gazed out across the fields.

"Jin has a LURP team keeping an eye on them," the captain said now. "We can't get close enough to tell exactly what's going on, even with the directional mikes, but it sure sounds like they're having some sort of deep and meaningful discussion, complete with lots of threats. I imagine they're discussing a possible change in the chain of command, and, frankly, nothing would please me better. This Camsan character is much too flexible and innovative a barbarian to make me happy."

"You really think they'll come at us again in the morning?" Roger waved at the heaps of Boman bodies, clearly visible to both of them thanks to the magnification of their light-gathering helmet visors. "After we did that to them in the open field?"

"I've done everything I can think of to encourage them to, at any rate," Pahner replied. "We used up almost a dozen charges for the plasma cannon blowing those nice, wide breaches in the wall, and I'll be extremely disappointed if it doesn't occur to any of them that they've got all sorts of ways into the city now. And the fact that all their women and children are in here should suggest to them that it would be a good idea for them to come and rescue them."

"And if they don't?" Roger asked. "What do we do then?"

"If they won't come to us, then we go to them—in a manner of speaking. I'll blow the Great Bridge behind us to maroon them on the other bank of the river, then head south with their women and children in the middle of a pike square, if I have to. They'll probably find a way across the river eventually—I'm sure they'll build rafts, if nothing else—but I figure we can make it almost all the way to D'Sley before they can get onto this side in any strength. There's enough left of the walls there, especially with the repairs Tor Flain, Fullea, and their people have been making, to hold easily with the rifles and the new artillery, and we'll still have their women and children as bargaining counters.

"In some ways, I'd have preferred to do that from the beginning, because whatever happens, it's going to be ugly if they come at us tomorrow. If we could get their dependents back to D'Sley and *make* them talk to us, and if it were handled right, by someone like Eleanora, it would probably offer the best way to settle this whole thing without huge additional casualties for somebody. Unfortunately, I didn't think we'd have time to hang around and handle the negotiations ourselves, which would have meant leaving it all up to the K'Vaernians, and much as I've come to like and respect most of them, I don't think that would've been a good idea. Even the best of them are still a bit too prone to simply slaughter their enemies and be done with it for me to feel comfortable about leaving so many thousands of noncombatants in their hands. Now that Dobrescu's come through with his *coll* liver oil extract, we could probably take the slower route . . . except that everything is already dug in and ready here, and there's too good a chance the bastards would manage to get across and swarm us in the open on the way back to D'Sley."

Roger turned his head and gazed at the captain's profile. Armand Pahner, he had discovered, was as complex a human being as he'd ever met. The captain was one of the most deadly people the prince could imagine, with a complete willingness to destroy anything or anyone he had to in order to complete his mission and deliver Roger alive to Earth once more. Yet for all his ruthlessness, the Marine was equally determined *not* to destroy anything he could avoid destroying. The prince had discovered enough about his own dark side, here on Marduk, to know how easy it would have been for someone in Pahner's place to become callous and uncaring. The Boman were only barbarians, after all. Why should their fate matter to a civilized man whose entire objective was to get off their planet in the first place?

Yet it did matter to him. As he stood there on the battlements beside Roger, Pahner had all the pieces in place to trap and destroy the Boman host. Not simply defeat it, but *destroy* it, in a massacre which would make today's casualties look like a children's pillow fight. The captain had worked for weeks to plan this operation, driven his Marines and his allies mercilessly to prepare and execute it, and he was determined to drive it through to a conclusion. No doubt many people would have believed that his determination sprang from a desire to stamp out the Boman once and for all, but Roger knew better. That determination sprang, in fact, from a desire to *spare* all the Boman that he possibly could. It was a recognition that the Boman would never concede defeat until they were made to do so, and that the only way to make them was to crush them militarily, with all the casualties and carnage that entailed. But the only way to prevent Pahner's allies from truly destroying the Boman by massacring the women and children who represented the continuation of the clans, was to force the warriors to admit defeat.

And so, in a way, the only way to save the warriors' families was to kill the warriors themselves, and that was precisely what Armand Pahner was prepared to do.

CHAPTER FORTY-TWO

Kny Camsan turned his face to the North as the gray light of a rainy Mardukan dawn filled the skies. Somewhere up there, young warriors were being born. In the far hills, shamans were placing their infant false-hands on the hilts of knives and slicing the palms of their true-hands to introduce them to the pleasure and the pain of battle. Somewhere, young hunters were tracking *atul* for their first kill.

Somewhere, life went on.

The ax didn't quite sever his head from his shoulders. That was a bad omen, but it wasn't allowed to delay the ceremony of investment of the new war leader, and Tar Tin, the new paramount war leader of the clans of the Boman, was anointed in the blood of his fallen predecessor, as tradition demanded.

Tar Tin lifted the blood-smeared ceremonial ax over his head and waved it at the far battlements.

"We will destroy the shit-sitters who befoul this land! We will retake the city, retake our women and our children, retake all that booty they would plunder from us! We will destroy this shit-sitter army to the last soul and level K'Vaern's Cove to the very earth and sow it with salt! We shall cleanse these lands so that treacherous shit-sitters across the world tremble at the very name of the Boman and know that treachery against us is the way of *death!*"

The chieftains and subchiefs assembled around him cheered and brandished their battle axes, and he pointed once more at the battered walls of Sindi.

"*Kill the shit-sitters!*"

"They seem upset," Pahner observed.

The captain, Roger, and Julian's entire surviving squad stood in the cellar of a large, demolished house in the northern portion of Sindi. The hurricane of the rocket bombardment had turned this entire part of the city into uneven mounds and hills of rubble, and the flourishes which Rus From's engineers had inflicted, with artful assistance from touches of Gronningen's plasma cannon, only completed the air of devastation. There was absolutely nothing in the area to attract the attention of any Boman warrior, which, of course, was the entire object.

"I think you might say 'upset' was just a *bit* of an understatement," Roger said judiciously, striving to match the Marine's clinical tone.

"You're probably right," Pahner conceded, "but what really matters is that they seem to have themselves a new commander, and, as Poertena would say, he's a 'pocking idiot.'"

This time, Roger only grunted in agreement. There wasn't much of anything else to say, as the two of them watched their pads display the torrent of red hostile icons streaming towards the breaches left so invitingly in Sindi's walls.

Roger watched them for a few more moments, but

his eyes were drawn inexorably towards the clusters of blue icons waiting for them. Those icons represented the rifle and pike battalions who had the hardest job of all, and he wondered what was going through their minds as they hunkered down in their rough fieldworks and waited for the onslaught.

Krindi Fain was quite certain that it was an enormous honor to be selected as the commander of Bistem Kar's personal bodyguard. With a whole three hours of sleep behind him, he almost felt alive enough to appreciate the honor, as a matter of fact. Unfortunately, there was a downside to his new assignment, as the echoing war cries and the thunder of the Boman's drums brought forcibly to mind.

The general wasn't quite in the most advanced position his troops occupied, but his dugout of rubble and sandbags came close enough to make Fain very, very nervous. Of course, the lieutenant—his "acting" rank had been confirmed before he turned in last night—understood why Kar had to be where he was. After yesterday, the Guard commander enjoyed the total trust—one might almost say adulation—of his troops, and their confidence in their commander had to be absolute for this to work. Which meant they had to know that "the Kren" was there, sticking his own neck into the noose right along with them.

This leadership crap, Fain thought, for far from the first time, was an excellent way to get killed.

"They're coming through about where we figured, General," Gunnery Sergeant Jin announced. The gunny and his LURP teams had been called in during the night and redistributed to put at least one Marine with helmet, pad, and communicator with each regimental commander and Kar. Now the noncom pointed to the pad open on the rickety table at the center of the dugout, and Fain managed—somehow—not to crane his neck in an effort to see the display himself. Not that it would have helped much if he'd been able to see it; unlike Kar and his staff, Fain hadn't learned to read the display icons the others were now peering at so intently.

"They seem to be throwing more of their weight on the west side than we'd anticipated, General," one of Kar's aides pointed out, and the huge K'Vaernian grunted in agreement.

"Doesn't matter in the long run," he said, after a moment. "They still have to come to the bridge if they want to get to the other side. Still, we'd better warn Colonel Tarm to expect more pressure sooner than he anticipated."

"On it," Jin said laconically, and Fain watched his lips move soundlessly as he passed the message to the Marine attached to Colonel Tarm's regimental CP.

"Looks like they're slowing up a little," someone else observed, and the entire command group grunted with laughter which held a certain undeniable edge of tension.

"No doubt they're confused about why no one's shooting at them," Kar said after a moment. "What a pity. Still, they should be running into the expected resistance just about . . . now."

A distant crackle of rifle fire broke out with perfect timing, as if the general's comment had been the cue both sides awaited.

"Contact," Julian murmured so quietly that Roger was certain the intel sergeant didn't even realize he'd spoken aloud. Not that any of the Marines in the cellar had needed to be told. They were watching their pad displays as the probing tentacles of Boman warriors ran into the first strongpoints and battle was joined.

"What do you make the numbers, Julian?" Pahner asked.

"Hard to say exactly, Sir," the NCO replied, "but I don't see how it can be much more than sixty, sixty-five thousand."

"Did we really whittle them down by forty percent in one day?" Roger wasn't quite able to keep the disbelief out of his voice.

"Probably not," Pahner said. "Oh, we could have come close to that, but it's more likely that they've got a lot of stragglers who are still heading in. They might even have a few chieftains or subchiefs who've decided not to participate in this little party, whatever the new management wants. Still, it's enough to get the job done, don't you think?"

The leading waves of Boman ran into a blizzard of rifle fire and died.

Rus From's engineers had sited the strongpoints with care. Wherever possible, they'd placed the rubble revetments where sunken lanes through the ruins would inevitably channel the heads of any invading columns into heavy interlocking fires, and the riflemen and spearmen manning those entrenchments took brutal advantage of their positions. The broken streets of Sindi ran red with barbarian blood, and fresh clouds of smoke and brimstone rose above the ruins as torrents of bullets hammered through flesh and bone.

The Boman shrieked enraged war cries as their point elements recoiled, but *all* they did was recoil. The clans had experienced what the new rifles could do the day before, and they were as prepared as anyone could be for the carnage they faced today. No one had ever accused the Boman of cowardice, and their frantic need to rescue their women and children drove them forward even more savagely than usual.

But for all Tar Tin's determination to storm the shit-sitter positions regardless of cost, he wasn't an utter fool, and even if he had been, many of his chiefs and subchiefs were not. They knew that driving directly into the fire zones of their entrenched enemies would invite casualties not even they could endure, and so they drew back and probed, looking for ways to bypass the dug-in defenders and get behind them.

As it turned out, there were many bypass routes. Sindi had been an enormous city, by Mardukan standards, and the full strength of the K'Vaernian army would hardly have sufficed to cover its interior in depth once the walls were lost. There simply weren't enough bodies in Bistem Kar's divisions to do that, which was why he and Pahner had placed his people in nodal positions covering primarily the approaches to the Great Bridge. They'd also paid meticulous care to planning and marking retreat routes through the rubble, complete with two alternates, for every unit. When the Boman managed to begin working their way around a position's flank through the broken stone and wreckage, the infantry manning it simply fell back—promptly—to the next prepared position on its list.

It was a dangerously complicated maneuver, requiring discipline, communication, and perfect timing, and only the army's faith in Bistem Kar and the electronic wizardry of the Marine communication links and remote sensors scattered through the ruins made it possible.

"All right, gentlemen," Kar said, looking around his command group as the last infantry battalion between them and the Boman began to fall back, "it's time we were going, too. Lieutenant Fain, if you please?"

"Yes, Sir!" Fain threw the general a salute he hoped didn't look *too* relieved and nodded to his top sergeant. The top nodded back, jerked his head at First Platoon, and Delta Company formed up in a ferocious, bayonet-bristling moving perimeter around the command group as it fell back towards its first alternate position.

"We're on our way, Captain," Fain heard Kar telling Pahner over the communicator clipped to the general's harness. "So far, they don't seem to suspect a thing."

The long morning wore away in a nightmare of thundering rifles, screams, smoke clouds, and carnage. It was impossible for any Boman chieftain to form a clear picture of everything that was happening, but certain essentials were clear enough.

Whatever the shit-sitters had done to Mnb Trag and his warriors when they took the city away from him, it had changed the northern portion of Sindi beyond all recognition. The Boman were hardly city dwellers to begin with, but the tortured wasteland of broken walls and roofs, heaps of rubble, and fallen timbers had obliterated the landmarks many of them had learned to recognize during their months in the city.

Yet in many ways, that actually favored them, for the burned-out shells of buildings and the haphazard heaps of stone helped to conceal and cover them as they probed for ways around the shit-sitter strongpoints. They were taking losses—hideous losses—as they stumbled into one entrenched position after another, but they were also driving the shit-sitters inexorably back. The broken city deprived the shit-sitter riflemen of extended fire lanes and left no place for those deadly pikes to deploy, and the force of Boman numbers gradually forced Bistem Kar's troops back, and back again, and back yet again.

Exactly as Armand Pahner had planned.

❖   ❖   ❖

"And now," Bistem Kar murmured, "comes the *difficult* part."

Krindi Fain could hardly believe his ears, yet he knew the general was serious. The long, bitter battle had reached the approaches to the Great Bridge. In fact, most of the surviving infantry had already retreated across it. But Kar had retained his own First Division to cover the final withdrawal, and Colonel Ni's regiment had the honor of forming the division's rearguard.

The afternoon was mostly gone, and evening was coming on quickly, but the Boman seemed inexhaustible. The God only knew how many thousands of them had already been killed, but it seemed not to have fazed them in the least. Probably that was because, despite their casualties, they'd been so successful in driving back the K'Vaernian forces. Whatever their losses here in the city had been so far, they were lower than the casualties they'd taken in the jungle the day before, and unlike yesterday, they had a clear meterstick—the ground they'd gained—to prove they were winning.

They had also been killing K'Vaernians, Diasprans, and Northerners. Fain didn't know what total casualties were, but he knew they'd been painful. The worst had been the loss of the entire rifle battalion from the Tonath Regiment when a Boman thrust broke through more quickly than anticipated and cut its carefully planned retreat route. The rest of the regiment had tried desperately to cut its way through to rescue its comrades, but the attempt had failed, and General Kar had ordered the surviving Tonath battalions to fall back. It had taken his direct order—repeated twice—to convince them to break off, and they'd retreated only sullenly even then, but they must have known it was the only thing they could do.

The loss of four hundred riflemen, along with the regimental commander and the human Marine private who'd been his communication link to headquarters, had been more than merely painful, but they were scarcely the only losses the army had suffered. The best estimate currently available was that the defenders had so far lost almost twelve hundred men, almost as many casualties as they'd suffered in the all-day fight in the jungle. Yet severe as those losses might be, they were a mere fraction of the casualties the Boman had taken, and they were also the grim but necessary price the army had to pay to bait Captain Pahner's trap. Coupled with the ground the Boman had recaptured, they "proved" that the "shit-sitters" were being driven back, with no option but to continue to yield ground.

Now the trick was to get the rearguard across the Great Bridge intact and without discouraging the barbarians' enthusiasm for keeping up their attack.

The command group was already at the northern end of the bridge, awaiting Colonel Ni's troops. Captain Pahner had been pressing General Kar to fall back earlier, but the K'Vaernian Guard commander had politely but firmly resisted the human's pressure. He would retreat only with the last of his own troops, and that was the way it was.

Fortunately for Fain's peace of mind, those final troops were falling back rapidly, and the moment of the general's departure was at hand.

The lieutenant looked out over the Great Bridge and shook his head in admiration. The troops retreating across it presented a picture of absolute chaos, obviously jostling and shoving one another in their desperate haste to escape the oncoming Boman. Of course, the effect would probably have been somewhat spoiled for an observer with an eye to detail, because none of those "fleeing" soldiers had thrown away their weapons, which was almost always the first thing troops did when they'd truly been routed. Aside from that minor detail, however, the picture could hardly have been more convincing, and Fain hoped that whoever was in command of the Boman had an excellent view of it.

But the rearguard couldn't afford to present the same picture of confusion, and as Colonel Ni's reinforced regiment came into sight, it was obvious that it wasn't going to.

The northern end of the Great Bridge opened into a large plaza or square, and the Marton Regiment moved slowly but steadily backward across it. Both pike battalions were in line, facing north and three ranks deep to hold the Boman beyond hand-to-hand range. The assegai companies had each been reinforced by a hundred and fifty dismounted, revolver-armed League cavalry, each with at least two pistols, which gave each of the assegai companies almost as much close-in firepower as the regiment's rifle battalion. One of the reinforced companies of spearmen covered each flank of the pike line, while the rifle battalion moved wherever it was needed to pour in a heavy fire and drive back particularly enterprising Boman thrusts.

"Nice, very nice," Kar commented to an aide, and Fain was forced to agree. Which didn't keep him from clearing his own throat pointedly from his position at the general's elbow. The K'Vaernian turned and cocked his head at the lieutenant, and Fain gestured at the bridge.

"Sir, I imagine that Colonel Ni would be just as happy if we would get out of his way and give him room to maneuver his troops."

"My, how tactfully phrased," the towering Guard commander murmured with a grunting chuckle. But he also nodded, much to Fain's relief, and the Diaspran lieutenant muttered a silent prayer of gratitude to the God of Water and nodded to Sergeant Knever once again.

The command group moved out onto the bridge, conspicuously isolated from the rest of the army as the "panicked retreat" of the previous units streamed towards the southern bank of the Tam. Fain would have been considerably happier if the general had kept a bit closer to the troops who'd preceded them across the bridge, but Kar was in no hurry. In fact, he had a distinct tendency to lag behind even his aides-de-camp and his message runners while he watched Ni's troops falling back to the bridgehead. The barbarians seemed determined to prevent this final group of shit-sitters from escaping their vengeance, and groups of them charged forward despite the surf roll of rifle and revolver bullets, screaming their war cries and hurling throwing axes even as they were hammered down. Troopers were going down, as well, most wounded, rather than killed, especially among the pikemen, but the regiment's discipline held, and the Boman were losing at least three for every casualty they inflicted, even now.

Which didn't mean that they couldn't still overwhelm the regiment by sheer weight of numbers, Fain reflected, and dropped back beside Kar once again.

"Sir, the General might want to move along a bit faster," the lieutenant suggested diffidently.

"In a moment," Kar replied with an impatient wave.

"Sir, the General keeps saying that," Fain pointed out. He watched another wave of Boman crest and die less than twenty meters in front of the retreating pikes, and beckoned unobtrusively to Erkum Pol, who sidled closer.

"I'll retreat when I'm ready to, Lieutenant," Kar rumbled in a deep, repressive tone. "It's not going to do the Regiment's morale any good to see me go scampering off to safety, you know."

"Sir, with all due respect," Fain said diffidently, "I'm

sure the Regiment would be very relieved to know you were out of harm's way. And whether they would or not, Sergeant Julian told me that Captain Pahner wants your butt at the reserve command post *before* the Boman come across the fucking bridge. That's almost a direct quote, Sir," the lieutenant added in an apologetic but politely firm tone.

"I said I'll come in a moment," Kar said even more repressively, and Fain shook his head.

"Erkum?"

"Yeah, Krindi?"

"Escort the General across the bridge," the lieutenant said flatly.

Bistem Kar's head snapped up, and for an instant, his eyes narrowed dangerously. Then they swiveled to Pol, who stood a full head taller than even his own formidable stature, and something like an unwilling chuckle escaped him.

"All right, Lieutenant," he told Fain wryly. "I'll go. I'll go! Who am I to argue with the mighty Erkum Pol? I don't want to get laid out with a plank!"

"I wouldn't hit *you*, General," the private said reproachfully.

"No doubt," Kar said, laying one hand on the towering Diaspran's upper shoulder, and then gathered up the rest of his command group with his eyes. "Gentlemen, Lieutenant Fain would appreciate it if we'd all step briskly along." He made a shooing gesture with both false-hands and flashed a bare-toothed human-style grin. "No dawdling, now!"

"Press them! *Press them!*" Tar Tin howled as the final band of shit-sitters retreated onto the bridge. The new war leader was trapped well back from the van of the host, but he could see the Great Bridge from his vantage point atop a collapsed house. And if he couldn't get at the shit-sitter rearguard now, he'd been in the forefront of the warriors who'd overwhelmed the trapped arquebusiers, and his ceremonial battle ax ran red with their blood.

The battle frenzy hadn't quite claimed him, but he felt the exaltation and the fire blazing in his own blood. They were only Southern shit-sitters, true, yet they'd stood and fought as courageously as any iron head—indeed, as any *Boman*—and the honor of their deaths filled his soul.

It had been a good battle, a great one whose grim glory the bards would sing for generations, and despite the host's losses, victory was within their grasp. However courageously the shit-sitter arquebusiers might have died, Tar Tin himself had seen the panic and terror with which the other shit-sitters had fled across the bridge. He knew the signs—he'd seen them often enough on many another battlefield. That was a broken force, one whose leaders would never convince it to stand if he could only hit it again, quickly, before it had time to untangle itself and find its courage once more.

"Once across the bridge, and the city is ours once more!" he shouted, brandishing his battle ax and waving still more of his warriors into the assault on the stubborn shit-sitter rearguard.

The host attacked with redoubled fury, but the shit-sitters were fully onto the bridge now, and it was no longer possible to threaten their flanks. The ones armed with those long, dreadful spears thickened their ranks, presenting an impenetrable thicket of needle-sharp points, and withdrew at a slow, steady pace. It was impossible to get to hand strokes with them, but at least the thicker formation also blocked their infernal arquebusiers, and the Boman pressed them harder, showering them with throwing axes. The shit-sitters' raised shields were a roof, rattling under the keen-edged rain of steel, and here and there one of them went down. But there were always other shit-sitters ready to drag the wounded to safety, and the slow, sullen retreat continued without breaking or wavering.

Tar Tin snarled, for he wanted that rearguard crushed, yet despite his frustration, he was satisfied enough. The shit-sitter rearguard might be retreating in good order, but it *was* retreating, and rapidly enough that the host would still arrive on the other bank before the rest of their broken army could reform.

"All right, people, let's get into our party dresses," Pahner said, and the squad of Marines around him reached for their helmets.

Roger reached for his along with them, and reflected that it was just as well that he'd spent so many days marching around the jungle in his own powered armor before the company left Q'Nkok. It had given him the opportunity to thoroughly familiarize himself with the armor's capabilities and limitations. He was still far from competent by the standards of the Imperial Marine Corps, and he knew it, but at least he was confident of his ability to move wearing the stuff.

The Marines obviously shared his reservations about his other abilities where the armor was concerned, for the plasma cannon with which his armor had originally been armed had been replaced with a bead cannon. The "stutter gun" was a thoroughly lethal piece of hardware, but its current loads, although ruinously effective against unarmored barbarians, would *not* take out a suit of IMC combat armor. He supposed that he might have felt a little offended by their evident concern over where his fire might go, but all he really felt was relieved.

All around him, helmets were being affixed, and he

watched the HUD come up in his own visor as the helmet sealed to its locking ring. Most of the really power-intensive systems remained on off-line standby, but the armor was live, and a slight shiver ran through his nerves as he reflected upon the destructive power massed in this cellar.

As Pahner had told Rastar on the day the Northern cavalry first joined forces with the Marines, they had sufficient spares and power for two uses of the armor, and this, the captain decided, was the right place to expend one of them. Roger knew that the Marine had considered using the armor in an open field fight, but the Boman had been too dispersed. The Marines would have exhausted their power packs before they could have covered even a fraction of the host's geographic dispersal.

Which had been the entire reason Pahner had constructed the elaborate trap called Sindi.

The Marton Regiment passed the midpoint of the Great Bridge. From its central span to the northern bank, the bridge was a solid mass of Boman, pushing and shoving at one another in their determination to reach the hated shit-sitters. It was a terrifying sight, viewed from the south side of the river, and Bogess and Rus From stood watching it with a sort of awed disbelief.

The bridge was clear between the retreating K'Vaernians and the south bank, and the reinforced regiment was a minuscule force opposed to the thousands upon thousands of barbarian warriors struggling to reach and kill it. The fact that it was exactly what they had planned for and wanted to see didn't make the sight one bit less frightening, and the two Diaspran leaders turned their backs upon it by unspoken mutual consent.

Instead of watching the grim, steady retreat, they let their eyes sweep over the surprise awaiting the Boman on this side of the river.

The original architects of Sindi had built a massive, separate gatehouse and bastioned keep to cover the Great Bridge's southern end. Beyond the gatehouse was another square, even larger than the one at the northern end, and beyond that were the first rows of houses and shops. The city's street net was as tangled and convoluted as that of any other Mardukan city, and even the broader boulevards were scarcely anything which might have been called wide open, but the designers had seen no reason to build massive curtain walls along the southern bank of the Tam. The only way an attacker could reach that part of the city was across the Great Bridge itself, so the powerful gatehouse blocking access to and from the bridge was really all the protection the city had required against assault from that direction.

The current landlords had made a few changes, however. Rus From's engineers had used old fashioned sledgehammers and charges of the black powder liberated from Sindi's own magazines to demolish whole blocks of buildings on the southern side of the square, effectively extending the plaza almost another full kilometer to the south. But if they'd given it more space to the south, they'd compensated by using the rubble produced by their demolition exercises to build stone walls, six meters high and three meters deep across every street and alleyway giving access to the square. Then they'd loopholed the inward-facing wall of every building still standing around the entire perimeter of the square and reinforced most of *those* walls from the inside with sandbags, for good measure. They'd left two of the main boulevards unblocked on the square's south side to permit the retreat of their own troops, and aside from the Marton Regiment, the entire army had now disappeared through those openings.

Through those *previous* openings, to be more precise. No sooner had the last "fleeing" infantryman passed through than the engineers had sprung into action once more. The walls of sandbags they'd assembled across the boulevards weren't quite as tall as the stone walls blocking the other streets, but they were just as thick . . . and each of them had embrasures for six of the new "Napoleons" from the cannon foundries of K'Vaern's Cove.

The general and the cleric regarded those grim preparations one last time, and, almost despite themselves, felt a moment of something very like pity for their enemies.

Krindi Fain heaved a sigh of relief as General Kar and his command group climbed the steep stairs to the top of the bastion and joined Bishop From and General Bogess. He would have been even more relieved if the gates and gate tunnel hadn't taken their own share of damage from the humans' plasma cannon. Although he understood why it was just as important for the defenses on this side of the river to have been "wrecked," it still would have been nice to be able to close a good, sturdy gate of bronze-sheathed ironwood against the shrieking hordes of Boman warriors, especially with the security of both senior Mardukan generals and their chief engineer to worry about.

He made a quick inspection of his troops' positions and felt a surge of pride. His men had to be at least as nervous as he was, given that they'd been less thoroughly briefed on the plan than he, but every one of them was exactly where he was supposed to be, already laying out his cartridge box. If everything went the way it was supposed to, the rest of the regiment would retreat into the gatehouse bastions along with Fain's own company, and if the main gateway had been blasted to bits, the gates and firing slits protecting the bastions were completely intact. They certainly ought to be able to hold out against anything the Boman could do for hours, at the very least, and that should be ample time . . . assuming the plan worked the way it was supposed to.

"Now! Drive them *now!*"

Tar Tin's shout was as hoarse as the scream of a newly branded *sorn*, but he was hardly alone in that. Every chieftain and subchief was shrieking the same message, goading their warriors on, and the war leader laughed in savage triumph as the host's leading warriors drew closer and closer to the southern gatehouse. Even from his own position on the north bank, the damage that gatehouse had suffered when the shit-sitters seized the city was clearly evident. What should have been an all but impenetrable barrier had been opened like a gutted *basik*. All they had to do was to drive these last, stubborn shit-sitters through the shattered tunnel and the city would be *theirs*.

"About *now*, I think," Captain Armand Pahner murmured as the blue icons of the Marton Regiment crossed the green safety line projected onto his HUD, and his toot transmitted the detonation code over his armor's com.

The micromolecular detonator had been designed to handle anything from highly sophisticated chemical explosives to small thermonuclear devices. The design team which had produced it had never even considered the possibility that it might be used for something as crude as black powder weapons, and they might have been offended by such a plebeian misuse of their ultrasophisticated brainchild.

Pahner could not have cared less about that. All he cared about was that it did precisely what he wanted it to do and ignited the quick match fuse running to the five hundred black powder claymore mines emplaced along the west side of the bridge.

The mines didn't detonate simultaneously. Instead, a rolling wall of fire and smoke raced clear across the bridge from just beyond its midpoint all the way to the northern bank of the river.

"Now!"

Colonel Ni's deep-voiced shout rang out, and every one of his pikemen squatted as if simultaneously stricken by diarrhea. The six hundred or so Boman who'd been outside the claymores' kill zone were too stunned by the cataclysm behind them to react, although there was very little they could have done, anyway. As the squatting pikemen cleared their line of fire, four hundred riflemen and three hundred revolver-armed cavalrymen opened fire at point-blank range. The bridge was so narrow that the K'Vaernians' and Northerners' ranks could be only twenty men across, but they could fire three ranks deep, and as each group of sixty fired, it squatted in turn to clear the fire of the group behind it. The firing sequence began with the cavalrymen; by the time it reached the second group of riflemen, there was not a single living, unwounded Boman on the entire length of the Great Bridge.

Sergeant Major Eva Kosutic paced back and forth along the gun line atop the rubble-built wall on the western side of the square. She hadn't been happy about being stuck here in the city while the troops were actually engaged in the field, especially when Roger and his Mobile Force had been fighting for their lives. But she was about to make up for her recent inactivity, she thought, listening to the crashing thunder of the Marton Regiment's volleys with a cold, thin smile.

"Load with grape," she told the gunners she and her initial cadre of naval artillerists had trained, and her smile turned even colder and thinner as she considered the surprise present they had for the Boman.

"Beware of Armaghans," she told the distant barbarians softly. "Especially when they bear gifts."

Tar Tin stared in horror at the Great Bridge.

Half a kilometer of Boman warriors—almost six thousand of them—had been ripped apart and strewn in bloody wreckage all along the northern half of the bridge. No doubt the host had lost many more than that during the fighting across the city, but not in such an eyeblink of time. Not so . . . horrifically. One moment they'd been living warriors, fierce and proud, screaming their war cries as they surged forward to close with their shit-sitter enemies; the next, they were so much shredded meat and blood, blown and splattered across the paved roadway. Blood ran from the bridge's storm drains, not in trickles but in streams that *splashed* into the river below and dyed it until it looked as if the Tam itself were bleeding to death.

And even as he stared at the carnage and destruction, even as the shit-sitter rearguard turned and jogged into the shadows of the broken gate tunnel, yet another huge explosion roared through the humid air. He watched the cloud of smoke and dust billowing up from the middle of the center span and hammered the edge of his ceremonial ax on the heaped stone upon which he stood, screaming his fury. The accursed shit-sitters had blown up the bridge behind themselves! Despite the panicked rout of almost their entire army, they were going to escape him because some demon among them had planned even for this contingency!

Curses and howls of baffled rage rose from thousands of other throats as the rest of the host realized the same thing. Warriors shrieked promises of dire vengeance, promised the gods the slow, lingering death of whatever shit-sitter had planned that ambush and that escape from their wrath.

But then the dust and smoke began to dissipate, and all of the curses, all of the shouts, faded into a breathless silence as the Great Bridge emerged slowly from the haze once more.

Tar Tin realized that he was holding his own breath, leaning forward, staring with hungry eyes as the bridge reemerged, pace by pace. Perhaps, if the gap wasn't too wide they would still be able to get across. Perhaps a temporary span, or—

A shout of triumph arose—first from one throat, then from a dozen, and finally from thousands. *The bridge stood!* The shit-sitter explosion had blasted away the raised stone guard walls on both sides, and taken a ragged bite out of the eastern side of the roadbed, but that was all. *All!*

"Now you will all die, shit-sitters!" Tar Tin screamed jubilantly. "So clever you were—so brilliant! But nothing stands between you and our axes now!" The paramount war leader of the clans raised his ax of office overhead in both true-hands, and his voice rang out like the trumpet of the war god.

"Forward the clans! *Kill the shit-sitters!*"

Armand Pahner inhaled in deep satisfaction as a fresh wave of Boman began thundering out onto the gore-splashed roadway of the bridge. His greatest fear had been that the barbarians would refuse to thrust their heads into the trap awaiting them on the south bank of the river. He'd had no choice but to set up the claymore ambush, because it had been imperative that there be a clean break between the K'Vaernian rearguard and the first ranks of barbarians to cross the bridge. The rearguard had to have time to file through the bastions' gates and bar those openings behind them, because he'd dared not let them into the killing ground with the enemy still in contact. Any force small enough to fit onto the bridge would have been easily outflanked and destroyed once the Boman had room to deploy around them, and the rest of the waiting troops couldn't have fired on the Boman without killing their own rearguard. Not to mention the fact that any premature firing might warn the barbarians of what was coming in time for them to refuse to cooperate. Yet even though he'd had no option but to place the claymores, he'd been more than half afraid that if the ambush worked, the Boman would recoil, refusing to continue their advance lest they run into additional, similar ambushes.

The only answer he'd been able to think of was to make the Boman think the defenders had done their level best to destroy the bridge entirely. The theory had been that the barbarians would figure that they wouldn't have tried to destroy the bridge, unless they'd been afraid of being pursued. From which it followed that this was the ideal time *to* pursue them. And so Corporal Aburia had worked with exquisite care to prepare a black powder "demolition charge" which would look spectacular as hell, do a fair amount of superficial damage, but leave the bridge structurally intact. He'd been a bit anxious about asking the corporal to tailor that precise a charge with something as crude as black powder, but she'd come through with flying colors.

Now he watched the bridge filling once again with close-packed Boman, and keyed his communicator.

"Here they come, Eva," he announced over the dedicated channel to the sergeant major. "Don't let anyone get too eager."

Honal stood peering through the firing slit in the wall of what once had been a shop of some sort. He had no idea what sort of goods it had sold, nor were there any clues to give him a hint. All that was left was a large, square, empty room with heavily reinforced stone walls. Well, that and the swivels, mounted on heavy timbers, driven into the ground, which the K'Vaernian Navy had contributed to the campaign.

The Sheffan nobleman rested one proprietary false-hand on the swivel beside him. For all intents and purposes, it was a small muzzle-loading cannon with a shot weight of no more than a single human kilo which took its name from the way it was mounted aboard K'Vaernian warships, which had a habit of mounting a dozen or so of them along each rail as antipersonnel weapons. Julian had taken one look at them and pronounced that they were the galaxy's biggest muzzle-loading "shotguns"—whatever a "shotgun" was. Honal didn't really know about that. All he knew was that this particular swivel was going to help him extract his long awaited vengeance for murdered Sheffan, and he showed his teeth in a snarl any human might have envied.

Bistem Kar watched from atop the gatehouse bastion as the unending tide of Boman swept towards him down the bridge. It scarcely even hesitated when it reached the area Aburia's charge had damaged, and the general's growl of satisfaction rumbled deep in his throat as the barbarians kept right on coming.

"Lieutenant Fain!"

"Yes, Sir?"

"Lieutenant, those bastards may get suspicious if we just welcome them into our parlor, but I don't want to put down enough fire to discourage them, either. I think one company of really good shots ought to be just about right. Would you happen to know where I might find one which would be interested in the job?"

"As a matter of fact, General," the Diaspran lieutenant told him with a slow smile, "I do. Company! Action front!"

Tar Tin snarled as the first shit-sitter arquebus fire began to crackle from the bastions to either side of the broken gatehouse. So, some of the rearguard had had the presence of mind to position themselves there in an effort to delay the host's pursuit of their fleeing fellows! It was a courageous decision, he conceded, since they could not have an unlimited supply of ammunition and whatever happened to the rest of their army *they* were certain to be dug out of their positions eventually and killed. But it was obvious that there weren't enough of them to stop the Boman. Dozens of warriors fell, or plunged over the side of the bridge into the Tam, as bullets struck them down, but even as dozens fell, hundreds continued to charge forward at a run, and already the host's fleetest warriors were passing through the broken gatehouse.

The bridge was theirs! The bridge was theirs—and soon all the rest of the city, and their families, and their stolen booty would be theirs once more and K'Vaern's Cove would be doomed!

Eva Kosutic watched the barbarians spilling into the enlarged plaza like a dark, living tide pouring into a dry lake bed from a sluice gate. They came onward, waving their axes, screaming their war cries, and she felt her gunners stirring uneasily. Not nervously, really—more . . . impatiently. They wanted to open fire *now*, but she only stood there, hands clasped behind her, and waited for the lake to fill.

Sna Hulf of the Ternolt Clan of the Boman charged through the ruined gate tunnel, howling his war cry. The exultation of battle carried him forward like a man possessed, eager to prove his courage and punish all shit-sitter treachery. He'd never experienced anything quite like the charge across the bridge, never been part of such a focused, unstoppable surge. It was as if the bridge were a narrow streambed, and the host a mighty tide driving through it, gaining speed as its bed narrowed until it erupted from the far end of the channel with a force nothing could resist! The weight of all his fellow warriors, of all the clans, thrust him forward with the massive momentum of literally kilotons of bone and blood and muscle.

Yet even in his exalted mood, he realized there was something strange and different about the square at this end of the bridge. It was larger than it had been the last time he was here, and all of the streets leading off of it seemed to have disappeared. And there were *holes* in the walls of all the buildings. And what were those shit-sitters doing on the platform atop the wall where the main boulevard had been?

He stared at the shit-sitters—the only ones he could see—while the momentum of his fellows propelled him forward into the square. They stood behind some sort of strange, two-wheeled carts which supported metal tubes of what looked like dark bronze. The tubes were long, and slender, unlike anything he'd ever seen before, yet there was something about them . . . something familiar, if only he could place it . . .

❖   ❖   ❖

"I've never seen so many Boman in such a small space in my entire life," Honal remarked to Rastar and Chim Pri.

"Like a stock pen full of *turom* at branding time," Pri agreed, rechecking the priming caps on one of his revolvers.

"And one big pocking target," Turkol Bes added. The commander of the Carnan Battalion had borrowed one of the Marines' repeating rifles and had at least forty magazines piled up in front of him. The weapon was ridiculously small for him, but that was all right with Bes.

"And one big pocking target," Rastar agreed grimly.

"They're starting to slow down, General," Krindi Fain remarked, and Kar nodded in agreement. The general had Dell Mir's telescope back out, and was peering towards the northern end of the bridge.

"I imagine the square is beginning to fill up, Lieutenant," he said almost absently. "Even with all the pressure coming from behind them, they can only cram so many bodies into so much space." He chuckled evilly. "Of course, we're about ready to begin making room for more of them, aren't we?"

"General, Colonel Ni reports that some of the Boman are beginning to try to force the gates into the bastion," one of Kar's staffers announced, and the general shrugged.

"I suggest you tell him not to let them do that," he said in mild tones, still peering through his telescope. "Although," he added dryly, "I imagine they'll have something else to distract them very shortly."

"Armand, we're just about full here."

Pahner grinned at Kosutic's pointed tone. The sergeant major would never come out and admit that she was feeling antsy, but her use of his first name in front of the troops, even over the dedicated command circuit, was a dead giveaway. And looking at the congested horde of red icons packing tighter and tighter together in the square, he could hardly blame her. The remote imagery from her helmet showed him a vast sea of Boman, surging this way and that while those closest to the edges of the huge mob began to hack at the barricades with their battle axes. They weren't going to get through that stone any time soon, but he didn't want them to get any ideas about helping one another swarm over their tops, either.

"How many do you figure are still on our side of the river or the bridge, Julian?" he asked.

"Call it ten or twelve thousand on the bridge, and another ten or so on the approaches," Julian replied after a moment.

Pahner frowned slightly. He'd calculated that the Boman could fit a maximum of about forty or forty-five thousand into the square beyond the gatehouse, but he didn't really think there were that many already in it. Call it thirty thousand, he decided. If Julian's estimate was correct—and Pahner rather thought it was—then the Boman were down to no more than fifty-two thousand, little more than half the size of their host before the campaign began. If things went according to plan, those on the bridge and already in the square were toast, but there was no way the limited number of suits of powered armor available to him was going to be able to simultaneously seal the bridge and round up anyone who wasn't already on it. Which meant that at least ten thousand of the barbarians were going to escape, and he hated that.

His frown turned into a grimace and a snort as he realized he was actually upset by the idea of inflicting "only" ninety percent casualties on his enemy.

Hubris, he decided, wasn't something a Marine needed to go around encouraging, and a mere ninety percent casualty rate ought to be enough to encourage even Boman to behave themselves in the future.

"All right, Eva," he said soothingly. "If it will make you feel any better, go ahead and get started."

"Gee, thanks," she said sarcastically, then turned to the gunners on the platform with her, and the captain heard her over the still-open com-link.

"Open fire!"

Sna Hulf had been shoved almost directly up against one of the stone walls fronting the square by the unendurable pressure of the warriors behind him. One or two of his fellows had already lost their footing and disappeared under the shrieking, ax-waving ocean of warriors. He had no doubt that they'd been trampled into paste, and the pressure around him was becoming distinctly unpleasant, but he couldn't take his mind off those bronze tubes.

If they'd been fatter and ringed with reinforcing hoops or bands of metal, he would have been tempted to think they were bombards. But no one had ever mounted a bombard on a carriage like *that*, and no one had ever cast a bombard that skinny for its length. It was ridiculous. And yet . . . and yet . . .

He was still pondering the conundrum when Eva Kosutic's order reached her gunners.

The gun platforms had been very carefully designed. Aside from the twelve guns in the sandbagged barriers built to close the two avenues by which the retreating K'Vaernians had cleared the square, each battery was at least six meters above ground level, and the gun platforms themselves sloped upward towards the rear, so that the guns' point of aim, at maximum depression,

was well below the level of the batteries on the opposite side of the square. After all, no one wanted any
friendly fire casualties.

But if no one wanted friendly casualties, there were
going to be plenty of *unfriendly* ones. Each round of
grapeshot consisted of nine individual shot, each fifty
millimeters in diameter, and there were a hundred and
eighty-two guns. Just over sixteen hundred iron balls,
each seventy percent the size of a pre-space baseball,
ripped into the packed Boman. Anyone who got in the
way of one of them simply exploded in a spray of
crimson and shredded flesh, and each of them blasted
its way well over four hundred meters into the stunned
mass of warriors.

No one ever knew how many thousands of Boman
died in that first salvo, and it didn't really matter. Even
as the artillery opened fire, riflemen and revolver-armed
cavalry rose atop the walls around the square, or
stepped up to the loopholes, and the six hundred Navy
swivels mounted behind other loopholes belched fire
and smoke. The swivels were loaded with canister, not
grape, and each of them sent one hundred and thirty-
five musket balls screaming into the Boman.

Honal shouted with delight as he touched off the
swivel. The concussion as hundreds of field guns and
swivels and thousands of rifles and revolvers simultaneously opened fire was like the blow from some
mighty hammer. The deafening waves of sound and
overpressure seemed to squeeze the air out of his
lungs, and the brimstone stench was shot through with
lurid tongues of flame, like some demon's paradise
turned loose on mortal beings.

To either side of him, Rastar, Chim Pri, and Turkol
Bes stood at their own loopholes, blazing away with
the same manic grins. Honal's assistants stepped

forward and began reloading the swivel, and the cavalryman drew two of his own revolvers and emptied them through the swivel's firing slit while they worked.

Shrieks and screams of terrified agony came from the slaughter pen into which the Boman had been herded, and hell-spawned night enveloped the scene of horror as choking clouds of smoke devoured the light.

Tar Tin was halfway across the bridge when the terrible explosions began on the far side of the gatehouse. The mighty stone structure of the Great Bridge itself seemed to quiver and pulse underfoot with the fury of the shit-sitters' fire, yet even through the dreadful thunder he could hear the despairing shrieks of the warriors trapped and dying under it.

Horrified understanding smote him as the choking pall of powder smoke rose above the far end of the bridge, and a fist seemed to close about his heart as he realized Kny Camsan had been right all along. To charge headlong against the shit-sitters' new weapons was to die, and he had been fooled—duped by shit-sitter cunning into doing just that! He still couldn't see what was happening in the square ahead, but he didn't need to see to know that the disaster to which he had led the clans was complete.

All about him, other warriors heard the sounds of slaughter and realized, as he, that the shit-sitters *wanted* them to continue their charge forward to their deaths. For a few moments, the pressure of those behind kept them moving forward anyway, but then even those at the very rear of the column realized, however imperfectly, what was happening. The pressure eased, and the flow of movement across the bridge began to reverse itself.

❖   ❖   ❖

"Okay, troops," Pahner said to the armored members of Julian's squad. "Time to push the little dogies along."

The true purpose of the armor was far less to wipe the Boman out of existence than to break the back of the remnant's morale.

It worked.

The armored Marines, concealed by the sophisticated chameleon systems of their armor, had actually passed through the rearmost stragglers of the Boman host without being detected. They'd split up, spreading out to cover as many as possible of the streets, alleys, and avenues leading into the square on the north bank of the Tam with at least one Marine, and now they advanced, firing as they came.

A tidal wave of flechettes, cannon beads, and plasma bolts erupted out of nowhere, tearing lethal holes through the Boman who had just begun to retreat from the holocaust on the *other* side of the river, and it was too much. Not even Boman battle frenzy could support them in the midst of such supernatural devastation and horror, and the warriors began throwing down their weapons and groveling on the ground, anything to get out of the hail of terrible, terrible death from the invisible demons.

Honal sent yet another charge of canister blazing through the loophole, and reached for another pair of revolvers. He stepped up to the opening and opened fire, watching still more of the trapped, screaming Boman fly back from his fire in splashes of red, and he laughed with an edge of hysteria. It was like killing *basik*. He could probably have wandered in with a *club* and killed the Boman—they were that broken.

His revolvers clicked empty, and he snarled in

frustration at the interruption of the terrible frenzy of slaughter. He swung out the cylinders and began stuffing fresh cartridges into the chambers. He recapped them, closed them, and began firing yet again.

"Cease fire, Honal," someone said in his ear.

"What?" he asked, picking another target and squeezing the trigger. The Boman blew sideways, disappearing into the heaped and piled corpses of his fellows, and someone hit Honal on the shoulder.

"Cease fire!" Rastar shouted in his ear.

Honal gave his cousin an incredulous glance, unable to believe what he was hearing, then looked back out the firing slit. The terrifying warriors of the Boman were a pitiful sight, most of them trying desperately to cower behind and under the piles of their own dead, and Rastar shook him by the shoulder.

"Cease fire," he said in a more nearly normal voice. "Despreaux says to cease fire. It's all over."

"But—" Honal began, and Rastar shook his head.

"She's right, cousin," the last prince of Therdan said. "Look at them, Honal. Look at them, and remember them as they were when they came over our walls . . . and as they will never, *ever* be again." He shook his head again, slowly. "The League is avenged, cousin. The League is avenged."

Tar Tin stood trapped in the center of the bridge, watching the destruction of his people's soul. The pride of the warrior people who had always triumphed, for whom defeat had never been more than a temporary setback and a spur to still greater triumph, died that day before his very eyes, and he knew it. Whatever might become of the pitiful survivors of the clans, they would never forget this disaster, never again find the courage to take the shit-sitters by the throat and teach them fear. *They* were the ones who would cower in terror from this day forth, hiding in the shadows lest the terrible shit-sitters come upon them and complete their destruction.

And it was he, Tar Tin, who had led them to this.

He knew what the clans would require of him—if they still possessed the spirit to demand a war leader's death. And he knew what they would *expect* of him, yet try as he might, he could not force a way through the defeated warriors about him to attack the shit-sitters and force them to kill him. He could not even sing his death song, for there was no enemy to give him death with honor. There was only shame, and the knowledge that the warrior people, terror of the North, would be warriors no more forever.

He looked down at the ceremonial ax in his true-hands—the ax which had been borne by the war leaders of the clans for fifteen generations, and which had finally known defeat and humiliation. His hands tightened on the shaft as he pictured the shit-sitters' gloating pleasure at claiming that emblem of Boman pride as a trophy to hang upon a palace wall in some stinking city, far from the free winds of the hills of the North.

No! That much, at least, he would prevent. In this, if in nothing else, he would prove himself worthy of his war leader's title.

Tar Tin, last paramount war leader of the clans of the Boman, clutched his ax of office to his chest with all four hands and climbed upon the parapet of the Great Bridge of Sindi. The water of the Tam ran red with the blood of his people below him, and he closed his eyes as he gave himself to the river.

CHAPTER FORTY-THREE

Poertena tossed down a single card.

"Gimme."

"Never draw to an inside straight," Fain said, flipping a card across the table. "It just won't work."

"A week," Tratan said. "A *week* he's been playing, and already he's an expert."

"It won't," the company commander said.

"We've got the masts almost finished," Tratan said, changing the subject, "and the last of the spars will be ready next week. Now if you hull pussies would ever get finished . . ."

"Real woodwork takes time," Trel Pis said. The old K'Vaernian shipbuilder scratched his right horn as he contemplated his cards. "You can't rush perfection."

"We gots tee last load o' planking from tee mills yestiday," Poertena said. "Tomorrow we starts putting it up. Every swingin' . . . whatever gets to put up planks til we done. T'en we parties."

"So next week the Prince has his yacht?" Fain asked. "Call. Pair of twos."

"Or tee week after," Poertena said. "We gots to set up tee rigging, an' t'at takes time. An' tee new canvas ain't ready yet, neither. Four eights. Gimme."

"If he was a Diaspran, I'd never believe it," Tratan said, throwing down his hand.

"Natural four?" Fain said in disbelieving tones.

"Hey," Poertena said. "If you gots tee cards, you don't have to draw to a straight. It's only when you pocked you gots to do t'at."

"Sergeant, could you take a look at this?"

The humans hadn't tried to explain the nature of the listening post to their hosts. The Mardukans had remarkable facility with gross manufacture, but the minute the word "electronics" was used, it became supernatural. So instead of trying to explain, Pahner had just asked for a high, open spot on the western wall, and left it at that.

Julian walked over from the open tower where the rest of the squad was lounging in the shade and checked the reading on the pad.

"Shit," he said quietly.

"What's it mean?" Cathcart asked, tapping a querying finger on the flashing icon.

"Encrypted voice transmission," Julian said, crouching down to run expertly through the analysis.

"From a recon flight?"

There was an unmistakable nervous note in the corporal's voice, and Julian didn't blame him. The entire company had known since the day they left Marshad that someone from the port had discovered the abandoned assault shuttles in which they'd reached the planet. The scrap of com traffic they'd picked up from the pinnace which had spotted them had been in the clear, which hadn't left much room for doubts. But it had also been *only* a scrap, and what no one knew was what whoever was in control of the port had done about that discovery since. It was unlikely that anyone would believe a single company of Marines could survive to get this far, but it certainly wasn't impossible.

"Don't know if it's a recon flight," he told Cathcart after a moment, "but whatever it is, we're close enough to pick it up. Which means they're close enough to see us . . . if they look. Or hear us, if we're careless with our radio traffic. "

"Saint?" the corporal asked, glancing at the sky.

"Civilian," Julian replied. "Standard program you can download off any planet's Infonet."

"That's good, right?" Cathcart said. "That means the Saint blockade might have been lifted. It might be a freighter or something."

"Yeah," Julian said. "Maybe." He tapped the icon, and it flashed red and yellow. "On the other hand, pirates use the same program."

Cord had considered himself a scholar in his day. And a poet. So when O'Casey set her toot to the task of accurately translating the long-ago log of the only ship known ever to have crossed the ocean, it was as a scholar that Cord had offered his assistance.

But it was with the mind of a shaman that he finally read the words which had been written on the crumbling leather leaves of the ancient log.

"Upon the forty-sixth day of the voyage, in the first quarter after light, there was a vast boiling upon the sea, as of a giant swell of water. All who were not employed upon the oars gathered on the starboard side to observe as another boil came up, and still another, each closer to the ship and apparently approaching rapidly.

"Just as the fourth boil of water was observed near alongside the starboard beam, there was a great

shudder from below, as if the ship had struck a hidden reef.

"Master Kindar called to back all oars, but before any action could be taken, a vast mouth, as wide as the ship was long, opened up, and the bow of the vessel dropped into its maw.

"The jaws closed upon the ship, tearing it asunder and taking away many who had run forward to see the apparition. Many others, especially those along the sides, were thrown from the shattered remnants.

"I stood my post upon the rudder deck as the ship began to roll to the side. There was more screaming forward, as the ship shuddered again, and it was apparent that the beast had taken another bite, but it was out of my view.

"I clung to the rudder as the ship rolled, and then lashed myself to the starboard bulwark as the fragment continued to float. Forward, I could hear the screams of others caught in the water, and again and again the creature crashed against the remnant of the ship, until it became either sated or disgusted with the fare. Perhaps it was the latter, for it has been ten days now, and it has not returned.

"The cook and I are the only survivors of the good ship *Nahn Cibell*. The wind and tide drive us slowly onward across the endless ocean. I have written all that I know. I hope to speak to my wife at the end of this voyage, and to see my young.

"But it is very hot upon the sea. And we have no water."

Roger sat on the end of the dock and looked out over the small cove. He could hear the party getting into swing behind him, but for the moment he was content just to watch the sun descending over the K'Vaern Sea.

He rubbed the cover of the bag, and unrolled it. The jeweled badge of an imperial servitor glittered in the fading light, and he unpinned it from the bag and held it up in one hand. He ran the forefinger of his other hand lightly, gently, across it, then drew a deep breath and pinned it very carefully to the breast of his own chameleon suit. He gave it a single, almost tender pat, and then returned to the bag.

One end held a lump, and he unsealed the bag and gently picked out a handful of fine ash.

"Oh, Danny boy," he whispered, and his hand moved, sending the fine drift of ashes out over the water while the words of the ancient paean to love and loss whispered out under the cry of four-winged avians whose like had never been dreamed of on Earth.

"Oh Danny boy, the pipes, the pipes are calling,
From glen to glen, and down the mountainside.
The summer's gone, and all the flowers are dying.
'Tis you, 'tis you must go, and I must bide.
But come ye back when summer's in the meadow,
Or when the valley's hushed and white with snow.
'Tis I'll be here in sunshine or in shadow,
Oh Danny boy, oh Danny boy, I love you so."

"Roger?" Nimashet put her hand on his shoulder. "Are you coming? This is your party, too."

"I'm coming." He stood and dusted off his hands. "I suppose that food is as good a way to celebrate him as any."

Prince Roger Ramius Sergei Alexander Chiang MacClintock, Heir Tertiary to the Throne of Man, took one last look at the gentle swell surging across the reef at the entrance to the cove. Then he turned and walked back to the restaurant, hand in hand with a sergeant of Marines, and the fine film of ash still clinging to his palm mingled and spread between their hands, unnoticed.

Behind them, the ashes slowly mixed with the salty sea and floated out on the tide of two moons. Floated out on the tide to wash upon distant shores.

**THE SMALL STREAM LEADING
OUT OF THE TOP OF RAN TAI LAKE
BECOMES THE CHASTEN**

K'VAERN'S COVE

TO D'SLEY

BATTLE OF THE FIELDS

SINDI

GATHERED MATERIALS

TO D'SLEY

ROGER'S STAND

TO THE

KRANOS MINES

excerpt from

MARCH TO THE STARS

available from Baen Books
January 2003
0-7434-3562-1, hardcover, $26.00

PROLOGUE

The body was in a state of advanced decomposition. Time, and the various insect analogues of Marduk, had worked their way with it, and what was left was mostly skeleton with a few bits of clinging tendon and skin. Temu Jin would have liked to say it was the worst thing he'd ever seen, but that would've been a lie.

He turned over one of the skeletal hands and ran a sensor wand across it. The catacomb-like tomb was hot and close, especially with three more team members and one of the gigantic Mardukans packed into it with him. The heat on Marduk was always bad—the "temperate" regions were a fairly constant thirty-five degrees—but in the tomb, with the remnant stink of decomposition (not to mention the smell of the unwashed assholes he'd arrived with), it was like an antechamber to Hell.

One that was already inhabited.

There was no question that its occupants had been Imperial Marines. Or, at least, people with Marine nano packs. The trace materials and surviving nanites were coded, and the sensor practically screamed "Imperials." But the questions were how they had gotten here . . . and *why* they were here? He could think of several reasons, and he liked the stink of all of them less than he did the stench in this room.

"Ask them again, geek," Dara said in a tight voice. The survey team leader choked for a second—again—then hawked, spat, and finished by blowing out his nose on the floor. Marduk was hell on his sinuses. "Talk gook. Make sure this is all there was."

Jin looked up at the towering Mardukan and ran the translation through his "toot." The tutorial implant, lodged just inside his mastoid bone, took his chosen words, translated them into the local Mardukan dialect, and adjusted his speaking voice to compensate.

"My illustrious leader wishes to ensure, once again, that there were no survivors."

Mardukan expressions were not the same as those of humans. Among other things, their faces had fewer muscles, and much of their expressiveness came from eloquent gestures of their four arms. But the body language of this Mardukan was closed, as well. Part of that might be from the fact that he was missing one arm from the elbow down. Currently, there was a rather nice prosthetic hook in its place, razor-sharp on both sides. So Dara had to be either stupid, arrogant, or both to ask, for the fifth time, if the Voitan representative was lying.

"Alas," T'leen Targ said with a sorrowful but cautious sweep of his arms (and hook), "there were no survivors. A few lasted a pair of days, but then they, too, succumbed. We did all we could for them. That we had been only a day sooner! The battle was great; your friends warred upon more Kranolta than the stars in the sky! They stacked them against the walls of the city and cut them down with their powerful fire-lances! Had our relief force but been sooner, some might have survived! Woe! But we were too late, alas. However, they did break the power of the Kranolta, and for that Voitan was and is eternally thankful. It was because of that gratitude that we interred them here, with our own honored dead, in hopes that someday others of their kind might come for them. And . . . here you are!"

"Same story," Jin said, turning back to the team leader.

"Where's the weapons? Where's the gear?" Dara demanded. Unlike the commo-puke's, his toot was an off-the-shelf civilian model and couldn't handle the only translation program available. It was loaded with the local patois used around the distant starport, but handling multiple dialects was beyond its capability, and Jin's system couldn't cross load the translation files.

"*Some* of that stuff should have survived," the team leader continued. "And there were supposed to be more of them at the last city. Where'd the rest of 'em go?"

"My illustrious leader asks about our dear friends' weapons and equipment," Jin said. The communications technician had had fairly extensive dealings with the natives, both back at the distant starport and on the hellish odyssey to this final resting place of the human castaways. And of them all, this one made him the most nervous. He'd almost rather be in the jungles again. Which was saying a lot.

Marduk was an incredibly hot and stable planet. The result was a nearly worldwide jungle, filled with the most vicious predators in the known worlds. And it seemed that the search team—or assassination team, depending on how one viewed it—had run into all of them on its journey here.

The starport's atmospheric puddle-jumpers had flown them to the dry lakebed where the four combat shuttles had landed. There was no indication, anywhere, of what unit had flown those shuttles, or where they had come from. All of them had been stripped of any information, and their computers purged. Just four shuttles, totally out of fuel, in the middle of five thousand square kilometers of salt.

There had, however, been a clear trail off the lakebed, leading up into the mountains. The search team had followed it, flying low, until it reached the lowland jungles. After that it had just . . . disappeared into the green hell.

Their initial request to return to base had been denied. It was unlikely, to say the very least, that the shuttle crews might survive to reach civilization. Even taking the local flora and fauna out of the equation, the landing site was on the far side of the planet from the starport, and unless they had brought along enough dietary supplements, they would starve to death long before they could make the trip. But unlikely or not, their fate had to be known. Not so much because anyone would ever ask, or care, about them. Because if there was *any* shred of a possibility that they could reach the base, or worse, get off planet, they had to be eliminated.

That consideration had been unstated, and it was also one of the reasons that the tech wasn't sure he would survive the mission. The "official" reason for the search was simply to rescue the survivors. But the composition of the team made it much more likely that the real reason was to eliminate a threat. Dara was the Governor's official bully-boy. Any minor "problem" that could be fixed with a little muscle or a discreetly disappearing body tended to get handed to the team leader. Otherwise, he was pretty useless. As demonstrated by his inability to see what was right in front of his eyes.

The rest of the team was cut from the same cloth. All fourteen of them—there'd been sixteen . . . before the local fauna got a shot at them on the trek here—were from the locally hired "guard" force, and all were wanted on one planet or another. Aware that maintaining forces on Class Three planets was difficult, at best, the distant Imperial capital allowed local governors wide latitude in the choice of personnel. Governor Moser had, by and large, hired what were still known as "Schultzes," guards who could be trusted to see, do, and hear nothing. Still, there were those special occasions when a real problem cropped up. And to deal with those problems, he had secured a "special reaction force" composed of what could graciously be called "scum." If, of course, one wanted to insult scum.

Jin was well aware that he was not an "official" member of the Special Force. As such, this mission might be a test for entry, and in many ways, that could be a good thing. There was one huge issue associated with the mission even so, however: it might involve fighting the Marines. He had several reasons, not the least of which was the likelihood of being blasted into plasma, to not want to fight Marines. But the mission had been angling steadily that way.

Now, however, it seemed all his worry had been for naught. The last of the Marines had died here, in this lonely outpost, overrun by barbarians before their friendly "civilized" supporters could arrive to save them!

Sure they did, he thought, and snorted mentally. *Either they wandered off and these guys are covering for them . . . or else the locals finished them off themselves and are graciously willing to give these 'Kranolta' the credit. The only problem at this point is figuring out which.*

"Alas," the local said yet again. He seemed remarkably fond of that word, Jin thought cynically as Trag gestured in the direction of the distant jungle somewhere outside the tomb. "The Kranolta took all their equipment with them. There was nothing left for us to give to their friends. That is, to you."

And you can believe as much or as little of that as you like, Jin thought. But the answer left a glaring hole he had to plug. And hope his efforts never came to light.

"The scummy says the barbs threw all the gear into the river," he mistranslated.

"Poth!" Dara snarled. "That means it's all trashed. *And* we can't trace the power packs! Even trashed, we could've gotten something for them."

What an imbecile, Jin thought. Dara must have been hiding behind the door when brains were given out.

When a body is looted, the looters very rarely take *every scrap* of clothing. Nor was that the only peculiarity. There was one clinging bit of skin on the corpse before him which had clearly been cut away in an oval, as if to remove a tattoo after the person was dead . . . and there were no weapons or even bits of weapons anywhere in sight. For that matter, the entire battle site had been meticulously picked over to remove every trace of evidence. Some of the scars from plasma gun fire had even been covered up. The barbarians, according to the locals' time line, could not possibly have swept the battlefield that well, no matter how addicted to trophy-taking they might be, before the "civilized" forces arrived to finish driving them off.

The last city they'd passed through had also been remarkably reticent about the actions the objects of the search team's curiosity had taken on their way through. The crews of the downed shuttles had apparently swept into town, destroyed and looted a selected few of the local "Great Houses," and then swept out again, just as rapidly. According to the local king and the very few nobles they'd been permitted to question, at least. And in that town, the search team had been followed everywhere by a large enough contingent of guards to make attempts to question anyone else contraindicated.

All of that proved one thing to Jin, and it took a sadistic, snot-filled idiot like Dara not to see it.

The bodies had been sterilized.

Somebody wanted to make *damn* sure that no one could determine who these Marines had been without a DNA database. The dead Marines' toots were already a dead issue, of course. Their built-in nanites had obediently reduced them to half-crumbled wreckage once their owners were dead. That was a routine security measure, but the rest of this definitely went far beyond "routine." Which meant these particular people were something other than standard Marines. Either Raiders or . . . something else. And since the locals were covering for them so assiduously, it was glaringly obvious that all of them *hadn't* died.

All of which meant that there was a short company—from the number of shuttles, Jin had put their initial force at a company—of an Imperial special operations unit out there wandering in the jungle. And the only reasonable target for their wandering was a certain starport.

Lovely.

He pushed aside a bit of the current corpse's hair, looking for any clue. The Marine had been female, with longish, dishwater blond hair. That was the only thing about the skeletal remains which would have been recognizable to anyone but a forensic pathologist, which Jin was not. He had some basic training in forensics, but all he could tell about this corpse was that a blade had half-severed the left arm. However, under the cover of the hair, there was a tiny earring. Just a scrap of bronze, with one ten-letter word on it.

Jin was unable to keep his eyes from widening, but he didn't freeze. He was far too well trained to do something so obvious. He simply moved his hand in a smooth motion, and the tiny earring was ripped from the decaying ear, a scrap of skin still dangling from it.

"I'm not finding anything," he said, getting to his feet as he willed his face to total immobility.

He looked at the native, who returned his regard impassively. The local "king" was named T'Kal Vlan. He'd greeted the search team as long-lost cousins, all the time giving the impression that he wanted to sell them a rug. For T'leen Targ, though, it always seemed to be a tossup between selling them a rug and burying them in one. Now the local scratched his horn with his hook and nodded . . . in a distinctly human fashion.

"I take it that you did not find anything," Targ said. "I'm *so* sorry. Will you be taking the bodies with you?"

"I think not," Jin replied. Standing as they were, the team leader was behind the local. Jin reached out with his left hand, and the Mardukan took it automatically, another example of acculturation to Terrans. Jin wondered if the Marines had realized how many clues they were unavoidably leaving behind. Given who they apparently were, it was probable, for all the proof of how hard they'd worked to avoid it. As he shook the Mardukan's slime-covered hand, a tiny drop of bronze was left behind, stuck in the mucus.

"I don't think we'll be back," the commo tech said. "But you might want to melt this down so nobody else finds it."

In the palm of the native's hand, the word "BARBARIANS" was briefly impressed into the mucus.

Then it disappeared.

CHAPTER ONE

"It's a halyard."

"No, it's a stay. T'e headstay."

The thirty-meter schooner *Ima Hooker* swooped closehauled into aquamarine swells so perfect they might have been drawn from a painting by the semi-mythical Maxfield Parrish. Overhead, the rigging sang in a faint but steady breeze. That gentle zephyr, smelling faintly of brine, was the only relief for the sweltering figures on her deck.

Julian mopped his brow and pointed to the offending bit of rigging.

"Look, there's a rope—"

"A line," Poertena corrected pedantically.

"Okay, there's a line and a pulley—"

"T'at's a block. Actually, it's a deadeye."

"Really? I thought a block was one of those with cranks."

"No, t'at's a windlass."

Six other schooners kept formation on *Hooker*. Five of them were identical to the one on whose deck Julian and Poertena stood: low, trim hulls with two masts of equal height and what was technically known as a "topsail schooner rig." What that meant was that each mast carried a "gaff sail," a fore-and-aft sail cut like a truncated triangle with its head set from an angled yard—the "gaff"—while the foremast also carried an entire set of conventional square sails. The after gaff sail—the "mainsail," Julian mentally corrected; after all, he had to get *something* right—had a boom; the forward gaff sail did not. Of course, it was called the foresail whereas the lowest square sail on that mast was called the "fore *course*," which struck him as a weird name for any sail. Then there were the "fore topsail," "fore topgallant," and "fore royal," all set above the fore course.

The second mast (called the "mainmast" rather than the "aftermast," for some reason Julian didn't quite understand, given that the ship had only two masts to begin with and that it carried considerably less canvas than the foremast), carried only a single square topsail, but compensated by setting a triangular "leg of mutton" fore-and-aft sail above the mainsail. There were also staysails set between the masts, not to mention a flying jib, outer jib, and inner jib, all set between the foremast and the bowsprit.

The sixth schooner was different—a much bigger, less agile, somehow unfinished-looking vessel with a far deeper hull and no less than five masts—and, at the insistence of Captain Armand Pahner, Imperial Marines, rejoiced in the name of *Snarleyow*. The smaller, more nimble ships seemed to regard their larger sister with mixed emotions. No one would ever have called *Snarleyow* anything so gauche as *clumsy*, perhaps, but she was clearly less fleet of foot, and her heavier, more deliberate motion almost seemed to hold the others back.

All six of the ships carried short-barreled cannon along their sides. *Snarleyow* mounted fifteen of them to a side, which gave her a quarter again the broadside armament of any of her consorts, but all of them carried a single, much larger cannon on a pivot mount towards the bow, as well. And every single one of them had ropes everywhere. Which was the problem.

"Okay." Julian drew a deep breath, then continued in a tone of massive calm. "There's a line and a pu—block. So why isn't it a halyard?"

"Halyard hauls up t'e sail. T'e stay, it hold t'e pocking mast up."

The Pinopan had grown up around the arcane terminology of the sea. Despite the impression of landsmen—that the arcana existed purely to cause them confusion—there was a real necessity for the distinct terminology. Ships constantly encounter situations where clear and unambiguous orders may mean the difference between life and death. Thus the importance of being able to tell hands to pull upon a certain "rope" in a certain way. Or, alternatively, to let it out slowly, all the while maintaining tension.

Thus such unambiguous and unintelligible orders as "Douse the mainsail and make fast!" Which does *not* mean throw water on it to increase speed.

"So which one's the halyard?" Julian asked plaintively.

"Which halyard? Countin' t'e stays'ils, t'ere's seventeen pocking halyards on t'is ship. . . ."

Hooker's design had been agreed upon as the best possible for the local conditions. She and her consorts had been created, through human design and local engineering, to carry Prince Roger and his bodyguards—now augmented by various local forces—across a previously unexplored ocean. Not that there hadn't, as always, been the odd, unanticipated circumstance requiring last-minute improvisation.

The fact that a rather larger number of Mardukan allies than originally anticipated had been added to Roger's force had created the need for more sealift capacity. Especially given the sheer size of the Mardukan cavalry's mounts. *Civan* were fast, tough, capable of eating almost anything, and relatively intelligent. One thing they were *not*, however, was petite. Hardly surprising, since the cavalrymen who rode into battle on their backs averaged between three and three and a half meters tall.

Carrying enough of them to sea aboard the six original schooners had turned out to be impossible once the revised numbers of local troopers had been totaled up. So just when everyone had thought they were done building, they—and somewhere around a quarter of the total shipbuilding force of K'Vaern's Cove—had turned to to build the *Snarleyow*. Fortunately, the local labor force had learned a lot about the new building techniques working on the smaller ships, but it had still been a backbreaking, exhausting task no one had expected to face. Nor had Poertena been able to spend as much time refining her basic design, which was one reason she was ugly, slabsided, and slow, compared to her smaller sisters. She was also built of green timber, which had never been seasoned properly and could be expected to rot with dismaying speed in a climate like Marduk's. But that was all right with Prince Roger and his companions. All they really cared about was that she last long enough for a single voyage.

Although she was scarcely in the same class for speed or handiness as Poertena's original, twin-masted design, *Snarleyow* was still enormously more efficient than any native Mardukan design. She had to be. The nature of the local weather was such that there was an almost unvarying wind from the northeast, yet that was the very direction in which the ships had to sail. That was the reason for their triangular sails. Their fore-and-aft rig—a technology the humans had introduced—made it possible for them to sail much more sharply into the wind than any local vessel, with its clumsy and inefficient, primitive square-rigged design, had ever been able to do. Similar ships had sailed the seas of Earth all the way up to the beginning of the Information Age, and they remained the mainstay for water worlds like Pinopa.

"Now I'm really confused," Julian moaned. "All right. Tying something down is 'making fast.' A rope attached to a sail is a 'sheet.' A rope tied to the mast is a 'stay.' And a bail is the iron thingamajig on the mast."

"T'e boom," Poertena corrected, wiping away a drop of sweat. The day, as always, was like a steambath, even with the light wind that filled the sails. "T'e bail is on t'e boom. Unless you're taking on water. T'en you bail it out."

"I give up!"

"Don' worry about it," the Pinopan said with a chuckle. "You only been at t'is a few weeks. Besides, you got me an' all t'ose four-armed monstrosities to do t'e sailing. You jus' pull when we say 'heave,' and stop when we say 'avast.'"

"And hold on when you say 'belay.'"

"And hold on *tight* when we say belay."

"I blame Roger for this," Julian said with another shake of his head.

"You blame Roger for what?" a cool female voice asked from behind him.

Julian looked over his shoulder and grinned at Nimashet Despreaux. The female sergeant was frowning at him, but it slid off the irrepressible NCO like water off a duck.

"It's all Roger's fault that we're in this predicament,"

he replied. "If it wasn't for him, I wouldn't have to learn this junk!"

Despreaux opened her mouth, but Julian held up a hand before she could retort.

"Calmly, Nimashet. I know it's not Roger's fault. It was a joke, okay?"

Despreaux's frown only underscored the classical beauty of her face, but it was dark with worry.

"Roger's . . . still not taking Kostas' death very well, Adib. I just don't. . . . I don't want anybody even *joking* about this being his fault," she said, and Poertena nodded in agreement.

"T'e Prince didn't maroon us here, Julian. T'e Saints an' whoever set t'at pocking tombie on us marooned us." The diminutive armorer shrugged. "I guess it wasn't very pocking punny."

"Okay," a chagrined Julian said. "You've got a point. Roger has been sort of dragging around, hasn't he?"

"He's been in a funk, is what you mean," Despreaux said.

"Well, I'm sure there's some way you could cheer him up," Julian suggested with an evil grin.

"Oh, pock," Poertena muttered, and backed up quickly. After a crack like that the fecal matter was about to hit the impeller.

"Now this is a mutinous crew, if ever I've seen one," Sergeant Major Kosutic said. She looked from Despreaux's furious face to Julian's "butter-wouldn't-melt-in-my-mouth" expression and frowned. "All right, Julian. What did you say this time?"

"Me?" Julian asked with enormous innocence but little real hope of evading the consequences. The sergeant major had an almost miraculous sense of timing; she always turned up just as the action was hottest. Which come to think of it, described her in bed as well. "What would I have said?"

Now he looked from the sergeant major to the fulminating Despreaux, decided that coming clean offered his best chance of survival, and shrugged with a repentant expression.

"I just suggested that there might be a way to cheer Roger up," he admitted, then, unable to help himself, grinned again. "I guarantee I'm right. God knows I've been more cheerful lately."

The sergeant major rolled her eyes and crossed her arms.

"Well if that's your attitude, you'll damned well be less cheerful for a while!" She looked at the three noncoms and shook her head. "This is a clear case of His Evilness' finding work for idle hands. Poertena, I thought you were supposed to be conducting a class in rigging."

"I was trying to get Julian up to speed, Sergeant Major," the Pinopan said, tossing a length of rope to the deck. "T'at's not going too good."

"I've got all the stuff loaded in my toot," Julian said with a shrug. "But some of the data seems to be wrong, and the rest just seems to be hitting and bouncing. I mean, what's 'luff' mean?"

"It's when the sail flaps," Kosutic replied, shaking her head. "Even I know that, and I hate sailing. I guess we should've known better than to try to teach Marines to be sailors."

"We don't really need them, Sergeant Major," Poertena told her. "We've got plenty of Mardukans."

"We need to work on our entry techniques, anyway," Julian pointed out. "We've been engaging in all these open-field maneuvers, but when we take the spaceport, it's going to be mostly close quarters. Whole different style, Smaj. And we haven't really done any of that since Q'Nkok."

The sergeant major frowned, then nodded. She was

sure Julian had come up with that because it was more fun than learning to sail. But that didn't mean he was wrong.

"Okay. Concur. If we wanted sailors, we should've left you on the *DeGlopper* and brought Navy pukes. I'll talk the change over with the Old Man. If he approves, we'll start working on close combat techniques for the rest of the voyage."

"Besides," Poertena pointed out gloomily, "we might need them before then. I've never seen a place like t'is t'at *didn't* have pirates."

"And then there's the 'fish of unusual size.'" Julian chuckled and gestured out over the emerald waters. "So far, so good, right?"

"Don't laugh," Despreaux muttered. "I read that log. I do *not* want to tangle with something big enough to bite a boat in half, even a small one."

"Well," Kosutic said, with a tug on her earlobe. "If worse comes to worst, we can always give Roger a pocket knife and throw him at it."

"Ooooo!" Julian shook his head. "You haven't even *met* one of these little fishies and you hate them *that* much?"

Prince Roger Ramius Sergei Alexander Chiang MacClintock, Heir Tertiary to the Throne of Man, turned away from the creaming waves to look across the shipboard bustle. The sergeant major had just broken up the huddle around Julian, and the four NCOs were headed in four different directions, and he took a moment extra to watch Despreaux make for the fo'c'sle. He knew his depression was beginning to affect her, and that he needed to snap out of it. But the loss of Kostas was the one wound that would not seem to heal, and he'd had too much time to think about it since the frantic haste of getting all seven ships built had eased into the voyage itself. For the first time in what seemed forever, he wasn't engaged in frantic efforts to train native troops, or build ships, or simply hike through endless jungle. For that matter, nothing was actively attempting to kill him, devour him, assassinate him, or kidnap him, and a part of him was distantly amazed to discover just how much having that respite depressed him. Having time to think, he had discovered, was not always a good thing.

He supposed he could pull up the list of casualties on his implanted toot. But there wouldn't be much point. When they'd first landed, the Marines of Bravo Company, Bronze Battalion, had been just so many faces. And the officers and crew of the Assault Ship *DeGlopper*, long since expanding plasma, had just been blurs. But since sometime after the pilots of the shuttles had brought them to deadstick landings on this backward hell, sometime between the internecine fighting that had erupted at the first city they'd visited and the furious battles with the Kranolta barbarians, the Marines had become more than faces. In many ways, they had become more than family—as close as a part of his own body.

And each loss had been like flaying skin.

First the loss of half the company in Voitan, fighting the Kranolta. Then the constant low-level seepage as they battled their way across the rest of the continent. More good troops killed in Diaspra against the Boman, and then a handful more in Sindi against the main Boman force. The ones that fell to the damnbeasts and the vampire moths. And the crocs. The ever-bedamned damncrocs.

And one of those had been Kostas.

Kostas. Not a Marine, or even one of the Navy shuttle pilots. Not one of the Mardukan mercenaries who had become welded to the Bronze Barbarians.

Roger could, to an extent, justify their losses. The entire purpose of Bravo Company, and of the mercenaries, was to protect the once lily-white skin of Prince Roger Ramius Sergei Alexander Chiang MacClintock. But that wasn't Kostas' purpose. He was just a valet. A nobody. A nonentity. Just . . . Kostas.

Just the man who had stood by Roger when the rest of the world thought he was a complete loss. Just the man who, thrown the responsibility for feeding and clothing the Company on its march, had taken it on without a qualm. Just the man who had found food where there was none, and prepared sumptuous dishes from swamp water and carnivores. Only the man who had been a father figure to him.

Only Kostas.

And not even lost to enemy action. Lost to a damncroc, five meters of rubbery skin and teeth. One of the innumerable hazards of the damned jungles of Marduk. Roger had killed the croc almost immediately, but it had been too late. He'd killed dozens of them since, but all of them were too late for Kostas. Too late for his . . . friend.

He hadn't had many friends growing up. Even as the least little scion of the Imperial Family, Roger had faced a future of power and wealth. And from the youngest age, there had been sycophants aplenty swarming around the prince. The innumerable Byzantine plots of Imperial City had sought constantly to co-opt one self-absorbed prince. And from the time he was a teenager, it had been Kostas—cautious, mousy Kostas—who had helped him thread the rocks and shoals. Often without Roger ever knowing it.

And now, he was gone. Just . . . gone. Like Hooker and Bilali and Pentzikis and . . . gods. The list went on and on.

Oh, they'd left a few widows on the other side in

their wake. They'd made alliances when and where they could, even passed without a ripple in a few places. But more often than not, it had been plasma guns and bead rifles, swords and pikes and a few thousand years of technical and tactical expertise, blasting a swath of destruction a blind man could track because they had no choice. Which created its own problem, because they scarcely needed to be leaving any bread crumb trails behind them. Especially when they already knew they didn't face only "casual" enemies on the planet. True, there were more than enough foes who had become dangers solely because they felt . . . argumentative when the Company had needed to cross their territory, but beyond them, Roger and the Barbarians faced the sworn enemies of the Empire and the Imperial House.

The planet Marduk was, technically, a fief of the Empire of Man. In fact, it was officially personally held by the Empress herself, since it had been discovered a few hundred years before by the expanding Empire and promptly claimed in the name of the House of MacClintock. For almost a hundred years, the planet had been no more than a notation on a survey somewhere, though. Then, early in the reign of Roger's grandfather, plans had been advanced for the Sagittarius Sector. Settlers were going to be sent out to the planets in the region, and a "new day of hope" would dawn for the beleaguered poor of the inner worlds. In preparation for the projected wave of expansion, outposts had been established on several of the habitable planets and provided with bare-bones starports. The Imperial government had put some additional seed money into establishing a limited infrastructure and offered highly attractive concessions to some of the Empire's biggest multi-stellar corporations to help produce more, but by and large, the planets in this sector had been earmarked strictly as new homes for the "little people" of the Empire.

Roger supposed the plans had spoken well for his grandfather's altruistic side. Of course, it was that same misplaced altruism and his tendency to trust advisers because of what he *thought* their characters were which had created most of the problems Roger's Empress Mother had been dealing with, first as Heir Primus and then as Empress, for longer than Roger had been alive. And it had also been an altruism whose hopes had been frustrated more often than not.

As they had been in the case of the Sagittarius Sector project.

Unfortunately for Grandfather's plans, the "poor" of the inner worlds were relatively comfortable with their low-paid work or government stipends. Given a choice between a small but decent apartment in Imperial City or Metrocal or New Glasgow or Delcutta and a small but decent house in a howling wilderness, the "poor" knew which side of their bread was buttered. Especially when the howling wilderness in question was on a planet like Marduk. For one thing, even in Delcutta, people rarely had to worry about being eaten.

So, despite all of the government's plans (and Emperor Andrew's), the sector had languished. Oh, two or three of the star systems in the area had attracted at least limited colonization, and the Sandahl System had actually done fairly well. But Sandahl was on the very fringe of the Sagittarius Sector, more of an appendage of the neighboring Handelmann Sector. For the most part, though, the Sagittarius planetary outposts and their starports had discovered that they were the designated hosts for a party no one came to. Except for the Saints.

One of the less altruistic reasons for the effort to

colonize the sector in the first place had been the fact that the Cavaza Empire was expanding in that direction. Unfortunately, the plan to build up a countervailing Imperial presence had failed, and eventually, as the Saints continued their expansion, they had noticed the port installed on the small, mountainous subcontinent of Marduk.

In many ways, Marduk was perfect for the Saints' purposes. The "untouched" world would require very little in "remedy" to return it to its "natural state." Or to colonize. With their higher birthrate, and despite their "green" stand, the Saints were notably expansionist. It was one of the many little inconsistencies which somehow failed to endear them to their interstellar neighbors. And in the meantime, the star system was well placed as a staging point for clandestine operations deeper into the Empire of Man.

Roger and his Marines were unsure of the conditions on the ground. But after their assault ship/transport, HMS *DeGlopper*, had been crippled by a programmed "toombie" saboteur, they had needed the closest port to which they could divert, and Marduk had been elected. Unfortunately, they had arrived only to be jumped by two Saint sublight cruisers which had been working in-system along with their globular "tunnel-drive" FTL carrier mother ship. The presence of Cavazan warships had told the Marines that whatever else was going on here, the planetary governor and his "locally" recruited Colonial Guards were no longer working for the Empire. That could be because they were all dead, but it was far more likely that the governor had reached some sort of accommodation with the Saints.

Whatever the fate of the governor might have been, the unpalatable outlines of the Bronze Barbarians' new mission had been abundantly clear. *DeGlopper* had managed to defeat the two cruisers, but she'd been destroyed in action with all hands herself in the process. Fortunately, the Prince and his Marine bodyguards had gotten away undetected in the assault ship's shuttles while she died to cover their escape and conceal the secret of Roger's presence aboard her. *Un*fortunately, the only way for the Marines to get Roger home would be to take the spaceport from whoever controlled it and then capture a ship. Possibly in the face of the remaining Cavazan carrier.

It was a tall order, especially for one understrength Marine company, be it ever so elite, shipwrecked on a planet whose brutal climate ate high-tech equipment like candy. The fact that they'd had only a very limited window of time before their essential dietary supplements ran out had only made the order still taller. But Bravo Company of the Empress' Own, was the force which had hammered fifteen thousand screaming Kranolta barbarians into offal. The force which had smashed every enemy in its path across half the circumference of the planet.

Whether it was turncoat Colonial Guards or a Saint carrier wouldn't matter. The Bronze Barbarians, and His Highness' Imperial Mardukan Guards, were going to hammer them into dust, as well.

Of course, that didn't mean all of the hammers were going to survive.

Armand Pahner chewed a sliver of mildly spicy *bisti* root and watched the prince out of one eye as Kosutic approached. She was probably going to suggest a change in the training program, and he was going to approve it, since it had become abundantly clear that they were never going to make the Marines "real" sailors in the short voyage across the Northern Sea. They were just about on the last leg of the journey they had begun so many months before, and he couldn't be more pleased. There would be a hard fight at the end. Taking the spaceport and, even more importantly, a functional ship would take some solid soldiering. But compared to the rest of the journey, it ought to be a picnic.

He chuckled grimly to himself, not for the first time, at how easily and completely a "routine" voyage could go wrong. Assuming they got back to report, this would definitely be one for the security school to study. Murphy's fell presence was obvious everywhere, from the helplessly programmed saboteur secreted within the loyal ship's company to the poor choices of potential emergency diversion planets, to the presence of Saint forces in the supposedly loyal system.

Once they'd reached the planet's actual surface, of course, things had only gone downhill. The sole redeeming quality of the trip was that they had left Earth guarding what was surely the weakest link in the Imperial Family. Now . . . he wasn't. The foppish, useless prince who had left Earth had died somewhere in the steaming jungles of Marduk. The MacClintock warrior who had replaced him had some problems of his own: most seriously, a tendency to brood and an even more dangerous tendency to look for answers in the barrel of a gun. But no one could call him a fop anymore. Not to his face, at least. Not and survive.

In a way, looked at with cold logic, the trip had been enormously beneficial, shipwreck, deaths, and all. Eventually, the old prince—unthinking, uncommitted, subject to control or manipulation by the various factions in the Imperial Palace—would probably have caused the deaths of far more than a company of Marines. So the loss of so many of Pahner's Barbarians could almost be counted as a win.

If you looked at it with cold enough logic.

But it was hard to be logical when it was *your* Marines doing the dying.

Kosutic smiled at the company commander. She knew damned well what he was pondering, in general, if not specifically. But it never hurt to ask.

"Penny for your thoughts, Captain."

"I'm not absolutely sure what his mother is going to say," the captain replied. It wasn't exactly what he'd been thinking about, but it was part and parcel of his thought process.

"Well, initially, she'll be dealing with disbelief," Kosutic snorted. "Not only that we, and Prince Roger in particular, are alive, but at the change in him. It'll be hard for her to accept. There've been times it seemed the Unholy One Himself was doing the operational planning, but between you and me, he's shaping up pretty well."

"True enough," Pahner said softly, then chuckled and changed the subject. "Speaking of shaping up, though, I take it you don't think we can turn Julian into a swabbie?"

"More along the lines of its not being worth the trouble," Kosutic admitted. "Besides, Julian just pointed out that we've gotten awful shabby at close combat work, and I have to agree. I'd like to set the Company to training on that, and maybe some cross-training with the Mardukan infantry."

"Works for me," Pahner agreed. "Despreaux took the Advanced Tactical Assault Course," he added after double-checking with his toot implant. "Make her NCOIC."

"Ah, Julian took it, too," the sergeant major said. Pahner glanced at her, and she shrugged. "It's not official, because he took it 'off the books.' That's why it's not in his official jacket."

"How'd that happen?" Pahner asked. After this long together, he'd thought he knew everything there was to know about the human troops. But there was always another surprise.

"ATAC is taught by contractors," Kosutic pointed out. "When he couldn't get a slot for the school, he took leave and paid his own way."

"Hmmm." Pahner shook his head doubtfully. "I don't know if I can approve using him for an instructor if he didn't take it through approved channels. Which contractor was it?"

"Firecat, LLC. It's the company Sergeant Major Catrone started after he got out."

"Tomcat?" Pahner shook his head again, this time with a laugh. "I can just see him teaching that class. A couple of times in the jungle, it was like I heard his voice echoing in my head. 'You think *this* is hot? Boy, you'd best wait to complain in HELL! And that's where you're gonna be if you don't get your head out of your ass!'"

"When in the Unholy One's Fifth Name did you deal with Sergeant Major Catrone?" Kosutic asked. "He'd been retired for at least a decade when I joined the Raiders."

"He was one of my basic training instructors at Brasilia Base," Pahner admitted. "That man made duralloy look soft. We swore that the way they made ChromSten armor was to have him eat nails for breakfast, then collect it from the latrines, because his anus compressed it so hard the atoms got crushed. If Julian passed the course with Tomcat teaching it, he's okay by me. Decide for yourself who should lead the instruction."

"Okay. Consider it done." Kosutic gave a wave that could almost have been classified as a salute, then turned away and beckoned for the other NCOs to cluster back around her.

Pahner nodded as he watched her sketching a plan on the deck. Not be all there was to war, but it was damned well half. And—

His head jerked up and he looked towards the *Sea Skimmer* as a crackle of rifle fire broke out, but then he relaxed with a crooked, approving grin. It looked as if the Marines weren't the only ones doing some training.